GREAT AMERICAN GHOST STORIES

Volumes in the American Ghost Series:

Dixie Ghosts
Eastern Ghosts
Ghosts of the Heartland
Hollywood Ghosts
New England Ghosts
Western Ghosts

GREAT AMERICAN GHOST STORIES

Edited by
Frank D. McSherry, Jr., Charles G. Waugh,
and Martin H. Greenberg

Rutledge Hill Press
Nashville, Tennessee

Published in Nashville, Tennessee, by Rutledge Hill Press, Inc.,
513 Third Avenue South, Nashville, Tennessee 37210

Typography by Bailey Typography, Nashville, Tennessee
Cover design by Harriette Bateman

Library of Congress Cataloging-in-Publication Data

Great American ghost stories / edited by Frank D. McSherry, Jr.,
    Charles G. Waugh, and Martin H. Greenberg.
        p.   cm.
    ISBN 1-55853-146-7
    1. Ghost stories, America.   I. McSherry, Frank D.   II. Waugh,
Charles G.   III. Greenberg, Martin Harry.
PS648.G48G7   1991
813'.0873308—dc20   91-24148
                                                                CIP

Manufactured in the United States of America

1 2 3 4 5 6 7 8 — 97 95 94 93 92 91

Table of Contents

The Borders of the Unknown 7

New Jersey
1. Double Vision (*Mary Higgings Clark*) 9

Connecticut
2. This Is Death (*Donald E. Westlake*) 39

Nevada
3. Pretty Maggie Moneyeyes (*Harlan Ellison*) 53

Iowa
4. Little Jimmy (*Lester del Rey*) 75

Georgia
5. Poor Little Saturday (*Madeleine L'Engle*) 91

Massachusetts
6. On 202 (*Jeff Hecht*) 109

New Jersey
7. Ransom Cowl Walks the Road
   (*Nancy Varian Berberick*) 119

North Dakota
8. School for the Unspeakable
   (*Manly Wade Wellman*) 137

West Virginia
9. The Stormsong Runner (*Jack L. Chalker*) 149

California
10. Harry's Ghost (*Talmage Powell*) 161

Massachusetts
11. Herbert West—Reanimator (*H. P. Lovecraft*) 177

Pennsylvania
12. Caller in the Night (*Burton Kline*) 209

Oklahoma
13. Professor Kate (*Margaret St. Clair*) 225

Texas
14. The Guns of William Longley
         (*Donald Hamilton*) 233

New York
15. Clay-Shuttered Doors (*Helen R. Hull*) 249

Arizona
16. The Stranger (*Ambrose Bierce*) 269

Massachusetts
17. Night-Side (*Joyce Carol Oates*) 275

North Carolina
18. Drawer 14 (*Talmage Powell*) 301

New Jersey
19. The Jest of Warburg Tantavul (*Seabury Quinn*) 313

California
20. One of the Dead (*William Wood*) 343

Maine
21. Emmett (*Dahlov Ipcar*) 373

Alabama
22. Night Court (*Mary Elizabeth Counselman*) 389

Ohio
23. The Boarded Window (*Ambrose Bierce*) 409

Washington
24. The Ghosts of Steamboat Coulee
         (*Arthur J. Burks*) 415

Ohio
25. He Walked By Day (*Julius Long*) 443

Maine
26. The Phantom Farmhouse (*Seabury Quinn*) 451

Minnesota
27. Stillwater, 1896 (*Michael Cassutt*) 475

Kentucky
28. Ride the Thunder (*Jack Cady*) 487

New Mexico
29. The Resting Place (*Oliver LaFarge*) 499

The Borders of the Unknown

Here he comes. Right at you.

Nice looking, well dressed, pleasant enough. A complete stranger. But—

Why do you feel you've seen him before—somewhere? Why does an icy shiver run down your spine, like a black spider the size of your palm scuttling down between your shoulder blades? Cold and dead and *moving*—

Suddenly you know. He's your double. An exact double.

It's like looking in a mirror. A doppelganger.

A *ghost*.

Ghosts come in many kinds.

Drifting misty white at night over smoking battlefields, strolling real as rock among guests at a harvest ball, a whispered voice warning a ship captain to change course, even a pale image of a skull in a White House mirror warning President Abraham Lincoln of his coming death—

Some are light as air, immaterial enough to walk through as vapor from a river at twilight. Others—well, there's the case of Flying Officer Ronald Davidson. Davidson saw his fellow squadron member, pilot Johnny Holmes, take off in his Sopwith biplane during the Battle of the Marne on September 17, 1914, and promptly dive nose-first into the ground, as if committing suicide. Holmes and his observer were killed instantly.

Davidson took off next, without an observer. He was hardly off the earth when he felt the plane suddenly dip, as if a heavy weight had dropped onto it. As Davidson glanced back, his eyes met those of his dead friend in the back seat. Holmes, or whatever it was, seized the stick and dove the plane into the ground. Davidson died in the hospital an hour later, after living just long enough to tell what happened.

The fascinating and eerie variety of ghosts is reflected in the twenty-nine tales collected in this volume. All are American ghosts. Each story is set in a state whose territory and history is

7

integral to the story and provides an additional bonus for the reader.

The authors include that queen of heart-stopping suspense, Mary Higgins Clark, whose many bestsellers include *Where Are the Children?* and *A Cry in the Night*; Harlan Ellison, winner of multiple Hugos ("Jeffty Is Five"), Nebulas ("A Boy and His Dog"), and Edgars ("Soft Monkey"), as well as the most popular "Star Trek" episode, "City of the Edge of Forever"; Donald Hamilton, creator of popular counterspy Matt Helm, whose ghostly tale deals with a famous gunslinger of the Old West; Civil War veteran Ambrose Bierce, whose life ended as mysteriously as his classic stories; H. P. Lovecraft, the most famous horror writer of his generation; and new writers such as the rising star of sword-and-sorcery writer Nancy Varian Berberick.

Their ghosts gleam and glimmer—and sometimes kill—in such places as witch-haunted Massachusetts, a pine-surrounded phantom farmhouse of Maine, and a small, quiet boys' school of North Dakota where, unknown to the administrators, a terrible lore is being secretly taught. They haunt the dusty streets of Texas cowtowns; a dead woman's soul inhabits a slot machine in Las Vegas; and the night court judge and jury in a sleepy southern town are out of this world.

These mysterious beings appear in every time, in every place. Are they all the results of superstition, of terror, misunderstanding, wishful thinking?

It is understandable that a grieving mother, looking at a filmy curtain blowing in the rain from an open window at night, could see a dead child returning. It should cause no surprise that in his last moment of life a wounded soldier might try to see his loved ones again . . . and that he might possibly succeed.

These stories are provided for your entertainment only. They are intended to provide a delicious thrill. So one should not worry if they remind us that we live in a strange universe within whose borders of darkness are things for which, even now, with all our scientific wisdom, we have no slightest explanation. . . .

So pay no attention to that person coming down the street. The one you've never met but seems somehow familiar.

Haven't you seen him somewhere?

Him, the one whose face just turned into a skull—

—Frank D. McSherry

When Jimmy Cleary killed the wrong twin, he knew he had to correct his mistake. What he didn't know was exactly how close identical twins can be.

ONE

Double Vision

Mary Higgins Clark

Jimmy Cleary crouched in the bushes outside Caroline's garden apartment in Princeton. His thick brown hair fell on his forehead and he pushed it back with the studied gesture that had become a mannerism. The May evening was unseasonably raw and chilly. Even so, perspiration soaked his sweat suit. He moistened his lips with the tip of his tongue. His whole body tingled with nervous exhilaration.

Five years ago tonight he had made the blunder of a lifetime. He had killed the wrong girl. He, the best actor in the entire world, had fouled up his ultimate scene. Now he was going to rectify that error. This time there would be no mistakes.

The back door of Caroline's apartment opened onto the parking lot. For the last few nights he'd been studying the area. Last night he'd unscrewed the light bulb outside her apartment, so now the back entrance was in deep shadows. It was 8:15; time to go in.

From his pocket he took out a spikelike tool, inserted it in the keyhole, and twisted it until he heard the click of the cylinder. With gloved hands he turned the knob and opened the door just wide enough to slip in. He closed and relocked it. There was an inside chain that she probably fastened at night. That was fine. Tonight she'd lock the two of them in. It gave Jimmy distinct pleasure to contemplate Caroline carefully securing the place. It would be like the ghost story that ended, "Now, we're locked in for the night."

He was in the kitchen, which opened directly from an

9

archway into the living room. Last night he'd hidden out-side the kitchen window and observed Caroline. There were plants on the sill, so the shade didn't go all the way down. At ten o'clock, she came out of the bedroom wearing red-and-white-striped pajamas. While she watched the news, she exercised, bending from the waist so that her blond hair flew from shoulder to shoulder.

She went back to her bedroom where she probably read for a while because the light stayed on for about an hour. He could just as easily have finished her then, but his sense of drama wanted him to wait for the exact anniversary.

The only light came from the outside streetlamps, but there weren't many places to hide in the apartment. He could fit under her bed, which had a velvet dust ruffle. It was an interesting idea: He could wait there, while she read, got sleepy, turned off the light; wait until she stopped moving and her breath became even. Then he could silently ease his body out, kneel beside her, watch her the way he had watched the other girl, and then wake her up. But be-fore he decided, he'd check other possibilities.

When he opened the door of the bedroom closet, a light went on automatically. Jimmy caught a glimpse of an almost full traveling bag. Quickly he closed the door. There was no place to hide here.

Imagine a woman who has less than two hours to live. Does she sense it? Does she go about her normal routine? These were the hypothetical questions Cory Zola had thrown at the acting class one night. Cory was a famous teacher who only took on students he thought had the po-tential to become stars. He put me in his private class the first time I auditioned for him, Jimmy reminded himself now. *He knows talent.*

There was no place to hide in the living room. The front door, however, opened directly into it, and there was a closet at a right angle. The closet door was open a couple of inches. Swiftly he moved over to inspect it.

This closet didn't have an automatic light. He pulled a pencil-thin flashlight from his pocket and shone the beam on the interior, which was unexpectedly deep. A heavy dress bag, encased in voluminous layers of plastic, hung at the front. This was the reason the door wasn't closed. It would have squashed the dress. He'd bet anything it was her wedding gown. Last night when he'd followed her, she'd stopped at a bridal shop and stayed nearly half an hour, probably for a final fitting. Maybe they'd bury her in this dress.

The cascade of plastic created a perfect hiding place. Jimmy stepped into the closet, slid between two winter coats and pulled them together. Suppose Caroline went into his closet and found him? The worst that could happen would be that he couldn't kill her exactly as he'd planned. But those traveling bags in the other closet were almost full. She probably was just about packed. He knew she was flying to St. Paul in the morning. She was getting married next week. She *thought* she was getting married next week.

Jimmy eased out of the closet. At five o'clock, in his rented car, he'd been waiting for Caroline outside the State House in Trenton. She'd worked late. He'd followed her to the restaurant where she met Wexford. He'd stood outside, and didn't leave until, through the window, he'd seen them order. Then he came directly here. She wouldn't be back for another hour at least. He helped himself to a can of soda from the refrigerator and settled on the couch. It was time to prepare himself for the third act.

It had begun five and a half years ago, that last semester at Rawlings College of Fine Arts in Providence. He'd been in the theater program studying acting. Caroline had majored in directing. He'd been in a couple of the plays she directed. As a junior he'd played Biff in *Death of a Salesman*. He'd been so fantastic that half the school started calling him Biff.

Jimmy sipped the soda. In memory he was back at college on the set of the senior play. He had the lead. The president of the college had invited an old friend, a Paramount producer, as his guest for opening night, and the word was out that the producer was looking for new talent. From the beginning he and Caroline hadn't seen eye to eye on his interpretation of the part. Then two weeks before opening night, she'd taken the part from him and given it to Brian Kent. He could still see her, her blond hair in a Psyche knot, her plaid shirt tucked inside her jeans, her earnest, worried look. "You're just not quite right, Jimmy. But I think you'd be perfect as the second lead, the brother."

Second lead. The brother had about six lines. He'd wanted to plead, to beg, but had known it was useless. When Caroline Marshall made a casting change she couldn't be budged. And he'd known in his gut that somehow being the lead in that play was crucial to his career. In that split second he'd made up his mind to kill her, and right away started performing. He'd laughed, a lighthearted, chagrined chuckle, and said, "Caroline, I've been working up the courage to tell you I'm so far behind in term papers, I can't even think about acting."

She'd fallen for it. And looked relieved. The Paramount producer had come. He'd invited Brian Kent to the Coast to test for a new series. The rest, as we say in Hollywood, Jimmy thought, was history. After nearly five years, the series was still in the top-ten ratings, and Brian Kent had just signed to do a movie for three million bucks.

Two weeks after graduation Jimmy had gone to St. Paul. Caroline's family's home was practically a mansion, but he'd quickly found that the side door was unlocked. He'd made his way along the downstairs floor, up the wide, sweeping staircase, past the master bedroom suite. The door was ajar. The bed was empty. Then he'd opened the next bedroom door and seen her: lying there asleep. He could still see the outlines of her room, the brass four-poster bed, the silky sheen of the soft, expensive percale sheets. He remembered how he'd bent over her as she lay there curled up in bed, her blond hair gleaming on the pillowcase. He'd whispered, "Caroline," and she'd opened her eyes, looked at him, and said "No."

He'd thrown his arms over her and covered her mouth with his hands. She'd listened, her eyes panicking, while he whispered that he was going to kill her, that if she hadn't taken the lead from him, he'd have been seen by the Paramount producer instead of Brian Kent. Finally he'd said, "You're not going to direct anything anymore, Caroline. You've got a new role. You're the victim."

She'd tried to pull away from him, but he yanked her back and twisted the cord around her neck. Her eyes had widened, blazing out at him. Her hands had lifted, palms outstretched begging him, then had fallen limp on the sheet.

The next morning he couldn't wait to read the newspapers. "Daughter of Prominent St. Paul Banker Slain." He remembered how he'd laughed, then cried with frustration when he read the first few sentences. *The body of twenty-one-year-old Lisa Marshall was found by her twin sister this morning.*

Lisa Marshall. Twin sister.

The story continued: *The young woman had been strangled. The twins were alone in the family home. Police have been unable to question Caroline Marshall. At the sight of her sister's body, she went into profound shock and is under heavy sedation.*

He'd tell Caroline about that later on tonight. All these years in Los Angeles he'd had a subscription to the Minneapolis-St. Paul papers, watching for any news about the case. Then he read that Caroline was engaged and would be married on May 30—next week. Caroline Marshall, who was a lawyer on the staff of the Attorney General in Trenton, New Jersey, was marrying an associate professor from Princeton University, Dr. Sean Wexford. Wexford had been a graduate student when Jimmy was at Rawlings. Jimmy had him for a psychology course. He wondered when Caroline and Wexford got together. They weren't going around when Caroline was a student at Rawlings. He was sure of that.

Jimmy shook his head. He took the empty soda can out to the kitchen and tossed it in the wastebasket. Caroline might be coming along anytime now. He went into the bathroom and winced at the noisy flush of the toilet. Then with infinite care he stepped into the closet and pulled the winter coats around him. He felt for the length of cord in the pocket of his sweat suit. It was cut from the same roll of heavy fishing tackle he'd used on her sister. He was ready.

"Cappuccino, darling?" Sean smiled across the candlelit table. Caroline's dark blue eyes were pensive with that look of absolute sadness that sometimes came into them. Understandable tonight. It was the anniversary of the last night she'd spent with Lisa.

To try to distract her, he said, "I felt like a bull in a china shop when I picked up your gown this afternoon."

Caroline raised her eyebrows. "You didn't look at it? That's bad luck."

"They didn't let me get near it. The saleslady kept apologizing that they couldn't send it."

"I've been rushing around so much this last month I've lost weight. They had to take it in."

"You're too thin. We'll have to fatten you up in Italy. Pasta three times a day."

"I can hardly wait." Caroline smiled across the table. She loved the bigness of Sean, the way his sandy hair always looked a bit disheveled, the humor in his gray eyes. "My mother phoned this morning. She's still worried that my dress doesn't have sleeves. She reminded me twice that the joke in Minnesota is, 'Which day was summer?'"

"I volunteer to keep you warm. Your dress is in the front closet. By the way, I'd better give you back your extra keys."

"Keep them. If I forget anything, you can bring it out with you next week."

When they left the restaurant Caroline followed him to the roomy Victorian house that would be theirs when they returned from the honeymoon. She was leaving her car in the second garage while they were away. Sean drove his car into the driveway, parked it, and got into hers. She slid over and he drove her home, his arm around her.

Jimmy was proud that even after an hour of standing still, he felt fine. That was because he was in shape from the gym and all the dancing lessons.

He'd spent the past five years studying, knocking on doors, trying to see casting people, getting close and then shut out. To get a good agent, you needed to show you'd had some good roles. To get sent to the good casting people, you needed a hotshot agent. And sometimes he'd hear the ultimate killer: "You're a Brian Kent type, and that isn't helping you."

The memory infuriated Jimmy, and he shook his head.

And all of this after his mother had persuaded his father to stake him to a year of what he called "trying to act."

Jimmy felt the old anger again. His father had never liked what he did. When Jimmy was so great in *Death of a Salesman,* had his father been proud? No. He wanted to cheer for a son who was the quarterback, a Heisman Trophy contender.

Jimmy hadn't bothered to ask for more when the money from his father ran out. Every month or so his mother sent him whatever she could squeeze from the house money. The old man might have plenty, but he sure was tight. But boy, would he have loved it if James Junior had been the one to sign Brian Kent's three-million-dollar contract last week. "That's my boy," he'd be yelling.

That's the way the scene would have been played if five years ago Caroline hadn't yanked him from the part and given it to Brian Kent.

Jimmy stiffened. There was a sound of voices at the front door. Caroline. *She wasn't alone.* A man's voice. Jimmy shrank against the wall. As the door opened and the light was snapped on, he glanced down and froze. The light filtered into the closet. He was sure he couldn't be seen, but the tips of his beat-up running shoes, pointing outward, screamed their presence.

Caroline glanced around the living room as the light went on. Tonight, for some reason, the apartment seemed different, alien. But of course that was only because it was tonight. Lisa's anniversary. She put her arms around Sean and he gently kneaded the back of her neck. "You do know that all evening you've been miles away."

"I always hang on your every word." It was an attempt at lightheartedness that failed. Her voice broke.

"Caroline, I don't want you to be alone tonight. Let me stay with you. Look, I know why you want to be by yourself, and I understand. Go into the bedroom. I'll stretch out on the couch."

Caroline tried to smile. "No, I'm really okay." She wrapped her arms around his neck. "Just hold me tight for one minute and then get out of here," she said. "I'm setting the alarm for six-thirty. I'm better off doing final packing in the morning. You know me. Sharp in the A.M. Fade in the P.M."

"I hadn't noticed." Sean's lips caressed her neck, her forehead, found her lips. He held her, feeling the tension in her slender body.

Tonight she had told him, "Once the anniversary is over, I'm really okay. It's just that the couple of days before, it's as though Lisa is with me. It's a feeling that builds and builds. Like today. But I know it will be fine tomorrow, and I'll go home and get ready for the wedding and be happy."

Reluctantly, Sean released Caroline from his arms. She looked so tired now, and oddly that made her look so young. Twenty-six, and at this moment she could have passed for one of the kids in his freshman class. He told her that. "But you're much prettier than any of them," he concluded. "It's going to be awfully nice to wake up and look at you first thing in the morning for the rest of my life."

Jimmy Cleary's body was soaked with perspiration. Suppose she let Wexford spend the night here. They'd surely see him in the morning when Caroline took the wedding dress from the closet. They were wrapped up in each other less than a foot from where he was standing. Suppose one of them smelled the perspiration from his body. But Wexford was leaving.

"I'll be here at seven, love," he told Caroline.

And you'll find her the way she found her sister, Jimmy thought. That's how you'll envision her in the morning for the rest of your life.

Caroline bolted the door behind Sean. For an instant she was tempted to reopen it immediately, call out to him, tell him yes, stay with me. I don't want to be alone. But I'm not alone, she thought as she took her hand from the knob. Lisa is so close to me tonight. Lisa. Lisa.

She went into the bedroom and undressed quickly. A hot shower helped to relieve some of the tension she felt in the muscles of her neck and back. She remembered the way Sean's hands had kneaded those muscles. I love him so much, she thought. Her red-and-white-striped pajamas were on the hook on the bathroom door. She'd been shopping for lingerie and nightgowns in a Madison Avenue boutique when she'd spotted them. "If you like them, better make up your mind fast," the salesgirl had said. "We only got in one pair in red. They're comfortable and awfully cute."

One pair. That had decided Caroline. One of the hardest things in these past five years was to break the habit of buying *two* of everything. For years if she saw something she liked, she'd automatically buy two. Lisa had done the same thing. They were exactly the same size, same height, same weight. Even their parents had trouble telling them apart. When they were juniors in high school, Mother had urged them to buy different gowns for the prom. They'd shopped separately in different stores and arrived home with exactly the same blue and white dotted-swiss gown.

The next year, they'd tearfully agreed with their parents and the school psychologist that they'd be doing themselves a favor if they attended different colleges and did not discuss being an identical twin. "Being close is wonderful," the psychologist had said, "but you've got to think of yourselves as individuals. You're not going to grow to your full capacity unless you give yourselves and each other space."

Caroline had gone to Rawlings, Lisa to Southern Cal. In college it secretly delighted Caroline that people thought she had inscribed her own picture, "To my best friend." They'd even graduated on the same day. Mother had gone to be with Lisa. Dad had come to Caroline's commencement.

Caroline went into the living room, remembered to fasten the chain on the back door, turned on the television, and halfheartedly began bending from side to side. A commercial for life insurance came on. "Isn't it a comfort to know that your family will be taken care of after you're gone?" Caroline snapped off the television. Turning off the livingroom light, she rushed into the bedroom and slipped under the covers. Lying on her side, she pulled her legs against her body and buried her face in her hands.

Sean Wexford could not shake off the feeling that he should have flatly refused to leave Caroline. He sat in the car for a few minutes looking at her door. But she needed to be alone. Shaking his head, Sean reached for the car keys.

On the drive home his emotions seesawed between his

concern for Caroline and anticipation that a week from tomorrow they'd be married. How astonished he'd been last year when he'd seen her jogging ahead of him on the Princeton campus. She'd been in only one of his classes in Rawlings. In those days he'd been working so hard on his doctoral thesis, he hadn't even thought about dating. That morning a year ago, she'd told him about going to Columbia Law School, clerking for a New Jersey Superior Court judge, and then going to work in the Attorney General's office in Trenton. And, Sean thought, as he steered the car into his driveway, over that first cup of coffee we both knew what was happening to us. He parked Caroline's car behind his own and went into the house smiling at the realization that soon their cars would always be together in the driveway.

Jimmy Cleary was surprised that Caroline had turned off the television so abruptly. He thought again of the questions Cory Zola had thrown at the acting class: *Imagine a woman who has less than two hours to live. Does she sense it? Does she go about her normal routine?* Caroline might be sensing danger. When he was back in class, he'd bring up that question again. "In my opinion," he would say, "there is a quickening of the spirit as it prepares to leave the body." He had a feeling that Zola would find his insight profound.

Jimmy felt a cramp in his leg. He wasn't used to standing perfectly still for so long, but he could do it for as long as necessary. If Caroline's intuition was warning her of danger, she'd be listening for even the smallest sound. These garden-apartment walls weren't thick. One scream and someone might hear her. He was glad she'd left the bedroom door open. He wouldn't have to worry about the door creaking when he went to her.

Jimmy closed his eyes. He wanted to duplicate the exact stance he'd been in when he woke her sister. One knee on the floor beside the bed, his arms ready to wrap around her, his hands in position to clamp over her mouth. Actually he'd knelt for a minute or two before he awakened the other girl. He probably wouldn't chance that luxury now. Caroline would be sleeping lightly. Her spirit would be pounding at her to beware.

Beware. A beautiful word. A word to whisper from the stage. He would have a stage career now. Broadway. Not nearly the pay you got for a film, but prestige. His name on the marquee.

Caroline was his jinx, and she was about to be removed.

Caroline lay curled up in bed, shivering. The soft down comforter could not stop the trembling. She was afraid. So terribly afraid. Why? "Lisa," she whispered, "Lisa, was this the way you felt? Did you wake up? Did you know what was happening to you?" *Did I hear you cry out that night and go back to sleep?*

She still didn't know. It was only an impression, a blurred, dreamy image that came to her in the weeks after Lisa's death. She and Sean had talked it through. "I think I might have heard her. Maybe if I had forced myself awake. . . ."

Sean had made her understand that her reaction was typical of families of victims. The "if only" syndrome. In this last year, through him and with him, she'd begun to experience peace, a healing. Except for now.

Caroline turned in the bed and forced herself to stretch out her legs and arms. "Irrational anxiety and profound sadness are symptoms of depression," she had read. Sadness, okay, she thought. It is the anniversary, but I won't give in to the anxiety. Think of the happy times with Lisa. That last evening.

Mother and Dad had left for a bankers' seminar in San Francisco. She and Lisa had ordered pizza with everything on it, drunk wine, and talked their heads off. Lisa's decision to go to law school. Caroline had taken the law school admittance exams too but still wasn't sure what she wanted to do.

"I really loved being in the theater group," she'd told Lisa. "I'm not a good actress but I can sense good acting. I think I could make a pretty fair director. The play went over well, and Brian Kent, who I just knew was right for the lead, was picked up by a producer. Still, if I get a law degree maybe we can open an office and tell people they're getting double their money's worth."

They'd gone to bed about eleven o'clock. Their rooms adjoined. Usually they left the door open, but Lisa wanted to watch a television show and Caroline was sleepy, so they blew kisses and Caroline closed the door. If only I'd left it open, she thought. I would surely have heard her if she'd had a chance to cry out.

The next morning, she hadn't waked up until after eight. She remembered sitting up, stretching, thinking how good it felt to have college behind her. As a graduation present, she and Lisa had been given a trip to Europe that summer.

Caroline remembered how she'd jumped out of bed, deciding to get coffee and juice and bring it up on a tray to Lisa. She squeezed fresh juice while the coffee perked, then put the glasses and cups and coffeepot on a tray and went up the stairs.

Lisa's door was open a crack. She'd kicked it open and called, "Wake up, my girl. We've got a tennis date in an hour."

And then she'd seen Lisa. Her head slumped unnaturally, the cord biting her neck, her eyes wide open and filled with fear, her palms extended as though trying to push something back. Caroline had dropped the tray, splashing her legs with the coffee, had managed to stumble to the phone and dial 911 and then scream, scream until her throat broke into a harsh, guttural sound. She awakened in the hospital three days later. She was told that the police found her lying beside Lisa, Lisa's head on her shoulder.

The only clue, the muddied partial print of a running shoe just inside the side door. "And then," as the chief of detectives told them later, "he, or she, was polite enough to scrape the rest of the mud off on the mat."

If only they had found Lisa's murderer, Caroline thought as she lay in the darkness. The detectives all believed that it was someone who had known Lisa. There was no attempt at robbery. No attempt to rape. They'd exhaustively questioned Lisa's friends, her dates at college. There was one young man in her class who had been obsessed by her. He'd remained a strong suspect, but the police could never prove he was in St. Paul that night.

They'd looked into mistaken identity, especially when they learned that neither girl had told her college friends she had an identical twin. "At first we didn't tell because we promised not to. It became a game with us," Caroline said.

"How about friends from college visiting your home?"

"We just didn't bring college friends home. We were glad to have time together during holidays and school breaks."

Oh, Lisa, Caroline thought now. If I only knew why. If I only could have helped you that night. She was not sleepy but was suddenly weary.

At last her eyelids began closing on their own. Oh, Lisa, she thought, I wanted you to have happiness like mine too. If only I could make it up to you.

The window was open a few inches from the bottom. Protective side locks kept it from being raised higher. Now a sharp gust of wind made the shade rattle. Caroline jumped up, realized what had happened, and forced herself to lie back against the pillows. Stop it, she told herself, stop it. Deliberately she closed her eyes and after a while fell into a light dream-filled sleep, a sleep in which Lisa was trying to call her, trying to warn her.

It was time. Jimmy Cleary could sense it. The rustling of the sheets had stopped. There was absolutely no sound coming from the bedroom. He slipped between the garments that had concealed him and eased aside the bag containing Caroline's gown. The hinges gave off a faint rubbing noise when he pushed the closet door open, but there was no reaction from inside the bedroom. He made his way across the living room to the side of the bedroom door. Caroline had a nightlight plugged into one of the sockets, and it threw off just enough light so that he could tell she was sleeping restlessly. Her breathing was even but shallow. Several times she turned her head from side to side as though she was protesting something.

Jimmy felt in his pocket for the cord. It was strangely satisfying to know it came from the same roll of tackle he'd used on the sister. This was even the same jogging suit he'd worn five years ago and the same running shoes. He'd known it was a little risky to keep them, just in case the cops ever questioned him, but he'd never been able to throw them away. Instead he'd put them with other stuff in a storage space he rented where nobody asked questions. Of course he'd used a different name.

He tiptoed to the side of Caroline's bed and knelt down.

He was able to savor a full minute of watching her before her eyes fluttered open and his hands snapped around her mouth.

Sean watched the ten o'clock news, realized he had absolutely no sleep in him, and opened a book he'd been wanting to read. A few minutes later he tossed it aside impatiently. Something was wrong. He could feel it as tangibly as though he could see smoke pouring from the next room and know that there was a fire blazing in the house. He'd phone Caroline. See how she was doing. On the other hand, maybe she'd managed to get to sleep. He walked over to the liquor cabinet and poured a generous amount of scotch into a tumbler. A few sips helped him to realize that he was probably acting like a nervous old biddy.

Caroline opened her eyes as she heard her name whispered. It's a nightmare, she thought, I've been dreaming. She started to cry out, then felt a hand clasped on her mouth, a hard, muscular hand that squeezed her cheekbones, that clamped her lips together, that half covered her nostrils. She gasped, fighting for breath. The hand slid down a fraction of an inch and she was able to breathe. She tried to pull away, but now the man was holding her with his other arm. His face was close to hers. "Caroline," he whispered, "I've come to correct my mistake."

The night-light sent eerie shadows onto the bed. That voice. She'd heard it before. The outline of his bold forehead, the square jaw. The powerful shoulders. Who?

"Caroline, the hotshot director."

Now she recognized the voice. Jimmy Cleary. Jimmy Cleary, and in that same instant she knew why. Like a scene from a movie, the moment when she'd told Jimmy he simply wasn't right for the part flashed through Caroline's mind. He'd taken it so well. Too well. She hadn't wanted to know he was acting. It had been easier to pretend that he agreed with her decision. *And he killed Lisa when he wanted to kill me. It's my fault.* A moan slipped past her lips, disappeared against his palm. My fault. My fault.

And then she heard Lisa's voice as clearly as though Lisa was whispering in her ear, telling secrets again, the way they had as children. *It's not your fault, but it's your fault if you let him kill again. Don't let this happen to Mother and Dad. Don't let it happen to Sean. Grow old for me. Have babies. Name one after me. You've got to live. Listen to me. Tell him he didn't make a mistake. Tell him you hated me too. I'll help you.*

Jimmy Cleary's breath was hot on her cheek. He was talking about the part, about Brian Kent being signed up by the producer, about Brian's new contract. "I'm going to kill you exactly the way I killed your sister. An actor keeps at his role until he has it perfect. You want to hear the last thing I said to your sister?" He lifted his hand a fraction so she could mouth an answer.

Tell him you're me.

For a split second Caroline was six again. She and Lisa were playing on the foundation of a house being built near theirs. Lisa, always more daring, always surefooted, was leading the way over the piles of cinder block. "Don't be a scaredy-cat," she'd urged. "Just follow me."

She heard herself whisper, "I'd love to hear all about it. I want to know how she died, so I can laugh. You did murder Caroline. I'm Lisa."

She felt the hand slap her mouth with savage force.

Someone had rewritten the script. Furiously, Jimmy dug his fingers into her cheekbones. Whose cheekbones? Caroline's? If he'd already killed her, why hadn't his luck changed? Without moving the arm that lay over her chest, he reached into the breast pocket of his sweat suit for the cord. Get it over with, he told himself. If they're both dead, you'll be sure you got Caroline.

But it was like being on stage in the third act without knowing how the play ended. If the actor didn't know the climax, how could you expect the audience to feel any tension? Because there was an audience, an invisible audience named fate. He had to be sure. "If you try to scream, you won't even get so far as a yelp," he told her. "That's all your sister got out."

She *had* heard Lisa that night.

"So nod if you promise not to scream. I'll talk to you. Maybe if you convince me, I'll let you live. Wexford wants to look at you first thing in the morning for the rest of his life, doesn't he? I heard him say so."

Jimmy Cleary had been here when they came in. Caroline felt darkness close over her.

Do as he says! Don't you dare pass out. Lisa's bossy voice. "The Duchess has spoken," Caroline used to tell her, and they'd laugh together.

Jimmy angled the arm that lay across Caroline's body, yanked the cord around her neck, and tied it in a slipknot. It was twice the length of the section he'd used last time. It had occurred to him that this time he'd make a double knot, a grand final gesture as he exited from the spotlight of death.

The extra length gave him the ability to manipulate her. Calmly he told her to get out of bed, that he was hungry— he wanted her to fix him a sandwich and coffee—that he'd be holding the end of the cord and would pull it till she strangled if she raised her voice or tried anything funny.

Do as he says.

Obediently Caroline sat up as Jimmy lifted the weight of his arm from across her body. Her feet touched the cool wood of the floor. Automatically she fumbled for her slippers. I may be dead in seconds and I worry about bare feet, she thought. As she bent forward the cord bit into her neck. "No . . . please." She heard the panic in her voice.

"Shut up!" She felt Jimmy Cleary's hands on her neck, loosening the cord. "Don't move so fast and don't raise your voice again."

Side by side they walked through the living room and into the kitchen. His hand rested on the back of her neck. His fingers gripped the cord. Even loosened, she could feel its pressure, like a band of steel. In her mind she could see the grayish stripe embedded in Lisa's throat. For the first time she began to remember the rest of that morning. She'd dialed 911 and begun to scream. Then she'd dropped the receiver. Lisa's body was almost on the edge of the bed as though in that last moment she'd tried to escape. Her skin was so blue, I was thinking she was cold, I had to warm her, Caroline recalled as she opened the refrigerator door. I ran around the bed and got in and put my arms around her and began to talk to her and I tried to get the cord from around her neck and then I felt as though I was falling.

Now the cord was around her neck. In the morning would Sean find her as she had found Lisa?

No. It mustn't happen. Make the sandwich. Make him coffee. Act as though you two are playing a great scene. Tell him how bossy I was. Come on. Take all the good things and turn them around. Blame me the way he's blaming you.

Caroline looked inside the refrigerator and had a swift feeling of gratitude that she'd put off emptying it. She'd always kept sandwich makings for Sean on hand; the cleaning woman was coming in the morning to take them home. She pulled out ham and cheese and turkey, lettuce, mayonnaise, and mustard. She remembered that at school when the cast went out for a late snack Jimmy Cleary always ordered a hero.

How would I have known that? Ask him what he wants.

She looked up. The only light came from the refrigerator but her eyes were adjusting to the darkness. She could clearly see the unmistakable square jaw that toughened Jimmy Cleary's face, and the anger and confusion in his expression. Her mouth dry with fear, she whispered, "What kind of sandwich do you want? Turkey? Ham? I've got whole wheat bread or Italian rolls."

She could sense that she passed the first test.

"Everything. The works on a roll."

She felt the cord loosen slightly. She put the kettle on to boil. She made the sandwich swiftly, piling turkey and ham on top of cheese, spreading the lettuce, gobbing mayonnaise and mustard across the roll.

He made her sit next to him at the table. She poured coffee for herself, forced herself to sip. The cord was biting into her neck. She moved her hand to loosen it.

"Don't touch that." He released it slightly.

"Thank you." She watched him wolf the sandwich.

Talk to him. You've got to convince him before it's too late.

"I think you told me your name but I didn't really get it."

He swallowed the last bit of sandwich. "On the marquee it's James Cleary. My agent and my friends call me Jimmy."

He was gulping the coffee. How could she make him believe her, trust her? From where she was sitting Caroline

25

could see the outline of the front closet. It had been almost closed before. That was where he must have been hiding. Sean had wanted to stay with her. If only she had let him stay. In those first couple of years after Lisa's death, there had been times when it seemed too much of a struggle to get through the day. Only the harsh demands of law school had kept her from sinking into suicidal depression. Now she could see Sean's face, so inexpressibly dear. I want to live, she thought. I want the rest of my life.

Jimmy Cleary felt better. He hadn't realized how hungry he was. In a way this was better than last time. Now he was acting out a cat-and-mouse scene. Now he was the judge. Was this Caroline? Maybe he hadn't made a mistake last time. But if he'd wasted Caroline, why hadn't the jinx been lifted? He finished the coffee. His fingers curled around the end of the cord, drawing it a hairbreadth tighter. Reaching over, he turned on the table lamp. He wanted to be able to study her face. "So tell me," he said easily. "Why should I believe you? And if I believe you, why should I let you live?"

Sean undressed and showered. In the bathroom mirror he looked at himself intently. He'd be thirty-four in ten days. Caroline would be twenty-seven the next day. They'd celebrate their birthdays in Venice. It would be good to sit in St. Mark's Square with her, to sip wine and hear the sweet sounds of the violins and watch the gondolas glide by. It was an image that had occurred to him several times in the past few weeks. Tonight it was as though he was drawing a blank. That picture simply wouldn't form.

He *had* to talk to Caroline. Wrapping a thick bath towel around him, he went to the bedside phone. It was nearly midnight. Even so, he dialed her number. The blazes with making excuses, he thought. I'll just tell her that I love her.

"It's not easy to be a twin." Caroline tilted her head so she could look directly into Jimmy Cleary's face. "My sister and I fought a lot. I used to call her the Duchess. She was so bossy. Even when we were little, she'd do things and blame me. I ended up hating her. That's why we went to colleges at opposite ends of the continent. I wanted to get away from her. I was her shadow, her mirror image, a nonperson. That last night she wanted to watch television and her set was broken, so she made me change rooms. When I found her that morning, I guess I just collapsed. But you see, even my mother and father didn't realize the mistake."

Caroline widened her eyes. She dropped her voice, making it intimate, confidential. "You're an actor, Jimmy. You can understand. When I came to they were calling me Caroline. You know the first words my mother said when I woke up were 'Oh, Caroline, we thank God it wasn't you.'"

Very good. You're getting to him.

She was six again. They were playing on the foundation. Lisa was running faster and faster. Caroline had looked down and gotten dizzy. But she'd still tried to keep up with her.

Jimmy was enjoying himself. He felt like a casting agent telling a hopeful to give him a cold reading. "So just like that you decided to be Caroline. How did you get away with it? Caroline went to Rawlings. What happened when Caroline's friends from Rawlings showed up?"

Caroline finished her own coffee. She could see the glints of madness in Jimmy Cleary's eyes. "It really wasn't hard. Shock. That was the excuse. I pretended not to remember lots of people we both knew. The doctors called it psychological amnesia. Everyone was very understanding."

Either she was a darn good actress or she was telling the truth. Jimmy was intrigued. He started to feel some of his anger fading. This girl was different from Caroline. Softer. Nicer. He felt a kinship with her, a regretful kinship. No matter what, he couldn't let her live. The only trouble was that if he had killed Caroline, if she wasn't lying—and he still wasn't sure—why hadn't the jinx been lifted five years ago?

Those cute red-and-white pajamas she was wearing. He laid his hand on her arm, then withdrew it. He had a sudden thought. "How about Wexford? How come you got together with him?"

"We just bumped into each other. I heard him call 'Caroline,' and I knew it was someone I was supposed to know. He told me his name as soon as he caught up with me jogging and in the next breath said something about having me in class, so I just faked it."

27

Remind Jimmy that Sean didn't bother with the real Caroline at Rawlings. Point out that he fell for you right away.

Jimmy shifted restlessly. Caroline said, "I can't tell you how many times Sean has said that I'm a much nicer person now. That's because I'm not the same person. Don't you love it? I'm glad you're sharing my secret, Jimmy. For the last five years you've been my secret benefactor, and at last I'm getting to know you. Would you like more coffee?"

Was she trying to snow him? Did she mean it? He touched her elbow. "More coffee sounds fine." He stood behind her, slightly to the side, as she turned the heat under the kettle. A very pretty girl. But he realized he couldn't let her live. He'd finish the coffee, bring her back into the bedroom and kill her. First he'd explain to her about the jinx. He glanced at the clock. It was 12:30. He'd killed the other sister at 12:40, so the timing was perfect. An image came into his mind of how the other girl had reached out her hands as though she wanted to claw him, how her eyes had blazed and bulged. Sometimes he dreamed about that. In the daytime the memory made him feel good. At night it made him break into a sweat.

The phone rang.

Caroline's hand gripped the handle of the kettle convulsively. She knew it would be Sean. Other nights when he'd sensed that she was terribly down and probably not sleeping, he'd phoned.

Convince Jimmy you've got to answer the telephone. You've got to let Sean know that you need him.

The phone rang a second, a third time.

Sweat glistened on Jimmy's forehead and upper lip. "Forget it," he said.

"Jimmy, I'm sure it's Sean. If I don't answer he'll think there's something wrong. I don't want him here. I want to talk to you."

Jimmy considered. If that was Wexford she was probably telling the truth. The phone rang again. It was attached to an answering machine. Jimmy pushed the button that made the conversation audible, picked up the receiver and handed it to her. He tightened the cord so that it bit into her throat.

Caroline knew she could not allow her voice to sound

shaky. "Hello." She managed to sound sleepy and was rewarded by a slight relaxing of the pressure on her neck.

"Caroline, honey, you were asleep. I'm sorry. I was worried that you were feeling pretty low. I know what tonight means to you."

"No, I'm glad you called. I wasn't really asleep. I was just starting to drift off." What can I tell him? Caroline wondered desperately.

The dress. Your wedding dress.

"It's kind of late," she heard Sean say. "Did you finish packing tonight after all?"

Jimmy tapped her shoulder and nodded.

"Yes. I felt wide awake, so I finished it."

Jimmy was looking impatient. He signaled for her to cut it short. Caroline bit her lip. If she didn't carry this off, it was the end. "Sean, I love you for calling and I'm really fine. I'll be ready at seven-thirty. Just one thing. When they packed my dress, did you remember to ask them to be sure to put lots of tissue in the sleeves so they wouldn't wrinkle?" She thought, don't let Sean give me away.

Sean felt his fingers holding the receiver go clammy. The dress. Caroline's dress did not have sleeves. And there was something else. Her voice had a hollow sound. She wasn't in bed. She was on the kitchen phone and the conference button was on. She wasn't alone. With a supreme effort he kept his voice steady. "Honey, I can swear on a stack of Bibles that the saleslady said something about that. I think your mother had called to remind her too. Now listen, get some sleep. I'll see you in the morning and remember, I love you." He managed to put the receiver down without letting it bang, then dropped the towel and pulled his sweat suit from the closet. The keys to Caroline's apartment were on the dresser with his car keys. Should he take the time to call the police? The phone in his car. He'd call them while he was on the way. Dear God, he thought, please. . . .

Sean had understood. Caroline replaced the receiver and looked at Jimmy. "You did a good job," he told her. "And you know, I'm starting to believe you." He led her back into the bedroom and forced her to lie down. He laid his arm across her, exactly as he had held down the sister. Then he

29

explained what his teacher, Cory Zola, had told him about the jinx. "We were doing a dueling scene in class last week, and I guess I was pretty mad. I cut the other student. Zola really got upset with me. I tried to explain that I'd been thinking about this jinx someone put on me and how it's spoiling everything. He told me to stay away from class until I'd gotten rid of it. So, even if I believe you that I got Caroline last time, I still have to get rid of that feeling because I can't go back to class until I'm free of it. And in my book, Lisa—that's the real name, huh?—you inherited it."

His eyes glittered. The expression was vacant, cold. He is mad, Caroline thought. It will take Sean fifteen minutes to get here. Three minutes gone. Twelve minutes more. Lisa, help me.

Brian Kent is the jinx. Strangers on a Train.

Her mouth was so dry. His face was so near hers. She could smell the perspiration that was dripping from his body. She felt his fingers begin to pull the cord. She managed to sound matter-of-fact. "Killing me won't solve anything. Brian Kent is the jinx, not me. If he's out of the way, you'll have your chance. And if I kill him you'll have just as big a hold on me as I have on you."

The astonished sucking in of his breath gave her hope. She touched his hand. "Stop fooling with that cord, Jimmy, and listen to me for two minutes. Let me sit up." Again the memory of playing follow-the-leader on the foundation of that new house ran through her mind. At one point they'd come to a gaping space left for a window. Lisa had jumped over. Caroline, a few steps behind her, had hesitated, closed her eyes, and jumped, barely clearing the opening. She was taking a jump now. If she failed, it was all over. Sean was coming. She knew it. She had to stay alive for the next eleven minutes.

Jimmy released his arm, allowing her to sit up. She drew her legs against her body and locked her hands around her knees. The cord was digging against her neck muscles but she didn't dare ask him to ease it. "Jimmy, you told me that your big problem is that you're too much like Brian Kent. Suppose something happened to Brian? They'd need to have a replacement. So, become him. Replace him the way I became Caroline. He has a sudden accident, they'll be frantic to find someone to step into that movie. Why shouldn't it be you?"

Jimmy shook the sweat from his forehead. She was suggesting a new interpretation of the role Brian was playing in his life. He'd always concentrated on becoming a star, becoming bigger than Brian, surpassing him, getting a better table in the restaurants, watching him fade. Never once had he thought about Brian just disappearing from the scene. And even if he killed this girl, this Lisa, because now he believed she was Lisa, Brian Kent would still be signing contracts, posing for spreads in *People* magazine. And worse, agents would still be telling him that he was a Brian Kent type.

Did he believe her? With her tongue, Caroline tried to moisten her lips. They were so dry it was hard to talk. "If you kill me now, they'll find you. Jimmy, the cops aren't dumb. They always questioned whether or not the wrong twin was killed."

He was listening.

"Jimmy, we can bring off *Strangers on a Train*. You remember the plot. Two people exchange murders. There's no motive. The difference is, we'll carry it off. You've already done your part. You got Caroline out of the way for me. Now let me get rid of Brian Kent for you."

Strangers on a Train. Jimmy had done a scene from that movie in class. He'd been great. Cory Zola had said, "Jimmy, you're a natural." His eyes flickered over her face. Look at her, smiling at him. She was a cool one. If she'd gotten away with convincing her family she was Caroline, she might be capable of setting up Brian Kent and pulling it off. But what insurance did he have that she wouldn't scream for the cops the minute he left her? He asked her that.

"Why, Jimmy, you have the best insurance in the world. You know I'm Lisa. They never checked Caroline's fingerprints against our birth records. You could give me away. Do you know what that would do to my parents, to Sean? Do you think they'd ever forgive me?" She looked directly into Jimmy's eyes, awaiting his judgment.

Sean ran from the house, then bit his lip in wild frustration. Caroline's car was blocking his. He wanted to be able to phone the police on the way. He ran back into the house, grabbed her car keys, pulled her car out of the way and got into his own. As he backed with furious speed onto the road, he ripped the car phone off its cradle and dialed 911.

Jimmy was experiencing a dazzling sense of rebirth. How many times in L.A. had he seen Brian Kent drive by in that Porsche of his? They'd gone to school together for four years, but Brian never gave him more than a cool nod if they bumped into each other. How much better if Brian didn't exist. And Lisa—she was Lisa, he was convinced of that—was right. He would have a hold on her. Deliberately he released his grip on the cord but did not remove it from her neck. "Let's say I believe you. How would you get him?"

Caroline fought to keep back the lightheaded sensation that came with hope. What could she tell him?

You'll go to the Coast. Look up Brian.

Desperately she searched for a plausible plot. Again she was six, skimming over the foundation. The gaping spaces between the cinder blocks were getting wider.

Poison. Poison.

"Sean has a friend, a professor who specializes in the history of medicine. Last week at dinner, he was talking about how many absolutely undetectable poisons there are. He described one of them, exactly how to prepare it from things you have in your medicine chest. A few drops is all it takes. Next month when I come back from my honeymoon, I have to go to California to depose a witness. I'll call Brian. After all, I—I mean Caroline gave him his big break. Right?"

Be careful.

She had slipped. But Jimmy didn't seem to notice. He was listening intently. The perspiration had caused his hair to curl so that it lay in damp ringlets on his forehead. She didn't remember that his hair was that curly. He must have had a body wave. Now it was cut exactly like the recent picture she'd seen of Brian Kent. "I'm sure he'd be glad to see me," she continued. As though stretching her legs from cramping, she eased them over the side of the bed.

His hand reached for and encircled the end of the cord. She slipped her hand over his. "Jimmy, there's a poison that takes a week, ten days to act. The symptoms don't even begin for three or four days. Even if there's an inquiry, who would connect the fact that Brian had coffee with an old college friend, who just married a Princeton professor, with a murderer? It's the perfect scenario."

Jimmy realized he was nodding in assent. The night had turned into a dream, a dream that would start his whole life all over. He could trust her. With dazzling clarity he accepted the truth of what she had pointed out to him. As long as Brian Kent was alive, he, who was the greatest actor in the world, would go unnoticed. The night-light in the bedroom became a footlight. The darkened living room was the theater where the audience was sitting. He was standing on stage. The audience was clapping its approval. He savored the moment, then chucked Caroline—no, Lisa—under the chin. "I do believe you," he whispered. "When exactly are you coming to California?"

Hang on. You're almost safe.

They were running faster and faster over the foundation. She couldn't keep up. Caroline heard her voice crack as she answered, "The second week in July."

Jimmy's remaining doubts vanished. Kent was due to start his new movie the first of August. If he was dead by then, they'd be frantic looking for a replacement.

He stood up and pulled Caroline to her feet. "Let me get that thing off your neck. Just remember it's right here in my pocket in case I ever need it again. I'm leaving now. We've got a deal. But if you don't keep your part of the bargain, some night when your professor is away or some afternoon when you stop for a red light, I'll be there."

Caroline felt the cord loosen, felt him pull it over her head. Hysterical sobs of relief were breaking in her throat. "It's a deal," she managed to say.

He dug his fingers into her shoulders and kissed her on the mouth. "I don't seal agreements with handshakes," he said. "Too bad I haven't got more time. I could go for you." His caricature of a smile became a bemused, wide-toothed grin. "I feel like the jinx is lifted already. Come on." He walked her to the back door. He reached up his hand to unfasten the chain.

Caroline caught a glimpse of the clock on the kitchen

wall. It was twelve minutes since Sean had phoned. In the next thirty seconds Jimmy would be gone and she could chain and barricade the door. In the next few minutes Sean would be there.

Again the memory of being six, running on the foundation. She had glanced down. It was eight or ten feet to the ground. Jutting pieces of broken concrete were lying there. Lisa had made the last jump over a wide space left for a door. . . .

Jimmy opened the door. She could feel the cool rush of night air on her face. He turned to her. "I know you never had the chance to see me perform, but I am a truly great actor."

"I know you're a great actor," Caroline heard herself say. "After *Death of a Salesman,* didn't everyone in school call you Biff?"

On the foundation she had hesitated that one moment before she made the final jump after Lisa. She had lost momentum. She had tumbled and her forehead had smashed against the concrete. With sickening fear she knew she had once again failed to follow Lisa.

The door slammed shut. For a split second she and Jimmy stared at each other. "Lisa couldn't have known that," Jimmy whispered. "You've been lying to me. You *are* Caroline." His hands lunged for her neck. She tried to scream as she backed away from him, turned and stumbled toward the front door. But only a low moan came from her lips.

Sean raced through the quiet streets. The 911 operator was asking him his name, where he was calling from, what was the nature of the emergency. "Get a squad car to eighty-one Priscilla Lane, apartment one-A," he shouted. "Never mind how I know there's something wrong. Get a car there."

"And what is the nature of the emergency?" the operator repeated.

Jimmy's hand slammed onto the front door as she tried to turn the lock. Caroline ducked past him and ran around the club chair. In the shadowy light she caught a glimpse of herself in the mirror over the couch, his looming presence behind her. His breath was hot on her neck. If she could only live for a minute more, Sean would be here. Before she could complete the thought, Jimmy had vaulted over the club chair. He was in front of her. She saw the cord in his hands. He spun her around. She felt her hair pulled back, the cord on her neck, saw their reflection in the mirror over the couch. She dropped to her knees and the cord tightened. She tried to crawl away from him, felt him leaning over her. "It's all over, Caroline. It's really your turn to be the victim."

Sean turned into Caroline's street. The brakes screeched as he jammed them on in front of her house. From a distance he could hear sirens. He ran to the door and tried the knob. With one fist he pounded on the door while he groped in his pocket for her keys. He remembered that the damn security lock had not been installed properly. You had to pull the door toward you before it would turn. In his anxiety, he could not match up the cylinder and the lock. It took three turns of the key before the lock released. Then the other key for the regular lock. Please. . . .

She was on her knees, clawing at the cord. It was choking her. She could hear Sean pounding on the door, calling her. So close, so close. Her eyes widened as the cord cut off her breath. Waves of blackness were rolling over her. Lisa . . . Lisa . . . I tried.

Don't pull away. Lean backward. Lean backward, I tell you.

In a final effort to save her life, Caroline forced herself to bend backward, to slide her body toward Jimmy instead of pulling away from him. For an instant the pressure on her throat eased. She gulped in one breath before the cord began to tighten again.

Jimmy shut out the sounds of the pounding and shouting. Nothing in the whole world mattered except to kill this woman who had ruined his career. Nothing.

The key turned. Sean slammed the door open. His gaze fell on the mirror over the couch, and the blood drained from his face.

Her eyes were blazing, bulging, her mouth was open and

35

gaping, her palms extended, her fingernails like claws. A bulky figure in a sweat suit was bending over her, strangling her with a cord. For an instant Sean was rooted, unable to move. Then the intruder looked up. Their eyes met in the mirror. As Sean watched, in that one second, still unable to move, he saw the horrified expression that came into the other man's face, watched him drop the cord from his hands, throw his arms over his face.

"Stay away from me!" Jimmy screamed. "Don't come any nearer. Stay away."

Sean spun around. Caroline was on the floor, clawing at the cord that was choking her. Sean dove across the room, butted the man who had been attacking her. The force of the blow sent Jimmy back against the window. The sound of shattering glass mingled with his screams and the wail of sirens as patrol cars screeched to a halt.

Caroline felt hands yanking at the cord. She heard a low moaning sound come from her throat. Then the cord released and a rush of air filled her lungs. Darkness, sweet, welcome darkness, enveloped her.

When she awoke, she was lying on the couch, an icy cloth around her neck. Sean was sitting by her, chafing her hands. The room was filled with policemen. "Jimmy?" her voice was a harsh croaking sound.

"They took him away. Oh, my darling." Sean lifted her up, wrapped her in his arms, laid her head against his chest, smoothed her hair.

"Why did he start screaming?" she whispered. "What happened? In another few seconds I'd have been dead."

"He saw the same thing I did. You were reflected in the mirror over the couch. He's completely nuts. He thought that he was seeing Lisa. He thought she was coming for revenge."

Sean would not leave her. After the policemen were gone, he lay beside her on the roomy couch, pulled the afghan over them and held her close. "Try to get some sleep." Safe in his arms, beyond exhaustion, she did manage to drift off.

At 6:30 he woke her up. "You'd better start getting ready," he told her. "If you're sure you're okay, I'll run home and get showered and dressed." Brilliant sunlight spilled through the room.

Five years ago this morning, she had walked into Lisa's room and found her. This morning, she had awakened in Sean's arms. She reached up and held his face in her hands, loving the faint stubble on his cheeks. "I'm all right. Really."

When Sean left, she went into the bedroom. Deliberately she stared at the bed, remembering how it had felt to open her eyes and see Jimmy Cleary. She showered, letting the hot water run for long minutes over her body, her hair, wanting all trace of his presence to be washed away. She dressed in a khaki-colored jumpsuit, cinching a braided belt around her waist. As she brushed her hair, she saw the reddish-purple welt around her neck. Quickly she turned away.

It was as though time were in abeyance, waiting for her to complete what must be completed. She packed her suitcase, set it with her handbag near the door. Then she did what she knew she had to do.

She knelt on the floor just as she had been kneeling when Jimmy Cleary tried to strangle her. She arched her body backward and stared at the mirror. It was as she had expected. The bottom of the mirror was a fraction of an inch above her hairline. There was no way she could have been reflected there. Jimmy had been right: He had seen Lisa.

"Lisa, Lisa, thank you," she whispered. There was no feeling of an answer. Lisa was gone, as Caroline had known she would be gone. For the last time the thought that she had been the cause of Lisa's death filled her consciousness and then was vanquished. It had been an act of fate, and she would not insult Lisa's memory by dwelling on it. She stood up, and now she was reflected in the mirror. Tenderly she raised her fingertips to her lips and blew a kiss. "Goodbye. I love you," she said aloud.

In the street she heard a car pull up. Sean's car. Caroline hurried to the door, flung it open, pushed out her suitcase and purse, reached for the plastic-wrapped garment bag that enveloped her wedding gown, and carrying it cradled in her arms, slammed the door behind her and ran to meet him.

*Mary Higgins Clark was born in New York in 1929, was edu-
cated at Ward Secretarial School and Fordham University, and worked
as a stewardess for Pan American Airways before starting
as a radio writer. She produced her first novel,* Where Are the
Children? *in 1975, which—along with her other novels* A Cry in
the Night *and* Stillwatch—*hit the best seller lists. She added the
icy touch of the supernatural to her work in* The Anastasia Syndrome and Other Stories, *in which her heroines deal with murderous ghosts of the past.*

When Ed thought that by committing suicide he was putting an end to his troubles, he didn't realize that his real problems were just beginning.

TWO

This Is Death
Donald E. Westlake

It's hard not to believe in ghosts when you are one. I hanged myself in a fit of truculence—stronger than pique, but not so dignified as despair—and regretted it before the thing was well begun. The instant I kicked the chair away, I wanted it back, but gravity was turning my former wish to its present command; the chair would not right itself from where it lay on the floor, and my 193 pounds would not cease to urge downward from the rope thick around my neck.

There was pain, of course, quite horrible pain centered in my throat, but the most astounding thing was the way my cheeks seemed to swell. I could barely see over their round red hills, my eyes staring in agony at the door, *willing* someone to come in and rescue me, though I knew there was no one in the house, and in any event the door was carefully locked. My kicking legs caused me to twist and turn, so that sometimes I faced the door and sometimes the window, and my shivering hands struggled with the rope so deep in my flesh I could barely find it and most certainly could not pull it loose.

I was frantic and terrified, yet at the same time my brain possessed a cold corner of aloof observation. I seemed now to be everywhere in the room at once, within my writhing body but also without, seeing my frenzied spasms, the thick rope, the heavy beam, the mismatched pair of lit bedside lamps throwing my convulsive double shadow on the walls, the closed locked door, the white-curtained window with its shade drawn all the way down. *This is death,* I thought, and I no longer wanted it, now that the choice was gone forever.

My name is—was—Edward Thornburn, and my dates are 1938-1977. I killed myself just a month before my fortieth birthday, though I don't believe the well-known pangs of that milestone had much if anything to do with my action. I blame it all (as I blamed most of the errors and failures of my life) on my sterility. Had I been able to father children my marriage would have remained strong, Emily would not have been unfaithful to me, and I would not have taken my own life in a final fit of truculence.

The setting was the guestroom in our house in Barnstaple, Connecticut, and the time was just after seven P.M.; deep twilight, at this time of year. I had come home from the office—I was a realtor, a fairly lucrative occupation in Connecticut, though my income had been falling off recently— shortly before six, to find the note on the kitchen table: "Antiquing with Greg. Afraid you'll have to make your own dinner. Sorry. Love, Emily."

Greg was the one; Emily's lover. He owned an antique shop out on the main road toward New York, and Emily filled a part of her days as his ill-paid assistant. I knew what they did together in the back of the shop on those long midweek afternoons when there were no tourists, no antique collectors to disturb them. I knew, and I'd known for more than three years, but I had never decided how to deal with my knowledge. The fact was, I blamed myself, and therefore I had no way to *behave* if the ugly subject were ever to come into the open.

So I remained silent, but not content. I was discontent, unhappy, angry, resentful—truculent.

I'd tried to kill myself before. At first with the car, by steering it into an oncoming truck (I swerved at the last second, amid howling horns) and by driving it off a cliff into the Connecticut River (I slammed on the brakes at the very brink, and sat covered in perspiration for half an hour before backing away) and finally by stopping athwart one of the few level crossings left in this neighborhood. But no train came for twenty minutes, and my truculence wore off, and I drove home.

Later I tried to slit my wrists, but found it impossible to push sharp metal into my own skin. Impossible. The vision of my naked wrist and that shining steel so close together washed my truculence completely out of my mind. Until the next time.

With the rope; and then I succeeded. Oh, totally, oh, fully I succeeded. My legs kicked at air, my fingernails clawed at my throat, my bulging eyes stared out over my swollen purple cheeks, my tongue thickened and grew bulbous in my mouth, my body jigged and jangled like a toy at the end of a string, and the pain was excruciating, horrible, not to be endured. I can't endure it, I thought, it can't be endured. Much worse than knife slashings was the knotted strangled pain in my throat, and my head ballooned with pain, pressure outward, my face turning black, my eyes no longer human, the pressure in my head building and building as though I would explode. Endless horrible pain, not to be endured, but going on and on.

My legs kicked more feebly. My arms sagged, my hands dropped to my side, my fingers twisted uselessly against my sopping trouser legs, my head hung at an angle from the rope, I turned more slowly in the air, like a broken windchime on a breezeless day. The pains lessened, in my throat and head, but never entirely stopped.

And now I saw that my distended eyes had become lusterless, gray. The moisture had dried on the eyeballs, they were as dead as stones. And yet I could see them, my own eyes, and when I widened my vision I could see my entire body, turning, hanging, no longer twitching, and with horror I realized I was dead.

But *present*. Dead, but still present, with the scraping ache still in my throat and the bulging pressure still in my head. Present, but no longer in that used-up clay, that hanging meat; I was suffused through the room, like indirect lighting, everywhere present but without a source. What happens now? I wondered, dulled by fear and strangeness and the continuing pains, and I waited, like a hovering mist, for whatever would happen next.

But nothing happened. I waited; the body became utterly still; the double shadow on the wall showed no vibration; the bedside lamps continued to burn; the door remained shut and the window shade drawn; and nothing happened.

What *now*? I craved to scream the question aloud, but I could not. My throat ached, but I had no throat. My mouth burned, but I had no mouth. Every final strain and struggle of my body remained imprinted in my mind, but I had no body and no brain and no *self,* no substance. No power to speak, no power to move myself, no power to remove myself from this room and this suspended corpse. I could only wait here, and wonder, and go on waiting.

There was a digital clock on the dresser opposite the bed, and when it first occurred to me to look at it the numbers were 7:21—perhaps twenty minutes after I'd kicked the chair away, perhaps fifteen minutes since I'd died. Shouldn't something happen, shouldn't some *change* take place?

The clock read 9:11 when I heard Emily's Volkswagen drive around to the back of the house. I had left no note, having nothing I wanted to say to anyone and in any event believing my own dead body would be eloquent enough, but I hadn't thought I would be *present* when Emily found me. I was justified in my action, however much I now regretted having taken it, I was justified, I knew I was justified, but I didn't want to see her face when she came through that door. She had wronged me, she was the cause of it, she would have to know that as well as I, but I didn't want to see her face.

The pains increased, in what had been my throat, in what had been my head. I heard the back door slam, far away downstairs, and I stirred like air currents in the room, but I didn't leave. I couldn't leave.

"Ed? Ed? It's me, hon!"

I know it's you. I must go away now, I can't stay here, I must go away. Is there a God? Is this my soul, this hovering presence? *Hell* would be better than this, take me away to Hell or wherever I'm to go, don't leave me here!

She came up the stairs, calling again, walking past the closed guestroom door. I heard her go into our bedroom, heard her call my name, heard the beginnings of apprehension in her voice. She went by again, out there in the hall, went downstairs, became quiet.

What was she doing? Searching for a note perhaps, some message from me. Looking out the window, seeing again my Chevrolet, knowing I must be home. Moving through the rooms of this old house, the original structure a barn nearly 200 years old, converted by some previous owner just after the Second World War, bought by me twelve years ago, furnished by Emily—and Greg—from their interminable, damnable, awful antiques. Shaker furniture, Colonial furniture, hooked rugs and quilts, the old yellow pine tables, the faint sense always of being in some slightly shabby minor museum, this house that I had bought but never loved. I'd bought it for Emily, I did everything for Emily, because I knew I could never do the one thing for Emily that mattered. I could never give her a child.

She was good about it, of course. Emily *is* good, I never blamed her, never completely blamed *her* instead of myself. In the early days of our marriage she made a few wistful references, but I suppose she saw the effect they had on me, and for a long time she has said nothing. But I have known.

The beam from which I had hanged myself was a part of the original building, a thick hand-hewed length of aged timber eleven inches square, chevroned with the marks of the hatchet that had shaped it. A strong beam, it would support my weight forever. It would support my weight until I was found and cut down. Until I was found.

The clock read 9:23 and Emily had been in the house twelve minutes when she came upstairs again, her steps quick and light on the old wood, approaching, pausing, stopping. "Ed?"

The doorknob turned.

The door was locked, of course, with the key on the inside. She'd have to break it down, have to call someone else to break it down, perhaps she wouldn't be the one to find me after all. Hope rose in me, and the pains receded.

"Ed? Are you in there?" She knocked at the door, rattled the knob, called my name several times more, then abruptly turned and ran away downstairs again, and after a moment I heard her voice, murmuring and unclear. She had called someone, on the phone.

Greg, I thought, and the throat-rasp filled me, and I wanted this to be the end. I wanted to be taken away, dead body and living soul, taken away. I wanted everything to be finished.

She stayed downstairs, waiting for him, and I stayed upstairs, waiting for them both. Perhaps she already knew what she'd find up here, and that's why she waited below.

I didn't mind about Greg, about being present when he came in. I didn't mind about *him*. It was Emily I minded.

The clock read 9:44 when I heard tires on the gravel at the side of the house. He entered, I heard them talking down there, the deeper male voice slow and reassuring, the lighter female voice quick and frightened, and then they came up together, neither speaking. The doorknob turned, jiggled, rattled, and Greg's voice called, "Ed?"

After a little silence Emily said, "He wouldn't— He wouldn't *do* anything, would he?"

"Do anything?" Greg sounded almost annoyed at the question. "What do you mean, do anything?"

"He's been so depressed, he's— Ed!" And forcibly the door was rattled, the door was shaken in its frame.

"Emily, don't. Take it easy."

"I shouldn't have called you," she said. "Ed, *please!*"

"Why not? For heaven's sake, Emily—"

"Ed, *please* come out, don't scare me like this!"

"Why *shouldn't* you call me, Emily?"

"Ed isn't stupid, Greg. He's—"

There was then a brief silence, pregnant with the hint of murmuring. They thought me still alive in here, they didn't want me to hear Emily say, "He *knows,* Greg, he know about us."

The murmurings sifted and shifted, and then Greg spoke loudly, "That's ridiculous. Ed? Come out, Ed, let's talk this over." And the doorknob rattled and clattered, and he sounded annoyed when he said, "We must get in, that's all. Is there another key?"

"I think all the locks up here are the same. Just a minute."

They were. A simple skeleton key would open any interior door in the house. I waited, listening, knowing Emily had gone off to find another key, knowing they would soon come in together, and I felt such terror and revulsion for Emily's entrance that I could feel myself shimmer in the room, like a reflection in a warped mirror. Oh, can I at least stop seeing? In life I had eyes, but also eyelids, I could shut out the intolerable, but now I was only a presence, a total presence, I *could not* stop my awareness.

The rasp of key in lock was like rough metal edges in my throat; my memory of a throat. The pain flared in me, and through it I heard Emily asking what was wrong, and Greg answering, "The key's in it, on the other side."

"Oh, dear God! Oh, Greg, what has he done?"

"We'll have to take the door off its hinges," he told her. "Call Tony. Tell him to bring the toolbox."

"Can't you push the key through?"

Of course he could, but he said, quite determinedly, "Go on, Emily," and I realized then he had no intention of taking the door down. He simply wanted her away when the door was first opened. Oh, very good, *very* good!

"All right," she said doubtfully, and I heard her go away to phone Tony. A beetle-browed young man with great masses of black hair and olive complexion, Tony lived in Greg's house and was a kind of handyman. He did work around the house and was also (according to Emily) very good at restoration of antique furniture; stripping paint, re-assembling broken parts, that sort of thing.

There was now a renewed scraping and rasping at the lock, as Greg struggled to get the door open before Emily's return. I found myself feeling unexpected warmth and liking toward Greg. He wasn't a bad person. Would he marry her now? They could live in this house, he'd had more to do with its furnishing than I. Or would this room hold too grim a memory, would Emily have to sell the house, live else-where? She might have to sell at a low price; as a realtor, I knew the difficulty in selling a house where a suicide has taken place. No matter how much they may joke about it, people are still afraid of the supernatural. Many of them would believe this room was haunted.

It was then I finally realized the room *was* haunted. With me! *I'm a ghost,* I thought, thinking the word for the first time, in utter blank astonishment. I'm a ghost.

Oh, how dismal! To hover here, to be a boneless fleshless aching *presence* here, to be a kind of ectoplasmic mildew seeping through the days and nights, alone, unending, a stupid pain-racked misery-filled observer of the comings and goings of strangers—she *would* sell the house, she'd have to, I was sure of that. Was this my punishment? The punishment of the suicide, the solitary hell of him who takes his own life. To remain forever a sentient nothing, bound by a force greater than gravity itself to the place of one's finish.

I was distracted from this misery by a sudden agitation in the key on this side of the lock. I saw it quiver and jiggle like something alive, and then it popped out—it seemed to *leap* out, itself a suicide leaping from a cliff—and clattered to the floor, and an instant later the door was pushed open and Greg's ashen face stared at my own purple face, and after the astonishment and horror, his expression shifted to revulsion—and contempt?—and he backed out, slamming the door. Once more the key turned in the lock, and I heard him hurry away downstairs.

The clock read 9:58. *Now* he was telling her. *Now* he was giving her a drink to calm her. *Now* he was phoning the police. *Now* he was talking to her about whether or not to admit their affair to the police; what would they decide?

"Noooooooooo!"

The clock read 10:07. What had taken so long? Hadn't he even called the police yet?

She was coming up the stairs, stumbling and rushing, she was pounding on the door, screaming my name. I shrank into the corners of the room, I *felt* the thuds of her fists against the door, I cowered from her. She can't come in, dear God don't let her in! I don't care what she's done, I don't care about anything, just don't let her see me! *Don't let me see her!*

Greg joined her. She screamed at him, he persuaded her, she raved, he argued, she demanded, he denied. "Give me the key. Give me the key."

Surely he'll hold out, surely he'll take her away, surely he's stronger, more forceful.

He gave her the key.

No. *This* cannot be endured. *This* is the horror beyond all else. She came in, she walked into the room, and the sound she made will always live inside me. That cry wasn't human; it was the howl of every creature that has *ever* despaired. *Now* I know what despair is, and why I called my own state mere truculence.

Now that it was too late, Greg tried to restrain her, tried to hold her shoulders and draw her from the room, but she pulled away and crossed the room toward—not toward *me*.

I was everywhere in the room, driven by pain and remorse, and Emily walked toward the carcass. She looked at it almost tenderly, she even reached up and touched its swollen cheek. "Oh, Ed," she murmured.

The pains were as violent now as in the moments before my death. The slashing torment in my throat, the awful distension in my head, they made me squirm in agony all over again; but I *could not* feel her hand on my cheek.

Greg followed her, touched her shoulder again, spoke her name, and immediately her face dissolved, she cried out once more and wrapped her arms around the corpse's legs and clung to it, weeping and gasping and uttering words too quick and broken to understand. Thank *God* they were too quick and broken to understand!

Greg, that fool, did finally force her away, though he had great trouble breaking her clasp on the body. But he succeeded, and pulled her out of the room and slammed the door, and for a little while the body swayed and turned, until it became still once more.

That was the worst. Nothing could be worse than that. The long days and nights here—how long must a stupid creature like myself *haunt* his death-place before release?—would be horrible, I knew that, but not so bad as this. Emily would survive, would sell the house, would slowly forget. (Even I would slowly forget.) She and Greg could marry. She was only 36, she could still be a mother.

For the rest of the night I heard her wailing, elsewhere in the house. The police did come at last, and a pair of grim silent white-coated men from the morgue entered the room to cut me—it—down. They bundled it like a broken toy into a large oval wicker basket with long wooden handles, and they carried it away.

I had thought I might be forced to stay with the body, I had feared the possibility of being buried with it, of spending eternity as a thinking nothingness in the black dark of a casket, but the body left the room and I remained behind.

A doctor was called. When the body was carried away the room door was left open, and now I could plainly hear the voices from downstairs. Tony was among them now, his characteristic surly monosyllable occasionally rumbling, but the main thing for a while was the doctor. He was trying to give Emily a sedative, but she kept wailing, she kept speaking high hurried frantic sentences as though she had too little time to say it all. "I did it!" she cried, over and over. "I did it! I'm to blame!"

Yes. That was the reaction I'd wanted, and expected, and here it was, and it was horrible. Everything I had desired in the last moments of my life had been granted to me, and they were all ghastly beyond belief. I *didn't* want to die! I *didn't* want to give Emily such misery! And more than all the rest I didn't want to be here, seeing and hearing it all.

They did quiet her at last, and then a policeman in a rumpled blue suit came into the room with Greg, and listened while Greg described everything that had happened. While Greg talked, the policeman rather grumpily stared at the remaining length of rope still knotted around the beam, and when Greg had finished the policeman said, "You're a close friend of his?"

"More of his wife. She works for me. I own The Bibelot, an antique shop out on the New York road."

"Mm. Why on earth did you let her in here?"

Greg smiled; a sheepish embarrassed expression. "She's stronger than I am," he said. "A more forceful personality. That's always been true."

It was with some surprise I realized it *was* true. Greg was something of a weakling, and Emily was very strong. (*I* had been something of a weakling, hadn't I? Emily was the strongest of us all.)

The policeman was saying, "Any idea why he'd do it?"

"I think he suspected his wife was having an affair with me." Clearly Greg had rehearsed this sentence, he'd much earlier come to the decision to say it and had braced himself for the moment. He blinked all the way through the statement, as though standing in a harsh glare.

The policeman gave him a quick shrewd look. "Were you?"

"Yes."

"She was getting a divorce?"

"No. She doesn't love me, she loved her husband."

"Then why sleep around?"

"Emily wasn't sleeping *around,*" Greg said, showing offense only with that emphasized word. "From time to time, and not very often, she was sleeping with me."

"Why?"

"For comfort." Greg too looked at the rope around the beam, as though it had become me and he was awkward speaking in its presence. "Ed wasn't an easy man to get along with," he said carefully. "He was moody. It was getting worse."

"Cheerful people don't kill themselves," the policeman said.

"Exactly. Ed was depressed most of the time, obscurely angry now and then. It was affecting his business, costing him clients. He made Emily miserable but she wouldn't leave him, she loved him. I don't know what she'll do now."

"You two won't marry?"

"Oh, no." Greg smiled, a bit sadly. "Do you think we murdered him, made it look like suicide so we could marry?"

"Not at all," the policeman said. "But what's the problem? You already married?"

"I am homosexual."

The policeman was no more astonished than I. He said, "I don't get it."

"I live with my friend; that young man downstairs. I am—capable—of a wider range, but my preferences are set. I am very fond of Emily, I felt sorry for her, the life she had with Ed. I told you our physical relationship was infrequent. And often not very successful."

Oh, Emily. Oh, poor Emily.

The policeman said, "Did Thornburn know you were, uh, that way?"

"I have no idea. I don't make a public point of it."

"All right." The policeman gave one more half-angry look around the room, then said, "Let's go."

They left. The door remained open, and I heard them continue to talk as they went downstairs, first the policeman asking, "Is there somebody to stay the night? Mrs. Thornburn shouldn't be alone."

"She has relatives in Great Barrington. I phoned them earlier. Somebody should be arriving within the hour."

"You'll stay until then? The doctor says she'll probably sleep, but just in case—"

"Of course."

That was all I heard. Male voices murmured a while longer from below, and then stopped. I heard cars drive away.

How complicated men and women are. How stupid are simple actions. I had never understood anyone, least of all myself.

The room was visited once more that night, by Greg, shortly after the police left. He entered, looking as offended and repelled as though the body were still here, stood the chair up on its legs, climbed on it, and with some difficulty untied the remnant of rope. This he stuffed partway into his pocket as he stepped down again to the floor, then returned the chair to its usual spot in the corner of the room, picked the key off the floor and put it in the lock, switched off both bedside lamps and left the room, shutting the door behind him.

Now I was in darkness, except for the faint line of light under the door, and the illuminated numerals of the clock. How long one minute is! That clock was my enemy, it dragged out every minute, it paused and waited and paused and waited till I could stand it no more, and then it waited longer, and *then* the next number dropped into place. Sixty times an hour, hour after hour, all night long. I couldn't stand one night of this, how could I stand eternity?

And how could I stand the torment and torture inside my brain? That was much worse now than the physical pain, which never entirely left me. I had been right about Emily and Greg, but at the same time I had been hopelessly brainlessly wrong. I had been right about my life, but wrong; right about my death, but wrong. How *much* I wanted to make amends, and how impossible it was to do anything any more, anything at all. My actions had all tended to this, and ended with this: black remorse, the most dreadful pain of all.

I had all night to think, and to feel the pains, and to wait without knowing what I was waiting for or when—or if— my waiting would ever end. Faintly I heard the arrival of Emily's sister and brother-in-law, the murmured conversation, then the departure of Tony and Greg. Not long afterward the guestroom door opened, but almost immediately closed again, no one having entered, and a bit after that the hall light went out, and now only the illuminated clock broke the darkness.

When next would I see Emily? Would she ever enter this room again? It wouldn't be as horrible as the first time, but it would surely be horror enough.

Dawn grayed the window shade, and gradually the room appeared out of the darkness, dim and silent and morose. Apparently it was a sunless day, which never got very bright. The day went on and on, featureless, each protracted minute marked by the clock. At times I dreaded someone's entering this room, at other times I prayed for something, anything—even the presence of Emily herself—to break this unending boring *absence*. But the day went on with no event, no sound, no activity anywhere—they must be keeping Emily sedated through this first day—and it wasn't until twilight, with the digital clock reading 6:52, that the door again opened and a person entered.

At first I didn't recognize him. An angry-looking man, blunt and determined, he came in with quick ragged steps, switched on both bedside lamps, then shut the door with rather more force than necessary, and turned the key in the lock. Truculent, his manner was, and when he turned from the door I saw with incredulity that he was *me*. Me! I wasn't dead, I was alive! But how could that be?

And what was that he was carrying? He picked up the chair from the corner, carried it to the middle of the room, stood on it—

No! No!

He tied the rope around the beam. The noose was already in the other end, which he slipped over his head and tightened around his neck.

Good God, *don't*!

He kicked the chair away.

The instant I kicked the chair away I wanted it back, but gravity was turning my former wish to its present command; the chair would not right itself from where it lay on the floor, and my 193 pounds would not cease to urge downward from the rope thick around my neck.

51

There was pain, of course, quite horrible pain centered in my throat, but the most astounding thing was the way my cheeks seemed to swell. I could barely see over their round red hills, my eyes staring in agony at the door, *willing* some-one to come in and rescue me, though I knew there was no one in the house, and in any event the door was carefully locked. My kicking legs caused me to twist and turn, so that sometimes I faced the door and sometimes the window, and my shivering hands struggled with the rope so deep in my flesh I could barely find it and most certainly could not pull it loose.

I was frantic and horrified, yet at the same time my brain possessed a cold corner of aloof observation. I seemed now to be everywhere in the room at once, within my writhing body but also without, seeing my frenzied spasms, the thick rope, the heavy beam, the mismatched pair of lit bedside lamps throwing my convulsive double shadow on the walls, the closed locked door, the white-curtained window with its shade drawn all the way down. *This is death.*

One of the masters of the hard-boiled detective mystery, Donald E. Westlake was born in New York in 1933. Educated at the State University of New York, Plattsburg, and Binghamton, he started writing full time after two years in the Air Force. In 1962, he be-gan the sixteen novels of the Parker series, starting with The Hunter, *and including* The Mourner, Deadly Edge, *and* Butcher's Moon. *His comedies include* God Save the Mark, *which won the Mystery Writers of America's Edgar. Westlake has also written works of fantasy and science fiction, including this one.*

Kostner wanted more than money—he got less.

THREE

Pretty Maggie Moneyeyes

Harlan Ellison

With an eight hole-card and a queen showing, with the dealer showing a four up, Kostner decided to let the house do the work. So he stood, and the dealer turned up. Six.

The dealer looked like something out of a 1935 George Raft film: Arctic diamond-chip eyes, manicured fingers long as a brain surgeon's, straight black hair slicked flat away from the pale forehead. He did not look up as he peeled them off. A three. Another three. Bam. A five. Bam. Twenty-one, and Kostner saw his last thirty dollars—six five-dollar chips—scraped on the edge of the cards, into the dealer's chip racks. Busted. Flat. Down and out in Las Vegas, Nevada. Playground of the Western World.

He slid off the comfortable stool-chair and turned his back on the blackjack table. The action was already starting again, like waves closing over a drowned man. He had been there, was gone, and no one had noticed. No one had seen a man blow the last tie with salvation. Kostner now had his choice: he could bum his way into Los Angeles and try to find something that resembled a new life . . . or he could go blow his brains out through the back of his head.

Neither choice showed much light or sense.

He thrust his hands deep into the pockets of his worn and dirty chinos, and started away down the line of slot machines clanging and rattling on the other side of the aisle between blackjack tables.

He stopped. He felt something in his pocket. Beside him, but all-engrossed, a fiftyish matron in electric lavender capris, high heels and Ship 'n' Shore blouse was working two

53

slots, loading and pulling one while waiting for the other to clock down. She was dumping quarters in a seemingly inexhaustible supply from a Dixie cup held in her left hand. There was a surrealistic presence to the woman. She was almost automated, not a flicker of expression on her face, the eyes fixed and unwavering. Only when the gong rang, someone down the line had pulled a jackpot, did she look up. And at that moment Kostner knew what was wrong and immoral and deadly about Vegas, about legalized gambling, about setting the traps all baited and open in front of the average human. The woman's face was gray with hatred, envy, lust and dedication to the game—in that timeless instant when she heard another drugged soul down the line winning a minuscule jackpot. A jackpot that would only lull the player with words like *luck* and *ahead of the game.* The jackpot lure; the sparkling, bobbling, many-colored wiggler in a sea of poor fish.

The thing in Kostner's pocket was a silver dollar.

He brought it out and looked at it.

The eagle was hysterical.

But Kostner pulled to an abrupt halt, only one half-footstep from the sign indicating the limits of Tap City. He was still with it. What the high-rollers called the *edge,* the *vigerish,* the fine hole-card. One buck. One cartwheel. Pulled out of the pocket not half as deep as the pit into which Kostner had just been about to plunge.

What the hell, he thought, and turned to the row of slot machines.

He had thought they'd all been pulled out of service, the silver dollar slots. A shortage of coinage, said the United States Mint. But right there, side by side with the nickel and quarter bandits, was one cartwheel machine. Two thousand dollar jackpot. Kostner grinned foolishly. If you're gonna go out, go out like a champ.

He thumbed the silver dollar into the coin slot and grabbed the heavy, oiled handle. Shining cast aluminum and pressed steel. Big black plastic ball, angled for arm ease, pull it all day and you won't get weary.

Without a prayer in the universe, Kostner pulled the handle.

*   *   *

*She had been born in Tucson, mother full-blooded Cher-
okee, father a bindlestiff on his way through. Mother had
been working a truckers' stop, father had popped for
spencer steak and sides. Mother had just gotten over a bad
scene, indeterminate origins, unsatisfactory culminations.
Mother had popped for bed. And sides. Margaret Annie
Jessie had come nine months later; black of hair, fair of face,
and born into a life of poverty. Twenty-three years later, a
determined product of Miss Clairol and Berlitz, a dream-
image formed by Vogue and intimate association with the
rat race, Margaret Annie Jessie had become a contraction.*

Maggie.

*Long legs, trim and coltish; hips a trifle large, the kind that
promote that specific thought in men, about getting their
hands around it; belly flat, isometrics; waist cut to the bone,
a waist that works in any style from dirndl to disco-slacks;
no breasts—all nipple, but no breast, like an expensive
whore (the way O'Hara pinned it)—and no padding . . .
forget the cans, baby, there's other, more important action;
smooth, Michelangelo-sculpted neck, a pillar, proud; and all
that face.*

*Outthrust chin, perhaps a tot too much belligerence, but
if you'd walloped as many gropers, you too, sweetheart;
narrow mouth, petulant lower lip, nice to chew on, a lower
lip as though filled with honey, bursting, ready for things to
happen; a nose that threw the right sort of shadow, flaring
nostrils, the acceptable words—aquiline, patrician, classic,
allathat; cheekbones as stark and promontory as a spit of
land after ten years of open ocean; cheekbones holding
darkness like narrow shadows, sooty beneath the taut-
fleshed bone-structure; amazing cheekbones, the whole
face, really; an ancient kingdom's uptilted eyes, the touch of
the Cherokee, eyes that looked out at you, as you looked in
at them, like someone peering out of the keyhole as you
peered in; actually, dirty eyes, they said you can get it.*

*Blonde hair, a great deal of it, wound and rolled and
smoothed and flowing, in the old style, the pageboy thing
men always admire; no tight little cap of slicked plastic; no
ratted and teased Annapurna of bizarre coiffure; no ironed-
flat discothèque hair like number 3 flat noodles. Hair, the
way a man wants it, so he can dig his hands in at the base of*

the neck and pull all that face very close.

An operable woman, a working mechanism, a rigged and sudden machinery of softness and motivation.

Twenty-three, and determined as hell never to abide in that vale of poverty her mother had called purgatory for her entire life; snuffed out in a grease fire in the last trailer, somewhere in Arizona, thank God no more pleas for a little money from babygirl Maggie hustling drinks in a Los Angeles topless joint. (There ought to be some remorse in there somewhere, for a Mommy gone where all the good grease-fire victims go. Look around, you'll find it.)

Maggie.

Genetic freak. Mommy's Cherokee uptilted eye-shape, and Polack quickscrewing Daddy WithoutaName's blue as innocence color.

Blue-eyed Maggie, dyed blonde, alla that face, alla that leg, fifty bucks a night can get it and it sounds like it's having a climax.

Irish-innocent blue-eyed-innocent French-legged-innocent Maggie. Polack. Cherokee. Irish. All-woman and going on the market for this month's rent on the stucco pad, eighty bucks' worth of groceries, a couple months' worth for a Mustang, three appointments with the specialist in Beverly Hills about that shortness of breath after a night on the hustle bump the sticky thigh the disco lurch the gotcha sweat: woman minutes. Increments under the meat; perspiration purchases, yeah it does.

Maggie, Maggie, Maggie, pretty Maggie Moneyeyes, who came from Tucson and trailers and rheumatic fever and a surge to live that was all kaleidoscope frenzy of clawing scrabbling no-nonsense. If it took lying on one's back and making sounds like a panther in the desert, then one did it, because nothing, but nothing was as bad as being dirt-poor, itchy-skinned, soiled-underwear, scuff-toed, hairy and ashamed lousy with the no-gots. Nothing!

Maggie. Hooker. Hustler. Grabber. Swinger. If there's a buck in it, there's rhythm and the onomatopoeia is Maggie Maggie Maggie.

She who puts out. For a price, whatever that might be.

Maggie was dating Nuncio. He was Sicilian. He had dark eyes and an alligator-grain wallet with slip-in pockets for

*credit cards. He was a spender, a sport, a high-roller. They
went to Vegas.*

*Maggie and the Sicilian. Her blue eyes and his slip-in
pockets. But mostly her blue eyes.*

The spinning reels behind the three long glass windows
blurred, and Kostner knew there wasn't a chance. Two
thousand dollar jackpot. Round and round, whirring. Three
bells or two bells and a jackpot bar, get 18; three plums or
two plums and a jackpot bar, get 14; three oranges or two
oranges and a jac—

Ten, five, two bucks for a single cherry cluster in first position. Something . . . I'm drowning . . . Something . . .

The whirring . . .

Round and round . . .

As something happened that was not considered in the
pit-boss manual.

The reels whipped and snapped to a stop, clank clank
clank, tight in place.

Three bars looked up at Kostner. But they did not say
JACKPOT. They were three bars from which stared three
blue eyes. Very blue, very immediate, very JACKPOT!!

Twenty silver dollars clattered into the payoff trough at the
bottom of the machine. An orange light popped on in the
casino cashier's cage, bright orange on the jackpot board.
And the gong began clanging overhead.

The Slot Machine Floor Manager nodded once to the Pit
Boss, who pursed his lips and started toward the seedy-
looking man still standing with his hand on the slot's handle.

The token payment—twenty silver dollars—lay untouched in the payoff trough. The balance of the jackpot—
one thousand nine hundred and eighty dollars—would be
paid manually, by the casino cashier. And Kostner stood,
dumbly, as the three blue eyes stared up at him.

There was a moment of idiotic disorientation, as Kostner
stared back at the three blue eyes; a moment in which the
slot machine's mechanisms registered to themselves; and
the gong was clanging furiously.

All through the hotel's casino people turned from their
games to stare. At the roulette tables the white-on-white
players from Detroit and Cleveland pulled their watery eyes

away from the clattering ball and stared down the line for a second, at the ratty-looking guy in front of the slot machine. From where they sat, they could not tell it was a two grand pot, and their rheumy eyes went back into billows of cigar smoke, and that little ball.

The blackjack hustlers turned momentarily, screwing around in their seats, and smiled. They were closer to the slot-players in temperament, but they knew the slots were a dodge to keep the old ladies busy, while the players worked toward their endless twenty-ones.

And the old dealer, who could no longer cut it at the fast-action boards, who had been put out to pasture by a grateful management, standing at the Wheel of Fortune near the entrance to the casino, even he paused in his zombie-murmuring ("Annnnother winner onna Wheel of For-chun!") to no one at all, and looked toward Kostner and that incredible gong-clanging. Then, in a moment, still with no players, he called *another* nonexistent winner.

Kostner heard the gong from far away. It had to mean he had won two thousand dollars, but that was impossible. He checked the payoff chart on the face of the machine. Three bars labeled JACKPOT meant JACKPOT. Two thousand dollars.

But these three bars did not say JACKPOT. They were three gray bars, rectangular in shape, with a blue eye directly in the center of each bar.

Blue eyes?

Somewhere, a connection was made, and electricity, a billion volts of electricity, shot through Kostner. His hair stood on end, his fingertips bled raw, his eyes turned to jelly, and every fiber in his musculature became radioactive. Somewhere, out there, in a place that was not this place, Kostner had been inextricably bound to—to someone. Blue eyes?

The gong had faded out of his head, the constant noise level of the casino, chips chittering, people mumbling, dealers calling plays, it had all gone, and he was embedded in silence.

Tied to that someone else, out there somewhere, through those three blue eyes.

Then in an instant, it had passed, and he was alone again, as though released by a giant hand, the breath crushed out of him. He staggered up against the slot machine.

"You all right, fellah?"

A hand gripped him by the arm, steadied him. The gong was still clanging overhead somewhere, and he was breathless from a journey he had just taken. His eyes focused and he found himself looking at the stocky Pit Boss who had been on duty while he had been playing blackjack.

"Yeah . . . I'm okay, just a little dizzy is all."

"Sounds like you got yourself a big jackpot, fellah." The Pit Boss grinned; it was a leathery grin; something composed of stretched muscles and conditioned reflexes, totally mirthless.

"Yeah . . . great . . ." Kostner tried to grin back. But he was still shaking from that electrical absorption that had kidnapped him.

"Let me check it out," the Pit Boss was saying, edging around Kostner, and staring at the face of the slot machine. "Yeah, three jackpot bars, all right. You're a winner."

Then it dawned on Kostner! Two thousand dollars! He looked down at the slot machine and saw—

Three bars with the word JACKPOT on them. No blue eyes, just words that meant money. Kostner looked around frantically, was he losing his mind? *From somewhere, not in the casino, he heard a tinkle of rhodium-plated laughter.*

He scooped up the twenty silver dollars. The Pit Boss dropped another cartwheel into the Chief, and pulled the jackpot off. Then the Pit Boss walked him to the rear of the casino, talking to him in a muted, extremely polite tone of voice. At the cashier's window, the Pit Boss nodded to a weary-looking man at a huge Rolodex cardfile, checking credit ratings.

"Barney, jackpot on the cartwheel Chief; slot five-oh-oh-one-five." He grinned at Kostner, who tried to smile back. It was difficult. He felt stunned.

The cashier checked a payoff book for the correct amount to be drawn and leaned over the counter toward Kostner. "Check or cash, sir?"

Kostner felt buoyancy coming back to him. "Is the casino's check good?" They all three laughed at that. "A check's fine," Kostner said. The check was drawn, and the Check-Riter punched out the little bumps that said two thousand. "The twenty cartwheels are a gift," the cashier said, sliding the check through to Kostner.

He held it, looked at it, and still found it difficult to believe. Two grand, back on the golden road.

As he walked back through the casino with the Pit Boss, the stocky man asked pleasantly, "Well, what are you going to do with it?" Kostner had to think a moment. He didn't really have any plans. But then the sudden realization came to him: "I'm going to play that slot machine again." The Pit Boss smiled: a congenital sucker. He would put all twenty of those silver dollars back into the Chief, and then turn to the other games. Blackjack, roulette, faro, baccarat . . . in a few hours he would have redeposited the two grand with the hotel casino. It always happened.

He walked Kostner back to the slot machine, and patted him on the shoulder. "Lotsa luck, fellah."

As he turned away, Kostner slipped a silver dollar into the machine, and pulled the handle.

The Pit Boss had only taken five steps when he heard the incredible sound of the reels clicking to a stop, the clash of twenty token silver dollars hitting the payoff trough, and that goddamned gong went out of its mind again.

She had known that sonofabitch Nuncio was a perverted swine. A walking filth. A dungheap between his ears. Some kind of monster in nylon undershorts. There weren't many kinds of games Maggie hadn't played, but what that Sicilian de Sade wanted to do was outright vomity!

She nearly fainted when he suggested it. Her heart— which the Beverly Hills specialist had said she should not tax—began whumping frantically. "You pig!" she screamed. "You filthy dirty ugly pig you, Nuncio you pig!" She had bounded out of the bed and started to throw on clothes. She didn't even bother with a brassiere, pulling the poorboy sweater on over her thin breasts, still crimson with the touches and love-bites Nuncio had showered on them.

He sat up in the bed, a pathetic-looking little man, gray hair at the temples and no hair atall on top, and his eyes were moist. He was porcine, was indeed the swine she had called him, but he was helpless before her. He was in love with his hooker, with the tart whom he was supporting. It had been the first time for the swine Nuncio, and he was helpless. Back in Detroit, had it been a floozy, a bimbo, a chippy broad, he would have gotten out of the double bed and rapped her around pretty good. But this Maggie, she tied him in knots. He had suggested . . . that, what they should do together . . . because he was so consumed with her. But she was furious with him. It wasn't that bizarre an idea!

"Gimme a chanct'a talk t'ya, honey . . . Maggie . . ."

"You filthy pig, Nuncio! Give me some money, I'm going down to the casino, and I don't want to see your filthy pig face for the rest of the day, remember that!"

And she had gone in his wallet and pants, and taken eight hundred and sixteen dollars, while he watched. He was helpless before her. She was something stolen from a world he knew only as "class" and she could do what she wanted with him.

Genetic freak Maggie, blue-eyed posing mannequin Maggie, pretty Maggie Moneyeyes, who was one-half Cherokee and one-half a buncha other things, had absorbed her lessons well. She was the very model of a "class broad."

"Not for the rest of the day, do you understand?" She stared at him till he nodded; then she went downstairs, furious, to fret and gamble and wonder about nothing but years of herself.

Men stared after her as she walked. She carried herself like a challenge, the way a squire carried a pennon, the way a prize bitch carried herself in the judge's ring. Born to the blue. The wonders of mimicry and desire.

Maggie had no lust for gambling, none whatever. She merely wanted to taste the fury of her relationship with the swine Sicilian, her need for solidity in a life built on the edge of the slide area, the senselessness of being here in Las Vegas when she could be back in Beverly Hills. She grew angrier and more ill at the thought of Nuncio upstairs in the room, taking another shower. She bathed three times a day. But it was different with him. He knew she resented his smell; he had the soft odor of wet fur sometimes, and she had told him about it. Now he bathed constantly, and hated

61

it. He was a foreigner to the bath. His life had been marked by various kinds of filths, and baths for him now were more of an obscenity than dirt could ever have been. For her, bathing was different. It was a necessity. She had to keep the patina of the world off her, had to remain clean and smooth and white. A presentation, not an object of flesh and hair. A chromium instrument, something never pitted by rust and corrosion.

When she was touched by them, by any one of them, by the men, by all the Nuncios, they left little pitholes of bloody rust on her white, permanent flesh; cobwebs, sooty stains. She had to bathe. Often.

She strolled down between the tables and the slots, carrying eight hundred and sixteen dollars. Eight one hundred dollar bills and sixteen dollars in ones.

At the change booth she got cartwheels for the sixteen ones. The Chief waited. It was her baby. She played it to infuriate the Sicilian. He had told her to play the nickel slots, the quarter or dime slots, but she always infuriated him by blowing fifty or a hundred dollars in ten minutes, one coin after another, in the big Chief.

She faced the machine squarely, and put in the first silver dollar. She pulled the handle that swine Nuncio. Another dollar, pulled the handle how long does this go on? The reels cycled and spun and whirled and whipped in a blurringspinning metalhumming overandoverandoverandover as Maggie blue-eyed Maggie hated and hated and thought of hate and all the days and nights of swine behind her and ahead of her and if only she had all the money in this room in this casino in this hotel in this town right now this very instant just an instant thisinstant it would be enough to whirring and humming and spinning and overandoverandover and she would be free free free free free and all the world would never touch her body again the swine would never touch her white flesh again and then suddenly as dollarafterdollarafterdollar went aroundaroundaround hummmmmming in reels of cherries and bells and bars and plums and oranges there was suddenly painpainpain a SHARP pain!pain!pain! in her chest, her heart, her center, a needle, a lancet, a burning, a pillar of flame that was purest pure purer PAIN!

Maggie, pretty Maggie Moneyeyes, who wanted all that money in that cartwheel Chief slot machine, Maggie who had come from filth and rheumatic fever, who had come all the way to three baths a day and a specialist in Very Expensive Beverly Hills, that Maggie suddenly had a seizure, a flutter, a slam of a coronary thrombosis and fell instantly dead on the floor of the casino. Dead.

One instant she had been holding the handle of the slot machine, willing her entire being, all that hatred for all the swine she had ever rolled with, willing every fiber of every cell of every chromosome into that machine, wanting to suck out every silver vapor within its belly, and the next instant—so close they might have been the same—her heart exploded and killed her and she slipped to the floor . . . still touching the Chief.

On the floor.
Dead.
Struck dead.
Liar. All the lies that were her life.
Dead on a floor.

[A moment out of time ■ lights whirling and spinning in a cotton candy universe ■ down a bottomless funnel roundly sectioned like a goat's horn ■ a cornucopia that rose up cuculiform smooth and slick as a worm's belly ■ endless nights that pealed ebony funeral bells ■ out of fog ■ out of weightlessness ■ suddenly total cellular knowledge ■ memory running backward ■ gibbering spastic blindness ■ a soundless owl of frenzy trapped in a cave of prisms ■ sand endlessly draining down ■ billows of forever ■ edges of the world as they splintered ■ foam rising drowning from inside ■ the smell of rust ■ rough green corners that burn ■ memory for gibbering spastic blind memory ■ seven rushing vacuums of nothing ■ yellow ■ pinpoints cast in amber straining and elongating running like live wax ■ chill fevers ■ overhead the odor of stop ■ this is the stopover before hell or heaven ■ this is limbo ■ trapped and doomed alone in a mist-eaten nowhere ■ a soundless screaming a soundless whirring a soundless spinning spinning spinning ■ spinning ■ spinning ■ spinning ■ spinning ■ spinninggggggggggg]

> Maggie had wanted all the silver in the machine. She had died, willing herself into the machine. Now, looking out from within, from inside the limbo that had become her own purgatory, Maggie was trapped, in the oiled and anodized interior of the silver dollar slot machine. The prison of her final desires, where she had wanted to be, completely trapped in that last instant of life between life/death. Maggie, gone inside, all soul now, trapped for all eternity in the cage soul of the machine. Limbo. Trapped Trapped.

"I hope you don't mind if I call over one of the slot men," the Slot Machine Floor Manager was saying, from a far distance. He was in his late fifties, a velvet-voiced man whose eyes held nothing of light and certainly nothing of kindness. He had stopped the Pit Boss as the stocky man had turned in mid-step to return to Kostner and the jackpotted machine; he had taken the walk himself. "We have to make sure, you know how it is: somebody didn't fool with the slot, you know, maybe it's outta whack or something, you know."

He lifted his left hand and there was a clicker in it, the kind children use at Halloween. He clicked half a dozen times, like a rabid cricket, and there was a scurrying in the pit between the tables.

Kostner was only faintly aware of what was happening. Instead of being totally awake, feeling the surge of adrenaline through his veins, the feeling any gambler gets when he is ahead of the game, a kind of desperate urgency when he has hit it for a boodle, he was numb, partaking of the action around him only as much as a drinking glass involves itself in the alcoholic's drunken binge.

All color and sound had been leached out of him.

A tired-looking, resigned-weary man wearing a gray porter's jacket, as gray as his hair, as gray as his indoor skin, came to them, carrying a leather wrap-up of tools. The slot repairman studied the machine, turning the pressed steel body around on its stand, studying the back. He used a key on the back door and for an instant Kostner had a view of gears, springs, armatures and the clock that ran the slot mechanism. The repairman nodded silently over it, closed and relocked it, turned it around again and studied the face of the machine.

"Nobody's been spooning it," he said, and went away.

Kostner stared at the Floor Manager.

"Gaffing. That's what he meant. Spooning's another word for it. Some guys use a little piece of plastic, or a wire, shove it down through the escalator, it kicks the machine. Nobody thought that's what happened here, but you know, we have to make sure, two grand is a big payoff, and twice . . . well, you know, I'm sure you'll understand. If a guy was doing it with a boomerang—"

Kostner raised an eyebrow.

"—uh, yeah, a boomerang, it's another way to spoon the machine. But we just wanted to make a little check, and now everybody's satisfied, so if you'll just come back to the casino cashier with me—"

And they paid him off again.

So he went back to the slot machine, and stood before it for a long time, staring at it. The change girls and the dealers going off-duty, the little old ladies with their canvas work gloves worn to avoid calluses when pulling the slot handles, the men's room attendant on his way up front to get more matchbooks, the floral tourists, the idle observers, the hard drinkers, the sweepers, the busboys, the gamblers with poached-egg eyes who had been up all night, the showgirls with massive breasts and diminutive sugar daddies, all of them conjectured mentally about the beat-up walker who was staring at the silver dollar Chief. He did not move, merely stared at the machine . . . and they wondered.

The machine was staring back at Kostner.

Three blue eyes.

The electric current had sparked through him again, as the machine had clocked down and the eyes turned up a second time, as he had *won* a second time. But this time he knew there was something more than luck involved, for no one else had seen those three blue eyes.

So now he stood before the machine, waiting. It spoke to him. Inside his skull, where no one had ever lived but himself, now someone else moved and spoke to him. A girl. A beautiful girl. Her name was Maggie, and she spoke to him.

I've been waiting for you. A long time, I've been waiting for you, Kostner. Why do you think you hit the jackpot? Because I've been waiting for you, and I want you. You'll

65

win all the jackpots. Because I want you, I need you. Love me, I'm Maggie, I'm so alone, love me.

Kostner had been staring at the slot machine for a very long time, and his weary brown eyes had seemed to be locked to the blue eyes on the jackpot bars. But he knew no one else could see the blue eyes, and no one else could hear the voice, and no one else knew about Maggie.

He was the universe to her. Everything to her.

He thumbed in another silver dollar, and the Pit Boss watched, the slot machine repairman watched, the Slot Machine Floor Manager watched, three change girls watched, and a pack of unidentified players watched, some from their seats.

The reels whirled, the handle snapped back, and in a second they flipped down to a halt, twenty silver dollars tokened themselves into the payoff trough and a woman at one of the crap tables belched a fragment of hysterical laughter.

And the gong went insane again.

The Floor Manager came over and said, very softly, "Mr. Kostner, it'll take us about fifteen minutes to pull this machine and check it out. I'm sure you understand." As two slot repairmen came out of the back, hauled the Chief off its stand, and took it into the repair room at the rear of the casino.

While they waited, the Floor Manager regaled Kostner with stories of spooners who had used intricate magnets inside their clothes, of boomerang men who had attached their plastic implements under their sleeves so they could be extended on spring-loaded clips, of cheaters who had come equipped with tiny electric drills in their hands and wires that slipped into the tiny drilled holes. And he kept saying he knew Kostner would understand.

But Kostner knew the Floor Manager would not understand.

When they brought the Chief back, one of the repairmen nodded assuredly. "Nothing wrong with it. Works perfectly. Nobody's been boomin' it."

But the blue eyes were gone on the jackpot bars.

Kostner knew they would return.

They paid him off again.

He returned and played again. And again. And again. They put a "spotter" on him. He won again. And again. And again. The crowd had grown to massive proportions. Word had spread like the silent communications of the telegraph vine, up and down the Strip, all the way to downtown Vegas and the sidewalk casinos where they played night and day every day of the year, and the crowd surged in a tide toward the hotel, and the casino, and the seedy-looking walker with his weary brown eyes. The crowd moved to him inexorably, drawn like lemmings by the odor of the luck that rose from him like musky electrical cracklings. And he won. Again and again. Thirty-eight thousand dollars. And the three blue eyes continued to stare up at him. Her lover was winning. Maggie and her Moneyeyes.

Finally, the casino decided to speak to Kostner. They pulled the Chief for fifteen minutes, for a supplemental check by experts from the slot machine company in downtown Vegas, and while they were checking it, they asked Kostner to come to the main office of the hotel.

The owner was there. His face seemed faintly familiar to Kostner. Had he seen it on television? The newspapers?

"Mr. Kostner, my name is Jules Hartshorn."

"I'm pleased to meet you."

"Quite a string of luck you're having out there."

"It's been a long time coming."

"You realize, this sort of luck is impossible."

"I'm compelled to believe it, Mr. Hartshorn."

"Um. As am I. It's happening to my casino. But we're thoroughly convinced of one of two possibilities, Mr. Kostner; one, either the machine is inoperable in a way we can't detect; or two, you are the cleverest spooner we've ever had in here."

"I'm not cheating."

"As you can see, Mr. Kostner, I'm smiling. The reason I'm smiling is at your naïveté in believing I would take your word for it. I'm perfectly happy to nod politely and say of course you aren't cheating. But no one can win thirty-eight thousand dollars on nineteen straight jackpots off one slot machine; it doesn't even have mathematical odds against its happening, Mr. Kostner. It's on a cosmic scale of improbability with three dark planets crashing into our sun within the next twenty minutes. It's on a par with the Pentagon, the Forbidden City and the Kremlin all three pushing the red button at the same microsecond. It's an impossibility, Mr. Kostner. An impossibility that's happening to me."

"I'm sorry."

"Not really."

"No, not really. I can use the money."

"For what, exactly, Mr. Kostner?"

"I hadn't thought about it, really."

"I see. Well, Mr. Kostner, let's look at it this way. I can't stop you from playing, and if you continue to win, I'll be required to pay off. And no stubble-chinned thugs will be waiting in an alley to jackroll you and take the money. The checks will be honored. The best I can hope for, Mr. Kostner, is the attendant publicity. Right now, every high-roller in Vegas is in that casino, waiting for you to drop cart-wheels into that machine. It won't make up for what I'm losing, if you continue the way you've been; but it'll help. Every sucker in town likes to rub up next to luck. All I ask is that you cooperate a little."

"The least I can do, considering your generosity."

"An attempt at humor."

"I'm sorry. What is it you'd like me to do?"

"Get about ten hours' sleep."

"While you pull the slot and have it worked over thoroughly?"

"Yes."

"If I wanted to keep winning, that might be a pretty stupid move on my part. You might change the thingamajig inside so I couldn't win if I put back every dollar of that thirty-eight grand."

"We're licensed by the state of Nevada, Mr. Kostner."

"I come from a good family, too, and take a look at me. I'm a bum with thirty-eight thousand dollars in my pocket."

"Nothing will be done to that slot machine, Kostner."

"Then why pull it for ten hours?"

"To work it over thoroughly in the shop. If something as undetectable as metal fatigue or a worn escalator tooth or—we want to make sure this doesn't happen with other machines. And the extra time will get the word around town;

we can use the crowd. Some of those tourists will stick to our fingers, and it'll help defray the expense of having you break the bank at this casino—on a slot machine."

"I have to take your word."

"This hotel will be in business long after you're gone, Kostner."

"Not if I keep winning."

Hartshorn's smile was a stricture. "A good point."

"So it isn't much of an argument."

"It's the only one I have. If you want to get back out on that floor, I can't stop you."

"No Mafia hoods ventilate me later?"

"I beg your pardon?"

"I said: no Maf—"

"You have a picturesque manner of speaking. In point of fact, I haven't the faintest idea what you're talking about."

"I'm sure you haven't."

"You've got to stop reading *The National Enquirer.* This is a legally run business. I'm merely asking a favor."

"Okay, Mr. Hartshorn, I've been three days without any sleep. Ten hours will do me a world of good."

"I'll have the desk clerk find you a quiet room on the top floor. And thank you, Mr. Kostner."

"Think nothing of it."

"I'm afraid that will be impossible."

"A lot of impossible things are happening lately."

He turned to go, as Hartshorn lit a cigarette.

"Oh, by the way, Mr. Kostner?"

Kostner stopped and half-turned. "Yes?"

His eyes were getting difficult to focus. There was a ringing in his ears. Hartshorn seemed to waver at the edge of his vision like heat lightning across a prairie. Like memories of things Kostner had come across the country to forget. Like the whimpering and pleading that kept tugging at the cells of his brain. The voice of Maggie. Still back in there, saying . . . things . . .

They'll try to keep you from me.

All he could think about was the ten hours of sleep he had been promised. Suddenly it was more important than the money, than forgetting, than anything. Hartshorn was talking, was saying things, but Kostner could not hear him. It was as if he had turned off the sound and saw only the silent rubbery movement of Hartshorn's lips. He shook his head trying to clear it.

There were half a dozen Hartshorns all melting into and out of one another. And the voice of Maggie.

I'm warm here, and alone. I could be good to you, if you can come to me. Please come, please hurry.

"Mr. Kostner?"

Hartshorn's voice came draining down through exhaustion as thick as velvet flocking. Kostner tried to focus again. His extremely weary brown eyes began to track.

"Did you know about that slot machine?" Hartshorn was saying. "A peculiar thing happened with it about six weeks ago."

"What was that?"

"A girl died playing it. She had a heart attack, a seizure while she was pulling the handle, and died right out there on the floor."

Kostner was silent for a moment. He wanted desperately to ask Hartshorn what color the dead girl's eyes had been, but he was afraid the owner would say blue.

He paused with his hand on the office door. "Seems as though you've had nothing but a streak of bad luck on that machine."

Hartshorn smiled an enigmatic smile. "It might not change for a while, either."

Kostner felt his jaw muscles tighten. "Meaning I might die, too, and wouldn't *that* be bad luck."

Hartshorn's smile became hieroglyphic, permanent, stamped on him forever. "Sleep tight, Mr. Kostner."

In a dream, she came to him. Long, smooth thighs and soft golden down on her arms; blue eyes deep as the past, misted with a fine scintillance like lavender spiderwebs; taut body that was the only body Woman had ever had, from the very first. Maggie came to him.

Hello, I've been traveling a long time.

"Who are you?" Kostner asked, wonderingly. He was standing on a chilly plain, or was it a plateau? The wind curled around them both, or was it only around him? She was exquisite, and he saw her clearly, or was it through a

mist? *Her voice was deep and resonant, or was it light and warm as night-blooming jasmine?*

I'm Maggie. I love you. I've waited for you.

"You have blue eyes."

Yes. *With love.*

"You're very beautiful."

Thank you. *With female amusement.*

"But why me? Why let it happen to me? Are you the girl who—are you the one that was sick—the one who—?"

I'm Maggie. And you, I picked you, because you need me. You've needed someone for a long long time.

Then it unrolled for Kostner. The past unrolled and he saw who he was. He saw himself alone. Always alone. As a child, born to kind and warm parents who hadn't the vaguest notion of who he was, what he wanted to be, where his talents lay. So he had run off, when he was in his teens, and alone always alone on the road. For years and months and days and hours, with no one. Casual friendships, based on food, or sex, or artificial similarities. But no one to whom he could cleave, and cling, and belong. It was that way till Susie, and with her he had found light. He had discovered the scents and aromas of a spring that was eternally one day away. He had laughed, really laughed, and known with her it would at last be all right. So he had poured all of himself into her, giving her everything; all his hopes, his secret thoughts, his tender dreams; and she had taken them, taken him, all of him, and he had known for the first time what it was to have a place to live, to have a home in someone's heart. It was all the silly and gentle things he laughed at in other people, but for him it was breathing deeply of wonder.

He had stayed with her for a long time, and had supported her, supported her son from the first marriage; the marriage Susie never talked about. And then one day, he had come back, as Susie had always known he would. He was a dark creature of ruthless habits and vicious nature, but she had been his woman, all along, and Kostner realized he had been used as a stop-gap, as a bill-payer till her wandering terror came home to nest. Then she had asked him to leave. Broke, and tapped out in all the silent inner ways a man can be drained, he had left, without even a

71

fight, for all the fight had been leached out of him. He had left, and wandered west, and finally come to Las Vegas, where he had hit bottom. And found Maggie. In a dream, with blue eyes, he had found Maggie.

I want you to belong to me. I love you. Her truth was vibrant in Kostner's mind. She was his, at last someone who was special, was his.

"Can I trust you? I've never been able to trust anyone before. Women, never. But I need someone. I really need someone."

It's me, always. Forever. You can trust me.

And she came to him, fully. Her body was a declaration of truth and trust such as no other Kostner had ever known before. She met him on a windswept plain of thought, and he made love to her more completely than he had known any passion before. She joined with him, entered him, mingled with his blood and his thought and his frustration, and he came away clean, filled with glory.

"Yes, I can trust you, I want you, I'm yours," he whispered to her, when they lay side by side in a dream nowhere of mist and soundlessness. "I'm yours."

She smiled, a woman's smile of belief in her man; a smile of trust and deliverance. And Kostner woke up.

The Chief was back on its stand, and the crowd had been penned back by velvet ropes. Several people had played the machine, but there had been no jackpots.

Now Kostner came into the casino, and the "spotters" got themselves ready. While Kostner had slept, they had gone through his clothes, searching for wires, for gaffs, for spoons or boomerangs. Nothing.

Now he walked straight to the Chief, and stared at it.

Hartshorn was there. "You look tired," he said gently to Kostner, studying the man's weary brown eyes.

"I am, a little." Kostner tried a smile; it didn't work. "I had a funny dream."

"Oh?"

"Yeah . . . about a girl. . . ." He let it die off.

Hartshorn's smile was understanding. Pitying, empathic and understanding. "There are lots of girls in this town. You shouldn't have any trouble finding one with your winnings."

Kostner nodded, and slipped his first silver dollar into the slot. He pulled the handle. The reels spun with a ferocity Kostner had not heard before and suddenly everything went whipping slantwise as he felt a wrenching of pure flame in his stomach, as his head was snapped on its spindly neck, as the lining behind his eyes was burned out. There was a terrible shriek, of tortured metal, of an express train ripping the air with its passage, of a hundred small animals being gutted and torn to shreds, of incredible pain, of night winds that tore the tops off mountains of lava. And a keening whine of a voice that wailed and wailed and wailed as it went away from there in blinding light—

Free! Free! Heaven or Hell it doesn't matter! Free!

The sound of a soul released from an eternal prison, a genie freed from a dark bottle. And in that instant of damp soundless nothingness, Kostner saw the reels snap and clock down for the final time:

One, two, three. Blue eyes.

But he would never cash his checks.

The crowd screamed through one voice as he fell sidewise and lay on his face. The final loneliness . . .

The Chief was pulled. Bad luck. Too many gamblers resented its very presence in the casino. So it was pulled. And returned to the company, with explicit instructions it was to be melted down to slag. And not till it was in the hands of the ladle foreman, who was ready to dump it into the slag furnace, did anyone remark on the final tally the Chief had clocked.

"Look at that, ain't that weird," said the ladle foreman to his bucket man. He pointed to the three glass windows.

"Never saw jackpot bars like that before," the bucket man agreed. "Three eyes. Must be an old machine."

"Yeah, some of these old games go way back," the foreman said, hoisting the slot machine onto the conveyor track leading to the slag furnace.

"Three eyes, huh? How about that. Three brown eyes." And he threw the knife-switch that sent the Chief down the track, to puddle in the roaring inferno of the furnace.

Three brown eyes.

Three brown eyes that looked very very weary. That

*looked very very trapped. That looked very very betrayed.
Some of these old games go way back.*

*Born angry in Ohio, 1934, Harlan Ellison has written that he's lived his
life—by most reports as fascinating as his fiction—by two admonitions:
"Chance favors the prepared mind" (Pasteur) and "How vain it is to sit
down to write when you have not stood up to live" (Thoreau). His
passion for experience has led him to cover race riots for Time; earn his
living at such varied jobs as hanging upside-down in a leather cradle
servicing the underside of the Brooklyn-Manhattan Bridge with rust-
resistant paint, working as a hired gun for a wealthy neurotic, and driving a dynamite truck in North Carolina; joining a street gang to gain
background for a novel on juvenile delinquency; and getting expelled
from Ohio State University when his English professor smugly advised
him he had no talent and could not write, and Ellison responded,
"@*%#&) (+#!" His ongoing response has been a thirty-six-year career in which he has written or edited fifty-six books, won the Mystery
Writers Edgar Allan Poe award twice, the Nebula three times, the Hugo
eight and a half times, the PEN Silver Pen for journalism . . . and on
and on.*

A. J. thought his mother was senile, until he discovered he had left the best part of himself behind.

FOUR

Little Jimmy

Lester del Rey

I've always thought that meeting a ghost would be a pretty comforting thing. By the time a man is past fifty and old enough to realize death, anything that will prove he doesn't come to a final, meaningless end should be a help. Even being doomed to haunt some place in solitude through all eternity doesn't have the creeping horror of just not being!

Of course, religion offers hope to some—but most of us don't have the faith of our forefathers. A ghost should be proof against the unimaginable finality of death.

That's the way I used to feel. Now, I don't know. If I could only explain little Jimmy. . . .

We heard him, all right. At Mother's death, the whole family heard him, right down to my sister Agnes, who's the most complete atheist I know. Even her youngest daughter, downstairs at the time, came running up to see who the other child was. It wasn't a case of collective hallucination, any more than it was something that can be explained by any natural laws we know.

The doctor heard it, too, and from the way he looked, I suppose he'd heard little Jimmy more than once before. He won't talk about it, though, and the others had never been around for a previous chance. I'm the only one who will admit to hearing little Jimmy more than that single time. I wish I didn't have to admit it, even to myself.

We were a big family, though the tradition for such families was already dying at the turn of the century. Despite the four girls who died before they had a chance to live, Mother and Dad wanted lots of children. Six of us boys and three girls lived, and that justified it all to Mother. There would have been more, I guess, if Dad hadn't been killed by an angry bull while I was away saving the world for Democracy. Mother could have had other husbands, maybe—the big Iowa farm with its huge old house would have guaranteed that—but she was dead set against it. And we older kids drifted into city jobs, helping the others through college until they had jobs of their own. Eventually, Mother was left alone in the old house, while the town outgrew itself until the farm was sold for lots around it.

That left her with a small fortune, particularly after the second war. She didn't seem to need us, and she was getting "sot" in her ways and hard to get along with. So little by little, we began visiting her less and less. I was the nearest, working in Des Moines, but I had my own life, and she seemed happy and capable, even at well past seventy. We're a long-lived, tough clan.

I sent her birthday and holiday notes—or at least Liza sent them for me—and kept meaning to see her. But my oldest boy seemed to go to pieces after the second war. My daughter married a truck driver and had a set of twins before they found a decent apartment. My youngest boy was taken prisoner in Korea. I was promoted to president of the roofing company. And a new pro at the club was coaching me into breaking ninety most of the time.

Then Mother began writing letters—the first real ones in years. They were cheerful enough, filled with chit-chat about some neighbors, the new drapes on the windows, a recipe for lemon cream pie, and such. At first, I thought they were a fine sign. Then something in them began to bother me. It wasn't until the fifth one, though, that I could put my finger on anything definite.

In that, she wrote a few words about the new teacher at the old schoolhouse. I went over it twice before realizing that the school building had been torn down fifteen years before. When that registered, other things began connecting. The drapes were ones she had put up years before, and the recipe was her first one—the one that always tasted too sweet, before she changed it! There were other strange details.

They kept bothering me, and I finally put through a call.

Mother sounded fine, though a little worried for fear something had gone wrong with me. She talked for a couple of minutes, muttered something about lunch on the stove, and hung up quickly. It couldn't have been more normal. I got out my clubs and was halfway down the front steps before something drove me back to her letters.

Then I called Doctor Matthews. After half a minute identifying myself, I asked about Mother.

His voice assumed a professional tone at once. She was fine—remarkably good physical condition for a woman of her age. No, no reason I should come down at once. There wasn't a thing wrong with her.

He overdid it, and he couldn't quite conceal the worry in his voice. I suppose I'd been thinking of taking a few days off later to see her. But when he hung up, I put the clubs back in the closet and changed my clothes. Liza was out at some civic betterment club, and I left a note for her. She'd taken the convertible though, so I was in luck. The new Cadillac was just back from a tune-up and perfect for a stiff drive. There'd also be less chance of picking up a ticket if I beat the speed limit a little; most cops are less inclined to be tough on a man who's driving one of those cars. I made good time all the way.

Matthews was still at the same address, but his white hair gave me a shock. He frowned at me, lifting his eyes from my waistline to what hair I had left, then back to my face. Then he stuck out his hand slowly, stealing a quick glance at the Cadillac.

"I suppose they all call you A. J. now," he said. "Come on in, since you're here!"

He took me back through the reception room and into his office, his eyes going to the car outside again. From somewhere, he drew out a bottle of good Scotch. At my nod, he mixed it with water from a cooler. He settled back, studying me as he took his own seat. "A. J., heh?" he commented again, sounding a sour note here, somehow. "That sounds like success. Thought your mother mentioned something about your having some trouble a few years back?"

"Not financial," I told him. I'd thought only Liza remembered it. She must have written to Mother at the time, since I'd kept it out of the papers. And after I'd agreed to buy the trucking line for our son-in-law, she'd finally completely forgiven me. It was none of Matthews' business—but out here, I remembered, doctors considered everything their business. "Why, Doc?"

He studied me, let his eyes sweep over the car again, and then tipped up the glass to finish the whisky. "Just curiosity. No, damn it, I might as well be honest. You'll see her anyhow, now. She's an old woman, Andrew, and she has what might be called a tidy fortune. When children who haven't worried about her for years turn up, it might not be affection. And I'm not going to have anything happen to Martha now!"

The hints in his remarks too closely matched my own suspicions. I could feel myself tightening up, tensing with annoyance and a touch of fear. I didn't want to ask the question. I wanted to get mad at him for being an interfering old meddler. But I had to know. "You mean—senile dementia?"

"No," he answered quickly, with a slightly lifted eyebrow. "No, Andrew, she isn't crazy! She's in fine physical shape, and sane enough to take care of herself for the next fifteen years she'll probably live. And she doesn't need any fancy doctors and psychiatrists. Just remember that, and remember she's an old woman. Thirteen children in less than twenty years! A widow before she was forty. Lonely all these years, even if she is too independent to bother you kids. An old woman's entitled to whatever kind of happiness she can get! And don't forget that!"

He stopped, seeming surprised at himself. Then he stood up and reached for his hat. "Come on, I'll ride out with you."

He kept up a patter of local history as we drove down the streets where corn had grown when I last saw this section. There was a hospital where the woods had been, and the old spring was covered by an apartment building. The big house where we had been born stood out, sprawling in ugly warmth among the facsimile piano-boxes they were calling houses nowadays.

I wanted to turn back, but Matthews motioned me after him up the walk. The front door was still unlocked, and he went in, tilting his head toward the stairs. "Martha! Hey, Martha!"

"Jimmy's out back, Doc," a voice called down. It was Mother's voice, unchanged except for a puzzling lilt I'd never heard before, and I drew a quick breath of relief.

"Okay, Martha," Matthews called up. "I'll just see him, then, and call you up later. You won't want me around when you see who I brought you! It's Andrew!"

"How nice! Tell him to sit down and I'll be dressed in a minute!"

Doc shrugged. "I'll sit out in the garden a few minutes," he told me. "Then I'll catch a cab back. But remember—your mother deserves any happiness she can get. Don't you ruin it!"

He went through the back door, and I found the parlor and dropped onto the old sofa. Then I frowned. It had been stored in the attic in 1913, when Dad bought the new furniture. I stared through the soft dimness, making out all the old pieces. Even the rug was the way it had been when I was a child. I walked into the other rooms, finding them the same as they had been forty years before, except for the television set in the dining room and the completely modern kitchen, with a pot of soup bubbling on the back of the stove.

I was getting a thick feeling in my throat and the anxiety I'd had before when the sound of steps on the stairs brought my eyes up.

Mother came down, a trifle slowly, but without any sign of weakness. She didn't rest her hand on the banister. She might have been the woman to match the furnishings of the house, except for the wrinkles and the white hair. And the dress was new, but a perfect copy of one she'd worn when I was still a child!

She seemed not to hear my gasp. Her hand came out to catch mine, and she bent forward, kissing me on the cheek. "You look real good, Andrew. There, now, let's see. Umm-hmm. Liza's been feeding you right, I can see that. But I'll bet you could eat some real home-made soup and pie, eh? Come out in the kitchen. I'll fix it in a minute."

She wasn't only in fine physical shape—she was like a woman fifteen years younger than her age. And she'd even

remembered to call me Andrew, instead of the various nick-
names she'd used during my growing up. That wasn't senility! A senile woman would have turned back to the
earliest one, as I remembered it—particularly since I'd had
to work hard to get her to drop the childhood names. Yet
the house. . . .

She bustled about the kitchen, dishing out some of the
rich, hot soup. She hadn't been a good cook when I was a
kid, but she'd grown steadily better, and this was super-
lative. "I guess Doc must have pronounced Jimmy well,"
she said casually. "He's gone running off somewhere now.
Well, after two weeks cooped up here with the measles, I
can't blame him. I remember how you were when you had
them. Notice how I had the house fixed up, Andrew?"

I nodded, puzzling over her words. "I noticed the old furniture. But this Jimmy. . . .?"

"Oh, you never met him, did you? Never mind, you will.
How long you staying, Andrew?"

I tried to figure things out, cursing Matthews for not warning me of this. Of course, I'd heard somehow that one of my
various nephews had lost his wife. Was he the one who'd
had the young boy? And hadn't he gone up to Alaska? No,
that was Frank's son. And why would anyone hand over a
youngster to Mother, anyhow? There were enough younger
women in the family.

I caught her eyes on me, and pulled myself together. "I'll
be leaving in a couple of hours, Mother. I just. . . ."

"It was real nice of you to drop over," she interrupted me,
as she had always cut into our answers. "I've been meaning
to see you and Liza soon, but fixing the house kept me kind
of busy. Two men carried the furniture down, but I did the
rest myself. Makes me feel younger somehow, having the
old furniture here."

She dished out a quarter of a peach cobbler and put it in
front of me, with a cup of steaming coffee. She took another
quarter for herself and filled her big cup. I had a mental
picture of Liza with her vitamins and diets. Who was senile?

"Jimmy's going to school now," she said. "He's got a
crush on his teacher, too. More pie, Andrew? I'll have to
save a piece for little Jimmy, but there are two left."

From outside, there was a sudden noise, and she jumped

up, to walk quickly toward the back door. Then she came into the kitchen again. "Just a neighbor kid taking a short cut. I wish they'd be a little nicer, though, and play with Jimmy. He gets lonesome sometimes. Like my kitchen, Andrew?"

"Nice," I said carefully, trying to keep track of the threads of conversation. "But it's kind of modern."

"That and the television set," she agreed cheerfully. "Some new things are nice. And some old ones. I've got a foam rubber mattress for my bed, but the rest of the room. . . . Andrew, you come up. I'll show you something I think's real elegant."

The house was clean, and no rooms were closed off. I wondered about that as we climbed the stairs. I hadn't seen a maid. But she sniffed in contempt when I mentioned it. "Of course I take care of it myself. That's a woman's job, ain't it? And then, little Jimmy helps some. He's getting to be mighty handy."

The bedroom was something to see. It reminded me of what I'd seen of the nineties in pictures and movies, complete with frills and fripperies. The years had faded the upholstery and wallpaper in the rest of the house. But here everything seemed bright and new.

"Had a young decorator fellow from Chicago fix it," she explained proudly. "Like what I always wanted when I was a young girl. Cost a fortune, but Jimmy told me I had to do it, because I wanted it." She chuckled fondly. "Sit down, Andrew. How are you and Liza making out? Still fighting over that young hussy she caught you with, or did she take my advice? Silly, letting you know she knew. Nothing makes a man more loving than a little guilt, I always found—especially if the woman gets real sweet about then."

We spent a solid hour discussing things, and it felt good. I told her how they were finally shipping my youngest back to us. I let her bawl me out for the way the oldest boy was using me and for what she called my snootiness about my son-in-law. But her idea of making him only junior partner in the trucking line at first wasn't bad. I should have thought of it myself. She also told me all the gossip about the family. Somehow, she'd kept track of things. I hadn't even known that Pete had died, though I had heard of the other two deaths. I'd meant to go to the funerals, but there'd been that big deal with Midcity Asphalt and then that trouble getting our man into Congress. Things like that had a habit of coming up at the wrong times.

When I finally stood up to go, I wasn't worried about any danger of a family scandal through Mother. If Matthews thought I'd be bothered about her switching back to the old furniture and having this room decorated period style—no matter what it cost—he was the senile one. I felt good, in fact. It had been better than a full round of golf, with me winning. I started to tell her I'd get back soon. I was even thinking of bringing Liza and the family out for our vacation, instead of taking the trip to Bermuda we'd talked about.

She got up to kiss me again. Then she caught herself. "Goodness! Here you're going, and you haven't met Jimmy yet. You sit down a minute, Andrew!"

She threw up the window quickly, letting in the scent of roses from the back. "*Jimmy!* Oh, *Jim-my!* It's getting late. Come on in. And wash your face before you come up. I want you to meet your Uncle Andrew."

She turned back, smiling a little apologetically. "He's my pet, Andrew. I always tried to be fair about my children, but I guess I like Jimmy sort of special!"

Downstairs, I could hear a door close faintly, and the muffled sounds of a boy's steps moving toward the kitchen. Mother sat beaming, happier than I'd seen her for years—since Dad died, in fact. Then the steps sounded on the stairs. I grinned myself, realizing that little Jimmy must be taking two steps at a time, using the banister to pull himself up. I'd always done that when I was a kid. I was musing on how alike boys are when the footsteps reached the landing and headed toward the room.

I started to look toward the door, but the transformation on Mother's face caught my attention. She suddenly looked almost young, and her eyes were shining, while her gaze was riveted on the door behind.

There was a faint sound of it opening and closing, and I started to turn. Something prickled up my backbone. Something was wrong! And then, as I turned completely, I recognized it. When a door opens, the air in the room stirs. We never notice it, unless it doesn't happen. Then the stillness tells us at once the door can't have really opened. This time, the air hadn't moved.

In front of me, the steps sounded, uncertainly, like those of a somewhat shy boy of six. But there was no one there! The thick carpet didn't even flatten as the soft sound of the steps came closer and stopped, just in front of me!

"This is Uncle Andrew, Jimmy," Mother announced happily. "Shake hands like a good boy, now. He came all the way from Des Moines to see you."

I put my hand out, dictated by some vague desire to please her, while I could feel cold sweat running down my arms and legs. I even moved my hand as if it were being shaken. Then I stumbled to the door, yanked it open, and started down the stairs.

Behind me, the boy's footsteps sounded uncertainly, following out to the landing. Then Mother's steps drowned them, as she came quickly down the stairs after me.

"Andrew, I think you're shy around boys! You're not fooling me. You're just running off because you don't know how to talk to little Jimmy!" She was grinning in amusement. Then she caught my hand again. "You come again real soon, Andrew."

I must have said the right things, somehow. She turned to go up the stairs, just as I heard the steps creak from above, where no one was standing! Then I stumbled out and into my car. I was lucky enough to find a few ounces of whisky in a bottle in the glove compartment. But the liquor didn't help much.

I avoided Matthews' place. I cut onto the main highway and opened the big engine all the way, not caring about cops. I wanted all the distance I could get between myself and the ghost steps of little Jimmy. Ghost? Not even that! Just steps and the weak sound of a door that didn't open. Jimmy wasn't even a ghost—he couldn't be.

I had to slow down as the first laughter tore out of my throat. I swung off the road and let it rip out of me, until the pain in my side finally cut it off.

Things were better after that. And when I started the Cadillac again, I was beginning to think. By the time I reached the outskirts of Des Moines, I had it licked.

It was hallucination, of course. Matthews had tried to

warn me that Mother was going through a form of dotage. She'd created a child for herself, going back to her youth for it. The school that wasn't there, the crush on the teacher, the measles—all were real things she was reliving through little Jimmy. But because she was so unlike other women in keeping firmly sane about everything except this one fantasy, she'd fooled me. She'd made me think she was completely rational. When she'd explained the return of the old furniture, she'd wiped out all my doubts, which had centered on that.

She'd made me take it for granted that Jimmy was real. And she had made me expect to hear steps when her own listening had prepared me for them. I'd been cued by her own faint reactions to her imagination—I must have seen some little gesture and followed her timing. It had been superbly real to her—and my senses had tricked me.

It wasn't impossible. It was the secret of many of the great stage illusions, aided by my own memories of the old house, and given life by the fact that she believed in the steps, as no stage trickster could believe.

I convinced myself of it almost completely. I had to do that. And finally I nearly dismissed the steps from my mind and concentrated on Mother. Matthews' words came back to me, and I nodded to myself. It was a harmless fantasy, and Mother was entitled to her pleasure. She was sane enough to care for herself, without any doubt, and physically far better than she had any right to be. With Matthews' interest in her, there was no reason for me to worry about anything.

By the time I pulled the car into the garage, I was making plans for setting up the trucking concern again, following Mother's advice about making myself the senior partner. It hadn't been a wasted day, after all.

Life went on, pretty much as usual. My younger boy was back home for a while. I'd looked forward to that, but somehow the Army had broken the old bonds between us. Even when I had time, there wasn't much we could talk about. I guess it was something of a relief when he left for some job in New York; anyhow, I was busy straightening out a brawl the older one got mixed up in. My daughter was expecting again, and her husband was showing a complete inability to coöperate with me. I didn't have much time to think about little Jimmy. Mercifully, Liza hadn't asked me about my trip; there was nothing to keep me from forgetting most of it.

I wrote Mother once in a while, now. Her letters grew longer, and sometimes Jimmy's name appeared, along with quite a bit of advice on the trucking business. Most of that was useless, naturally, but she knew more than I'd suspected about the ways of business. It gave me something to write back about.

I paid a fat fee to a psychiatrist for a while, but mostly he only confirmed what I'd already reasoned out. I wasn't interested in some of the other nonsense he tried to sell me, so I stopped going after a while.

And then I forgot the whole thing when the first tentative feeler from New Mode Roofing and Asphalt suggested a merger. I'd been planting the seed for the idea for months, but getting it set to put control in my hands was a tricky problem. I finally had to compromise by agreeing to move the headquarters to Akron, tearing up my roots overnight and resettling. Liza made a scene over that, and my daughter flatly refused to come. I had to agree to turn the trucking concern over to my son-in-law completely, just when it was beginning to show a profit. But the rift had been coming ever since he'd refused to fire my oldest boy from the job of driving one of the trailers.

Maybe it was just as well. The boy seemed to like it. We'd be in Akron, nobody would know about it, and he'd be better off than he was hanging around with some of the friends he'd had before. I meant to write Mother about that, since she'd suggested it once, and I suspected she'd had something to do with it. But the move took all my attention. After that, there was the problem of organizing the new firm.

I decided to see Mother, instead of writing to her. I wasn't going to be fooled again with the same hallucination. The new psychiatrist assured me of that, and advised the trip. I had already marked off the date on my calendar for the visit next month.

It didn't work out. Matthews called me at two o'clock in the morning with the news, after wasting two days tracing me down through acquaintances. Nobody thought of looking me up in a business directory, of course.

Mother had pneumonia and the prognosis was unfavorable.

"At her age, these things are serious," he said. His voice wasn't professional this time. "You'd better get here as quickly as you can. She's been asking for you."

"I'll charter a plane at once," I told him. This would raise the deuce with the voting of stock we'd scheduled, but I couldn't stay away, obviously. I'd almost convinced myself Mother would go on for another twenty years. Now. . . . "How'd it happen?"

"The big storm last week. She went out in it with rubbers and an umbrella to fetch little Jimmy from school! She got sopping wet. When I reached her, she already had a fever. I've been trying everything, but. . . . "

I hung up, sick. Little Jimmy! For a minute, I wanted him to be real enough to strangle.

I pounded on Liza's door and got her to charter the plane while I packed and roused out my secretary on the other phone. Liza drove me to the airport where the plane was warmed up and waiting. I turned to say good-by, but she was dragging out a second bag from the back.

"I'm going," she announced flatly.

I started to argue, saw her expression, and gave up. A few minutes later, we took off.

Most of the rest of the family was already there, hovering around outside the newly decorated bedroom where Mother lay under an oxygen tent; huddles of the family and their children were in every other room on the second floor, staring at the closed door and discussing things in the harsh whispers people use for a scene of death.

Matthews motioned them back and came over to me at once. "No hope, I'm afraid, Andrew," he said, and there were tears in his eyes.

"Isn't there anything we can do?" Liza asked, her voice dropping to the hoarse whisper of the others. "Anything at all, Doctor?"

He shook his head. "I've already talked to the best men in the country. We've tried everything. Even prayer."

From one side of the hall, Agnes sniffed loudly. Her militant atheism couldn't be downed by anything, it seemed. It didn't matter. There was death in the house, thick enough to smell. I had always hated the waste and futility of dying. Now it had a personal meaning, and it was worse. Behind that closed door, Mother lay dying, and nothing I could do would help.

"Can I go in?" I asked, against my wishes.

Matthews nodded. "It can't hurt now. And she wanted to see you."

I went in after him, with the eyes of the others thrusting at me. Matthews waved the nurse out and went over to the window; the choking sound from his throat was louder than the faint hiss of the oxygen. I hesitated, then drew near the bed.

Mother lay there, and her eyes were open. She turned them toward me, but there was no recognition in them. One of her thin hands was poking at the transparent tent over her. I looked toward Matthews, who nodded slowly. "It won't matter now."

He helped me move it aside. Her hand groped out, while the wheezing sound of her breathing grew louder. I tried to follow her pointing finger. But it was Matthews who picked up the small picture of a young boy, put it into her hands for her to clasp to her.

"Mother!" It ripped out of me, louder than I had intended. "Mother, it's Andy! I'm here!"

Her eyes turned again, and she moved her parched lips. "Andrew?" she asked weakly. Then a touch of a smile came briefly. She shook her head slightly. "Jimmy! Jimmy!"

The hands lifted the picture until she could see it. *"Jimmy!"* she repeated.

From below, there was the sound of a door closing weakly and steps moving across the lower floor. They took the stairs, two steps at a time, but quickly now, without need of the banister. They crossed the landing. The door remained closed, but there was the sound of a knob turning, a faint squeak of hinges, then another sound of a door closing. Young footsteps moved across the rug, invisible, a sound that seemed to make all other sounds fade to silence. The steps reached the bed and stopped.

Mother turned her eyes, and the smile quickened again.

One hand lifted. Then she dropped back and her breathing stopped.

The silence was broken by the sound of feet again— heavier, surer feet that seemed to be planted on the floor beside the bed. Two sets of footsteps sounded. One might have been those of a small boy. The others were the quick, sharp sounds that only a young woman can make as she hurries along with her first-born beside her. They moved across the room.

There was no hesitation at the door this time, nor any sound of opening or closing. The steps went on, across the landing and down the stairs. As Matthews and I followed into the hall, they seemed to pick up speed toward the back door. Now finally there was a soft, deliberate sound of a door closing, and then silence.

I jerked my gaze back, to see the eyes of all the others riveted on the back entrance, while emotions I had never seen washed over the slack faces. Agnes rose slowly, her eyes turned upwards. Her thin lips opened, hesitated, and closed into a tight line. She sat down like a stick woman folding, glancing about to see whether the others had noticed.

From below, her daughter came running up the stairs. "Mother! Mother, who was the little boy I heard?"

I didn't wait for the answer, nor the thick words with which Matthews confirmed the news of Mother's death. I was back beside the poor old body, taking the picture from the clasped hands.

Liza had followed me in, with the color just beginning to return to her face. "Ghosts," she said thickly. Then she shook her head, and her voice softened. "Mother and one of the babies, come back to get her. I always thought. . . ."

"No," I told her. "Not one of my sisters who died too young. Nothing that easy, Liza. Nothing that good. It was a boy. A boy who had measles when he was six, who took the stairs two at a time—a boy named Jimmy. . . ."

She stared at me doubtfully, then down at the picture I held—the picture of me when I was six. "But you—" she began. Then she turned away without finishing, while the others began straggling in.

We had to stay for the ceremony, of course, though I

guess Mother didn't need me at the funeral. She already had her Jimmy.

She'd wanted to name me James for her father, and Dad had insisted on Andrew for his. He'd won, and Andrew came first. But until I was ten, I'd always been called Jimmy by Mother. Jimmy, Andy, Andrew, A. J. A man's name was part of his soul, I remembered, in the old beliefs.

But it didn't make sense, no matter how I figured it out by myself. I tried to talk it over with Matthews, but he wouldn't comment. I made another effort with Liza when we were on the plane going back.

"I can believe in Mother's spirit," I finished. I'd been over it all so often in my own mind that I had accepted that finally. "But who was Jimmy? We all heard him—even Agnes's daughter heard him from downstairs. So he wasn't a delusion. But he can't be a ghost. A ghost is a returned spirit—the soul of a man who has died!"

"Well?" Liza asked coldly. I waited, but she went on staring out of the plane window, not saying another word.

I used to think meeting a ghost would offer reassurance to a man. Now I don't know. If I could only explain little Jimmy. . . .

One of the luminaries of the Golden Age of science fiction, Lester del Rey was born in Minnesota in 1915. A sharecropper's son, the Great Depression ended his higher education after two years at George Washington University (1932–33). His first story, "The Faithful" (1938), led to a remarkable career as a writer. In his grim novella, Nerves *(1942), he was the first to write of the possible consequences of a nuclear power accident. He is currently editor of the Del Rey Books line of Ballantine in New York.*

There was more than one way to look at the lonely witch woman in the sleepy south Georgia town who befriended the little boy who haunted the lonely plantation. . . .

FIVE

Poor Little Saturday
Madeleine L'Engle

The witch woman lived in a deserted, boarded-up plantation house, and nobody knew about her but me. Nobody in the nosey little town in south Georgia where I lived when I was a boy knew that if you walked down the dusty main street to where the post office ended it, and then turned left and followed that road a piece until you got to the rusty iron gates of the drive to the plantation house, you could find goings on would make your eyes pop out. It was just luck that I found out. Or maybe it wasn't luck at all. Maybe the witch woman wanted me to find out because of Alexandra. But now I wish I hadn't because the witch woman and Alexandra are gone forever and it's much worse than if I'd never known them.

Nobody'd lived in the plantation house since the Civil War when Colonel Londermaine was killed and Alexandra Londermaine, his beautiful young wife, hung herself on the chandelier in the ball room. A while before I was born some northerners bought it but after a few years they stopped coming and people said it was because the house was haunted. Every few years a gang of boys or men would set out to explore the house but nobody ever found anything, and it was so well boarded up it was hard to force an entrance, so by and by the town lost interest in it. No one climbed the wall and wandered around the grounds except me.

I used to go there often during the summer because I had bad spells of malaria when sometimes I couldn't bear to lie on the iron bedstead in my room with the flies buzzing around my face, or out on the hammock on the porch with the screams and laughter of the other kids as they played torturing my ears. My aching head made it impossible for me to read, and I would drag myself down the road, scuffling my bare sunburned toes in the dust, wearing the tattered straw hat that was supposed to protect me from the heat of the sun, shivering and sweating by turns. Sometimes it would seem hours before I got to the iron gates near which the brick wall was lowest. Often I would have to lie panting on the tall prickly grass for minutes until I gathered strength to scale the wall and drop down on the other side.

But once inside the grounds it seemed cooler. One funny thing about my chills was that I didn't seem to shiver nearly as much when I could keep cool as I did at home where even the walls and the floors, if you touched them, were hot. The grounds were filled with live oaks that had grown up unchecked everywhere and afforded an almost continuous green shade. The ground was covered with ferns which were soft and cool to lie on, and when I flung myself down on my back and looked up, the roof of leaves was so thick that sometimes I couldn't see the sky at all. The sun that managed to filter through lost its bright pitiless glare and came in soft yellow shafts that didn't burn you when they touched you.

One afternoon, a scorcher early in September, which is usually our hottest month (and by then you're fagged out by the heat anyhow), I set out for the plantation. The heat lay coiled and shimmering on the road. When you looked at anything through it, it was like looking through a defective pane of glass. The dirt road was so hot that it burned even through my calloused feet and as I walked clouds of dust rose in front of me and mixed with the shimmying of the heat. I thought I'd never make the plantation. Sweat was running into my eyes but it was cold sweat, and I was shivering so that my teeth chattered as I walked. When I managed finally to fling myself down on my soft green bed of ferns inside the grounds I was seized with one of the worst chills I'd ever had in spite of the fact that my mother had given me an extra dose of quinine that morning and some 666 Malaria Medicine to boot. I shut my eyes tight and clutched the ferns with my hands and teeth to wait until the chill had passed, when I heard a soft voice call:

"Boy."

I thought at first I was delirious, because sometimes I got lightheaded when my bad attacks came on; only then I remembered that when I was delirious I didn't know it; all the strange things I saw and heard seemed perfectly natural. So when the voice said, "Boy," again, as soft and clear as the mocking bird at sunrise, I opened my eyes.

Kneeling near me on the ferns was a girl. She must have been about a year younger than I. I was almost sixteen so I guess she was fourteen or fifteen. She was dressed in a blue and white gingham dress; her face was very pale, but the kind of paleness that's supposed to be, not the sickly pale kind that was like mine showing even under the tan. Her eyes were big and very blue. Her hair was dark brown and she wore it parted in the middle in two heavy braids that were swinging in front of her shoulders as she peered into my face.

"You don't feel well, do you?" she asked. There was no trace of concern or worry in her voice. Just scientific interest.

I shook my head. "No," I whispered, almost afraid that if I talked she would vanish, because I had never seen anyone here before, and I thought that maybe I was dying because I felt so awful, and I thought maybe that gave me the power to see the ghost. But the girl in blue and white checked gingham seemed as I watched her to be good flesh and blood.

"You'd better come with me," she said. "She'll make you all right."

"Who's she?"

"Oh—just Her," she said.

My chill had begun to recede by now, so when she got up off her knees, I scrambled up, too. When she stood up her dress showed a white ruffled petticoat underneath it, and bits of green moss had left patterns on her knees and I didn't think that would happen to the knees of a ghost, so I followed her as she led the way towards the house. She did not go up the sagging, half-rotted steps which led to the veranda about whose white pillars wisteria vines climbed in wild profusion, but went around to the side of the house where there were slanting doors to a cellar. The sun and rain had long since blistered and washed off the paint, but the doors looked clean and were free of the bits of bark from the eucalyptus tree which leaned nearby and which had dropped its bits of dusty peel on either side; so I knew that these cellar stairs must frequently be used.

The girl opened the cellar doors. "You go down first," she said. I went down the cellar steps which were stone, and cool against my bare feet. As she followed me she closed the cellar doors after her and as I reached the bottom of the stairs we were in pitch darkness. I began to be very frightened until her soft voice came out of the black.

"Boy, where are you?"

"Right here."

"You'd better take my hand. You might stumble."

We reached out and found each other's hands in the darkness. Her fingers were long and cool and they closed firmly around mine. She moved with authority as though she knew her way with the familiarity born of custom.

"Poor Sat's all in the dark," she said, "but he likes it that way. He likes to sleep for weeks at a time. Sometimes he snores awfully. Sat, darling!" she called gently. A soft, bubbly, blowing sound came in answer, and she laughed happily. "Oh, Sat, you are sweet!" she said, and the bubbly sound came again. Then the girl pulled at my hand and we came out into a huge and dusty kitchen. Iron skillets, pots, and pans were still hanging on either side of the huge stove, and there was a rolling pin and a bowl of flour on the marble topped table in the middle of the room. The girl took a lighted candle off the shelf.

"I'm going to make cookies," she said as she saw me looking at the flour and the rolling pin. She slipped her hand out of mine. "Come along." She began to walk more rapidly. We left the kitchen, crossed the hall, went through the dining room, its old mahogany table thick with dust although sheets covered the pictures on the walls. Then we went into the ball room. The mirrors lining the walls were spotted and discolored; against one wall was a single delicate gold chair, its seat cushioned with pale rose and silver woven silk; it seemed extraordinarily well preserved. From the ceiling hung the huge chandelier from which Alexandra Londermaine had hung herself, its prisms catching and breaking up into a hundred colors the flickering of the candle and the few shafts of light that managed to slide in through the boarded-up windows. As we crossed the ball room the girl began to dance by herself, gracefully, lightly, so that her full blue and white checked gingham skirts flew out around her. She looked at herself with pleasure in the old mirrors as she danced, the candle flaring and guttering in her right hand.

"You've stopped shaking. Now what will I tell Her?" she said as we started to climb the broad mahogany staircase. It was very dark so she took my hand again, and before we had reached the top of the stairs I obliged her by being seized by another chill. She felt my trembling fingers with satisfaction. "Oh, you've started again. That's good." She slid open one of the huge double doors at the head of the stairs.

As I looked in to what once must have been Colonel Londermaine's study I thought that surely what I saw was a scene in a dream or a vision in delirium. Seated at the huge table in the center of the room was the most extraordinary woman I had ever seen. I felt that she must be very beautiful, although she would never have fulfilled any of the standards of beauty set by our town. Even though she was seated I felt that she must be immensely tall. Piled up on the table in front of her were several huge volumes, and her finger was marking the place in the open one in front of her, but she was not reading. She was leaning back in the carved chair, her head resting against a piece of blue and gold embroidered silk that was flung across the chair back, one hand gently stroking a fawn that lay sleeping in her lap. Her eyes were closed and somehow I couldn't imagine what color they would be. It wouldn't have surprised me if they had been shining amber or the deep purple of her velvet robe. She had a great quantity of hair, the color of mahogany in firelight, which was cut quite short and seemed to be blown wildly about her head like flame. Under her closed eyes were deep shadows, and lines of pain about her mouth. Otherwise there were no marks of age on her face

95

but I would not have been surprised to learn that she was any age in the world—a hundred, or twenty-five. Her mouth was large and mobile and she was singing something in a deep, rich voice. Two cats, one black, one white, were coiled up, each on a book, and as we opened the doors a leopard stood up quietly beside her, but did not snarl or move. It simply stood there and waited, watching us.

The girl nudged me and held her finger to her lips to warn me to be quiet, but I would not have spoken—could not, anyhow, my teeth were chattering so from my chill which I had completely forgotten, so fascinated was I by this woman sitting back with her head against the embroidered silk, soft deep sounds coming out of her throat. At last these sounds resolved themselves into words, and we listened to her as she sang. The cats slept indifferently, but the leopard listened, too:

> I sit high in my ivory tower,
>   The heavy curtains drawn.
> I've many a strange and lustrous flower,
>   A leopard and a fawn
>
> Together sleeping by my chair
>   And strange birds softly winging,
> And ever pleasant to my ear
>   Twelve maidens' voices singing.
>
> Here is my magic maps' array,
>   My mystic circle's flame.
> With symbol's art He lets me play,
>   The unknown my domain,
>
> And as I sit here in my dream
>   I see myself awake,
> Hearing a torn and bloody scream,
>   Feeling my castle shake . . .

Her song wasn't finished but she opened her eyes and looked at us. Now that his mistress knew we were here the leopard seemed ready to spring and devour me at one gulp, but she put her hand on his sapphire-studded collar to restrain him.

"Well, Alexandra," she said, "Who have we here?"

The girl, who still held my hand in her long, cool fingers, answered, "It's a boy."

"So I see. Where did you find him?"

The voice sent shivers up and down my spine.

"In the fern bed. He was shaking. See? He's shaking now. Is he having a fit?" Alexandra's voice was filled with pleased interest.

"Come here, boy," the woman said.

As I didn't move, Alexandra gave me a push, and I advanced slowly. As I came near, the woman pulled one of the leopard's ears gently, saying, "Lie down, Thammuz." The beast obeyed, flinging itself at her feet. She held her hand out to me as I approached the table. If Alexandra's fingers felt firm and cool, hers had the strength of the ocean and the coolness of jade. She looked at me for a long time and I saw that her eyes were deep blue, much bluer than Alexandra's, so dark as to be almost black. When she spoke again her voice was warm and tender: "You're burning up with fever. One of the malaria bugs?" I nodded. "Well, we'll fix that for you."

When she stood and put the sleeping fawn down by the leopard, she was not as tall as I had expected her to be; nevertheless she gave an impression of great height. Several of the bookshelves in one corner were emptied of books and filled with various shaped bottles and retorts. Nearby was a large skeleton. There was an acid stained wash basin, too; that whole section of the room looked like part of a chemist's or physicist's laboratory. She selected from among the bottles a small amber colored one, and poured a drop of the liquid it contained into a glass of water. As the drop hit the water there was a loud hiss and clouds of dense smoke arose. When it had drifted away she handed the glass to me and said, "Drink. Drink, my boy!"

My hand was trembling so that I could scarcely hold the glass. Seeing this, she took it from me and held it to my lips.

"What is it?" I asked.

"Drink it," she said, pressing the rim of the glass against my teeth. On the first swallow I started to choke and would have pushed the stuff away, but she forced the rest of the burning liquid down my throat. My whole body felt on fire. I

felt flame flickering in every vein and the room and everything in it swirled around. When I had regained my equi-
librium to a certain extent I managed to gasp out again,
"What is it?"

She smiled and answered:

Nine peacocks' hearts, four bats' tongues,
A pinch of moondust and a hummingbird's lungs.

Then I asked a question I would never have dared ask if it
hadn't been that I was still half drunk from the potion I had
swallowed, "Are you a witch?"

She smiled again, and answered, "I make it my profession."

Since she hadn't struck me down with a flash of lightning,
I went on. "Do you ride a broomstick?"

This time she laughed. "I can when I like."

"Is it—is it very hard?"

"Rather like a bucking bronco at first, but I've always
been a good horsewoman, and now I can manage very
nicely. I've finally progressed to sidesaddle, though I still feel
safer astride. I always rode my horse astride. Still, the best
witches ride sidesaddle, so . . . Now run along home. Alexandra has lessons to study and I must work. Can you hold
your tongue or must I make you forget?"

"I can hold my tongue."

She looked at me and her eyes burnt into me like the
potion she had given me to drink. "Yes, I think you can,"
she said. "Come back tomorrow if you like. Thammuz will
show you out."

The leopard rose and led the way to the door. As I hesitated, unwilling to tear myself away, it came back and pulled
gently but firmly on my trouser leg.

"Good-bye, boy," the witch woman said. "And you
won't have any more chills and fever."

"Good-bye," I answered. I didn't say thank you. I didn't
say good-bye to Alexandra. I followed the leopard out.

She let me come every day. I think she must have been
lonely. After all I was the only thing there with a life apart
from hers. And in the long run the only reason I have had a
life of my own is because of her. I am as much a creation of

the witch woman's as Thammuz the leopard was, or the two cats, Ashtaroth and Orus (it wasn't until many years after the last day I saw the witch woman that I learned that those were the names of the fallen angels).

She did cure my malaria, too. My parents and the townspeople thought that I had outgrown it. I grew angry when they talked about it so lightly and wanted to tell them that it was the witch woman, but I knew that if ever I breathed a word about her I would be eternally damned. Mamma thought we should write a testimonial letter to the 666 Malaria Medicine people, and maybe they'd send us a couple of dollars.

Alexandra and I became very good friends. She was a strange, aloof creature. She liked me to watch her while she danced alone in the ball room or played on an imaginary harp—thought sometimes I fancied I could hear the music. One day she took me into the drawing room and uncovered a portrait that was hung between two of the long boarded up windows. Then she stepped back and held her candle high so as to throw the best light on the picture. It might have been a picture of Alexandra herself, or Alexandra as she might be in five years.

"That's my mother," she said. "Alexandra Londermaine."

As far as I knew from the tales that went about town, Alexandra Londermaine had given birth to only one child, and that still-born, before she had hung herself on the chandelier in the ball room—and anyhow, any child of hers would have been Alexandra's mother or grandmother. But I didn't say anything because when Alexandra got angry she became ferocious like one of the cats, and was given to leaping on me, scratching and biting. I looked at the portrait long and silently.

"You see, she has on a ring like mine," Alexandra said, holding out her left hand, on the fourth finger of which was the most beautiful sapphire and diamond ring I had ever seen, or rather, that I could ever have imagined, for it was a ring apart from any owned by even the most wealthy of the townsfolk. Then I realized that Alexandra had brought me in here and unveiled the portrait simply that she might show me the ring to better advantage, for she had never worn a ring before.

"Where did you get it?"

"Oh, she got it for me last night."

"Alexandra," I asked suddenly, "how long have you been here?"

"Oh, a while."

"But how long?"

"Oh, I don't remember."

"But you must remember."

"I don't. I just came—like Poor Sat."

"Who's Poor Sat?" I asked, thinking for the first time of whoever it was that had made the gentle bubbly noises at Alexandra the day she found me in the fern bed.

"Why, we've never shown you Sat, have we!" she exclaimed. "I'm sure it's all right, but we'd better ask Her first."

So we went to the witch woman's room and knocked. Thammuz pulled the door open with his strong teeth and the witch woman looked up from some sort of experiment she was making with test tubes and retorts. The fawn, as usual, lay sleeping near her feet. "Well?" she said.

"Is it all right if I take him to see Poor Little Saturday?" Alexandra asked her.

"Yes, I suppose so," she answered. "But no teasing," and turned her back to us and bent again over her test tubes as Thammuz nosed us out of the room.

We went down to the cellar. Alexandra lit a lamp and took me back to the corner furthest from the doors, where there was a stall. In the stall was a two-humped camel. I couldn't help laughing as I looked at him because he grinned at Alexandra so foolishly, displaying all his huge buck teeth and blowing bubbles through them.

"She said we weren't to tease him," Alexandra said severely, rubbing her cheek against the preposterous splotchy hair that seemed to be coming out, leaving bald pink spots of skin on his long nose.

"But what—" I started.

"She rides him sometimes." Alexandra held out her hand while he nuzzled against it, scratching his rubbery lips against the diamond and sapphire of her ring. "Mostly She talks to him. She says he is very wise. He goes up to Her

100

room sometimes and they talk and talk. I can't understand a word they say. She says it's Hindustani and Arabic. Sometimes I can remember little bits of it, like: *iderow, sorcabatcha,* and *anna bihed bech.* She says I can learn to speak with them when I finish learning French and Greek."

Poor Little Saturday was rolling his eyes in delight as Alexandra scratched behind his ears. "Why is he called Poor Little Saturday?" I asked.

Alexandra spoke with a ring of pride in her voice. "I named him. She let me."

"But why did you name him that?"

"Because he came last winter on the Saturday that was the shortest day of the year, and it rained all day so it got light later and dark earlier than it would have if it had been nice, so it really didn't have as much of itself as it should, and I felt so sorry for it I thought maybe it would feel better if we named him after it . . . she thought it was a nice name!" she turned on me suddenly.

"Oh, it is! It's a fine name!" I said quickly, smiling to myself as I realized how much greater was this compassion of Alexandra's for a day than any she might have for a human being. "How did She get him?" I asked.

"Oh, he just came."

"What do you mean?"

"She wanted him so he came. From the desert."

"He *walked!*"

"Yes. And swam part of the way. She met him at the beach and flew him here on the broom stick. You should have seen him. She was still all wet and looked so funny. She gave him hot coffee with things in it."

"What things?"

"Oh, just things."

Then the witch woman's voice came from behind us. "Well, children?"

It was the first time I had seen her out of her room. Thammuz was at her right heel, the fawn at her left. The cats, Ashtaroth and Orus, had evidently stayed upstairs. "Would you like to ride Saturday?" she asked me.

Speechless, I nodded. She put her hand against the wall and a portion of it slid down into the earth so that Poor Little Saturday was free to go out. "She's sweet, isn't she?" the witch woman asked me, looking affectionately at the strange, bumpy-kneed, splay-footed creature. "Her grandmother was very good to me in Egypt once. Besides, I love camel's milk."

"But Alexandra said she was a he!" I exclaimed.

"Alexandra's the kind of woman to whom all animals are he except cats, and all cats are she. As a matter of fact, Ashtaroth and Orus are she, but it wouldn't make any difference to Alexandra if they weren't. Go on out, Saturday. Come on!"

Saturday backed out, bumping her bulging knees and ankles against her stall, and stood under a live oak tree. "Down," the witch woman said. Saturday leered at me and didn't move. "Down, sorcabatcha!" the witch woman commanded, and Saturday obediently got down on her knees. I clambered up onto her, and before I had managed to get at all settled she rose with such a jerky motion that I knocked my chin against her front hump and nearly bit my tongue off. Round and round Saturday danced while I clung wildly to her front hump and the witch woman and Alexandra rolled on the ground with laughter. I felt as though I were on a very unseaworthy vessel on the high seas, and it wasn't long before I felt violently seasick as Saturday pranced among the live oak trees, sneezing delicately.

At last the witch woman called out, "Enough!" and Saturday stopped in her tracks, nearly throwing me, and kneeling laboriously. "It was mean to tease you," the witch woman said, pulling my nose gently. "You may come sit in my room with me for a while if you like."

There was nothing I liked better than to sit in the witch woman's room and to watch her while she studied from her books, worked out strange looking mathematical problems, argued with the zodiac, or conducted complicated experiments with her test tubes and retorts, sometimes filling the room with sulphurous odors or flooding it with red or blue light. Only once was I afraid of her, and that was when she danced with the skeleton in the corner. She had the room flooded with a strange red glow and I almost thought I could see the flesh covering the bones of the skeleton as they danced together like lovers. I think she had forgotten that I was sitting there, half hidden in the wing chair, because when they had finished dancing and the skeleton stood in the corner again, his bones shining and polished, devoid of any living trappings, she stood with her forehead against one of the deep red velvet curtains that covered the boarded-up windows and tears streamed down her cheeks. Then she went back to her test tubes and worked feverishly. She never alluded to the incident and neither did I.

As winter drew on she let me spend more and more time in the room. Once I gathered up courage enough to ask her about herself, but I got precious little satisfaction.

"Well, then, are you maybe one of the northerners who bought the place?"

"Let's leave it at that, boy. We'll say that's who I am. Did you know that my skeleton was old Colonel Londermaine? Not so old, as a matter of fact; he was only thirty-seven when he was killed at the battle of Bunker Hill—or am I getting him confused with his great-grandfather, Rudolph Londermaine? Anyhow he was only thirty-seven, and a fine figure of a man, and Alexandra only thirty when she hung herself for love of him on the chandelier in the ballroom. Did you know that the fat man with the red mustaches has been trying to cheat your father? His cow will give sour milk for seven days. Run along now and talk to Alexandra. She's lonely."

When the winter had turned to spring and the camellias and azaleas and Cape Jessamine had given way to the more lush blooms of early May, I kissed Alexandra for the first time, very clumsily. The next evening when I managed to get away from the chores at home and hurried out to the plantation, she gave me her sapphire and diamond ring which she had swung for me on a narrow bit of turquoise satin. "It will keep us both safe," she said, "if you wear it always. And then when we're older we can get married and you can give it back to me. Only you mustn't let anyone see it, ever, ever, or She'd be very angry."

I was afraid to take the ring but when I demurred Alexandra grew furious and started kicking and biting and I had to give in.

Summer was almost over before my father discovered the ring hanging about my neck. I fought like a witch boy to keep him from pulling out the narrow ribbon and seeing the ring, and indeed the ring seemed to give me added strength and I had grown, in any case, much stronger during the winter than I had ever been in my life. But my father was still stronger than I, and he pulled it out. He looked at it in dead silence for a moment and then the storm broke. That was the famous Londermaine ring that had disappeared the night Alexandra Londermaine hung herself. That ring was worth a fortune. Where had I got it?

No one believed me when I said I had found it in the grounds near the house—I chose the grounds because I didn't want anybody to think I had been in the house or indeed that I was able to get in. I don't know why they didn't believe me; it still seems quite logical to me that I might have found it buried among the ferns.

It had been a long, dull year, and the men of the town were all bored. They took me and forced me to swallow quantities of corn liquor until I didn't know what I was saying or doing. When they had finished with me I didn't even manage to reach home before I was violently sick and then I was in my mother's arms and she was weeping over me. It was morning before I was able to slip away to the plantation house. I ran pounding up the mahogany stairs to the witch woman's room and opened the heavy sliding doors without knocking. She stood in the center of the room in her purple robe, her arms around Alexandra who was weeping bitterly. Overnight the room had completely changed. The skeleton of Colonel Londermaine was gone, and books filled the shelves in the corner of the room that had been her laboratory. Cobwebs were everywhere, and broken glass lay on the floor; dust was inches thick on her work table. There was no sign of Thammuz, Ashtaroth or Orus, or the fawn, but four birds were flying about her, beating their wings against her hair.

She did not look at me or in any way acknowledge my presence. Her arm about Alexandra, she led her out of the room and to the drawing room where the portrait hung. The birds followed, flying around and around them. Alexandra had stopped weeping now. Her face was very proud and pale and if she saw me miserably trailing behind them she gave no notice. When the witch woman stood in front of the portrait the sheet fell from it. She raised her arm; there was a great cloud of smoke; the smell of sulphur filled my nostrils, and when the smoke was gone, Alexandra was gone, too. Only the portrait was there, the fourth finger of the left hand now bearing no ring. The witch woman raised her hand again and the sheet lifted itself up and covered the portrait. Then she went, with the birds, slowly back to what had once been her room, and still I tailed after, frightened as I had never been before in my life, or have been since.

She stood without moving in the center of the room for a long time. At last she turned and spoke to me.

"Well, boy, where is the ring?"

"They have it."

"They made you drunk, didn't they?"

"Yes."

"I was afraid something like this would happen when I gave Alexandra the ring. But it doesn't matter . . . I'm tired . . ." She drew her hand wearily across her forehead.

"Did I—did I tell them everything?"

"You did."

"I—I didn't know."

"I know you didn't know, boy."

"Do you hate me now?"

"No, boy, I don't hate you."

"Do you have to go away?"

"Yes."

I bowed my head. "I'm so sorry . . ."

She smiled slightly. "The sands of time . . . Cities crumble and rise and will crumble again and breath dies down and blows once more . . ."

The birds flew madly about her head, pulling at her hair, calling into her ears. Downstairs we could hear a loud pounding, and then the crack of boards being pulled away from a window.

"Go, boy," she said to me. I stood rooted, motionless, unable to move. "GO!" she commanded, giving me a mighty push so that I stumbled out of the room. They were waiting for me by the cellar doors and caught me as I climbed out. I had to stand there and watch when they came out with her. But it wasn't the witch woman, my witch woman. It was *their* idea of a witch woman, someone thousands of years old, a disheveled old creature in rusty black, with long wisps of gray hair, a hooked nose, and four wiry black hairs springing out of the mole on her chin. Behind her flew the four birds and suddenly they went up, up, into the sky, directly in the path of the sun until they were lost in its burning glare.

Two of the men stood holding her tightly, although she wasn't struggling, but standing there, very quiet, while the others searched the house, searched it in vain. Then as a group of them went down into the cellar I remembered, and by a flicker of the old light in the witch woman's eyes I could see that she remembered, too. Poor Little Saturday had been forgotten. Out she came, prancing absurdly up the cellar steps, her rubbery lips stretched back over her gigantic teeth, her eyes bulging with terror. When she saw the witch woman, her lord and master, held captive by two dirty, insensitive men, she let out a shriek and began to kick and lunge wildly, biting, screaming with the blood-curdling, heart-rending screams that only a camel can make. One of the men fell to the ground, holding a leg in which the bone had snapped from one of Saturday's kicks. The others scattered in terror, leaving the witch woman standing on the veranda supporting herself by clinging to one of the huge wisteria vines that curled around the columns. Saturday clambered up onto the veranda, and knelt while she flung herself between the two humps. Then off they ran, Saturday still screaming, her knees knocking together, the ground shaking as she pounded along. Down from the sun plummeted the four birds and flew after them.

Up and down I danced, waving my arms, shouting wildly until Saturday and the witch woman and the birds were lost in a cloud of dust, while the man with the broken leg lay moaning on the ground beside me.

Born in New York City in 1917, Madeleine L'Engle was educated at Smith College and Columbia University. During World War II she taught for the Committee for Refugee Education, helping victims of Nazi terror settle in the United States; later she taught at St. Hugh's School in New York. A specialist in children's books, she is best known for her science fiction novel A Wrinkle in Time, *which won the Newbery Medal in*

1963, the Hans Christian Andersen Runner-Up Award in 1964, the Sequoyah Award in 1965, and the Lewis Carroll Shelf Award in 1965. She has also written a number of shorter works, such as the charming— and somewhat sinister—"Poor Little Saturday."

Sandy knew Wayne only listened to the music of the 1960s, but she never expected him to become obsessed with the music of the dead.

SIX

On 202

Jeff Hecht

The leaves skittered across the road as the cold November wind blew out of the western Massachusetts hills. They were a familiar sight to Sandy, but the first time the headlights of the old Volvo caught them, Wayne started to brake the car and stalled the engine. He muttered an obscenity.

"Why did you do that? You're going to get us stuck out here," Sandy grumbled. "I told you we should have stayed the night in Amherst." Even though they were both tired and it was nearly midnight before they'd left Sandy's friends' apartment, Wayne had insisted on making the two-hour trip to her parents' home in Lowell that night.

"There were animals running across the road," Wayne replied as he shifted into neutral and steered the slowing car toward the side of the road. The engine caught, and he shifted back into drive. "Didn't you see them? They were little dark things, rats I think." He accelerated and pulled the car back toward the middle of the empty road.

"They were just leaves, blown by the wind. It's something you never see in California."

"Then I'm glad I missed them. California's always had everything I wanted."

"Except me."

"Sometimes I wonder about that."

It was an old line of banter that, like many other things, was souring on them both, but Wayne's twisting of it hurt Sandy. The trip had been her idea—she'd wanted to visit family and friends back East, and hoped that the trip would help bring her and Wayne back together. But nothing had gone right; even the old car she'd brought West with her years ago was dying. "Come on, Wayne. You agreed to come back with me. You said you wanted to see the East, remember?"

"Yeah, I guess I did. There was nothing better to do. But it's so damn alien here."

Sandy stared out the windshield, trying to find a way to snap Wayne out of his foul mood. The wind was picking up, bringing with it some snowflakes which were settling on the empty road that would take them to Pelham, where they would pick up Route 202 and drive north for miles to Route 2, then to Route 495, and finally into Lowell. She knew the route well from her college years, but she'd never taken it so late at night.

In the silence, Wayne reached over and turned on the radio. He punched two buttons and got only static, but the third brought Jimi Hendrix's voice into the car: "Two riders were approaching, and the wind began to howl . . ." The last word echoed down the road with them and the wind, then faded back into static as they went down a hill.

Sandy shuddered. "Turn it off, Wayne, please."

"Why? I like it; I haven't heard it in ages."

"It bothers me. Hendrix has been dead for ten years now. To hear him now is like—like a ghost singing."

Wayne laughed. "Don't be silly. It's just electronics, just music. It's grooves on a record being translated electromechanically into signals that can make a speaker move. There's nothing supernatural about it." He stared out into the thickening snow. "The only thing that's spooky around here is the country."

"What do you mean?"

"It's strange, that's all. Ancient and foreboding and now—" he pointed to the bare trees beside the road, "—barren."

"You call this barren after living around Los Angeles?" Sandy thought of the scraggly shrubs that failed to cover the dry soil of the Angeles National Forest, and of the sandy desert east of San Bernardino.

"No, I mean empty, menacing. You remember that book we read by Lovecraft? He lived in New England, and this is his kind of country. Even the names match. I remember the name of one of his characters—Whateley, Wilbur Whateley.

There's a town named after him. We drove through it, re-member?"

"The town spells it differently—W-h-a-t-e-l-y. Lovecraft had an extra *e* in it. I checked."

Wayne shrugged. "It doesn't matter. It's still a horror-story kind of place, a dark and sleepy town that time and the highway passed by."

Sandy watched the snowflakes as she tried to sort through her thoughts. "I don't understand." She saw a single light on the hillside; outside of their headlights it seemed to be the only light in the world. "Why does it bother you?"

"It's empty, it's—" he groped for words. "Well, I can't really find the words, but it's just not right."

"For God's sake, Wayne, it sounds like you're taking those old horror stories seriously!"

He turned from the road and looked at her. "So how many horror stories have they written about Los Angeles?" They came up over a hill and saw a handful of lights among the snowflakes and the dark houses of Pelham. "Look, Sandy," he stated, but was interrupted by John Lennon singing from the radio: "All we are saying, is give peace a chance."

Sandy shivered. "Please turn it off."

"But it's good music—great music. It takes me back to the good years, back when the Movement was alive."

"Lennon is dead," she said, realizing as the words came from her mouth that they would have no more impact than reminding Wayne that the Movement had died, too. He had never been able to cope with that reality, and music had become his way of tuning out the world. At times—often when she was out working—he would sit for hours listening over headphones. "Just listening," he would say when she came home and asked. He insisted that the only reason he used the headphones was that they sounded better than the speakers, but she suspected that he really was trying to keep his beloved old music to himself. Perhaps he wanted to slip back a decade to when the music was being made, and to when he wasn't the only one drifting aimlessly through life.

Wayne shifted into neutral and kept his foot on the gas while braking for the flashing red light at the end of the road. It wasn't the best treatment for an automatic transmission, but it was the only way they'd found to keep the car from stalling when they slowed it. This time it worked.

"We don't have to worry about that again for a while," Sandy said as they coasted through the left turn and Wayne began accelerating on Route 202. "It's probably twenty miles before the next stop light."

"That far?"

"There's not much out this way. We're going through the watershed of the Quabbin Reservoir—Boston's water supply. There aren't any houses for miles." They were out of the village of Pelham before they realized it. The snow was coming down heavily now, and Wayne eased off the gas. With the snow blowing outside and the speedometer light out, Sandy couldn't estimate their speed. The trees seemed to meet overhead at places, and it looked as if they were driving through an endless tunnel defined by their headlights.

Wayne stared out into the snow, trying to see the road. "The snow's early, isn't it?"

"A little. But it does this sometimes." The sad, flabby voice of Elvis Presley sang meaningless words in the background. Sandy tuned them out automatically.

"It's a desolate land, Sandy, and these are desolate times." Wayne's voice seemed remote, as if he was speaking from the other end of a tunnel rather than from the other side of the car. "The music helps me hold off the worst of it, lets me try to recapture the magic that's gone. Sometimes it seems like I'm the only one left who remembers it all, you know, like everybody else had forgotten peace and love and copped out and voted for Ronnie Reagan."

"What do you mean?" Sandy kept her question short, hoping it would keep Wayne from drifting back into the silent brooding that she dreaded the most.

"Even the music has become a big business. Take Elvis—or Lennon. What did they say Lennon was worth when that guy shot him—two hundred million? What did he do to deserve all of that? And how many people could he have fed with his money?"

It was a familiar tirade. Wayne had always been jealous of people who had money because he wished he had some, and Sandy told him so once again. She didn't expect him to become a businessman, but there were times that she did get tired of supporting him.

"It's not the money, dammit, it's the waste. Lennon and Yoko rode around in chauffeured Rolls Royces while people starved to death. And look at your friends out there in that little town with all that land. They have a great big lawn, some pasture for a couple of horses, and forty acres of woods. That land could be feeding people like it used to. Now it's covered by the darkness of the forest because the rich think it's pretty."

The tone of the words scared Sandy. "That soil is awfully rocky, Wayne; you can't farm it very well."

"But people did a hundred years ago. That quaint little house used to be a farmhouse that housed real working people, and those woods used to be a farm that gave them a living. Your friends seemed so proud of that. Why waste land that could be used? Why hand it over to the darkness of the forest?"

"What's the matter with the forest? We need trees; they can be lovely."

"They cut out the sun and hide the light. The forest breeds bugs and decay and disease."

"That's where you had your bad trip, wasn't it. Out in the woods in Oregon somewhere? You're not getting a flash-back now, are you? Not after all these years?"

Wayne stared through the windshield at the tunnel of snow illuminated by the cold light of the headlamps. "No." He seemed to be switching his attention back to the road. The wind had died down, and enough of the heavy snow had accumulated to make the surface slippery.

The distorted voice of a disk jockey cut through the static, a strange voice that Sandy felt sure she'd heard years before. "In Enfield this is WEND, 666 on your AM dial. That's the number of the beast, folks, you come to it and it comes to you, via the miracle of Mr. Marconi and others long dead. And you're listening to the voices of the dead tonight—"

Sandy leaned forward and punched another button on the radio. There was only static.

"Turn it back. I want to hear it."

"It fits your mood tonight, doesn't it? Voices of the dead from the dead past."

"Come on, dammit. I'm driving; I can pick what I want to listen to. I need it to keep awake—you're not going to find anything else on the air out here at this hour, are you?"

"I thought you wanted to talk."

"I did, for a while." He reached over to the radio and pushed the button that brought the music back. Jim Morrison's voice was singing: "Break . . . break . . . break on through . . . to the other side." Wayne turned the volume up.

"What's the matter?" Sandy asked, but Wayne didn't seem to hear her. She forced her voice to shout, trying to make herself heard over the music. "Turn it down!" When there was no response, she did. Wayne appeared to frown at her, but it was hard to be sure. With the dashboard lights out, the only light inside the car was the reflection of the headlights from the snow, and the feeble blue glow of the high-beam indicator. While she was looking at him, Wayne switched to low beams.

"Damn snow freaks me out," he muttered. "I can't see much out there, just the snowflakes and the darkness. The trees look like claws reaching into the night. I wish I was back in California."

Sandy turned her eyes to the heavy snow. The latticework of flakes drifting to the ground, dancing in front of the windshield, drew her attention. After she strained for a while, she could focus her eyes on the road. The car seemed to be crawling, probably going only about ten miles an hour. "Do you want me to drive? I can see in this—"

"No," Wayne snapped. "You said you were tired, and I told you I'd get you there."

"What about stopping?"

"We'd freeze out here."

"Maybe in Orange or Athol. There's got to be a motel somewhere around there. You're not going to make it this way, you know."

Wayne said nothing as the song drew to its crescendo and closed. He was being drawn into the music as Sandy had seen a hundred times before. He was nodding his head to it; she couldn't see his face, but she saw his head silhouetted against the snow. Jim Croce began singing "Bad, Bad Leroy Brown."

Wayne settled down for a moment. "It's the newest one they've played all night."

"It's not that new. Croce died years ago." Sandy couldn't remember when Croce's plane had crashed; it had faded into the haze that she identified as the middle seventies. "All the disco bands picked it up and turned it into mush."

Wayne was looking out into the snow, still bobbing his head faintly to the music. "It's good music, Sandy. Croce was one of the greats. I'd like to hear him now, you know, him and the others. But so many of them are gone— Hendrix and Elvis and Lennon and Morrison and—"

"Can you see where you're going, Wayne?"

"Of course not, not in this snow."

"Then let me drive. You're too tired, too far spaced out on something. You were smoking grass before we left, weren't you?"

"I'm okay," Wayne replied without taking his eyes from the falling snow. "You couldn't do any better in this mess. I'll make it—I always have."

Sandy didn't see how Wayne could see the road through the snow. They seemed to be alone in a world of whiteness, drifting through the space defined by their headlights. She hadn't seen another car moving since they'd left Amherst, but she wasn't surprised by that. The natives knew better than to drive on a country road in a nighttime snowstorm. And even if Route 202 was a U.S. highway, it was still a country road. "I'm scared," she said.

"So am I. I see the dark out there, I see the cold. I see things lurking in the trees, waiting for us. I see snow that would trap us here and freeze us to death. I see time, I see emptiness. I've never sensed an emptiness like this before. Even when we drove across the desert, it was on an interstate highway full of trucks and cars and at night there were at least other headlights. But this . . ."

Wayne's voice drifted away as the disk jockey returned. ". . . not the Grateful Dead, this night or ever here on Enfield Radio WEND, just the ungrateful dead . . ."

"Snap out of it, please, Wayne!" Sandy tried to shout, but the car seemed to muffle the words.

". . . Janis Joplin," were the disk jockey's words, tumbling out of the speaker. "You remember how she overdosed and they found her and we were all so scared that death had come to our beautiful world. . . ."

"Wayne!"

"I can see the road now, Sandy. Don't worry, don't worry. I can steer across the trackless waste between the vampire trees."

Sandy closed her eyes, bowed her head, and made the sign of the cross on her breast. It was the first time in years, since her grandmother had dragged her to church a few days after her seventeenth birthday. She tried to recapture the strand of faith that she'd let slip from her hands years before, tried to shut her eyes and ears to the outside and to pray.

Joplin's words drifted her into awareness—"Me and Bobby McGee," a song that had always reminded Sandy of people that once had been precious to her but now were gone. When the familiar voice of the dead woman she had never met came to the words "I let him slip away," Sandy broke into sobs. She thought of losing Wayne, and before him of losing Michael and Barney and Andy. She thought of her grandmother and her uncle Bill, both alive when she'd left Massachusetts, now both dead. She thought of the 4 A.M. phone call from her mother, begging her to come back home and see her grandmother before she died and how, standing naked in the tiny apartment in the cool California morning, she had begged off, trying to avoid telling her mother or admitting to herself how shaken she was.

As her tears began to subside, the music drifted back into her awareness. It was Morrison's voice again, louder than before and badly distorted: "This is the end, my only friend, the end . . ."

She looked at Wayne. He seemed rigid, hypnotized by the snow, but his arms still moved just enough to steer the car around curves. The flakes were coming at them faster— the car seemed to be speeding up. "Wayne, turn it off!" she demanded. He said nothing; Morrison's ghost voice sang of "a desperate land."

She reached to push a button, but couldn't make the dial move. When she moved her hand toward the volume control, Wayne's hand pushed hers away.

Sandy shivered. "Please, Wayne, please let me turn it off. It's scaring me, it's terrifying me, it's trying to kill me."

"I need it on." His voice was flat, almost calm except for its rigidity. "I can't see where I'm going without it." He steered the car around a curve and up a hill.

Sandy couldn't make herself believe that he knew what he was doing. In front of the car, she saw only snowflakes; to the side she knew there must be trees. She crossed herself, not recognizing the motion until she'd completed it. She tried to pray, to force the music out of her awareness, to push away Morrison's dead plea: "Ride the snake, he's old and his skin is cold. . . ."

The song evoked the fears that had haunted Sandy in the lonely, desolate years a decade earlier. It made her remember her last night with Barney, of lying sleeplessly beside him with the song haunting her long after the record had ended and the turntable shut itself off, leaving her alone with the silence and the certainty that she never wanted to see Barney again.

She prayed, trying to hold herself away from tears and the music. The words reached again for her attention after the long instrumental passage ended. A phrase touched her: "It hurts to set you free, but you'll never follow me." She would follow Wayne no more; she'd stay in Massachusetts and have someone send her things back from California.

"This . . ." the refrain repeated in the last line seemed to drag on forever and ". . . is . . ." tried to seize her, although ". . . the . . ." words were deceptively soft. The last of them ". . . ennnnnd . . ." stretched on to the end of the world as she tried to flee from it.

The force of the impact threw her against the seat and shoulder belts and knocked her unconscious.

She woke as two men in hunting jackets bundled her into a blanket. One was big and paunchy, an awkward man trying to handle her gently. The other was thinner and looked about twenty years older. "Does it hurt anywhere?" the older man asked when he saw her eyes were open.

She ignored the pain in her chest. "Wayne—what about Wayne?"

"The man in the car?" he asked, then realized that he didn't have to ask. "I'm afraid—afraid he's dead, ma'am."

"He's messed up real bad—stuck in there," the younger man said as they eased her into the back seat of their big old car.

Sandy cried then, cried as the older man laid something more over her, and cried as they started the car and drove on in the night. Much later, when she got control of herself, she asked them where Enfield was.

"Nothing there anymore, ma'am," the older man replied. "They drowned it more than forty years ago; it's under the Quabbin."

"There's an Enfield in Connecticut, Dad, down by Hartford," the younger man added.

Sandy heard him, but it didn't matter anymore.

Born in Connecticut in 1947, Jeff Hecht attended schools all over the United States before getting a degree in electronic engineering from the California Institute of Technology, followed by two years of graduate study at the University of Massachusetts at Amherst. After editing a trade magazine, Laser Focus, *for seven years, he became a full time writer in 1981. Co-author of* Laser: Super Tool for the '80s, *he has now turned to fiction such as "On 202."*

Karen thought the skip-rope rhyme about mass murderer Ransom Cowl was just part of a child's game—until the night someone dug up his grave.

SEVEN

Ransom Cowl Walks the Road
Nancy Varian Berberick

Dre: my husband's name has always held the magic to make me smile. Bowdre Carson. I can still hear his mother calling him. She would stand at the back door of the enormous old house. "Bowdre!" she would call, pause, and then louder: "Bowdree!" The *dreee!* would rise, skirling into the summer blue sky, losing none of its demand for distance. Dre would stop what he was doing at once. He'd grin sheepishly, and shrug, then scramble off to answer the summons. And always, before he left, he would stop to pull one of my long black braids and then dance away laughing. I didn't know it then, of course, but I probably loved Dre even in those golden days when being eight made the summer last forever.

I never longed, as many of my friends did, to leave our little town in the hills of western New Jersey. For me there were no bigger and better things to find than Dre and little Petersons Run. The years spent away at college were obligatory and I quickly put them behind me. Returning to Petersons Run to teach seemed right. I like completed circles. And after my first year at the grammar school "Karen Keller" became "Karen Carson" and I was happy.

My days moved to the songs of children, skip-rope rhymes, and learning tunes. *"A" my name is Alice and my husband's name is Al*—and *Lincoln, Lincoln, I've been thinkin', what's that stuff that you been drinkin'*—or *I before E except after C*. And, still, as it had been during the time

119

that Dre and I watched the years move along outside the wide classroom windows: *Ransom Cowl walks the road, Ransom Cowl can see! Ransom Cowl walks the road, and he comes for thee!* and the *thee!* would rise, high, almost hysterically high, and end in giggles and gasps.

Ransom Cowl was Petersons Run's own mass murderer.

He haunted the nights of the town's children with a delicious fear, mitigated by the nearness of parents murmuring in soft conversation, and the completed ending of the terrible story. Ransom Cowl had met justice. Strapped into a huge, ungainly wooden chair he went, assisted by killing voltage, to a quicker death than any of his victims had met. And each child knew that when a story is ended, it is ended. No one seemed to remember that the little rhyme chanted in schoolyards to the cadence of a skip rope was the curse of Beckon Cowl, spat out into the hot July dust the day her grandson was executed.

Jason's Meadow was named for Dre's maternal great-grandfather. The house, one hundred fifty years old and still in good condition, had been in his family since it was built to hold his great-grandfather's brood of seven children. It was a large, neatly laid-out clapboard at the edge of the four acres of Jason's Meadow that remained to Dre's family. The house came to Dre in the normal course of things, and both of us were happy to continue our lives together in this place where we'd played during our childhood. Another circle complete, I would think, as I went about cleaning the many rooms. Our children would grow up here, and theirs. My roots, when they are set, are set deeply.

I listened to the sighing of the snow in December, the insistent piping of cardinals in May, and the winding *chirrrr* of cicadas in July. These were the songs of my life until dirges came to replace them.

That year, though I was grateful for the summer school classes that provided extra money, I was also grateful that they would soon be over. Two more weeks, I thought as I took the steps of the front porch. Two more weeks!

I could sense Dre's mood before I saw him. I knew he was in the kitchen at the back of the house, brooding over a beer, before I called out. "Too many years together," he used to say when I did what he called reading his mind. He'd laugh and shake his head and swear that there was no use keeping secrets from me. I didn't read his mind, of course, and we both knew it. It was just cumulative knowledge. He could do the trick, too, but didn't very often.

"Dre?"

"Back here, honey." His voice was flat, dull, empty of anything that would tell me his mood. Still, I knew.

"You're home early." I dropped my book bag onto the sofa in the living room, scooped up the mail from the coffee table, and went through into the kitchen. July sunlight splashed soft squares of gold across the wide planked floor. The earthy scents of basil, thyme, and oregano interlaced under the sun's heat with the marigolds' musk and drifted in from the kitchen garden.

Dre pushed his beer aside and sat back. His dark thick hair was rumpled, his wide mouth, usually so generous with his smile, was a grim, hard line.

"Bad day," he sighed.

It was a standing joke between us: how bad could a day be on a police force of four men when two of them took turns napping from boredom? But there was no laughter in Dre's green eyes today.

"What happened, hon?"

"The cemetery's been vandalized."

"Oh, no."

"Yeah." His eyes were filled now with disgust.

"Badly?" I filled a tall glass with ice and poured myself a soda.

"One grave's been dug up."

"Ugh! Any ideas?"

"Not a one. That's why I'm home early. Just stopped in to get a bite to eat. I'll be out late tonight, Karen."

"Why?"

Dre shook his head. "It's not going to be fun, but Pete and I have drawn what you might call a graveyard shift tonight." For the first time a smile, wry at his own bad pun, lighted his face.

"I'll fix you a sandwich. Want something to take for tonight?"

"I don't think I could eat a thing tonight. Coffee would be nice, though."

I didn't know where the thermos was, but I got to my feet, determined to root through attic and cellar until I found it.

"Thanks, Karen."

"Sure." I paused in the doorway. "Which one? Which grave?"

Dre pulled in a chest full of air and let it out in a gusting sigh. "Ransom Cowl's."

I didn't say "ugh" this time. Chills crawled up my arms, my stomach was suddenly too tight and full of an old childhood fear. I heard, in my mind, the rhythmic slap-slap-slap of a school yard skip rope and the voices of young girls singing an old song that was peculiar to Petersons Run alone.

My determination to search through the dark attic and the musty cellar flagged a little, but I would not send him out into the night without his coffee. Dre must have seen the squaring of my shoulders because his "atta girl" followed me down the hall.

A lovely New Jersey night can turn threatening and ugly in only an hour. The dusk's promise of a clear evening went unfulfilled. Grey clouds hung, leaden and sulking, over Jason's Meadow. The approaching storm's power breathed in the air. The potent humidity of a steamy night crept into the house. In the hall the old Regulator clock groaned once and struck three times.

Startled by the weighty, echoing bongs, I realized that the volume of Shakespeare had fallen, unnoticed, from my hand. Though the night was warm, I shivered. I was listening. I had been listening, though not consciously, through the last scenes of the fourth act of Hamlet. The words, lovely, amusing, intricately woven, had passed through my mind, leaving little mark. My breathing had become soft, cautious. Polonius went to his death unremarked by me, and Hamlet made his discourse with his uncle about the fate of men and worms unheeded by me.

I was listening, and now I knew what it was that I listened for. Dre was not due back yet from his cemetery stakeout.

But like the night waiting for the storm, I waited and listened for his return.

Even as I realized this, I heard his car, the soft hum of the Volvo's engine on the long driveway that wound from the road to the house. Relief gusted through me and my breath came in a choppy sigh. I closed the book and went to the front door to watch the swinging arc of the Volvo's headlights sweep the elms that huddled near the garage.

The car's door chunked closed. A moment later I heard Dre's feet crunching on the driveway's gravel, the only sound in the thick, hot night.

"Honey?" I called.

He was a dark patch of night, moving closer to the house, his head down, his shoulders hunched.

"Dre?"

A cicada started up its whirring somewhere nearby. I gasped; my hand flew to my throat. A cricket piped its monotonous song, high, higher, high, under the front porch. My pulse jerked and thumped under my fingertips. The insects sounded too loud in the waiting stillness.

"How'd you make out, Dre?" Thunder growled in the western sky, lightning flashed, throwing the garage and the elms into startling silhouette. Close on that flash came another, and I saw Dre's face, pale and drawn. His eyes were dark pits of shadow. This time I could not read his mood. I shivered again in the hot night air and stepped out onto the porch.

"Come on in, honey, I'll fix you some coffee."

"I'm tired, Karen. I just want to go to bed."

He did look tired. His feet were dragging, his shoulders slumped. When he passed me I heard the soft slither of dirt dropping from his shoes. He smelled of dark earth and sunless places; the pungent scent of crushed weeds clung to him.

I followed him up to bed and didn't think to ask why he had abandoned his graveyard shift early.

The voice was high and thin, an echo of voices I had heard drifting in from the playground through the open windows of my classroom.

"Ransom Cowl walks the road! Ransom Cowl can see!"

In my dream I shuddered. Cold sweat traced clammy paths down my neck, between my breasts.

"Ransom Cowl walks the road!" Now the tinny echoing quality of the voice was gone. The words were spoken in a quavering old voice filled with groaning and hatred. I could not breathe. It was as though a hand pressed down upon my chest.

"And he comes for *theeeee!*"

I screamed. And behind my scream I heard the crackling old voice tell me that I could scream until my throat bled, I could scream until my eyes, clenched against the dread and terror, threatened to burst. It makes no difference; Ransom Cowl still comes.

He was filthy with evil, he wore it like a shroud, bore it like a shield. He laughed, and that laughter was the knell of church bells, tolling in mourning. He howled, and the howling was the sound of Death triumphant.

Putrid and stinking of hopeless, midnight places, rotting grave clothes still clinging to his wasted body, he shambled to the bed. His lifelessness chilled me to the bone, sucking from me all that was warm and alive. My heart slammed hard against my ribs, a terrified rabbit in a cage of bones. My ears were filled with the sound of my own racing blood. His scabrous hand, scraps of decayed flesh shivering on the white bones of his fingers, touched my lips.

"Lovely," he said. I heard the word as a doom pronounced, a sentence handed down. Nausea twisted my stomach and bile burned a searing path to my throat.

Thunder growled in the distance. A storm prowled close to the valley.

His face came close to mine and I could smell the rotten stench that gusted from his decaying, gap-toothed mouth. It was the stink of something long dead in the bushes, moldering and putrefying. Then I saw, the shock of the sight racing through me like an electrical current, that he had only empty, gaping sockets where his eyes should have been.

"Oh, God, no!" I screamed, and I was, at last, awake.

As though my scream had been the power that called it, lightning danced at the window, tossing huge, unrecognized shadows across the walls of my familiar bedroom.

There was a hand on my face.

"Karen." Dre's voice was soft, inquiring. His fingers stroked my cheek, moved up to brush my hair back from my face.

"Dre—I—it was—"

"It's all right," he whispered, leaning closer to me, curling his leg over mine beneath the sheet. "It's all right, it's all right."

"A—a nightmare—" I shivered, trembling hard as if from a bone freezing cold.

"I know. It's all right." He tucked his chin over my shoulder and buried his face in my hair, offering the comfort of his nearness, of his body. But when his hand moved up to my breast, when his lips brushed gently against my ear as he murmured, "Lovely," my blood turned to ice.

"Dre."

"Lovely Karen." He sighed.

"No. No, Dre." I turned away from him and felt his leg move away, his hand draw back to my shoulder.

"It was just a dream, Karen."

"I know," I said, my voice a quivering whisper. I did know. And he had always called me "lovely" just before his lips moved from my ear to my neck, to my shoulder. But "lovely" had new echoes that I hated and feared.

I told myself that the dream would be gone in the morning, leaving not even a shadow of fear to be remembered by. I apologized silently to Dre, knowing that he would understand.

And he must have understood, for I heard his even, gentle breathing before long. I did not sleep that night, but listened to the rolling progress of the storm as it marched into our little valley.

When the phone rang my mouth was full of toothpaste. "Dre?" I called through clenched teeth. He didn't answer me, but must have answered the phone because it went silent after three rings. I finished brushing my teeth, washed up quickly, and pulled my robe closer around me. As I racketed down the stairs, I cursed the alarm clock I hadn't heard and decided that Dre and I were getting no better a breakfast than juice and cold cereal this morning. He was already

125

in the kitchen, slouched in a chair. His elbows were on the table, his hands covered his eyes. It was not an unfamiliar pose: Dre tried to protect himself from the morning for as long as possible.

"OJ, honey?" I asked.

"No."

"Cereal?"

"No."

"Who was on the phone?"

"Pete's wife."

"Clare? What's up?" Yet even as I asked the question, I recalled, from some odd tangent of memory, that I hadn't asked Dre why he'd come home so early last night. I nudged the refrigerator door closed behind me and put the orange juice on the table. "Sure you won't have any juice, honey?"

"No!" The word was a bullet fired through the morning silence. Startled, I dropped the glass I'd been holding. The little bright shards scattered across the wooden floor, glittering in the sunlight. I held my breath and watched them spin and tumble.

"I'm sorry, Karen. I'm sorry."

He might have been, but I saw nothing of it in his eyes. They were dark holes in a face that was too pale. There wasn't enough room for apology in those eyes, crowded as they were with confusion and a haunted fear. Quietly, I swept the broken glass from the floor.

"Dre? What is it?"

"Pete didn't get home last night."

"Well, but—didn't you drop him off?"

His answer came fast. "Yes, of course I did."

"At the house?"

"At the road. He wanted to walk in."

"But—" I shook my head and took another tack. "You guys didn't stay very late last night."

"I think the wrong one of us is the cop in this house," Dre said coldly. He didn't look at me when he spoke. His eyes, those pits of confusion, were riveted to the table. The forefinger of his right hand traced the ancient pattern of some child's homework, engraved long ago into the soft pine planking.

"Dre."

"Leave me alone, will you, Karen? I'm tired, and I don't know where Pete is. Clare is upset. Will you stop by to see her on your way to school?"

I was late already, and for a moment my conscience warred between declaring a convenient illness so that I could spend the day with Clare, and the fact that my students would be dismissed early today because I couldn't find a substitute teacher at this hour. Clare—or perhaps it was the students—won.

"I'll call in sick, Dre. They can spare me for a day, I'm sure."

His "atta girl" was perfunctory, barely grunted. I put it down to his concern for Pete and kissed him briefly on the top of his head. He moved his hand as though to touch mine, but the gesture died with his sigh.

Clare hadn't immediately fallen into the "My God, He's Dead" syndrome. She worked her way toward it through the "My God, He's Cheating on Me" syndrome first.

By the time she'd reached the point of aggressively asserting that Pete was "a good man, a wonderful husband, he'd never cheat on me—*never!*—he loves me, loves the kids—" we'd gone through too many pots of coffee and eaten too many cookies. The evening sun slanted in through her kitchen windows, seven o'clock mellow. There was nothing left to face now but the fear that Pete was dead. When she finally acknowledged that fear, Clare's voice was a cracked whisper from which hope leaked fast.

"He's *not* dead, Clare."

"But where is he then? Where?"

I didn't know. I didn't know where Dre was either. He hadn't called at all that day. I snatched at this and patted Clare's trembling hand with an assurance I hardly felt.

"We haven't heard from Dre yet. Surely we'd have heard if something were wrong. Come on, come on, now."

She'd sent the two children to stay with her mother. I didn't know whether or not she'd told them that their father hadn't come home the night before. I thought now that the children would be just the comfort she needed. But when I offered to pick them up and drop them off she only shook her head.

"No, Karen, not now. Not yet."

Her thick blonde hair was a tumbled mess. She'd piled it carelessly atop her head this morning and it fell now, in fits and straggles about her face and neck. She'd been plowing her fingers through it all day. Her face, one I'd always thought of as pretty and plump, looked haggard and bloated now. Without her makeup, in fear's harsh light, she appeared far older than forty-two.

"Karen, call the station for me? Call them to see what's going on? I can't stand this waiting anymore."

I didn't want to do it. I didn't want to hear the dispatcher's patient kindness. But I couldn't watch Clare gnawing at herself, either, poised to leap for a phone that hadn't rung all day.

The dispatcher's voice sounded like that of a mother who assures her frightened child that it was only a dream, only a nightmare, that there's really nothing to worry about. She hadn't heard from Dre all day, but, yes, he'd been out with the others looking for Pete.

"There are lots of people looking for him, Clare," I assured her as I hung up the phone. "The police, the whole auxiliary staff." It didn't make her feel better. Though Clare hadn't wept all day, tears threatened now in eyes bruised from exhaustion. Her lips trembled, her hands moved in unconscious jerks through her hair. I made a quick decision.

"Come with me,"

She looked puzzled. "Where?"

"Home. We'll wait there."

"No."

"Clare."

"No! I want to be *here*."

"Then I'm going to run home and leave a note for Dre. I'll get a few things and spend the night."

She didn't refuse that. Her gratitude poured from her eyes in the first tears I had seen all day.

The storm was a terrible one. Between the house-shaking blasts of thunder I heard rain lashing against the window of Clare's guest room. Lightning splashed the room with a baleful glare, threw the furniture into huge silhouette. Shadows staggered across the walls. I'd asked Clare if she wanted me to sleep with her, thinking she would want the comfort of another person nearby. I regretted her refusal more for my own sake than hers. It was a long time before I slept.

"Ransom Cowl walks the road."

The dream was upon me, smothering me like a thick woolen blanket. The tremorous old voice whispered in my ears, drifted around in my sleeping mind.

"Ransom Cowl can see."

In my dream I moaned.

It had been on all the local news stations, even the national news had carried the story for one day. *In the small New Jersey town of Petersons Run a local man is accused of murdering six women.* A serious, grim voice, newscaster-perfect in its enunciation, rolled through the dream.

And yet, how did I know this? How could the words of a broadcast that was older than I am whisper now in my dream?

My dream world began to rumble, to shake, like the quavering old voice that spoke the rhyme. "Ransom Cowl walks the road."

The six women had been butchered. It was a term too frequently used these days to mean brutally murdered. These women *had* been butchered. Like heifers for market, they had been neatly, cleanly taken apart. There had been no evidence of a killing wound. They'd been butchered alive.

"And he comes for *theee!*"

Death-awkward, he staggered across the guest room and stopped at the bedside. His fingers were ice upon my face. His nails, longer in death than they should have been in life, rested lightly on my cheek. A relentless, dread-filled ache seeped through me as his lifeless chill passed through skin and blood and bone. It touched deep inside me, reaching for the core of who I was.

Ransom Cowl scratched against the surface of my soul, chipped away shards of reality. I could not have screamed had I wanted to. And I did not want to this time. It seemed then that everything within me, my heart, my lungs, my mind, everything that *was* me, halted, paused, listened. Horror was crouched, ready, waiting to burst the boundaries of the thing I call my soul. It never did. My pent breath, ready to erupt in a ranting scream, sighed tremblingly away.

"Lovely," he said, his voice a grating rasp. "Lovely." He leaned nearer, filling my whole dream with the stench of his breath, and the rotting stink of his body. The white bone of his skull gaped in places through the putrefying flesh that had once been his face. Then, as on the night before, I did scream.

And, as on the night before, I was suddenly awake. My husband stood at my bedside.

"Dre!"

"Right here, Karen."

"How—how did you get here?"

His smile was slow and familiar. "I found your note, of course. I didn't want to spend the night alone."

I couldn't blame him. I sat up and reached for his arms. The storm had passed, leaving behind a sweet, clean breeze. It plucked now at the curtains, made their yellow rosebud pattern dance like a field of flowers in the wind.

"How did you get in?"

"Pete had his key."

"Pete! You found him!"

"Sure did."

"Where?"

"Tomorrow, Karen. It's late and I'm tired."

"What time is it?"

He sat on the edge of the bed, pulled off his shoes, and rose to unzip his pants. "Four. Now hush and let me in."

I moved over in the little double bed, made room for him, and cuddled next to him. I had turned away from his comfort the night before. I wouldn't tonight.

But he made no advance, simply settled down beneath the sheets and turned his back to me. "Good night," he mumbled.

Fair is fair, I thought wryly, and turnabout, they say, is fair play. I kissed the back of his head. "Good night."

I dreamed again, and heard only whispering, murmuring, and laughing. Snatches of the old rhyme drifted in and around these sounds, but I didn't wake until morning.

*   *   *

Bacon sizzled and spat in the pan. Coffee sent its familiar comfortable smell throughout the house. Despite the hour he'd arrived, Dre was up and humming around the kitchen, lurking near the stove for the first cup of coffee.

"You must be exhausted," I said, giving the bacon a final shake.

"Too wired to sleep."

I could understand that. It was why I was awake, rambling around in an unfamiliar kitchen, making breakfast. "I've made enough for Clare and Pete. Should I wake them?"

Dre shrugged.

"Where did you finally find Pete?"

Dre poured his coffee and took a seat at the table. "It's a long story, Karen. Wait until he's had a chance to explain to Clare. I'll tell you when we get home."

Had Pete been with some woman? Had he been cheating on Clare? I felt a sudden flare of anger, remembering her torment of fear. The anger must have shown on my face because Dre chuckled a little.

"Don't go jumping to conclusions, Karen."

"No, you're right." I smiled at him, feeling suddenly sheepish, and noticed that there was a smear of mud near the counter where he stood. "Dre, you're tracking up Clare's kitchen."

He glanced down at his feet and shrugged again. "Sorry."

His shoes were filthy, and dark stains smeared the legs of his pants. Where had he found Pete, anyway? "Oh, Dre, what a mess! See if you can find a broom. I'm going to see if Clare and Pete are awake."

My light tap at the bedroom door went unanswered. I knocked a little harder and waited. There was no sound from within. Maybe we should just have breakfast, I thought, leave a note, and call them later. I was anxious to get home anyway. But I tried one more time.

"Clare?"

I tapped again at the door. "Pete?" Nothing, not even snoring. The door was ajar, and as I turned to go back down the stairs my shoulder brushed against it. It opened with a creak and a sigh. A yellow line of sunlight from the bedroom window widened on the floor at my feet.

"Anybody awake?"

No one stirred. Shrugging, I reached for the doorknob, thinking to pull the door shut. I caught a glimpse of the room and saw only Clare lying still in the middle of the large bed, her hand flung over the side.

Was Pete up already? I listened, but heard no sound from the bathroom. "Clare?"

She didn't move. The morning breeze stirred at her window, fluttering the curtains. I wondered, suddenly, if she was all right. I'd made enough noise out here to wake the—

"Clare?"

I stepped into the room, not caring now that I was invading private territory. The white shag carpet was splashed with mud and something red.

"My God." My throat was tight and dry, my blood hummed and pounded in my head. Clare's blood was splattered all over the carpet. She was not all right.

The room spun around me, nausea churned in my stomach. The once-good smells of bacon and coffee drifted up from the kitchen, sickening me. I clamped my hands across my mouth as vomit rushed up against my teeth with its acid sting.

No one part of Clare was connected to another. The pieces of her lay on the bed, like parts of a toy ready for assembly. Everything was laid out neatly, arms near the torso, legs where they should be, her head upon the pillow. Her lovely blonde hair splayed across sheets that were crimsoned with her blood.

I wailed. "Dre! Dre! Dreeeee!"

I bolted from the room, gasping, moaning, a "no-no-no" chant of denial. I dashed my knee against the door. Pain burst like a fireball and raced along my leg but I did not stop. I scrambled for the stairs and took them running, stumbling twice. My leg screamed pain from my ankle to my knee but I righted myself, still gasping "No-no-no!" I could not think about what I had just seen, I could not allow those pictures back into my mind. My only thought was to get to the kitchen and Dre.

"Dreee!" I gasped, falling to my knees at the bottom of

the stairs. *No-no-no!* My mind coughed the words over and over, stuck in a groove of repetition. *No-no-no!*

His back was to me when I staggered into the kitchen. I fell against the table, grasping its edge as though it were the edge of a cliff. I heard the fat spattering in the frying pan, smelled the acrid stink of bacon burning.

"Dre! My God, my God, Dre! She's dead!"

When he turned he was Dre. And yet he was not Dre.

"I know." His voice was hollow, deep and cold. His eyes, Dre's eyes, were pits, holes, empty of any emotion. Even as fear's icy finger skipped up my spine my stomach clenched against a sudden flood of adrenaline. His face was changing before my eyes, shifting, wavering.

"Dre—"

The flesh of his face thinned. His jaw became more square now, his face longer. Dre's dark hair turned, before my horrified eyes, to slatey grey. His straight white teeth became ravaged by decay. I could smell the stink of his breath from across the kitchen.

I'd seen the pictures, grainy black and white newspaper photos. Every child in Petersons Run had sought them out at one time or another. When I was young it was almost a rite of passage: find a picture of Ransom Cowl, look at it, and try to suppress the giggling squeal of fear that you hoped your friends thought was only pretended. But I'd seen more than pictures. I'd seen him two nights running in my dreams.

No-no-no! The chant started up in my mind again. Breathless and terrified, it was a child's denial.

"Yes," he said, his voice as cold as winter's ice. His fingers gently caressed the shining edge of a carving knife. "Yes, yes."

He did not shamble now. He had the strength of Dre's body, Dre's strong legs, powerful and muscled. He leaped for me, throwing himself across the table, the knife gleaming silver in the sunlight.

I scrambled around the table, keeping it between him and me. "No! Dre! Dre!"

But he was no longer my Dre, and there was no emotion to respond to my pleading. There was only Ransom Cowl, muttering "Lovely, lovely, lovely," and a voice, ghostly and cracked with age, whispering that Ransom Cowl could see.

My knee throbbed where I had smashed it against Clare's bedroom door. My hands shook, palsied with fear. Breathing in short, panting gasps, I wrapped my fingers around the back of a chair and took two retreating steps until the small of my back touched the counter. Fat from the burning bacon spattered against my arm, bit my skin with needle-sharp, fiery teeth.

"Lovely, lovely."

Dre's prelude to love, growled from the rotting throat of the thing before me, made me furious. It was violation, a rape of moments that had been beautiful. My fury gave me the strength I needed to act. Clutching the chair with one hand, I reached for the frying pan with the other.

The thing laughed, a guttural sound, and lunged around the table.

No-no-no! my mind gibbered. No-no-no! I hurled the spitting frying pan at the thing's face, laughed and screamed to hear its howl of pain. It could be hurt! My heart cringed at the knowledge. Of course it could be hurt; it was, in some awful way, Dre.

It still had the knife, grasped in fingers that were rotting before my eyes. It leaped from where it was crouched on the floor, hitting me low. I crashed to the floor, my elbow smashed against the stove, my head thumped against the floor.

No-no-no! I clawed at its face and pieces of skin came off in my hands. Bile rushed up my throat. I spat it out and forced my heaving stomach to calm. The Dre-thing lay across me full length, its face touching mine, its knees thrusting in attenuated kicks against my ribs. The knife in its right hand caught the light. The gleaming blade was all that I could see.

"Lovely, lovely, lovely."

It was going to kill me and my death would be a horrible one.

I thrust upward with all my strength but I could not move the thing. I twisted, screamed, kicked, but I could not free myself. My hand, in its flailing, found the frying pan. I clutched at its handle, raised it, and brought it crashing down on the thing's skull. The stinking face snapped away from mine, the body sagged and rolled off me. It was stunned, and I scrambled to my feet.

The knife! It lay a few inches from the creature's hand. *No-no-no!* It seemed that the screaming child in my mind already knew what I was about to do. *No-no-no!*

But I couldn't listen to it now. I couldn't take the time to consider what I was about to do. I simply did it.

The knife made horrible thudding sounds when I plunged it into the Dre-thing's chest, and wet, sucking sounds when I pulled it out. I did not butcher it—though the word would later be used to describe what I did. I killed it. I sent it back to the unholy grave it had come from, howling and screaming like a sidhe wailing across Irish moors.

And when I was done, it was not Ransom Cowl who lay beneath my hands. It was Dre. My Dre whom I'd loved from childhood, who had been all I'd ever asked from life. His head was smashed, his eyes seemed to stare, still frozen with terror, at my hands. His blood spattered in sticky drops from my fingers, tapping the first faint beat of a dirge that would haunt me all my days.

I wept for him, and wept for myself. Then I climbed to my feet. I staggered across the blood-smeared kitchen, moving numbly to the phone. *Police,* I thought, *I must call the police—.* Victim, bereaved, and killer, I did not know what else to do.

I lifted the receiver. The dial tone sounded like the first whimpering echo in a long, black tunnel of loneliness.

Born in New Jersey in 1951 and educated there, Nancy Varian Berberick began writing full time in 1984. Her first novel, Storm-blade, *was published in 1988, and a grim tale, "Cairn and Pyre," appeared in* Amazing Stories *in 1989. "My work," she says, "Is essentially optimistic and mystical." Her novel,* The Jewels of Elvish, *is available from TSR and two more will follow from Berkley—Shadow of the Seventh Moon in 1991 and Children of the Smoke, a sequel to* The Jewels of Elvish, *in 1992.*

Bart expected someone from the new boarding school to meet him at the train station. He didn't expect the school to be so unusual . . .

EIGHT

School for the Unspeakable

Manly Wade Wellman

Bart Setwick dropped off the train at Carrington and stood for a moment on the station platform, an honest-faced, well-knit lad in tweeds. This little town and its famous school should be his home for the next eight months; but which way to the school? The sun had set, and he could barely see the shop signs across Carrington's modest main street. He hesitated, and a soft voice spoke at his very elbow:

"Are you for the school?"

Startled, Bart Setwick wheeled. In the gray twilight stood another youth, smiling thinly and waiting as if for an answer. The stranger was all of nineteen years old—that meant maturity to young Setwick, who was fifteen—and his pale face had shrewd lines to it. His tall, shambling body was clad in high-necked jersey and unfashionably tight trousers. Bart Setwick skimmed him with the quick, appraising eye of young America.

"I just got here," he replied. "My name's Setwick."

"Mine's Hoag." Out came a slender hand. Setwick took it and found it froggy-cold, with a suggestion of steel-wire muscles. "Glad to meet you. I came down on the chance someone would drop off the train. Let me give you a lift to the school."

Hoag turned away, felinely light for all his ungainliness, and led his new acquaintance around the corner of the little wooden railway station. Behind the structure, half hidden in

137

its shadow, stood a shabby buggy with a lean bay horse in the shafts.

"Get in," invited Hoag, but Bart Setwick paused for a moment. His generation was not used to such vehicles. Hoag chuckled and said, "Oh, this is only a school wrinkle. We run to funny customs. Get in."

Setwick obeyed. "How about my trunk?"

"Leave it." The taller youth swung himself in beside Setwick and took the reins. "You'll not need it tonight."

He snapped his tongue and the bay horse stirred, drew them around and off down a bush-lined side road. Its hoof-beats were oddly muffled.

They turned a corner, another, and came into open country. The lights of Carrington, newly kindled against the night, hung behind like a constellation settled down to Earth. Setwick felt a hint of chill that did not seen to fit the September evening.

"How far is the school from town?" he asked.

"Four or five miles," Hoag replied in his hushed voice. "That was deliberate on the part of the founders—they wanted to make it hard for the students to get to town for larks. It forced us to dig up our own amusements." The pale face creased in a faint smile, as if this were a pleasantry. "There's just a few of the right sort on hand tonight. By the way, what did you get sent out for?"

Setwick frowned his mystification. "Why, to go to school. Dad sent me."

"But what for? Don't you know that this is a high-class prison prep? Half of us are lunkheads that need poking along, the other half are fellows who got in scandals somewhere else. Like me." Again Hoag smiled.

Setwick began to dislike his companion. They rolled a mile or so in silence before Hoag again asked a question: "Do you go to church, Setwick?"

The new boy was afraid to appear priggish, and made a careless show with, "Not very often."

"Can you recite anything from the Bible?" Hoag's soft voice took on an anxious tinge.

"Not that I know of."

"Good," was the almost hearty response. "As I was saying, there's only a few of us at the school tonight—only three, to be exact. And we don't like Bible-quoters."

Setwick laughed, trying to appear sage and cynical. "Isn't Satan reputed to quote the Bible to his own—"

"What do you know about Satan?" interrupted Hoag. He turned full on Setwick, studying him with intent, dark eyes. Then, as if answering his own question: "Little enough, I'll bet. Would you like to know about him?"

"Sure I would," replied Setwick, wondering what the joke would be.

"I'll teach you after a while," Hoag promised cryptically, and silence fell again.

Half a moon was well up as they came in sight of a dark jumble of buildings.

"Here we are," announced Hoag, and then, throwing back his head, he emitted a wild, wordless howl that made Setwick almost jump out of the buggy. "That's to let the others know we're coming," he explained. "Listen!"

Back came a seeming echo of the howl, shrill, faint and eery. The horse wavered in its muffled trot, and Hoag clucked it back into step. They turned in at a driveway well grown up in weeds, and two minutes more brought them up to the rear of the closest building. It was dim gray in the wash of moonbeams, with blank inky rectangles for windows. Nowhere was there a light, but as the buggy came to a halt Setwick saw a young head pop out of a window on the lower floor.

"Here already, Hoag?" came a high, reedy voice.

"Yes," answered the youth at the reins, "and I've brought a new man with me."

Thrilling a bit to hear himself called a man, Setwick alighted.

"His name's Setwick," went on Hoag. "Meet Andoff, Setwick. A great friend of mine."

Andoff flourished a hand in greeting and scrambled out over the windowsill. He was chubby and squat and even paler than Hoag, with a low forehead beneath lank, wet-looking hair, and black eyes set wide apart in a fat, stupid-looking face. His shabby jacket was too tight for him, and beneath worn knickers his legs and feet were bare. He might have been an overgrown thirteen or an undeveloped eighteen.

"Felcher ought to be along in half a second," he volunteered.

"Entertain Setwick while I put up the buggy," Hoag directed him.

Andoff nodded, and Hoag gathered the lines in his hands, but paused for a final word.

"No funny business yet, Andoff," he cautioned seriously. "Setwick, don't let this lard-bladder rag you or tell you wild stories until I come back."

Andoff laughed shrilly. "No, no wild stories," he promised. "You'll do the talking, Hoag."

The buggy trundled away, and Andoff swung his fat, grinning face to the new arrival.

"Here comes Felcher," he announced. "Felcher, meet Setwick."

Another boy had bobbed up, it seemed, from nowhere. Setwick had not seen him come around the corner of the building, or slip out of a door or window. He was probably as old as Hoag, or older, but so small as to be almost a dwarf, and frail to boot. His most notable characteristic was his hairiness. A great mop covered his head, bushed over his neck and ears, and hung unkemptly to his bright, deep-set eyes. His lips and cheeks were spread with a rank down, and a curly thatch peeped through the unbuttoned collar of his soiled white shirt. The hand he offered Setwick was almost simian in its shagginess and in the hardness of its palm. Too, it was cold and damp. Setwick remembered the same thing of Hoag's handclasp.

"We're the only ones here so far," Felcher remarked. His voice, surprisingly deep and strong for so small a creature, rang like a great bell.

"Isn't even the headmaster here?" inquired Setwick, and at that the other two began to laugh uproariously, Andoff's fife-squeal rendering an obbligato to Felcher's bell-boom. Hoag, returning, asked what the fun was.

"Setwick asks," groaned Felcher, "why the headmaster isn't here to welcome him."

More fife-laughter and bell-laughter.

"I doubt if Setwick would think the answer was funny," Hoag commented, and then chuckled softly himself.

Setwick, who had been well brought up, began to grow nettled.

"Tell me about it," he urged, in what he hoped was a bleak tone, "and I'll join your chorus of mirth."

Felcher and Andoff gazed at him with eyes strangely eager and yearning. Then they faced Hoag.

"Let's tell him," they both said at once, but Hoag shook his head.

"Not yet. One thing at a time. Let's have the song first."

They began to sing. The first verse of their offering was obscene, with no pretense of humor to redeem it. Setwick had never been squeamish, but he found himself definitely repelled. The second verse seemed less objectionable, but it hardly made sense:

> All they tried to teach here
> Now goes untaught.
> Ready, steady, each here,
> Knowledge we sought.
> What they called disaster
> Killed us not, O master!
> Rule us, we beseech here,
> Eye, hand and thought.

It was something like a hymn, Setwick decided; but before what altar would such hymns be sung? Hoag must have read that question in his mind.

"You mentioned Satan in the buggy on the way out," he recalled, his knowing face hanging like a mask in the half-dimness close to Setwick. "Well, that was a Satanist song."

"It was? Who made it?"

"I did," Hoag informed him. "How do you like it?"

Setwick made no answer. He tried to sense mockery in Hoag's voice, but could not find it. "What," he asked finally, "does all this Satanist singing have to do with the headmaster?"

"A lot," came back Felcher deeply, and "A lot," squealed Andoff.

Hoag gazed from one of his friends to the others, and for the first time he smiled broadly. It gave him a toothy look.

"I believe," he ventured quietly but weightily, "that we might as well let Setwick in on the secret of our little circle."

Here it would begin, the new boy decided—the school hazing of which he had heard and read so much. He had anticipated such things with something of excitement, even eagerness, but now he wanted none of them. He did not like his three companions, and he did not like the way they approached whatever it was they intended to do. He moved backward a pace or two, as if to retreat.

Swift as darting birds, Hoag and Andoff closed in at either elbow. Their chill hands clutched him and suddenly he felt light-headed and sick. Things that had been clear in the moonlight went hazy and distorted.

"Come on and sit down, Setwick," invited Hoag, as though from a great distance. His voice did not grow loud or harsh, but it embodied real menace. "Sit on that windowsill. Or would you like us to carry you?"

At the moment Setwick wanted only to be free of their touch, and so he walked unresistingly to the sill and scrambled up on it. Behind him was the blackness of an unknown chamber, and at his knees gathered the three who seemed so eager to tell him their private joke.

"The headmaster was a proper churchgoer," began Hoag, as though he were the spokesman for the group. "He didn't have any use for devils or devil worship. Went on record against them when he addressed us in chapel. That was what started us."

"Right," nodded Andoff, turning up his fat, larval face. "Anything he outlawed, we wanted to do. Isn't that logic?"

"Logic and reason," wound up Felcher. His hairy right hand twiddled on the sill near Setwick's thigh. In the moonlight it looked like a big, nervous spider.

Hoag resumed. "I don't know of any prohibition of his it was easier or more fun to break."

Setwick found that his mouth had gone dry. His tongue could barely moisten his lips. "You mean," he said, "that you began to worship devils?"

Hoag nodded happily, like a teacher at an apt pupil.

"One vacation I got a book on the cult. The three of us studied it, then began ceremonies. We learned the charms and spells, forward and backward—"

"They're twice as good backward," put in Felcher, and Andoff giggled.

"Have you any idea, Setwick," Hoag almost cooed, "what it was that appeared in our study the first time we burned wine and sulfur, with the proper words spoken over them?"

Setwick did not want to know. He clenched his teeth. "If you're trying to scare me," he managed to growl out, "it certainly isn't going to work."

All three laughed once more, and began to chatter out their protestations of good faith.

"I swear that we're telling the truth, Setwick," Hoag assured him. "Do you want to hear it, or don't you?"

Setwick had very little choice in the matter, and he realized it. "Oh, go ahead," he capitulated, wondering how it would do to crawl backward from the sill into the darkness of the room.

Hoag leaned toward him, with the air as of one confiding. "The headmaster caught us. Caught us red-handed."

"Book open, fire burning," chanted Felcher.

"He had something very fine to say about the vengeance of heaven," Hoag went on. "We got to laughing at him. He worked up a frenzy. Finally he tried to take heaven's vengeance into his own hands—tried to visit it on us, in a very primitive way. But it didn't work."

Andoff was laughing immoderately, his fat arms across his bent belly.

"He thought it worked," he supplemented between high gurgles, "but it didn't."

"Nobody could kill us," Felcher added. "Not after the oaths we'd taken, and the promises that had been made us."

"What promises?" demanded Setwick, who was struggling hard not to believe. "Who made you any promises?"

"Those we worshiped," Felcher told him. If he was simulating earnestness, it was a supreme bit of acting. Setwick, realizing this, was more daunted than he cared to show.

"When did all these things happen?" was his next question.

"When?" echoed Hoag. "Oh, years and years ago."

"Years and years ago," repeated Andoff.

"Long before you were born," Felcher assured him.

They were standing close together, their backs to the moon that shone in Setwick's face. He could not see their expressions clearly. But their three voices—Hoag's soft, Felcher's deep and vibrant, Andoff's high and squeaky—were absolutely serious.

"I know what you're arguing within yourself," Hoag announced somewhat smugly. "How can we, who talk about those many past years, seem so young? That calls for an explanation, I'll admit." He paused, as if choosing words. "Time—for us—stands still. It came to a halt on that very night, Setwick; the night our headmaster tried to put an end to our worship."

"And to us," smirked the gross-bodied Andoff, with his usual air of self-congratulation at capping one of Hoag's statements.

"The worship goes on," pronounced Felcher, in the same chanting manner that he had affected once before. "The worship goes on, and we go on, too."

"Which brings us to the point," Hoag came in briskly. "Do you want to throw in with us, Setwick?—make the fourth of this lively little party?"

"No, I don't," snapped Setwick vehemently.

They fell silent, and gave back a little—a trio of bizarre silhouettes against the pale moon glow. Setwick could see the flash of their staring eyes among the shadows of their faces. He knew that he was afraid, but hid his fear. Pluckily he dropped from the sill to the ground. Dew from the grass spattered his sock-clad ankles between oxfords and trouser-cuffs.

"I guess it's my turn to talk," he told them levelly. "I'll make it short. I don't like you, nor anything you've said. And I'm getting out of here."

"We won't let you," said Hoag, hushed but emphatic.

"We won't let you," murmured Andoff and Felcher together, as though they had rehearsed it a thousand times.

Setwick clenched his fists. His father had taught him to box. He took a quick, smooth stride toward Hoag and hit him hard in the face. Next moment all three had flung themselves upon him. They did not seem to strike or grapple or tug, but he went down under their assault. The shoulders of his tweed coat wallowed in sand, and he smelled crushed weeds. Hoag, on top of him, pinioned his arms with a knee on each bicep. Felcher and Andoff were stooping close.

Glaring up in helpless rage, Setwick knew once and for all that this was no schoolboy prank. Never did practical jokers gather around their victim with such staring, green-gleaming eyes, such drawn jowls, such quivering lips.

Hoag bared white fangs. His pointed tongue quested once over them.

"Knife!" he muttered, and Felcher fumbled in a pocket, then passed him something that sparkled in the moonlight.

Hoag's lean hand reached for it, then whipped back. Hoag had lifted his eyes to something beyond the huddle. He choked and whimpered inarticulately, sprang up from Setwick's laboring chest, and fell back in awkward haste. The others followed his shocked stare, then as suddenly cowered and retreated in turn.

"It's the master!" wailed Andoff.

"Yes," roared a gruff new voice. "Your old headmaster—and I've come back to master *you!*"

Rising upon one elbow, the prostrate Setwick saw what they had seen—a tall, thick-bodied figure in a long dark coat, topped with a square, distorted face and a tousle of white locks. Its eyes glittered with their own pale, hard light. As it advanced slowly and heavily it emitted a snigger of murderous joy. Even at first glance Setwick was aware that it cast no shadow.

"I am in time," mouthed the newcomer. "You were going to kill this poor boy."

Hoag had recovered and made a stand. "Kill him?" he quavered, seeming to fawn before the threatening presence. "No. We'd have given him life—"

"You call it life?" trumpeted the long-coated one. "You'd have sucked out his blood to teem your own dead veins, damned him to your filthy condition. But I'm here to prevent you!"

145

A finger pointed, huge and knuckly, and then came a torrent of language. To the nerve-stunned Setwick it sounded like a bit from the New Testament, or perhaps from the Book of Common Prayer. All at once he remembered Hoag's avowed dislike for such quotations.

His three erstwhile assailants reeled as if before a high wind that chilled or scorched. "No, no! Don't!" they begged wretchedly.

The square old face gaped open and spewed merciless laughter. The knuckly finger traced a cross in the air, and the trio wailed in chorus as though the sign had been drawn upon their flesh with a tongue of flame.

Hoag dropped to his knees. "Don't!" he sobbed.

"I have power," mocked their tormenter. "During years shut up I won it, and now I'll use it." Again a triumphant burst of mirth. "I know you're damned and can't be killed, but you can be tortured! I'll make you crawl like worms before I'm done with you!"

Setwick gained his shaky feet. The long coat and the blocky head leaned toward him.

"Run, you!" dinned a rough roar in his ears. "Get out of here—and thank God for the chance!"

Setwick ran, staggering. He blundered through the weeds of the driveway, gained the road beyond. In the distance gleamed the lights of Carrington. As he turned his face toward them and quickened his pace he began to weep, chokingly, hysterically, exhaustingly.

He did not stop running until he reached the platform in front of the station. A clock across the street struck ten, in a deep voice not unlike Felcher's. Setwick breathed deeply, fished out his handkerchief and mopped his face. His hand was quivering like a grass stalk in a breeze.

"Beg pardon!" came a cheery hail. "You must be Setwick."

As once before on this same platform, he whirled around with startled speed. Within touch of him stood a broad-shouldered man of thirty or so, with horn-rimmed spectacles. He wore a neat Norfolk jacket and flannels. A short briar pipe was clamped in a good-humored mouth.

"I'm Collins, one of the masters at the school," he introduced himself. "If you're Setwick, you've had us worried.

We expected you on that seven o'clock train, you know. I dropped down to see if I couldn't trace you."

Setwick found a little of his lost wind. "But I've—been to the school," he mumbled protestingly. His hand, still trembling, gestured vaguely along the way he had come.

Collins threw back his head and laughed, then apologized.

"Sorry," he said. "It's no joke if you really had all that walk for nothing. Why, that old place is deserted—used to be a catch-all for incorrigible rich boys. They closed it about fifty years ago, when the headmaster went mad and killed three of his pupils. As a matter of coincidence, the master himself died just this afternoon, in the state hospital for the insane."

A major writer of the supernatural, Manly Wade Wellman was born in Portugese West Africa, where his father was a medical missionary, in 1903. Brought to the United States at the age of six, he was educated at Wichita University and Columbia University and worked as a reporter until 1930, when he quit to become a full-time professional writer. In two decades more than 300,000 of his words were published in Weird Tales. *In 1946 his story,* "A Star for a Warrior," *won first prize in the first* Ellery Queen's Mystery Magazine *Annual Contest (William Faulkner came in second); the prize money permitted him to move to North Carolina, where he lived the rest of his life. Wellman published many full-length works, including two large collections of supernatural stories:* Worse Things Waiting *(1973) and* Lonesome Vigils *(1982). He died in 1986.*

When he came to educate them, he learned something from their "ignorant" superstitions. . . .

NINE

The Stormsong Runner

Jack L. Chalker

I wonder who's in charge of cold weather for this region. I'd like to talk to them. You see, I—no, I'm not crazy. Or maybe I am. It would simplify things enormously if I were.

Look, let me explain it to you. About three years ago, I graduated from college in Pittsburgh. There I was, twenty-two, fresh, eager, armed with a degree in elementary education. All scholarship, no problems. I sailed through.

And back then, as now, that degree and half a buck bought a large coffee to go.

So I drifted, bummed around, took any job I could get, while firing off applications to dozens of school districts. The baby boom's over, though—there were few openings, none that wouldn't make you cut your throat in a couple of years.

I was on the road to failing the most important course of all—life. I started drinking, blowing pot and sniffing coke, and was in and out involved with a bunch of flaky girls more into that than I was.

What rescued me was, oddly enough, an accident. I was driving a girlfriend's old clunker when this fellow ran a light and hit me broadside. A couple of weeks in the hospital, a lurking lawyer I'd known from high school, and I suddenly had a good deal of the other guy's insurance company's money.

I bought a place down in southern West Virginia, up in the hills in the middle of nowhere, and tried to get my head on straight. It was peaceful in those mountains, and quiet; the little town about three miles away had the few necessities of life available, and the people were friendly, if a little curious about why such a rich city feller would move down there. Grass is greener syndrome, I suppose.

As I wandered the trails of my first summer, I made some acquaintance with the people who lived further back, primitive, clannish, and isolated from even the tiny corner of the twentieth century that permeated the little town. I even got shot at when I discovered that they still do indeed have stills back there—and got blind stinking drunk when we straightened it out.

The grinding poverty of these people was matched only by their lack of knowledge about how destitute they really were. State social workers and welfare people sometimes trekked up there, but they encountered hostility mixed with pride. And, in a way, I admired the mountain folk all the more for it, for in some things they were richer than anyone in this uncertain world—their sense of family, the closeness between people, the love of nature and the placement of a person's worth above all else—these were things my own culture had long ago lost, called corny and hick.

Most of these people were illiterate, and so were their kids. Most of the time the kids were kept hidden when the state people came up—these folk were too poor to afford shoes, pens and pencils, and all the other costly paraphernalia of our "free" school system. They preferred to ignore the state laws on education as much as they did the federal ones on making moonshine.

Well, I talked to some of the state people, who knew of the problem but could do little about it, and convinced someone in the welfare department that I could make a contribution. They accepted my teaching certificate, and I became a *per diem* teacher to the hill people on the West Virginia State Department of Education. Not much, but it was a job, and I was needed here. The only way these people were ever going to break the bonds of poverty and isolation was through education, at least in the basics. I was determined that my students—perhaps a dozen at the start—would be able to read and write and do simple, practical sums before I was through—and that's more than most modern high school graduates in urban areas can do these days.

It was tough to get some of those parents to agree, but when the first snow fell in early October I had a group. We met in my house—a two-story actual log cabin, but with only two large rooms (one more than I needed). The kids were fun, and eager learners. I wound up with an ominous thirteen, but it was perfect—each one got individual attention from me, and I got to know them well. When they ran into trouble, I'd go up to their shacks, stomach lined as much as possible with yogurt or cream against the inevitable parental hospitality, and we'd have extra lessons. In this way I sneakily started teaching some of the parents as well.

Their ages ranged from nine to fourteen, but they all started off evenly—they were ignorant as hell. And I got help—the state was so pleased to make any kind of a dent in the region that they sent us everything from hot-lunch supplies to pens, pencils, crayons, and even some simple books, obviously years old and discovered in some Charleston elementary school's basement but perfect for us.

Schooling was erratic and unconventional. The snow was extremely deep at times, the weather as fierce as the Canadian northwoods, and there were whole weeks when contact was impossible. Yet, as spring approached progress had been made; their world was a little wider. They were mostly on Dick and Jane, but they were *reading,* and they were already adding and subtracting on a basic level.

And they taught me, too. We spent time in those woodlands watching deer and coon, and, as spring arrived, they showed me the best spots for viewing the wonderful flowers and catching the biggest fish.

They were close to nature and were, in fact, a part of it. It sometimes made me hesitate in what I was doing. "Poor" is such a relative term.

Only one of the students was a real puzzle—a girl of ten or eleven (who knew for sure?) named Cindy Lou Whittler, the only child of a poor woman who made out as best she could while tending the grave of her husband just out back. She was fat and acne-ridden, and awkward as hell; the other kids would have made her the butt of their cruel jokes in normal circumstances, but they steered clear of her. She sat off by herself, talked only haltingly and only when prompted—and you could cut the tension with a knife.

They were scared to death of her.

Finally I could stand it no longer, and had a talk with Billy Bushman. He was the oldest of the group, the most worldly-wise, and was the natural class leader.

"Billy," I asked him one day, "you've got to tell me. Why are you and everybody else scared of Cindy Lou?"

He shuffled uneasily and glanced around. "'Cause she a witcher woman," he replied softly. "You do somthang she don' liak, she sing th' stormsong an' thas all fo you."

A little more prompting brought the rest of the story. They thought—knew—she was a witch, and they believed she could cause lightning and thunder.

I felt sorry for the girl. Superstition is rampant among the ignorant (and some not so ignorant, come to think of it) and an idea based on it, once formed, is almost impossible to dislodge. Seems a couple of years back she and a boy had had a fight, and she threatened him. A couple of days later, he was struck by lightning and killed.

Such are legends born.

Shortly after, contemplating her sullen loneliness in the corner, I called her aside after class and talked to her about it. Getting any response from her was like pulling teeth.

"Cindy Lou, I know the others think you're a witch," I told her, feeling genuinely sorry for her, "and I know how lonely you must be."

She smiled a little, and the hurt that was always in her eyes seemed to lessen.

"I heard the story about the boy," I told her, trying to tread cautiously but to open her up.

"Didn't kill nobody," she replied at last. "Couldn't."

"I know," I told her. "I understand."

Finally she couldn't hold it in any longer, and started crying. I tried to soothe and comfort her, glad the hurt was coming out. To cure a boil—even one in the soul—it must first be lanced so tears can flow.

"I jest make 'em liak ah'm told ta," she sobbed. "Ah caint tell 'em what ta do."

This threw me for a loop. In my smug urban superiority it had never occurred to me that she might believe it, too.

"Who tells you?" I asked softly. "Who tells you to bring the thunderstorms?"

"Papa come sometimes," she replied, still sniffling. "He say ah got to make 'em. That everybody's got a reason for bein' heah an' mine's doin' this."

I understood now. I knew. An ugly, fat little girl *would* see her father, now two years dead, and she would rationalize her loneliness and ugliness somehow. This was in the character of these people so much a part of nature and the hills—she wasn't the ugly duckling, no, she was the most important person, most powerful person in the whole area.

She made the thunderstorms for southern West Virginia—and she was here for that purpose.

It made life livable.

The beginning of spring meant the onrush of thunderstorms as the warmer air now moving in struck the mountains; and as they increased in frequency, so did her loneliness, isolation—and pride. As the kids became more scared of her, she knew she had power—over them, over all.

She made the storms. She.

I tried to teach them a little basic meteorology, to sneakily dispel this fantasy for the rest of them, but they nodded, told me the answers I wanted to hear, and kept on believing that Cindy Lou made the storms. Outsiders couldn't understand. And this gave them some pride, too—for they were smugly confident that, for all my education, they knew for sure something that was beyond me.

It was the middle of May now, and my job had been among the most enjoyable and rewarding that I could imagine. I started to pick up other students as word got around, and began to travel as well, to teach some of the adults who managed to swallow just enough of that fierce pride to get me to help them.

One day I was coming back from one such student—he was seventy if he was a day, and I had him up to Dr. Seuss—when I passed near the Whittler house. I decided to stop by and see how Cindy Lou and her terribly suffering mother, the oldest thirty-six I had ever seen, were getting along. Classes were infrequent now; in spring these people planted and worked hard to eke out their subsistence.

As I approached the house, I thought I heard Cindy Lou's voice coming from inside, and I hesitated, as if a great hand were lain upon me. Frozen, her words drifted through the crude wooden shack to me.

"No, Papa!" she cried out fiercely. "Ah caint do this'n! You caint ask me! You know the wata's too high now. A big'n liak this'll flood the whole valley—maybe the town, too!"

And then there came the sound I'll never forget—the one that made the hairs on my neck stand up.

"You do liak yo' papa say!" came a deep, gravelly and oddly hollow man's voice. "Ah ain't got no choice in this mattah and neither do you. Leave them choices to them what knows bettah. You do it, now, heah? You know what happen if'n you don't!"

Suddenly the spell that seemed to hold me broke, and I stood for a moment, uneasily shivering. I considered not dropping in, just going on, but I finally decided it was my duty. I knew one thing for sure—somebody definitely *did* tell Cindy Lou to make the storms; she could never have made that voice outside a recording studio.

I had to know who was feeding her this. I knocked.

For a while there was no answer. Then, just as I was about to give up, the door creaked open and Cindy Lou peered out.

She'd been crying, I could see, but she was glad to see me and asked me in.

"Mama's gone ta town," she explained. "Cleanin' Mr. Summil's windas."

I walked into the one-room shack that I'd been in many times before. There was no back door, and only the most basic furnishings.

There was no one else in the shack but the two of us.

My stomach started turning a little, but I got a grip on myself.

"Cindy Lou?" I asked anxiously. "Where's the man who was just here? I heard voices."

She shrugged. "Papa dead, you know. Cain't hang around fo' long," she explained so matter-of-factly that it was more upsetting than the voice itself. I shifted subjects, the last refuge of the nervous.

"You've been crying," I noted.

She nodded seriously. "Papa want me t'do a big'n to-night. You been by the dam today?"

I shook my head slowly. There was a small earthen dam used to trap water. Part of it was tapped for town use, and the small lake it backed up made the best fishing in the area. I had walked by there only a half hour or so earlier; the water was already to the top, ready to spill over, this mostly from the runoff of melting snow from the hard winter.

"If'n it rain big, that dam'll bust," she said flatly.

Again I nodded. It was true—I'd complained to the county about that dam, pleaded with them to shore it up, but it was low on the priority list—not many voters in these parts.

"Ah din't kill that boy," she continued, getting more anxious, "but if'n I do what Papa want, ah'll kill a lot of folk sure."

And that, too, was true—if the dam burst and nobody heeded any warnings. I tried to think of an answer that would comfort her. I was terribly afraid of what would happen to her if that dam *did* break in a storm. She paid a heavy price for assumed guilt by others; this one she'd blame on herself, and I was sure she couldn't handle that.

"What happens if you don't bring the storm?" I asked gently.

She was grim, face set, and her voice sounded almost as dead and hollow as that man's eerie tones had been.

"Terrible thangs" was all she could tell me.

I didn't want to leave her, but when I heard that the storm was set for before midnight, and that her mother probably wouldn't come home until the next day, I decided I had to act. Cindy Lou refused to come with me, and I had little choice, I was afraid that she might kill herself to keep from doing her terrible task, and I needed reinforcement. I made for town and Mrs. Whittler.

It took me over an hour to get there, and another half hour to find her. She seemed extremely alarmed, and it was the first time I'd heard her curse, but she and I rushed back to where no cars could go as quickly as possible.

Clouds obscured the sky, and no stars showed through that low ceiling as sundown caught us still on the rutted path to the shack. Ordinarily, no problem—it was usually cloudy on this side of the mountains—but that deepening blackness seemed somehow alive, threatening now as we neared the shack.

We burst in suddenly, and I quickly lit a kerosene lantern. The shack was empty.

"My God! My God!" Mrs. Whittler moaned. "What has that rascal done to mah poor baby?"

"Think!" I urged her. "Where would she go?"

She shook her head sadly from side to side. "I dunno. Nowheres. Everywheres. Too dark to see her anyways if she din't wanta be seen."

It was true, but I didn't want to face it. Nothing is more terrible than knowing you are impotent in a crisis.

There was a noticeable lowering of the temperature. The barometer was falling so fast that you could feel it sink. There was a mild rumble off in the distance.

"There must be *something* we can do!" I almost screamed in frustration.

She chewed on her lower lip a moment. Then, suddenly, her head came up, and there was fire in her eyes. "There's one thang!" she said firmly, and walked out of the shack. I followed numbly.

We walked around to the back in the almost complete darkness. Small flashes of lightning gave a sudden, intermittent illumination, like a few frames of a black and white movie.

She stood there at the grave of her husband, the little wooden cross the only sign that someone was buried there.

"Jared Whittler!" she screamed. "You cain't do this to our daughta! She's ours! Ours! *Please,* oh, God! You was always a good man, Jared! *In the name of God, she's all I've got!*"

It seemed then that the lightning picked up, and thunder roared and echoed among the darkened hills.

Now, suddenly, there was a cosmic fireworks display; sharp, piercing streaks of lightning seemed to flash all around us, thunder boomed, and the wind picked up to tremendous force.

It started to rain, a few hard drops at first, then faster and faster, until we were engulfed in a terrible torrent.

And yet we stood there transfixed, in front of that little cross, and we prayed, and we pleaded, oblivious to the weather.

Suddenly, through it all, we heard a roaring sound unlike any of the storm. I turned slowly, the terror of reality in my soul.

"Oh, my God!" I managed. "There goes the dam!"

There was a sound like a tidal wave moving closer to us, then passing us somewhere to our backs, and continuing on down into the valley below.

As suddenly as it came on, the rain stopped. Both of us still stood there, soaked to the skin, now ankle-deep in mud. Now the storm was just a set of dull flashes in the distance to the east, and a few muted rumbles of what it had been.

She turned to me then. Though I couldn't really see her, I knew that she was stoic as all hill folk were in disaster.

"You're soaked," she said quietly. "Come in and git dried off. There'll be work to do in the town tonight."

I was shocked, numb, and silently, without thought, I followed her into the shack where, by the light of the kerosene lantern, she fished out some ragged towels for me to use.

We said nothing to each other. There was nothing left to say.

Suddenly there was a noise outside, and slowly, hesitantly, the old door opened on creaking hinges.

"Cindy Lou!" her mother almost whispered, and then ran and hugged her, holding the child to her bosom. Cindy Lou cried and hugged her mother all the more.

After a time, Mrs. Whittler turned her loose and looked at her. "Lord! You a mess!" she exclaimed, and went over and threw the girl a towel.

I stood there dumbly, trying to think of something to say. She sensed it, and looked up at me.

"Ah went to the dam," she said softly. "If'n it was gonna go, ah wanted to be goin' with it. Papa come to me then, say, 'These things hav'ta happen sometimes.' He say you goes when th' time comes, but it wasn't mah time, that you an' Mama was heah, callin' fo' me."

"It had to happen—your papa's right about that. If it hadn't been this time, then a few days from now," I consoled.

She shrugged.

"Ah couldn't do it. Papa got the man in charge of eastern Kentucky to do it," she said. "Papa say he don't want me doin' this no mo'. He gon' try ta git me changed to handlin' warm days."

And that was it.

We spent days cleaning up the mess; my cabin was the highest ground near the town, so it became rescue headquarters and temporary shelter. It'll take months to dig that silt out of the town itself, but, miraculously, no lives had been lost.

The state says they'll do something real soon now. By that time I'll be dead of old age, of course—but, no, I'll die of helping everybody with the red tape first.

Cindy Lou? Well, she seems happier now, convinced that she's switched jobs to something potentially less lethal. I go up there often. The kids still aren't all that friendly, but I take Cindy Lou with me on my rounds; realistically, I know I'm the father figure she craves, and she is almost like a daughter to me, but, what the hell. You get to analyzing why you do something and you go nuts.

And my students? More each day seem to show up, ages five to eighty-five. No teacher can find more satisfaction in his work than I do.

Every time there's a thunderstorm, though, I get to thinking—and I'm not sure that's good, either.

The weather bureau had predicted that storm; the Charleston paper showed a front right where a front should have been, and I looked at back issues and that front had been moving across the country for three days. Anybody used to this mountain country could tell a storm was brewing that day.

And that man's voice? I don't know. I'm not sure whether Cindy Lou's voice can go that low or not, but . . . it must have, mustn't it? She hasn't seen Papa much these days, she tells me. He's mad at her, and she doesn't care at all.

And yet, creeping into my mind some lonely, storm-tossed nights, I can't help thinking; what if it's true? Is it truly a disturbing thought or is it, in some way, equally comforting, for if such things actually are it gives some meaning to practically everyone's usually dull life.

Does each of us have a specific purpose here on Earth? Are some of us teachers to those who need us, and others stormsong runners?

Born in Virginia in 1944 and educated at Towson State College and Johns Hopkins University, Jack L. Chalker is a science fiction fan turned publisher turned writer. In 1960 he founded Mirage fiction. Chalker's first novel, A Jungle of Stars *(1976) earned him the John Campbell Award as Best New Writer in 1977. Recent titles include* Children of Flux and Anchor *and* When the Changewinds Blow.

Most people don't want ghosts in their homes, but Miss Annie would do anything to keep hers. Anything.

TEN

Harry's Ghost
Talmage Powell

Harry's ghostly visitations became the focus of Miss Annie's unhappy life. She anticipated his ectoplasm with the breathlessness of a schoolgirl, and if several evenings passed without a sign from him, she was more miserably lonely than before.

Now that she was in the twilight of her life, she'd had nothing but memories bleak and barren of all the years BH (Before Harry).

It could have been so different, she would think bitterly. Certainly no spot on earth should have been more conducive to happiness than the southern California, Pasadena to be precise, into which she had been born.

It was the Eden in those days, the irresistible lure that had drawn, like flies to the honey pot, the despoiling millions who had cut the flower-quilted hillsides, smothered the orange groves in concrete, piled the spaghetti-tangled morass of freeways for the insane rushing multitudes, and blanketed the friendliest sun on earth with a poisonous curtain of smog.

Those days . . . a lazy interurban between Pasadena and downtown Los Angeles, strollers window shopping on Colorado Avenue, where the bus station was furnished with over-stuffed couches and chairs like a friendly living room, radishes two cents a bunch, avocados for a nickle, families dining on the front porch of a house that had been converted into a neighborhood cafe, a war between oil companies reducing gasoline prices to nothing for the guzzling Stutz or Dusenberg or Cadillac, a morning tobogganing on

161

pristine snow in the mountains and driving past olive and date groves on your way home that evening to the perfume of flowers and the welcoming nod of palm trees.

But only in retrospect was Miss Annie aware . . . the shadow of papa, from her first squalling breath to the end of his days, had been her reality.

Why couldn't he have died early-on, that martinet she called papa, when she still had time to realize that she, too, was a person? But he hadn't, and she hadn't. And she couldn't at last explain how it had all happened, this process she called her life. The years had somehow simply crept away, in his shadow, in the sound of his voice, cautioning, warning of the evils of the world, opening her eyes to the filth of the young males, claiming her time and attention, making her aware of how much she owed him, how dutiful she must be, how he was poor, dear papa.

And when he had finally died, it had been too late. And her reward had been endless hours of days in which to dwell on the past, her only security three small houses in an old section.

Life had certainly changed for Miss Annie after the advent of Harry. It was no longer a dull gray abyss. Nothing in this three-dimensional realm could equal the experience of having a real live ghost for one's own, especially one as nice as Harry. And only the confirmed addict of an hallucinatory drug might have comprehended Miss Annie's wracking anxieties during those periods when Harry refused to appear.

Then, just as Miss Annie was about to succumb to despair, the first swirl of ectoplasm would glimmer in the narrow, dark hallway or in a corner of the kitchen.

Miss Annie would rise from her inner ashes, blood stirring in her old, stiff veins, the most delicious fright and fascination searing through her brittle bones and wrinkled-parchment tissues.

Neither her reaction nor Harry's existence perturbed her in the least. It was inconceivable that anyone could fail to respond to such a dear as Harry. And on the second point, Harry's existence, to Miss Annie's way of thinking, was no more surprising than this year's rebirth of the tiger lily that had died last autumn.

"Harry?" she would say through the pulse beating in her

thin, bony neck. Then her dentures would click as her soft, chiding smile belied her sternly wagging finger: "You've been a very naughty young man, Harry, staying away so long. I was on the point of moving out, like the others. How would you like that?"

The quick shimmering of ectoplasm hinted that he wouldn't like it at all. He partially succeeded in materializing there in the dim hallway, a quivering, uncertain image of a tall, thin, clean cut young man with dark hair and the imprint of deep sorrow on his gaunt face.

He was trying to tell her something. He was always trying to tell her.

She stood with eyes enrapt, her heart beating in wild excitement. From crown to toe she came to tingling life. Emotions, long banked like embers of half-forgotten fires, sputtered and flamed. She ached with the desire to know his secret, but she was in the same moment torn with the fear that if he ever managed to reveal it he would go away forever.

"Harry. . . ." She could barely whisper above her shortness of breath. "What is it like? Is there day and night? Cold and hot? Harry, please!"

But his grip weakened on forces beyond her own space-time continuum, and his already-fuzzy image melted and slipped away, until there was just a wisp of ectoplasm coiling and writhing a dozen feet from her face.

"Oh, Harry . . . Harry . . ." she sobbed faintly, and then the hallway was quite empty.

Miss Annie returned to limp awareness of her surroundings. With a petulant little sigh, she turned toward the living room. It hadn't been a good visitation, not at all. If Harry would only try as hard to get here as she expended the effort to bring him—

She started slightly as the front door chimes sounded. Frowning at the unexpected event of someone calling on her, she crossed the living room.

She opened the door on a tall, lean young man who was dressed in dark denim slacks and a blue peajacket.

"Miss Annie Loxton?"

She nodded, struck by the strange sense of familiarity aroused by his gaunt face and shock of dark hair.

"I'm Horace Grimshaw," he said. "Harry's brother."

That explained it. She expelled a tiny breath. Peered at closely, he wasn't Harry at all. Though similar on the surface, the cast of Horace's features, the charisma, contrasted with Harry. Horace was tougher, that was the word. Harder bitten. More capable of meeting the world's cruelty head-on.

"If you don't mind, Miss Annie," he was saying, "I'd like to talk to you."

"Of course," she said quickly. "Do come in."

He surveyed the modest living room with a glance as he entered. This was the first time he'd been in the house where Harry had died, and a tightness tugged the corner of his mouth.

"Please sit down, Mr. Grimshaw. Would you like some coffee?"

"No, thanks. Just some talk about Harry, if it's okay."

She nodded, watching him sit down in the barrel-backed chair near the window. He was bigger boned than Harry. Big knuckles. Big wrists thrusting a half-inch from the sleeves of the worn seaman's jacket as he bent his arms and rested his elbows on the chair arms.

"I didn't know that Harry had a brother," she said.

"We haven't seen each other in a long while. I was working on a scabby island freighter in the Celebes and Banda Seas when news of his death finally reached me."

She slipped into a chair opposite him, blue-veined, chicken-claw old hands folded tightly in her lap. She saw the grief-darkness in his face, and she felt she should say something. But she didn't know what would be entirely appropriate. The dull gray years, devoid of human fellowship and communication, had hardly trained her in the art of consoling a saddened stranger.

He pushed aside his remote moment, lifting his eyes. "They say that Harry killed himself."

"Yes," she murmured.

"Here in this house. In the basement. They say he hanged himself in the basement."

"Please, Mr. Grimshaw. It happened weeks ago. It's all over and done."

His weather-tanned young face studied her a moment.

His lips had the look of being chiseled from ice. For an instant, he was just a little frightening.

"I knew my brother, Miss Annie. I don't believe he would have done such a thing. I don't honestly think he had the guts."

Her watery blue eyes glanced away. She was beginning to dislike Harry's brother. To talk of Harry in such terms, as if it was Horace who possessed all the intestinal fortitude in the family.

"You rented the house to him," Horace said.

"Yes," Miss Annie nodded. "To him and his wife. She left him shortly afterward, for another man, I think. He continued on in a bachelor existence, with a cleaning woman in twice a week. It was she who found him—the cleaning woman, I mean. Later, Harry's ex-wife came and claimed their things."

"Do you know where she is now?"

"No, Mr. Grimshaw. Such affairs are not my business. She had a legal paper. She took their belongings. That's the last I've seen of her."

He'd assessed Miss Annie's tone.

"Good riddance?" he suggested.

She refolded her hands.

"If you wish to put it that way," she said stiffly. "I think your brother was a far finer person than his wife was."

"Were you here when she took the things away?"

"Naturally, and so was a detective. I rented the house partially furnished, and I had to watch after my own things. Later. . . ."

"Yes, Miss Annie?"

She straightened her thin shoulders an inch. "Well, the next two tenants didn't stay long. They—they claimed Harry was still here, making little noises in the plaster and sometimes glowing in the dark. Well, not glowing exactly. Kind of a shower of sparks. Like those childrens' toys, sparklers."

He waited, and she felt the need to break the sudden silence.

She stifled her sense of aggravation with him and forced herself to speak calmly. "I didn't believe it myself, Mr. Grimshaw. But the tenants kept running, so to speak, and I

165

had to have my rents. My father left me three little cottages like this one. It's all I have. So, if I could not keep this one rented, I decided to move in myself and rent out the one in which I'd lived. It worked out nicely. Good tenants in the other places, and I like it here, very much."

"Even with Harry around?"

She bristled inwardly at the faint scorn in his voice, but before she could tell him how much she liked having Harry around, he was on a new tack.

"My brother worked for an outfit called Happy Havens, I believe."

"An executive director," Miss Annie said proudly. "And a wonderful organization it is, too. They build and support nursing homes, for helpless senior citizens without kin or money."

"They'd conducted a big fund drive just before Harry's death," Horace said. "Is that correct?"

"Yes, that is true."

"And forty thousand dollars showed up short when all the collections were in and the kitty totaled up."

Miss Annie looked at the pulsing blue veins on her tight knuckles and wished Horace would go away.

Remorse over the forty thousand in embezzled funds was what had killed Harry. Too nice. Too fine. Too decent and honest to go against his own conscience, no matter what had been his reasons in his once-in-a-lifetime moment of weakness and temptation.

"The police tell me, Miss Annie, that they never did recover the forty thousand. Could Harry have reconciled with his wife? She's quite a beauty, I hear. Could she have talked to him, coaxed him, worn him down, conned him into taking the money?"

"A Jezebel," Miss Annie whispered. "Filthy creature of her sex!"

"What was that, Miss Annie?"

"I think," she said, lifting her eyes, "that Harry was deeply infatuated with her at one time, but I think he got over her when she left."

"You saw him often?"

"Whenever I collected the rents."

"But you noticed a change in him?"

"Yes. He seemed harried, absent-minded when I first rented them the house. After she left he seemed to find a sense of relief. His color was better. He gained a little weight."

He cut a side glance. "You seem to have noticed a lot, Miss Annie."

"I was fond of your brother, Mr. Grimshaw. He didn't treat me like a prune-faced landlady. In all my life—"

Again he waited. And she pinked, wondering how she could be so open to a perfect stranger.

"I won't trouble you with the details of my life, Mr. Grimshaw. Sufficient to say that I was a shy, sickly, ugly little girl. My mother died, and I never escaped the shadow of my father, who rather despised me and felt that I was incapable of coping with the world. To sum up, it hasn't been much of a life, and your brother was one of the rare people who looked at me and saw a person, who seemed to under-stand—"

She broke off. Horace, unlike his brother, lacked that par-ticular empathy. Horace's eyes held a nearly hidden chill, as if he found her soft voice repugnant.

"If there's nothing more, Mr. Grimshaw—"

But before she could rise and dismiss him, he said, "There is more. A lot more. In seaman's language, I'm not—but I'd better not use any seaman's language, Miss Annie. Let's just say that I'm not satisfied with a lot of things."

"As?"

"The note my brother was supposed to have left, for one thing. The suicide note, saying he had stolen the money, realized later that he was bound to get caught, and simply couldn't stand the prospect of scandal, shame, and prison." The chair creaked slightly under his shifting weight. "The note was typewritten, Miss Annie. Anyone can type a note."

"But it had his signature."

"Which gets us to the nitty-gritty," he said. "If Harry didn't take the money or write the note, then it had to be someone who had both access to the money and to Harry's signature so it could be copied."

"You're dismissing his wife?"

"For the moment. The other angle narrows down the suspects to people within or close to Happy Havens. How many people were there in executive directorships or posts above that?"

"Three at the time, I think. Harry, and a Mr. Philbin, and Mr. James Fellows who lives third house down the street," Miss Annie said. "Harry and Mr. Fellows used to take turns driving their cars and riding to work together."

"And while they're riding along," Horace said, "this guy Fellows, sick to death with the boring details and fawning over contributors and the low pay that goes with every charity job, this guy decides to grab a big fat plum while he's got the chance to use the trusting, dumb cluck on the car seat beside him for a fall guy."

"But the police—"

"Do their routine and are promptly swamped with a dozen, a hundred, a million other crimes. Sure, they look for the missing money. They figure every place Harry might have put it. They go over every crack here in the house he occupied. But he is hanging by the neck in his own basement and a note with his signature says he did it and the missing money is another unanswered detail in an already cluttered file."

"But they questioned the others!"

"For hours," Horace agreed. "Probably searched their premises, too. And no doubt really put the ex-wife over the coals. But the question of the money remains, and if I knew that soft-sister Harry he would have gone crawling back with it instead of killing himself."

Miss Annie thought: Philbin? She knew him only through Happy Havens publicity releases that had appeared in the newspapers. A frail little man, very old, very gray. Far too weak to have hanged Harry.

Fellows? James Fellows? A far different case, indeed! He had been here a time or two when she'd dropped by for the rent. Big, jovial. Too hearty, that was Fellows. The back-slapper. The glad-hander.

Oh, by all means, now that she came to think of it. Fellows. A big, broad smile for big contributors whose wealth he secretly envied. An ogling phony and four flusher, her instincts had told her that the first time she'd met him.

"A penny, Miss Annie?" Horace's words nudged into her thoughts.

"For my thoughts?" She arose stiffly, and crossed to the window. She slipped back the drape and looked at the Fellows house down the street. Modest, like the rest of them on the block. But the lawn needed cutting, and there was Mrs. Fellows coming out the front door. Sexpot blonde in those dreadful hotpants. Cheap and vulgar. Crossing to the Fellows car, which was too flashy for Mr. Fellows's salary.

Miss Annie recognized her suspicion as just that. A suspicion. But it was possible. Fellows was cunning enough and strong enough to have pulled it off. Fellows could have taken the money and before the theft was discovered he could have strolled over for a chat with Harry that unspeakable evening.

Fellows could easily have overpowered an unsuspecting Harry, knocked him out, carried him unconscious to the basement. When he departed, Fellows could have left the forged suicide note which he'd prepared in advance. And Harry, slowly turning left and slowly turning right, his neck secured by the rope to the overhead waterpipe . . . .

Then Fellows simply waits, bides his time until the "heat was off" as the late movies put it. In due time Fellows manages to get himself fired at Happy Havens and, quite naturally, fades from sight—with his blonde and the forty thousand dollars bought with Harry's life.

Miss Annie didn't know she was biting her knuckles until Horace tapped her shoulder and said sharply, "Miss Annie, what is this you're mumbling? About Harry being here, about Harry trying to tell you—?"

She turned, tears in irregular course on the bleached crocodile leather of her face. "He is here, Mr. Grimshaw. Harry really is here. If you don't believe me, ask the previous tenants, the ones who rented the house after he was hanged."

Horace was stilled for a moment. He crept a glance over his shoulder.

"I don't see him, Miss Annie."

"Oh, for heaven's sake," she shrilled, jerking away from his touch. "You're like so many other people. To you, I'm just an old prune-face. Pixillated now. Old, you know. A little cracked. Imagining things. Well, I don't imagine a blessed thing, you foolish and cruel young man. I don't see Harry, either, when he isn't there. Only when he is able to materialize. But not with creakings in the walls, not as a dime store sparkler in the dark. Not with me, young fellow! Harry and I understand each other, something that you would never comprehend. With understanding, Harry and I have almost bridged the gap."

She hobbled over to a chair, feeling suddenly weak.

"Miss Annie—"

"No! Just go. You don't believe and—"

"But maybe I do, Miss Annie." His shadow fell across her chair. "I've seen some kookie things in the Celebes. Things I can't account for. Things science can't explain. Miss Annie, let me come back. If my brother is present, you owe me the privilege of coming back."

She didn't want him to come back. She didn't want him around. She was content to be alone in the house, with Harry's ghost.

She drew her head to one side, looking up at him from the corners of her eyes. He seemed quite serious, not making fun of her at all.

"Harry was all the kin I had, Miss Annie. Parents dead. No wife. No real friends. Just some guys and chicks I knew knocking around in the south seas. Nobody but Harry, Miss Annie."

"Very well," she relented reluctantly. "You may come and see him—if he appears."

"Does he favor certain times?"

"Not precisely. He doesn't call by appointment."

"Certain places here in the house?"

"The hallway, the kitchen, and the basement, where he was hanged."

"Murdered, Miss Annie."

"Murdered," she said.

They sat quietly in the confines of the basement with its earthen smell and feel of dusty cobwebs. It was the second evening in a row that they'd sat here for two-hour stretches. Eight o'clock to ten o'clock each night. Thinking back over the visitations, Miss Annie had concluded that Harry favored the hour of nine. It was the hour, the coroner had officially reported, when Harry's life had been surrendered to the length of rope and water pipe.

They sat on two old kitchen chairs that had been stored in the basement, just the two of them. Miss Annie near the foot of the narrow, steep stairs and Horace a few feet away. There was no sign of Harry, and nothing broke the silence, until Horace remarked, "Not like a regular seance, Miss Annie. No tilting table. No joining of hands and calling up the spirits."

"I don't believe in such humbug, Horace."

"Neither do I."

"Now and then a being such as Harry is forced to return. That's what I believe. And dishes fly off the shelves to make a poltergeist's presence known."

"It's happened in some well-authenticated instances," Horace agreed, "with even hard-headed cops and newspaper reporters on hand to witness the knockings."

Miss Annie's silence dropped the subject. In a moment, she stirred, watching the brief emergence of Horace's hard-bitten young face in the glow of his cigarette.

"Horace?"

"Yes, Miss Annie?"

"Was there bad blood between you and Harry?"

"Why do you ask, Miss Annie?"

"I'm not sure, except that he doesn't seem inclined to appear while you're present."

"No, Miss Annie. Nothing like that. Frankly, I used to make him out a sissy sometimes, but I think that deep down he knew that I did admire other qualities he had."

"Then we shall wait."

"Right on, Miss Annie."

He finished his cigarette and ground it under his heel.

"It's after nine, Miss Annie. I don't think—"

"Shhhh!" It was a softly barked expletive, cutting him short, freezing him in his chair. "I feel that strange warmth, Horace, that tingling of life, that sensation quite unlike any other I've ever known . . . There, Horace! Near the water heater!"

Horace stumbled to his feet, toppling his chair. In the dim corner at which Miss Annie was pointing the first thin tendril of ectoplasm threshed like the body of a headless, silvery glowing snake.

The manifestation eeled and crawled its way through the space-time warp. It grew, eddied, steadied. It strained itself into shape, shimmering unsteadily.

"Harry," Miss Annie said to the image, "your brother Horace has come all the way from the south seas to see you."

The image quivered a greeting to Horace, and Horace, supporting himself with one hand against a brick pillar, got his sea legs under him.

"Hello, Harry," Horace said. "I'm sorry it has to be like this, under these circumstances."

Harry darkened, sharing Horace's sentiment.

Horace had strength to push away from the basement support.

"I want to help you, Harry. I know it must be hell, trapped the way you are," Horace said.

Harry brightened perceptibly.

"Okay," Horace said on a deep breath, "I know you can't stick around long at a time, so let's hit the point. You can move up and down, and you can move side to side. I've got some questions. Move up and down for a yes answer, side to side for a no. Can do?"

Harry moved up and down fitfully.

"Swell," Horce said. "First off, were you murdered?"

Yes, Harry replied.

"By your wife?"

No.

"By someone at Happy Havens who wanted to steal money safely, using you for a patsy?"

Yes, Harry answered with a quick up-down bob of his disembodied reflection.

"Was it James Fellows?"

Yes, yes, yes!

Miss Annie was drawing to her feet, breathless spectator, her gaze dashing from brother to brother.

"Fellows is now just waiting his chance to leave without suspicion," Horace pressed on, "taking the forty thousand dollars with him?"

Yes, Harry replied.

"You must get around in a brand new way nowadays," Horace said. "Walls can't stop you. Have you looked in on the Fellowses?"

Yes.

"Do you know where he's got the money hidden?"

Yes.

Horace paused, taking breath. Harry could signal only positive or negative responses, and Horace spent a moment framing his questions.

"Is the money stashed in a safety deposit box?"

No.

"Bus station locker, maybe?" Horace said.

No.

"In his house?"

Yes, yes!

"None of the usual hiding places," Horace mused to himself, "or the cops would have found it."

"Horace," Miss Annie remarked, "Harry is slipping away. He's barely hanging on. I can tell."

"Harry, stick with us," Horace pleaded. "If all the furniture were taken out of the house, would the money still be in there?"

Yes.

"In the attic?"

No.

"Basement?"

No.

"In the walls?"

No.

Horace looked a bit helplessly at Miss Annie. "What other parts of a house—" He suddenly bit the words off, snapped his fingers. Then asked, "The floor, Harry?"

Yes.

"He spread the money and hid it with an inlay of fresh tile?"

No. And again No, as if Horace were the biggest dummy on the high seas.

"Then the carpet . . ." Horace said. "Sure! Fellows just loosened the edge of the carpet, rolled it back, spread the money, and then refastened the wall-to-wall carpeting!"

Yes. In capitals. A bob from floor to partially through the ceiling. Then the movement became a swirl, and the swirl a vortex, and the vortex was sucked into empty space. Harry was gone, and a silence came to the basement.

Miss Annie felt Horace's touch on her arm. They looked at each other in the dimness filtering down the narrow stairs. Then, silently, they started up, Miss Annie in the lead.

When they were halfway up, Horace remarked, "Somehow we've got to figure a way to get the police to roll back every inch of floor covering in the Fellows house. Can't very well tell them a ghost told us to do so."

"No, we can't," Miss Annie agreed. She struggled to the top of the stairs, reaching for the door jamb.

"We'll figure a way," Horace said confidently, "even if I have to sneak into the Fellows house when they're away and call the cops from there, after I've uncovered the money. And the money will put the guilt where it belongs."

"It surely will, Horace," said Miss Annie.

"And that will certainly balance whatever cosmic forces we're dealing with. Don't you see? Harry is trapped where he is, but when we restore the cosmic balance, it should release Harry, forever."

Framed in the doorway at the top of the stairs, Miss Annie stopped and turned.

"What is this you're saying, Horace?"

A couple of stair treads below her, he looked up at her wiry figure.

"I'm an amateur at this sort of thing, exorcising ghosts, getting messages from the great beyond," he admitted. "But we can be sure of one thing, Harry is stuck. And Harry is tormented with the need to see his murderer brought to justice. And while he was visible to us, he gave me the strongest impression that justice for his murderer would complete the equation, put things in balance. He was trying to let me, his brother, know that it was the one way I could help him get unstuck. I'm certain of that."

"Justice for his murderer," Miss Annie murmured, "and Harry is chased away for good."

"Released, Miss Annie," Horace corrected. "He'll never bother you again or chase away another tenant."

"I'm sorry, Horace," Miss Annie said in that instant that she put out her hands and pushed him with all her wiry old strength.

She saw the look of surprise on his face as Horace went over backward and fell all the way to the bottom, bumping and banging. She flinched when his head struck the bottom step and he came to rest in an awkward pile of outflung arms and twisted legs.

She slipped down the stairs quickly. She'd expected, at the very least, that the fall would stun him, give her the advantage, offer her time enough to grab the handaxe from the tool cabinet and finish the job. But as she knelt beside him, she saw that the most, not the least, had happened. He was dead. His skull had cracked and was seeping red.

Now all that remained was the burial of Horace, here in the basement. He had no relatives, no friends. He was a stranger in the city for whom no one would come asking. No one would ever know.

Then, still in her kneeling position beside Horace, she sensed a presence. She turned her head a few inches and in the further corner of the basement, she saw the first spark, a little burst of stardust against the darkness.

"Harry," she said, rising slowly and reaching out entreating hands, "I simply had to do it. I couldn't take a chance that Horace was right, that you'd go away if Fellows was brought to justice. I'd die, Harry, before I'd risk the destruction of the only relationship I ever had . . ."

Her words faltered. The nice, strange warmth had failed to come. Instead, a breath of inter-spacial zero oozed through the basement.

And she knew. As the form before her materialized, the full truth flowed suddenly through her mind. This wasn't Harry. This was Horace, trapped hellishly in cosmic imbalance. This was a Horace transformed to raw wrath and a dark, boundless thirst for revenge.

And Miss Annie started screaming.

A former reporter, Talmage Powell was born in North Carolina in 1920. A graduate of the University of North Carolina, he sold his first story, a mystery, in 1943; he has since sold more than six hundred short stories, as well as television and film scripts, children's books, and more than twenty novels. The author of Written for Hitchcock *(1989), his stories are tightly told, suspenseful, and filled with surprises.*

Herbert West knew he could bring the dead back to life, but where was he going to get fresh bodies?

ELEVEN

Herbert West— Reanimator

H. P. Lovecraft

From the Dark

Of Herbert West, who was my friend in college and in after life, I can speak only with extreme terror. This terror is not due altogether to the sinister manner of his recent disappearance, but was engendered by the whole nature of his life-work, and first gained its acute form more than seventeen years ago, when we were in the third year of our course at the Miskatonic University Medical School in Arkham. While he was with me, the wonder and diabolism of his experiments fascinated me utterly, and I was his closest companion. Now that he is gone and the spell is broken, the actual fear is greater. Memories and possibilities are ever more hideous than realities.

The first horrible incident of our acquaintance was the greatest shock I ever experienced, and it is only with reluctance that I repeat it. As I have said, it happened when we were in the medical school, where West had already made himself notorious through his wild theories on the nature of death and the possibility of overcoming it artificially. His views, which were widely ridiculed by the faculty and by his fellow students, hinged on the essentially mechanistic nature of life; and concerned means for operating the organic machinery of mankind by calculated chemical action after the failure of natural processes. In his experiments

177

with various animating solutions he had killed and treated immense numbers of rabbits, guinea pigs, cats, dogs, and monkeys, till he had become the prime nuisance of the college. Several times he had actually obtained signs of life in animals supposedly dead; in many cases violent signs; but he soon saw that the perfection of his process, if indeed possible, would necessarily involve a lifetime of research. It likewise became clear that, since the same solution never worked alike on different organic species, he would require human subjects for further and more specialized progress. It was here that he first came into conflict with the college authorities, and was debarred for future experiments by no less a dignitary than the dean of the medical school himself—the learned and benevolent Dr. Allan Halsey, whose work in behalf of the stricken is recalled by every old resident of Arkham.

I had always been exceptionally tolerant of West's pursuits, and we frequently discussed his theories, whose ramifications and corollaries were almost infinite. Holding with Haeckel that all life is a chemical and physical process, and that the so-called "soul" is a myth, my friend believed that artificial reanimation of the dead can depend only on the condition of the tissues; and that unless actual decomposition has set in, a corpse fully equipped with organs may with suitable measures be set going again in the peculiar fashion known as life. That the psychic or intellectual life might be impaired by the slight deterioration of sensitive brain cells which even a short period of death would be apt to cause, West fully realized. It had at first been his hope to find a reagent which would restore vitality before the actual advent of death, and only repeated failures on animals had shown him that the natural and artificial life-motions were incompatible. He then sought extreme freshness in his specimens, injecting his solutions into the blood immediately after the extinction of life. It was this circumstance which made the professors so carelessly skeptical, for they felt that true death had not occurred in any case. They did not stop to view the matter closely and reasoningly.

It was not long after the faculty had interdicted his work that West confided to me his resolution to get fresh human bodies in some manner, and continue in secret the experiments he could no longer perform openly. To hear him discussing ways and means was rather ghastly, for at the college we had never procured anatomical specimens ourselves. Whenever the morgue proved inadequate, two local Negroes attended to this matter, and they were seldom questioned. West was then a small, slender, spectacled youth with delicate features, yellow hair, pale blue eyes, and a soft voice, and it was uncanny to hear him dwelling on the relative merits of Christchurch Cemetery and the potter's field. We finally decided on the potter's field, because practically every body in Christchurch was embalmed; a thing of course ruinous to West's researches.

I was by this time his active and enthralled assistant, and helped him make all his decisions, not only concerning the source of bodies but concerning a suitable place for our loathsome work. It was I who thought of the deserted Chapman farmhouse beyond Meadow Hill, where we fitted up on the ground floor an operating room and a laboratory, each with dark curtains to conceal our midnight doings. The place was far from any road, and in sight of no other house, yet precautions were none the less necessary; since rumors of strange lights, started by chance nocturnal roamers, would soon bring disaster on our enterprise. It was agreed to call the whole thing a chemical laboratory if discovery should occur. Gradually we equipped our sinister haunt of science with materials either purchased in Boston or quietly borrowed from the college—materials carefully made unrecognizable save to expert eyes—and provided spades and picks for the many burials we should have to make in the cellar. At the college we used an incinerator, but the apparatus was too costly for our unauthorized laboratory. Bodies were always a nuisance—even the small guinea pig bodies from the slight clandestine experiments in West's room at the boarding house.

We followed the local death notices like ghouls, for our specimens demanded particular qualities. What we wanted were corpses interred soon after death and without artificial preservation; preferably free from malforming disease, and certainly with all organs present. Accident victims were our best hope. Not for many weeks did we hear of anything suitable; though we talked with morgue and hospital authorities, ostensibly in the college's interest, as often as we could without exciting suspicion. We found that the college had first choice in every case, so that it might be necessary to remain in Arkham during the summer, when only the limited summer school classes were held. In the end, though, luck favored us; for one day we heard of an almost ideal case in the potter's field: a brawny young workman drowned only the morning before in Sumner's Pond, and buried at the town's expense without delay or embalming. That afternoon we found the new grave, and determined to begin work soon after midnight.

It was a repulsive task that we undertook in the black small hours, even though we lacked at the time the special horror of graveyards which later experiences brought to us. We carried spades and oil dark lanterns, for although electric torches were then manufactured, they were not as satisfactory as the tungsten contrivances of today. The process of unearthing was slow and sordid—it might have been gruesomely poetical if we had been artists instead of scientists—and we were glad when our spades struck wood. When the pine box was fully uncovered West scrambled down and removed the lid, dragging out and propping up the contents. I reached down and hauled the contents out of the grave, and then both toiled hard to restore the spot to its former appearance. The affair made us rather nervous, especially the stiff form and vacant face of our first trophy, but we managed to remove all traces of our visit. When we had patted down the last shovelful of earth we put the specimen in a canvas sack and set out for the old Chapman place beyond Meadow Hill.

On an improvised dissecting-table in the old farmhouse, by the light of a powerful acetylene lamp, the specimen was not very spectral looking. It had been a sturdy and apparently unimaginative youth of wholesome plebeian type—large-framed, grey-eyed, and brown-haired—a sound animal without psychological subtleties, and probably having vital processes of the simplest and healthiest sort. Now, with the eyes closed, it looked more asleep than dead; though the expert test of my friend soon left no doubt on that score. We had at last what West had always longed for—a real dead man of the ideal kind, ready for the solution as prepared according to the most careful calculations and theories for human use. The tension on our part became very great. We knew that there was scarcely a chance for anything like complete success, and could not avoid hideous fears at possible grotesque results of partial animation. Especially were we apprehensive concerning the mind and impulses of the creature, since in the space following death some of the more delicate cerebral cells might well have suffered deterioration. I, myself, still held some curious notions about the traditional "soul" of man, and felt an awe at the secrets that might be told by one returning from the dead. I wondered what sights this placid youth might have seen in inaccessible spheres, and what he could relate if fully restored to life. But my wonder was not overwhelming, since for the most part I shared the materialism of my friend. He was calmer than I as he forced a large quantity of his fluid into a vein of the body's arm, immediately binding the incision securely.

The waiting was gruesome, but West never faltered. Every now and then he applied his stethoscope to the specimen, and bore the negative results philosophically. After about three-quarters of an hour without the least sign of life he disappointedly pronounced the solution inadequate, but determined to make the most of his opportunity and try one change in the formula before disposing of his ghastly prize. We had that afternoon dug a grave in the cellar, and would have to fill it by dawn—for although we had fixed a lock on the house we wished to shun even the remotest risk of a ghoulish discovery. Besides, the body would not be even approximately fresh the next night. So taking the solitary acetylene lamp into the adjacent laboratory, we left our silent guest on the slab in the dark, and bent every energy to the mixing of a new solution; the weighing and measuring supervised by West with an almost fanatical care.

The awful event was very sudden, and wholly unexpected. I was pouring something from one test tube to another, and West was busy over the alcohol blast lamp which had to answer for a Bunsen burner in this gasless edifice, when from the pitch black room we had left there burst the most appalling and demoniac succession of cries that either of us had ever heard. Not more unutterable could have been the chaos of hellish sound if the pit itself had opened to release the agony of the damned, for in one inconceivable cacophony was centered all the supernal terror and unnatural despair of animate nature. Human it could not have been—it is not in man to make such sounds—and without a thought of our late employment or its possible discovery both West and I leaped to the nearest window like stricken animals; overturning tubes, lamp, and retorts, and vaulting madly into the starred abyss of the rural night. I think we screamed ourselves as we stumbled frantically toward the town, though as we reached the outskirts we put on a semblance of restraint—just enough to seem like belated revelers staggering home from a debauch.

We did not separate, but managed to get to West's room, where we whispered with the gas up until dawn. By then we had calmed ourselves a little with rational theories and plans for investigation, so that we could sleep through the day— classes being disregarded. But that evening two items in the paper, wholly unrelated, made it again impossible for us to sleep. The old deserted Chapman house had inexplicably burned to an amorphous heap of ashes; that we could understand because of the upset lamp. Also, an attempt had been made to disturb a new grave in the potter's field, as if by futile and spadeless clawing at the earth. That we could not understand, for we had patted down the mold very carefully.

And for seventeen years after that West would look frequently over his shoulder, and complain of fancied footsteps behind him. Now he had disappeared.

The Plague Demon

I shall never forget that hideous summer sixteen years ago, when like a noxious afrite from the halls of Eblis typhoid stalked leeringly through Arkham. It is by the satanic scourge that most recall the year, for truly terror brooded with bat-wings over the piles of coffins in the tombs of Christchurch Cemetery; yet for me there is a greater horror in that time—a horror known to me alone now that Herbert West has disappeared.

West and I were doing post-graduate work in summer

classes at the medical school of Miskatonic University, and my friend had attained a wide notoriety because of his experiments leading toward the revivification of the dead. After the scientific slaughter of uncounted small animals the freakish work had ostensibly stopped by order of our skeptical dean, Dr. Allan Halsey; though West had continued to perform certain secret tests in his dingy boarding-house room, and had on one terrible and unforgettable occasion taken a human body from its grave in the potter's field to a deserted farmhouse beyond Meadow Hill.

I was with him on that odious occasion, and saw him inject into the still veins the elixir which he thought would to some extent restore life's chemical and physical processes. It had ended horribly—in a delirium of fear which we gradually came to attribute to our own overwrought nerves—and West had never afterward been able to shake off a maddening sensation of being haunted and hunted. The body had not been quite fresh enough; it is obvious that to restore normal mental attributes a body must be very fresh indeed; and the burning of the old house had prevented us from burying the thing. It would have been better if we could have known it was underground.

After that experience West had dropped his researches for some time; but as the zeal of the born scientist slowly returned, he again became importunate with the college faculty, pleading for the use of the dissecting-room and of fresh human specimens for the work he regarded as so overwhelmingly important. His pleas, however, were wholly in vain; for the decision of Dr. Halsey was inflexible, and the other professors all endorsed the verdict of their leader. In the radical theory of reanimation they saw nothing but the immature vagaries of a youthful enthusiast whose slight form, yellow hair, spectacled blue eyes, and soft voice gave no hint of the super-normal—almost diabolical—power of the cold brain within. I can see him now as he was then— and I shiver. He grew sterner of face, but never elderly. And now Sefton Asylum has had the mishap and West has vanished.

West clashed disagreeably with Dr. Halsey near the end of our last undergraduate term in a wordy dispute that did less credit to him than to the kindly dean in point of courtesy. He felt that he was needlessly and irrationally retarded in a supremely great work; a work which he could of course conduct to suit himself in later years, but which he wished to begin while still possessed of the exceptional facilities of the university. That the tradition-bound elders should ignore his singular results on animals, and persist in their denial of the possibility of reanimation, was inexpressibly disgusting and almost incomprehensible to a youth of West's logical temperament. Only greater maturity could help him understand the chronic mental limitations of the "professor doctor" type—the product of generations of pathetic Puritanism; kindly, conscientious, and sometimes gentle and amiable, yet always narrow, intolerant, custom-ridden, and lacking in perspective. Age has more charity for these incomplete yet high-souled characters, whose worst real vice is timidity, and who are ultimately punished by general ridicule for their intellectual sins—sins like Ptolemaism, Calvinism, anti-Darwinism, anti-Nietzscheism, and every sort of Sabbatarianism and sumptuary legislation. West, young despite his marvelous scientific acquirements, had scant patience with good Dr. Halsey and his erudite colleagues; and nursed an increasing resentment, coupled with a desire to prove his theories to these obtuse worthies in some striking and dramatic fashion. Like most youths, he indulged in elaborate daydreams of revenge, triumph, and final magnanimous forgiveness.

And then had come the scourge, grinning and lethal, from the nightmare caverns of Tartarus. West and I had graduated about the time of its beginning, but had remained for additional work at the summer school, so that we were in Arkham when it broke with full daemoniac fury upon the town. Though not as yet licensed physicians, we now had our degrees, and were pressed frantically into public service as the numbers of the stricken grew. The situation was almost past management, and deaths ensued too frequently for the local undertakers fully to handle. Burials without embalming were made in rapid succession, and even the Christchurch Cemetery receiving tomb was crammed with coffins of the unembalmed dead. This circumstance was not without effect on West, who thought often of the irony of the situation—so many fresh specimens, yet none for his persecuted researches! We were frightfully overworked, and the terrific mental and nervous strain made my friend brood morbidly.

But West's gentle enemies were no less harassed with prostrating duties. College had all but closed, and every doctor of the medical faculty was helping to fight the typhoid plague. Dr. Halsey in particular had distinguished himself in sacrificing service, applying his extreme skill with wholehearted energy to cases which many others shunned because of danger or apparent hopelessness. Before a month was over the fearless dean had become a popular hero, though he seemed unconscious of his fame as he struggled to keep from collapsing with physical fatigue and nervous exhaustion. West could not withhold admiration for the fortitude of his foe, but because of this was even more determined to prove to him the truth of his amazing doctrines. Taking advantage of the disorganization of both college work and municipal health regulations, he managed to get a recently deceased body smuggled into the university dissecting room one night, and in my presence injected a new modification of his solution. The thing actually opened its eyes, but only stared at the ceiling with a look of soul-petrifying horror before collapsing into an inertness from which nothing could rouse it. West said it was not fresh enough—the hot summer air does not favor corpses. That time we were almost caught before we incinerated the thing, and West doubted the advisability of repeating his daring misuse of the college laboratory.

The peak of the epidemic was reached in August. West and I were almost dead, and Dr. Halsey did die on the fourteenth. The students all attended the hasty funeral on the fifteenth, and bought an impressive wreath, though the latter was quite overshadowed by the tributes sent by wealthy Arkham citizens and by the municipality itself. It was almost a public affair, for the dean had surely been a public benefactor. After the entombment we were all somewhat depressed, and spent the afternoon at the bar of the Commercial House; where West, though shaken by the death of his chief opponent, chilled the rest of us with references to his notorious theories. Most of the students went home, or to various duties, as the evening advanced; but

West persuaded me to aid him in "making a night of it."
West's landlady saw us arrive at his room about two in the
morning, with a third man between us; and told her husband that we had all evidently dined and wined rather well.

Apparently this acidulous matron was right; for about
3:00 A.M. the whole house was aroused by cries coming
from West's room, where when they broke down the door
they found the two of us unconscious on the bloodstained
carpet, beaten, scratched, and mauled, and with the broken
remnants of West's bottles and instruments around us. Only
an open window told what had become of our assailant,
and many wondered how he himself had fared after the
terrific leap from the second story to the lawn which he
must have made. There were some strange garments in the
room, but West upon regaining consciousness said they did
not belong to the stranger, but were specimens collected for
bacteriological analysis in the course of investigations on the
transmission of germ diseases. He ordered them burnt as
soon as possible in the capacious fireplace. To the police we
both declared ignorance of our late companion's identity.
He was, West nervously said, a congenial stranger whom
we had met at some downtown bar of uncertain location.
We had all been rather jovial, and West and I did not wish to
have our pugnacious companion hunted down.

That same night saw the beginning of the second Arkham
horror—the horror that to me eclipsed the plague itself.
Christchurch Cemetery was the scene of a terrible killing; a
watchman having been clawed to death in a manner not
only too hideous for description, but raising a doubt as to
the human agency of the deed. The victim had been seen
alive considerably after midnight—the dawn revealed the
unutterable thing. The manager of a circus at the neigh-
boring town of Bolton was questioned, but he swore that no
beast had at any time escaped from its cage. Those who
found the body noted a trail of blood leading to the receiving tomb, where a small pool of red lay on the concrete just
outside the gate. A fainter trail led away toward the woods,
but it soon gave out.

The next night devils danced on the roofs of Arkham, and
unnatural madness howled in the wind. Through the fevered town had crept a curse which some said was greater

than the plague, and which some whispered was the embodied demon-soul of the plague itself. Eight houses were entered by a nameless thing which strewed red death in its wake—in all, seventeen maimed and shapeless remnants of bodies were left behind by the voiceless, sadistic monster that crept abroad. A few persons had half seen it in the dark, and said it was white and like a malformed ape or anthropomorphic fiend. It had not left behind quite all that it had attacked, for sometimes it had been hungry. The number it had killed was fourteen; three of the bodies had been in stricken homes and had not been alive.

On the third night frantic bands of searchers, led by the police, captured it in a house on Crane Street near the Miskatonic campus. They had organized the quest with care, keeping in touch by means of volunteer telephone stations, and when someone in the college district had reported hearing a scratching at a shuttered window, the net was quickly spread. On account of the general alarm and precautions, there were only two more victims, and the capture was effected without major casualties. The thing was finally stopped by a bullet, though not a fatal one, and was rushed to the local hospital amidst universal excitement and loathing.

For it had been a man. This much was clear despite the nauseous eyes, the voiceless simianism, and the demoniac savagery. They dressed its wound and carted it to the asylum at Sefton, where it beat its head against the walls of a padded cell for sixteen years—until the recent mishap, when it escaped under circumstances that few like to mention. What had most disgusted the searchers of Arkham was the thing they noticed when the monster's face was cleaned—the mocking, unbelievable resemblance to a learned and self-sacrificing martyr who had been entombed but three days before—the late Dr. Allan Halsey, public benefactor and dean of the medical school of Miskatonic University.

To the vanished Herbert West and to me the disgust and horror were supreme. I shudder tonight as I think of it; shudder even more than I did that morning when West muttered through his bandages,

"Damn it, it wasn't *quite* fresh enough!"

Six Shots by Moonlight

It is uncommon to fire all six shots of a revolver with great suddenness when one would probably be sufficient, but many things in the life of Herbert West were uncommon. It is, for instance, not often that a young physician leaving college is obliged to conceal the principles which guide his selection of a home and office, yet that was the case with Herbert West. When he and I obtained our degrees at the medical school of Miskatonic University, and sought to relieve our poverty by setting up as general practitioners, we took great care not to say that we chose our house because it was fairly well isolated, and as near as possible to the potter's field.

Reticence such as this is seldom without a cause, nor indeed was ours; for our requirements were those resulting from a life-work distinctly unpopular. Outwardly we were doctors only, but beneath the surface were aims of far greater and more terrible moment—for the essence of Herbert West's existence was a quest amid black and forbidden realms of the unknown, in which he hoped to uncover the secret of life and restore to perpetual animation the graveyard's cold clay. Such a quest demands strange materials, among them fresh human bodies; and in order to keep supplied with these indispensable things one must live quietly and not far from a place of informal interment.

West and I had met in college, and I had been the only one to sympathize with his hideous experiments. Gradually I had come to be his inseparable assistant, and now that we were out of college we had to keep together. It was not easy to find a good opening for two doctors in company, but finally the influence of the university secured us a practice in Bolton—a factory town near Arkham, the seat of the college. The Bolton Worsted Mills are the largest in the Miskatonic Valley, and their polyglot employees are never popular as patients with the local physicians. We chose our house with the greatest care, seizing at last on a rather run-down cottage near the end of Pond Street; five numbers from the closest neighbor, and separated from the local potter's field by only a stretch of meadow land, bisected by a narrow neck of the rather dense forest which lies to the north. The distance was greater than we wished, but we could get no nearer house without going on the other side of the field, wholly out of the factory district. We were not much displeased, however, since there were no people between us and our sinister source of supplies. The walk was a trifle long, but we could haul our silent specimens undisturbed.

Our practice was surprisingly large from the very first—large enough to please most young doctors, and large enough to prove a bore and a burden to students whose real interest lay elsewhere. The mill hands were of somewhat turbulent inclinations; and besides their many natural needs, their frequent clashes and stabbing affrays gave us plenty to do. But what actually absorbed our minds was the secret laboratory we had fitted up in the cellar—the laboratory with the long table under the electric lights, where in the small hours of the morning we often injected West's various solutions into the veins of the things we dragged from the potter's field. West was experimenting madly to find something which would start man's vital motions anew after they had been stopped by the thing we call death, but had encountered the most ghastly obstacles. The solution had to be differently compounded for different types—what would serve for guinea pigs would not serve for human beings, and different human specimens required large modifications.

The bodies had to be exceedingly fresh, or the slight decomposition of brain tissue would render perfect reanimation impossible. Indeed, the greatest problem was to get them fresh enough—West had had horrible experiences during his secret college researches with corpses of doubtful vintage. The results of partial or imperfect animation were much more hideous than were the total failures, and we both held fearsome recollections of such things. Ever since our first demonic session in the deserted farmhouse on Meadow Hill in Arkham, we had felt a brooding menace; and West, though a calm, blond, blue-eyed scientific automaton in most respects, often confessed to a shuddering sensation of stealthy pursuit. He half felt that he was followed—a psychological delusion of shaken nerves, enhanced by the undeniably disturbing fact that at least one of our reanimated specimens was still alive—a frightful carnivorous thing in a padded cell at Sefton. Then there was another— our first—whose exact fate we had never learned.

We had fair luck with specimens in Bolton—much better than in Arkham. We had not been settled a week before we got an accident victim on the very night of burial, and made it open its eyes with an amazingly rational expression before the solution failed. It had lost an arm—if it had been a perfect body we might have succeeded better. Between then and the next January we secured three more; one total failure, one case of marked muscular motion, and one rather shivery thing—it rose of itself and uttered a sound. Then came a period when luck was poor; interments fell off, and those that did occur were of specimens either too diseased or too maimed for use. We kept track of all the deaths and their circumstances with systematic care.

One March night, however, we unexpectedly obtained a specimen which did not come from the potter's field. In Bolton the prevailing spirit of Puritanism had outlawed the sport of boxing—with the usual result. Surreptitious and ill-conducted bouts among the mill workers were common, and occasionally professional talent of low grade was imported. This late winter night there had been such a match; evidently with disastrous results, since two timorous Poles had come to us with incoherently whispered entreaties to attend to a very secret and desperate case. We followed them to an abandoned barn, where the remnants of a crowd of frightened foreigners were watching a silent black form on the floor.

The match had been between Kid O'Brien—a lubberly and now quaking youth with a most un-Hibernian hooked nose—and Buck Robinson, "The Harlem Smoke." The Negro had been knocked out, and a moment's examination showed us that he would permanently remain so. He was a loathsome, gorilla-like thing, with abnormally long arms which I could not help calling fore legs, and a face that conjured up thoughts of unspeakable Congo secrets and tom-tom poundings under an eerie moon. The body must have looked even worse in life—but the world holds many ugly things. Fear was upon the whole pitiful crowd, for they did not know what the law would exact of them if the affair were not hushed up; and they were grateful when West, in spite of my involuntary shudders, offered to get rid of the thing quietly—for a purpose I knew too well.

There was bright moonlight over the snowless landscape, but we dressed the thing and carried it home between us through the deserted streets and meadows, as we had carried a similar thing one horrible night in Arkham. We approached the house from the field in the rear, took the specimen in the back door and down the cellar stairs, and prepared it for the usual experiment. Our fear of the police was absurdly great, though we had timed our trip to avoid the solitary patrolman of that section.

The result was wearily anticlimactic. Ghastly as our prize appeared, it was wholly unresponsive to every solution we injected in its black arm, solutions prepared from experience with white specimens only. So as the hour grew dangerously near to dawn, we did as we had done with the others—dragged the thing across the meadows to the neck of the woods near the potter's field, and buried it there in the best sort of grave the frozen ground would furnish. The grave was not very deep, but fully as good as that of the previous specimen—the thing which had risen of itself and uttered a sound. In the light of our dark lanterns we carefully covered it with leaves and dead vines, fairly certain that the police would never find it in a forest so dim and dense.

The next day I was increasingly apprehensive about the police, for a patient brought rumors of a suspected fight and death. West had still another source of worry, for he had been called in the afternoon to a case which ended very threateningly. An Italian woman had become hysterical over her missing child—a lad of five who had strayed off early in the morning and failed to appear for dinner—and had developed symptoms highly alarming in view of an always weak heart. It was a very foolish hysteria, for the boy had often run away before; but Italian peasants are exceedingly superstitious, and this woman seemed as much harassed by omens as by facts. About seven o'clock in the evening she had died, and her frantic husband had made a frightful scene in his efforts to kill West, whom he wildly blamed for not saving her life. Friends had held him when he drew a stiletto, but West departed amidst his inhuman shrieks, curses, and oaths of vengeance. In his latest affliction the fellow seemed to have forgotten his child, who was still missing as the night advanced. There was some talk of searching the woods, but most of the family's friends were busy with the dead woman and the screaming man. Altogether, the nervous strain upon West must have been tremendous. Thoughts of the police and of the mad Italian both weighed heavily.

We retired about eleven, but I did not sleep well. Bolton had a surprisingly good police force for so small a town, and I could not help fearing the mess which would ensue if the affair of the night before were ever tracked down. It might mean the end of all our local work—and perhaps prison for both West and me. I did not like those rumors of a fight which were floating about. After the clock had struck three the moon shone in my eyes, but I turned over without rising to pull down the shade. Then came the steady rattling at the back door.

I lay still and somewhat dazed, but before long heard West's rap on my door. He was clad in dressing gown and slippers, and had in his hands a revolver and an electric flashlight. From the revolver I knew that he was thinking more of the crazed Italian than of the police.

"We'd better both go," he whispered. "It wouldn't do not to answer it anyway, and it may be a patient—it would be like one of those fools to try the back door."

So we both went down the stairs on tiptoe, with a fear partly justified and partly that which comes only from the soul of the weird small hours. The rattling continued, growing somewhat louder. When we reached the door I cautiously unbolted it and threw it open, and as the moon streamed revealingly down on the form silhouetted there, West did a peculiar thing. Despite the obvious danger of attracting notice and bringing down on our heads the dreaded police investigation—a thing which after all was mercifully averted by the relative isolation of our cottage—my friend suddenly, excitedly, and unnecessarily emptied all six chambers of his revolver into the nocturnal visitor.

For that visitor was neither Italian nor policeman. Looming hideously against the spectral moon was a gigantic misshapen thing not to be imagined save in nightmares—a glass-eyed, ink-black apparition nearly on all fours, covered with bits of mold, leaves, and vines, foul with caked blood, and having between its glistening teeth a snowwhite, terrible, cylindrical object terminating in a tiny hand.

The Scream of the Dead

The scream of a dead man gave to me that acute and added horror of Dr. Herbert West which harassed the latter years of our companionship. It is natural that such a thing as a dead man's scream should give horror, for it is obviously not a pleasing or ordinary occurrence; but I was used to similar experiences, hence suffered on this occasion only because of a particular circumstance. And, as I have implied, it was not of the dead man himself that I became afraid.

Herbert West, whose associate and assistant I was, possessed scientific interests far beyond the usual routine of a village physician. That was why, when establishing his practice in Bolton, he had chosen an isolated house near the potter's field. Briefly and brutally stated, West's sole absorbing interest was a secret study of the phenomena of life and its cessation, leading toward the reanimation of the dead through injections of an excitant solution. For this ghastly experimenting it was necessary to have a constant supply of very fresh human bodies; very fresh because even the least decay hopelessly damaged the brain structure, and human because we found that the solution had to be compounded differently for different types of organisms. Scores of rabbits and guinea pigs had been killed and treated, but their trail was a blind one. West had never fully succeeded because he had never been able to secure a corpse sufficiently fresh. What he wanted were bodies from which vitality had only just departed; bodies with every cell intact and capable of receiving again the impulse toward that mode of motion called life. There was hope that this second and artificial life might be made perpetual by repetitions of the injection, but we had learned that an ordinary natural life would not respond to the action. To establish the artificial motion, natural life must be extinct—the specimens must be very fresh, but genuinely dead.

The awesome quest had begun when West and I were

students at the Miskatonic University Medical School in Arkham, vividly conscious for the first time of the thoroughly mechanical nature of life. That was seven years before, but West looked scarcely a day older now—he was small, blond, clean-shaven, soft-voiced, and spectacled, with only an occasional flash of a cold blue eye to tell of the hardening and growing fanaticism of his character under the pressure of his terrible investigations. Our experiences had often been hideous in the extreme; the results of defective reanimation, when lumps of graveyard clay had been galvanized into morbid, unnatural, and brainless motion by various modifications of the vital solution.

One thing had uttered a nerve shattering scream; another had risen violently, beaten us both to unconsciousness, and run amuck in a shocking way before it could be placed behind asylum bars; still another, a loathsome African monstrosity, had clawed out of its shallow grave and done a deed—West had had to shoot that object. We could not get bodies fresh enough to show any trace of reason when reanimated, so had perforce created nameless horrors. It was disturbing to think that one, perhaps two, of our monsters still lived—that thought haunted us shadowingly, till finally West disappeared under frightful circumstances. But at the time of the scream in the cellar laboratory of the isolated Bolton cottage, our fears were subordinate to our anxiety for extremely fresh specimens. West was more avid than I, so that it almost seemed to me that he looked half-covetously at any very healthy living physique.

It was in July, 1910, that the bad luck regarding specimens began to turn. I had been on a long visit to my parents in Illinois, and upon my return found West in a state of singular elation. He had, he told me excitedly, in all likelihood solved the problem of freshness through an approach from an entirely new angle—that of artificial preservation. I had known that he was working on a new and highly unusual embalming compound, and was not surprised that it had turned out well; but until he explained the details I was rather puzzled as to how such a compound could help in our work, since the objectionable staleness of the specimens was largely due to delay occurring before we secured them. This, I now saw, West had clearly recognized;

creating his embalming compound for future rather than immediate use, and trusting to fate to supply again some very recent and unburied corpse, as it had years before when we obtained the Negro killed in the Bolton prize fight. At last fate had been kind, so that on this occasion there lay in the secret cellar laboratory a corpse whose decay could not by any possibility have begun. What would happen on reanimation, and whether we could hope for a revival of mind and reason, West did not venture to predict. The experiment would be a landmark in our studies, and he had saved the new body for my return, so that both might share the spectacle in accustomed fashion.

West told me how he had obtained the specimen. It had been a vigorous man; a well-dressed stranger just off the train on his way to transact some business with the Bolton Worsted Mills. The walk through the town had been long, and by the time the traveler paused at our cottage to ask the way to the factories his heart had become greatly overtaxed. He had refused a stimulant, and had suddenly dropped dead only a moment later. The body, as might be expected, seemed to West a heaven sent gift. In his brief conversation the stranger had made it clear that he was unknown in Bolton, and a search of his pockets subsequently revealed him to be one Robert Leavitt of St. Louis, apparently without a family to make instant inquiries about his disappearance. If this man could not be restored to life, no one would know of our experiment. We buried our materials in a dense strip of woods between the house and the potter's field. If, on the other hand, he could be restored, our fame would be brilliantly and perpetually established. So without delay West had injected into the body's wrist the compound which would hold it fresh for use after my arrival. The matter of the presumably weak heart, which to my mind imperiled the success of our experiment, did not appear to trouble West extensively. He hoped at last to obtain what he had never obtained before—a rekindled spark of reason and perhaps a normal, living creature.

So on the night of July 18, 1910, Herbert West and I stood in the cellar laboratory and gazed at a white, silent figure beneath the dazzling arc light. The embalming compound had worked uncannily well, for as I stared fascinatedly at the sturdy frame which had lain two weeks without stiffening I was moved to seek West's assurance that the thing was really dead. This assurance he gave readily enough; reminding me that the reanimating solution was never used without careful tests as to life; since it could have no effect if any of the original vitality were present. As West proceeded to take preliminary steps, I was impressed by the vast intricacy of the new experiment; an intricacy so vast that he could trust no hand less delicate than his own. Forbidding me to touch the body, he first injected a drug in the wrist just beside the place his needle had punctured when injecting the embalming compound. This, he said, was to neutralize the compound and release the system to a normal relaxation so that the reanimating solution might freely work when injected. Slightly later, when a change and a gentle tremor seemed to affect the dead limbs, West stuffed a pillow-like object violently over the twitching face, not withdrawing it until the corpse appeared quiet and ready for our attempt at reanimation. The pale enthusiast now applied some last perfunctory tests for absolute lifelessness, withdrew satisfied, and finally injected into the left arm an accurately measured amount of the vital elixir, prepared during the afternoon with a greater care than we had used since college days, when our feats were new and groping. I cannot express the wild, breathless suspense with which we waited for results on this first really fresh specimen—the first we could reasonably expect to open its lips in rational speech, perhaps to tell of what it had seen beyond the unfathomable abyss.

West was a materialist, believing in no soul and attributing all the working of consciousness to bodily phenomena; consequently he looked for no revelation of hideous secrets from gulfs and caverns beyond death's barrier. I did not wholly disagree with him theoretically, yet held vague instinctive remnants of the primitive faith of my forefathers; so that I could not help eyeing the corpse with a certain amount of awe and terrible expectation. Besides—I could not extract from my memory that hideous, inhuman shriek we heard on the night we tried our first experiment in the deserted farmhouse at Arkham.

Very little time had elapsed before I saw the attempt was

not to be a total failure. A touch of color came to cheeks hitherto chalk-white, and spread out under the curiously ample stubble of sandy beard. West, who had his hand on the pulse of the left wrist, suddenly nodded significantly; and almost simultaneously a mist appeared on the mirror inclined above the body's mouth. There followed a few spasmodic muscular motions, and then an audible breathing and visible motion of the chest. I looked at the closed eyelids, and thought I detected a quivering. Then the lids opened, showing eyes which were grey, calm, and alive, but still unintelligent and not even curious.

In a moment of fantastic whim I whispered questions to the reddening ears; questions of other worlds of which the memory might still be present. Subsequent terror drove them from my mind, but I think the last one, which I repeated, was: "Where have you been?" I do not yet know whether I was answered or not, for no sound came from the well-shaped mouth; but I do know that at that moment I firmly thought the thin lips moved silently, forming syllables which I would have vocalized as "only now" if that phrase had possessed any sense or relevancy. At that moment, as I say, I was elated with the conviction that the one great goal had been attained; and that for the first time a reanimated corpse had uttered distinct words impelled by actual reason. In the next moment there was no doubt about the triumph; no doubt that the solution had truly accomplished, at least temporarily, its full mission of restoring rational and articulate life to the dead. But in that triumph there came to me the greatest of all horrors—not horror of the thing that spoke, but of the deed that I had witnessed and of the man with whom my professional fortunes were joined.

For that very fresh body, at last writhing into full and terrifying consciousness with eyes dilated at the memory of its last scene on earth, threw out its frantic hands in a life and death struggle with the air; and suddenly collapsing into a second and final dissolution from which there could be no return, screamed out the cry that will ring eternally in my aching brain:

"Help! Keep off, you cursed little towhead fiend—keep that damned needle away from me!"

The Horror from the Shadows

Many men have related hideous things, not mentioned in print, which happened on the battlefields of the Great War. Some of these things have made me faint, others have convulsed me with devastating nausea, while still others have made me tremble and look behind me in the dark; yet despite the worst of them I believe I can myself relate the most hideous thing of all—the shocking, the unnatural, the unbelievable horror from the shadows.

In 1915 I was a physician with the rank of First Lieutenant in a Canadian regiment in Flanders, one of many Americans to precede the government itself into the gigantic struggle. I had not entered the army on my own initiative, but rather as a natural result of the enlistment of the man whose indispensable assistant I was—the celebrated Boston surgical specialist, Dr. Herbert West. Dr. West had been avid for a chance to serve as surgeon in a great war, and when the chance had come he carried me with him almost against my will. There were reasons why I would have been glad to let the war separate us; reasons why I found the practice of medicine and the companionship of West more and more irritating; but when he had gone to Ottawa and through a colleague's influence secured a medical commission as Major, I could not resist the imperious persuasion of one determined that I should accompany him in my usual capacity.

When I say that Dr. West was avid to serve in battle, I do not mean to imply that he was either naturally warlike or anxious for the safety of civilization. Always an ice-cold intellectual machine; slight, blond, blue-eyed, and spectacled; I think he secretly sneered at my occasional martial enthusiasms and censures of supine neutrality. There was, however, something he wanted in embattled Flanders; and in order to secure it he had to assume a military exterior. What he wanted was not a thing which many persons want, but something connected with the peculiar branch of medical science which he had chosen quite clandestinely to follow, and in which he had achieved amazing and occasionally hideous results. It was, in fact, nothing more or less than an abundant supply of freshly killed men in every stage of dismemberment.

Herbert West needed fresh bodies because his life-work was the reanimation of the dead. This work was not known to the fashionable clientele who had so swiftly built up his fame after his arrival in Boston; but was only too well known to me, who had been his closest friend and sole assistant since the old days in Miskatonic University Medical School at Arkham. It was in those college days that he had begun his terrible experiments, first on small animals and then on human bodies shockingly obtained. There was a solution which he injected into the veins of dead things, and if they were fresh enough they responded in strange ways. He had had much trouble in discovering the proper formula, for each type of organism was found to need a stimulus especially adapted to it. Terror stalked him when he reflected on his partial failures; nameless things resulting from imperfect solutions or from bodies insufficiently fresh. A certain number of these failures had remained alive—one was in an asylum while others had vanished—and as he thought of conceivable yet virtually impossible eventualities he often shivered beneath his usual stolidity.

West had soon learned that absolute freshness was the prime requisite for useful specimens, and had accordingly resorted to frightful and unnatural expedients in body-snatching. In college, and during our early practice together in the factory town of Bolton, my attitude toward him had been largely one of fascinated admiration; but as his boldness in methods grew, I began to develop a gnawing fear. I did not like the way he looked at healthy living bodies; and then there came a nightmarish session in the cellar laboratory when I learned that a certain specimen had been a living body when he secured it. That was the first time he had ever been able to revive the quality of rational thought in a corpse; and his success, obtained at such a loathsome cost, had completely hardened him.

Of his methods in the intervening five years I dare not speak. I was held to him by sheer force of fear, and witnessed sights that no human tongue could repeat. Gradually I came to find Herbert West himself more horrible than anything he did—that was when it dawned on me that his once normal scientific zeal for prolonging life had subtly degenerated into a mere morbid and ghoulish curiosity and secret sense of charnel picturesqueness. His interest became a hellish and perverse addiction to the repellently and fiendishly abnormal; he gloated calmly over artificial monstrosities which would make most healthy men drop dead from fright and disgust; he became, behind his pallid intellectuality, a fastidious Baudelaire of physical experiment—a languid Elagabalus of the tombs.

Dangers he met unflinchingly; crimes he committed unmoved. I think the climax came when he had proved his point that rational life can be restored, and had sought new worlds to conquer by experimenting on the reanimation of detached parts of bodies. He had wild and original ideas on the independent vital properties of organic cells and nerve tissue separated from natural physiological systems; and achieved some hideous preliminary results in the form of never-dying, artificially nourished tissue obtained from the nearly hatched eggs of an indescribable tropical reptile. Two biological points he was exceedingly anxious to settle—first, whether any amount of consciousness and rational action be possible without the brain, proceeding from the spinal cord and various nerve-centers; and second, whether any kind of ethereal, intangible relation distinct from the material cells may exist to link the surgically separated parts of what has previously been a single living organism. All this research work required a prodigious supply of freshly slaughtered human flesh—and that was why Herbert West had entered the Great War.

The phantasmal, unmentionable thing occurred one midnight late in March, 1915, in a field hospital behind the lines at St. Eloi. I wonder even now if it could have been other than a daemoniac dream of delirium. West had a private laboratory in an east room of the barn-like temporary edifice, assigned him on his plea that he was devising new and radical methods for the treatment of hitherto hopeless cases of maiming. There he worked like a butcher in the midst of his gory wares—I could never get used to the levity with which he handled and classified certain things. At times he actually did perform marvels of surgery for the soldiers; but his chief delights were of a less public and philanthropic kind, requiring many explanations of sounds which seemed peculiar even amidst that babel of the damned. Among these sounds were frequent revolver shots—surely not uncommon on a battlefield, but distinctly uncommon in a hospital. Dr. West's reanimated specimens were not meant for long existence or a large audience. Besides human tissue, West employed much of the reptile embryo tissue which he had cultivated with such singular results. It was better than human material for maintaining life in organless fragments, and that was now my friend's chief activity. In a dark corner of the laboratory, over a queer incubating burner, he kept a large covered vat full of this reptilian cell matter; which multiplied and grew puffily and hideously.

On the night of which I speak we had a splendid new specimen—a man at once physically powerful and of such high mentality that a sensitive nervous system was assured. It was rather ironic, for he was the officer who had helped West to his commission, and who was now to have been our associate. Moreover, he had in the past secretly studied the theory of reanimation to some extent under West. Major Sir Eric Moreland Clapham-Lee, D.S.O., was the greatest surgeon in our division, and had been hastily assigned to the St. Eloi sector when news of the heavy fighting reached headquarters. He had come in an aëroplane piloted by the intrepid Lieut. Ronald Hill, only to be shot down when directly over his destination. The fall had been spectacular and awful; Hill was unrecognizable afterward, but the wreck yielded up the great surgeon in a nearly decapitated but otherwise intact condition. West had greedily seized the lifeless thing which had once been his friend and fellow scholar; and I shuddered when he finished severing the head, placed it in his hellish vat of pulpy reptile-tissue to preserve it for future experiments, and proceeded to treat the decapitated body on the operating table. He injected new blood, joined certain veins, arteries, and nerves at the headless neck, and closed the ghastly aperture with engrafted skin from an unidentified specimen which had borne an officer's uniform. I knew what he wanted—to see if this highly organized body could exhibit, without its head, any of the signs of mental life which had distinguished Sir Eric Moreland Clapham-Lee. Once a student of reanimation, this silent trunk was now gruesomely called upon to exemplify it.

I can still see Herbert West under the sinister electric light as he injected his reanimating solution into the arm of the headless body. The scene I cannot describe—I should faint if I tried it, for there is madness in a room full of classified charnel things, with blood and lesser human debris almost ankle deep on the slimy floor, and with hideous reptilian abnormalities sprouting, bubbling, and baking over a winking bluish-green specter of dim flame in a far corner of black shadows.

The specimen, as West repeatedly observed, had a splendid nervous system. Much was expected of it; and as a few twitching motions began to appear, I could see the feverish interest on West's face. He was ready, I think, to see proof of his increasingly strong opinion that consciousness, reason, and personality can exist independently of the brain—that man has no central connective spirit, but is merely a machine of nervous matter, each section more or less complete in itself. In one triumphant demonstration West was about to relegate the mystery of life to the category of myth. The body now twitched more vigorously, and beneath our avid eyes commenced to heave in a frightful way. The arms stirred disquietingly, the legs drew up, and various muscles contracted in a repulsive kind of writhing. Then the headless thing threw out its arms in a gesture which was unmistakably one of desperation—an intelligent desperation apparently sufficient to prove every theory of Herbert West. Certainly, the nerves were recalling the man's last act in life; the struggle to get free of the falling aëroplane.

What followed, I shall never positively know. It may have been wholly an hallucination from the shock caused at that instant by the sudden and complete destruction of the building in a cataclysm of German shellfire—who can gainsay it, since West and I were the only proved survivors? West liked to think that before his recent disappearance, but there were times when he could not; for it was queer that we both had the same hallucination. The hideous occurrence itself was very simple, notable only for what it implied.

The body on the table had risen with a blind and terrible groping, and we had heard a sound. I should not call that sound a voice, for it was too awful. And yet its timbre was not the most awful thing about it. Neither was its message—

it had merely screamed, "Jump, Ronald, for God's sake, jump!" The awful thing was its source.

For it had come from the large covered vat in that ghoulish corner of crawling black shadows.

The Tomb-Legions

When Dr. Herbert West disappeared a year ago, the Boston police questioned me closely. They suspected that I was holding something back, and perhaps suspected graver things; but I could not tell them the truth because they would not have believed it. They knew, indeed, that West had been connected with activities beyond the credence of ordinary men; for his hideous experiments in the reanimation of dead bodies had long been too extensive to admit of perfect secrecy; but the final soul-shattering catastrophe held elements of demoniac phantasy which make even me doubt the reality of what I saw.

I was West's closest friend and only confidential assistant. We had met years before, in medical school, and from the first I had shared his terrible researches. He had slowly tried to perfect a solution which, injected into the veins of the newly deceased, would restore life; a labor demanding an abundance of fresh corpses and therefore involving the most unnatural actions. Still more shocking were products of some of the experiments—grisly masses of flesh that had been dead, but that West waked to a blind, brainless, nauseous animation. These were the usual results, for in order to reawaken the mind it was necessary to have specimens so absolutely fresh that no decay could possibly affect the delicate brain cells.

This need for very fresh corpses had been West's moral undoing. They were hard to get, and one awful day he had secured his specimen while it was still alive and vigorous. A struggle, a needle, and a powerful alkaloid had transformed it to a very fresh corpse, and the experiment had succeeded for a brief and memorable moment; but West had emerged with a soul calloused and seared, and a hardened eye which sometimes glanced with a kind of hideous and calculating appraisal at men of especially sensitive brain and especially vigorous physique. Toward the last I became acutely afraid of West, for he began to look at me that way. People did not seem to notice his glances, but they noticed my fear; and after his disappearance used that as a basis for some absurd suspicions.

West, in reality, was more afraid than I; for his abominable pursuits entailed a life of furtiveness and dread of every shadow. Partly it was the police he feared; but sometimes his nervousness was deeper and more nebulous, touching on certain indescribable things into which he had injected a morbid life, and from which he had not seen that life depart. He usually finished his experiments with a revolver, but a few times he had not been quick enough. There was that first specimen on whose rifled grave marks of clawing were later seen. There was also that Arkham professor's body which had done cannibal things before it had been captured and thrust unidentified into a madhouse cell at Sefton, where it beat the walls for sixteen years. Most of the other possibly surviving results were things less easy to speak of— for in later years West's scientific zeal had degenerated to an unhealthy and fantastic mania, and he had spent his chief skill in vitalizing not entire human bodies but isolated parts of bodies, or parts joined to organic matter other than human. It had become fiendishly disgusting by the time he disappeared; many of the experiments could not even be hinted at in print. The Great War, through which both of us served as surgeons, had intensified this side of West.

In saying that West's fear of his specimens was nebulous, I have in mind particularly its complex nature. Part of it came merely from knowing of the existence of such nameless monsters, while another part arose from apprehension of the bodily harm they might under certain circumstances do him. Their disappearance added horror to the situation—of them all West knew the whereabouts of only one, the pitiful asylum thing. Then there was a more subtle fear—a very fantastic sensation resulting from a curious experiment in the Canadian army in 1915. West, in the midst of a severe battle, had reanimated Major Sir Eric Moreland Clapham-Lee, D.S.O., a fellow-physician who knew about his experiments and could have duplicated them. The head had been removed, so that the possibilities of quasi-intelligent life in the trunk might be investigated. Just as the building was wiped out by a German shell, there had been a success. The trunk had moved intelligently; and, unbelievable to relate, we were both sickeningly sure that articulate sounds had come from the detached head as it lay in a shadowy corner of the laboratory. The shell had been merciful, in a way—but West could never feel as certain as he wished, that we two were the only survivors. He used to make shuddering conjectures about the possible actions of a headless physician with the power of reanimating the dead.

West's last quarters were in a venerable house of much elegance, overlooking one of the oldest burying grounds in Boston. He had chosen the place for surely symbolic and fantastically aesthetic reasons, since most of the interments were of the colonial period and therefore of little use to a scientist seeking very fresh bodies. The laboratory was in a subcellar secretly constructed by imported workmen, and contained a huge incinerator for the quiet and complete disposal of such bodies, or fragments and synthetic mockeries of bodies, as might remain from the morbid experiments and unhallowed amusements of the owner. During the excavation of this cellar the workmen had struck some exceedingly ancient masonry; undoubtedly connected with the old burying ground, yet far too deep to correspond with any known sepulchre therein. After a number of calculations West decided that it represented some secret chamber beneath the tomb of the Averills, where the last interment had been made in 1768. I was with him when he studied the nitrous, dripping walls laid bare by the spades and mattocks of the men, and was prepared for the gruesome thrill which would attend the uncovering of centuried grave-secrets; but for the first time West's new timidity conquered his natural curiosity, and he betrayed his degenerating fibre by ordering the masonry left intact and plastered over. Thus it remained till that final hellish night; part of the walls of the secret laboratory. I speak of West's decadence, but must add that it was a purely mental and intangible thing. Outwardly he was the same to the last—calm, cold, slight, and yellow-haired, with spectacled blue eyes and a general aspect of youth which years and fears seemed never to change. He seemed calm even when he thought of that clawed grave and looked over his shoulder; even when he thought of the carnivorous thing that gnawed and pawed at Sefton bars.

The end of Herbert West began one evening in our joint study when he was dividing his curious glance between the newspaper and me. A strange headline item had struck at him from the crumpled pages, and a nameless titan claw had seemed to reach down through sixteen years. Something fearsome and incredible had happened at Sefton Asylum fifty miles away, stunning the neighborhood and baffling the police. In the small hours of the morning a body of silent men had entered the grounds and their leader had aroused the attendants. He was a menacing military figure who talked without moving his lips and whose voice seemed almost ventriloquially connected with an immense black case he carried. His expressionless face was handsome to the point of radiant beauty, but had shocked the superintendent when the hall light fell on it—for it was a wax face with eyes of painted glass. Some nameless accident had befallen this man. A larger man guided his steps; a repellent hulk whose bluish face seemed half eaten away by some unknown malady. The speaker had asked for the custody of the cannibal monster committed from Arkham sixteen years before; and upon being refused, gave a signal which precipitated a shocking riot. The fiends had beaten, trampled, and bitten every attendant who did not flee; killing four and finally succeeding in the liberation of the monster. Those victims who could recall the event without hysteria swore that the creatures had acted less like men than like unthinkable automata guided by the wax-faced leader. By the time help could be summoned, every trace of the men and of their mad charge had vanished.

From the hour of reading this item until midnight, West sat almost paralyzed. At midnight the doorbell rang, startling him fearfully. All the servants were asleep in the attic, so I answered the bell. As I have told the police, there was no wagon in the street; but only a group of strange looking figures bearing a large square box which they deposited in the hallway after one of them had grunted in a highly unnatural voice, "Express—prepaid." They filed out of the house with a jerky tread, and as I watched them go I had an odd idea that they were turning toward the ancient cemetery on which the back of the house abutted. When I slammed the door after them West came downstairs and looked at the box. It was about two feet square, and bore West's correct name and present address. It also bore the inscription, "From Eric Moreland Clapham-Lee, St. Eloi, Flanders." Six years before, in Flanders, a shelled hospital had fallen upon the headless reanimated trunk of Dr. Clapham-Lee, and upon the detached head which—perhaps—had uttered articulate sounds.

West was not even excited now. His condition was more ghastly. Quickly he said, "It's the finish—but let's incinerate—this." We carried the thing down to the laboratory— listening. I do not remember many particulars—you can imagine my state of mind—but it is a vicious lie to say it was Herbert West's body which I put into the incinerator. We both inserted the whole unopened wooden box, closed the door, and started the electricity. Nor did any sound come from the box, after all.

It was West who first noticed the falling plaster on that part of the wall where the ancient tomb masonry had been covered up. I was going to run, but he stopped me. Then I saw a small black aperture, felt a ghoulish wind of ice, and smelled the charnel bowels of a putrescent earth. There was no sound, but just then the electric lights went out and I saw outlined against some phosphorescence of the nether world a horde of silent toiling things which only insanity—or worse—could create. Their outlines were human, semihuman, fractionally human, and not human at all—the horde was grotesquely heterogeneous. They were removing the stones quietly, one by one, from the centuried wall. And then, as the breach became large enough, they came out into the laboratory in single file; led by a stalking thing with a beautiful head made of wax. A sort of mad-eyed monstrosity behind the leader seized on Herbert West. West did not resist or utter a sound. Then they all sprang at him and tore him to pieces before my eyes, bearing the fragments away into that subterranean vault of fabulous abominations. West's head was carried off by the wax-headed leader, who wore a Canadian officer's uniform. As it disappeared I saw that the blue eyes behind the spectacles were hideously blazing with their first touch of frantic, visible emotion.

Servants found me unconscious in the morning. West was gone. The incinerator contained only unidentifiable ashes. Detectives have questioned me, but what can I say? The Sefton tragedy they will not connect with West; not that, nor the men with the box, whose existence they deny. I told them of the vault, and they pointed to the unbroken plaster wall and laughed. So I told them no more. They imply that I am either a madman or a murderer—probably I am mad. But I might not be mad if those accursed tomb-legions had not been so silent.

Called the greatest writer of the supernatural since Poe, H. P. Lovecraft was a gaunt, almost-reclusive writer born in Rhode Island in 1890. Precocious and largely self-educated, Lovecraft was writing a monthly astrology column at sixteen. Patterning his life after that of an English gentleman of the 1800s, Lovecraft became a ghost writer and revisionist to supplement his income as a writer of the macabre. His first professional sale was "Herbert West: Reanimator," and he is noted for his Cthulhu Mythos stories. After his death in 1936, Arkham House re-published most of his work, and his fame has grown immensely.

Mrs. Pollard knew the ruins of a nearby cabin held a terrible secret. She never expected to be the one to find out what it was.

TWELVE

The Caller in the Night
Burton Kline

By the side of a road which wanders in company of a stream across a region of Pennsylvania farmland that is called "Paradise" because of its beauty, you may still mark the ruins of a small brick cabin in the depths of a grove. In summertime ivy drapes its jagged fragments and the pile might be lost to notice but that at dusk the trembling leaves of the vine have a way of whispering to the nerves of your horse and setting them too in a tremble. And the people in the village beyond have a belief that three troubled human beings lie buried under those ruins, and that at night, or in a storm, they sometimes cry aloud in their unrest.

The village is Bustlebury, and its people have a legend that on a memorable night there was once disclosed to a former inhabitant the secret of that ivied sepulchre.

All the afternoon the two young women had chattered in the parlor, cooled by the shade of the portico, and lost to the heat of the day, to the few sounds of the village, to the passing hours themselves. Then of a sudden Mrs. Pollard was recalled to herself at the necessity of closing her front windows against a gust of wind that blew the curtains, like flapping flags, into the room.

"Sallie, we're going to get it again," she said, pausing for a glance at the horizon before she lowered the sash.

"Get what?" Her visitor walked to the other front window and stooped to peer out.

Early evening clouds were drawing a black cap over the fair face of the land.

"I think we're going to have some more of Old Screamer Moll this evening. I knew we should, after this hot—"

"There! Margie, that was the expression I've been trying to remember all afternoon. You used it this morning. Where did you get such a poetic nickname for a thunder— O-oh!"

For a second, noon had returned to the two women. From their feet two long streaks of black shadow darted back into the room, and vanished. Overhead an octopus of lightning snatched the whole heavens in its grasp, shook them, and disappeared.

The two women screamed, and threw themselves on the sofa. Yet in a minute it was clear that the world still rolled on, and each looked at the other and laughed at her fright—till the prospect of an evening of storm sobered them both.

"Mercy!" Mrs. Pollard breathed in discouragement. "We're in for another night of it. We've had this sort of thing for a week. And tonight of all nights, when I wanted you to see this wonderful country under the moon!"

Mrs. Pollard, followed by her guest, Mrs. Reeves, ventured to the window timidly again, to challenge what part of the sky they could see from under the great portico outside, and learn its portent for the night.

An evil visage it wore—a swift change from a noon day of beaming calm. Now it was curtained completely with blue-black cloud, which sent out mutterings, and then long brooding silences more ominous still in their very concealment of the night's intentions.

There was no defense against it but to draw down the blinds and shut out this angry gloom in the glow of the lamps within. And, with a half hour of such glow to cozen them, the two women were soon merry again over their reminiscences, Mrs. Pollard at her embroidery, Mrs. Reeves at the piano, strumming something from Chopin in the intervals of their chatter.

"The girl" fetched them their tea. "Five already!" Mrs. Pollard verified the punctuality of her servant with a glance at the clock. "Then John will be away for another night. I do hope he won't try to get back this time. Night before last he left his assistant with a case, and raced his horse ten miles in the dead of the night to get home," Mrs. Pollard proudly reported, "for fear I'd be afraid in the storm."

"And married four years!" Mrs. Reeves smilingly shook her head in indulgence of such long-lived romance.

In the midst of their cakes and tea the bell announced an impatient hand at the door.

"Well, 'speak of angels!'" Mrs. Pollard quoted, and flew to greet her husband. But she opened the door upon smiling old Mr. Barber, instead, from the precincts across the village street.

Mr. Barber seemed to be embarrassed. "I—I rather thought you might be wanting something," he said in words. By intention he was making apology for the night. "I saw the doctor drive away, but I haven't seen him come back. So I—I thought I'd just run over and see—see if there wasn't something you wanted." He laughed uneasily.

Mr. Barber's transparent diplomacy having been rewarded with tea, they all came at once to direct speech. "It ain't going to amount to much," Mr. Barber insisted. "Better come out, you ladies, and have a look around. It may rain a bit, but you'll feel easier if you come and get acquainted with things, so to say." And gathering their resolution the two women followed him out on the portico.

They shuddered at what they saw.

Night was at hand, two hours before its time. Nothing stirred, not a vocal chord of hungry, puzzled, frightened chicken or cow. The whole region seemed to have caught its breath, to be smothered under a pall of stillness, unbroken except for some occasional distant earthquake of thunder from the inverted Switzerland of cloud that hung pendant from the sky.

Mr. Barber's emotions finally ordered themselves into speech as he watched. "Ain't it grand!" he said.

The two women made no reply. They sat on the steps to the portico, their arms entwined. The scene beat their more sophisticated intelligences back into silence. Some minutes they all sat there together, and then again Mr. Barber broke the spell.

"It do look fearful, like. But you needn't be afraid. It's better to be friends with it, you might say. And then go to bed and fergit it."

They thanked him for his goodness, bade him goodby, and he clinked down the flags of the walk and started across the street.

He had got midway across when they all heard a startling sound, an unearthly cry.

It came out of the distance, and struck the stillness like a blow.

"What is it? What is it, Margie?" Mrs. Reeves whispered excitedly.

Faint and quavering at its beginning, the cry grew louder and more shrill, and then died away, as the breath that made it ebbed and was spent. It seemed as if this unusual night had found at last a voice suited to its mood. Twice the cry was given, and then all was still as before.

At its first notes the muscles in Mrs. Pollard's arm had tightened. But Mr. Barber had hastened back at once with reassurance.

"I guess Mrs. Pollard knows what that is," he called to them from the gate. "It's only our old friend Moll, that lives down there in the notch. She gets lonesome, every thunderstorm, and lets it off like that. It's only her rheumatiz, I reckon. We wouldn't feel easy ourselves without them few kind words from Old Moll!"

The two women applauded as they could his effort toward humor. Then, "Come on, Sallie, quick!" Mrs. Pollard cried to her guest, and the two women bolted up the steps of the portico and flew like girls through the door, which they quickly locked between themselves and the disquieting night.

Once safe within, relief from their nerves came at the simple effort of laughter, and an hour later, when it was clear that the stars still held to their courses, the two ladies were at their ease again, beneath the lamp on the table, with speech and conversation to provide an escape from thought. The night seemed to cool its high temper as the hours wore on, and gradually the storm allowed itself to be forgotten.

Together, at bed time, the two made their tour of the house, locking the windows and doors, and visiting the pantry on the way for an apple. Outside all was truly calm and still, as, with mock and exaggerated caution, they peered through one last open window. A periodic, lazy flash from the far distance was all that the sky could muster of its earlier wrath. And they tripped upstairs and to bed, with that hilarity which always attends the feminine pursuit of repose.

But in the night they were awakened.

Not for nothing, after all, had the skies marshalled that afternoon array of their forces. Now they were as terribly vociferous as they had been terrifyingly still before. Leaves, that had drooped melancholy and motionless in the afternoon, were whipped from their branches at the snatch of the wind. The rain came down in a solid cataract. The thunder was a steady bombardment, and the frolic powers above, that had toyed and practiced with soundless flashes in the afternoon, had grown wanton at their sport, and hurlec' their electric shots at earth in appallingly accurate marksmanship. Between the flashes from the sky, the steady glare of a burning barn here and there reddened the blackness. The village dead, under the pelted sod, must have shuddered at the din. Even the moments of lull were saturate with terrors. In them rose audible the roar of waters, the clatter of frightened animals, the rattle of gates, the shouts of voices, the click of heels on the flags of the streets, as the villagers hurried to the succor of neighbors fighting fires out on the hills. For long afterward the tempest of that night was remembered. For hours while it lasted, trees were toppled over, and houses rocked to the blast.

And for as long as it would, the rain beat in through an open window and wetted the two women where they lay in their bed, afraid to stir, even to help themselves, gripped in a paralysis of terror.

Their nerves were not the more disposed to peace, either, by another token of the storm. All through the night, since their waking, in moments of stillness sufficient for it to be heard, they had caught that cry of the late afternoon. Doggedly it asserted itself against the uproar. It insisted upon being heard. It too wished to shriek relievingly, like the inanimate night, and publish its sickness abroad. They heard it far off, at first. But it moved, and came nearer. Once the two women quaked when it came to them, shrill and clear, from a point close at hand. But they bore its invasion along with the wind and the rain, and lay shameless and numb in the rude arms of the night.

They lay so till deliverance from the hideous spell came at last, in a vigorous pounding at the front door.

"It's John!" Mrs. Pollard cried in her joy. "And through such a storm!"

She slipped from the bed, threw a damp blanket about her, and groped her way out of the room and down the stair, her guest stumbling after. They scarcely could fly fast enough down the dark steps. At the bottom Mrs. Pollard turned brighter the dimly burning entry lamp, shot back the bolt with fingers barely able to grasp it in their eagerness, and threw open the door.

"John!" she cried.

But there moved into the house the tall and thin but heavily framed figure of an old woman, who peered about in confusion.

In a flash of recognition Mrs. Pollard hurled herself against the intruder to thrust her out.

"No!" the woman said. "No, you will not, on such a night!" And the apparition herself, looking with feverish curiosity at her unwilling hostesses, slowly closed the door and leaned against it.

Mrs. Pollard and her friend turned to fly, in a mad instinct to be anywhere behind a locked door. Yet before the instinct could reach their muscles, the unbidden visitor stopped them again.

"No!" she said. "I am dying. Help me!"

The two women turned, as if hypnotically obedient to her command. Their tongues lay thick and dead in their mouths. They fell into each other's arms, and their caller stood looking them over, with the same fevered curiosity. Then she turned her deliberate scrutiny to the house itself.

In a moment she almost reassured them with a first token of being human and feminine. On the table by the stairs lay a book, and she went and picked it up. "Fine!" she mused. Then her eye traveled over the pictures on the walls. "Fine!" she said. "So this is the inside of a fine house!" But suddenly, as her peering gaze returned to the two women, she was recalled to herself. "But you wanted to put me out—on a night like this! Hear it!"

For a moment she looked at them in frank hatred. And on an impulse she revenged herself upon them by sounding, in their very ears, the shrill cry they had heard in the afternoon, and through the night, that had mystified the villagers for years from the grove. The house rang with it, and with the hard peal of laughter that finished it.

All three of them stood there, for an instant, viewing each other. But at the end of it the weakest of them was the partly sibylline, partly mountebank intruder. She swayed back against the wall. Her head rolled limply to one side, and she moaned, "O God, how tired I am tonight!"

Frightened as they still were, their runaway hearts beating a tattoo that was almost audible, the two other women made a move to support her. But she waved them back with a suddenly returning air of command. "No!" she said. "You wanted to put me out!"

The creature wore some sort of thin skirt whose color had vanished in the blue-black of its wetness. Over her head and shoulders was thrown a ragged piece of shawl. From under it dangled strands of grizzled gray hair. Her dark eyes were hidden in the shadows of her impromptu hood. The hollows of her cheeks looked deeper in its shadows.

She loosed the shawl from her head, and it dropped to the floor, disclosing a face like one of the Fates. She folded her arms, and there was a rude majesty in the massive figure and its bearing as she tried to command herself and speak.

"I come here—in this storm. Hear it! Hear that! I want shelter. I want comfort. And what do you say to me! Well, then I take comfort from you. You thought I was your husband. You called his name. Well, I saw him this afternoon. He drove out. I called to him from the roadside. 'Let me tell your fortune! Only fifty cent!' But he whipped up his horse and drove away. You are all alike. But I see him now—in Woodman's Narrows. It rains there, same as here. Thunder and lightning, same as here. Trees fall. The wind blows. The wind blows!"

The woman had tilted her head and fixed her eyes, shining and eager, as if on some invisible scene, and she half intoned her words as if in a trance.

"I see your husband now. His wagon is smashed by a

tree. The horse is dead. Your husband lies very still. He does not move. There!"—she turned to them alert again to their presence—"there is the husband that you want. If you don't believe me, all I say is, wait! He is there. You will see!"

She ended in a peal of laughter, which itself ended in a weary moan. "Oh, why can't you help me!" She came toward them, her arms outstretched. "*Don't* be afraid of me. I want a woman to know me—to comfort me. I die to-night. It's calling me, outside. Don't you hear?"

"Listen to me, you women!" she went on, and tried to smile, to gain their favor. "I lied to you, to get even with you. You want your husband. Well, I lied. He isn't dead. For all you tried to shut me out. Do you never pity? Do you never help? O-oh—"

Her hand traveled over her brow, and her eyes wandered.

"No one knows what I need now! I got to tell it, I got to tell it! Hear that?" There had been a louder and nearer crash outside. "That's my warning. That says I got to tell it, before it's too late. No storm like this for forty years—not since one night forty years ago. My God, that night!" Another heavy rumble interrupted her. "Yes, yes!" she turned and called. "I'll tell it! I promise!"

She came toward her audience and said pleadingly, "Listen—even if it frightens you. You've got to listen. That night, forty years ago"—she peered about her cautiously— "I think—I think I hurt two people—hurt them very bad. And ever since that night—"

The two women had once again tried to fly away, but again she halted them. "Listen! You have no right to run away. You got to comfort me! You hear? Please, please, don't go."

She smiled, and so seemed less ugly. What could her two auditors do but cling to each other and hear her through, dumb and helpless beneath her spell?

"Only wait. I'll tell you quickly. Oh, I was not always like this. Once I could talk—elegant too. I've almost forgotten now. But I never looked like this then. I was not always ugly—no teeth—gray hair. Once I was beautiful too. You laugh? But yes! Ah, I was young, and tall, and had long black hair. I was Mollie, then. Mollie Morgan. That's the first time I've said my name for years. But that's who I was. Ask Bruce—he knows."

She had fallen back against the wall again, her eyes roaming as she remembered. Here she laughed. "But Bruce is dead these many years. He was my dog." A long pause. "We played together. Among the flowers—in the pretty cottage—under the vines. Not far from here. But all gone now, all gone. Even the woods are gone—the woods where Bruce and I hunted berries. And my mother!"

Again the restless hands sought the face and covered it.

"My mother! Almost as young as I. And how *she* could talk! A fine lady. As fine as you. And oh, we had good times together. Nearly always. Sometimes mother got angry—in a rage. She'd strike me, and say I was an idiot like my father. The next minute she'd hug me, and cry, and beg me to forgive her. It all comes back to me. Those were the days when she'd bake a cake for supper—the days when she cried, and put on a black dress. But mostly she wore the fine dresses—all bright, and soft, and full of flowers. Oh, how she would dance about in those, sometimes. And always laughed when I stared at her. And say I was Ned's girl to my fingertips. I never understood what she meant—then."

The shrill speaker of a moment before had softened suddenly. The creature of the woods sniffed eagerly this atmosphere of the house, and faint vestiges of a former personage returned to her, summoned along with the scene she had set herself to recall.

"But oh, how good she was to me! And read to me. And taught me to read. And careful of me? Ha! Never let me go alone to the village. Said I was too good for such a place. Some day we would go back to the world—whatever she meant by that. Said people there would clap the hands when they saw me—more than they had clapped the hands for her. Once she saw a young man walk along the road with me. Oh, how she beat my head when I came home! Nearly killed me, she was so angry. Said I mustn't waste myself on such trash. My mother—I never understood her then.

"She used to tell me stories—about New York, and Phil'delph. Many big cities. There they applaud, and clap the hands, when my mother was a queen, or a beggar girl, in the theatre, and make love and kill and fight. Have grand supper in hotel afterward. And I'd ask my mother how soon I too may be a queen. And she'd give me to learn the words they say, and I'd say them. Then she'd clap me on the head again and tell me, 'Oh, you're Ned's girl. You're a blockhead, just like your father!' And I'd say, 'Where is my father? Why does he never come?' And after that my mother would always sit quiet, and never answer when I talked.

"And then she'd be kind again, and make me proud, and tell me I'm a very fine lady, and have fine blood. And she'd talk about the day when we'd go back to the world, and she'd buy me pretty things to wear. But I thought it was fine where we were—there in the cottage, I with the flowers, and Bruce. In those days, yes," the woman sighed, and left them to silence for a space,—for silent seemed the wind and rain, on the breaking of her speech.

A rumble from without started her on again.

"Yes, yes! I'm telling! I'll hurry. Then I grow big. Seventeen. My mother call me her little giantess, her handsome darling, her conceited fool, all at the same time. I never understood my mother—then.

"But then, one day, it came!"

The woman pressed her fingers against her eyes, as if to shut out the vision her mind was preparing.

"Everything changed then. Everything was different. No more nights with stories and books. No more about New York and Phil'delph. Never again.

"I was out in the yard one day, on my knees, with the flowers. It was Springtime, and I was digging and fixing. And I heard a horse's hoofs on the road. A runaway, I thought at first. I stood up to look, and—" She faltered, and then choked out, "I stood up to look, and the man came!" And with the words came a crash that rocked the house.

"Hear that!" the woman almost shrieked. "That's him— that's the man. I hear him in every storm!

"He came," she went on more rapidly. "A tall man— fine—dressed in fine clothes—brown hair—brown eyes! Oh, I often see those brown eyes. I know what they are like. He came riding along the bye-road. When he caught sight of my mother he almost fell from his horse. The horse nearly fell, the man pulled him in so sharp. 'Good God!' the man said. 'Fanny! Is this where you are! Curse you, old girl, is this where you are!' Funny, how I remember his words. And then he came in.

"And he talked to my mother a long time. Then he looked round and said, 'So this is where you've crawled to!' And he petted Bruce. And then he came to me, and looked into my face a long time, and said, 'So this is his girl, eh? Fanny junior, down to the last eyelash! Come here, puss!' he said. And I made a face at him. And he put his hands to his sides and laughed and laughed at me. And he turned to my mother and said, 'Fanny, Fanny, what a queen!' I thought he meant be a queen in the theatre. But he meant something else. He came to me again, and squeezed me and pressed his face against mine. And my mother ran and snatched him away. And I ran behind the house.

"And by-and-by my mother came to find me, and said, 'Oho, my little giantess! So here you are! What are you trembling for!' And she kicked me. 'Take that!' she said.

"And I didn't understand—not then. But I understand now.

"Next day the man came again, and talked to my mother. But I saw him look and look at me. And by-and-by he reached for my hand. And my mother said, 'Stop that! None of that, my little George! One at a time, if you please!' And he laughed and let me go. And they went out and sat on a bench in the yard. And the man stroked my mother's hair. And I watched and listened. They talked a long time till it was night. And I heard George say, 'Well, Fanny, old girl, we did for him, all right, didn't we?' I've always remembered it. And they laughed and they laughed. Then the man said, 'God, how it does scare me, sometimes!' And my mother laughed at him for that. And George said, 'Look what I've had to give up. And you penned up here! But never mind. It will blow over. Then we'll crawl back to the old world, eh, Fanny?'"

All this the woman had rattled off like a child with a recitation, as something learned long ago and long rehearsed against just this last contingency and confession.

"Oh, I remember it!" she said, as if her volubility needed an explanation. "It took me a long time to understand. But one day I understood.

"He came often, then—George did. And I was not afraid of him any more. He was fine, like my mother. Every time I saw him come my stomach would give a jump. And I liked to have him put his face against mine, the way I'd seen him do to mother. And every time he went away I'd watch him from the hilltop till I couldn't see him any more. And at night I couldn't sleep. And George came very often—to see me, he told me, and not my mother.

"And my mother was changed then. She never hit me again, because George said he'd kill her if she did. But she acted very strange when he told her that, and looked and looked at me. And didn't speak to me for days and days. But I didn't mind—I could talk to George. And we'd go for long walks, and he'd tell me more about New York and Phil'delph—more than my mother could tell. Oh, I loved to hear him talk. And he said such nice things to me—such nice things to me! Bruce—I forgot all about Bruce. Oh, I was happy! But that was because I knew nothing.

"Yes, I pleased George. But by-and-by he changed too. Then I couldn't say anything that he liked. 'Stupid child!' he called me. I tried, ever so hard, to please him. But it was like walking against a wind, that you can't push aside. You women, you just guess how I felt then! You just guess! You want your husband. It was the same with me. I want George. But he wouldn't listen to me no more."

The woman seemed to sink, to shrivel, under the weight of her recollection. Finding her not a monster but a woman after all, her two hearers were moved to another slight token of sympathy. They were "guessing," as she commanded. But still, with a kind of weary magnanimity, she waved them back, away from the things she had yet to make clear.

"But one day I saw it. One day I saw something. I came home with my berries, and George was there. His breath was funny, and he talked funny, and walked funny. I'd seen people in the village that way. But—my mother was that way, too. She looked funny—had very red cheeks, and talked very fast. Very foolish. And her breath was the same as George's. And she laughed and laughed at me, and made fun of me.

"I said nothing. But I didn't sleep that night. I wondered what would happen. Many days I thought of what was happening. Then I knew. My mother was trying to get George away from me. That was what had happened.

"Another day I came back with my berries, and my mother was not there. Neither was George there. So! She had taken George away. My George. Well! I set out to look. No rest for me till I find them. I knew pretty well where they might be. I started for George's little brick house down in the hollow. That's where he had taken to living—hunting and fishing. It was late—the brick house was far away—I was very tired. But I went. And—"

She had been speaking more rapidly. Here she stopped to breathe, to swallow, to collect herself for the final plunge.

"I heard a runaway horse. 'George's horse!' I said. 'George is coming back to me, after all! George is coming back to me! She can't keep him!' And, yes, it was George's horse. But nobody on him. I was so scared I could hardly stand. Something had happened to George. Only then did I know how much I wanted him—when something had happened to him. I almost fell down in the road, but I crawled on. And presently I came to him, to George. He was walking in the road, limping and stumbling and rolling—all muddy—singing to himself. He didn't know me at first. I ran to him—to my George. And he grabbed me, and stumbled, and fell. And he grabbed my ankle. 'Come to me, li'l one!' he said. 'Damn the old hag!' he said. 'It's the girl I want— Ned's own!' he said. 'Come here to me, Ned's own. I want you!' And he pinched me. He bit my hand. And—and I— all of a sudden I was afraid.

"And I snatched myself loose. 'George!' I screamed. 'No!' I said—I don't know why. I was very scared. I was wild. I kicked away—and ran—ran, ran—away—I don't know where—to the woods. And oh, a long time I heard George laugh at me. 'Just like the very old Ned!' I heard him shout. But I ran, till I fell down tired. And there I sat and thought.

"And all of a sudden I understood. All at once I knew many things. I knew then what my mother had said about Ned sometimes. He was my father. He was dead. Somebody had killed him, I knew—I knew it from what they said. George knew my father, then, too. What did he know? That was it! He—he was the man that killed my father. He was after my mother then—he had been after her before, and made her breathe funny, made a fool of her. That was why my beautiful mother was so strange to me sometimes. That's why there was no more New York and Phil'delph. George did that—spoiled everything. Now he was back—making a fool of her again—my mother! And wanted to make a fool of me. Oh, then I knew! That man! And I had liked him. His brown hair, his brown eyes! But oh, I understood, I understood.

"I got up from the ground. Everything reeled and fell apart. There was nothing more for me. Everything spoiled. Our pretty cottage—the stories—all gone. Spoiled. So I ran back. Maybe I could bring my mother back. Maybe I could save something. Oh, I was sick. The trees, they bent and rolled the way George walked. The wind bent them double. They held their stomachs, as if they were George, laughing at me. They seemed to holler 'Ned's girl!' at me. I was dizzy, and the wind nearly blew me over. But I had to hurry home.

"I got near. No one there. Not even George. But I had to find my beautiful little mother. All round I ran. The brambles threw me down. I fell over a stump and struck my face. I could feel the blood running down over my cheeks. It was warmer than the rain. No matter, I had to find my mother. My poor little mother.

"Bruce growled at me when I got to the house. He didn't know me. That's how I looked! But there was a light in the house. Yes, my mother was there! But George was there, too. That man! They had bundles all ready to go away. They weren't glad to see me. I got there too soon. George said, 'Damn her soul! Always that girl of Ned's! I'll show her!' And he kicked me.

"George kicked me!

"But my mother—she didn't laugh when she saw me. She was very scared. She shook George, and said, 'George! Come away, quick! Look at her face! Look at her eyes!' she said.

"Oh, my mother, my little mother. She thought I would hurt her. Even when she'd been such a fool. I was the one that had to take care of her, then. But she wanted to go away—with that man! That made me wild.

"'You, George!' I said, 'You've got to go! You've—

you've done too much to us!' I said. 'You go!' And 'Mother!' I said. 'You've got to leave him! He's done too much to us!' I said.

"She only answered, 'George, come, quick!' And she dragged George toward the door. And George laughed at me. Laughed and laughed—till he saw my eyes. He didn't laugh then. Nor my mother. My mother screamed when she saw my eyes. 'Shut up, George!' she screamed. 'She's not Ned's girl now!' And George said, 'No, by God! She's *your* brat now, all right! She's the devil's own!'

"And they ran for the door. I tried to get there first, to catch my little mother. My mother only screamed, as if she were wild. And they got out—out in the dark. 'Mother!' I cried. 'Mother! Come back, come back!' No answer. My mother was gone.

"Oh, that made me feel, somehow, very strong. 'I'll bring you back!' I shouted. 'You, George! I'll send you away. Wait and see!' They never answered. Maybe they never heard. The wind was blowing, like tonight.

"But I knew where I could find them. I knew where to go to find George. And I ran to my loft, for my knife. But, O my God, when I saw poor Mollie in the glass! Teeth gone. I wasn't beautiful any more. And my eyes!—they came out of the glass at me, like two big dogs jumping a fence. I ran from them. I didn't know myself. I ran out of the door, in the night. I went after that man. He had done too much. That storm—the lightning that night! Awful! But no storm kept me back. Rain—hail—but I kept on. Trees fell—but I went on. I called out. I laughed then, myself. I'll get him! I say, 'Look out for Ned's girl! Look out for Ned's girl!' I say—

Unconsciously the woman was re-enacting every gesture, repeating every phrase and accent of her journey through the night, that excursion out of the world, from which there had been no return for her. "Look out for Ned's girl!"—the house rang with the cry. But this second journey, of the memory, ended in a moan and a faint.

"I said I would tell it! Help me!" she said.

In some fashion they worked her heavy bulk out of its crazy wrappings and into a bed. John arrived, to help them. Morning peered timidly over the eastern hills, as if fearful of beholding what the night had wrought. In its smiling calm the noise of the storm was already done away. But the storm in the troubled mind raged on.

For days it raged, in fever and delirium. Then they buried the rude minister of justice in the place where she commanded—under the pile of broken stones and bricks among the trees in the hollow. And it is said that the inquisitive villagers who had a part in the simple ceremonies stirred about till they made the discovery of two skeletons under the ruins. And to this day there are persons in Bustlebury with a belief that at night, or in a storm, they sometimes hear a long-drawn cry issuing from that lonely little hollow.

Little seems to be known about Burton Kline, but he was a frequent contributor to magazines in the early 1900s. Many of his stories appeared in O'Brien's Best Short Stories of the Year *volumes. They often dealt with the supernatural, as in "In the Open Code" and "The Caller in the Night."*

Kate's family was running from an unspeakable horror, but only Kate realized why they weren't getting away.

THIRTEEN

Professor Kate

Margaret St. Clair

"The boy that directed us on this road, pa," Kate said, leaning forward to speak to the man in the front seat, "—do you think he was real?"

John Bender Senior turned and regarded her. "What you mean by that, Käter?" he asked sternly. He had to raise his voice to be heard over the rumble of the wagon wheels.

Kate's fingers moved nervously over the bosom of her shirtwaist. "Why that . . . that he might be one of them we left in the orchard, back on the farm. This road ain't like a road that goes anywhere."

Her father's lean face grew dark with anger. "Stop dot talk, Käter. Stop your mouth."

"*Ja*, stop it, daughter," Mrs. Bender said. Her blue eyes were hard in her large white face. "Is nonsense, unsinn. How could it be one of dem? Didn't we bind dem to stay before we left?"

Kate sighed and sank back in her seat. Her brother John, who was sitting beside her (he was only her half-brother, she was wont to say with a touch of defiance), slipped his arm around her waist. "You're tired, Kate," he said. "It ain't them dead ones I'm afraid of. I'm afraid of a posse coming after us."

"Oh, do you think there'll be one?" Kate answered vaguely. Once more her hands were moving on her dress.

"Dead sure. Colonel York suspicioned us about his brother. They traced him as far as our farm."

"He didn't come back for the seance, though," Kate replied.

"No. But we knew he'd be back later for sure, with more men. Things was getting hot. That's why we left."

Kate laughed suddenly, a bold, ringing laugh. "Why we left! Didn't we look out the bedroom window that morning and see the ground heaving below in the orchard? Didn't you hear her little voice crying 'Mama! Mama!' the way she did when we buried her? Why we left!"

"I didn't hear or see nothing, Kate. I only said that to . . . to agree with you."

Once more Kate laughed. "You didn't hear anything? Why, you turned as white as a sheet!"

"As a ghost," her brother corrected after a moment had passed. "Make it a ghost, while you're doing it."

They jounced on. Bender, hunched over the reins, clucked now and then at the team. Once John said out of a long silence, "This here ain't much of a road, for a fact." Kate looked at him sideways without saying anything.

The sun began to sink. The air, which had been warm with spring earlier in the day, grew colder. A light breeze ruffled the long grass of the prairie. Kate, shivering, let John embrace her without resistance.

Old man Bender turned round to face them. "Hope we find dose houses soon," he said uneasily. "That boy said we'd get to them before night."

Kate raised her head from John's shoulder and looked him full in the eyes. His gaze wavered. He coughed and turned back to the team.

They stopped at last. "Is too dark to drive more," old man Bender said, his voice loud in the sudden silence. "Ve got to sleep here." He looked around the vacant flatness of the prairie, frowning, and then began to unharness the team.

John jumped from the wagon and then turned to help Kate. She was stiff from the long sitting; she almost fell into his arms. Mrs. Bender, meantime, was getting sacks and crocks of provisions out from under the front seat.

"Have an apple, son," she said, holding one out to the young man.

"No. I can't say as I care for the fruit from them trees."

Mrs. Bender began to munch the apple herself. Kate had

taken advantage of the distraction to withdraw from John's embrace and wander off. He looked after her, his forehead wrinkled. Then he began to help his mother with the preparations for the evening meal.

Suddenly Kate screamed. It was a high sound, not very loud. John dropped the bread he was holding and ran toward her.

He found her sitting on her heels, her black bombazine skirt drawn tightly around her haunches. She was holding a long thigh bone in one hand.

"It scared me when I first saw it," she said, looking up at him brightly. "The skull, I mean. And look, over there in the grass, there's another one."

John followed her gesture. He kicked the grass apart. After a short time he found the second skeleton, gleaming whitely even in the dim light. He stooped over, hunting, and came up at last with something in his hand.

"It was an Indian," he announced to Kate. "This here's what killed him. An arrow." He showed it to her.

She seemed to lose interest. "Oh, an Indian. Must of been a long time ago." She cocked her head and listened intently. "John, I hear voices. Not like them on the farm, though. Maybe it's the Indians. Listen!" She held up a hand, warning him.

There was the rustle of the grass, the plaintive note of a mourning dove. "I don't hear nothing," he said. He pulled at his mustache.

"You wouldn't 'fess up to it if you did," she said. She giggled. "I want to have a seance, John. 'Member how they called me Professor Kate in the Parsons paper that time I lectured there on spiritualism?" She rose to her feet and faced him. "Maybe a seance would quiet the voices. On the farm it used to. Professor Kate wants to have a seance."

He slapped her. His hand left a red mark on her face, but she made no sign of having felt it. "Stop it, Kate. You want to drive all of us crazy? Why stir them up? And anyhow, it ain't nothing. We'll sleep in the wagon tonight and tomorrow start early. It's only two Indians. Ain't you used to dead people?"

He took her by the hand and led her back to the wagon. Sighing, she stumbled after him. "Do you think we'll get to

Vinita tomorrow, John?" she asked. "I'm so tired of riding. Father said we could leave the wagon and take the train once we got to the Indian Territory."

"Sure thing, you bet," he answered, without looking at her. "Get up early, ride all day. It ain't far."

John woke early, while it was still dark. He found water and washed in a cupful of it. After a moment he heard Kate getting down from the wagon. She came up to him, yawning and shivering.

He poured water for her and she scrubbed her face with a handkerchief. She straightened her hair with her hands. "How did you sleep, John?" she asked, putting her head on one side. "Did you rest well?"

"Naw. Why ask? I had dreams."

"Like my dreams, I guess. This ain't a good place. Listen, paw and maw are getting up."

They breakfasted on slabs of bread and cold pork. Old man Bender harnessed up the team and turned the wagon around. "We make a fine quick start," he said. "De stars ain't set yet. Before sun-up, we be back on the right road."

The pursuers rose nearly as early as the Benders did. The Benders were moved by fear, the posse by hate. As Captain Sanders swung into the saddle, he said to the lieutenant, "Today or tomorrow, sure. We're getting close."

The lieutenant (he, like Sanders, had gained his rank in the Grand Army of the Republic less than ten years before) said flatly, "We're not going to take them back to the county for trial."

"No. You don't try rattlers. We found eleven bodies in the orchard. But what I remember most is the body of the little girl. She must have been still alive when they buried her." The sun rose. The day wore on. At noon the Benders stopped at a farmhouse for water and learned that they were on the right road. They might be able to make Vinita by dark. Kate, sighing with relief, did not resist when John drew her down under the wagon seat.

Afterward they chatted idly over plans, what they should do with the money they had taken from the travelers who had stopped at the Bender farmhouse. John wanted to start a restaurant in Denison, Kate wanted to keep on with the seances and the lecturing. She spoke of the good luck she'd had curing deafness and epileptic fits. Or the four of them might buy another farm. Why not? They had plenty of rhino, John said.

As the sun began to wester, Kate dozed. She leaned against John, her body swaying to the steady jogging. Once she said petulantly, "Vinita sure is a long way off."

At sundown the posse reached a crossroads. Sanders dismounted to check the wagon tracks. As he grasped the pommel again he was frowning. "They've turned," he told the men with him, gesturing to the right. "They're headed back."

"Why?" asked the lieutenant after a moment.

Sanders shrugged. "The devil knows. May be trying to throw us off the track."

It was quite dark when the wagon stopped, Vinita still unreached. Kate was drunk with sleepiness. John roused her and helped her out.

"Vinita?" she asked as she reached the ground.

"No, Kate. Not yet. First thing tomorrow, I guess."

She stood looking around her. The moon had not risen; it was difficult to see anything. Suddenly she gathered up her skirts and ran like a wild thing. After a moment they heard her screaming, "John! John! We've come back. This is the same place!"

When he got up to her she pointed at the skeleton. She picked up the arrow and handed it to him. "They've brought us back to the same place."

He let the point fall from his fingers. "What do you mean? Who has?"

"The Indians. They wouldn't let us get away. They brought us back. The dead—don't you see, John?—the dead stick together."

He stared at her in the darkness. Then he grasped her by the shoulder and began to pull her after him with desperate energy. "Hurry! Hurry! The wagon! We've got to get away!"

But as they neared the wagon they heard a thunder and a plunging, and then old man Bender's voice crying despairingly, "Whoa! Whoa! Damn you, come back!"

"The team's run off," Kate said simply. "I knew they wouldn't let us get away."

He began to wrench at the wagon sides, tearing off planking. "We'll make a fire, a big fire. They can't get past it. And paw will get out the guns."

"That's right," Kate said, cheering. "And we'll stay awake, all of us, Maybe if. . . ."

There were noises on the other side of the wagon as the night got older. Once old man Bender said, "What's dot whooping!" and Kate laughed.

The fire died down and was replenished with the wagon seats. Kate yawned, and then John and the others. He said, "We've got to stay awake."

About two in the morning Professor Kate realized abruptly that the others were sleeping. She ran from one to the other, shaking them, screaming their names. They wouldn't wake.

Morning came. John said, "Guess we must have gone to sleep, h'um, Kate?"

"I guess so. I remember dreaming. I'm awful tired."

John Bender yawned. "Well, anyway, we're all right. We was silly to worry. And look, the team's come back."

Old man Bender was silently harnessing the horses. When he was done, they climbed in the wagon. The front seat was still intact, but John and his sister had to sit on the floor. After they had driven for about a mile, Kate said, "Where are we going, paw?"

"To—I can't call the name to mind, daughter."

"Bin—Binecia," she answered, stumbling over the syllables. "I wish we'd hurry up and get there."

"Stop it, Kate," John said. "We will."

In the afternoon Kate said, "I wish we'd pass some houses." Later, when it was almost sunset, she turned to her brother. "Do you know what's going to happen, John?" she asked.

"What?" he replied. It was the first word he had spoken to her since early morning.

"It's going to get dark. And then we'll stop and we'll be back by the Indians. Back by the ashes of our fire. Back where we spent last night." She began to cry.

"No. You're crazy. We must be almost to Venita."

"Venita? We'll never get there. We'll just keep driving, driving, driving. Something's gone wrong with time."

"Be quiet, damn you. I hear horses, voices." He laid his hand over her mouth.

Old Man Bender had stopped the wagon. "Something ahead," he said softly. "You two go look."

They stole forward, tiptoeing. "I can't see good," Kate whispered.

"Hush. It's men with horses. They're bending over something. But I can't see what they're doing. There's a mist."

Kate had turned away. "Let's go back to the wagon," she whispered.

"Why? I want to know what they're doing."

"Oh, I know already."

"Then tell me."

"You know without telling. What they're bending over—"

"Is us. Is our bodies. No! No! I won't have it!"

She was wringing her hands and wailing. "Oh, but it is! Last night—last night the Indians didn't let us get away," said Professor Kate.

Born in Kansas in 1911, Margaret St. Clair is known for her stories of distant futures both adventurous and beautiful. The daughter of an attorney, she was educated at the University of California and worked as a horticulturalist from 1938 to 1941. Nearly all her work is in the field of fantasy, including Vulcan's Dolls *(1952) and* The Shadow People *(1976). She also writes under the pen name Idris Seabright.*

When Waco gave Jim Anderson the guns Bill Longley had worn, neither man really believed the legends about them. . . .

FOURTEEN

The Guns of William Longley

Donald Hamilton

We'd been up north delivering a herd for old man Butcher the summer I'm telling about. I was nineteen at the time. I was young and big, and I was plenty tough, or thought I was, which amounts to the same thing up to a point. Maybe I was making up for all the years of being that nice Anderson boy, back in Willow Fork, Texas. When your dad wears a badge, you're kind of obliged to behave yourself around home so as not to shame him. But Pop was dead now, and this wasn't Texas.

Anyway, I was tough enough that we had to leave Dodge City in something of a hurry after I got into an argument with a fellow who, it turned out, wasn't nearly as handy with a gun as he claimed to be. I'd never killed a man before. It made me feel kind of funny for a couple of days, but like I say, I was young and tough then, and I'd seen men I really cared for trampled in stampedes and drowned in rivers on the way north. I wasn't going to grieve long over one belligerent stranger.

It was on the long trail home that I first saw the guns one evening by the fire. We had a blanket spread on the ground, and we were playing cards for what was left of our pay— what we hadn't already spent on girls and liquor and general hell-raising. My luck was in, and one by one the others dropped out, all but Waco Smith, who got stubborn and went over to his bedroll and hauled out the guns.

"I got them in Dodge," he said. "Pretty, ain't they? Fellow I bought them from claimed they belonged to Bill Longley."

233

"Is that a fact?" I said, like I wasn't much impressed. "Who's Longley?"

I knew who Bill Longley was, all right, but a man's got a right to dicker a bit, and besides I couldn't help deviling Waco now and then. I liked him all right, but he was one of those cocky little fellows who asks for it. You know the kind. They always know everything.

I sat there while he told me about Bill Longley, the giant from Texas with thirty-two killings to his credit, the man who was hanged twice. A bunch of vigilantes strung him up once for horse-stealing he hadn't done, but the rope broke after they'd ridden off and he dropped to the ground, kind of short of breath but alive and kicking.

Then he was tried and hanged for a murder he had done, some years later, in Giddings, Texas. He was so big that the rope gave way again and he landed on his feet under the trap, making six-inch-deep footprints in the hard ground—they're still there in Giddings to be seen, Waco said, Bill Longley's footprints—but it broke his neck this time and they buried him nearby. At least a funeral service was held, but some say there's just an empty coffin in the grave.

I said, "This Longley gent can't have been so much, to let folks keep stringing him up that way."

That set Waco off again, while I toyed with the guns. They were pretty, all right, in a big carved belt with two carved holsters, but I wasn't much interested in leatherwork. It was the weapons themselves that took my fancy. They'd been used, but someone had looked after them well. They were handsome pieces, smooth-working, and they had a good feel to them. You know how it is when a firearm feels just right. A fellow with hands the size of mine doesn't often find guns to fit him like that.

"How much do you figure they're worth?" I asked, when Waco stopped for breath.

"Well, now," he said, getting a sharp look on his face, and I came home to Willow Fork with the Longley guns strapped around me. If that's what they were.

I got a room and cleaned up at the hotel. I didn't much feel like riding clear out to the ranch and seeing what it looked like with Ma and Pa gone two years and nobody looking after things. Well, I'd put the place on its feet again one of these days, as soon as I'd had a little fun and saved a little money. I'd buckle right down to it, I told myself, as soon as Junellen set the date, which I'd been after her to do since before my folks died. She couldn't keep saying forever we were too young.

I got into my good clothes and went to see her. I won't say she'd been on my mind all the way up the trail and back again, because it wouldn't be true. A lot of the time I'd been too busy or tired for dreaming, and in Dodge City I'd done my best *not* to think of her, if you know what I mean. It did seem like a young fellow engaged to a beautiful girl like Junellen Barr could have behaved himself better up there, but it had been a long dusty drive and you know how it is.

But now I was home, and it seemed like I'd been missing Junellen every minute since I left, and I couldn't wait to see her. I walked along the street in the hot sunshine feeling light and happy. Maybe my leaving my guns at the hotel had something to do with the light feeling, but the happiness was all for Junellen, and I ran up the steps to the house and knocked on the door. She'd have heard we were back, and she'd be waiting to greet me, I was sure.

I knocked again and the door opened and I stepped forward eagerly. "Junellen—" I said, and stopped foolishly.

"Come in, Jim," said her father, a little turkey of a man who owned the drygoods store in town. He went on smoothly: "I understand you had quite an eventful journey. We are waiting to hear all about it."

He was being sarcastic, but that was his way, and I couldn't be bothered with trying to figure what he was driving at. I'd already stepped into the room, and there was Junellen with her mother standing close, as if to protect her, which seemed kind of funny. There was a man in the room, too, Mr. Carmichael from the bank, who'd fought with Pa in the war. He was tall and handsome as always, a little heavy nowadays but still dressed like a fashion plate. I couldn't figure what he was doing there.

It wasn't going at all the way I'd hoped, my reunion with Junellen, and I stopped, looking at her.

"So you're back, Jim," she said. "I heard you had a real exciting time. Dodge City must be quite a place."

There was a funny hard note in her voice. She held herself very straight, standing there by her mother, in a blue-flowered dress that matched her eyes. She was a real little lady, Junellen. She made kind of a point of it, in fact, and Martha Butcher, old man Butcher's kid, used to say about Junellen Barr that butter wouldn't melt in her mouth, but that always seemed like a silly saying to me, and who was Martha Butcher anyway, just because her daddy owned a lot of cows?

Martha'd also remarked about girls who had to drive two front names in harness, as if one wasn't good enough, and I'd told her it surely wasn't if it was a name like Martha, and she'd kicked me on the shin. But that was a long time ago when we were all kids.

Junellen's mother broke the silence in her nervous way: "Dear, hadn't you better tell Jim the news?" She turned to Mr. Carmichael. "Howard, perhaps you should—"

Mr. Carmichael came forward and took Junellen's hand, "Miss Barr has done me the honor to promise to be my wife," he said.

I said, "But she can't. She's engaged to me."

Junellen's mother said quickly, "It was just a childish thing, not to be taken seriously."

I said, "Well, I took it seriously!"

Junellen looked up at me. "Did you, Jim? In Dodge City, did you?" I didn't say anything. She said breathlessly, "It doesn't matter. I suppose I could forgive. . . . But you have killed a man. I could never love a man who has taken a human life."

Anyway, she said something like that. I had a funny feeling in my stomach and a roaring sound in my ears. They talk about your heart breaking, but that's where it hit me, the stomach and the ears. So I can't tell you exactly what she said, but it was something like that.

I heard myself say, "Mr. Carmichael spent the war peppering Yanks with a peashooter, I take it."

"That's different—"

Mr. Carmichael spoke quickly. "What Miss Barr means is that there's a difference between a battle and a drunken brawl, Jim. I am glad your father did not live to see his son wearing two big guns and shooting men down in the street.

He was a fine man and a good sheriff for this county. It was only for his memory's sake that I agreed to let Miss Barr break the news to you in person. From what we hear of your exploits up north, you have certainly forfeited all right to consideration from her."

There was something in what he said, but I couldn't see that it was his place to say it. "You agreed?" I said. "That was mighty kind of you sir, I'm sure." I looked away from him. "Junellen—"

Mr. Carmichael interrupted. "I do not wish my fiancée to be distressed by a continuation of this painful scene. I must ask you to leave, Jim."

I ignored him. "Junellen," I said, "is this what you really—"

Mr. Carmichael took me by the arm. I turned my head to look at him again. I looked at the hand with which he was holding me. I waited. He didn't let go. I hit him and he went back across the room and kind of fell into a chair. The chair broke under him. Junellen's father ran over to help him up. Mr. Carmichael's mouth was bloody. He wiped it with a handkerchief.

I said, "You shouldn't have put your hand on me, sir."

"Note the pride," Mr. Carmichael said, dabbing at his cut lip. "Note the vicious, twisted pride. They all have it, all these young toughs. You are too big for me to box, Jim, and it is an undignified thing, anyway. I have worn a sidearm in my time. I will go to the back and get it, while you arm yourself."

"I will meet you in front of the hotel, sir," I said, "if that is agreeable to you."

"It is agreeable," he said, and went out.

I followed him without looking back. I think Junellen was crying, and I know her parents were saying one thing and another in high, indignant voices, but the funny roaring was in my ears and I didn't pay too much attention. The sun was very bright outside. As I started for the hotel, somebody ran up to me.

"Here you are, Jim." It was Waco, holding out the Longley guns in their carved holsters. "I heard what happened. Don't take any chances with the old fool."

I looked down at him and asked, "How did Junellen and her folks learn about what happened in Dodge?"

He said, "It's a small town, Jim, and all the boys have been drinking and talking, glad to get home."

"Sure," I said, buckling on the guns. "Sure."

It didn't matter. It would have got around sooner or later, and I wouldn't have lied about it if asked. We walked slowly toward the hotel.

"Dutch LeBaron is hiding out back in the hills with a dozen men," Waco said. "I heard it from a man in a bar."

"Who's Dutch LeBaron?" I asked. I didn't care, but it was something to talk about as we walked.

"Dutch?" Waco said. "Why Dutch is wanted in five states and a couple of territories. Hell, the price on his head is so high now even Fenn is after him."

"Fenn?" I said. He sure knew a lot of names. "Who's Fenn?"

"You've heard of Old Joe Fenn, the bounty hunter. Well, if he comes after Dutch, he's asking for it. Dutch can take care of himself."

"Is that a fact?" I said, and then I saw Mr. Carmichael coming, but he was a ways off yet and I said, "You sound like this Dutch fellow was a friend of yours—"

But Waco wasn't there any more. I had the street to myself, except for Mr. Carmichael, who had a gun strapped on outside his fine coat. It was an army gun in a black army holster with a flap, worn cavalry style on the right side, butt forward. They wear them like that to make room for the saber on the left, but it makes a clumsy rig.

I walked forward to meet Mr. Carmichael, and I knew I would have to let him shoot once. He was a popular man and a rich man and he would have to draw first and shoot first or I would be in serious trouble. I figured it all out very coldly, as if I had been killing men all my life. We stopped, and Mr. Carmichael undid the flap of the army holster and pulled out the big cavalry pistol awkwardly and fired and missed, as I had known, somehow, that he would.

Then I drew the right-hand gun, and as I did so I realized that I didn't particularly want to kill Mr. Carmichael. I mean, he was a brave man coming here with his old cap-and-ball pistol, knowing all the time that I could outdraw and outshoot him with my eyes closed. But I didn't want to be killed, either, and he had the piece cocked and was about to fire again. I tried to aim for a place that wouldn't kill him, or cripple him too badly, and the gun wouldn't do it.

I mean, it was a frightening thing. It was like I was fighting the Longley gun for Mr. Carmichael's life. The old army revolver fired once more and something rapped my left arm lightly. The Longley gun went off at last, and Mr. Carmichael spun around and fell on his face in the street. There was a cry, and Junellen came running and went to her knees beside him.

"You murderer!" she screamed at me. "You hateful murderer!"

It showed how she felt about him, that she would kneel in the dust like that in her blue-flowered dress. Junellen was always very careful of her pretty clothes. I punched out the empty and replaced it. Dr. Sims came up and examined Mr. Carmichael and said he was shot in the leg, which I already knew, being the one who had shot him there. Dr. Sims said he was going to be all right, God willing.

Having heard this, I went over to another part of town and tried to get drunk. I didn't have much luck at it, so I went into the place next to the hotel for a cup of coffee. There wasn't anybody in the place but a skinny girl with an apron on.

I said, "I'd like a cup of coffee, ma'am," and sat down.

She said, coming over, "Jim Anderson, you're drunk. At least you smell like it."

I looked up and saw that it was Martha Butcher. She set a cup down in front of me. I asked, "What are you doing here waiting tables?"

She said, "I had a fight with Dad about . . . well, never mind what it was about. Anyway, I told him I was old enough to run my own life and if he didn't stop trying to boss me around like I was one of the hands, I'd pack up and leave. And he laughed and asked what I'd do for money, away from home, and I said I'd earn it, so here I am."

It was just like Martha Butcher, and I saw no reason to make a fuss over it like she probably wanted me to.

"Seems like you are," I agreed. "Do I get sugar, too, or does that cost extra?"

She laughed and set a bowl in front of me. "Did you have a good time in Dodge?" she asked.

"Fine," I said, "Good liquor. Fast games. Pretty girls. Real pretty girls."

"Fiddlesticks," she said. "I know what you think is pretty. Blond and simpering. You big fool. If you'd killed him over her, they'd have put you in jail, at the very least. And just what are you planning to use for an arm when that one gets rotten and falls off? Sit still."

She got some water and cloth and fixed up my arm where Mr. Carmichael's bullet had nicked it.

"Have you been out to your place yet?" she asked.

I shook my head. "Figure there can't be much out there by now. I'll get after it one of these days."

"One of these days!" she said. "You mean when you get tired of strutting around with those big guns and acting dangerous—." She stopped abruptly.

I looked around, and got to my feet. Waco was there in the doorway, and with him was a big man, not as tall as I was, but wider. He was a real whiskery gent, with a mat of black beard you could have used for stuffing a mattress. He wore two gunbelts, crossed, kind of sagging low at the hips.

Waco said, "You're a fool to sit with your back to the door, Jim. That's the mistake Hickok made, remember? If instead of us it had been somebody like Jack McCall—"

"Who's Jack McCall?" I asked innocently.

"Why, he's the fellow shot Wild Bill in the back. . . ." Waco's face reddened. "All right, all right. Always kidding me. Dutch, this big joker is my partner, Jim Anderson. Jim, Dutch LeBaron. He's got a proposition for us."

I tried to think back to where Waco and I had decided to become partners, and couldn't remember the occasion. Well, maybe it happens like that, but it seemed like I should have had some say in it.

"Your partner tells me you're pretty handy with those guns," LeBaron said, after Martha'd moved off across the room. "I can use a man like that."

"For what?" I asked.

"For making some quick money over in New Mexico territory," he said.

The Guns of William Longley

I didn't ask any fool questions, like whether the money was to be made legally or illegally. "I'll think about it," I said.

Waco caught my arm. "What's to think about? We'll be rich, Jim!"

I said, "I'll think about it, Waco."

LeBaron said, "What's the matter, sonny, are you scared?"

I turned to look at him. He was grinning at me, but his eyes weren't grinning, and his hands weren't too far from those low-slung guns.

I said, "Try me and see."

I waited a little. Nothing happened. I walked out of there and got my pony and rode out to the ranch, reaching the place about dawn. I opened the door and stood there, surprised. It looked just about the way it had when the folks were alive, and I half expected to hear Ma yelling at me to beat the dust off outside and not bring it into the house. Somebody had cleaned the place up for me, and I thought I knew who. Well, it certainly was neighborly of her, I told myself. It was nice to have somebody show a sign that they were glad to have me home, even if it was only Martha Butcher.

I spent a couple of days out there, resting up and riding around. I didn't find much stock. It was going to take money to make a going ranch of it again, and I didn't figure any credit at Mr. Carmichael's bank was anything to count on. I couldn't help giving some thought to Waco and LeBaron and the proposition they'd put before me. It was funny. I'd think about it most when I had the guns on. I was out back practicing with them one day when the stranger rode up.

He was a little, dry elderly man on a sad-looking white horse he must have hired at the livery stable for not very much, and he wore his gun in front of his left hip with butt to the right for a cross draw. He didn't make any noise coming up. I'd fired a couple of times before I realized he was there.

"Not bad," he said when he saw me looking at him. "Do you know a man named LeBaron, son?"

"I've met him," I said.

"Is he here?"

"Why should he be here?"

"A bartender in town told me he'd heard you and your sidekick, Smith, had joined up with LeBaron, so I thought you might have given him the use of your place. It would be more comfortable for him than hiding out in the hills."

"He isn't here," I said. The stranger glanced toward the house. I started to get mad, but shrugged instead. "Look around if you want to."

"In that case," he said, "I don't figure I want to." He glanced toward the target I'd been shooting at, and back to me. "Killed a man in Dodge, didn't you, son? And then stood real calm and let a fellow here in town fire three shots at you, after which you laughed and pinked him neatly in the leg."

"I don't recall laughing," I said. "And it was two shots, not three."

"It makes a good story, however," he said. "And it is spreading. You have a reputation already, did you know that, Anderson? I didn't come here just to look for LeBaron. I figured I'd like to have a look at you, too. I always like to look up fellows I might have business with later."

"Business?" I said, and then I saw that he'd taken a tarnished old badge out of his pocket and was pinning it on his shirt. "Have you a warrant, sir?" I asked.

"Not for you," he said. "Not yet."

He swung the old white horse around and rode off. When he was out of sight, I got my pony out of the corral. It was time I had a talk with Waco. Maybe I was going to join LeBaron and maybe I wasn't, but I didn't much like his spreading it around before it was true.

I didn't have to look for him in town. He came riding to meet me with three companions, all hard ones if I ever saw any.

"Did you see Fenn?" he shouted as he came up. "Did he come this way?"

"A little old fellow with some kind of badge?" I said. "Was that Fenn? He headed back to town, about ten minutes ahead of me. He didn't look like much."

"Neither does the devil when he's on business," Waco said. "Come on, we'd better warn Dutch before he rides into town."

I rode along with them, and we tried to catch LeBaron on the trail, but he'd already passed with a couple of men. We saw their dust ahead and chased it, but they made it before us, and Fenn was waiting in front of the cantina that was LeBaron's hangout when he was in town.

We saw it all as we came pounding after LeBaron, who dismounted and started into the place, but Fenn came forward, looking small and inoffensive. He was saying something and holding out his hand. LeBaron stopped and shook hands with him, and the little man held onto LeBaron's hand, took a step to the side, and pulled his gun out of that cross-draw holster left-handed, with a kind of twisting motion.

Before LeBaron could do anything with his free hand, the little old man had brought the pistol barrel down across his head. It was as neat and coldblooded a thing as you'd care to see. In an instant, LeBaron was unconscious on the ground, and Old Joe Fenn was covering the two men who'd been riding with him.

Waco Smith, riding beside me, made a sort of moaning sound as if he'd been clubbed himself. "Get him!" he shouted, drawing his gun. "Get the dirty, sneaking bounty hunter!"

I saw the little man throw a look over his shoulder, but there wasn't much he could do about us with those other two to handle. I guess he hadn't figured us for reinforcements riding in. Waco fired and missed. He never could shoot much, particularly from horseback. I reached out with one of the guns and hit him over the head before he could shoot again. He spilled from the saddle.

I didn't have it all figured out. Certainly it wasn't a very nice thing Mr. Fenn had done, first taking a man's hand in friendship and then knocking him unconscious. Still, I didn't figure LeBaron had ever been one for giving anybody a break; and there was something about the old fellow standing there with his tarnished old badge that reminded me of Pa, who'd died wearing a similar piece of tin on his chest. Anyway, there comes a time in a man's life when he's got to make a choice, and that's the way I made mine.

Waco and I had been riding ahead of the others. I turned my pony fast and covered them with the guns as they came charging up—as well as you can cover anybody from a plunging horse. One of them had his pistol aimed to shoot. The left-handed Longley gun went off and he fell to the ground. I was kind of surprised. I'd never been much at shooting left-handed. The other two riders veered off and headed out of town.

By the time I got my pony quieted down from having that gun go off in his ear, everything was pretty much under control. Waco had disappeared, so I figured he couldn't be hurt much; and the new sheriff was there, old drunken Billy Bates who'd been elected after Pa's death by the gambling element in town, who hadn't liked the strict way Pa ran things.

"I suppose it's legal," Old Billy was saying grudgingly. "But I don't take it kindly, Marshal, your coming here to serve a warrant without letting me know."

"My apologies, Sheriff," Fenn said smoothly. "An oversight, I assure you. Now, I'd like a wagon. He's worth seven-hundred and fifty dollars over in New Mexico Territory."

"No decent person would want that kind of money," Old Billy said sourly, swaying on his feet.

"There's only one kind of money," Fenn said. "Just as there's only one kind of law, even though there's different kinds of men enforcing it." He looked at me as I came up. "Much obliged, son."

"Por nada," I said. "You get in certain habits when you've had a badge in the family. My daddy was sheriff here once."

"So? I didn't know that." Fenn looked at me sharply. "Don't look like you're making any plans to follow in his footsteps. That's hardly a lawman's rig you wearing."

I said, "Maybe, but I never yet beat a man over the head while I was shaking his hand, Marshal."

"Son," he said, "my job is to enforce the law and maybe make a small profit on the side, not to play games with fair and unfair." He looked at me for a moment longer. "Well, maybe we'll meet again. It depends."

"On what?" I asked.

"On the price," he said. "That price on your head."

"But I haven't got—"

"Not now," he said. "But you will, wearing those guns. I know the signs. I've seen them before, too many times. Don't count on having me under obligation to you, when your time comes. I never let personal feelings interfere with business. . . . Easy, now," he said, to a couple of fellows who were lifting LeBaron, bound hand and foot, into the wagon that somebody had driven up. "Easy. Don't damage the merchandise. I take pride in delivering them in good shape for standing trial, whenever possible."

I decided I needed a drink, and then I changed my mind in favor of a cup of coffee. As I walked down the street, leaving my pony at the rail back there, the wagon rolled past and went out of town ahead of me. I was still watching it, for no special reason, when Waco stepped from the alley behind me.

"Jim!" he said. "Turn around, Jim!"

I turned slowly. He was a little unsteady on his feet, standing there, maybe from my hitting him, maybe from drinking. I thought it was drinking. I hadn't hit him very hard. He'd had time for a couple of quick ones, and liquor always got to him fast.

"You sold us out, you damn traitor!" he cried. "You took sides with the law!"

"I never was against it," I said. "Not really."

"After everything I've done for you!" he said thickly. "I was going to make you a great man, Jim, greater than Longley or Hickok or any of them. With my brains and your size and speed, nothing could have stopped us! But you turned on me! Do you think you can do it alone? Is that what you're figuring, to leave me behind now that I've built you up to be somebody?"

"Waco," I said, "I never had any ambitions to be—"

"You and your medicine guns!" he sneered. "Let me tell you something. Those old guns are just something I picked up in a pawnshop. I spun a good yarn about them to give you confidence. You were on the edge, you needed a push in the right direction, and I knew once you started wearing a flash rig like that, with one killing under your belt already, somebody'd be bound to try you again, and we'd be on our way to fame. But as for their being Bill Longley's guns, don't make me laugh!"

I said, "Waco—"

"They's just metal and wood like any other guns!" he said. "And I'm going to prove it to you right now! I don't need you, Jim! I'm as good a man as you, even if you laugh at me and make jokes at my expense. . . . *Are you ready, Jim?*"

He was crouching, and I looked at him, Waco Smith, with whom I'd ridden up the trail and back. I saw that he was no good and I saw that he was dead. It didn't matter whose guns I was wearing, and all he'd really said was that he didn't know whose guns they were. But it didn't matter, they were my guns now, and he was just a little runt who never could shoot for shucks, anyway. He was dead, and so were the others, the ones who'd come after him, because they'd come, I knew that.

I saw them come to try me, one after the other, and I saw them go down before the big black guns, all except the last, the one I couldn't quite make out. Maybe it was Fenn and maybe it wasn't. . . .

I said, "To hell with you, Waco. I've got nothing against you, and I'm not going to fight you. Tonight or any other time."

I turned and walked away. I heard the sound of his gun behind me an instant before the bullet hit me. Then I wasn't hearing anything for a while. When I came to, I was in bed, and Martha Butcher was there.

"Jim!" she breathed. "Oh, Jim . . . . !"

She looked real worried, and kind of pretty, I thought, but of course I was half out of my head. She looked even prettier the day I asked her to marry me, some months later, but maybe I was a little out of my head that day, too. Old Man Butcher didn't like it a bit. It seems his fight with Martha had been about her cleaning up my place, and his ordering her to quit and stay away from that young troublemaker, as he'd called me after getting word of all the hell we'd raised up north after delivering his cattle.

He didn't like it, but he offered me a job, I suppose for Martha's sake. I thanked him and told him I was much obliged, but I'd just accepted an appointment as Deputy

U.S. Marshal. Seems like somebody had recommended me for the job, maybe Old Joe Fenn, maybe not. I got my old gun out of my bedroll and wore it tucked inside my belt when I thought I might need it. It was a funny thing how seldom I had any use for it, even wearing a badge. With that job, I was the first in the neighborhood to hear about Waco Smith. The news came from New Mexico Territory. Waco and a bunch had pulled a job over there, and a posse has trapped them in a box canyon and shot them to pieces.

I never wore the other guns again. After we moved into the old place, I hung them on the wall. It was right after I'd run against Billy Bates for sheriff and won that I came home to find them gone. Martha looked surprised when I asked about them.

"Why," she said, "I gave them to your friend, Mr. Williams. He said you'd sold them to him. Here's the money."

I counted the money, and it was a fair enough price for a pair of second-hand guns and holsters, but I hadn't met any Mr. Williams.

I started to say so, but Martha was still talking. She said, "He certainly had an odd first name, didn't he? Who'd christen anybody Long Williams? Not that he wasn't big enough. I guess he'd be as tall as you, wouldn't he, if he didn't have that trouble with his neck?"

"His neck?" I said.

"Why, yes," she said. "Didn't you notice when you talked to him, the way he kept his head cocked to the side. Like this."

She showed me how Long Williams had kept his head cocked to the side. She looked real pretty doing it, and I couldn't figure how I'd ever thought her plain, but maybe she'd changed. Or maybe I had. I kissed her and gave her back the gun money to buy something for herself, and went outside to think. Long Williams, William Longley. A man with a wry neck and a man who was hanged twice. It was kind of strange, to be sure, but after a time I decided it was just a coincidence. Some drifter riding by just saw the guns through the window and took a fancy to them.

I mean, if it had really been Bill Longley, if he was alive and had his guns back, we'd surely have heard of him by now down at the sheriff's office, and we never have.

The creator of secret agent Matthew Helm, Donald Hamilton was born in Sweden in 1916 and immigrated to the United States in 1924. Educated at the University of Chicago, he has been a full-time writer since 1946. Many of Hamilton's novels have been made into films, including The Big Country *(1957), starring Gregory Peck and Charlton Heston. The two worlds of the ruthless killer and the Western combine in the haunting "The Guns of William Longley."*

Thalia Corson should have died on the Brooklyn Bridge, but her husand's love called her back. Or was it love?

FIFTEEN

Clay-Shuttered Doors
Helen R. Hull

For months I have tried not to think about Thalia Corson. Anything may invoke her, with her langorous fragility, thin wrists and throat, her elusive face with its long eyelids. I can't quite remember her mouth. When I try to visualize her sharply I get soft pale hair, the lovely curve from her temple to chin, and eyes blue and intense. Her boy, Fletcher, has eyes like hers.

Today I came back to New York, and my taxi to an uptown hotel was held for a few minutes in Broadway traffic where the afternoon sunlight fused into a dazzle a great expanse of plateglass and elaborate show motor cars. The "Regal Eight"—Winchester Corson's establishment. I huddled as the taxi jerked ahead, in spite of knowledge that Winchester would scarcely peer out of that elegant setting into taxi cabs. I didn't wish to see him, nor would he care to see me. But the glimpse had started the whole affair churning again, and I went through it deliberately, hoping that it might have smoothed out into some rational explanation. Sometimes things do, if you leave them alone, like logs submerged in water that float up later, encrusted thickly. This affair won't add to itself. It stays unique and smooth, sliding through the rest of life without annexing a scrap of seaweed.

I suppose, for an outsider, it all begins with the moment on Brooklyn Bridge; behind that are the years of my friendship with Thalia. Our families had summer cottages on the Cape. She was just enough older, however, so that not until I had finished college did I catch up to any intimacy with her. She had married Winchester Corson, who at that time

249

fitted snugly into the phrase "a rising young man." During those first years, while his yeast sent up preliminary bubbles, Thalia continued to spend her summers near Boston, with Winchester coming for occasional weekends. Fletcher was, unintentionally, born there; he began his difficult existence by arriving as a seven-months baby. Two years later Thalia had a second baby to bring down with her. Those were the summers which gave my friendship for Thalia its sturdy roots. They made me wonder, too, why she had chosen Winchester Corson. He was personable enough; tall, with prominent dark eyes and full mouth under a neat mustache, restless hands, and an uncertain disposition. He could be a charming companion, sailing the catboat with dash, managing lobster parties on the shore; or he would, unaccountably, settle into a foggy grouch, when everyone—children and females particularly—was supposed to approach only on tiptoe, bearing burnt offerings. The last time he spent a fortnight there, before he moved the family to the new Long Island estate, I had my own difficulties with him. There had always been an undertone of sex in his attitude toward me, but I had thought "that's just his male conceit." That summer he was a nuisance, coming upon me with his insistent, messy kisses, usually with Thalia in the next room. They were the insulting kind of kisses that aren't at all personal, and I could have ended them fast enough if there hadn't been the complication of Thalia and my love for her. If I made Winchester angry he'd put an end to Thalia's relation to me. I didn't, anyway, want her to know what a fool he was. Of course she did know, but I thought then that I could protect her.

There are, I have decided, two ways with love. You can hold one love, knowing that, if it is a living thing, it must develop and change. That takes maturity, and care, and a consciousness of the other person. That was Thalia's way. Or you enjoy the beginning of love and, once you're past that, you have to hunt for a new love, because the excitement seems to be gone. Men like Winchester, who use all their brains on their jobs, never grow up; they go on thinking that preliminary stir and snap is love itself. Cut flowers, that was Winchester's idea, while to Thalia love was a tree.

But I said Brooklyn Bridge was the point at which the

affair had its start. It seems impossible to begin there, or anywhere, as I try to account for what happened. Ten years after the summer when Winchester made himself such a nuisance—that last summer the Corsons spent at the Cape—I went down at the end of the season for a week with Thalia and the children at the Long Island place. Winchester drove out for the weekend. The children were mournful because they didn't wish to leave the shore for school; a sharp September wind brought rain and fog down the Sound, and Winchester nourished all that Sunday a disagreeable grouch. I had seen nothing of them for most of the ten intervening years, as I had been first in France and then in China, after feature article stuff. The week had been pleasant: good servants, comfortable house, a half-moon of white beach below the drop of lawn; Thalia a stimulating listener, with Fletcher, a thin, eager boy of twelve, like her in his intensity of interest. Dorothy, a plump, pink child of ten, had no use for stories of French villages or Chinese temples. Nug, the wire-haired terrier, and her dolls were more immediate and convincing. Thalia was thin and noncommittal, except for her interest in what I had seen and done. I couldn't, for all my affection, establish any real contact. She spoke casually of the town house, of dinners she gave for Winchester, of his absorption in business affairs. But she was sheathed in polished aloofness and told me nothing of herself. She did say, one evening, that she was glad I was to be in New York that winter. Winchester, like his daughter Dorothy, had no interest in foreign parts once he had ascertained that I hadn't even seen the Chinese quarters of the motor company in which he was concerned. He had an amusing attitude toward me: careful indifference, no doubt calculated to put me in my place as no longer alluring. Thalia tried to coax him into listening to some of my best stories. "Tell him about the bandits, Mary"—but his sulkiness brought, after dinner, a casual explanation from her, untinged with apology. "He's working on an enormous project, a merging of several companies, and he's so soaked in it he can't come up for a breath."

In the late afternoon the maid set out high tea for us, before our departure for New York. Thalia suggested that perhaps one highball was enough if Winchester intended to drive over the wet roads. Win immediately mixed a second, asking if she had ever seen him in the least affected. "Be better for you than tea before a long damp drive, too." He clinked the ice in his glass. "Jazz you up a bit." Nug was begging for food and Thalia, bending to give him a corner of her sandwich, apparently did not hear Winchester. He looked about the room, a smug, owning look. The fire and candlelight shone in the heavy waxed rafters, made silver beads of the rain on the French windows. I watched him—heavier, more dominant, his prominent dark eyes and his lips sullen, as if the whiskey banked up his temper rather than appeased it.

Then Jim, the gardener, brought the car to the door; the children scrambled in. Dorothy wanted to take Nug, but her father said not if she wanted to sit with him and drive.

"How about chains, sir?" Jim held the umbrella for Thalia.

"Too damned noisy. Don't need them." Winchester slammed the door and slid under the wheel. Thalia and I, with Fletcher between us, sat comfortably in the rear.

"I like it better when Walter drives, don't you, Mother?" said Fletcher as we slid down the drive out to the road.

"Sh—Father likes to drive. And Walter likes Sunday off, too." Thalia's voice was cautious.

"It's too dark to see anything."

"I can see lots," announced Dorothy, whereupon Fletcher promptly turned the handle that pushed up the glass between the chauffeur's seat and the rear.

The heavy car ran smoothly over the wet narrow road, with an occasional rumble and flare of headlights as some car swung past. Not till we reached the turnpike was there much traffic. There Winchester had to slacken his speed for other shiny beetles slipping along through the rain. Sometimes he cut past a car, weaving back into line in the glaring teeth of a car rushing down on him, and Fletcher would turn inquiringly toward his mother. The gleaming, wet darkness and the smooth motion made me drowsy, and I paid little heed until we slowed in a congestion of cars at the approach to the bridge. Far below on the black river, spaced red and white stars suggested slow-moving tugs, and beyond, faint lights splintered in the rain hinted at the city.

"Let's look for the cliff dwellers, Mother."

Thalia leaned forward, her fine, sharp profile dimly outlined against the shifting background of arches, and Fletcher slipped to his feet, his arm about her neck. "There!"

We were reaching the New York end of the bridge, and I had a swift glimpse of their cliff dwellers—lights in massed buildings, like ancient camp fires along a receding mountain side. Just then Winchester nosed out of the slow line, Dorothy screamed, the light from another car tunnelled through our windows, the car trembled under the sudden grip of brakes, and like a crazy top spun sickeningly about, with a final thud against the stone abutment. A shatter of glass, a confusion of motor horns about us, a moment while the tautness of shock held me rigid.

Around me that periphery of turmoil—the usual recriminations, "what the hell you think you're doing?"—the shriek of a siren on an approaching motor cycle. Within the circle I tried to move across the narrow space of the car. Fletcher was crying; vaguely I knew that the door had swung open, that Thalia was crouching on her knees, the rain and the lights pouring on her head and shoulders; her hat was gone, her wide fur collar looked like a drenched and lifeless animal. "Hush, Fletcher." I managed to force movement into my stiff body. "Are you hurt? Thalia—" Then outside Winchester, with the bristling fury of panic, was trying to lift her drooping head. "Thalia! My God, you aren't hurt!" Someone focussed a searchlight on the car as Winchester got his arms about her and lifted her out through the shattered door.

Over the springing line of the stone arch I saw the cliff dwellers' fires and I thought as I scrambled out to follow Winchester, "She was leaning forward, looking at those, and that terrific spin of the car must have knocked her head on the door as it lurched open."

"Lay her down, man!" An important little fellow had rushed up, a doctor evidently. "Lay her down, you fool!" Someone threw down a robe, and Winchester, as if Thalia were a drowned feather, knelt with her, laid her there on the pavement. I was down beside her and the fussy little man also. She did look drowned, drowned in that beating sea of tumult, that terrific honking of motors, unwilling to stop an instant even for—was it death? Under the white glare of headlights her lovely face had the empty shallowness, the husklikeness of death. The little doctor had his pointed beard close to her breast; he lifted one of her long eyelids. "She's just fainted, eh, doctor?" Winchester's angry voice tore at him.

The little man rose slowly. "She your wife? I'm sorry. Death must have been instantaneous. A blow on the temple."

With a kind of roar Winchester was down there beside Thalia, lifting her, her head lolling against his shoulder, his face bent over her. "Thalia! Thalia! Do you hear? Wake up!" I think he even shook her in his baffled fright and rage. "Thalia, do you hear me? I want you to open your eyes. You weren't hurt. That was nothing." And then, "Dearest, you must!" and more words, frantic, wild words, mouthed close to her empty face. I touched his shoulder, sick with pity, but he staggered up to his feet, lifting her with him. Fletcher pressed shivering against me, and I turned for an instant to the child. Then I heard Thalia's voice, blurred and queer, "You called me, Win?" and Winchester's sudden, triumphant laugh. She was standing against his shoulder, still with that husklike face, but she spoke again, "You did call me?"

"Here, let's get out of this." Winchester was again the efficient, competent man of affairs. The traffic cops were shouting, the lines of cars began to move. Winchester couldn't start his motor. Something had smashed. His card and a few words left responsibility with an officer, and even as an ambulance shrilled up, he was helping Thalia into a taxi. "You take the children, will you?" to me, and "Get her another taxi, will you?" to the officer. He had closed the taxi door after himself, and was gone, leaving us to the waning curiosity of passing cars. As we rode off in a second taxi, I had a glimpse of the little doctor, his face incredulous, his beard wagging, as he spoke to the officer.

Dorothy was, characteristically, tearfully indignant that her father had left her to me. Fletcher was silent as we bumped along under the elevated tracks, but presently he tugged at my sleeve, and I heard his faint whisper. "What is it?" I asked.

"Is my mother really dead?" he repeated.

"Of course not, Fletcher. You saw her get into the cab with your father."

"Why didn't Daddy take us too?" wailed Dorothy, and I had to turn to her, although my nerves echoed her question.

The house door swung open even as the taxi bumped the curb, and the butler hurried out with an umbrella which we were too draggled to need.

"Mr. Corson instructed me to pay the man, madam." He led us into the hall, where a waiting maid popped the children at once into the tiny elevator.

"Will you wait for the elevator, madam? The library is one flight." The butler led me up the stairs, and I dropped into a low chair near the fire, vaguely aware of the long, narrow room, with discreet gold of the walls giving back light from soft lamps. "I'll tell Mr. Corson you have come."

"Is Mrs. Corson—does she seem all right?" I asked.

"Quite, madam. It was a fortunate accident, with no one hurt."

Well, perhaps it had addled my brain! I waited in a kind of numbness for Winchester to come.

Presently he strode in, his feet silent on the thick rugs.

"Sorry," he began, abruptly. "I wanted to look the children over. Not a scratch on them. You're all right, of course?"

"Oh, yes. But Thalia—"

"She won't even have a doctor. I put her straight to bed—she's so damned nervous, you know. Hot-water bottles—she was cold. I think she's asleep now. Said she'd see you in the morning. You'll stay here, of course." He swallowed in a gulp the whiskey he had poured. "Have some, Mary? Or would you like something hot?"

"No, thanks. If you're sure she's all right I'll go to bed."

"Sure?" His laugh was defiant. "Did that damn fool on the bridge throw a scare into you? He gave me a bad minute, I'll say. If that car hadn't cut in on me— I told Walter last week the brakes needed looking at. They shouldn't grab like that. Might have been serious."

"Since it wasn't—" I rose, wearily, watching him pour

amber liquid slowly into his glass—"if you'll have someone show me my room—"

"After Chinese bandits, a little skid ought not to matter to you." His prominent eyes gleamed hostilely at me; he wanted some assurance offered that the skidding wasn't his fault, that only his skill had saved all our lives.

"I can't see Thalia?" I said.

"She's asleep. Nobody can see her." His eyes moved coldly from my face, down to my muddy shoes. "Better give your clothes to the maid for a pressing. You're smeared quite a bit."

I woke early, with clear September sun at the windows of the room, with blue sky behind the sharp city contours beyond the windows. There was none too much time to make the morning train for Albany, where I had an engagement that day, an interview for an article. The maid who answered my ring insisted on serving breakfast to me in borrowed elegance of satin negligee. Mrs. Corson was resting, and would see me before I left. Something—the formality and luxury, the complicated household so unlike the old days at the Cape—accented the queer dread which had filtered all night through my dreams.

I saw Thalia for only a moment. The heavy silk curtains were drawn against the light and in the dimness her face seemed to gather shadows.

"Are you quite all right, Thalia?" I hesitated beside her bed, as if my voice might tear apart the veils of drowsiness in which she rested.

"Why, yes—" as if she wondered. Then she added, so low that I wasn't sure what I heard, "It is hard to get back in."

"What, Thalia?" I bent toward her.

"I'll be myself once I've slept enough." Her voice was clearer. "Come back soon, won't you, Mary?" Then her eyelids closed and her face merged into the shadows of the room. I tiptoed away, thinking she slept.

It was late November before I returned to New York. Free-lancing has a way of drawing herrings across your trail and, when I might have drifted back in early November, a younger sister wanted me to come home to Arlington for her marriage. I had written to Thalia, first a note of courtesy for my week with her, and then a letter begging for news. Like many people of charm, she wrote indifferent letters, stiff and childlike, lacking in her personal quality. Her brief reply was more unsatisfactory than usual. The children were away in school, lots of cold rainy weather, everything was going well. At the end, in writing unlike hers, as if she scribbled the line in haste, "I am lonely. When are you coming?" I answered that I'd show up as soon as the wedding was over.

The night I reached Arlington was rainy, too, and I insisted upon a taxi equipped with chains. My brother thought that amusing, and at dinner gave the family an exaggerated account of my caution. I tried to offer him some futile sisterly advice and, to point up my remarks, told about that drive in from Long Island with the Corsons. I had never spoken of it before; I found that an inexplicable inhibition kept me from making much of a story.

"Well, nothing happened, did it?" Richard was triumphant.

"A great deal might have," I insisted. "Thalia was stunned, and I was disagreeably startled."

"Thalia was stunned, was she?" An elderly cousin of ours from New Jersey picked out that item. I saw her fitting it into some pigeon hole, but she said nothing until late that evening when she stopped at the door of my room.

"Have you seen Thalia Corson lately?" she asked.

"I haven't been in New York since September."

She closed the door and lowered her voice, a kind of avid curiosity riding astride the decorous pity she expressed.

"I called there, one day last week. I didn't know what was the matter with her. I hadn't heard of that accident."

I waited, an old antagonism for my proper cousin blurring the fear that shot up through my thoughts.

"Thalia was always *individual*, of course." She used the word like a reproach. "But she had *savoir faire*. But now she's—well—*queer*. Do you suppose her head was affected?"

"How is she queer?"

"She looks miserable, too. Thin and white."

"But how—"

"I am telling you, Mary. She was quite rude. First she didn't come down for ever so long, although I sent up word that I'd come up to her room if she was resting. Then her whole manner—well, I was really offended. She scarcely heard a word I said to her, just sat with her back to a window so I couldn't get a good look at her. When I said, 'You don't look like yourself,' she actually sneered. 'Myself?' she said. 'How do you know?' Imagine! I tried to chatter along as if I noticed nothing. I flatter myself I can manage awkward moments rather well. But Thalia sat there and I am sure she muttered under her breath. Finally I rose to go and I said, meaning well, 'You'd better take a good rest. You look half dead.' Mary, I wish you'd seen the look she gave me! Really I was frightened. Just then their dog came in, you know, Dorothy's little terrier. Thalia used to be silly about him. Well, she actually tried to hide in the folds of the curtain, and I don't wonder! The dog was terrified at her. He crawled on his belly out of the room. Now she must have been cruel to him if he acts like that. I think Winchester should have a specialist. I didn't know how to account for any of it; but of course a blow on the head can affect a person."

Fortunately my mother interrupted us just then, and I didn't, by my probable rudeness, give my cousin reason to suppose that the accident had affected me, too. I sifted through her remarks and decided they might mean only that Thalia found her more of a bore than usual. As for Nug, perhaps he retreated from the cousin! During the next few days the house had so much wedding turmoil that she found a chance only for a few more dribbles: one that Thalia had given up all her clubs—she had belonged to several—the other that she had sent the children to boarding schools instead of keeping them at home. "Just when her husband is doing so well, too!"

I was glad when the wedding party had departed, and I could plan to go back to New York. Personally I think a low-caste Chinese wedding is saner and more interesting than a modern American affair. My cousin "should think I could stay home with the family," and "couldn't we go to New York together, if I insisted upon gadding off?" We couldn't. I saw to that. She hoped that I'd look up Thalia. Maybe I could advise Winchester about a specialist.

I did telephone as soon as I got in. That sentence "I am lonely," in her brief note kept recurring. Her voice sounded thin and remote, a poor connection, I thought. She was sorry. She was giving a dinner for Winchester that evening. The next day?

I had piles of proof to wade through that next day, and it was late afternoon when I finally went to the Corson house. The butler looked doubtful but I insisted, and he left me in the hall while he went off with my card. He returned, a little smug in his message: Mrs. Corson was resting and had left word she must not be disturbed. Well, you can't protest to a perfect butler, and I started down the steps, indignant, when a car stopped in front of the house, a liveried chauffeur opened the door, and Winchester emerged. He glanced at me in the twilight and extended an abrupt hand.

"Would Thalia see you?" he asked.

"No." For a moment I hoped he might convoy me past the butler. "Isn't she well? She asked me to come to-day."

"I hoped she'd see you." Winchester's hand smoothed at his little mustache. "She's just tired from her dinner last night. She overexerted herself, was quite the old Thalia." He looked at me slowly in the dusk, and I had a brief feeling that he was really looking at me, no, *for* me, for the first time in all our meetings, as if he considered me without relation to himself for once. "Come in again, will you?" He thrust away whatever else he thought of saying. "Thalia really would like to see you. Can I give you a lift?"

"No, thanks. I need a walk." As I started off I knew the moment had just missed some real significance. If I had ventured a question—but, after all, what could I ask him? He had said that Thalia was "just tired." That night I sent a note to her, saying I had called and asking when I might see her.

She telephoned me the next day. Would I come in for Thanksgiving? The children would be home, and she wanted an old-fashioned day, everything but the sleigh ride New York couldn't furnish. Dinner would be at six, for the children; perhaps I could come in early. I felt a small grievance at being put off for almost a week, but I promised to come.

That was the week I heard gossip about Winchester, in the curious devious way of gossip. Atlantic City, and a gaudy lady. Someone having an inconspicuous fortnight of convalescence there had seen them. I wasn't surprised, except perhaps that Winchester chose Atlantic City. Thalia was too fine; he couldn't grow up to her. I wondered how much she knew. She must, years ago, with her sensitiveness, have discovered that Winchester was stationary so far as love went and, being stationary himself, was inclined to move the object toward which he directed his passion.

On Thursday, as I walked across Central Park, gaunt and deserted in the chilly afternoon light, I decided that Thalia probably knew more about Winchester's affairs than gossip had given me. Perhaps that was why she had sent the children away. He had always been conventionally discreet, but discretion would be a tawdry coin among Thalia's shining values.

I was shown up to the nursery, with a message from Thalia that she would join me there soon. Fletcher seemed glad to see me, in a shy, excited way, and stood close to my chair while Dorothy wound up her phonograph for a dance record and pirouetted about us with her doll.

"Mother keeps her door tight locked all the time," whispered Fletcher doubtfully. "We can't go in. This morning I knocked and knocked but no one answered."

"Do you like your school?" I asked cheerfully.

"I like my home better." His eyes, so like Thalia's with their long, arched lids, had young bewilderment under their lashes.

"See me!" called Dorothy. "Watch me do this!"

While she twirled I felt Fletcher's thin body stiffen against my arm, as if a kind of panic froze him. Thalia stood in the doorway. Was the boy afraid of her? Dorothy wasn't. She cried, "See me, Mother! Look at me!" and in her lusty confusion, I had a moment to look at Thalia before she greeted me. She was thin, but she had always been that. She did not heed Dorothy's shrieks, but watched Fletcher, a kind of slanting dread on her white, proud face. I had thought, that week on Long Island, that she shut herself away from me, refusing to restore the intimacy of ten years earlier. But now a stiff loneliness hedged her as if she were rimmed in ice and

snow. She smiled. "Dear Mary," she said. At the sound of
her voice I lost my slightly cherished injury that she had
refused earlier to see me. "Let's go down to the library," she
went on. "It's almost time for the turkey." I felt Fletcher
break his intent watchfulness with a long sigh, and as
the children went ahead of us, I caught at Thalia's arm.
"Thalia—" She drew away, and her arm, under the soft
flowing sleeve of dull blue stuff, was so slight it seemed brittle. I thought suddenly that she must have chosen that gown
because it concealed so much beneath its lovely embroidered folds. "You aren't well, Thalia. What *is* it?"

"Well enough! Don't fuss about me." And even as I
stared reproachfully she seemed to gather vitality, so that
the dry pallor of her face became smooth ivory and her eyes
were no longer hollow and distressed. "Come."

The dinner was amazingly like one of our old holidays.
Winchester wore his best mood, the children were delighted
and happy. Thalia, under the gold flames of the tall black
candles, was a gracious and lovely hostess. I almost forgot
my troublesome anxiety, wondering whether my imagination hadn't been playing me tricks.

We had coffee by the library fire and some of Winchester's old Chartreuse. Then he insisted upon exhibiting
his new radio. Thalia demurred, but the children begged for
a concert. "This is their party, Tally!" Winchester opened
the doors of the old teakwood cabinet which housed the
apparatus. Thalia sank back into the shadows of a wing
chair, and I watched her over my cigarette. Off guard, she
had relaxed into strange apathy. Was it the firelight or my
unaccustomed Chartreuse? Her features seemed blurred as
if a clumsy hand trying to trace a drawing made uncertain
outlines. Strange groans and whirrs from the radio.

"Win, I can't stand it!" Her voice dragged from some
great distance. "Not tonight." She swayed to her feet, her
hands restless under the loose sleeves.

"Static," growled Winchester. "Wait a minute."

"No!" Again it was as if vitality flowed into her. "Come,
children. You have had your party. Time to go upstairs. I'll
go with you."

They were well trained, I thought. Kisses for their father, a
curtsy from Dorothy for me, and a grave little hand ex-

tended by Fletcher. Then Winchester came toward the fire as the three of them disappeared.

"You're good for Thalia," he said, in an undertone. "She's—well, what do you make of her?"

"Why?" I fenced, unwilling to indulge him in my vague anxieties.

"You saw how she acted about the radio. She has whims like that. Funny, she was herself at dinner. Last week she gave a dinner for me, important affair, pulled it off brilliantly. Then she shuts herself up and won't open her door for days. I can't make it out. She's thin—"

"Have you had a doctor?" I asked, banally.

"That's another thing. She absolutely refuses. Made a fool of me when I brought one here. Wouldn't unlock her door. Says she just wants to rest. But—" he glanced toward the door—"do you know that fool on the bridge—that little runt? The other night, I swear I saw him rushing down the steps as I came home. Thalia just laughed when I asked about it."

Something clicked in my thoughts, a quick suspicion, drawing a parallel between her conduct and that of people I had seen in the East. Was it some drug? That lethargy, and the quick spring into vitality? Days behind a closed door—

"I wish you'd persuade her to go off for a few weeks. I'm frightfully pressed just now, in an important business matter, but if she'd go off—maybe you'd go with her?"

"Where, Winchester?" We both started, with the guilt of conspirators. Thalia came slowly into the room. "Where shall I go? Would you suggest—Atlantic City?"

"Perhaps. Although some place farther south this time of year—" Winchester's imperturbability seemed to me far worse than some slight sign of embarrassment; it marked him as so rooted in successful deceit whether Thalia's inquiry were innocent or not. "If Mary would go with you. I can't get away just now."

"I shall not go anywhere until your deal goes through. Then—" Thalia seated herself again in the wing chair. The hand she lifted to her cheek, fingers just touching her temple beneath the soft drift of hair, seemed transparent against the firelight. "Have you told Mary about your deal? Winchester plans to be the most important man on Auto-

mobile Row." Was there mockery in her tone? "I can't tell
you the details, but he's buying out all the rest."

"Don't be absurd. Not all of them. It's a big merging of
companies, that's all."

"We entertain the lords at dinner, and in some mysterious
way that smooths the merging. It makes a wife almost necessary."

"Invite Mary to the next shebang, and let her see how
well you do it." Winchester was irritated. "For all your scoff-
ing, there's as much politics to being president of such a
concern as of the United States."

"Yes, I'll invite Mary. Then she'll see that you don't really
want to dispense with me—yet."

"Good God, I meant for a week or two."

As Winchester, lighting a cigarette, snapped the head
from several matches in succession, I moved my chair a little
backward, distressed. There was a thin wire of significance
drawn so taut between the two that I felt at any moment it
might splinter in my face.

"It's so lucky—" malice flickered on her thin face—"that
you weren't hurt in that skid on the bridge, Mary.
Winchester would just have tossed you in the river to conceal your body."

"If you're going over that again!" Winchester strode out
of the room. As Thalia turned her head slightly to watch
him, her face and throat had the taut rigidity of pain so great
that it congeals the nerves.

I was silent. With Thalia I had never dared intrude except
when she admitted me. In another moment she too had
risen. "You'd better go home, Mary," she said, slowly. "I
might tell you things you wouldn't care to live with."

I tried to touch her hand, but she retreated. If I had been
wiser or more courageous, I might have helped her. I shall
always have that regret, and that can't be much better to live
with than whatever she might have told me. All I could say
was stupidly, "Thalia, if there's anything I can do! You know
I love you."

"Love? That's a strange word," she said, and her laugh in
the quiet room was like the shrilling of a grasshopper on a
hot afternoon. "One thing I will tell you." (She stood now
on the stairway above me.) "Love has no power. It never

shouts out across great space. Only fear and self-desire are strong."

Then she had gone, and the butler appeared silently, to lead me to the little dressing room.

"The car is waiting for you, madam," he assured me, opening the door. I didn't want it, but Winchester was waiting, too, hunched angrily in a corner.

"That's the way she acts," he began. "Now you've seen her I'll talk about it. Thalia never bore grudges, you know that."

"It seems deeper than a grudge," I said cautiously.

"That reference to the—the accident. That's a careless remark I made. I don't even remember just what I said. Something entirely inconsequential. Just that it was damned lucky no one was hurt when I was putting this merger across. You know if it'd got in the papers it would have queered me. Wrecking my own car—there's always a suspicion you've been drinking. She picked it up and won't drop it. It's like a fixed idea. If you can suggest something. I want her to see a nerve specialist. What does she do behind that locked door?"

"What about Atlantic City?" I asked, abruptly. I saw his dark eyes bulge, trying to ferret out my meaning, there in the dusky interior of the car.

"A week there with you might do her good." That was all he would say, and I hadn't courage enough to accuse him, even in Thalia's name.

"At least you'll try to see her again," he said, as the car stopped in front of my apartment house.

I couldn't sleep that night. I felt that just over the edge of my squirming thoughts there lay clear and whole the meaning of it all, but I couldn't reach past thought. And then, stupidly enough, I couldn't get up the next day. Just a feverish cold, but the doctor insisted on a week in bed and subdued me with warnings about influenza.

I had begun to feel steady enough on my feet to consider venturing outside my apartment when the invitation came, for a formal dinner at the Corson's. Scrawled under the engraving was a line, "Please come. T." I sent a note, explaining that I had been ill, and that I should come—the dinner was a fortnight away—unless I stayed too wobbly.

I meant that night to arrive properly with the other guests, but my watch, which had never before done anything except lose a few minutes a day, had gained an unsuspected hour. Perhaps the hands stuck—perhaps— Well, I was told I was early, Thalia was dressing, and only the children, home for the Christmas holidays, were available. So I went again to the nursery. Dorothy was as plump and unconcerned as ever, but Fletcher had a strained, listening effect and he looked too thin and white for a little boy. They were having their supper on a small table, and Fletcher kept going to the door, looking out into the hall. "Mother promised to come up," he said.

The maid cleared away their dishes, and Dorothy, who was in a beguiling mood, chose to sit on my lap and entertain me with stories. One was about Nug the terrier; he had been sent out to the country because Mother didn't like him any more.

"I think," interrupted Fletcher, "she likes him, but he has a queer notion about her."

"She doesn't like him," repeated Dorothy. Then she dismissed that subject, and Fletcher too, for curiosity about the old silver chain I wore. I didn't notice that the boy had slipped away, but he must have gone down stairs; for presently his fingers closed over my wrist, like a frightened bird's claw, and I turned to see him, trembling, his eyes dark with terror. He couldn't speak but he clawed at me, and I shook Dorothy from my knees and let him pull me out to the hall.

"What is it, Fletcher?" He only pointed down the stairway, toward his mother's door, and I fled down those stairs. *What* had the child seen?

"The door wasn't locked—" he gasped behind me—"I opened it very still and went in—"

I pushed it ajar. Thalia sat before her dressing table, with the threefold mirrors reiterating like a macabre symphony her rigid, contorted face. Her gown, burnished blue and green like peacock's feathers, sheathed her gaudily, and silver, blue, and green chiffon clouded her shoulders. Her hands clutched at the edge of the dressing table. For an instant I could not move, thrust through with a terror like the

265

boy's. Then I stumbled across the room. Before I reached her, the mirrors echoed her long shudder, her eyelids dragged open, and I saw her stare at my reflection wavering toward her. Then her hands relaxed, moved quickly toward the crystal jars along the heavy glass of the table and, without a word, she leaned softly forward, to draw a scarlet line along her white lips.

"How cold it is in here," I said, stupidly, glancing toward the windows, where the heavy silk damask, drawn across, lay in motionless folds. "Fletcher said—" I was awkward, an intruder.

"He startled me." Her voice came huskily. She rouged her hollow cheeks. It was as if she drew another face for herself. "I didn't have time to lock the door." Then turning, she sought him out, huddled at the doorway, like a moth on a pin of fear. "It wasn't nice of you, Son. It's all right now. You see?" She rose, drawing her lovely scarf over her shoulders. "You should never open closed doors." She blew him a kiss from her finger tips. "Now run along and forget you were so careless."

The icy stir of air against my skin had ceased. I stared at her, my mind racing back over what I knew of various drugs and the stigmata of their victims. But her eyes were clear and undilated, a little piteous. "This," she said, "is the last time. I can't endure it." And then, with that amazing flood of vitality, as if a sudden connection had been made and current flowed again, "Come, Mary. It is time we were down stairs."

I thought Fletcher peered over the railing as we went down. But a swift upward glance failed to detect him.

The dinner itself I don't remember definitely except that it glittered and sparkled, moving with slightly alcoholic wit through elaborate courses, while I sat like an abashed poor relation at a feast, unable to stop watching Thalia, wondering whether my week of fever had given me a tendency to hallucinations. At the end a toast was proposed, to Winchester Corson and his extraordinary success. "It's done, then?" Thalia's gaiety had sudden malice—as she looked across at Winchester, seating himself after a slightly pompous speech. "Sealed and cemented forever?"

"Thanks to his charming wife, too," cried a plump, bald man, waving his glass. "A toast to Mrs. Corson!"

Thalia rose, her rouge like flecked scarlet on white paper. One hand drew her floating scarf about her throat, and her painted lips moved without a sound. There was an instant of agitated discomfort, as the guests felt their mood broken so abruptly, into which her voice pierced, thin, high. "I—deserve—such a toast—"

I pushed back my chair and reached her side.

"I'll take her—" I saw Winchester's face, wine-flushed, angry rather than concerned. "Come, Thalia."

"Don't bother. I'll be all right—now." But she moved ahead of me so swiftly that I couldn't touch her. I thought she tried to close her door against me, but I was too quick for that. The silver candelabra still burned above the mirrors. "Mary!" Her voice was low again as she spoke a telephone number. "Tell him *at once.*" She stood away from me, her face a white mask with spots of scarlet, her peacock dress ashimmer. I did as I was bid and when I had said, "Mrs. Corson wishes you at once," there was an emptiness where a man's voice had come which suggested a sudden leap out of a room somewhere.

"I can never get in again!" Her fingers curled under the chiffon scarf. "Never! The black agony of fighting back— If he—" She bent her head, listening. "Go down to the door and let him in," she said.

I crept down the stairs. Voices from the drawing-room. Winchester was seeing the party through. Almost as I reached the door and opened it I found him there: the little doctor with the pointed beard. He brushed past me up the stairs. He knew the way, then! I was scarcely surprised to find Thalia's door fast shut when I reached it. Behind it came not a sound. Fletcher, like an unhappy sleepwalker, his eyes heavy, slipped down beside me, clinging to my hand. I heard farewells, churring of taxis and cars. Then Winchester came up the stairs.

"She's shut you out?" He raised his fist and pounded on the door. "I'm going to stop this nonsense!"

"I sent for a doctor," I said. "He's in there."

"Is it—" his face was puffy and gray—"that same fool?"

Then the door opened, and the man confronted us.

"It is over," he said.

"What have you done to her?" Winchester lunged toward the door, but the little man's lifted hand had dignity enough somehow to stop him.

"She won't come back again." He spoke slowly. "You may look if you care to."

"She's dead?"

"She died—months ago. There on the bridge. But you called to her, and she thought you wanted—*her.*"

Winchester thrust him aside and strode into the room. I dared one glance and saw only pale hair shining on the pillow. Then Fletcher flung himself against me, sobbing, and I knelt to hold him close against the fear we both felt.

What Winchester saw I never knew. He hurled himself past us, down the stairs. And Thalia was buried with the coffin lid fast closed under the flowers.

A publisher's granddaughter, Helen Hull said she can't "remember when I did not intend to write." Born in Michigan in about 1889, she was educated at Michigan State College, the University of Michigan, and the University of Chicago. Her mystery novel, A Tapping on the Wall, *won a college writing prize in 1960. Her best known work is the story "Clay-Shuttered Doors."*

No one wants to die unknown.

SIXTEEN

The Stranger
Ambrose Bierce

A man stepped out of the darkness into the little illuminated circle about our failing campfire and seated himself
upon a rock.

"You are not the first to explore this region," he said,
gravely.

Nobody controverted his statement; he was himself proof
of its truth, for he was not of our party and must have been
somewhere near when we camped. Moreover, he must
have companions not far away; it was not a place where one
would be living or traveling alone. For more than a week we
had seen, besides ourselves and our animals, only such living things as rattlesnakes and horned toads. In an Arizona
desert one does not long coexist with only such creatures as
these: one must have pack animals, supplies, arms—"an
outfit." And all these imply comrades. It was perhaps a
doubt as to what manner of men this unceremonious
stranger's comrades might be, together with something in
his words interpretable as a challenge, that caused every
man of our half-dozen "gentlemen adventurers" to rise to
a sitting posture and lay his hand upon a weapon—an act
signifying, in that time and place, a policy of expectation.
The stranger gave the matter no attention and began again
to speak in the same deliberate, uninflected monotone in
which he had delivered his first sentence:

"Thirty years ago Ramon Gallegos, William Shaw,
George W. Kent and Berry Davis, all of Tucson, crossed the
Santa Catalina mountains and traveled due west, as nearly
as the configuration of the country permitted. We were
prospecting and it was our intention, if we found nothing, to

269

push through to the Gila River at some point near Big Bend, where we understood there was a settlement. We had a good outfit but no guide—just Ramon Gallegos, William Shaw, George W. Kent and Berry Davis.

The man repeated the names slowly and distinctly, as if to fix them in the memories of his audience, every member of which was now attentively observing him, but with a slackened apprehension regarding his possible companions somewhere in the darkness that seemed to enclose us like a black wall; in the manner of this volunteer historian was no suggestion of an unfriendly purpose. His act was rather that of a harmless lunatic than an enemy. We were not so new to the country as not to know that the solitary life of many a plainsman had a tendency to develop eccentricities of conduct and character not always easily distinguishable from mental aberration. A man is like a tree: in a forest of his fellows he will grow as straight as his generic and individual nature permits; alone in the open, he yields to the deforming stresses and torsions that environ him. Some such thoughts were in my mind as I watched the man from the shadow of my hat, pulled low to shut out the firelight. A witless fellow, no doubt, but what could he be doing there in the heart of a desert?

Having undertaken to tell this story, I wish that I could describe the man's appearance; that would be a natural thing to do. Unfortunately, and somewhat strangely, I find myself unable to do so with any degree of confidence, for afterward no two of us agreed as to what he wore and how he looked; and when I try to set down my own impressions they elude me. Anyone can tell some kind of story; narration is one of the elemental powers of the race. But the talent for description is a gift.

Nobody having broken silence the visitor went on to say:

"This country was not then what it is now. There was not a ranch between the Gila and the Gulf. There was a little game here and there in the mountains, and near the infrequent waterholes grass enough to keep our animals from starvation. If we should be so fortunate as to encounter no Indians we might get through. But within a week the purpose of the expedition had altered from discovery of wealth to preservation of life. We had gone too far to go back, for what was ahead could be no worse than what was behind; so we pushed on, riding by night to avoid Indians and the intolerable heat, and concealing ourselves by day as best we could. Sometimes, having exhausted our supply of wild meat and emptied our casks, we were days without food or drink; then a water-hole or a shallow pool in the bottom of an arroyo so restored our strength and sanity that we were able to shoot some of the wild animals that sought it also. Sometimes it was a bear, sometimes an antelope, a coyote, a cougar—that was as God pleased; all were food.

"One morning as we skirted a mountain range, seeking a practicable pass, we were attacked by a band of Apaches who had followed our trail up a gulch—it is not far from here. Knowing that they outnumbered us ten to one, they took none of their usual cowardly precautions, but dashed upon us at a gallop, firing and yelling. Fighting was out of the question: we urged our feeble animals up the gulch as far as there was footing for a hoof, then threw ourselves out of our saddles and took to the chaparral on one of the slopes, abandoning our entire outfit to the enemy. But we retained our rifles, every man—Ramon Gallegos, William Shaw, George W. Kent and Berry Davis."

"Same old crowd," said the humorist of our party. He was an Eastern man, unfamiliar with the decent observances of social intercourse. A gesture of disapproval from our leader silenced him and the stranger proceeded with his tale:

"The savages dismounted also, and some of them ran up the gulch beyond the point at which we had left it, cutting off further retreat in that direction and forcing us on up the side. Unfortunately the chaparral extended only a short distance up the slope, and as we came into the open ground above we took the fire of a dozen rifles; but Apaches shoot badly when in a hurry, and God so willed it that none of us fell. Twenty yards up the slope, beyond the edge of the brush, were vertical cliffs, in which, directly in front of us, was a narrow opening. Into that we ran, finding ourselves in a cavern about as large as an ordinary room in a house. Here for a time we were safe: a single man with a repeating rifle could defend the entrance against all the Apaches in

271

the land. But against hunger and thirst we had no defense. Courage we still had, but hope was a memory.

"Not one of those Indians did we afterward see, but by the smoke and glare of their fires in the gulch we knew that by day and by night they watched with ready rifles in the edge of the bush—knew that if we made a sortie not a man of us would live to take three steps into the open. For three days, watching in turn, we held out before our suffering became insupportable. Then—it was the morning of the fourth day—Ramon Gallegos said:

"'Señores, I know not well of the good God and what please him. I have live without religion, and I am not acquaint with that of you. Pardon, señores, if I shock you, but for me the time is come to beat the game of the Apache.'

"He knelt upon the rock floor of the cave and pressed his pistol against his temple. 'Madre de Dios,' he said, 'comes now the soul of Ramon Gallegos.'

"And so he left us—William Shaw, George W. Kent and Berry Davis.

"I was the leader: it was for me to speak.

"'He was a brave man,' I said—'he knew when to die, and how. It is foolish to go mad from thirst and fall by Apache bullets, or be skinned alive—it is in bad taste. Let us join Ramon Gallegos.'

"'That is right,' said William Shaw.

"'That is right,' said George W. Kent.

"I straightened the limbs of Ramon Gallegos and put a handkerchief over his face. Then William Shaw said: 'I should like to look like that—a little while.'

"And George W. Kent said that he felt that way, too.

"'It shall be so,' I said: 'the red devils will wait a week. William Shaw and George W. Kent, draw and kneel.'

"They did so and I stood before them.

"'Almighty God, our Father,' said I.

"'Almighty God, our Father,' said William Shaw.

"'Almighty God, our Father,' said George W. Kent.

"'Forgive us our sins,' said I.

"'Forgive us our sins,' said they.

"'And receive our souls.'

"'And receive our souls.'

"'Amen!'

"'Amen!'

"I laid them beside Ramon Gallegos and covered their faces."

There was a quick commotion on the opposite side of the campfire: one of our party had sprung to his feet, pistol in hand.

"And you!" he shouted—"*you* dared to escape?—you dare to be alive? You cowardly hound, I'll send you to join them if I hang for it!"

But with the leap of a panther the captain was upon him, grasping his wrist. "Hold it in, Sam Yountsey, hold it in!"

We were now all upon our feet—except the stranger, who sat motionless and apparently inattentive. Someone seized Yountsey's other arm.

"Captain," I said, "there is something wrong here. This fellow is either a lunatic or merely a liar—just a plain, every-day liar whom Yountsey has no call to kill. If this man was of that party it had five members, one of whom—probably himself—he has not named."

"Yes," said the captain, releasing the insurgent, who sat down, "there is something—unusual. Years ago four dead bodies of white men, scalped and shamefully mutilated, were found about the mouth of that cave. They are buried there; I have seen the graves—we shall all see them to-morrow."

The stranger rose, standing tall in the light of the expiring fire, which in our breathless attention to his story we had neglected to keep going.

"There were four," he said—"Ramon Gallegos, William Shaw, George W. Kent and Berry Davis."

With this reiterated roll-call of the dead he walked into the darkness and we saw him no more.

At that moment one of our party, who had been on guard, strode in among us, rifle in hand and somewhat excited.

"Captain," he said, "for the last half-hour three men have been standing out there on the mesa." He pointed in the direction taken by the stranger. "I could see them distinctly, for the moon is up, but as they had no guns and I had them covered with mine I thought it was their move. They have made none, but, damn it! they have got on to my nerves."

"Go back to your post, and stay till you see them again," said the captain. "The rest of you lie down again, or I'll kick you all into the fire."

The sentinel obediently withdrew, swearing, and did not return. As we were arranging our blankets the fiery Yountsey said: "I beg your pardon, Captain, but who the devil do you take them to be?"

"Ramon Gallegos, William Shaw and George W. Kent."

"But how about Berry Davis? I ought to have shot him."

"Quite needless; you couldn't have made him any deader. Go to sleep."

Ambrose Bierce was one of the first American short story writers to gain international fame. Born in Ohio in 1842, he served with distinction in the Union army during the Civil War. As a newspaperman for the San Francisco Examiner, *the handsome, fearless Bierce was noted for his bitter remarks (for instance, "Friendship—a barque that will hold two in fair weather but only one in foul) collected in* The Devil's Dictionary *(1906), his grim tales of the Civil War* Tales of Soldiers and Civilians *(1891), and such horrifying stories as "The Damned Thing" and the classic "An Occurrence at Owl Creek Bridge." He vanished somewhere in Mexico in 1914; his fate is unknown to this day.*

Perry Moore was a scientist, an objective researcher into fraudulent psychic mediums—until a voice from his own past spoke out of the darkness.

SEVENTEEN

Night-Side
Joyce Carol Oates

6 *February 1887. Quincy, Massachusetts. Montague House.*

Disturbing experience at Mrs. A——'s home yesterday evening. Few theatrics—comfortable though rather pathetically shabby surroundings—an only mildly sinister atmosphere (especially in contrast to the Walpurgis Night presented by that shameless charlatan in Portsmouth: the Dwarf Eustace who presumed to introduce me to Swedenborg himself, under the erroneous impression that I am a member of the Church of the New Jerusalem—*I!*). Nevertheless I came away disturbed, and my conversation with Dr. Moore afterward, at dinner, though dispassionate and even, at times, a bit flippant, did not settle my mind. Perry Moore is of course a hearty materialist, an Aristotelian-Spencerian with a love of good food and drink, and an appreciation of the more nonsensical vagaries of life; when in his company I tend to support that general view, as I do at the University as well—for there is a terrific pull in my nature toward the gregarious that I cannot resist. (That I do not wish to resist.) Once I am alone with my thoughts, however, I am accursed with doubts about my own position and nothing seems more precarious than my intellectual "convictions."

The more hardened members of our Society, like Perry Moore, are apt to put the issue bluntly: Is Mrs. A—— of Quincy a conscious or unconscious fraud? The conscious frauds are relatively easy to deal with; once discovered, they prefer to erase themselves from further consideration. The unconscious frauds are not, in a sense, "frauds" at all. It would certainly be difficult to prove criminal intention. Mrs. A—— for instance, does not accept money or gifts so far as we have been able to determine, and both Perry Moore and I noted her courteous but firm refusal of the Judge's offer to send her and her husband (presumably ailing?) on holiday to England in the spring. She is a mild, self-effacing, rather stocky woman in her mid-fifties who wears her hair parted in the center, like several of my maiden aunts, and whose sole item of adornment was an old-fashioned cameo brooch; her black dress had the appearance of having been homemade, though it was attractive enough, and freshly ironed. According to the Society's records she has been a practicing medium now for six years. Yet she lives, still, in an undistinguished section of Quincy, in a neighborhood of modest frame dwellings. The A——s' house is in fairly good condition, especially considering the damage routinely done by our winters, and the only room we saw, the parlor, is quite ordinary, with overstuffed chairs and the usual cushions and a monstrous horsehair sofa and, of course, the oaken table; the atmosphere would have been so conventional as to have seemed disappointing had not Mrs. A—— made an attempt to brighten it, or perhaps to give it a glamourously occult air, by hanging certain watercolors about the room. (She claims that the watercolors were "done" by one of her contact spirits, a young Iroquois girl who died in the seventeen seventies of smallpox. They are touchingly garish—mandalas and triangles and stylized eyeballs and even a transparent Cosmic Man with Indian-black hair.)

At last night's sitting there were only three persons in addition to Mrs. A——. Judge T—— of the New York State Supreme Court (now retired); Dr. Moore; and I, Jarvis Williams. Dr. Moore and I came out from Cambridge under the aegis of the Society for Psychical Research in order to make a preliminary study of the kind of mediumship Mrs. A—— affects. We did not bring a stenographer along this time though Mrs. A—— indicated her willingness to have the sitting transcribed; she struck me as being rather warmly cooperative, and even interested in our formal procedures, though Perry Moore remarked afterward at dinner that she had struck him as "noticeably reluctant." She was, however, flustered at the start of the séance and for a while it seemed as if we and the Judge might have made the trip for nothing. (She kept waving her plump hands about like an embarrassed hostess, apologizing for the fact that the spirits were evidently in a "perverse uncommunicative mood tonight.")

She did go into a trance eventually, however. The four of us were seated about the heavy round table from approximately 6:50 P.M. to 9:00 P.M. For nearly forty-five minutes Mrs. A—— made abortive attempts to contact her Chief Communicator and then slipped abruptly into trance (dramatically, in fact: her eyes rolled back in her head in a manner that alarmed me at first), and a personality named Webley appeared. "Webley's" voice appeared to be coming from several directions during the course of the sitting. At all times it was at least three yards from Mrs. A——; despite the semi-dark of the parlor I believe I could see the woman's mouth and throat clearly enough, and I could not detect any obvious signs of ventriloquism. (Perry Moore, who is more experienced than I in psychical research, and rather more casual about the whole phenomenon, claims he has witnessed feats of ventriloquism that would make poor Mrs. A—— look quite shabby in comparison.) "Webley's" voice was raw, singsong, peculiarly disturbing. At times it was shrill and at other times so faint as to be nearly inaudible. Something brattish about it. Exasperating. "Webley" took care to pronounce his final g's in a self-conscious manner, quite unlike Mrs. A——. (Which could be, of course, a deliberate ploy.)

This Webley is one of Mrs. A——'s most frequent manifesting spirits, though he is not the most reliable. Her Chief Communicator is a Scots patriarch who lived "in the time of Merlin" and who is evidently very wise; unfortunately he did not choose to appear yesterday evening. Instead, Webley presided. He is supposed to have died some seventy-five years ago at the age of nineteen in a house just up the street from the A——s'. He was either a butcher's helper or an apprentice tailor. He died in a fire—or by a "slow dreadful crippling disease"—or beneath a horse's hooves, in a freakish accident; during the course of the sitting he alluded self-pityingly to his death but seemed to have forgotten the exact details. At the very end of the evening he addressed me directly as Dr. Williams of Harvard University, saying that since I had influential friends in Boston I could help him with his career—it turned out he had written hundreds of songs and poems and parables but none had been published; would I please find a publisher for his work? Life had treated him so unfairly. His talent— his genius—had been lost to humanity. I had it within my power to help him, he claimed, was I not *obliged* to help him . . .? He then sang one of his songs, which sounded to me like an old ballad; many of the words were so shrill as to be unintelligible, but he sang it just the same, repeating the verses in a haphazard order:

> This ae nighte, this ae nighte,
> —*Every nighte and alle,*
> Fire and fleet and candle-lighte,
> And Christe receive thy saule.
>
> When thou from hence away art past,
> —*Every nighte and alle,*
> To Whinny-muir thou com'st at last:
> And Christe receive thy saule.
>
> From Brig o' Dread when thou may'st pass,
> —*Every nighte and alle,*
> The whinnes sall prick thee to the bare bane:
> And Christe receive thy saule.

The elderly Judge T—— had come up from New York City in order, as he earnestly put it, to "speak directly to his deceased wife as he was never able to do while she was living"; but Webley treated the old gentleman in a high-handed, cavalier manner, as if the occasion were not at all serious. He kept saying, "Who is there tonight? *Who* is there? Let them introduce themselves again—I don't *like* strangers! I tell you I don't *like* strangers!" Though Mrs. A—— had informed us beforehand that we would witness no physical phenomena, there were, from time to time, glimmerings of light in the darkened room, hardly more than the tiny pulsations of light made by fireflies; and both Perry Moore and I felt the table vibrating beneath our fingers. At about the time when Webley gave way to the spirit

278

of Judge T——'s wife, the temperature in the room seemed to drop suddenly and I remember being gripped by a sensation of panic—but it lasted only an instant and I was soon myself again. (Dr. Moore claimed not to have noticed any drop in temperature and Judge T—— was so rattled after the sitting that it would have been pointless to question him.)

The séance proper was similar to others I have attended. A spirit—or voice—laid claim to being the late Mrs. T——; this spirit addressed the survivor in a peculiarly intense, urgent manner, so that it was rather embarrassing to be present. Judge T—— was soon weeping. His deeply creased face glistened with tears like a child's.

"Why Darrie! *Darrie!* Don't cry! Oh, don't cry!" the spirit said. "No one is dead, Darrie. There is no death. No death! . . . Can you hear me, Darrie? Why are you so frightened? So upset? No need, Darrie, no need! Grandfather and Lucy and I are together here—happy together. Darrie, look up! Be brave, my dear! My poor frightened dear! We never knew each other, did we? My poor dear! My love! . . . I saw you in a great transparent house, a great burning house; poor Darrie, they told me you were ill, you were weak with fever; all the rooms of the house were aflame and the staircase was burnt to cinders, but there were figures walking up and down, Darrie, great numbers of them, and you were among them, dear, stumbling in your fright—so clumsy! Look up, dear, and shade your eyes, and you will see me. Grandfather helped me—did you know? Did I call out his name at the end? My dear, my darling, it all happened so quickly—we never knew each other, did we? Don't be hard on Annie! Don't be cruel! Darrie? Why are you crying?" And gradually the spirit voice grew fainter; or perhaps something went wrong and the channels of communication were no longer clear. There were repetitions, garbled phrases, meaningless queries of "Dear? Dear?" that the Judge's replies did not seem to placate. The spirit spoke of her gravesite, and of a trip to Italy taken many years before, and of a dead or unborn baby, and again of Annie—evidently Judge T——'s daughter; but the jumble of words did not always make sense and it was a great relief when Mrs. A—— suddenly woke from her trance.

Judge T—— rose from the table, greatly agitated. He wanted to call the spirit back; he had not asked her certain crucial questions; he had been overcome by emotion and had found it difficult to speak, to interrupt the spirit's monologue. But Mrs. A—— (who looked shockingly tired) told him the spirit would not return again that night and they must not make any attempt to call it back.

"The other world obeys its own laws," Mrs. A—— said in her small, rather reedy voice.

We left Mrs. A——'s home shortly after 9:00 P.M. I too was exhausted; I had not realized how absorbed I had been in the proceedings.

Judge T—— is also staying at Montague House, but he was too upset after the sitting to join us for dinner. He assured us, though, that the spirit was authentic—the voice had been his wife's, he was certain of it, he would stake his life on it. She had never called him "Darrie" during her lifetime, wasn't it odd that she called him "Darrie" now?—and was so concerned for him, so loving?—and concerned for their daughter as well? He was very moved. He had a great deal to think about. (Yes, he'd had a fever some weeks ago—a severe attack of bronchitis and a fever; in fact, he had not completely recovered.) What was extraordinary about the entire experience was the wisdom revealed: There is no death.

There is no death.

Dr. Moore and I dined heartily on roast crown of lamb, spring potatoes with peas, and buttered cabbage. We were served two kinds of bread—German rye and sour cream rolls; the hotel's butter was superb; the wine excellent; the dessert—crepes with cream and toasted almonds—looked marvelous, though I had not any appetite for it. Dr. Moore was ravenously hungry. He talked as he ate, often punctuating his remarks with rich bursts of laughter. It was his opinion, of course, that the medium was a fraud—and not a very skillful fraud, either. In his fifteen years of amateur, intermittent investigations he had encountered far more skillful mediums. Even the notorious Eustace with his levitating table and hobgoblin chimes and shrieks was cleverer than Mrs. A——; one knew of course that Eustace was a cheat, but one was hard pressed to explain his method. Whereas Mrs. A—— was quite transparent.

Dr. Moore spoke for some time in his amiable, dogmatic way. He ordered brandy for both of us, though it was nearly midnight when we finished our dinner and I was anxious to get to bed. (I hoped to rise early and work on a lecture dealing with Kant's approach to the problem of Free Will, which I would be delivering in a few days.) But Dr. Moore enjoyed talking and seemed to have been invigorated by our experience at Mrs. A——'s.

At the age of forty-three Perry Moore is only four years my senior, but he has the air, in my presence at least, of being considerably older. He is a second cousin of my mother, a very successful physician with a bachelor's flat and office in Louisburg Square; his failure to marry, or his refusal, is one of Boston's perennial mysteries. Everyone agrees that he is learned, witty, charming, and extraordinarily intelligent. Striking rather than conventionally handsome, with a dark, lustrous beard and darkly bright eyes, he is an excellent amateur violinist, an enthusiastic sailor, and a lover of literature—his favorite writers are Fielding, Shakespeare, Horace, and Dante. He is, of course, the perfect investigator in spiritualist matters since he is detached from the phenomena he observes and yet he is indefatigably curious; he has a positive love, a mania, for facts. Like the true scientist he seeks facts that, assembled, may possibly give rise to hypotheses: he does not set out with a hypothesis in mind, like a sort of basket into which certain facts may be tossed, helter-skelter, while others are conveniently ignored. In all things he is an empiricist who accepts nothing on faith.

"If the woman is a fraud, then," I say hesitantly, "you believe she is a self-deluded fraud? And her spirits' information is gained by means of telepathy?"

"Telepathy indeed. There can be no other explanation," Dr. Moore says emphatically. "By some means not yet known to science—by some uncanny means she suppresses her conscious personality—and thereby releases other, secondary personalities that have the power of seizing upon others' thoughts and memories. It's done in a way not understood by science at the present time. But it will be understood eventually. Our investigations into the unconscious powers of the human mind are just beginning; we're on the threshold, really, of a new era."

"So she simply picks out of her clients' minds whatever they want to hear," I say slowly. "And from time to time she can even tease them a little—insult them, even: she can unloose a creature like that obnoxious Webley upon a person like Judge T—— without fear of being discovered. Telepathy . . . Yes, that would explain a great deal. Very nearly everything we witnessed tonight."

"*Everything*, I should say," Dr. Moore says.

In the coach returning to Cambridge I set aside Kant and my lecture notes and read Sir Thomas Browne: *Light that makes all things seen, makes some things invisible. The greatest mystery of Religion is expressed by adumbration.*

19 March 1887. Cambridge. 11 P.M.

Walked ten miles this evening; must clear cobwebs from mind.

Unhealthy atmosphere. Claustrophobic. Last night's sitting in Quincy—a most unpleasant experience.

(Did not tell my wife what happened. Why is she so curious about the Spirit World?—about Perry Moore?)

My body craves more violent physical activity. In the summer, thank God, I will be able to swim in the ocean: the most strenuous and challenging of exercises.

Jotting down notes re the Quincy experience:

I. Fraud

Mrs. A——, possibly with accomplices, conspires to deceive: she does research into her clients' lives beforehand, possibly bribes servants. She is either a very skillful ventriloquist or works with someone who is. (Husband? Son? The husband is a retired cabinetmaker said to be in poor health; possibly consumptive. The son, married, lives in Waterbury.)

Her stated wish to avoid publicity and her declining of payment may simply be ploys; she may intend to make a great deal of money at some future time.

(Possibility of blackmail?—might be likely in cases similar to Perry Moore's.)

II. Non-fraud

Naturalistic
1. Telepathy. She reads minds of clients.
2. "Multiple personality" of medium. Aspects of her own buried psyche are released as her conscious personality is suppressed. These secondary beings are in mysterious rapport with the "secondary" personalities of the clients.

Spiritualistic
1. The controls are genuine communicators, intermediaries between our world and the world of the dead. These spirits give way to other spirits, who then speak through the medium; or
2. These spirits *influence* the medium, who relays their messages using her own vocabulary. Their personalities are then filtered through and limited by hers.
3. The spirits are not those of the deceased; they are perverse, willful spirits. (Perhaps demons? But there are no demons.)

III. Alternative hypothesis
Madness: the medium is mad, the clients are mad, even the detached, rationalist investigators are mad.

Yesterday evening at Mrs. A——'s home, the second sitting Perry Moore and I observed together, along with Miss Bradley, a stenographer from the Society, and two legitimate clients—a Brookline widow, Mrs. P——, and her daughter Clara, a handsome young woman in her early twenties. Mrs. A—— exactly as she appeared to us in February; possibly a little stouter. Wore black dress and cameo brooch. Served Lapsang tea, tiny sandwiches, and biscuits when we arrived shortly after 6:00 P.M. Seemed quite friendly to Perry, Miss Bradley, and me; fussed over us, like any hostess, chattered a bit about the cold spell. Mrs. P—— and her daughter arrived at six-thirty and the sitting began shortly thereafter.

Jarring from the very first. A babble of spirit voices. Mrs.

A—— in trance, head flung back, mouth gaping, eyes rolled upward. Queer. Unnerving. I glanced at Dr. Moore but he seemed unperturbed, as always. The widow and her daughter, however, looked as frightened as I felt.

Why are we here, sitting around this table?

What do we believe we will discover?

What are the risks we face . . .?

"Webley" appeared and disappeared in a matter of minutes. His shrill, raw, aggrieved voice was supplanted by that of a creature of indeterminate sex who babbled in Gaelic. This creature in turn was supplanted by a hoarse German, a man who identified himself as Felix; he spoke a curiously ungrammatical German. For some minutes he and two or three other spirits quarreled. (Each declared himself Mrs. A——'s Chief Communicator for the evening.) Small lights flickered in the semi-dark of the parlor and the table quivered beneath my fingers and I felt, or believed I felt, something brushing against me, touching the back of my head. I shuddered violently but regained my composure at once. An unidentified voice proclaimed in English that the Spirit of our Age was Mars: there would be a catastrophic war shortly and most of the world's population would be destroyed. All atheists would be destroyed. Mrs. A—— shook her head from side to side as if trying to wake. Webley appeared, crying "Hello? Hello? I can't see anyone! Who is there? Who has called me?" but was again supplanted by another spirit who shouted long strings of words in a foreign language. [Note: I discovered a few days later that this language was Walachian, a Romanian dialect. Of course Mrs. A——, whose ancestors are English, could not possibly have known Walachian, and I rather doubt that the woman has ever heard of the Walachian people.]

The sitting continued in this chaotic way for some minutes. Mrs. P—— must have been quite disappointed, since she had wanted to be put in contact with her deceased husband. (She needed advice on whether or not to sell certain pieces of property.) Spirits babbled freely in English, German, Gaelic, French, even in Latin, and at one point Dr. Moore queried a spirit in Greek, but the spirit retreated at once as if not equal to Dr. Moore's wit. The atmosphere was alarming but at the same time rather manic; almost jocular. I found myself suppressing laughter. Something touched the back of my head and I shivered violently and broke into perspiration, but the experience was not altogether unpleasant; it would be very difficult for me to characterize it.

And then . . .

And then, suddenly, everything changed. There was complete calm. A spirit voice spoke gently out of a corner of the room, addressing Perry Moore by his first name in a slow, tentative, groping way. "Perry? Perry . . .?" Dr. Moore jerked about in his seat. He was astonished; I could see by his expression that the voice belonged to someone he knew.

"Perry . . .? This is Brandon. I've waited so long for you, Perry, how could you be so selfish? I forgave you. Long ago. You couldn't help your cruelty and I couldn't help my innocence. Perry? My glasses have been broken . . . I can't see. I've been afraid for so long, Perry, please have mercy on me! I can't bear it any longer. I didn't *know* what it would be like. There are crowds of people here, but we can't see one another, we don't know one another, we're strangers, there is a universe of strangers. . . . I can't see anyone clearly . . . I've been lost for twenty years, Perry. I've been waiting for you for twenty years! You don't dare turn away again, Perry! Not again! Not after so long!"

Dr. Moore stumbled to his feet, knocking his chair aside. "No . . . Is it . . . I don't believe . . ."

"Perry? Perry? Don't abandon me again, Perry! Not again!"

"What is this?" Dr. Moore cried.

He was on his feet now; Mrs. A—— woke from her trance with a groan. The women from Brookline were very upset and I must admit that I was in a mild state of terror, my shirt and my underclothes drenched with perspiration.

The sitting was over. It was only seven-thirty.

"Brandon?" Dr. Moore cried. "Wait. Where are . . .? Brandon? Can you hear me? Where are you? Why did you do it, Brandon? Wait! Don't leave! Can't anyone call him back—Can't anyone help me . . .?"

Mrs. A—— rose unsteadily. She tried to take Dr. Moore's hands in hers but he was too agitated.

"I heard only the very last words," she said. "They're always that way . . . so confused, so broken . . . the poor

285

things. . . . Oh, what a pity! It wasn't murder, was it? Not murder! Suicide . . .? I believe suicide is even worse for them! The poor broken things, they wake in the other world and are utterly, utterly lost—they have no guides, you see— no help in crossing over. . . . They are completely alone for eternity . . ."

"Can't you call him back?" Dr. Moore asked wildly. He was peering into a corner of the parlor, slightly stooped, his face distorted as if he were staring into the sun. "Can't someone help me? . . . Brandon? Are you here? Are you here somewhere? For God's sake can't someone help!"

"Dr. Moore, please, the spirits are gone—the sitting is over for tonight—"

"You foolish old woman, leave me alone! Can't you see I . . . I . . . I must not lose him . . . Call him back, will you? I insist! I insist!"

"Dr. Moore, please . . . You mustn't shout . . ."

"I said call him back! At once! *Call him back!*"

Then he burst into tears. He stumbled against the table and hid his face in his hands and wept like a child; he wept as if his heart had been broken.

And so today I have been reliving the séance. Taking notes, trying to determine what happened. A brisk windy walk of ten miles. Head buzzing with ideas. Fraud? Deceit? Telepathy? Madness?

What a spectacle! Dr. Perry Moore calling after a spirit, begging it to return . . . and then crying, afterward, in front of four astonished witnesses.

Dr. Perry Moore of all people.

My dilemma: whether I should report last night's incident to Dr. Rowe, the president of the Society, or whether I should say nothing about it and request that Miss Bradley say nothing. It would be tragic if Perry's professional reputation were to be damaged by a single evening's misadventure; and before long all of Boston would be talking.

In his present state, however, he is likely to tell everyone about it himself.

At Montague House the poor man was unable to sleep. He would have kept me up all night had I had the stamina to endure his excitement.

There *are* spirits! There have always been spirits!

His entire life up to the present time has been misspent! And of course, most important of all . . . there is no death!

He paced about my hotel room, pulling at his beard nervously. At times there were tears in his eyes. He seemed to want a response of some kind from me but whenever I started to speak he interrupted; he was not really listening.

"Now at last I know. I can't undo my knowledge," he said in a queer hoarse voice. "Amazing, isn't it, after so many years . . . so many wasted years . . . Ignorance has been my lot, darkness . . . and a hideous complacency. My God, when I consider my deluded smugness! I am so ashamed, so ashamed. All along people like Mrs. A—— have been in contact with a world of such power . . . and people like me have been toiling in ignorance, accumulating material achievements, expending our energies in idiotic transient things. . . . But all that is changed now. Now I know. I *know*. There is no death, as the Spiritualists have always told us."

"But, Perry, don't you think. . . Isn't it possible that . . . "

"I *know*," he said quietly. "It's as clear to me as if I had crossed over into that other world myself. Poor Brandon! He's no older now than he was *then*. The poor boy, the poor tragic soul! To think that he's still living after so many years . . . Extraordinary . . . It makes my head spin," he said slowly. For a moment he stood without speaking. He pulled at his beard, then absently touched his lips with his fingers, then wiped at his eyes. He seemed to have forgotten me. When he spoke again his voice was hollow, rather ghastly. He sounded drugged. "I . . . I had been thinking of him as . . . as dead, you know. As dead. Twenty years. Dead. And now, tonight, to be forced to realize that . . . that he isn't dead after all . . . It was laudanum he took. I found him. His rooms on the third floor of Weld Hall. I found him. I had no real idea, none at all, not until I read the note . . . and of course I destroyed the note . . . I had to, you see: for his sake. For his sake more than mine. It was because he realized there could be no . . . no hope . . . Yet he called me cruel! You heard him, Jarvis, didn't you? Cruel! I suppose I was. Was I? I don't know what to think. I must talk with him again. I . . . I don't know what to . . . what to think. I . . . . "

"You look awfully tired, Perry. It might be a good idea to go to bed," I said weakly.

". . . recognized his voice at once. Oh at once: no doubt. None. What a revelation! And my life so misspent . . . Treating people's *bodies*. Absurd. I know now that nothing matters except that other world . . . nothing matters except our dead, our beloved dead . . . who are *not dead*. What a colossal revelation . . . ! Why, it will change the entire course of history. It will alter men's minds throughout the world. You were there, Jarvis, so you understand. You were a witness . . . "

"But . . . "

"You'll bear witness to the truth of what I am saying?"

He stared at me, smiling. His eyes were bright and threaded with blood.

I tried to explain to him as courteously and sympathetically as possible that his experience at Mrs. A——'s was not substantially different from the experiences many people have had at séances. "And always in the past psychical researchers have taken the position . . . "

"You were *there*," he said angrily. "You heard Brandon's voice as clearly as I did. Don't deny it!"

". . . have taken the position that . . . the phenomenon can be partly explained by the telepathic powers of the medium . . . "

"That was Brandon's *voice*," Perry said. "I felt his presence, I tell you! *His*. Mrs. A—— had nothing to do with it . . . nothing at all. I feel as if . . . as if I could call Brandon back by myself. . . . I feel his presence even now. Close about me. He isn't dead, you see; no one is dead, there's a universe of . . . of people who are not dead . . . Parents, grandparents, sisters, brothers, everyone . . . everyone . . . How can you deny, Jarvis, the evidence of your own senses? You were there with me tonight and you know as well as I do . . . "

"Perry, I don't *know*. I did hear a voice, yes, but we've heard voices before at other sittings, haven't we? There are always voices. There are always 'spirits.' The Society has taken the position that the spirits could be real, of course, but that there are other hypotheses that are perhaps more likely . . . "

"Other hypotheses indeed!" Perry said irritably. "You're like a man with his eyes shut tight who refuses to open them out of sheer cowardice. Like the cardinals refusing to look through Galileo's telescope! And you have pretensions of being a man of learning, of science. . . . Why, we've got to destroy all the records we've made so far; they're a slander on the world of the spirits. Thank God we didn't file a report yet on Mrs. A——! It would be so embarrassing to be forced to call it back . . ."

"Perry, please. Don't be angry. I want only to remind you of the fact that we've been present at other sittings, haven't we? . . . and we've witnessed others responding emotionally to certain phenomena. Judge T——, for instance. He was convinced he'd spoken with his wife. But you must remember, don't you, that you and I were not at all convinced . . . ? It seemed to us more likely that Mrs. A—— is able, through extrasensory powers we don't quite understand, to read the minds of her clients, and then to project certain voices out into the room so that it sounds as if they are coming from other people. . . . You even said, Perry, that she wasn't a very skillful ventriloquist. You said—"

"What does it matter what, in my ignorance, I said?" he cried. "Isn't it enough that I've been humiliated? That my entire life has been turned about? Must you insult me as well . . . sitting there so smugly and insulting *me?* I think I can make claim to being someone whom you might respect."

And so I assured him that I did respect him. And he walked about the room, wiping at his eyes, greatly agitated. He spoke again of his friend, Brandon Gould, and of his own ignorance, and of the important mission we must undertake to inform men and women of the true state of affairs. I tried to talk with him, to reason with him, but it was hopeless. He scarcely listened to me.

". . . must inform the world . . . crucial truth. . . . There is no death, you see. Never was. Changes civilization, changes the course of history. Jarvis?" he said groggily. "You see? *There is no death.*"

25 March 1887. Cambridge.

Disquieting rumors re Perry Moore. Heard today at the University that one of Dr. Moore's patients (a brother-in-law of Dean Barker) was extremely offended by his behavior during a consultation last week. Talk of his having been drunk . . . which I find incredible. If the poor man appeared to be excitable and not his customary self, it was not because he was *drunk,* surely.

Another far-fetched tale told me by my wife, who heard it from her sister Maude: Perry Moore went to church (St. Aidan's Episcopal Church on Mount Street) for the first time in a decade, sat alone, began muttering and laughing during the sermon, and finally got to his feet and walked out, creating quite a stir. *What delusions! What delusions!* . . . he was said to have muttered.

I fear for the poor man's sanity.

31 March 1887. Cambridge. 4 A.M.
Sleepless night. Dreamed of swimming . . . swimming in the ocean . . . enjoying myself as usual when suddenly the water turns thick . . . turns to mud. Hideous! Indescribably awful. I was swimming nude in the ocean, by moonlight, I believe, ecstatically happy, entirely alone, when the water turned to mud. . . . Vile, disgusting mud; faintly warm; sucking at my body. Legs, thighs, torso, arms. Horrible. Woke in terror. Drenched with perspiration: pajamas wet. One of the most frightening nightmares of my adulthood.

A message from Perry Moore came yesterday just before dinner. Would I like to join him in visiting Mrs. A—— sometime soon, in early April perhaps, on a noninvestigative basis . . . ? He is uncertain now of the morality of our "investigating" Mrs. A—— or any other medium.

4 April 1887. Cambridge.
Spent the afternoon from two to five at William James's home on Irving Street, talking with Professor James of the inexplicable phenomenon of consciousness. He is robust as always, rather irreverent, supremely confident in a way I find enviable; rather like Perry Moore before his conversion. (Extraordinary eyes—so piercing, quick, playful; a graying beard liberally threaded with white; close-cropped graying hair; a large, curving, impressive forehead; a manner intelligent and graceful and at the same time rough-edged, as if he anticipates or perhaps even hopes for recalcitration in his

listeners.) We both find conclusive the ideas set forth in Binét's *Alterations of Personality*—unsettling as these ideas may be to the rationalist position. James speaks of a *peculiarity* in the constitution of human nature: this is, the fact that we inhabit not only our ego-consciousness but a wide field of psychological experience (most clearly represented by the phenomenon of memory, which no one can adequately explain) over which we have no control whatsoever. In fact, we are not generally aware of this field of consciousness.

We inhabit a lighted sphere, then; and about us is a vast penumbra of memories, reflections, feelings, and stray uncoordinated thoughts that "belong" to us theoretically, but that do not seem to be part of our conscious identity. (I was too timid to ask Professor James whether it might be the case that we do not inevitably own these aspects of the personality . . . that such phenomena belong as much to the objective world as to our subjective selves.) It is quite possible that there is an element of some indeterminate kind: oceanic, timeless, and living, against which the individual being constructs temporary barriers as part of an ongoing process of unique, particularized survival; like the ocean itself, which appears to separate islands that are in fact not "islands" at all, but aspects of the earth firmly joined together below the surface of the water. Our lives, then, resemble these islands. . . . All this is no more than a possibility, Professor James and I agreed.

James is acquainted, of course, with Perry Moore. But he declined to speak on the subject of the poor man's increasingly eccentric behavior when I alluded to it. (It may be that he knows even more about the situation than I do—he enjoys a multitude of acquaintances in Cambridge and Boston.) I brought our conversation round several times to the possibility of the *naturalness* of the conversion experience in terms of the individual's evolution of self, no matter how his family, his colleagues, and society in general viewed it, and Professor James appeared to agree; at least he did not emphatically disagree. He maintains a healthy skepticism, of course, regarding Spiritualist claims, and all evangelical and enthusiastic religious movements, though he is, at the same time, a highly articulate foe of the "rationalist" position and he believes that psychical research of the kind some of us are attempting will eventually unearth riches . . . revealing aspects of the human psyche otherwise closed to our scrutiny.

"The fearful thing," James said, "is that we are at all times vulnerable to incursions from the 'other side' of the personality. . . . We cannot determine the nature of the total personality simply because much of it, perhaps most, is hidden from us. . . . When we are invaded, then, we are overwhelmed and surrender immediately. Emotionally charged intuitions, hunches, guesses, even ideas may be the least aggressive of these incursions; but there are visual and auditory hallucinations, and forms of automatic behavior not controlled by the conscious mind. . . . Ah, you're thinking I am simply describing insanity?"

I stared at him, quite surprised.

"No. Not at all. Not at all," I said at once.

Reading through my grandfather's journals, begun in East Anglia many years before my birth. Another world then. Another language, now lost to us. *Man is sinful by nature. God's justice takes precedence over His mercy.* The dogma of Original Sin: something brutish about the innocence of that belief. And yet consoling. . . .

Fearful of sleep since my dreams are so troubled now. The voices of impudent spirits (Immanuel Kant himself come to chide me for having made too much of his categories!), stray shouts and whispers I cannot decipher, the faces of my own beloved dead hovering near, like carnival masks, insubstantial and possibly fraudulent. Impatient with my wife, who questions me too closely on these personal matters; annoyed from time to time, in the evenings especially, by the silliness of the children. (The eldest is twelve now and should know better.) Dreading to receive another lengthy letter—sermon, really—from Perry Moore re his "new position," and yet perversely hoping one will come soon.

I must know.

(Must know *what?*)

I must know.

10 April 1887. Boston. St. Aidan's Episcopal Church.

Funeral service this morning for Perry Moore; dead at forty-three.

17 April 1887. Seven Hills, New Hampshire.
A weekend retreat. No talk. No need to think.

Visiting with a former associate, author of numerous books. Cartesian specialist. Elderly. Partly deaf. Extraordinarily kind to me. (Did not ask about the Department or about my work.) Intensely interested in animal behavior now, in observation primarily; fascinated with the phenomenon of hibernation.

He leaves me alone for hours. He sees something in my face I cannot see myself.

The old consolations of a cruel but just God: ludicrous today.

In the nineteenth century we live free of God. We live in the illusion of freedom-of-God.

Dozing off in the guest room of this old farmhouse and then waking abruptly. *Is someone here? Is someone here?* My voice queer, hushed, childlike. *Please: is someone here?*
Silence.

Query: Is the penumbra outside consciousness all that was ever meant by "God"?

Query: Is inevitability all that was ever meant by "God"?

God—the body of fate we inhabit, then; no more and no less.

God pulled Perry down into the body of fate: into Himself. (Or Itself.) As Professor James might say, Dr. Moore was "vulnerable" to an assault from the other side.

At any rate he is dead. They buried him last Saturday.

25 April 1887. Cambridge.
Shelves of books. The sanctity of books. Kant, Plato, Schopenhauer, Descartes, Hume, Hegel, Spinoza. The others. All. Nietzsche, Spencer, Leibnitz (on whom I did a torturous Master's thesis). Plotinus. Swedenborg. *The Transactions of the American Society for Psychical Research.* Voltaire. Locke. Rousseau. And Berkeley: the good Bishop adrift in a dream.

An etching by Halbrech above my desk, "The Thames 1801." Water too black. Inky-black. Thick with mud . . .? Filthy water in any case.

Perry's essay, forty-five scribbled pages, "The Challenge of the Future." Given to me several weeks ago by Dr. Rowe, who feared rejecting it for the *Transactions* but could not, of course, accept it. I can read only a few pages at a time, then push it aside, too moved to continue. Frightened also.

The man had gone insane.

Died insane.

Personality broken: broken bits of intellect.

His argument passionate and disjointed, with no pretense of objectivity. Where some weeks ago he had taken the stand that it was immoral to investigate the Spirit World, now he took the stand that it was imperative we do so. We are on the brink of a new age . . . new knowledge of the universe . . . comparable to the stormy transitional period between the Ptolemaic and the Copernican theories of the universe. . . . More experiments required. Money. Donations. Subsidies by private institutions. All psychological research must be channeled into a systematic study of the Spirit World and the ways by which we can communciate with that world. Mediums like Mrs. A—— must be brought to centers of learning like Harvard and treated with the respect their genius deserves. Their value to civilization is, after all, beyond estimation. They must be rescued from arduous and routine lives where their genius is drained off into vulgar pursuits . . . they must be rescued from a clientele that is mainly concerned with being put into contact with deceased relatives for utterly trivial, self-serving reasons. Men of learning must realize the gravity of the situation. Otherwise we will fail, we will stagger beneath the burden, we will be defeated, ignobly, and it will remain for the twentieth century to discover the existence of the Spirit Universe that surrounds the Material Universe, and to determine the exact ways by which one world is related to another.

Perry Moore died of a stroke on the eighth of April; died instantaneously on the steps of the Bedford Club shortly after 2:00 P.M. Passers-by saw a very excited, red-faced gentleman with an open collar push his way through a small gathering at the top of the steps . . . and then suddenly fall, as if shot down.

In death he looked like quite another person: his features sharp, the nose especially pointed. Hardly the handsome Perry Moore everyone had known.

He had come to a meeting of the Society, though it was suggested by Dr. Rowe and by others (including myself) that he stay away. Of course he came to argue. To present his "new position." To insult the other members. (He was contemptuous of a rather poorly organized paper on the medium Miss E——of Salem, a young woman who works with objects like rings, articles of clothing, locks of hair, et cetera; and quite angry with the evidence presented by a young geologist that would seem to discredit, once and for all, the claims of Eustace of Portsmouth. He interrupted a third paper, calling the reader a "bigot" and an "ignorant fool.")

Fortunately the incident did not find its way into any of the papers. The press, misunderstanding (deliberately and maliciously) the Society's attitude toward Spiritualism, delights in ridiculing our efforts.

There were respectful obituaries. A fine eulogy prepared by Reverend Tyler of St. Aidan's. Other tributes. *A tragic loss . . . Mourned by all who knew him . . .* (I stammered and could not speak. I cannot speak of him, of it, even now. Am I mourning, am I aggrieved? Or merely shocked? Terrified?) Relatives and friends and associates glossed over his behavior these past few months and settled upon an earlier Perry Moore, eminently sane, a distinguished physician and man of letters. I did not disagree, I merely acquiesced; I could not make any claim to have really known the man.

And so he has died, and so he is dead. . . .

Shortly after the funeral I went away to New Hampshire for a few days. But I can barely remember that period of time now. I sleep poorly. I yearn for summer, for a drastic change of climate, of scene. It was unwise for me to take up the responsibility of psychical research, fascinated though I am by it; my classes and lectures at the University demand most of my energy.

How quickly he died, and so young: so relatively young. No history of high blood pressure, it is said.

At the end he was arguing with everyone, however. His personality had completely changed. He was rude, impetuous, even rather profane; even poorly groomed. (Rising to challenge the first of the papers, he revealed a shirtfront that appeared to be stained.) Some claimed he had been drinking all along, for years. Was it possible . . . ? (He had clearly enjoyed the wine and brandy in Quincy that evening, but I would not have said he was intemperate.) Rumors, fanciful tales, outright lies, slander. . . . It is painful, the vulnerability death brings.

Bigots, he called us. Ignorant fools. Unbelievers . . . atheists . . . traitors to the Spirit World . . . heretics. Heretics! I believe he looked directly at me as he pushed his way out of the meeting room: his eyes glaring, his face dangerously flushed, no recognition in his stare.

After his death, it is said, books continue to arrive at his home from England and Europe. He spent a small fortune on obscure, out-of-print volumes . . . commentaries on the Kabbala, on Plotinus, medieval alchemical texts, books on astrology, witchcraft, the metaphysics of death. Occult cosmologies. Egyptian, Indian, and Chinese "wisdom." Blake, Swedenborg, Cozad. *The Tibetan Book of the Dead.* Datsky's *Lunar Mysteries.* His estate is in chaos because he left not one but several wills, the most recent made out only a day before his death, merely a few lines scribbled on scrap paper, without witnesses. The family will contest, of course. Since in this will he left his money and property to an obscure woman living in Quincy, Massachusetts, and since he was obviously not in his right mind at the time, they would be foolish indeed not to contest.

Days have passed since his sudden death. Days continue to pass. At times I am seized by a sort of quick, cold panic; at other times I am inclined to think the entire situation has been exaggerated. In one mood I vow to myself that I will never again pursue psychical research because it is simply too dangerous. In another mood I vow I will never again pursue it because it is a waste of time and my own work, my own career, must come first.

Heretics, he called us. Looking straight at me.

Still, he was mad. And is not to be blamed for the vagaries of madness.

19 June 1887. Boston.

Luncheon with Dr. Rowe, Miss Madeleine van der Post, young Lucas Matthewson; turned over my personal records and notes re the mediums Dr. Moore and I visited. (Destroyed jottings of a private nature.) Miss van der Post and Matthewson will be taking over my responsibilities. Both are young, quickwitted, alert, with a certain ironic play about their features; rather like Dr. Moore in his prime. Matthewson is a former seminary student now teaching physics at the Boston University. They questioned me about Perry Moore, but I avoided answering frankly. Asked if we were close, I said *No*. Asked if I had heard a bizarre tale making the rounds of Boston salons . . . that a spirit claiming to be Perry Moore has intruded upon a number of séances in the area. . . . I said honestly that I had not; and I did not care to hear about it.

Spinoza: *I will analyze the actions and appetites of men as if it were a question of lines, of planes, and of solids.*

It is in this direction, I believe, that we must move. Away from the phantasmal, the vaporous, the unclear; toward lines, planes, and solids.

Sanity.

8 July 1887. Mount Desert Island, Maine.

Very early this morning, before dawn, dreamed of Perry Moore: a babbling, gesticulating spirit, bearded, bright-eyed, obviously mad. Jarvis? Jarvis? Don't deny me! he cried. I am so . . . so bereft. . . .

Paralyzed, I faced him: neither awake nor asleep. His words were not really *words* so much as unvoiced thoughts. I heard them in my own voice; a terrible raw itching at the back of my throat yearned to articulate the man's grief.

Perry?

You don't dare deny me! Not now!

He drew near and I could not escape. The dream shifted, lost its clarity. Someone was shouting at me. Very angry, he was, and baffled . . . as if drunk . . . or ill . . . or injured.

Perry? I can't hear you—

. . . our dinner at Montague House, do you remember? Lamb, it was. And crepes with almond for dessert. You remember! You remember! You can't deny me! We were both nonbelievers then, both abysmally ignorant . . . you can't deny me!

(I was mute with fear or with cunning.)

. . . that idiot Rowe, how humiliated he will be! All of them! All of you! The entire rationalist bias, the . . . the conspiracy of . . . of fools . . . bigots . . . In a few years . . . In a few short years . . . Jarvis, where are you? Why can't I see you? Where have you gone? . . . My eyes can't focus: will someone help me? I seem to have lost my way. Who is here? Who am I talking with? You remember me, don't you?

(He brushed near me, blinking helplessly. His mouth was a hole torn into his pale ravaged flesh.)

Where are you? Where is everyone? I thought it would be crowded here but . . . but there's no one . . . I am forgetting so much! My name—what was my name? Can't see. Can't remember. Something very important . . . something very important I must accomplish—can't remember—Why is there no God? No one here? No one in control? We drift this way and that way, we come to no rest, there are no landmarks . . . no way of judging . . . everything is confused . . . disjointed . . . Is someone listening? Would you read to me, please? Would you read to me?—anything!—that speech of Hamlet's—*To be or not*—a *sonnet of Shakespeare's—any sonnet, anything—That time of year thou may in me behold*—is that it?—is that how it begins? *Bare ruin'd choirs where the sweet birds once sang.* How does it go? Won't you tell me? I'm lost—there's nothing here to see, to touch—isn't anyone listening? I thought there was someone nearby, a friend: isn't anyone here?

(I stood paralyzed, mute with caution: he passed by.)

. . . *When in the chronicle of wasted time—the wide world dreaming of things to come*—is anyone listening?—can anyone help?—I am forgetting so much . . . my name, my life . . . my life's work . . . to penetrate the mysteries . . . the veil . . . to do justice to the universe of . . . of what . . . what I had intended? . . . am I in my place of repose now, have I come home? Why is it so empty here? Why is no one in control? My eyes—my head—mind broken and blown about—slivers—shards—annihilating all that's made to a . . . a green thought . . . a green shade—Shakespeare?

Plato? Pascal? Will someone read me Pascal again? I seem to have lost my way. . . . I am being blown about—Jarvis, was it? My dear young friend Jarvis? But I've forgotten your last name. . . . I've forgotten so much . . .

(I wanted to reach out to touch him—but could not move, could not wake. The back of my throat ached with sorrow. Silent! Silent! I could not utter a word.)

. . . my papers, my journal—twenty years—a key somewhere hidden—where?—ah yes: the bottom drawer of my desk—do you hear?—my desk—house—Louisburg Square—the key is hidden there—wrapped in a linen handkerchief—the strongbox is—the locked box is—hidden—my brother Edward's house—attic—trunk—steamer trunk—initials R. W. M.—Father's trunk, you see—strongbox hidden inside—my secret journals—life's work—physical and spiritual wisdom—must not be lost—are you listening?—is anyone listening? I am forgetting so much, my mind is in shreds—but if you could locate the journal and read it to me—if you could salvage it—me—I would be so very grateful—I would forgive you anything, all of you—Is anyone there? Jarvis? Brandon? No one?—My journal, my soul: will you salvage it? Will—

(He stumbled away and I was alone again.)

Perry—?

But it was too late: I awoke drenched with perspiration.

Nightmare.

Must forget.

Best to rise early, before the others. Mount Desert Island lovely in July. Our lodge on a hill above the beach. No spirits here: wind from the northeast, perpetual fresh air, perpetual waves. Best to rise early and run along the beach and plunge into the chilly water.

Clear the cobwebs from one's mind.

How beautiful the sky, the ocean, the sunrise!

No spirits here on Mount Desert Island. Swimming: skillful exertion of arms and legs. Head turned this way, that way. Eyes half shut. The surprise of the cold rough waves. One yearns almost to slip out of one's human skin at such times . . .! Crude blatant beauty of Maine. Ocean. Muscular exertion of body. How alive I am, how living, how invulnerable; what a triumph in my every breath . . .

Everything slips from my mind except the present moment. I am living. I am alive, I am immortal. Must not weaken: must not sink. Drowning? No. Impossible. Life is the only reality. It is not extinction that awaits but a hideous dreamlike state, a perpetual groping, blundering—far worse than extinction—incomprehensible: so it is life we must cling to, arm over arm, swimming, conquering the element that sustains us.

Jarvis? someone cried. *Please hear me—*

How exquisite life is, the turbulent joy of life contained in flesh! I heard nothing except the triumphant waves splashing about me. I swam for nearly an hour. Was reluctant to come ashore for breakfast, though our breakfasts are always pleasant rowdy sessions: my wife and my brother's wife and our seven children thrown together for the month of July. Three boys, four girls: noise, bustle, health, no shadows, no spirits. No time to think. Again and again I shall emerge from the surf, face and hair and body streaming water, exhausted but jubilant, triumphant. Again and again the children will call out to me, excited, from the dayside of the world that they inhabit.

I will not investigate Dr. Moore's strongbox and his secret journal; I will not even think about doing so. The wind blows words away. The surf is hypnotic. I will not remember this morning's dream once I sit down to breakfast with the family. I will not clutch my wife's wrist and say *We must not die! We dare not die!*—for that would only frighten and offend her.

Jarvis? she is calling at this very moment.

And I say *Yes—? Yes, I'll be there at once.*

Born in 1938 in New York and educated at Syracuse University and the University of Wisconsin, Joyce Carol Oates is an English teacher, currently at Princeton. Her first book By the North Gate, was published in 1963. Strongly influenced by William Faulkner, Oates sets many of her works in her fictional Eden County. She has been called "the finest Southern writer that ever came out of the North."

EIGHTEEN

Drawer 14

Talmage Powell

No cracks about my job, please. I've already taken more than enough ribbing from campus cutups. I don't relish being night attendant at the Asheville city morgue, but there are compensations.

For one thing, the job gave me a chance to complete my college work in daytime and do considerable studying at night between catnaps and the light, routine duties.

In their tagged and numbered drawers, the occupants weren't going to disturb me while I was cracking a brain cell on a problem in calculus. Or so I thought.

This particular night I relieved Olaf Daly, like always. Olaf was a man stuck with a job because of his age and a game leg. He lived each day only for the moment when he could flee his profession, as it were. Like always, he grunted a hello and a goodbye in the same breath, the game leg assisting him out of the morgue with surprising alacrity.

Alone in the deep silence of the anteroom, I dropped my thermos, transistor radio, and a couple of textbooks on the desk. I pulled the heavy record book toward me to give it a rundown.

Olaf had made his daily entries in his neat, spidery handwriting. Male victim of drowning. Man and woman dead in auto crash. Wino who didn't wake up when his bed caught fire. Male loser of a knife fight. Woman found dead in river.

Olaf's day had been routine. Nothing had come in like the dilly of last week.

She had been a pitiful, dirty, lonely old woman who had lived in a hovel. Crazy as a scorched moth, she had slipped into a dream world where she wasn't dirty, or old, or forsaken at all. Instead, she had believed she was the Fourth Witch of Endor, with power over the forces of darkness.

The slum section being a breeding ground for ignorance and superstition, some of her neighbors had taken the Fourth Witch of Endor seriously. She had looked the part, with a skull-like face, a beaked nose with a wart on the end, a toothless mouth accenting a long and pointed chin, and strings of dirty hair hanging lank about her sunken cheeks. She had eked out a half-starved living by telling fortunes, performing incantations, predicting winning numbers, and selling love potions and spells. To her credit, she never had gone in for the evil eye, her neighbors reported. If she couldn't put a good hex on a person, she had refused to hex him at all.

On a very hot and humid night, the Fourth Witch of Endor had mounted the roof of her tenement. Nobody knew for sure whether she had slipped or maybe taken a crack at flying to the full moon. Anyhow, she had been scraped off the asphalt six stories below, brought here, and deposited in drawer 14. She had lain in the refrigerated cubicle for four days before an immaculate son had flown in from a distant state to claim the body.

She hadn't departed a moment too soon for Olaf Daly. "I swear," the old man had said, "there's a hint of a smell at drawer 14, like you'd figure sulphur and brimstone to smell."

I hadn't noticed. The only smells assailing my nostrils were those in a chem lab where I was trying hard to keep up with the class.

I turned from the record book for a routine tour of the building.

Lighted brightly, the adjoining room was large, chill, and barren. The floor was spotless gray tile with a faint, antiseptic aroma. Across the room was the double doorway to the outside ramp where the customers were brought in. Near the door was the long, narrow, marble-topped table mounted on casters. Happily, it was empty at the moment, scrubbed clean, waiting for inevitable use. The refrigeration equipment made a low, whispering sound, more felt than heard.

To my right, like an outsized honeycomb, was the bank of drawers where the dead were kept for the claiming, or eventual burial at city expense.

Each occupied drawer was tagged, like with a shipping ticket or baggage check, the tag being attached with thin wire to the proper drawer handle when the body was checked in.

I whistled softly between my teeth, just for the sake of having some sound, as I started checking the tags against my mental tally from the record book.

As I neared drawer 14, I caught myself on the point of sniffing. Instead of sniffing, I snorted. "That Olaf Daly," I muttered. "He and his smell of sulphur and brimstone!"

A couple steps past drawer 14 I rocked up on my toes, turned my head, then my whole body around.

Olaf had not listed an occupant for drawer 14, but the handle was tagged. I bent forward slightly, reached. The whistle sort of dripped to nothing off my lips.

I turned the tag over casually the first time; then a second and third time, considerably faster.

I straightened and gave my scalp a scratch. Both sides of the tag were blank. Olaf was old, but far from senile. This wasn't like him at all, forgetting to fill in a drawer tag.

Then I half grinned to myself. The old coot was playing a joke on me. I didn't know he had it in him.

The whistle returned to my lips with a wise note, but not exactly appreciative. I took hold of the handle and gave it a yank. The drawer slid open on its rollers. The whistle keened to a thin wail and broke.

The girl in the drawer was young. She was blonde. She was beautiful, even in death.

I stood looking at her with my toes curling away from the soles of my shoes. The features of her face were lovely, the skin like pale tan satin. Her eyes were closed as if she were merely sleeping, her long lashes like dark shadows. She was clothed in a white nylon uniform with a nurse's pin on the collar. The only personal adornment was an I.D. bracelet of delicate golden chain and plaque. The plaque was engraved with initials: Z. L.

I broke my gaze away from the blonde girl and hurried back to the anteroom. At the desk, I jerked the record book toward me. I didn't want to misjudge old man Daly.

I moved my finger down the day's entries. Hesitated. Repeated the process. Went to the previous day by turning a page. Then to the day before that. Nobody, definitely, had been registered in drawer 14.

I puckered, but couldn't find a whistle as I turned again to the door of the morgue room. There was a glass section in the upper portion of the door. I looked through the glass. I didn't have to open the door. I'd left drawer 14 extended, and blonde Z. L. was still there, bigger than life, as big as death.

Carefully, I sat down at the desk, took out my handkerchief, wiped my forehead.

I took a long, deliberate breath, picked up the phone and dialed Olaf Daly's number. While his phone rang, I sneaked a glance in the direction of the morgue room.

Olaf's wife answered sleepily, along about the sixth or seventh ring. No, I couldn't speak to Olaf because he hadn't come home yet.

Then she added suddenly, in a kindlier tone, "Just a minute. I think I hear him coming now."

Olaf got on the line with a clearing of his throat. "Yah, what is it?"

"This is Tully Branson, Mr. Daly."

"I ain't available for stand-in duty if some of your college pals have cracked a keg someplace."

"No, sir," I said. "I understand, Mr. Daly. It's just that I need the information on the girl in drawer 14."

"Ain't nobody in drawer 14, Tully."

"Yes, sir. There's a girl in drawer 14. A blonde girl, Mr. Daly, far too young and nice looking to have to die. I'm sure you remember. Only you forgot the record book when she was brought in."

I heard Mrs. Daly asking Olaf what was it. The timber of his voice changed as he spoke in the direction of his wife. "I think young Branson brought straight whisky in his thermos tonight."

"No, sir," I barked at Olaf. "I need it, but I haven't got any whisky. All I've got is a dead blonde girl in drawer 14 that you forgot to make a record of."

"How could I do a thing like that?" Olaf demanded.

"I don't know," I said, "but you did. She's right here. If you don't believe me, come down and have a look."

"I think I'll do just that, son! You're accusing me of a mighty serious thing!"

He slammed the phone down so hard it stabbed me in the eardrum. I hung up with a studied gentleness, lighted a cigarette, poured some coffee from the thermos, lighted a cigarette, took a sip of coffee, and lighted a cigarette.

I had another swallow of coffee, reached for the package, and discovered I already had three cigarettes spiraling smoke from the ashtray. I gave myself a sickly grin and butted out two of the cigarettes to save for later.

With his game leg, Olaf arrived with the motion of a schooner mast on a stormy sea. I returned his glare with a smile that held what smug assurance I was able to muster. Then I bowed him into the morgue room.

He went through the swinging door, with me following closely. Drawer 14 was still extended. He didn't bother to cross all the way to it. Instead, after one look, he whirled on me.

"Branson," he snarled in rage, "if I was twenty years younger I'd bust your nose! You got a nerve, dragging a tired old man back to this stinking place. And just when I'd decided you was one of the nicer members of the younger generation too!"

"But Mr. Daly . . ."

"Don't 'but' me, you young pup! I'll put you on report for this!"

I took another frantic look at drawer 14. She was there, plain as anything. Blonde, and beautiful, and dead.

Olaf started past me, shoving me aside. I caught hold of his arm. I was chicken—and just about ready to molt. "Old man," I yelled, "you see her. I know you do!"

"Get your mitts offa me," he yelled back. "I see exactly what's there. I see an empty drawer. About as empty as your head."

I clutched his arm, not wanting to let go. "I don't know what kind of joke this is . . ."

"And neither do I," he said, shouting me down. "But it's a mighty poor one!"

"Then look at that drawer, old man, and quit horsing around."

"I've looked all I need to. Nothing but an overgrown juvenile delinquent would think up such a shoddy trick to oust a poor old man out of his house!"

He jerked his arm free of my grip, stormed through the door, past the anteroom. At the front door of the building, which was down a short corridor, he stopped, turned, and shook his finger at me.

"You cruel young crumb," he said, "you better start looking for another job tomorrow, if I have anything to do with it!" With that, he was gone.

I'd followed him as far as the anteroom. I turned slowly, looked through the glass pane into the morgue room. A dismal groan came from me. Z. L. still occupied drawer 14.

"Be a good girl," I heard myself mumbling, "and go away. I'll close my eyes, and you just go away."

I closed my eyes, opened them. But she hadn't gone away.

I groped to the desk chair and collapsed. I didn't sit long, on account of a sudden flurry of business which was announced by the buzzer at the service door.

The skirling sound, coming suddenly, lifted me a couple feet off the desk chair. When I came down, I was legging it across the morgue room.

Smith and Macklin, from the meat wagon, were sliding an old guy in tattered clothing from a stretcher to the marble-topped table.

"He walked in front of a truck," Smith said.

"No I.D.," Macklin said. "Ice him as a John Doe."

"Kinda messy, ain't he, Branson?" Smith grinned at me as he pulled the sheet over the John Doe. Smith was always egging me because he knew my stomach wasn't the strongest.

"Yeah," I said. "Kinda." I blew some sweat off my upper lip. "Not like the girl. No marks on her."

"Girl?"

"Sure," a note of eagerness slipped into my voice. "The beautiful blonde. The one in drawer 14."

Smith and Macklin both looked at the open, extended drawer. Then they looked at each other.

"Tully, old boy," Macklin said, "how you feeling these days?"

"Fine," I said, a strip of ice forming where my forehead was wrinkling.

"No trouble sleeping? No recurrent nightmares?"

"Nope," I said. "But the blonde in 14 . . . if you didn't bring her in, then maybe Collins and Snavely can give me the rundown on her."

Smith and Macklin sort of edged from me. Then Smith's guffaw broke the morgue stillness. "Beautiful blonde, drawer 14, where the poor old demented woman was . . . Sure, Branson, I get it."

Macklin looked at his partner uncertainly. "You do?"

"Simple," Smith said, sounding relieved. "Old Tully here gets bored. Just thought up a little gag to rib us, huh, Tully?"

It was obvious they didn't see the girl and weren't going to see her. If I insisted, I knew suddenly, I was just asking for trouble. So I let out a laugh about as strong as skimmed milk. "Sure," I said. "Got to while away the tedium, you know."

Smith punched me in the ribs with his elbow. "Don't let your corpses get warm, Tully old pal." He departed with another belly laugh. But Macklin was still throwing worried looks over his shoulder at me as he followed Smith out.

I hated to see the outside door close behind them. I sure needed some company. For the first time, being the only living thing in the morgue caused my stomach to shrink to the size of a cold, wrinkled prune.

I skirted drawer 14 like I was crossing a deep gorge on a bridge made of brittle glass.

"Go away," I muttered to Z. L. "You're not real. Not even a dead body. Just a—an *image* that nobody can see but me. So go away!"

My words had no effect whatever on the image. They merely frightened me a little when I caught the tone in which I was conversing with a nonexistent dead body.

Back at the anteroom desk, I sat and shivered for several seconds. Then an idea glimmered encouragingly in my mind. Maybe Olaf Daly, Smith, and Macklin were all in on the gag. Maybe Z. L. had been brought in by Collins and Snavely, who tooled the meat wagon on the dayshift, and everybody had thought it would be a good joke to scare the pants off the bright young college man.

Feeling slightly better, I reached for the phone and called Judd Lawrence. A golfing pal of my father's, Judd was a plainclothes detective attached to homicide. He'd always seemed to think well of me; had, in fact, recommended me for the job here.

Judd wasn't home. He was pulling a three-to-eleven P.M. tour of duty. I placed a second call to police headquarters. Judd had signed out, but they caught him in the locker room.

"Tully Branson, Mr. Lawrence."

"How goes it, Tully?"

"I got a problem."

"Shoot." There was no hesitation in his big, hearty voice.

"Well, uh . . . seems like the record is messed up on one of our transients. A girl. Blonde girl. A nurse. Her initials are Z. L."

"You ought to call Olaf Daly, Tully."

"Yes, sir. But you know how Olaf is when he gets away from here. Anyhow, he's in dreamland by this time and I sure hate to get him riled up. He gets real nasty."

Judd boomed a laugh. "Can't say that I blame him. That all you've got on the girl?"

"Just what I've given you. She's certainly no derelict, furthest thing in the world from that. Girl like her, dead from natural causes, would be in a private funeral home, not here."

"So the fact that she's in the morgue means she died violently," Judd said.

"I guess it has to mean that."

"Murder?"

"Can't think of anything else," I said. "It has to be a death under suspicious circumstances."

"Okay, Tully. I'll see what I can turn up for you."

"Sure hate to put you to the trouble."

"Trouble?" he said. "No trouble. Couple phone calls is all it should take."

"I sure appreciate it, Mr. Lawrence."

I hung up. While I was waiting for Judd Lawrence to call me back, I sneaked to the door of the morgue room and let my gaze creep to the glass pane to make sure the image was still in drawer 14.

It was. I shuffled back to the desk, feeling like I was a tired old man.

When the phone rang finally, I snatched it up. "City morgue. Tully Branson speaking."

"Judd here, Tully."

"Did you . . ."

"Negative from homicide, Tully. No blondes with initials Z. L., female, have been murdered in the last twenty-four hour period."

"Oh," I said, gagging, giving vent to a moan of real anguish.

"Checked with nurse's registry," Judd was saying. "There is a nurse answering your description. Young, blonde, just finished training. Her name is Zella Langtry. Lives at 711 Eastland Avenue. She recently went to work at City Hospital. But if any violence occurred to her, it's been in the past half-hour. She just checked off duty when the graveyard shift reported on."

His words, coupled with the image in drawer 14, left one crazy, wild possibility. The inspiration was so weird it turned the hair on my scalp to needles.

"Mr. Lawrence, I have the most terrible feeling Zella Langtry will never reach home alive."

"What is that? What are you saying, Tully?"

"The Fourth Witch of Endor . . ." I gabbled. "She was a kindly soul at heart. Never put a bad hex on anybody. Just good ones."

"What in the blathering world are you carrying on about?" Judd asked sharply. "Tully, you been drinking?"

"No, sir."

"Feel all right?"

"I—uh . . . Yes, sir, and thanks a lot, Mr. Lawrence."

Twenty minutes later, my jalopy rolled to a stop on Eastland Avenue. I got out, started walking along looking for numbers. I knew I was in the right block, and I located number 711 easily enough. It was a small, white cottage with a skimpy yard that attempted to look more wholesome than its lower-class surroundings.

The place was dark, quiet, peaceful.

I was standing there feeling like seventy kinds of fool when the whir of a diesel engine at the street intersection caught my attention. I looked toward the sound, saw a municipal bus lumbering away.

From the shadows of a straggly maple tree, I watched the shadowy figure of a girl coming along Eastland in my direction. But she wasn't the only passenger who had got off the bus. Behind her was a taller, heavier shadow, that of a man. My breathing thinned as I took in the scene.

She realized he was behind her. She started walking faster. So did the man. She looked over her shoulder. She stepped up the pace even more, almost running now.

The man's shoes slapped quick and hard against the sidewalk. The girl's scream was choked off as the man slammed against her.

They were struggling on the sidewalk, the man locking her throat in the crook of his elbow, the girl writhing and kicking.

I went from under the maple tree like invisible trumpets were urging me on with a blood-rousing fanfare. The man heard me coming, released the girl. I piled into him with a shoulder in his midsection.

He brought a knee up hard. It caught me on the point of the chin. I sat down on the sidewalk, and the man turned and ran away.

Firm but gentle hands helped me to my feet. I looked into the eyes of Zella Langtry for the first time. They were very nice, smoky and grateful in the shadowy night.

"You all right?" I asked, getting my breath back.

"I am now, thanks to you. And you?"

"Fine," I said. "Just fine now."

She was regaining her composure. "Lucky thing for me you were around at the right moment!"

"I—uh—just happened to be passing," I said. "Maybe I'd better walk you to your destination. Won't do any good to report that guy now. Didn't get a look at him. Never would catch him."

"I was going home," she said. "I live just down the street."

We walked along, and she told me her name was Zella, and I told her mine was Tully. When we got to her front door, we looked at each other, and I asked if I could call her some time, and she said any time a phone was handy.

I watched her go inside. I was whistling as I returned to the jalopy.

Inside the morgue, I headed straight for drawer 14. If my theory was correct, the image of Zella Langtry wouldn't be in the drawer, now that she had been rescued from the jaws of death, as it were.

I stood at drawer 14, taking a good, long look. My theory was right as far as it went.

The image of Zella Langtry was no longer in the drawer. The new one was quite a lovely redhead.

The author of more than six hundred short stories, mostly mystery and suspense, Talmage Powell was born in North Carolina in 1920. Except for a short stint as police reporter, he has been a professional writer all his life. His first novel, The Smasher, *appeared in 1959; his Florida private eye, Ed Rivers, stars in five novels, including* The Girl's Number Doesn't Answer *(1959). His fast-moving stories are ingenious and frequently peopled with a large cast of characters.*

Warburg Tantavul had refused to permit his son to marry cousin Arabella. So why did his will promise such a great reward for the birth of their first child?

NINETEEN

The Jest of Warburg Tantavul

Seabury Quinn

Warburg Tantavul was dying. Little more than skin and bones, he lay propped up with pillows in the big sleigh bed and smiled as though he found the thought of dissolution faintly amusing.

Even in comparatively good health the man was never prepossessing. Now, wasted with disease, that smile of self-sufficient satisfaction on his wrinkled face, he was nothing less than hideous. The eyes, which nature had given him, were small, deep-set and ruthless. The mouth, which his own thoughts had fashioned through the years, was wide and thin-lipped, almost colorless, and even in repose was tightly drawn against his small and curiously perfect teeth. Now, as he smiled, a flickering light, lambent as the quick reflection of an unseen flame, flared in his yellowish eyes, and a hard white line of teeth showed on his lower lip, as if he bit it to hold back a chuckle.

"You're still determined that you'll marry Arabella?" he asked his son, fixing his sardonic, mocking smile on the young man.

"Yes, Father, but—"

"No buts, my boy"—this time the chuckle came, low and muted, but at the same time glassy-hard—"no buts. I've told you I'm against it, and you'll rue it to your dying day if you should marry her; but"—he paused, and breath rasped in his wizened throat—"but go ahead and marry her, if your heart's set on it. I've said my say and warned you—heh, boy, never say your poor old father didn't warn you!"

313

He lay back on his piled-up pillows for a moment, swallowing convulsively, as if to force the fleeting life-breath back, then, abruptly: "Get out," he ordered. "Get out and stay out, you poor fool; but remember what I've said."

"Father," young Tantavul began, stepping toward the bed, but the look of sudden concentrated fury in the old man's tawny eyes halted him in midstride.

"Get—out—I—said," his father snarled, then, as the door closed softly on his son:

"Nurse—hand—me—that—picture." His breath was coming slowly, now, in shallow labored gasps, but his withered fingers writhed in a gesture of command, pointing to the silver-framed photograph of a woman which stood upon a little table in the bedroom windowbay.

He clutched the portrait as if it were some precious relic, and for a minute let his eyes rove over it. "Lucy," he whispered hoarsely, and now his words were thick and indistinct, "Lucy, they'll be married, 'spite of all that I have said. They'll be married, Lucy, d'ye hear?" Thin and high-pitched as a child's, his voice rose to a piping treble as he grasped the picture's silver frame and held it level with his face. "They'll be married, Lucy dear, and they'll have—"

Abruptly as a penny whistle's note is stilled when no more air is blown in it, old Tantavul's cry hushed. The picture, still grasped in his hands, fell to the tufted coverlet, the man's lean jaw relaxed and he slumped back on his pillows with a shadow of the mocking smile still in his glazing eyes.

Etiquette requires that the nurse await the doctor's confirmation at such times, so, obedient to professional dictates, Miss Williamson stood by the bed until I felt the dead man's pulse and nodded; then with the skill of years of practice she began her offices, bandaging the wrists and jaws and ankles that the body might be ready when the representative of Martin's Funeral Home came for it.

My friend de Grandin was annoyed. Arms akimbo, knuckles on his hips, his black-silk kimono draped round him like a mourning garment, he voiced his plaint in no uncertain terms. In fifteen little so small minutes he must leave for the theatre, and that son and grandson of a filthy swine who was the florist had not delivered his gardenia. And was it not a fact that he could not go forth without a fresh gardenia for his lapel? But certainly. Why did that *sale chameau* procrastinate? Why did he delay delivering that unmentionable flower till this unspeakable time of night? He was Jules de Grandin, he, and not to be oppressed by any species of a goat who called himself a florist. But no. It must not be. It should not be, by blue! He would—

"Axin' yer pardon, sir," Nora McGinnis broke in from the study door, "there's a Miss an' Mr. Tantavul to see ye, an'—"

"Bid them be gone, *ma charmeuse*. Request that they jump in the bay—*Grand Dieu*"—he cut his oratory short—*"les enfants dans le bois!"*

Truly, there was something reminiscent of the Babes in the Wood in the couple who had followed Nora to the study door. Dennis Tantavul looked even younger and more boyish than I remembered him, and the girl beside him was so childish in appearance that I felt a quick, instinctive pity for her. Plainly they were frightened, too, for they clung hand to hand like frightened children going past a graveyard, and in their eyes was that look of sick terror I had seen so often when the X-ray and blood test confirmed preliminary diagnosis of carcinoma.

"Monsieur, Mademoiselle!" The little Frenchman gathered his kimono and his dignity about him in a single sweeping gesture as he struck his heels together and bowed stiffly from the hips. "I apologize for my unseemly words. Were it not that I have been subjected to a terrible, calamitous misfortune, I should not so far have forgotten myself—"

The girl's quick smile cut through his apology. "We understand," she reassured. "We've been through trouble, too, and have come to Dr. Trowbridge—"

"Ah, then I have permission to withdraw?" he bowed again and turned upon his heel, but I called him back.

"Perhaps you can assist us," I remarked as I introduced the callers.

"The honor is entirely mine, Mademoiselle," he told her as he raised her fingers to his lips. "You and Monsieur your brother—"

315

"He's not my brother," she corrected. "We're cousins. That's why we've called on Dr. Trowbridge."

De Grandin tweaked the already needle-sharp points of his small blond mustache. *"Pardonnez-moi?"* he begged. "I have resided in your country but a little time; perhaps I do not understand the language fluently. It is because you and Monsieur are cousins that you come to see the doctor? Me, I am dull and stupid like a pig; I fear I do not comprehend."

Dennis Tantavul replied: "It's not because of the relationship, Doctor—not entirely, at any rate, but—"

He turned to me: "You were at my father's bedside when he died; you remember what he said about marrying Arabella?"

I nodded.

"There was something—some ghastly, hidden threat concealed in his warning, Doctor. It seemed as if he jeered at me—dared me to marry her, yet—"

"Was there some provision in his will?" I asked.

"Yes, sir," the young man answered. "Here it is." From his pocket he produced a folded parchment, opened it and indicated a paragraph:

> "To my son Dennis Tantavul I give, devise and bequeath all my property of every kind and sort, real, personal and mixed, of which I may die seized and possessed, or to which I may be entitled, in the event of his marrying Arabella Tantavul, but should he not marry the said Arabella Tantavul, then it is my will that he receive only one half of my estate, and that the residue thereof go to the said Arabella Tantavul, who has made her home with me since childhood and occupied the relationship of daughter to me."

"H'm," I returned the document, "this looks as if he really wanted you to marry your cousin, even though—"

"And see here, sir," Dennis interrupted, "here's an envelope we found in Father's papers."

Sealed with red wax, the packet of heavy, opaque parchment was addressed:

"To my children, Dennis and Arabella Tantavul, to
be opened by them upon the occasion of the birth
of their first child."

De Grandin's small blue eyes were snapping with the
flickering light they showed when he was interested.
"Monsieur Dennis," he took the thick envelope from the
caller, "Dr. Trowbridge has told me something of your father's death-bed scene. There is a mystery about this business. My suggestion is you read the message now—"

"No, sir. I won't do that. My father didn't love me—
sometimes I think he hated me—but I never disobeyed a
wish that he expressed, and I don't feel at liberty to do so
now. It would be like breaking faith with the dead. But"—
he smiled a trifle shamefacedly—"Father's lawyer Mr.
Bainbridge is out of town on business, and it will be his duty
to probate the will. In the meantime I'd feel better if the will
and this envelope were in other hands than mine. So we
came to Dr. Trowbridge to ask him to take charge of them till
Mr. Bainbridge gets back, meanwhile—"

"Yes, Monsieur, meanwhile?" de Grandin prompted as
the young man paused.

"You know human nature, Doctor," Dennis turned to
me; "no one can see farther into hidden meanings than the
man who sees humanity with its mask off, the way a doctor
does. D'ye think Father might have been delirious when he
warned me not to marry Arabella, or—" His voice trailed
off, but his troubled eyes were eloquent.

"H'm," I shifted uncomfortably in my chair, "I can't see
any reason for hesitating, Dennis. That bequest of all your
father's property in the event you marry Arabella seems to
indicate his true feelings." I tried to make my words convincing, but the memory of old Tantavul's dying words
dinned in my ears. There had been something gloating in
his voice as he told the picture that his son and niece would
marry.

De Grandin caught the hint of hesitation in my tone.
"Monsieur," he asked Dennis, "will not you tell us of the
antecedents of your father's warning? Dr. Trowbridge is
perhaps too near to see the situation clearly. Me, I have no

knowledge of your father or your family. You and Mademoiselle are strangely like. The will describes her as having lived with you since childhood. Will you kindly tell us how it came about?"

The Tantavuls were, as he said, strangely similar. Anyone might easily have taken them for twins. Like as two plaster portraits from the same mold were their small straight noses, sensitive mouths, curling pale-gold hair.

Now, once more hand in hand, they sat before us on the sofa, and as Dennis spoke I saw the frightened, haunted look creep back into their eyes.

"Do you remember us as children, Doctor?" he asked me.

"Yes, it must have been some twenty years ago they called me out to see you youngsters. You'd just moved into the old Stephens house, and there was a deal of gossip about the strange gentleman from the West with his two small children and Chinese cook, who greeted all the neighbors' overtures with churlish rebuffs and never spoke to anyone."

"What did you think of us, sir?"

"H'm; I thought you and your sister—as I thought her then—had as fine a case of measles as I'd ever seen."

"How old were we then, do you remember?"

"Oh, you were something like three; the little girl was half your age, I'd guess."

"Do you recall the next time you saw us?"

"Yes, you were somewhat older then; eight or ten, I'd say. That time it was the mumps. You were queer, quiet little shavers. I remember asking if you thought you'd like a pickle, and you said, 'No, thank you, sir, it hurts.'"

"It did, too, sir. Every day Father made us eat one; stood over us with a' whip till we'd chewed the last morsel."

"What?"

The young folks nodded solemnly as Dennis answered, "Yes, sir; every day. He said he wanted to check up on the progress we were making."

For a moment he was silent, then: "Dr. Trowbridge, if anyone treated you with studied cruelty all your life—if you'd never had a kind word or gracious act from that person in all your memory, then suddenly that person offered you a favor—made it possible for you to gratify your dearest wish, and threatened to penalize you if you failed to do so, wouldn't you be suspicious? Wouldn't you suspect some sort of dreadful practical joke?"

"I don't think I quite understand."

"Then listen: in all my life I can't remember ever having seen my father smile, not really smile with friendliness, humor or affection, I mean. My life—and Arabella's, too—was one long persecution at his hands. I was two years or so old when we came to Harrisonville, I believe, but I still have vague recollections of our Western home, of a house set high on a hill overlooking the ocean, and a wall with climbing vines and purple flowers on it, and a pretty lady who would take me in her arms and cuddle me against her breast and feed me ice cream from a spoon, sometimes. I have a sort of recollection of a little baby sister in that house, too, but these things are so far back in babyhood that possibly they were no more than childish fancies which I built up for myself and which I loved so dearly and so secretly they finally came to have a kind of reality for me.

"My real memories, the things I can recall with certainty, begin with a hurried train trip through hot, dry, uncomfortable country with my father and a strangely silent Chinese servant and a little girl they told me was my cousin Arabella.

"Father treated me and Arabella with impartial harshness. We were beaten for the slightest fault, and we had faults a-plenty. If we sat quietly we were accused of sulking and asked why we didn't go and play. If we played and shouted we were whipped for being noisy little brats.

"As we weren't allowed to associate with any of the neighbors' children we made up our own games. I'd be Geraint and Arabella would be Enid of the dovewhite feet, or perhaps I'd be King Arthur in the Castle Perilous, and she'd be the kind Lady of the Lake who gave him back his magic sword. And though we never mentioned it, both of us knew that whatever the adventure was, the false knight or giant I contended with was really my father. But when actual trouble came I wasn't an heroic figure.

"I must have been twelve or thirteen when I had my last thrashing. A little brook ran through the lower part of our land, and the former owners had widened it into a lily pond. The flowers had died out years before, but the outlines of the pool remained, and it was our favorite summer play place. We taught ourselves to swim—not very well, of course, but well enough—and as we had no bathing suits we used to go in in our underwear. When we'd finished swimming we'd lie in the sun until our underthings were dry, then slip into our outer clothing. One afternoon as we were splashing in the water, happy as a pair of baby otters, and nearer to shouting with laughter than we'd ever been before, I think, my father suddenly appeared on the bank.

" 'Come out o' there!' he shouted to me, and there was a kind of sharp, dry hardness in his voice I'd never heard before. "So this is how you spend your time?' he asked as I climbed up the bank. 'In spite of all I've done to keep you decent, you do a thing like this!'

" 'Why, Father, we were only swimming—' I began, but he struck me on the mouth.

" 'Shut up, you little rake!' he roared. 'I'll teach you!' He cut a willow switch and thrust my head between his knees; then while he held me tight as in a vice he flogged me with the willow till the blood came through my skin and stained my soaking cotton shorts. Then he kicked me back into the pool as a heartless master might a beaten dog.

"As I said, I wasn't an heroic figure. It was Arabella who came to my rescue. She helped me up the slippery bank and took me in her arms. 'Poor Dennie,' she said. 'Poor, poor Dennie. It was my fault, Dennie, dear, for letting you take me into the water!' Then she kissed me—the first time anyone had kissed me since the pretty lady of my half-remembered dreams. 'We'll be married on the very day that Uncle Warburg dies,' she promised, 'and I'll be so sweet and good to you, and you'll love me so dearly that we'll both forget these dreadful days.'

"We thought my father'd gone, but he must have stayed to see what we would say, for as Arabella finished he stepped from behind a rhododendron bush, and for the first time I heard him laugh. 'You'll be married, will you?' he asked. 'That would be a good joke—the best one of all. All right, go ahead—see what it gets you.'

"That was the last time he ever actually struck me, but from that time on he seemed to go out of his way to invent mental tortures for us. We weren't allowed to go to school, but he had a tutor, a little rat-faced man named Ericson, come in to give us lessons, and in the evening he'd take the book and make us stand before him and recite. If either of us failed a problem in arithmetic or couldn't conjugate a French or Latin verb he'd wither us with sarcasm, and always as a finish to his diatribe he'd jeer at us about our wish to be married, and threaten us with something dreadful if we ever did it.

"So, Dr. Trowbridge, you see why I'm suspicious. It seems almost as if this provision in the will is part of some horrible practical joke my father prepared deliberately—as if he's waiting to laugh at us from the grave."

"I can understand your feelings, boy," I answered, "but—"

" 'But' be damned and roasted on the hottest griddle in hell's kitchen!" Jules de Grandin interrupted. "The wicked dead one's funeral is at two tomorrow afternoon, n'est-ce-pas?

"*Très bien.* At eight tomorrow evening—or earlier, if it will be convenient—you shall be married. I shall esteem it a favor if you permit that I be best man; Dr. Trowbridge will give the bride away, and we shall have a merry time, by blue! You shall go upon a gorgeous honeymoon and learn how sweet the joys of love can be—sweeter for having been so long denied! And in the meantime we shall keep the papers safely till your lawyer returns.

"You fear the so unpleasant jest? *Mais non,* I think the jest is on the other foot, my friends, and the laugh on the other face!"

Warburg Tantavul was neither widely known nor popular, but the solitude in which he had lived had invested him with mystery; now the bars of reticence were down and the walls of isolation broken, upward of a hundred neighbors, mostly women, gathered in the Martin funeral chapel as the services began. The afternoon sun beat softly through the stained glass windows and glinted on the polished mahogany of the casket. Here and there it touched upon bright spots of color that marked a woman's hat or a man's tie. The solemn hush was broken by occasional whispers: "What'd he die of? Did he leave much? Were the two young folks his only heirs?"

Then the burial office: "Lord, Thou hast been our refuge from one generation to another . . . for a thousand years in Thy sight are but as yesterday . . . Oh teach us to number our days that we may apply our hearts unto wisdom. . . ."

As the final Amen sounded one of Mr. Martin's frock-coated young men glided forward, paused beside the casket, and made the stereotyped announcement: "Those who wish to say goodbye to Mr. Tantavul may do so at this time."

The grisly rite of the passing by the bier dragged on. I would have left the place; I had no wish to look upon the man's dead face and folded hands; but de Grandin took me firmly by the elbow, held me till the final curiosity-impelled female had filed past the body, then steered me quickly toward the casket.

He paused a moment at the bier, and it seemed to me there was a hint of irony in the smile that touched the corners of his mouth as he leant forward. *"Eh bien,* my old one; we know a secret, thou and I, *n'est-ce-pas?"* he asked the silent form before us.

I swallowed back an exclamation of dismay. Perhaps it was a trick of the uncertain light, perhaps one of those ghastly, inexplicable things which every doctor and embalmer meets with sometimes in his practice—the effect of desiccation from formaldehyde, the pressure of some tissue gas within the body, or something of the sort—at any rate, as Jules de Grandin spoke the corpse's upper lids drew back the fraction of an inch, revealing slits of yellow eye which seemed to glare at us with mingled hate and fury.

"Good heavens; come away!" I begged. "It seemed as if he *looked* at us, de Grandin!"

"Et puis—and if he did? I damn think I can trade him look for look, my friend. He was clever, that one, I admit it; but do not be mistaken, Jules de Grandin is nobody's imbecile."

The wedding took place in the rectory of St. Chrysostom's. Robed in stole and surplice, Dr. Bentley glanced benignly from Dennis to Arabella, then to de Grandin and me as he began: "Dearly beloved, we are gathered together here in the sight of God and in the face of this company to join together this man and this woman in holy matrimony. . . ." His round and ruddy face grew slightly stern as he admonished, "If any man can show just cause why they should not lawfully be joined together, let him now speak or else hereafter for ever hold his peace."

He paused the customary short, dramatic moment, and I thought I saw a hard, grim look spread on de Grandin's face. Very faint and far-off seeming, so faint that we could scarcely hear it, but gaining steadily in strength, there came a high, thin, screaming sound. Curiously, it seemed to me to resemble the long-drawn, wailing shriek of a freight train's whistle heard miles away upon a still and sultry summer night, weird, wavering and ghastly. Now it seemed to grow in shrillness, though its volume was no greater.

I saw a look of haunted fright leap into Arabella's eyes, saw Dennis' pale face go paler as the strident whistle sounded shriller and more shrill; then, as it seemed I could endure the stabbing of that needle sound no longer, it ceased abruptly, giving way to blessed, comforting silence. But through the silence came a burst of chuckling laughter, half breathless, half hysterical, wholly devilish: *Huh—hu-u-uh—hu-u-u-uh!* the final syllable drawn out until it seemed almost a groan.

"The wind, *Monsieur le Curé;* it was nothing but the wind," de Grandin told the clergyman sharply. "Proceed to marry them, if you will be so kind."

"Wind?" Dr. Bentley echoed. "I could have sworn I heard somebody laugh, but—"

"It is the wind, Monsieur; it plays strange tricks at times," the little Frenchman insisted, his small blue eyes as hard as frozen iron. "Proceed, if you will be so kind. We wait on you."

"Forasmuch as Dennis and Arabella have consented to be joined together in holy wedlock, I pronounce them man and wife," concluded Dr. Bentley, and de Grandin, ever gallant, kissed the bride upon the lips, and before we could restrain him, planted kisses on both Dennis' cheeks.

"*Cordieu,* I thought that we might have the trouble, for a time," he told me as we left the rectory.

"What *was* that awful shrieking noise we heard?" I asked.

"It was the wind, my friend," he answered in a hard, flat, toneless voice. "The ten times damned, but wholly ineffectual wind."

* * *

"So, then, little sinner, weep and wail for the burden of mortality you have assumed. Weep, wail, cry and breathe, my small and wrinkled one! Ha, you will not? *Pardieu,* I say you shall!"

Gently, but smartly, he spanked the small red infant's small red posterior with the end of a towel wrung out in hot water, and as the smacking impact sounded the tiny toothless mouth opened and a thin, high, piping squall of protest sounded. "Ah, that is better, *mon petit ami,*" he chuckled. "One cannot learn too soon that one must do as one is told, not as one wishes, in this world which you have just entered. Look to him, Mademoiselle," he passed the wriggling, bawling morsel of humanity to the nurse and turned to me as I bent over the table where Arabella lay. "How does the little mother, Friend Trowbridge?" he asked.

"U'm'mp," I answered noncommittally. "Bear a hand, here, will you? The perineum's pretty badly torn—have to do a quick repair job—"

"But in the morning she will have forgotten all the pain," laughed de Grandin as Arabella, swathed in blankets, was trundled from the delivery room. "She will gaze upon the little monkey-thing which I just caused to breathe the breath of life and vow it is the loveliest of all God's lovely creatures. She will hold it at her tender breast and smile on it, she will—*Sacré nom d'un rat vert,* what is that?"

From the nursery where, ensconced in wire trays, a score of newborn fragments of humanity slept or squalled, there came a sudden frightened scream—a woman's cry of terror.

We raced along the corridor, reached the glass-walled room and thrust the door back, taking care to open it no wider than was necessary, lest a draft disturb the carefully conditioned air of the place.

Backed against the farther wall, her face gone gray with fright, the nurse in charge was staring at the skylight with terror-widened eyes, and even as we entered she opened her lips to emit another scream.

"Desist, *ma bonne,* you are disturbing your small charges!" de Grandin seized the horrified girl's shoulder and administered a shake. Then: "What is it, Mademoiselle?" he whispered. "Do not be afraid to speak; we shall respect your confidence—but speak softly."

"It—it was up there!" she pointed with a shaking finger toward the black square of the skylight. "They'd just brought Baby Tantavul in, and I had laid him in his crib when I thought I heard somebody laughing. Oh"—she shuddered at the recollection—"it was awful! not really a laugh, but something more like a long-drawn-out hysterical groan. Did you ever hear a child tickled to exhaustion—you know how he moans and gasps for breath, and laughs, all at once? I think the fiends in hell must laugh like that!"

"Yes, yes, we understand," de Grandin nodded, "but tell us what occurred next."

"I looked around the nursery, but I was all alone here with the babies. Then it came again, louder, this time, and seemingly right above me. I looked up at the skylight, and—there it was!"

"It was a face, sir—just a face, with no body to it, and it seemed to float above the glass, then dip down to it, like a child's balloon drifting in the wind, and it looked right past me, down at Baby Tantavul, and laughed again."

"A face, you say, Mademoiselle—"

"Yes, sir, yes! The awfullest face I've ever seen. It was thin and wrinkled—all shriveled like a monkey—and as it looked at Baby Tantavul its eyes stretched open till their whites glared all around the irises, and the mouth opened, not widely, but as if it were chewing something it relished—and it gave that dreadful, cackling, jubilating laugh again. That's it! I couldn't think before, but it seemed as if that bodiless head were laughing with a sort of evil triumph, Dr. de Grandin!"

"H'm," he tweaked his tightly waxed mustache, "I should not wonder if it did, Mademoiselle." To me he whispered, "Stay with her, if you will, my friend, I'll see the supervisor and have her send another nurse to keep her company. I shall request a special watch for the small Tantavul. At present I do not think the danger is great, but mice do not play where cats are wakeful."

"Isn't he just lovely?" Arabella looked up from the small bald head that rested on her breast, and ecstasy was in her eyes. "I don't believe I ever saw so beautiful a baby!"

"*Tiens*, Madame, his voice is excellent, at any rate," de

Grandin answered with a grin, "and from what one may observe his appetite is excellent, as well."

Arabella smiled and patted the small creature's back. "You know, I never had a doll in my life," she confided. "Now I've got this dear little mite, and I'm going to be so happy with him. Oh, I wish Uncle Warburg were alive. I know this darling baby would soften even his hard heart.

"But I mustn't say such things about him, must I? He really wanted me to marry Dennis, didn't he? His will proved that. You think he wanted us to marry, Doctor?"

"I am persuaded that he did, Madame. Your marriage was his dearest wish, his fondest hope," the Frenchman answered solemnly.

"I felt that way, too. He was harsh and cruel to us when we were growing up, and kept his stony-hearted attitude to the end, but underneath it all there must have been some hidden stratum of kindness, some lingering affection for Dennis and me, or he'd never have put that clause in his will—"

"Nor have left this memorandum for you," de Grandin interrupted, drawing from an inner pocket the parchment envelope Dennis had entrusted to him the day before his father's funeral.

She started back as if he menaced her with a live scorpion, and instinctively her arms closed protectively around the baby at her bosom. "The—that—letter?" she faltered, her breath coming in short, smothered gasps. "I'd forgotten all about it. Oh, Dr. de Grandin, burn it. Don't let me see what's in it. I'm afraid!"

It was a bright May morning, without sufficient breeze to stir the leaflets on the maple trees outside the window, but as de Grandin held the letter out I thought I heard a sudden sweep of wind around the angle of the hospital, not loud, but shrewd and keen, like wind among the graveyard evergreens in autumn, and, curiously, there seemed a note of soft malicious laughter mingled with it.

The little Frenchman heard it, too, and for an instant he looked toward the window, and I thought I saw the flicker of an ugly sneer take form beneath the waxed ends of his mustache.

"Open it, Madame," he bade. "It is for you and Monsieur Dennis, and the little *Monsieur Bébé* here."

"I—I daren't—"

"*Tenez,* then Jules de Grandin does!" With his penknife he slit the heavy envelope, pressed suddenly against its ends so that its sides bulged, and dumped its contents on the counterpane. Ten fifty-dollar bills dropped on the coverlet. And nothing else.

"Five hundred dollars!" Arabella gasped. "Why—"

"A birthday gift for *petit Monsieur Bébé,* one surmises," laughed de Grandin. "*Eh bien,* the old one had a sense of humor underneath his ugly outward shell, it seems. He kept you on the tenterhooks lest the message in this envelope contained dire things, while all the time it was a present of congratulation."

"But such a gift from Uncle Warburg—I can't understand it!"

"Perhaps that is as well, too, Madame. Be happy in the gift and give your ancient uncle credit for at least one act of kindness. *Au 'voir.*"

"Hanged if I can understand it, either," I confessed as we left the hospital. "If that old curmudgeon had left a message berating them for fools for having offspring, or even a new will that disinherited them both, it would have been in character, but such a gift—well, I'm surprised."

Amazingly, he halted in midstep and laughed until the tears rolled down his face. "*You* are surprised!" he told me when he managed to regain his breath, "*Cordieu,* my friend, I do not think that you are half as much surprised as Monsieur Warburg Tantavul!"

Dennis Tantavul regarded me with misery-haunted eyes. "I just can't understand it," he admitted. "It's all so sudden, so utterly—"

"*Pardonnez-moi,*" de Grandin interrupted from the door of the consulting room, "I could not help but hear your voice, and if it is not an intrusion—"

"Not at all, sir," the young man answered. "I'd like the benefit of your advice. It's Arabella, and I'm terribly afraid she's—"

"Non, do not try it, *mon ami,"* de Grandin warned. "Do you give us the symptoms, let us make the diagnosis. He who acts as his own doctor has a fool for a patient, you know."

"Well, then, here are the facts: this morning Arabella woke me up, crying as if her heart would break. I asked her what the trouble was, and she looked at me as if I were a stranger—no, not exactly that, rather as if I were some dreadful thing she'd suddenly found at her side. Her eyes were positively round with horror, and when I tried to take her in my arms to comfort her she shrank away as if I were infected with the plague.

" 'Oh, Dennie, don't!' she begged and positively cringed away from me. Then she sprang out of bed and drew her kimono around her as if she were ashamed to have me see her in her pajamas, and ran out of the room.

"Presently I heard her crying in the nursery, and when I followed her in there—" He paused and tears came to his eyes. "She was standing by the crib where little Dennis lay, and in her hand she held a long sharp steel letter-opener. 'Poor little mite, poor little flower of unpardonable sin,' she said. 'We've got to go, Baby darling; you to limbo, I to hell—oh, God wouldn't, *couldn't* be so cruel as to damn you for our sin!—but we'll all three suffer torment endlessly, because we didn't know!"

"She raised the knife to plunge it in the little fellow's heart, and he stretched out his hands and laughed and cooed as the sunlight shone on the steel. I was on her in an instant, wrenching the knife from her with one hand and holding her against me with the other, but she fought me off.

" 'Don't touch me, Dennie, please, *please* don't,' she begged. I know it's mortal sin, but I love you so, my dear, that I just can't resist you if I let you put your arms about me.'

"I tried to kiss her, but she hid her face against my shoulder and moaned as if in pain when she felt my lips against her neck. Then she went limp in my arms, and I carried her, unconscious but still moaning piteously, into her sitting room and laid her on the couch. I left Sarah the nursemaid with her, with strict orders not to let her leave the room. Can't you come over right away?"

De Grandin's cigarette had burned down till it threatened his mustache, and in his little round blue eyes there was a look of murderous rage. *"Bête!"* he murmured savagely. *"Sale chameau;* species of a stinking goat! This is his doing, undoubtlessly. Come, my friends, let us rush, hasten, fly. I would talk with Madame Arabella."

"No, sir, she's done gone," the portly nursemaid told us when we asked for Arabella. "The baby started squealing something awful right after Mister Dennis left, and I knew it was time for his breakfast, so Miss Arabella was laying nice and still on the sofa, and I said, 'You lay still there, honey, whilst I see after your baby;' so I went to the nursery, and fixed him all up, and carried him back to the setting room where Miss Arabella was, and she ain't there no more. No, sir."

"I thought I told you—" Dennis began furiously, but de Grandin laid a hand upon his arm.

"Do not upbraid her, *mon ami,* she did wisely, though she knew it not; she was with the small one all the while, so no harm came to him. Was it not better so, after what you witnessed in the morning?"

"Ye-es," the other grudgingly admitted, "I suppose so. But Arabella—"

"Let us see if we can find a trace of her," the Frenchman interrupted. "Look carefully, do you miss any of her clothing?"

Dennis looked about the pretty chintz-hung room. "Yes," he decided as he finished his inspection, "her dress was on that lounge and her shoes and stockings on the floor beneath it. They're all gone."

"So," de Grandin nodded. "Distracted as she seemed, it is unlikely she would have stopped to dress had she not planned on going out. Friend Trowbridge, will you kindly call police headquarters and inform them of the situation? Ask to have all exits to the city watched."

As I picked up the telephone he and Dennis started on a room-by-room inspection of the house.

"Find anything?" I asked as I hung up the 'phone after talking with the missing persons bureau.

"Corbleu, but I should damn say yes!" de Grandin an-

swered as I joined them in the upstairs living room. "Look yonder, if you please, my friend."

The room was obviously the intimate apartment of the house. Electric lamps under painted shades were placed beside deep leather-covered easy chairs, ivory-enameled bookshelves lined the walls to a height of four feet or so, upon their tops was a litter of gay, unconsidered trifles— cinnabar cigarette boxes, bits of hammered brass. Old china, blue and red and purple, glowed mellowly from open spaces on the shelves, its colors catching up and accenting the muted blues and reds of antique Hamadan carpet. A Paisley shawl was draped scarfwise across the baby grand piano in one corner.

Directly opposite the door a carven crucifix was standing on the bookcase top. It was an exquisite bit of Italian work, the cross of ebony, the corpus of old ivory, and so perfectly executed that though it was a scant six inches high, one could note the tense, tortured muscles of the pendent body, the straining throat which overfilled with groans of agony, the brow all knotted and bedewed with the cold sweat of torment. Upon the statue's thorn-crowned head, where it made a bright iridescent halo, was a band of gem-encrusted platinum, a woman's diamond-studded wedding ring.

"*Hélas,* it is love's crucifixion!" whispered Jules de Grandin.

Three months went by, and though the search kept up unremittingly, no trace of Arabella could be found. Dennis Tantavul installed a fulltime highly-trained and recommended nurse in his desolate house, and spent his time haunting police stations and newspaper offices. He aged a decade in the ninety days since Arabella left; his shoulders stooped, his footsteps lagged, and a look of constant misery lay in his eyes. He was a prematurely old and broken man.

"It's the most uncanny thing I ever saw," I told de Grandin as we walked through West Forty-second Street toward the West Shore Ferry. We had gone over to New York for some surgical supplies, and I do not drive my car in the metropolis. Truck drivers there are far too careless and repair bills for wrecked mudguards far too high. "How a fullgrown woman would evaporate this way is something I can't understand. Of course, she may have done away with herself, dropped off a ferry, or—"

"S-s-st," his sibilated admonition cut me short. "That woman there, my friend, observe her, if you please." He nodded toward a female figure twenty feet or so ahead of us.

I looked, and wondered at his sudden interest at the draggled hussy. She was dressed in tawdry finery much the worse for wear. The sleazy silken skirt was much too tight, the cheap fur jaquette far too short and snug, and the high heels of her satin shoes were shockingly run over. Makeup was fairly plastered on her cheeks and lips and eyes, and short black hair bristled untidily beneath the brim of her abbreviated hat. Written unmistakably upon her was the nature of her calling, the oldest and least honorable profession known to womanhood.

"Well," I answered tartly, "what possible interest can you have in a—"

"Do not walk so fast," he whispered as his fingers closed upon my arm, "and do not raise your voice. I would that we should follow her, but I do not wish that she should know."

The neighborhood was far from savory, and I felt uncomfortably conspicuous as we turned from Forty-second Street into Eleventh Avenue in the wake of the young strumpet, followed her provocatively swaying hips down two malodorous blocks, finally pausing as she slipped furtively into the doorway of a filthy, unkempt "rooming house."

We trailed her through a dimly lighted barren hall and up a flight of shadowy stairs, then up two further flights until we reached a sort of oblong foyer bounded on one end by the stairwell, on the farther extremity by a barred and very dirty window, and on each side by sagging, paint-blistered doors. On each of these was pinned a card, handwritten with the many flourishes dear to the chirography of the professional card-writer who still does business in the poorer quarters of our great cities. The air was heavy with the odor of cheap whiskey, bacon rind and fried onions.

We made a hasty circuit of the hall, studying the cardboard labels. On the farthest door the notice read *Miss Sieglinde*.

"*Mon Dieu,*" he exclaimed as he read it, "*c'est le mot propre!*"

"Eh?" I returned.

"Sieglinde, do not you recall her?"

"No-o, can't say I do. The only Sieglinde I remember is the character in Wagner's *Die Walküre* who unwittingly became her brother's paramour and bore him a son—"

"*Précisément.* Let us enter, if you please." Without pausing to knock he turned the handle of the door and stepped into the squalid room.

The woman sat upon the unkempt bed, her hat pushed back from her brow. In one hand she held a cracked teacup, with the other she poised a whiskey bottle over it. She had kicked her scuffed and broken shoes off; we saw that she was stockingless, and her bare feet were dark with long-accumulated dirt and black-nailed as a miner's hands. "Get out!" she ordered thickly. "Get out o' here. I ain't receivin'—" a gasp broke her utterance, and she turned her head away quickly. Then: "Get out o' here, you lousy bums!" she screamed. "Who d'ye think you are, breakin' into a lady's room like this? Get out, or—"

De Grandin eyed her steadily, and as her strident command wavered: "Madame Arabella, we have come to take you home," he announced softly.

"Good God, man, you're crazy!" I exclaimed. "Arabella? This—"

"Precisely, my old one; this is Madame Arabella Tantavul whom we have sought these many months in vain." Crossing the room in two quick strides he seized the cringing woman by the shoulders and turned her face up to the light. I looked, and felt a sudden swift attack of nausea.

He was right. Thin to emaciation, her face already lined with the deep-bitten scars of evil living, the woman on the bed was Arabella Tantavul, though the shocking change wrought in her features and the black dye in her hair had disguised her so effectively that I should not have known her.

"We have come to take you home, *ma pauvre,*" he repeated. "Your husband—"

"My husband!" her reply was half a scream. "Dear God, as if I had a husband—"

"And the little one who needs you," he continued. "You cannot leave them thus, Madame."

"I can't? Ah, that's where you're wrong, Doctor, I can never see my baby again, in this world or the next. Please go away and forget you've seen me, or I shall have to drown myself—I've tried it twice already, but the first time I was rescued, and the second time my courage failed. But if you try to take me back, or if you tell Dennis you saw me—"

"Tell me, Madame," he broke in, "was not your flight caused by a visitation from the dead?"

Her faded brown eyes—eyes that had been such a startling contrast to her pale-gold hair—widened. "How did you know?" she whispered.

"*Tiens,* one may make surmises. Will not you tell us just what happened? I think there is a way out of your difficulties."

"No, no, there isn't; there can't be!" Her head drooped listlessly. "He planned his work too well; all that's left for me is death—and damnation afterward."

"But if there were a way—if I could show it to you?"

"Can you repeal the laws of God?"

"I am a very clever person, Madame. Perhaps I can accomplish an evasion, if not an absolute repeal. Now tell us, how and when did Monsieur your late but not at all lamented uncle come to you?"

"The night before—before I went away. I woke about midnight, thinking I heard a cry from Dennie's nursery. When I reached the room where he was sleeping I saw my uncle's face glaring at me through the window. It seemed to be illuminated by a sort of inward hellish light, for it stood out against the darkness like a jack-o'-lantern, and it smiled an awful smile at me. 'Arabella,' it said, and I could see its thin dead lips writhe back as if all the teeth were burning-hot, 'I've come to tell you that your marriage is a mockery and a lie. The man you married is your brother, and the child you bore is doubly illegitimate. You can't continue living with them, Arabella. That would be an even greater sin. You must leave them right away, or'—once more his lips crept back until his teeth were bare—'or I shall come to visit you each night, and when the baby has grown old enough to understand I'll tell him who his parents really are. Take your choice, my daughter. Leave them and let me go back to the grave, or stay and see me every night and know that I will tell your son when he is old enough to understand. If I do it he will loathe and hate you; curse the day you bore him.'

"'And you'll promise never to come near Dennis or the baby if I go?' I asked.

"He promised, and I staggered back to bed, where I fell fainting.

"Next morning when I wakened I was sure it had been a bad dream, but when I looked at Dennis and my own reflection in the glass I knew it was no dream, but a dreadful visitation from the dead.

"Then I went mad. I tried to kill my baby, and when Dennis stopped me I watched my chance to run away, came over to New York and took to this." She looked significantly around the miserable room. "I knew they'd never look for Arabella Tantavul among the city's whores; I was safer from pursuit right here than if I'd been in Europe or China."

"But, Madame," de Grandin's voice was jubilant with shocked reproof, "that which you saw was nothing but a dream; a most unpleasant dream, I grant, but still a dream. Look in my eyes, if you please!"

She raised her eyes to his, and I saw his pupils widen as a cat's do in the dark, saw a line of white outline the cornea, and, responsive to his piercing gaze, beheld her brown eyes set in a fixed stare, first as if in fright, then with a glaze almost like that of death.

"Attend me, Madame Arabella," he commanded softly. "You are tired—*grand Dieu*, how tired you are! You have suffered greatly, but you are about to rest. Your memory of that night is gone; so is all memory of the things which have transpired since. You will move and eat and sleep as you are bidden, but of what takes place around you till I bid you wake you will retain no recollection. Do you hear me, Madame Arabella?"

"I hear," she answered softly in a small tired voice.

"*Très bon.* Lie down, my little poor one. Lie down to rest and dreams of love. Sleep, rest, dream and forget.

"Will you be good enough to 'phone to Dr. Wyckoff?" he asked me. "We shall place her in his sanitorium, wash this *sacré* dye from her hair and nurse her back to health; then when all is ready we can bear her home and have her take up life and love where she left off. No one shall be the wiser. This chapter of her life is closed and sealed for ever.

"Each day I'll call upon her and renew hypnotic treatments that she may simulate the mild but curable mental case which we shall tell the good Wyckoff she is. When finally I release her from hypnosis her mind will be entirely cleared of that bad dream that nearly wrecked her happiness."

Arabella Tantavul lay on the sofa in her charming boudoir, an orchid negligée about her slender shoulders, an eiderdown rug tucked around her feet and knees. Her wedding ring was once more on her finger. Pale with a pallor not to be disguised by the most skillfully applied cosmetics, and with deep violet crescents underneath her amber eyes, she lay back listlessly, drinking in the cheerful warmth that emanated from the fire of apple-logs that snapped and crackled on the hearth. Two months of rest at Dr. Wyckoff's sanitorium had cleansed the marks of dissipation from her face, and the ministrations of beauticians had restored the pale-gold luster to her hair, but the listlessness that followed her complete breakdown was still upon her like the weakness from a fever.

"I can't remember anything about my illness, Dr. Trowbridge," she told me with a weary little smile, "but vaguely I connect it with some dreadful dream I had. And"—she wrinkled her smooth forehead in an effort at remembering—"I think I had a rather dreadful dream last night, but—"

"Ah-*ha?*" de Grandin leant abruptly forward in his chair. "What was it that you dreamed, Madame?"

"I—don't—know," she answered slowly. "Odd, isn't it, how you can remember that a dream was so unpleasant, yet not recall its details? Somehow, I connect it with Uncle Warburg; but—"

"*Parbleu,* do you say so? Has he returned? *Ah bah,* he makes me to be so mad, that one!"

*   *   *

"It is time we went, my friend," de Grandin told me as the tall clock in the hall beat out its tenth deliberate stroke; "we have important duties to perform."

"For goodness' sake," I protested, "at this hour o' night?"

"Precisely. At Monsieur Tantavul's I shall expect a visitor tonight, and—we must be ready for him.

"Is Madame Arabella sleeping?" he asked Dennis as he answered our ring at the door.

"Like a baby," answered the young husband. "I've been sitting by her all evening, and I don't believe she even turned in bed."

"And you did keep the window closed, as I requested?"

"Yes, sir; closed and latched."

"*Bien*. Await us here, *mon brave;* we shall rejoin you presently."

He led the way to Arabella's bedroom, removed the wrappings from a bulky parcel he had lugged from our house, and displayed the object thus disclosed with an air of inordinate pride. "Behold him," he commanded gleefully. "Is he not magnificent?"

"Why—what the devil?—it's nothing but an ordinary window screen," I answered.

"A window screen, I grant, my friend; but not an ordinary one. Can not you see it is of copper?"

"Well—"

"*Parbleu,* but I should say it is well," he grinned. "Observe him, how he works."

From his kit bag he produced a roll of insulated wire, an electrical transformer, and some tools. Working quickly he passe-patouted the screen's wooden frame with electrician's tape, then plugged a wire in a nearby lamp socket, connected it with the transformer, and from the latter led a double strand of cotton-wrapped wire to the screen. This he clipped firmly to the copper meshes and led a third strand to the metal grille of the heat register. Last of all he filled a bulb syringe with water and sprayed the screen, repeating the performance till it sparkled like a cobweb in the morning sun. "And now, *Monsieur le Revenant,*" he chuckled as he finished, "I damn think all is ready for your warm reception!"

For something like an hour we waited, then he tiptoed to the bed and bent over Arabella.

"Madame!"

The girl stirred slightly, murmuring some half-audible response, and:

"In half an hour you will rise," he told her. "You will put your robe on and stand by the window, but on no account will you go near it or lay hands on it. Should anyone address you from outside you will reply, but you will not remember what you say or what is said to you."

He motioned me to follow, and we left the room, taking station in the hallway just outside.

How long we waited I have no accurate idea. Perhaps it was an hour, perhaps less; at any rate the silent vigil seemed unending, and I raised my hand to stifle back a yawn when:

"Yes, Uncle Warburg, I can hear you," we heard Arabella saying softly in the room beyond the door.

We tiptoed to the entry: Arabella stood before the window, and from beyond it glared the face of Warburg Tantavul.

It was dead, there was no doubt about that. In sunken cheek and pinched-in nose and yellowish-gray skin there showed the evidence of death and early putrefaction, but dead though it was, it was also animated with a dreadful sort of life. The eyes were glaring horribly, the lips were red as though they had been painted with fresh blood.

"You hear me, do you?" it demanded. "Then listen, girl; you broke your bargain with me, now I'm come to keep my threat: every time you kiss your husband"—a shriek of bitter laughter cut his words, and his staring eyes half closed with hellish merriment—"or the child you love so well, my shadow will be on you. You've kept me out thus far, but some night I'll get in, and—"

The lean dead jaw dropped, then snapped up as if lifted by sheer will-power, and the whole expression of the corpse-faced changed. Surprise, incredulous delight, anticipation as before a feast were pictured on it. "Why"—its cachinnating laughter sent a chill up my spine—"why your window's open! You've changed the screen and I can enter!"

337

Slowly, like a child's balloon stirred by a vagrant wind, the awful thing moved closer to the window. Closer to the screen it came, and Arabella gave ground before it and put up her hands to shield her eyes from the sight of its hellish grin of triumph.

"*Sapristi,*" swore de Grandin softly. "Come on, my old and evil one, come but a little nearer—"

The dead thing floated nearer. Now its mocking mouth and shriveled, pointed nose were almost pressed against the copper meshes of the screen; now they began to filter through the meshes like a wisp of fog—

There was a blinding flash of blue-white flame, the sputtering gush of fusing metal, a wild, despairing shriek that ended ere it fairly started in a sob of mortal torment, and the sharp and acrid odor of burned flesh!

"Arabella—darling—is she all right?" Dennis Tantavul came charging up the stairs. "I thought I heard a scream—"

"You did, my friend," de Grandin answered, "but I do not think that you will hear its repetition unless you are unfortunate enough to go to hell when you have died."

"What was it?"

"*Eh bien,* one who thought himself a clever jester pressed his jest too far. Meantime, look to Madame your wife. See how peacefully she lies upon her bed. Her time for evil dreams is past. Be kind to her, *mon jeune.* Do not forget, a woman loves to have a lover, even though he is her husband." He bent and kissed the sleeping girl upon the brow. "*Au 'voir,* my little lovely one," he murmured. Then, to me:

"Come, Trowbridge, my good friend. Our work is finished here. Let us leave them to their happiness."

An hour later in the study he faced me across the fire. "Perhaps you'll deign to tell me what it's all about now?" I asked sarcastically.

"Perhaps I shall," he answered with a grin. "You will recall that this annoying Monsieur Who Was Dead Yet Not Dead appeared and grinned most horrifyingly through windows several times? Always from the outside, please remember. At the hospital, where he nearly caused the *guarde-malade* to have a fit, he laughed and mouthed at her through the glass skylight. When he first appeared and threatened Madame Arabella he spoke to her through the window—"

"But her window was open," I protested.

"Yes, but screened," he answered with a smile. "Screened with iron wire, if you please."

"What difference did that make? Tonight I saw him almost force his features through—"

"A copper screen," he supplied. "Tonight the screen was copper; me, I saw to that."

Then, seeing my bewilderment: "Iron is the most earthy of all metals," he explained. "It and its derivative, steel, are so instinct with the earth's essence that creatures of the spirit cannot stand its nearness. The legends tell us that when Solomon's Temple was constructed no tool of iron was employed, because even the friendly *jinn* whose help he had enlisted could not perform their tasks in close proximity to iron. The witch can be detected by the pricking of an iron pin—never by a pin of brass.

"Very well. When first I thought about the evil dead one's reappearances I noted that each time he stared outside the window. Glass, apparently, he could not pass—and glass contains a modicum of iron. Iron window-wire stopped him. 'He are not a true ghost, then,' I inform me. 'They are things of spirit only, they are thoughts made manifest. This one is a thing of hate, but also of some physical material as well; he is composed in part of emanations from the body which lies putrefying in the grave. *Voilà*, if he have physical properties he can be destroyed by physical means.'

"And so I set my trap. I procured a screen of copper through which he could effect an entrance, but I charged it with electricity. I increased the potential of the current with a step-up transformer to make assurance doubly sure, and then I waited for him like the spider for the fly, waited for him to come through that charged screen and electrocute himself. Yes, certainly."

"But is he really destroyed?" I asked dubiously.

"As the candle flame when one has blown it out. He was—how do you say it?—short-circuited. No malefactor in the chair of execution ever died more thoroughly than that one, I assure you."

"It seems queer, though, that he should come back from

the grave to haunt those poor kids and break up their marriage when he really wanted it," I murmured wonderingly.

"Wanted it? Yes, as the trapper wants the bird to step within his snare."

"But he gave them such a handsome present when little Dennis was born—"

"*La la,* my good, kind, trusting friend, you are *naïf.* The money I gave Madame Arabella was my own. I put it in that envelope."

"Then what was the real message?"

"It was a dreadful thing, my friend; a dreadful, wicked thing. The night that Monsieur Dennis left that package with me I determined that the old one meant to do him injury, so I steamed the cover open and read what lay within. It made plain the things which Dennis thought that he remembered.

"Long, long ago Monsieur Tantavul lived in San Francisco. His wife was twenty years his junior, and a pretty, joyous thing she was. She bore him two fine children, a boy and girl, and on them she bestowed the love which he could not appreciate. His surliness, his evil temper, his constant fault-finding drove her to distraction, and finally she sued for divorce.

"But he forestalled her. He spirited the children away, then told his wife the plan of his revenge. He would take them to some far off place and bring them up believing they were cousins. Then when they had attained full growth he would induce them to marry and keep the secret of their relationship until they had a child, then break the dreadful truth to them. Thereafter they would live on, bound together by their fear of censure, or perhaps of criminal prosecution, but their consciences would cause them endless torment, and the very love they had for each other would be like fetters forged of white-hot steel, holding them in odious bondage from which there was no escape. The sight of their children would be a reproach to them, the mere thought of love's sweet communion would cause revulsion to the point of nausea.

"When he had told her this his wife went mad. He thrust her into an asylum and left her there to die while he came with his babies to New Jersey, where he reared them together, and by guile and craftiness nurtured their love,

340

knowing that when finally they married he would have his so vile revenge."

"But, great heavens, man, they're brother and sister!" I exclaimed in horror.

"Perfectly," he answered coolly. "They are also man and woman, husband and wife, and father and mother."

"But—but—" I stammered, utterly at loss for words.

"But me no buts, good friend. I know what you would say. Their child? *Ah bah,* did not the kings of ancient times repeatedly take their own sisters to wife, and were not their offspring usually sound and healthy? But certainly cross-breeding produces inferior progeny only when defective recessive genes are matched. Look at little Monsieur Dennis. Were you not blinded by your silly, unrealistic training and tradition—did you not know his parents' near relationship—you would not hesitate to pronounce him an unusually fine, healthy child.

"Besides," he added earnestly, "they love each other, not as brother and sister, but as man and woman. He is her happiness, she is his, and little Monsieur Dennis is the happiness of both. Why destroy this joy—*le bon Dieu* knows they earned it by a joyless childhood—when I can preserve it for them by simply keeping silent?"

For a quarter of a century, Seabury Quinn's ghostly tales were almost always ranked first by the readers of Weird Tales, *where nearly all of his more than 160 stories appeared. Born in Washington, D.C., in 1889, Quinn graduated from the Law School of the Washington, D.C. Bar, saw military service in World War I, became the editor of trade journals for mortuary directors, and was an expert on mortuary law and science. He is best known, however, as the creator of Dr. Jules De Grandin, the dapper blond ghosthunter whose best cases are collected in* The Phantom-Fighter, *His best non-de Grandin tales appear in* Is the Devil a Gentleman?

Ted was suspicious when the lot in exclusive Clay Canyon was only $1500. What was the catch?

TWENTY

One of the Dead
William Wood

We couldn't have been more pleased. Deep in Clay Canyon we came upon the lot abruptly at a turn in the winding road. There was a crudely lettered board nailed to a dead tree which read, LOT FOR SALE—$1500 OR BEST OFFER, and a phone number.

"Fifteen hundred dollars—in Clay Canyon? I can't believe it," Ellen said.

"Or best offer," I corrected.

"I've heard you can't take a step without bumping into some movie person here."

"We've come three miles already without bumping into one. I haven't seen a soul."

"But there are the houses." Ellen looked about breathlessly.

There indeed were the houses—to our left and our right, to our front and our rear—low, ranch-style houses, unostentatious, prosaic, giving no hint of the gay and improbable lives we imagined went on inside them. But as the houses marched up the gradually climbing road there was not a single person to be seen. The cars—the Jaguars and Mercedeses and Cadillacs and Chryslers—were parked unattended in the driveways, their chrome gleaming in the sun; I caught a glimpse of one corner of a pool and a white diving board, but no one swam in the turquoise water. We climbed out of the car, Ellen with her rather large, short-haired head stooped forward as if under a weight. Except for the fiddling of a cicada somewhere on the hill, a profound hush lay over us in the stifling air. Not even a bird moved in the motionless trees.

343

"There must be something wrong with it," Ellen said.

"It's probably already been sold, and they just didn't bother to take down the sign. . . . There was something here once, though." I had come across several ragged chunks of concrete that lay about randomly as if heaved out of the earth.

"A house, do you think?"

"It's hard to say. If it was a house it's been gone for years."

"Oh, Ted," Ellen cried. "It's perfect! Look at the view!" She pointed up the canyon toward the round, parched hills. Through the heat shimmering on the road they appeared to be melting down like wax.

"Another good thing," I said. "There won't be much to do to get the ground ready except for clearing the brush away. This place has been graded once. We save a thousand dollars right there."

Ellen took both my hands. Her eyes shone in her solemn face. "What do you think, Ted? What do you think?"

Ellen and I had been married four years, having both taken the step relatively late—in our early thirties—and in that time had lived in two different places, first an apartment in Santa Monica, then, when I was promoted to office manager, in a partly furnished house in the Hollywood Hills, always with the idea that when our first child came we would either buy or build a larger house of our own. But the child had not come. It was a source of anxiety and sadness to us both and lay between us like an old scandal for which each of us took on the blame.

Then I made an unexpected killing on the stock market and Ellen suddenly began agitating in her gentle way for the house. As we shopped around she dropped hints along the way—"This place is really too small for us, don't you think?" or "We'd have to fence off the yard, of course"— that let me know that the house had become a talisman for her; she had conceived the notion that perhaps, in some occult way, if we went ahead with our accommodations for a child the child might come. The notion gave her happiness. Her face filled out, the gray circles under her eyes disappeared, the quiet gaiety, which did not seem like gaiety at all but a form of peace, returned.

As Ellen held on to my hands, I hesitated. I am convinced now that there was something behind my hesitation— something I felt then only as a quality of silence, a fleeting twinge of utter desolation. "It's so safe," she said. "There's no traffic at all."

I explained that. "It's not a through street. It ends somewhere up in the hills."

She turned back to me again with her bright, questioning eyes. The happiness that had grown in her during our months of house-hunting seemed to have welled into near rapture.

"We'll call the number," I said, "but don't expect too much. It must have been sold long ago."

We walked slowly back to the car. The door handle burned to the touch. Down the canyon the rear end of a panel truck disappeared noiselessly around a bend.

"No," Ellen said, "I have a feeling about this place. I think it was meant to be ours."

And she was right, of course.

Mr. Carswell Deeves, who owned the land, was called upon to do very little except take my check for $1500 and hand over the deed to us, for by the time Ellen and I met him we had already sold ourselves. Mr. Deeves, as we had suspected from the unprofessional sign, was a private citizen. We found his house in a predominantly Mexican section of Santa Monica. He was a chubby, pink man of indeterminate age dressed in white ducks and soft white shoes, as if he had had a tennis court hidden away among the squalid, asphalt-shingled houses and dry kitchen gardens of his neighbors.

"Going to live in Clay Canyon, are you?" he said. "Ros Russell lives up there, or used to." So, we discovered, did Joel McCrea, Jimmy Stewart and Paula Raymond, as well as a cross-section of producers, directors and character actors. "Oh, yes," said Mr. Deeves, "it's an address that will look extremely good on your stationery."

Ellen beamed and squeezed my hand.

Mr. Deeves turned out to know very little about the land other than that a house had been destroyed by fire there years ago and that the land had changed hands many times since. "I myself acquired it in what may strike you as a novel way," he said as we sat in his parlor—a dark, airless box which smelled faintly of camphor and whose walls were obscured with yellowing autographed photographs of movie stars. "I won it in a game of hearts from a makeup man on the set of *Quo Vadis*. Perhaps you remember me. I had a close-up in one of the crowd scenes."

"That was a number of years ago, Mr. Deeves," I said. "Have you been trying to sell it all this time?"

"I've nearly sold it dozens of times," he said, "but something always went wrong somehow."

"What kind of things?"

"Naturally, the fire-insurance rates up there put off a lot of people. I hope you're prepared to pay a high premium—"

"I've already checked into that."

"Good. You'd be surprised how many people will let details like that go till the last minute."

"What other things have gone wrong?"

Ellen touched my arm to discourage my wasting any more time with foolish questions.

Mr. Deeves spread out the deed before me and smoothed it with his forearm. "Silly things, some of them. One couple found some dead doves. . . "

"Dead doves?" I handed him the signed article. With one pink hand Mr. Deeves waved it back and forth to dry the ink. "Five of them, if I remember correctly. In my opinion they'd sat on a wire and were electrocuted somehow. The husband thought nothing of it, of course, but his wife became so hysterical that we had to call off the transaction."

I made a sign at Mr. Deeves to drop this line of conversation. Ellen loves animals and birds of all kinds with a devotion that turns the loss of a household pet into a major tragedy, which is why, since the death of our cocker spaniel, we have had no more pets. But Ellen appeared not to have heard; she was watching the paper in Mr. Deeves' hand fixedly, as if she were afraid it might vanish.

Mr. Deeves sprang suddenly to his feet. "Well!" he cried. "It's all yours now. I know you'll be happy there."

Ellen flushed with pleasure. "I'm sure we will," she said, and took his pudgy hand in both of hers.

"A prestige address," called Mr. Deeves from his porch as we drove away. "A real prestige address."

Ellen and I are modern people. Our talk in the evenings is generally on issues of the modern world. Ellen paints a little and I do some writing from time to time—mostly on technical subjects. The house that Ellen and I built mirrored our concern with present-day aesthetics. We worked closely with Jack Salmanson, the architect and a friend, who designed a steel module house, low and compact and private, which could be fitted into the irregularities of our patch of land for a maximum of space. The interior *décor* we left largely up to Ellen, who combed the home magazines and made sketches as if she were decorating a dozen homes.

I mention these things to show that there is nothing Gothic about my wife and me: We are as thankful for our common sense as for our sensibilities, and we flattered ourselves that the house we built achieved a balance between the aesthetic and the functional. Its lines were simple and clean; there were no dark corners, and it was surrounded on three sides by houses, none of which were more than eight years old.

There were, however, signs from the very beginning, ominous signs which can be read only in retrospect, though it seems to me now that there were others who suspected but said nothing. One was the Mexican who cut down the tree.

As a money-saving favor to us, Jack Salmanson agreed to supervise the building himself and hire small, independent contractors to do the labor, many of whom were Mexicans or Negroes with dilapidated equipment that appeared to run only by some mechanical miracle. The Mexican, a small, forlorn workman with a stringy moustache, had already burned out two chain-saw blades and still had not cut halfway through the tree. It was inexplicable. The tree, the same one on which Ellen and I had seen the original FOR SALE sign, had obviously been dead for years, and the branches that already lay scattered on the ground were rotted through.

"You must have run into a batch of knots," Jack said. "Try it again. If the saw gets too hot, quit and we'll pull it down with the bulldozer." As if answering to its name, the bulldozer turned at the back of the lot and lumbered toward us in a cloud of dust, the black shoulders of the Negro operator gleaming in the sun.

The Mexican need not have feared for his saw. He had scarcely touched it to the tree when it started to topple of its own accord. Startled, he backed away a few steps. The tree had begun to fall toward the back of the lot, in the direction of his cut, but now it appeared to arrest itself, its naked branches trembling as if in agitation; then with an awful rending sound it writhed upright and fell back on itself, gaining momentum and plunging directly at the bulldozer. My voice died in my throat, but Jack and the Mexican shouted, and the operator jumped and rolled on the ground just as the tree fell high on the hood, shattering the windshield to bits. The bulldozer, out of control and knocked off course, came directly at us, gears whining and gouging a deep trough in the earth. Jack and I jumped one way, the Mexican the other; the bulldozer lurched between us and ground on toward the street, the Negro sprinting after it.

"The car!" Jack shouted. "The car!"

Parked in front of the house across the street was a car, a car which was certainly brand-new. The bulldozer headed straight for it, its blade striking clusters of sparks from the pavement. The Mexican waved his chain saw over his head like a toy and shouted in Spanish. I covered my eyes with my hands and heard Jack grunt softly, as if he had been struck in the mid-section, just before the crash.

Two women stood on the porch of the house across the street and gaped. The car had caved in at the center, its steel roof wrinkled like tissue paper; its front and rear ends were folded around the bulldozer as if embracing it. Then with a low whoosh, both vehicles were enveloped in creeping blue flame.

"Rotten luck," Jack muttered under his breath as we ran into the street. From the corner of my eye I caught the curious sight of the Mexican on the ground, praying, his chain saw lying by his knees.

In the evening Ellen and I paid a visit to the Sheffits', Sondra and Jeff, our neighbors across the canyon road, where we met the owner of the ruined car, Joyce Castle, a striking blonde in lemon-colored pants. The shock of the

accident itself wore off with the passing of time and cock-
tails, and the three of them treated it as a tremendous joke.

Mrs. Castle was particularly hilarious. "I'm doing better,"
she rejoiced. "The Alfa-Romeo only lasted two days, but I
held on to this one a whole six weeks. I even had the permanent plates on."

"But you mustn't be without a car, Mrs. Castle," Ellen
said in her serious way. "We'd be glad to loan you our
Plymouth until you can—"

"I'm having a new car delivered tomorrow afternoon.
Don't worry about me. A Daimler, Jeff, you'll be interested
to know. I couldn't resist after riding in yours. What about
the poor bulldozer man? Is he absolutely wiped out?"

"I think he'll survive," I said. "In any case he has two
other 'dozers."

"Then you won't be held up," Jeff said.

"I wouldn't think so."

Sondra chuckled softly. "I just happened to look out the
window," she said. "It was just like a Rube Goldberg car-
toon. A chain reaction."

"And there was my poor old Cadillac at the end of it,"
Mrs. Castle sighed.

Suey, Mrs. Castle's dog, who had been lying on the floor
beside his mistress glaring dourly at us between dozes, suddenly ran to the front door barking ferociously, his red mane
standing straight up.

"Suey!" Mrs. Castle slapped her knee. "Suey! Come
here!"

The dog merely flattened its ears and looked from his
mistress toward the door again as if measuring a decision.
He growled deep in his throat.

"It's the ghost," Sondra said lightly. "He's behind the
whole thing." Sondra sat curled up in one corner of the sofa
and tilted her head to one side as she spoke, like a very
clever child.

Jeff laughed sharply. "Oh, they tell some very good
stories."

With a sigh Mrs. Castle rose and dragged Suey back by
his collar. "If I didn't feel so self-conscious about it I'd take

him to an analyst," she said. "Sit, Suey! Here's a cashew nut for you."

"I'm very fond of ghost stories," I said, smiling.

"Oh, well," Jeff murmured, mildly disparaging.

"Go ahead, Jeff," Sondra urged him over the rim of her glass. "They'd like to hear it."

Jeff was a literary agent, a tall, sallow man with dark oily hair that he was continually pushing out of his eyes with his fingers. As he spoke he smiled lopsidedly as if defending against the probability of being taken seriously. "All I know is that back in the late seventeenth century the Spanish used to have hangings here. The victims are supposed to float around at night and make noises."

"Criminals?" I asked.

"Of the worst sort," said Sondra. "What was the story Guy Relling told you, Joyce?" She smiled with a curious inward relish that suggested she knew the story perfectly well herself.

"Is that Guy Relling, the director?" I asked.

"Yes," Jeff said. "He owns those stables down the canyon."

"I've seen them," Ellen said. "Such lovely horses."

Joyce Castle hoisted her empty glass into the air. "Jeff, love, will you find me another?"

"We keep straying from the subject," said Sondra gently. "Fetch me another too, darling"—she handed her glass to Jeff as he went by—"like a good boy. . . . I didn't mean to interrupt, Joyce. Go on." She gestured toward us as the intended audience. Ellen stiffened slightly in her chair.

"It seems that there was one *hombre* of outstanding depravity," Joyce Castle said languidly. "I forgot the name. He murdered, stole, raped . . . one of those endless Spanish names with a 'Luis' in it, a nobleman I think Guy said. A charming sort. Mad, of course, and completely unpredictable. They hanged him at last for some unsavory escapade in a nunnery. You two are moving into a neighborhood rich with tradition."

We all laughed.

"What about the noises?" Ellen asked Sondra. "Have you heard anything?"

"Of course," Sondra said, tipping her head prettily. Every

inch of her skin was tanned to the color of coffee from afternoons by the pool. It was a form of leisure that her husband, with his bilious coloring and lank hair, apparently did not enjoy.

"Everywhere I've ever lived," he said, his grin growing crookeder and more apologetic, "there were noises in the night that you couldn't explain. Here there are all kinds of wildlife—foxes, coons, possums—even coyotes up on the ridge. They're all active after sundown."

Ellen's smile of pleasure at this news turned to distress as Sondra remarked in her offhand way, "We found our poor kitty-cat positively torn to pieces one morning. He was all blood. We never did find his head."

"A fox," Jeff put in quickly. Everything he said seemed hollow. Something came from him like a vapor. I thought it was grief.

Sondra gazed smugly into her lap as if hugging a secret to herself. She seemed enormously pleased. It occurred to me that Sondra was trying to frighten us. In a way it relieved me. She was enjoying herself too much, I thought, looking at her spoiled, brown face, to be frightened herself.

After the incident of the tree everything went well for some weeks. The house went up rapidly. Ellen and I visited it as often as we could, walking over the raw ground and making our home in our mind's eye. The fireplace would go here, the refrigerator here, our Picasso print there. "Ted," Ellen said timidly, "I've been thinking. Why don't we fix up the extra bedroom as a children's room?"

I waited.

"Now that we'll be living out here our friends will have to stay overnight more often. Most of them have young children. It would be nice for them."

I slipped my arm around her shoulders. She knew I understood. It was a delicate matter. She raised her face and I kissed her between her brows. Signal and counter-signal, the keystones of our life together—a life of sensibility and tact.

"Hey, you two!" Sondra Sheffits called from across the street. She stood on her front porch in a pink bathing suit, her skin brown, her hair nearly white. "How about a swim?"

"No suits!"

"Come on, we've got plenty."

Ellen and I debated the question with a glance, settled it with a nod.

As I came out onto the patio in one of Jeff's suits, Sondra said, "Ted, you're pale as a ghost. Don't you get any sun where you are?" She lay in a chaise lounge behind huge elliptical sunglasses encrusted with glass gems.

"I stay inside too much, writing articles," I said.

"You're welcome to come here any time you like"—she smiled suddenly, showing me a row of small, perfect teeth—"and swim."

Ellen appeared in her borrowed suit, a red one with a short, limp ruffle. She shaded her eyes as the sun, glittering metallically on the water, struck her full in the face.

Sondra ushered her forward as if to introduce my wife to me. "You look much better in that suit than I ever did." Her red nails flashed on Ellen's arm. Ellen smiled guardedly. The two women were about the same height, but Ellen was narrower in the shoulders, thicker through the waist and hips. As they came toward me it seemed to me that Ellen was the one I did not know. Her familiar body became strange. It looked out of proportion. Hairs that on Sondra were all but invisible except when the sun turned them to silver, lay flat and dark on Ellen's pallid arm.

As if sensing the sudden distance between us, Ellen took my hand. "Let's jump in together," she said gaily. "No hanging back."

Sondra retreated to the chaise lounge to watch us, her eyes invisible behind her outrageous glasses, her head on one side.

Incidents began again and continued at intervals. Guy Relling, whom I never met but whose pronouncements on the supernatural reached me through others from time to time like messages from an oracle, claims that the existence of the living dead is a particularly excruciating one as they hover between two states of being. Their memories keep the passions of life forever fresh and sharp, but they are able to relieve them only at a monstrous expense of will and energy which leaves them literally helpless for months or sometimes even years afterward. This was why materializations and other forms of tangible action are relatively rare. There are of course exceptions, Sondra, our most frequent translator of Relling's theories, pointed out one evening with the odd joy that accompanied all of her remarks on the subject; some ghosts are terrifically active—particularly the insane ones who, ignorant of the limitations of death as they were of the impossibilities of life, transcend them with the dynamism that is exclusively the property of madness. Generally, however, it was Relling's opinion that a ghost was more to be pitied than feared. Sondra quoted him as having said, "The notion of a haunted house is a misconception semantically. It is not the house but the soul itself that is haunted."

On Saturday, August 6, a workman laying pipe was blinded in one eye by an acetylene torch.

On Thursday, September 1, a rockslide on the hill behind us dumped four tons of dirt and rock on the half-finished house and halted work for two weeks.

On Sunday, October 9—my birthday, oddly enough—while visiting the house alone, I slipped on a stray screw and struck my head on a can of latex paint which opened up a gash requiring ten stitches. I rushed across to the Sheffits'. Sondra answered the door in her bathing suit and a magazine in her hand. "Ted?" She peered at me. "I scarcely recognized you through the blood. Come in, I'll call the doctor. Try not to drip on the furniture, will you?"

I told the doctor of the screw on the floor, the big can of paint. I did not tell him that my foot had slipped because I had turned too quickly and that I had turned too quickly because the sensation had grown on me that there was someone behind me, close enough to touch me, perhaps, because something hovered there, fetid and damp and cold and almost palpable in its nearness; I remember shivering violently as I turned, as if the sun of this burning summer's day had been replaced by a mysterious star without warmth. I did not tell the doctor this nor anyone else.

In November Los Angeles burns. After the long drought of summer the sap goes underground and the baked hills seem to gasp in pain for the merciful release of either life or death—rain or fire. Invariably fire comes first, spreading through the outlying parts of the country like an epidemic, till the sky is livid and starless at night and overhung with dun-colored smoke during the day.

There was a huge fire in Tujunga, north of us, the day Ellen and I moved into our new house—handsome, severe, aggressively new on its dry hillside—under a choked sky the color of earth and a muffled, flyspeck sun. Sondra and Jeff came over to help, and in the evening Joyce Castle stopped by with Suey and a magnum of champagne.

Ellen clasped her hands under her chin. "What a lovely surprise!"

"I hope it's cold enough. I've had it in my refrigerator since four o'clock. Welcome to the canyon. You're nice people. You remind me of my parents. God, it's hot. I've been weeping all day on account of the smoke. You'll have air conditioning I suppose?"

Jeff was sprawled in a chair with his long legs straight in front of him in the way a cripple might put aside a pair of crutches. "Joyce, you're an angel. Excuse me if I don't get up. I'm recuperating."

"You're excused, doll, you're excused."

"Ted," Ellen said softly. "Why don't you get some glasses?"

Jeff hauled in his legs. "Can I give you a hand?"

"Sit still, Jeff."

He sighed. "I hadn't realized I was so out of shape." He looked more cadaverous than ever after our afternoon of lifting and shoving. Sweat had collected in the hollows under his eyes.

"Shall I show you the house, Joyce? While Ted is in the kitchen?"

"I love you, Ellen," Joyce said. "Take me on the whole tour."

Sondra followed me into the kitchen. She leaned against the wall and smoked, supporting her left elbow in the palm of her right hand. She didn't say a word. Through the open door I could see Jeff's outstretched legs from the calves down.

"Thanks for all the help today," I said to Sondra in a voice unaccountably close to a whisper. I could hear Joyce and Ellen as they moved from room to room, their voices swelling and dying: "It's all steel? You mean everything? Walls and all? Aren't you afraid of lightning?"

"Oh, we're all safely grounded, I think."

Jeff yawned noisily in the living room. Wordlessly Sondra put a tray on the kitchen table as I rummaged in an unpacked carton for the glasses. She watched me steadily and coolly, as if she expected me to entertain her. I wanted to say something further to break a silence which was becoming unnatural and oppressive. The sounds around us seemed only to isolate us in a ring of intimacy. With her head on one side Sondra smiled at me. I could hear her rapid breathing.

"What's this, a nursery? Ellen, love!"

"No, no! It's only for our friends' children."

Sondra's eyes were blue, the color of shallow water. She seemed faintly amused, as if we were sharing in a conspiracy—a conspiracy I was anxious to repudiate by making some prosaic remark in a loud voice for all to hear, but a kind of pain developed in my chest as the words seemed dammed there, and I only smiled at her foolishly. With every passing minute of silence, the more impossible it became to break through and the more I felt drawn into the intrigue of which, though I was ignorant, I was surely guilty. Without so much as a touch she had made us lovers.

Ellen stood in the doorway, half turned away as if her first impulse had been to run. She appeared to be deep in thought, her eyes fixed on the steel, cream-colored doorjamb.

Sondra began to talk to Ellen in her dry, satirical voice. It was chatter of the idlest sort, but she was destroying, as I had wished to destroy, the absurd notion that there was something between us. I could see Ellen's confusion. She hung on Sondra's words, watching her lips attentively, as if this elegant, tanned woman, calmly smoking and talking of trifles, were her savior.

As for myself, I felt as if I had lost the power of speech entirely. If I joined in with Sondra's carefully innocent chatter I would only be joining in the deception against my wife; if I proclaimed the truth and ended everything by bringing it into the open . . . . but what truth? What was there in fact to bring into the open? What was there to end? A feeling in the air? An intimation? The answer was nothing, of course. I did not even like Sondra very much. There was something cold and unpleasant about her. There was nothing to proclaim because nothing had happened. "Where's Joyce?" I asked finally, out of a dry mouth. "Doesn't she want to see the kitchen?"

Ellen turned slowly toward me, as if it cost her a great effort. "She'll be here in a minute," she said tonelessly, and I became aware of Joyce's and Jeff's voices from the living room. Ellen studied my face, her pupils oddly dilated unter the pinkish fluorescent light, as if she were trying to penetrate to the bottom of a great darkness that lay beneath my chance remark. Was it a code of some kind, a new signal for her that I would shortly make clear? What did it mean? I smiled at her and she responded with a smile of her own, a tentative and formal upturning of her mouth, as if I were a familiar face whose name escaped her for the moment.

Joyce came in behind Ellen. "I hate kitchens. I never go into mine." She looked from one to the other of us. "Am I interrupting something?"

At two o'clock in the morning I sat up in bed, wide awake. The bedroom was bathed in the dark red glow of the fire which had come closer in the night. A thin, autumnal veil of smoke hung in the room. Ellen lay on her side, asleep, one hand cupped on the pillow next to her face as if waiting for something to be put in it. I had no idea why I was so fully awake, but I threw off the covers and went to the window to check on the fire. I could see no flame, but the hills stood out blackly against a turgid sky that belled and sagged as the wind blew and relented.

Then I heard the sound.

I am a person who sets store by precision in the use of words—in the field of technical writing this is a necessity. But I can think of no word to describe that sound. The closest I can come with a word of my own invention is "vlump." It came erratically, neither loud nor soft. It was, rather, pervasive and without location. It was not a *solid* sound. There was something vague and whispering about it, and from time to time it began with the suggestion of a sigh—a shuffling dissipation in the air that seemed to take form and die in the same instant. In a way I cannot define, it was mindless, without will or reason, yet implacable. Because I could not explain it immediately I went to seek an explanation.

I stepped into the hall and switched on the light, pressing the noiseless button. The light came down out of a fixture set flush into the ceilings and diffused through a milky plastic-like Japanese rice paper. The clean, indestructible walls rose perpendicularly around me. Through the slight haze of smoke came the smell of the newness, sweet and metallic— more like a car than a house. And still the sound went on. It seemed to be coming from the room at the end of the hall, the room we had designed for our friends' children. The door was open and I could see a gray patch that was a west window. Vlump . . . vlump . . . vlumpvlump. . . .

Fixing on the gray patch, I moved down the hall while my legs made themselves heavy as logs, and all the while I repeated to myself, "The house is settling. All new houses settle and make strange noises." And so lucid was I that I believed I was not afraid. I was walking down the bright new hall of my new steel house to investigate a noise, for the house might be settling unevenly, or an animal might be up to some mischief—raccoons regularly raided the garbage cans, I had been told. There might be something wrong with the plumbing or with the radiant-heating system that warmed our steel and vinyl floors. And now, like the responsible master of the house, I had located the apparent center of the sound and was going responsibly toward it. In a second or two, very likely, I would know. Vlump vlump. The gray of the window turned rosy as I came near enough to see the hillside beyond it. That black was underbrush and that pink the dusty swath cut by the bulldozer before it had run amok. I had watched the accident from just about the spot where I stood now, and the obliterated hole where the tree had been, laid firmly over with the prefabricated floor of the room whose darkness I would eradicate by touching with my right hand the light switch inside the door.

"Ted?"

Blood boomed in my ears. I had the impression that my heart had burst. I clutched at the wall for support. Yet of course I knew it was Ellen's voice, and I answered her calmly. "Yes, it's me."

"What's the matter?" I heard the bedclothes rustle.

"Don't get up, I'm coming right in." The noise had stopped. There was nothing. Only the almost inaudible hum of the refrigerator, the stirring of the wind.

Ellen was sitting up in bed. "I was just checking on the fire," I said. She patted my side of the bed and in the instant before I turned out the hall light I saw her smile.

"I was just dreaming about you," she said softly, as I climbed under the sheets. She rolled against me. "Why, you're trembling."

"I should have worn my robe."

"You'll be warm in a minute." Her fragrant body lay against mine, but I remained rigid as stone and just as cold, staring at the ceiling, my mind a furious blank. After a moment she said, "Ted?" It was her signal, always hesitant, always tremulous, that meant I was to roll over and take her in my arms.

Instead I answered, "What?" just as if I had not understood.

For a few seconds I sensed her struggling against her reserve to give me a further sign that would pierce my peculiar distraction and tell me she wanted love. But it was too much for her—too alien. My coldness had created a vacuum she was too unpracticed to fill—a coldness sudden and inexplicable, unless . . .

She withdrew slowly and pulled the covers up under her chin. Finally she asked, "Ted, is there something happening that I should know about?" She had remembered Sondra and the curious scene in the kitchen. It took, I knew, great courage for Ellen to ask that question, though she must have known my answer.

"No, I'm just tired. We've had a busy day. Good-night, dear." I kissed her on the cheek and sensed her eyes, in the shadow of the fire, searching mine, asking the question she could not give voice to. I turned away, somehow ashamed because I could not supply the answer that would fulfill her need. Because there was no answer at all.

The fire was brought under control after burning some eight hundred acres and several homes, and three weeks later the rains came. Jack Salmanson came out one Sunday to see how the house was holding up, checked the foundation, the roof and all the seams and pronounced it tight as a drum. We sat looking moodily out the glass doors onto the patio—a flatland of grayish mud which threatened to swamp with a thin ooze of silt and gravel the few flagstones I had set in the ground. Ellen was in the bedroom lying down; she had got into the habit of taking a nap after lunch, though it was I, not she, who lay stark awake night after night explaining away sounds that became more and more impossible to explain away. The gagging sound that sometimes accompanied the vlump and the strangled expulsion of air that followed it were surely the result of some disturbance in the water pipes; the footsteps that came slowly down the hall and stopped outside our closed door and then went away again with something like a low chuckle were merely the night contracting of our metal house after the heat of the day. Through all this Ellen slept as if in a stupor; she seemed to have become addicted to sleep. She went to bed at nine and got up at ten the next morning; she napped in the afternoon and moved about lethargically the rest of the time with a Mexican shawl around her shoulders, complaining of the cold. The doctor examined her for mononucleosis but found nothing. He said perhaps it was her sinuses and that she should rest as much as she wanted.

After a protracted silence Jack put aside his drink and stood up. "I guess I'll go along."

"I'll tell Ellen."

"What the hell for? Let her sleep. Tell her I hope she feels better." He turned to frown at the room of the house he had designed and built. "Are you happy here?" he asked suddenly.

"Happy?" I repeated the word awkwardly. "Of course we're happy. We love the house. It's . . . just a little noisy at night, that's all." I stammered it out, like the first word of a monstrous confession, but Jack seemed hardly to hear it. He waved a hand. "House settling." He squinted from one side of the room to the other. "I don't know. There's something about it. . . . It's not right. Maybe it's just the weather . . . the light. . . . It could be friendlier, you know what I mean? It seems cheerless."

I watched him with a kind of wild hope, as if he might magically fathom my terror—do for me what I could not do for myself, and permit it to be discussed calmly between two men of temperate mind. But Jack was not looking for the cause of the gloom but the cure for it.

"Why don't you try putting down a couple of orange rugs in this room?" he said.

I stared at the floor as if two orange rugs were an infallible charm. "Yes," I said, "I think we'll try that."

Ellen scuffed in, pushing back her hair, her face puffy with sleep. "Jack," she said, "when the weather clears and I'm feeling livelier, you and Anne and the children must come and spend the night."

"We'd like that. After the noises die down," he added satirically to me.

"Noises? What noises?" A certain blankness came over Ellen's face when she looked at me now. The expression was the same, but what had been open in it before was now merely empty. She had put up her guard against me; she suspected me of keeping things from her.

"At night," I said. "The house is settling. You don't hear them."

When Jack had gone, Ellen sat with a cup of tea in the chair where Jack had sat, looking out at the mud. Her long purple shawl hung all the way to her knees and made her look armless. There seemed no explanation for the two white hands that curled around the teacup in her lap. "It's a sad thing," she said tonelessly. "I can't help but feel sorry for Sondra."

"Why is that?" I asked guardedly.

"Joyce was here yesterday. She told me that she and Jeff have been having an affair off and on for six years." She turned to see how I would receive this news.

"Well, that explains the way Joyce and Sondra behave toward each other," I said, with a pleasant glance straight into Ellen's eyes; there I encountered only the reflection of the glass doors, even to the rain trickling down them, and I had the eerie sensation of having been shown a picture of the truth, as if she were weeping secretly in the depths of a soul I could no longer touch. For Ellen did not believe my innocence; I'm not sure I still believed in it myself; very likely

Jeff and Joyce didn't either. It is impossible to say what Sondra believed. She behaved as if our infidelity were an accomplished fact. In its way it was a performance of genius, for Sondra never touched me except in the most accidental or impersonal way; even her glances, the foundation on which she built the myth of our liaison, had nothing soft in them; they were probing and sly and were always accompanied by a furtive smile, as if we merely shared some private joke. Yet there was something in the way she did it—in the tilt of her head perhaps—that plainly implied that the joke was at everyone else's expense. And she had taken to calling me "darling."

"Sondra and Jeff have a feebleminded child off in an institution somewhere," Ellen said. "That set them against each other, apparently."

"Joyce told you all this?"

"She just mentioned it casually as if it were the most natural thing in the world—she assumed we must have known. . . . But I don't want to know things like that about my friends."

"That's show biz, I guess. You and I are just provincials at heart."

"Sondra must be a very unhappy girl."

"It's hard to tell with Sondra."

"I wonder what she tries to do with her life. . . . If she looks for anything—outside."

I waited.

"Probably not," Ellen answered her own question. "She seems very self-contained. Almost cold . . ."

I was treated to the spectacle of my wife fighting with herself to delay a wound that she was convinced would come home to her sooner or later. She did not want to believe in my infidelity. I might have comforted her with lies. I might have told her that Sondra and I rendezvoused downtown in a cafeteria and made love in a second-rate hotel on the evenings when I called to say that I was working late. Then the wound would be open and could be cleaned and cured. It would be painful of course, but I would have confided in her again and our old system would be restored. Watching Ellen torture herself with doubt, I was tempted to tell her those lies. The truth never tempted me: To have admitted that I knew what she was thinking would have been tantamount to an admission of guilt. How could I suspect such a thing unless it were true? And was I to explain my coldness by terrifying her with vague stories of indescribable sounds which she never heard?

And so the two of us sat on, dumb and chilled, in our watertight house as the daylight began to go. And then a sort of exultation seized me. What if my terror were no more real than Ellen's? What if both our ghosts were only ghosts of the mind which needed only a little common sense to drive them away? And I saw that if I could drive away my ghost, Ellen's would soon follow, for the secret that shut me away from her would be gone. It was a revelation, a triumph of reason.

"What's that up there?" Ellen pointed to something that looked like a leaf blowing at the top of the glass doors. "It's a tail, Ted. There must be some animal on the roof."

Only the bushy tip was visible. As I drew close to it I could see raindrops clinging as if by a geometrical system to each black hair. "It looks like a raccoon tail. What would a coon be doing out so early?" I put on a coat and went outside. The tail hung limply over the edge, ringed with white and swaying phlegmatically in the breeze. The animal itself was hidden behind the low parapet. Using the ship's ladder at the back of the house I climbed up to look at it.

The human mind, just like other parts of the anatomy, is an organ of habit. Its capabilities are bounded by the limits of precedent; it thinks what it is used to thinking. Faced with a phenomenon beyond its range it rebels, it rejects, sometimes it collapses. My mind, which for weeks had steadfastly refused to honor the evidence of my senses that there was Something Else living in the house with Ellen and me, something unearthly and evil, largely on the basis of insufficient evidence, was now forced to the subsequent denial by saying, as Jeff had said, "fox." It was, of course, ridiculous. The chances of a fox's winning a battle with a raccoon were very slight at best, let alone what had been done to this raccoon. The body lay on the far side of the roof. I didn't see the head at all until I had stumbled against it and it had rolled over and over to come to rest against the parapet where it pointed its masked, ferret face at me.

Only because my beleaguered mind kept repeating, like a voice, "Ellen mustn't know, Ellen mustn't know," was I able to take up the dismembered parts and hurl them with all my strength onto the hillside and answer when Ellen called out, "What is it, Ted?" "Must have been a coon. It's gone now," in a perfectly level voice before I went to the back of the roof and vomited.

I recalled Sondra's mention of their mutilated cat and phoned Jeff at his agency. "We will discuss it over lunch," I told myself. I had a great need to talk, an action impossible within my own home, where every day the silence became denser and more intractable. Once or twice Ellen ventured to ask, "What's the matter, Ted?" but I always answered, "Nothing." And there our talk ended. I could see it in her wary eyes; I was not the man she had married; I was cold, secretive. The children's room, furnished with double bunks and wallpaper figured with toys, stood like a rebuke. Ellen kept the door closed most of the time though once or twice, in the late afternoon, I had found her in there moving about aimlessly, touching objects as if half in wonder that they should still linger on after so many long, sterile months; a foolish hope had failed. Neither did our friends bring their children to stay. They did not because we did not ask them. The silence had brought with it a profound and debilitating inertia. Ellen's face seemed perpetually swollen, the features cloudy and amorphous, the eyes dull; her whole body had become bloated, as if an enormous cache of pain had backed up inside her. We moved through the house in our orbits like two sleepwalkers, going about our business out of habit. Our friends called at first, puzzled, a little hurt, but soon stopped and left us to ourselves. Occasionally we saw the Sheffitses. Jeff was looking seedier and seedier, told bad jokes, drank too much and seemed always ill at ease. Sondra did most of the talking, chattering blandly on indifferent subjects and always hinting by gesture, word or glance at our underground affair.

Jeff and I had lunch at the Brown Derby on Vine Street under charcoal caricatures of show folk. At a table next to ours an agent was eulogizing an actor in a voice hoarse with trumped-up enthusiasm to a large, purple-faced man who was devoting his entire attention to a bowl of vichyssoise.

"It's a crazy business," Jeff said to me. "Be glad you're not in it."

"I see what you mean," I replied. Jeff had not the faintest idea of why I had brought him there, nor had I given him any clue. We were "breaking the ice." Jeff grinned at me with that crooked trick of his mouth, and I grinned back. "We are friends"—presumably that is the message we were grinning at each other. Was he my friend? Was I his friend? He lived across the street; our paths crossed perhaps once a week; we joked together; he sat always in the same chair in our living room twisting from one sprawl to another; there was a straight white chair in his living room that I preferred. Friendships have been founded on less, I suppose. Yet he had an idiot child locked off in an asylum somewhere and a wife who amused herself with infidelity by suggestion; I had a demon loose in my house and a wife gnawed with suspicion and growing remote and old because of it. And I had said, "I see what you mean." It seemed insufferable. I caught Jeff's eye. "You remember we talked once about a ghost?" My tone was bantering; perhaps I meant to make a joke.

"I remember."

"Sondra said something about a cat of yours that was killed."

"The one the fox got."

"That's what you said. That's not what Sondra said." Jeff shrugged. "What about it?"

"I found a dead raccoon on our roof."

"Your roof!"

"Yes. It was pretty awful."

Jeff toyed with his fork. All pretense of levity was at an end. "No head?"

"Worse."

For a few moments he was silent. I felt him struggle with himself before he spoke. "Maybe you'd better move out, Ted," he said.

He was trying to help—I knew it. With a single swipe he had tried to push through the restraint that hung between us. He was my friend; he was putting out his hand to me.

And I suppose I must have known what he'd suggest. But I could not accept it. It was not what I wanted to hear. "Jeff, I can't do that," I said tolerantly, as if he had missed my point. "We've only been living there five months. It cost me twenty-two thousand to build that place. We have to live in it at least a year under the GI loan."

"Well, you know best, Ted." The smile dipped at me again.

"I just wanted to talk," I said, irritated at the ease with which he had given in. "I wanted to find out what you knew about this ghost business."

"Not very much. Sondra knows more than I do."

"I doubt that you would advise me to leave a house I had just built for no reason at all."

"There seems to be some sort of jinx on the property, that's all. Whether there's a ghost or not I couldn't tell you," he replied, annoyed in his turn at the line the conversation was taking. "How does Ellen feel about this?"

"She doesn't know."

"About the raccoon?"

"About anything."

"You mean there's more?"

"There are noises—at night. . . ."

"I'd speak to Sondra if I were you. She's gone into this business much more deeply than I. When we first moved in, she used to hang around your land a good deal . . . just snooping . . . particularly after that cat was killed . . ." He was having some difficulty with his words. It struck me that the conversation was causing him pain. He was showing his teeth now in a smiling grimace. Dangling an arm over the back of his chair he seemed loose to the point of collapse. We circled warily about his wife's name.

"Look, Jeff," I said, and took a breath, "about Sondra . . ."

Jeff cut me off with a wave of his hand. "Don't worry, I know Sondra."

"Then you know there's nothing between us?"

"It's just her way of amusing herself. Sondra's a strange girl. She does the same thing with me. She flirts with me but we don't sleep together." He picked up his spoon and stared at it unseeingly. "It started when she became pregnant. After she had the boy, everything between us stopped. You know we had a son? He's in a sanitarium in the Valley."

"Can't you do anything?"

"Sure. Joyce Castle. I don't know what I'd have done without her."

"I mean divorce."

"Sondra won't divorce me. And I can't divorce her. No grounds." He shrugged as if the whole thing were of no concern at all to him. "What could I say? I want to divorce my wife because of the way she looks at other men? She's scrupulously faithful."

"To whom, Jeff? To you? To whom?"

"I don't know—to herself, maybe," he mumbled.

Whether with encouragement he might have gone on I don't know, for I cut him off. I sensed that with the enigmatic remark he was giving me my cue and that if I had chosen to respond to it he would have told me what I had asked him to lunch to find out—and all at once I was terrified; I did not want to hear it; I did not want to hear it at all. And so I laughed in a quiet way and said, "Undoubtedly, undoubtedly," and pushed it behind the closed door of my mind where I had stored all the impossibilities of the last months—the footsteps, the sounds in the night, the mutilated raccoon—or else, by recognizing them, go mad.

Jeff suddenly looked me full in the face; his cheeks were flushed, his teeth clamped together. "Look, Ted," he said, "can you take the afternoon off? I've got to go to the sanitarium and sign some papers. They're going to transfer the boy. He has fits of violence and does . . . awful things. He's finally gotten out of hand."

"What about Sondra?"

"Sondra's signed already. She likes to go alone to visit him. She seems to like to have him to herself. I'd appreciate it, Ted—the moral support. . . . You don't have to come in. You can wait in the car. It's only about thirty miles from here, you'd be back by dinnertime. . . ." His voice shook, tears clouded the yellow-stained whites of his eyes. He looked like a man with fever. I noticed how shrunken his neck had become as it revolved in his collar, how his head caved in sharply at the temples. He fastened one hand on my arm, like a claw. "Of course I'll go, Jeff," I said. "I'll call the office. They can get along without me for one afternoon."

He collected himself in an instant. "I'd appreciate it, Ted. I promise you it won't be so bad."

The sanitarium was in the San Fernando Valley, a complex of new stucco buildings on a newly seeded lawn. Everywhere there were signs that read, PLEASE KEEP OFF, FOLKS. Midget saplings stood in discs of powdery earth along the cement walks angling white and hot through the grass. On these walks, faithfully observing the signs, the inmates strolled. Their traffic, as it flowed somnolently from one avenue to another, was controlled by attendants stationed at intersections, conspicuous in white uniforms and pith helmets.

After a time it became unbearably hot in the car, and I climbed out. Unless I wished to pace in the parking lot among the cars, I had no choice but to join the inmates and their visitors on the walks. I chose a nearly deserted walk and went slowly toward a building that had a yard attached to it surrounded by a wire fence. From the slide and the jungle gym in it I judged it to be for the children. Then I saw Jeff come into it. With him was a nurse pushing a kind of cart railed around like an oversized toddler. Strapped into it was "the boy."

He was human, I suppose, for he had all the equipment assigned to humans, yet I had the feeling that if it were not for the cart the creature would have crawled on his belly like an alligator. He had the eyes of an alligator too—sleepy, cold and soulless—set in a swarthy face and a head that seemed to run in a horizontal direction rather than the vertical, like an egg lying on its side. The features were devoid of any vestige of intelligence; the mouth hung open and the chin shone with saliva. While Jeff and the nurse talked, he sat under the sun, inert and repulsive.

I turned on my heel and bolted, feeling that I had intruded on a disgrace. I imagined that I had been given a glimpse of a diseased universe, the mere existence of which constituted a threat to my life; the sight of that monstrous boy with his cold, bestial eyes made me feel as if, by stumbling on this shame I somehow shared in it with Jeff. Yet I told myself that the greatest service I could do him was to pretend that I had seen nothing, knew nothing, and not place on him the hardship of talking about something which obviously caused him pain.

He returned to the car pale and shaky and wanting a drink. We stopped first at a place called Joey's on Hollywood Way. After that it was Cherry Lane on Vine Street, where a couple of girls propositioned us, and then a stop at the Brown Derby again, where I had left my car. Jeff downed the liquor in a joyless, businesslike way and talked to me in a rapid, confidential voice about a book he had just sold to Warner Brothers Studio for an exorbitant sum of money—trash in his opinion, but that was always the way—the parasites made it. Pretty soon there wouldn't be any good writers left: "There'll only be competent parasites and incompetent parasites." This was perhaps the third time we had had this conversation. Now Jeff repeated it mechanically, all the time looking down at the table where he was painstakingly breaking a red swizzle stick into ever tinier pieces.

When we left the restaurant, the sun had gone down, and the evening chill of the desert on which the city had been built had settled in. A faint pink glow from the vanished sun still lingered on the top of the Broadway Building. Jeff took a deep breath, then fell into a fit of coughing. "Goddamn smog," he said. "Goddamn city. I can't think of a single reason why I live here." He started toward his Daimler, tottering slightly.

"How about driving home with me?" I said. "You can pick your car up tomorrow."

He fumbled in the glove compartment and drew out a packet of small cigars. He stuck one between his teeth where it jutted unlit toward the end of his nose. "I'm not going home tonight, Ted friend," he said. "If you'll just drop me up the street at the Cherry Lane I'll remember you for life."

"Are you sure? I'll go with you if you want."

Jeff shook a forefinger at me archly. "Ted, you're a gentleman and a scholar. But my advice to you is to go home and take care of your wife. No, seriously. Take care of her, Ted. As for myself I shall go quietly to seed in the Cherry

Lane Café." I had started toward my car when Jeff called out to me again. "I just want to tell you, Ted friend. . . . My wife was once just as nice as your wife. . . ."

I had gone no more than a mile when the last glimmer of light left the sky and night fell like a shutter. The sky above the neon of Sunset Boulevard turned jet black, and a sickly half-moon rose and was immediately obscured by thick fog that lowered itself steadily as I traveled west, till at the foot of Clay Canyon it began to pat my windshield with little smears of moisture.

The house was dark, and at first I thought Ellen must have gone out, but then seeing her old Plymouth in the driveway I felt the grip of a cold and unreasoning fear. The events of the day seemed to crowd around and hover at my head in the fog; and the commonplace sight of that car, together with the blackness and silence of the house, sent me into a panic as I ran for the door. I pushed at it with my shoulder as if expecting it to be locked, but it swung open easily and I found myself in the darkened living room with no light anywhere and the only sound the rhythm of my own short breathing. "Ellen!" I called in a high, querulous voice I hardly recognized. "Ellen!" I seemed to lose my balance; my head swam; it was as if this darkness and silence were the one last iota that the chamber of horrors in my mind could not hold, and the door snapped open a crack, emitting a cloudy light that stank of corruption, and I saw the landscape of my denial, like a tomb. It was the children's room. Rats nested in the double bunks, mold caked the red wallpaper, and in it an insane Spanish don hung by his neck from a dead tree, his heels vlumping against the wall, his foppish clothes rubbing as he revolved slowly in invisible currents of bad air. And as he swung toward me, I saw his familiar reptile eyes open and stare at me with loathing and contempt.

I conceded: It is here and It is evil, and I have left my wife alone in the house with It, and now she has been sucked into that cold eternity where the dumb shades store their plasms against an anguished centenary of speech—a single word issuing from the petrified throat, a scream or a sigh or a groan, syllables dredged up from a lifetime of eloquence to slake the bottomless thirst of living death.

And then a light went on over my head, and I found myself in the hall outside the children's room. Ellen was in her nightgown, smilng at me. "Ted? Why on earth are you standing here in the dark? I was just taking a nap. Do you want some dinner? Why don't you say something? Are you all right?" She came toward me; she seemed extraordinarily lovely; her eyes, a deeper blue than Sondra's, looked almost purple; she seemed young and slender again; her old serenity shone through like a restored beacon.

"I'm all right," I said hoarsely. "Are you sure you are?"

"Of course I am," she laughed. "Why shouldn't I be? I'm feeling much, much better." She took my hand and kissed it gaily. "I'll put on some clothes and then we'll have our dinner." She turned and went down the hall to our bedroom, leaving me with a clear view into the children's room. Though the room itself was dark, I could see by the hall light that the covers on the lower bunk had been turned back and that the bed had been slept in. "Ellen," I said. "Ellen, were you sleeping in the children's room?"

"Yes," she said, and I heard the rustle of a dress as she carried it from the closet. "I was in there mooning around, waiting for you to come home. I got sleepy and lay down on the bunk. What were you doing, by the way? Working late?"

"And nothing happened?"

"Why? What should have happened?"

I could not answer; my head throbbed with joy. It was over—whatever it was, it was over. All unknowing Ellen had faced the very heart of the evil and had slept through it like a child, and now she was herself again without having been tainted by the knowledge of what she had defeated; I had protected her by my silence, by my refusal to share my terror with this woman whom I loved. I reached inside and touched the light button; there was the brave red wallpaper scattered over with toys, the red-and-white curtains, the blue-and-red bedspreads. It was a fine room. A fine, gay room fit for children.

Ellen came down the hall in her slip. "Is anything wrong, Ted? You seem so distraught. Is everything all right at the office?"

"Yes, yes," I said. "I was with Jeff Sheffits. We went to see his boy in the asylum. Poor Jeff; he leads a rotten life." I told Ellen the whole story of our afternoon, speaking freely in my house for the first time since we had moved there. Ellen listened carefully as she always did, and wanted to know, when I had finished, what the boy was like.

"Like an alligator," I said with disgust. "Just like an alligator."

Ellen's face took on an unaccountable expression of private glee. She seemed to be looking past me into the children's room, as if the source of her amusement lay there. At the same moment I shivered in a breath of profound cold, the same clammy draft that might have warned me on my last birthday had I been other than what I am. I had a sense of sudden dehydration, as if all the blood had vanished from my veins. I felt as if I were shrinking. When I spoke, my voice seemed to come from a throat rusty and dry with disuse. "Is that funny?" I whispered.

And my wife replied, "Funny? Oh, no, it's just that I'm feeling so much better. I think I'm pregnant, Ted." She tipped her head to one side and smiled at me.

All the editors know about William Wood is that he is the author of a fine story of dark, ghostly horrors invading a house in the rainswept California hills.

Everyone knows cats have nine lives, but what if each one is a little bigger and meaner than the one before?

TWENTY-ONE

Emmett

Dahlov Ipcar

Some of the things that happen in this world can be so crazy that you hate even to think about them. That's the way I feel about this business I've just been through with Artie. I'm just an ordinary guy with a wife and three kids and a nice quiet desk job, and I'm the last person in the world you'd expect to get mixed up in anything really weird.

But there I was in as deep as all hell, right up to my ears—and all I'd wanted was a nice quiet week of hunting in the Maine woods, same as I've had every year since I went to work for Eastern Bio Supplies. You see, I'm willing to stick around in August, when everyone else wants out of the city, so they give me this extra week in November or whenever the deer season opens up there in Sagadahoc County. Artie had this little old rundown farm way off in the woods, and he throws me a standing invitation. So every November that's where I'd head for. I just liked to get in a week away from the wife and kids, beating the brush, and boozing a little, and yacking with my old pal. Usually I'd come back with a whitetail tied to my fender—the Great Maine Hunter bit—playing it to the hilt for the kids. But it's not really the Call of the Wild with me, not really the Old Blood Lust and all that, I just like the chance to get out of the city and tramp around in the woods where it's nice and peaceful and smells good.

Artie always gave me a big welcome. I'd tell him all the off-color stories I'd picked up during the year, and he'd come up with a few good ones he'd collected, mostly from the vet who doctored his cows; because, believe it or not,

Artie really farmed. He had about twelve of these cows and a few hens and this little ol' beagle called Lady Anne, and he lived there in his old house by himself as happy as a clam at high water. I won't swear he lived a virtuous life. He boozed some, and he entertained lady friends; but he never let any of them move in on him. He'd always been a queer egg, sort of an odd-ball, a real hermit type. Didn't want to get tied down to a woman's apron strings, he said; though he sure was tied to those cows' tails, and that's a helluva lot worse. He couldn't go anywhere, even for a day. He always had to be back to milk those four-legged bosses of his—now I know why they call all cows "boss."

But old Artie, he thrived on the life; always looked healthy as an ox, made me feel like I was pale and flabby and going to pot sitting at a desk, though I jog eight blocks to work every morning. I guess it's a good thing I get that much exercise or a week in the woods would kill me. Sometimes I envied Artie; sometimes I thought he was nuts—the way he lived. But he had a good thing going for him there. Not that those twelve cows brought in much income, but they gave Artie something to write about. He wrote a lot of articles for magazines on "How to Be Happy with a Manure Pile and a Fly Swatter" and stuff like that, and it sold like hot cakes. So it seems he was doing okay. He sure always seemed brimming over with health and good spirits—that is until this November.

We'd been bosom pals ever since we were kids. We'd both been sent to this Manumassett School in New Jersey, a progressive-type boarding school. They had this beat-up farm set up—lots of lambkins sporting on the green, cocks treading hens, and cows producing milk and calves and manure like mad. The idea was to take us city kids and introduce us to Nature, elevate our minds by rubbing our noses in the dirt, teach us about the flowers and the bees so we wouldn't get stung, and all that hokum.

Most of it went over with me like a ton of lead, but Artie just ate it up, especially the farm bit. He was the kind of kid who'd follow around behind a cow and admire the beautiful plops she made. He used to tell me all kinds of weird stuff about what the animals were thinking, how they felt about us humans and all. He told me once when he was about nine that everything had a soul and feelings, even trees and vegetables. He claimed it hurt a tree to get chopped down, and that the sap that flowed out of it was just like tears. He had quite an imagination, that kid. I didn't put much stock in the crying vegetables, but sometimes it made kitchen duty a lot pleasanter if I just *pretended* that the carrots and potatoes were suffering as much as I was suffering at having to peel them. Because we all had to pitch in and work as well as keep up on our studies; that was part of the big deal.

But some of the Nature gimmick I really liked, and that was the times we took to the woods on biology walks, collecting specimens. There was this real mucky swamp nearby, where we used to go wading around, coming home with jars full of salamanders and centipedes as long as your arm, and snakes and tree toads and the worst cases of poison ivy on record. I guess that's where I learned to like tramping around in the woods, same as Artie got the rage to go live on a farm for the rest of his life. I know some of that stuff was supposed to rub off on us kids, but I kind of doubt if they expected us to apply it as literally as Artie did. I think they expected us to *sublimate our experience,* like me sitting here writing out orders for frogs in formaldehyde.

Artie and I roomed together for all of six years, and we got so damn close, we could just about read one another's minds. But the most important thing that happened to us there, I never even thought was important at all—until this business came up.

You see, there was this one teacher, Old Hoyle, who used to entertain us with stories on Friday nights. He'd hold a real session around the big fireplace in the main hall. All the lights would be out, just the fire flickering away, and he'd usually tell these real spooky ghost stories. We really ate it up, though sometimes he just about scared the pants off us. I never forgot one night when he got going on a series of tales about cats. One of them was Edgar Allan Poe's story "The Black Cat"—that one where the cat gets walled up in the cellar with the corpse and wails like crazy. That story really gave me the willies, and Artie got the willies worse than I did. He was so shook up he wouldn't let me turn out the light in our room that night. And for a whole month at least, he made me keep the light burning, though I'd got over the effects long before that.

We were just little kids about ten; but while I got over it, like I said—Artie never did get over it. He never went back to listen to any more storytelling—and he developed this real thing about cats. He never could stand to have a cat near him again. When he got older he told people he was allergic to them, but I knew better; I knew he was plain scared to death of them. I admit that black-cat story got me too, but it didn't make me hate cats. It just made me avoid reading any more Poe for about ten years.

After he grew up, Artie bummed around a while. He never could stick at any city job for long. Finally he bought this little farm in Maine. And then the guy was happy, just living there with his cows and his chickens and his beagle— and *no cats*. I guess he encouraged that beagle to be a cat-killer, because no stray cats ever moved in on him, that is—I never heard of any—before this November when I showed up for the opening of deer season.

The first thing that struck me as I got out of my car was how lousy Artie looked. He really looked sick, sort of nervous and haggard and run-down, his hands shaking and his eyes kind of haunted-looking. I really felt worried about him, but he swore he was in the best of health. He seemed awful glad to see me. We broke open a bottle of the bourbon I'd brought, and I told him a couple of my best stories that I'd been saving, and he seemed to cheer up.

But at four in the afternoon he got up to go milk his cows. This struck me as peculiar; because always, ever since I could remember, he'd milked the cows after supper— sometimes as late as ten or eleven at night. That way he didn't have to get up early to milk them again in the morning. That's the kind of farmer he was—casual.

"What's the idea?" I asked. "We going somewhere tonight or something?"

"No," he said. "No. I'm not going anywhere. *Not at night!*" He said this with such emphasis that it took me kind of aback. "I've just started milking the cows early lately, that's all," he said, sort of irritable. "I've reformed."

I didn't quite buy it, but anyhow, he had the cows all

milked by five-thirty. We ate supper and sat around and jawed and drank more bourbon, and then around nine o'clock I decided I'd turn in. I wanted to get an early start on the opening day of the season.

I'd left my gear in the car, so I went out to get it. I was standing alongside the car, just getting out the rifle and the shells, when I heard this peculiar noise, sort of a long hiss with a snarl in it. It seemed to come from the darkness not too far off, so I reached in and flicked on the headlights. And there in the lights was the biggest damn Canada lynx—a great big white long-legged bastard—sort of snarling at me. He seemed blinded by the headlights and just stood there for a full minute, and I stood there too, just as stupified. Then, suddenly I realized I had the rifle in my hand, and I slammed back the bolt and rammed in a shell. The cat seemed to recover himself too. He turned and leapt off into the darkness; but I could see him plain, a white shape bounding away, and I blasted him. He tumbled head over heels and lay there a while kicking.

Boy! I had never felt so excited in my life! I yelled for Artie, but he didn't come out. So I walked up on the cat cautiously, and when I was sure he was really dead, I dragged him back into the headlights and laid him out to admire. He was sure a helluva big one, all white and sort of freckled brownish all over—with long, tufted ears. As handsome an animal as I ever saw.

I ran back in the house, all excited. Artie was sitting there, his head in his hands. He looked up at me real wild-eyed. "You didn't kill him?" he asked. "Oh, God, you didn't, did you?"

"If you mean that lynx, I sure as hell did. Come look at him!" I tried to drag him up on his feet, but he was sort of shaking all over and moaning something about cats and a bigger one coming—none of which made any sense to me.

"Was that what had you so worried?" I asked, kind of beginning to catch on. "You mean that cat's been hanging around, and you've been scared to go out at night?" Hell, I didn't blame him, for a guy that was scared of cats this one was just the ticket. But what baffled me was why he seemed so upset that I had shot the damn thing. You'd think he'd be tickled pink.

But no, he kept moaning, "You shouldn't have shot him. You shouldn't have killed him." Sometimes he'd say something like, "I can't stay here. I've got to get away before the next one comes—" and he'd start shaking like a leaf again.

I got some more bourbon into him and calmed him down some, and he began to make sense after a fashion. Finally he told me the whole story about what was bothering him. It came out sort of bit by bit, but it seemed it had all started about a month before.

He'd been delivering milk to this house on his route, when this little boy had come out holding a little fuzzy white kitten. He shoved it right in Artie's face and said, "This is my kitten. His name is Emmett."

Well, Artie had been upset as hell and yelled at the kid to get the damn thing away from him, and the kid had cried, and he'd had to apologize to the kid's mother, and all that had really gotten him stirred up. Then just as he was ready to drive off, there was the damn kitten sitting right in the driveway. He said he could have blown his horn or waited until it ran off, but he was sore and he hated cats anyhow. So he just stepped on the gas and ran the kitten over, squashed it flat. He didn't even feel guilty doing it, he said. But the kid screamed and carried on, and he had to apologize some more. He said he remembered the little kid yelling at him, "You're a murderer! You murdered Emmett!" That had bothered him, because he may have hated cats, but he kind of liked kids.

Anyhow, that was the beginning. The next thing that happened was a small gray kitten showed up in his barn a few days later, and he didn't hesitate to bait it with milk and poison it. Then about three days after that another kitten appeared, a half-grown one. This one was more wary, but Artie laid for it and got it with his shotgun. Then another cat turned up. He heard this commotion among his hens, and there was this yellow cat running off with a half-grown chick in its mouth. He sicked the beagle on it, and the dog caught up with it halfway to the woods and broke its back.

That was four cats down, but it seems there were more to come. Artie had never been so plagued with cats before, but he didn't really put two and two together yet. He was beginning to get the feeling though, and he wasn't too surprised when a big black-and-white tom cat started hanging around his hen yard. This one was big enough to have a real scrap with the beagle and come out alive. But Artie and his shotgun caught up with him too.

There was about a week, Artie said, when everything seemed to be back to normal. And then one night he put Lady Anne out before he went to bed, and he heard this terrific row out in the yard, the dog yelping like mad and howling, and a snarling and spitting like all the cats of hell. He got out there with his shotgun as fast as he could, and there was this big brown bobcat tangling with old Lady Anne and getting much the best of it. Artie let him have it with both barrels. He killed the bobcat all right; but he wounded the beagle, who was pretty torn up anyhow, and she died at the vet's that night.

Artie was pretty shook up. He felt bad at losing his dog, and he was just beginning to think the thing through— about all those cats coming, one after the other, and each one bigger than the last. The real clincher was when he got back from the vet's that same night. As he pulled up in front of his house, there, sitting by the side of the road in the full glare of the headlights, was this big white Canada lynx—the same one I had killed.

That had really got through to him. He said he sat in his car all night with that animal prowling around in the darkness, letting out earsplitting yells. He didn't dare leave the car until morning when the big cat had gone. That had been two weeks ago, he told me, and that damn lynx had hung around all the time. He didn't dare step out of his door at night. It had raided his hen house and cleaned out all his hens, and he didn't dare let his cows out of the barn. Even in the daytime he walked around looking over his shoulder and getting back under cover as fast as he could.

"But why in hell didn't you try to shoot it?" I asked.

He looked at me pretty funny. "Don't you get it?" he asked. "Don't you understand? That damn cat has nine lives. There's always a bigger cat comes back! I didn't *want* to kill the lynx. I was scared to death of what would show up next. But now you've gone and done it. I've got to get out of here, that's all. I've got to get away—far away—before the next *bigger* cat comes. It may be out there now," he said, shivering as he stared at the black night outside the window.

I tried to reason with him. I thought it all sounded pretty damn silly. I told him it was probably just a coincidence, the lynx following the bobcat like that. "Maybe there's some condition up in the North woods," I told hm. "Something that's making the big cats move down this way." But that wasn't exactly the right thing to say.

"Oh, there's a *condition*, all right," he said; and he started giggling hysterically, sort of choking and shivering all over. It really got me to see him in such a state.

"Look," I said, as reasonably as I could. "There just isn't any bigger cat that can come now. You know damn well there isn't anything bigger than a Canada lynx around here. You know that!"

"It's got to come," he said. "It's got to come. I've counted them all up; there were only seven—there are still two more lives—still two more bigger cats."

"Oh for chrissake!" I said. I was getting kind of fed up with all the argument. "What you need is a real rest. Maybe you ought to see a doctor, get away from this place. You've been alone here too damn much."

"You bet your sweet life I'm getting away," he said. "The first thing in the morning!"

"Well, let's get some sleep," I said, "so we can get an early start."

An early start deer hunting, I meant. I wasn't going along with any of this midnight raving. So he turned in. And so did I, but first I went out and hung my big lynx up in the shed. It was the biggest and handsomest trophy I'd ever shot, and I wasn't going to let it get messed up no matter how nuts Artie was on the subject of cats.

I set the alarm for five to give me plenty of time to get dressed and out in the woods before sunup. But around 3:00 A.M. I woke up and remembered something I'd completely forgotten—one of those spooky cat tales that Old Hoyle had told us kids the night Artie got so bugged on the subject of cats. Before this I'd always thought it was that tale of Poe's that had got to him, same as it got me; but now I remembered another tale Hoyle had told that same night.

As a matter of fact, it wasn't much of a story. It was kind of a foolish thing without even much point. But, of course, Hoyle was a darn good storyteller, and to even a half-baked yarn, he'd given a lot of atmosphere and built up the suspense. As near as I can remember the story went something like this:

There was this young fellow walking alone through the hills at night, and it gets real dark, and a storm comes up, blowing a gale, and the boy starts looking for some shelter. Up on a high hill he sees this big old house, all dark and deserted-looking. He goes up there and knocks on the door, and nobody answers. But the door isn't locked, so he goes inside, and here is this big spooky old mansion, all full of cobwebs and stuff, and one big room with a huge fireplace in it. He's cold and wet, so he gathers some wood together and builds himself a fire. He's sitting there warming up and enjoying the blaze, when he hears a door creak on its hinges, and in walks this black cat. It walks up to the fire and sits down and looks at him. Then it yawns and sort of blinks its eyes and licks its chops, and it says, "Well, I'll just wait 'til Emmett comes."

He gets up and he says to the cat, "Good evening. I hope you don't mind me warming myself a little here by the fire."

But the cat just looks at him poisonous-like and sits there watching him. The boy sits down again and is sort of dozing off, when he hears the door creak again, and another bigger black cat walks in and sits down alongside the first one. And it too yawns and kind of licks its chops hungry-like, and it says, "Well, I'll just wait 'til Emmett comes."

Then one cat after another comes in and sits down alongside the others, and each one is bigger and blacker than the one before. And each one says in the same kind of ominous way, "Well, I'll just wait 'til Emmett comes."

Finally, a cat walks in, and even sitting down, it's all of six feet tall. It just sits there looking down at him with big green ferocious eyes, with a hungry look in them; and when that cat yawns at him, it's like looking into the mouth of a cave, and it, too, says, "Well, I'll just wait 'til Emmett comes."

But at this, the boy gets up, and he bows with great dignity, and he says to all the cats lined up there watching him, "When Emmett comes, will you all please tell him that I done set, and I done rested myself, and I done left!'' And he grabs his hat and lights out of there at a dead run.

Well, that's all there was to the story, and you can see it was pretty damn silly, not even real spooky. Heck, you'd think whoever made it up could've come up with a real spooky name instead of something as common-sounding as "Emmett."

But I figured, lying there half awake, that it was that little kid calling his kitten "Emmett" that had started poor old Artie off on this whole crazy bat. I figured I'd tell him in the morning, show him what had made him flip, and maybe he'd see there was nothing supernatural about it all. I was determined I was going to get in a week of deer hunting or else. So I turned over and went to sleep.

I slept so sound that I never heard the alarm; what woke me up was a whole barrage of rifle fire that sounded like it was right under my window. I jumped out of bed with the daylights scared out of me. The first thing that crossed my mind was that Artie had really gone berserk and was starting the day with some kind of crazy mayhem. But when I barged out into the hall in my pajamas, there was Artie coming out of his room looking as startled as I was.

"They've got their damn nerve," he said right off. It's not even sunup. If they've shot any of *my* deer on *my* place, I'll have the game warden on the whole lot of them!"

I was relieved, I'll tell you. He sounded like his old self. We looked out all the windows, but the shots must have come from the nearby woods, because no hunters were in sight. We neither of us mentioned cats, but got dressed and were just heating up some coffee, when there comes this knock at the door, and these two hunters are standing there all excited.

"Can we use your phone?" one of them asks. "You guys won't believe it, but we just shot the biggest damn mountain lion—right out here in your woods!"

And then Artie really went all to pieces. He started screaming at them, and at me, and practically frothing at the mouth.

I rushed those two guys outside as fast as I could. They must have thought he was nuts, and I'm not sure he wasn't.

But anyway, I went with these two guys, and they showed

me this cat they had killed. It was a mountain lion all right, big and gray with a black tip on his tail, and these two sad black stripes running down his muzzle. There'd always been rumors of mountain lions in Maine; but it was like UFOs, only nuts believed in them. Even standing there, looking down at that big cat, I didn't believe it.

"Listen," I said to those two guys, "I don't care what you do with this cat—take him off and get your pictures in the paper, or bury him right here, but for chrissake get him out of sight, and don't bring him around where my friend is!"

They really thought I was crazy. They tried to argue with me. Their car was parked four miles down the road, they said; all they wanted was to phone and have someone pick them up. They tried to persuade me to drive them down to their car, but I was in a hurry to get back to Artie.

"You get that cat out of here, if you have to drag it all the way!"

"Have a heart, Mac," they begged. "It must weigh three hundred pounds. We had a helluva time lugging it this far."

I didn't waste any more time with them; I just beat it back to the house. I found Artie busy packing, tearing open drawers and grabbing stuff and tossing it in suitcases.

He looked up real wild-eyed when I came in. "Don't try to talk me out of leaving!" he said. "I'm not waiting for any bigger cats!"

"Oh," I said. "You remember that story too."

"What story?" he said and went on throwing stuff around.

But I didn't think it would do any good to go over all that business about the story, not now. I made one last attempt. "You can't just walk out like this, Artie. What about your cows?"

"To hell with the cows," he said. Then he picked up the phone.

He really got pretty efficient there for a while. First he phoned a cattle dealer. "Come pick up the whole herd," he said. "Today. It's got to be today. Sixteen head, counting calves. No, I haven't got time to tell you about them! I'm getting out of here right now. I haven't fed or milked them this morning, so you better get down here today. You can send me a check, whatever the market price is. I'm not going to argue."

He hung up and phoned a real estate agent. "I want to sell my place," he said. "Sell or rent, I don't care. Yeh, lock, stock, and barrel, the works. I'll mail you the keys." That was that.

He phoned the power company and the phone company. Then he went back to packing, gathering up papers and stuff. He may have left something undone, but I don't know what. He even had me down in the cellar with a pipe wrench, draining the water system. It was the fastest house-closing I ever saw. Then we piled all our bags into my car—I wasn't trusting him to drive his own—and we got off, well inside of an hour.

We were tooling down the road, and damned if we didn't pass those two guys, sweating and staggering along, carrying that big lion slung on a pole between them. Here I'd wanted to keep Artie from seeing that cat, but it was too late now. He stared at it, his eyes bugging out, as we sailed by. And those two guys stared back, all grins until they saw who it was, then they looked like they really hated our guts.

Artie started shaking like a leaf. "You see the size of that thing?" he asked me in this queer dead voice. He turned and looked at me, just about as hateful as those two hunters. "You're the guy said there wasn't any bigger cat than that lynx!" He sucked in his breath, and I could hear his teeth chattering. The tears started running down his cheeks.

"Take it easy," I said. "Take it easy, Artie. We're getting out of here. You'll be all right." I went on talking to him like you talk to a kid that's had a nightmare, and after a while, he began to calm down again. I sure felt sorry for him, but I wasn't feeling any too good about it all myself. Things had been happening too fast. I'd even forgotten all about my own trophy I'd left hanging in the shed, but somehow, it didn't seem as wonderful as it had—I wished I'd never shot the damn thing.

We went along okay for about three hours, and I thought Artie was starting to relax at last. Then just outside Boston on the by-pass this cat dashes across the road in front of us.

It was just an ordinary cat. Hell, it wasn't even *black*—

and we missed it by a mile. But right away Artie goes all to pieces again. I mean he threw a real fit: he moaned and thrashed around, and spit ran out of his mouth, and he started breathing in this ghastly kind of way, and scared the living daylights out of me.

I pulled up alongside the road and tried to get some bourbon down him—he looked as gray as a corpse—but he just seemed to get more excited when I stopped the car. "Keep going," he managed to gasp. "Just keep going! Please—please keep going!"

So then I figured he was more than I could handle, and I decided to get him to a doctor as fast as I could. I left the turnpike at the next exit and stopped at the first house I came to. By then Artie had passed out on me.

"Where's the nearest doctor?" I asked this dame.

"Well," she says, real slow, and I could have booted her, "the *nearest* doctor is Dr. Vorbrichten, but he's retired."

"I don't want no doctors of divinity or doctors of philosophy," I said. "If he's a medical doctor just tell me where he is."

"Oh, he's a *medical* doctor. He lives about three miles down the road. But he doesn't *practice*. He's *retired*."

"I don't care how retired he is," I said, feeling real desperate. "This is an emergency!"

I finally got the directions out of her and went on down that road like a bat out of hell, with old Artie all slumped over and passed out beside me.

I found the house and ran up the steps and pounded on the door. This old lady answers it.

"I've got an awful sick friend out in the car," I tell her. "Please, I've got to have the doctor look at him. It's a matter of life or death!" Boy, was I right!

"Come in," she says. "The doctor is in his study. I'll ask him."

Well, she sounded so doubtful that as soon as she opened this study door, I barged right on in determined to convince this guy to get out there and help Artie. I stopped dead in my tracks.

There, standing in the middle of the Persian rug, was the biggest damn African lion I'd ever seen!

I dropped. I dropped like I was sandbagged, keeled right over, passed out cold.

When I came to, I was on this couch; and the doctor, a red-faced, white-haired old guy, was waving smelling salts under my nose and feeling my pulse and all.

"The lion!" I gasped. I tried to sit up. He pushed me back down.

"The lion is nothing to be afraid of, young man," he said. "It's an old, old pet, as gentle as a lamb. There's nothing to be afraid of."

And the damn lion was still there, sitting on his haunches now, looking at me with these mild, gold-colored eyes, very sad-like. But the end of his tail with that big black tassel on it kept sort of twitching, and then he opened his mouth and yawned—and brother!—you never saw such teeth. You could have made a powder horn out of any one of them.

I kind of grabbed onto the doctor and begged him please to take care of Artie out in the car. "But don't let him see that lion!" I almost screamed this. "For chrissake, Doc, I don't care how tame he is. Just don't let Artie see him!"

"Please calm yourself," the doctor said, like I was being unreasonable. "I will put the lion away in his den. You understand, I don't practice medicine any more, otherwise, I would not have such a pet. But there is really nothing, absolutely nothing, to fear."

"Just don't let my friend see him!" I begged, still clutching at his arm.

He managed to pry my fingers loose; and then, holding that lion by a hunk of his shaggy mane, he led him out of the room.

He was back in a few seconds with a pill and a glass of water, which he made me swallow. "That will calm you down," he said. "I'm sorry to have to tell you this, but your friend was beyond my help. I'm afraid he died of heart failure. Of course, it will be just as well to have him examined thoroughly—I have already phoned the hospital—but I'm sure you will find my diagnosis is correct."

"That lion!" I cried sitting up. "He saw that damn lion!"

"No," said the doctor. "No, that is impossible. It was not

the lion. I'm afraid he was dead *before* you ever reached my house."

"You mean he died *without* seeing the lion?" I couldn't believe it.

"Please," the doctor protested. "Why do you keep concerning yourself about the lion? I keep telling you: he is a family pet, as gentle as a kitten—Old Emmett wouldn't hurt a fly."

I wasn't so sure about that. There had been a kind of look in those dreamy gold eyes, and I didn't like that yawn—it was kind of a warning.

But the thing that really struck me then—the thing that really got me—was that like the guy in the story—Artie had gone *without waiting until Emmett came.*

Of course, I feel bad about Artie, but otherwise I'm not too sure how I feel about the whole crazy business. I kept thinking about all those cats until I began to get almost as psyched out as Artie. Finally, a couple of days after I got back, I phoned this Curator of Mammals up at the Museum of Natural History, and I asked him if there'd ever been any real proof that there were mountain lions in Maine. He said yes there had been, which made me feel a little better. But I didn't much like the evidence he cited. He said that as a matter of fact just ten days before, two men in southwest Maine had shot a big two hundred and twenty pound male lion *felis concolor.*

As far as I'm concerned that doesn't prove a damn thing!

Author and self-taught illustrator of children's books, Dahlov Ipcar was born in Vermont in 1917. Her parents gave her no training, hoping to keep her style free and fresh. She had the first of many one-woman shows in 1939 at the Museum of Modern Arts. Later shows were at the Cocoran Gallery and the Carnegie Institute. She specializes in children's books, mostly self-illustrated, such as The Marvelous Merry-Go-Round. *She also writes adult fiction for such magazines as* Argosy *and* Yankee, *and adult fantasy novels like* A Dark Wind Blowing.

Until Robert Trask realized whose face he had seen, it looked as if he never would learn. . . .

TWENTY-TWO

Night Court
Mary Elizabeth Counselman

Bob waited, humming to himself in the stifling telephone booth, his collar and tie loosened for comfort in the late August heat, his Panama tilted rakishly over one ear to make room for the instrument. Through it he could hear a succession of female voices: "Garyville calling Oak Grove thuh-ree, tew, niyun, six . . . collect . . ." "Oak Grove. What was that number . . . ?" "Thuh-ree, tew . . ."

He stiffened as a low, sweetly familiar voice joined the chorus:

"Yes, yes! I—I accept the charges . . . Hello? Bob . . . ?"

Instinctively he pressed the phone closer to his mouth, the touch of it conjuring up the feel of cool lips, soft blond hair, and eyes that could melt a steel girder.

"Marian? Sure it's me! . . . Jail? No! No, honey, that's all over. I'm free! Free as a bird, yeah! The judge said it was unavoidable. Told you, didn't I?" He mugged into the phone as though somehow, in this age of speed, she could see as well as hear him across the twenty-odd miles that separated them. "It was the postponement that did it. Then they got this new judge—and guess what? He used to go to school with Dad and Uncle Harry! It was a cinch after that . . . Huh?"

He frowned slightly, listening to the soft voice coming over the wire; the voice he could not wait to hear congratulating him. Only, she wasn't. She was talking to him—he grinned sheepishly—the way Mom talked to Dad sometimes, when he came swooping into the driveway. One drink too many at the country club after his Saturday golf . . .

"Say!" he snorted. "Aren't you *glad* I don't have to serve ten to twenty years for manslaughter . . . ?"

"Oh, Bob." There was a sadness in his fiancee's voice, a troubled note. "I . . . I'm glad. Of course I'm glad about it. But . . . it's just that you sound so smug, so . . . That poor old Negro . . ."

"Smug!" He stiffened, holding the phone away slightly as if it had stung him. "Honey . . . how can you say a thing like that! Why, I've done everything I could for his family. Paid his mortgage on that little farm! Carted one of his kids to the hospital *every week* for two months, like . . ." His voice wavered, laden with a genuine regret. "Like the old guy would do himself, I guess, if he was still . . . *Marian!* You think I'm not *sorry* enough; is that it?" he demanded.

There was a little silence over the wire. He could picture her, sitting there quietly in the Marshalls' cheery-chintz living room. Maybe she had her hair pinned back in one of those ridiculous, but oddly attractive, "horse-tails" the teen-agers were wearing this year. Her little cat-face would be tilted up to the lamp, eyes closed, the long fringe of lashes curling up over shadowy lids. Bob fidgeted, wanting miserably to see her expression at that moment.

"Well? Say something!"

The silence was broken by a faint sigh.

"Darling . . . What is there to say? You're so thoughtless! Not callous; I don't mean that. Just . . . *careless!* Bob, you've got to unlearn what they taught you in Korea. You're . . . you're home again, and this is what you've been fighting for, isn't it? For . . . for the people around us to be safe? For life not to be cheap, something to be thrown away just to save a little *time* . . ."

"Say, listen!" He was scowling now, anger hardening his mouth into ugly lines. "I've had enough lectures these past two months—from Dad, from the sheriff, from Uncle Harry. You'd think a guy twenty-two years old, in combat three years and got his feet almost frozen off, didn't know the score! What's the matter with *everybody*?" Bob's anger was mounting. "Listen! I got a medal last year for killing fourteen North Koreans. For gunning 'em down! Deliberately!

But now, just because I'm driving a little too fast and some old creep can't get his wagon across the highway . . ."

"Bob!"

". . . now, all at once, I'm not a hero, I'm a murderer! I don't know the value of human life! I don't give a hoot how many people I . . ."

"Darling!"

A strangled sob came over the long miles. That stopped him. He gripped the phone, uncertainty in his oddly tip-tilted eyes that had earned him, in service, the nickname of "Gook."

"Darling, you're all mixed up. Bob . . . ? Bob dear, are you listening? If I could just *talk* to you tonight . . . ! What time is it? Oh, it's after *six!* I . . . I don't suppose you could drive over here tonight . . ."

The hard line of his mouth wavered, broke. He grinned.

"No? Who says I can't?" His laughter, young, winged and exultant, floated up. "Baby, I'll burn the road . . . Oops! I mean . . ." He broke off, sheepishly. "No, no; I'll keep 'er under fifty. Honest!" Laughing, he crossed his heart— knowing Marian so well that he knew she would sense the gesture left over from their school days. "There's so much to talk over now," he added eagerly. "Uncle Harry's taking me into the firm. I start peddling real estate for him next week. No kiddin'! And . . . and that little house we looked at . . . It's for sale, all right! Nine hundred down, and . . ."

"Bob . . . Hurry! Please!" The voice over the wire held, again, the tone he loved, laughing and tender. "But drive carefully. Promise!"

"Sure, sure! Twenty miles, twenty minutes!"

He hung up, chuckling, and strode out into the street. Dusk was falling, the slow Southern dusk that takes its time about folding its dark quilt over the Blue Ridge foothills. With a light, springy step Bob walked to where his blue con-vertible was parked outside the drugstore, sandwiched between a pickup truck and a sedan full of people. As he climbed under the steering wheel, he heard a boy's piping voice, followed by the shushing monotone of an elder:

"Look! That's Bob Trask! He killed that old Negro last Fourth-o-July . . ."

"Danny, hush! Don't talk so loud! He can hear . . ."

"Benny Olsen told me it's his second bad wreck . . ."

"Danny!"

". . . and that's the third car he's tore up in two years. Boy, you oughta seen that roadster he had! Sideswiped a truck and tore off the whole . . ."

"Hmph! License was never revoked, either! Politics! If his uncle wasn't city commissioner . . ."

Bob's scowl returned, cloudy with anger. People! They made up their own version of how an accident happened. That business with the truck, for instance. Swinging out into the highway just as he had tried to pass! Who could blame him for *that?* Or the fact that, weeks later, the burly driver had happened to die? From a ruptured appendix! The damage suit had been thrown out of court, because nobody could prove the collision had been what caused it to burst.

Backing out of the parking space in a bitter rush, Bob drove the convertible south, out of Gareyville on 31, headed for Oak Grove. Accidents! Anybody could be involved in an accident! Was a guy supposed to be lucky all the time? Or a mind-reader, always clairvoyant about the other driver?

As the white ribbon of the highway unreeled before him, Bob's anger cooled. He smiled a little, settling behind the steering wheel and switching on the radio. Music poured out softly. He leaned back, soothed by its sound and the rush of wind tousling his dark hair.

The law had cleared him of reckless driving; and that was all that counted. The landscape blurred as the sun sank. Bob switched on his headlights, dimmed. There was, at this hour, not much traffic on the Chattanooga Road.

Glancing at his watch, Bob pressed his foot more heavily on the accelerator. Six-fifteen already? Better get to Marian's before that parent of hers insisted on dragging her off to a movie. He chuckled. His only real problem now was to win over Marian's mother, who made no bones of her disapproval of him, ever since his second wreck. *"Show me the way a man drives a car, and I'll tell you what he's like inside . . ."* Bob had laughed when Marian had repeated those words. A man could drive, he had pointed out, like an old-maid schoolteacher and still be involved in an accident that was not legally his fault. All right, *two* accidents! A guy could have lousy luck twice, couldn't be? Look at the statistics! Fatal accidentsd happened every day . . .

Yawning, at peace with himself and the lazy countryside sliding past his car window, Bob let the speedometer climb another ten miles an hour. Sixty-five? He smiled, amused. Marian was such an old grandma about driving fast! After they were married, he would have to teach her, show her. Why, he had had this old boat up to ninety on this same tree-shaded stretch of highway! A driver like himself, a good driver with a good car, had perfect control over his vehicle at any . . .

The child seemed to appear out of nowhere, standing in the center of the road. A little girl in a frilly pink dress, her white face turned up in sudden horror, picked out by the headlights' glare.

Bob's cry was instinctive as he stamped on the brakes, and wrenched at the steering wheel. The car careened wildly, skidding sidewise and striking the child broadside. Then, in a tangle of wheels and canvas top, it rolled into a shallow ditch, miraculously rightside up. Bob felt his head strike something hard—the windshield. It starred out with tiny shimmering cracks, but did not shatter. Darkness rushed over him; the sick black darkness of the unconscious; but through it, sharp as a knifethrust, bringing him back to hazy awareness, was the sound of a child screaming.

"Oh, no ohmygodohgod . . ." Someone was sobbing, whimpering the words aloud. Himself.

Shaking his head blurrily, Bob stumbled from the tilted vehicle and looked about. Blood was running from a cut in his forehead, and his head throbbed with a surging nausea. But, ignoring the pain, he sank to his knee and peered under the car.

She was there. A little girl perhaps five years old. Ditch water matted the soft blond hair and trickled into the half-closed eyes, tiptilted at a pixie-like angle and fringed with long silky lashes. Bob groaned aloud, cramming his knuckles into his squared mouth to check the sob that burst out of him like a gust of desperate wind. She was pinned under a front wheel. Such a lovely little girl, appearing out here, miles from town, dressed as for a party. A sudden thought struck him that he knew this child, that he had seen her somewhere, sometime. On a bus? In a movie lobby . . . ? Where?

He crawled under the car afraid to touch her, afraid not to. She did not stir. Was she dead? Weren't those frilly little organdy ruffles on her small chest moving, ever so faintly . . . ? If he could only get her out from under that wheel! Get the car moving, rush her to a hospital . . . ! Surely, surely there was some spark of life left in that small body . . . !

Bob stood up, reeling, rubbing his eyes furiously as unconsciousness threatened to engulf him again. It was at that moment that he heard the muffled roar of a motorcycle. He whirled. Half in eagerness, half in dread, he saw a shadowy figure approaching down the twilight-misted highway.

The figure on the motorcycle, goggled and uniformed as a state highway patrolman, braked slowly a few feet away. With maddening deliberateness of movement, he dismounted, flipped out a small report-pad, and peered at the convertible, jotting down its license number. Bob beckoned frantically, pointing at the child pinned under the car. But the officer made no move to help him free her; took no notice of her beyond a cursory glance and a curt nod.

Instead, tipping back his cap from an oddly pale face, he rested one booted foot on the rear bumper and beckoned Bob to his side.

"All right, buddy . . ." His voice, Bob noted crazily, was so low that he could scarcely hear it; a whisper, a lip-movement pronouncing sounds that might have been part of the wind soughing in the roadside trees. "Name: Robert Trask? I had orders to be on the lookout for you . . ."

"Orders?" Bob bristled abruptly, caught between anxiety for the child under his car and an instinct for self-preservation. "Now, wait! I've got no record of reckless driving. I . . . I was involved in a couple of accidents; but the charges were dropped . . . Look!" he burst out. "While you're standing here yapping, this child may be . . . Get on that scooter of yours and go phone an ambulance, you! I'll report you for dereliction of duty! . . . Say!" he yelled, as the officer did not move, but went on scribbling in his book. "What kind of man *are* you, anyway? Wasting time booking me, when there still may be time to save this . . . this poor little . . . !"

The white, goggle-obscured face lifted briefly, expressionless as a mask. Bob squirmed under the scrutiny of eyes hidden behind the green glass; saw the lips move . . . and noticed, for the first time, how queerly the traffic officer held his head. His pointed chin was twisted sidewise, meeting the left shoulder. When he looked up, his whole body turned, like a man with a crick in his neck . . .

"What kind of man are *you?*" said the whispering lips. "That's what we have to find out . . . And that's why I got orders to bring you in. *Now!*"

"Bring me in . . . ?" Bob nodded dully. "Oh, you mean I'm under arrest? Sure, sure . . . But the little girl!" He glared, suddenly enraged by the officer's stolid indifference to the crushed form under the car. "Listen, if you don't get on that motorbike and go for help, I . . . I'll knock you out and go myself! Resisting arrest; leaving the scene of an accident . . . Charge me with anything you like! But if there's still time to save her . . ."

The goggled eyes regarded him steadily for a moment. Then, nodding, the officer scribbled something else in his book.

"Time?" the windy whisper said, edged with irony. "Don't waste time, eh? . . . Why don't you speed-demons think about other people *before* you kill them off? Why? *Why?* That's what we want to find out, what we *have* to find out . . . *Come on!*" The whisper lashed out, sibilant as a striking snake. "Let's go, buddy! *Walk!*"

Bob blinked, swayed. The highway patrolman, completely ignoring the small body pinned under the convertible, had strode across the paved road with a peremptory beckoning gesture. He seemed headed for a little byroad that branched off the highway, losing itself among a thick grove of pine trees. It must, Bob decided eagerly, lead to some farmhouse where the officer meant to phone for an ambulance. Staggering, he followed, with a last anxious glance at the tiny form spread-eagled under his car wheel. Where had he seen that little face? *Where* . . . ? Some neighbor's child, visiting out here in the country . . . ?

"You . . . you think she's . . . dead?" he blurted, stumbling after the shadowy figure ahead of him. "Is it too late . . . ?"

The officer with the twisted neck half-turned, swiveling his whole body to look back at him.

"That," the whispering voice said, "all depends. Come on, you—snap it up! We got all night, but there's no sense wastin' time! Eh, buddy?" The thin lips curled ironically. "Time! That's the most important thing in the world . . . to them as still have it!"

Swaying dizzily, Bob hurried after him up the winding little byroad. It led, he saw with a growing sense of unease, through a country cemetery . . . Abruptly, he brought up short, peering ahead at a gray gleam through the pines. Why, there was no farmhouse ahead! A fieldstone chapel with a high peaked roof loomed against the dusk, its arched windows gleaming redly in the last glow of the sunset.

"Hey!" he snapped. "What *is* this? Where the hell are you taking me?"

The highway patrolman turned again, swiveling his body instead of his stiff, twisted neck.

"Night court," his whisper trailed back on a thread of wind.

"*Night* court!" Bob halted completely, anger stiffening his resolve not to be railroaded into anything, no matter what he had done to that lovely little girl back there in the ditch. "Say! Is this some kind of a gag? A kangaroo court, is it? You figure on lynching me after you've . . . ?"

He glanced about the lonely graveyard in swift panic, wondering if he could make a dash for it. This was no orderly minion of the law, this crazy deformed figure stalking ahead of him! A crank, maybe? Some joker dressed up as a highway patrolman . . . ? Bob backed away a few steps, glancing left and right. A crazy man, a crackpot . . . ?"

He froze. The officer held a gun leveled at his heart.

"Don't try it!" The whisper cracked like a whiplash. "Come on, bud. You'll get a fair trial in this court—fairer than the likes of you deserve!"

Bob moved forward, helpless to resist. The officer turned his back, almost insolently, and stalked on up the narrow road. At the steps of the chapel he stood aside, however, waving his gun for Bob to open the heavy doors. Swallowing on a dry throat, he obeyed—and started violently as the rusty hinges made a sound like a hollow groan.

Then, hesitantly, his heart beginning to hammer with apprehension, Bob stepped inside. Groping his way into the darker interior of the chapel, he paused for a moment to let his eyes become accustomed to the gloom. Row on row of hardwood benches faced a raised dais, on which was a pulpit. Here, Bob realized with a chill coursing down his spine, local funeral services were held for those to be buried in the churchyard outside. As he moved forward, his footsteps echoed eerily among the beamed rafters overhead . . .

Then he saw them. People in those long rows of benches! Why, there must be over a hundred of them, seated in silent bunches of twos and threes, facing the pulpit. In a little alcove, set aside for the choir, Bob saw another, smaller group—and found himself suddenly counting them with a surge of panic. There were twelve in the choir box. Twelve, the number of a jury! Dimly he could see their white faces, with dark hollows for eyes, turning to follow his halting progress down the aisle.

Then, like an echo of a voice, deep and reverberating, someone called his name.

"The defendant will please take the stand . . . !"

Bob stumbled forward, his scalp prickling at the ghostly resemblance of this mock-trial to the one in which he had been acquitted only that morning. As though propelled by unseen hands, he found himself hurrying to a seat beside the pulpit, obviously reserved for one of the elders, but now serving as a witness-stand. He sank into the big chair, peering through the half-darkness in an effort to make out some of the faces around him . . .

Then, abruptly, as the "bailiff" stepped forward to "swear him in," he stifled a cry of horror.

The man had no face. Where his features had been there was a raw, reddish mass. From this horror, somehow, a nightmare slit of mouth formed the words: ". . . to tell the truth, the whole truth, and nothing but the truth, so help you God?"

"I . . . I do," Bob murmured; and compared to the whispered tones of the bailiff, his own voice shocked him with its loudness.

"State your name."

"R-robert Trask . . ."

"Your third offense, isn't it, Mr. Trask?" the judge whispered drily. "A habitual reckless-driver . . ."

Bob was shaking now, caught in the grip of a nameless terror. What was this? Who were all these people, and why had they had him brought here by a motorcycle cop with a twisted . . . ?

He caught his breath again sharply, stifling another cry as the figure of a dignified elderly man became visible behind the pulpit, where before he had been half-shrouded in shadow. Bob blinked at him, sure that his stern white face was familiar—very familiar, not in the haunting way in which that child had seemed known to him, lying there crushed under his car. This man . . .

His head reeled all at once. Of course! Judge Abernathy! Humorous, lenient old Judge Ab, his father's friend, who had served in the Gareyville circuit court . . . Bob gulped. In 1932! Why, he had been only a youngster then! Twenty years would make this man all of ninety-eight years old, if . . . And it was suddenly that *"if"* which made Bob's scalp prickle with uneasiness. *If he were alive.* Judge Ab was *dead!* Wasn't he? Hadn't he heard his mother and dad talking about the old man, years ago; talking in hushed, sorrowful tones about the way he had been killed by a hit-and-run driver who had never been caught?

Bob shook his head, fighting off the wave of dizziness and nausea that was creeping over him again. It was crazy, the way his imagination was running away with him! Either this was not Judge Ab, but some old fellow who vaguely resembled him in this half-light . . . Or it *was* Judge Ab, alive, looking no older than he had twenty-odd years ago, at which time he was supposed to have been killed.

Squinting out across the rows of onlookers, Bob felt a growing sense of unreality. He could just make out, dimly, the features of the people seated in the first two rows of benches. Other faces, pale blurs against the blackness, moved restlessly as he peered at them . . . Bob gasped. His eyes made out things in the semi-gloom that he wished he had not seen. Faces mashed and cut beyond the semblance of a face! Bodies without arms! One girl . . . He swayed in his chair sickly; her shapely form was without a head!

He got a grip on his nerves with a tremendous effort. Of course! It wasn't real; it was all a horrible, perverted sort of practical joke! All these people were tricked up like corpses in a Chamber-of-Commerce "horror" parade. He tried to laugh, but his lips jerked with the effort . . . Then they quivered, sucking in breath.

The "prosecuting attorney" had stepped forward to question him—as, hours ago, he had been questioned by the attorney for Limestone County. Only . . . Bob shut his eyes quickly. It couldn't be! They wouldn't, whoever these people in this lonely chapel might be, they *wouldn't* make up some old Negro to look like the one whose wagon he had . . . had . . .

The figure moved forward, soundlessly. Only someone who had seen him on the morgue slab, where they had taken him after the accident, could have dreamed up that wooly white wig, that wrinkled old black face, and . . . And that gash at his temple, on which now the blood seemed to have dried forever . . .

"Hidy, Cap'm," the figure said in a diffident whisper. "I got to ast you a few questions. Don't lie, now! Dat's de *wust* thing you could do—tell a lie in dis-*yeah* court! . . . 'Bout how fast you figger you was goin' when you run over de girl-baby?"

"I . . . Pretty fast," he blurted. "Sixty-five, maybe seventy an hour."

The man he had killed nodded, frowning. "Yassuh. Dat's about right, sixty-five accordin' to de officer here." He glanced at the patrolman with the twisted neck, who gave a brief, grotesque nod of agreement.

Bob waited sickly. The old Negro—or whoever was dressed up as a dead man—moving toward him, resting his hand on the ornate rail of the chapel pulpit.

"Cap'm . . ." His soft whisper seemed to come from everywhere, rather than from the moving lips in that black face. "Cap'm . . . *why?* How come you was drivin' fifteen

miles over the speed limit on this-yeah road? Same road
where you run into my wagon . . ."

The listeners in the tiers of pews began to sway all at
once, like reeds in the wind. *"Why?"* someone in the rear
took up the word, and then another echoed it, until a faint,
rhythmic chant rose and fell over the crowded chapel:

"Why? Why? Why? . . . Why? Why? Why?"

"Order!" The "judge," the man who looked like a judge
long dead, banged softly with his gavel; or it could have
been a shutter banging at one of those arched chapel windows, Bob thought strangely.

The chanting died away. Bob swallowed nervously. For
the old Negro was looking up at him expectantly, waiting for
an answer to his simple question—the question echoed by
those looking and listening from that eery "courtroom."
Why? Why was he driving so fast? If he could only make up
something, some good reason . . .

"I . . . I had a date with my girl," Bob heard his own
voice, startling in its volume compared to the whispers
around him.

"Yassuh?" The black prosecutor nodded gently. "She
was gwine off someplace, so's you had to hurry to catch up
wid her? Or else, was she bad-off sick and callin' for
you . . . ?"

"I . . . No," Bob said, miserably honest. "No. There
wasn't any hurry. I just . . . didn't want to . . ." He gestured
futilely. "I wanted to be with her as quick as I could! Be-
because I love her . . ." He paused, waiting to hear a titter of
mirth ripple over the listeners.

There was no laughter. Only silence, sombre and accusing.

"Yassuh." Again the old Negro nodded his graying head,
the head with the gashed temple. "All of us wants to be wid
the ones we love. We don't want to waste no time doin' it
. . . Only, you got to remember de Lawd give each of us a
certain po'tion of time to use. And he don't aim for us to cut
off de supply dat belong to somebody else. They got a right
to live and love and be happy, too!"

The grave words hit Bob like a hammer blow—or like, he
thought oddly, words he had been forming in his own mind,
but holding off, not letting himself think because they might

hurt. He fidgeted in the massive chair, twisting his hands together in sudden grim realization. Remorse had not, up to this moment, touched him deeply. But now it brought tears welling up, acid-like, to burn his eyes.

"Oh . . . please!" he burst out. "Can't we get this over with, this . . . this crazy mock-trial? I don't know who you are, all you people here. But I know you've . . . you've been incensed because my . . . my folks pulled some wires and got me out of two traffic-accidents that I . . . I should have been punished for! Now I've . . . I've run over a little girl, and you're afraid if I go to regular court-trial, my uncle will get me free again; is that it? That's it, isn't it . . . ?" he lashed out, half-rising. "All this . . . masquerade! Getting yourselves up like . . . like people who are dead . . . ! You're doing it to scare me!" He laughed harshly. "But it doesn't scare me, kid tricks like . . . like . . ."

He broke off, aware of another figure that had moved forward, rising from one of the forward benches. A burly man in overalls, wearing a trucker's cap . . . One big square hand was pressed to his side, and he walked as though in pain. Bob recognized those rugged features with a new shock.

"Kid . . . listen!" His rasping whisper sounded patient, tired. "We ain't here to scare anybody . . . Hell, that's for Hallowe'en parties! The reason we hold court here, night after night, tryin' some thick-skinned jerk who thinks he owns the road . . . Look, we just want t' know *why;* see? Why we had to be killed. Why some nice joe like you, with a girl and a happy future ahead of 'im, can't understand that . . . that *we* had a right to live, too! Me! Just a dumb-lug of a truck jockey, maybe . . . But I was doin' all right. I was gettin' by, raisin' my kids right . . ." The square hand moved from the man's side, gestured briefly and pressed back again.

"I figured to have my fool appendix out, soon as I made my run and got back home that Sunday. Only, you . . . Well, gee! Couldn't you have spared me ten seconds, mac?" the hoarse whisper accused. "Wouldn't you loan me that much of your . . . your precious time, instead of takin' away all of mine? Mine, and this ole darkey's? And tonight . . ."

An angry murmur swept over the onlookers, like a rising wind.

"Order!" The gavel banged again, like a muffled heart beat. "The accused is not on trial for previous offenses. Remarks of the defense attorney—who is distinctly out of order—will be stricken from the record. Does the prosecution wish to ask the defendant any more questions to determine the *reason* for the accident?"

The old Negro shook his head, shrugging. "Nawsuh, Jedge. Reckon not."

Bob glanced sidewise at the old man who looked so like Judge Ab. He sucked in a quick breath as the white head turned, revealing a hideously crushed skull matted with some dark brown substance. Hadn't his father said something, years ago, about that hit-and-run driver running a wheel over his old friend's head? Were those . . . were those tire-tread marks on this man's white collar . . . ? Bob ground his teeth. How far would these Hallowe'en mummers go to make their macabre little show realistic . . . ?

But now, to his amazement, the burly man in trucker's garb moved forward, shrugging.

"Okay, Your Honor," his hoarse whisper apologized. "I . . . I know it's too late for justice, not for us here. And if the court appoints me to defend this guy, I'll try . . . Look buddy," his whisper softened. "You have reason to believe your girl was steppin' out on you? That why you was hurryin', jumpin' the speed-limit, to get there before she . . . ? You were out of your head, crazy-jealous?"

Bob glared. "Say!" he snapped. "This is going too far, dragging my financée's name into this . . . this fake trial . . . Go ahead! I'm guilty of reckless driving—three times! I admit it! There was no reason on this earth for me to be speeding, no excuse for running over that . . . that poor little kid! It's . . . it's just that I . . . ." His voice broke, "I didn't *see* her! Out here in the middle of nowhere—a child! How was I to know? The highway was clear, and then all at once, there she was right in front of my car . . . But . . . but I *was* going too fast. I deserve to be lynched! Nothing you do to me would be enough . . . ."

He crumpled in the chair, stricken with dry sobs of remorse. But fear, terror of this weirdly-made-up congregation, left him slowly, as, looking from the judge to the highway patrolman, from the old Negro to the trucker, he saw only pity in their faces, and a kind of sad bewilderment.

"But—why? Why need it happen?" the elderly judge asked softly, in a stern voice Bob thought he could remember from childhood. "Why does it go on and on? This senseless slaughter! If we could only *understand* . . . ! If we could only make the living understand, and stop and think, before it's too late for . . . another such as we. There is no such thing as an accidental death! Accidents are murders—because someone could have prevented them!"

The white-haired man sighed, like a soft wind blowing through the chapel. The sigh was caught up by others, until it rose and fell like a wailing gust echoing among the rafters.

Bob shivered, hunched in his chair. The hollow eyes of the judge fixed themselves on him, stern but pitying. He hung his head, and buried his face in his hands, smearing blood from the cut on his forehead.

"I . . . I . . . Please! Please don't say any more!" he sobbed. "I guess I just didn't realize, I was too wrapped up in my own selfish . . ." His voice broke. "And now it's too late . . ."

As one, the shadowy figures of the old Negro and the burly truck driver moved together in a kind of grim comradeship. They looked at the judge mutely as though awaiting his decision. The gaunt figure with the crushed skull cleared his throat in a way Bob thought he remembered . . .

"Too late? Yes . . . for these two standing before you. But the dead," his sombre whisper rose like a gust of wind in the dark chapel, "the dead can not punish the living. They are part of the past, and have no control over the present . . . or the future."

"Yet, sometimes," the dark holes of eyes bored into Bob's head sternly, "the dead can guide the living, by giving them a glimpse into the future. The future as it will be . . . unless the living use their power to change it! Do you understand, Robert Trask? Do you understand that you are on trial in this night court, not for the past but for the future . . . ?"

Bob shook his head, bewildered. "The . . . future? I don't understand. I . . ." He glanced up eagerly. "The little girl!

You . . . you mean, she's all right? She isn't dead . . . ? he pressed, hardly daring to hope.

"She is not yet born," the old man whispered quietly. "But one day you will see her, just as you saw her tonight, lying crushed under your careless wheels . . . unless . . ." The whisper changed abruptly; became the dry official voice of a magistrate addressing his prisoner. "It is therefore the judgment of this court that, in view of the defendant's plea of guilty and in view of his extreme youth and of his war record, sentence shall be suspended pending new evidence of criminal behavior in the driver's seat of a motor vehicle. If such new evidence should be brought to the attention of this court, sentence shall be pronounced and the extreme penalty carried out . . . Do you understand, Mr. Trask?" the grave voice repeated. "*The extreme penalty!* . . . Case dismissed."

The gavel banged. Bob nodded dazedly, again burying his face in his hands and shaking with dry sobs. A wave of dizziness swept over him. He felt the big chair tilt, it seemed, and suddenly he was falling, falling forward into a great black vortex that swirled and eddied . . .

Light snatched him back to consciousness, a bright dazzling light that pierced his eyeballs and made him gag with nausea. Hands were pulling at him, lifting him. Then, slowly, he became aware of two figures bending over him: a gnome-like little man with a lantern, and a tall, sunburned young man in the uniform of a highway patrolman. It was not, Bob noted blurrily, the same one, the one with the twisted neck . . . He sat up, blinking.

"My, my, young feller!" The gnome with the lantern was trying to help him up from where he lay on the chapel floor in front of the pulpit. "Nasty lump on your head there! I'm the sexton: live up the road a piece. I heard your car hit the ditch a while ago, and called the highway Patrol. Figgered you was drunk . . ." He sniffed suspiciously, then shrugged. "Don't smell drunk. What happened? You fall asleep at the wheel?"

Bob shut his eyes, groaning. He let himself be helped to one of the front pews and leaned back against it heavily before answering. Better tell the truth now. Get it over with . . .

"The . . . little girl. Pinned under my car—you found her?" He forced out the words sickly. "I . . . didn't see her, but . . . It was my fault. I was . . . driving too fast. Too fast to stop when she stepped out right in front of my . . ."

He broke off, aware that the tall tanned officer was regarding him with marked suspicion.

"What little girl?" he snapped. "There's nobody pinned under your car, buddy! I looked. Your footprints were the only ones leading away from the accident . . . and I traced them here! Besides, you were dripping blood from that cut on you . . . Say! You trying to kid somebody?"

"No, no!" Bob gestured wildly. "Who'd kid about a thing like . . . ? Maybe the other highway patrolman took her away on his motorcycle! He . . . All of them . . . There didn't seem any doubt that she'd been killed instantly. But then, the judge said she . . . she wasn't even born yet! They made me come here, to . . . to try me! In . . . night court, they called it! All of them pretending to be . . . dead people, accident victims. Blood all over them! Mangled . . ." He checked himself, realizing how irrational he sounded. "I fainted," his voice trailed uncertainly. "I guess when they . . . they heard you coming, they all ran away . . ."

"*Night* court?" The officer arched one eyebrow, tipped back his cap, and eyed Bob dubiously. "Say, you *sure* you're sober, buddy? Or maybe you got a concussion . . . There's been nobody here. Not a soul; has there, Pop?"

"Nope." The sexton lifted his lamp positively, causing shadows to dance weirdly over the otherwise empty chapel. A film of dust covered the pews, undisturbed save where Bob himself now sat. "Ain't been nary a soul here since the Wilkins funeral; that was Monday three weeks ago. My, you never saw the like o' flowers . . ."

The highway patrolman gestured him to silence, peering at Bob once more. "What was that you said about another speed cop? There was no report tonight. What was his badge number? You happen to notice?"

Bob shook his head vaguely; then dimly recalled numbers he had seen on a tarnished shield pinned to that shadowy uniform.

"Eight something . . . 84! That was it! And . . . and he had a kind of twisted set to his head . . ."

The officers scowled suddenly, hands on hips. "Sa-ay!" he said in a cold voice. "What're you tryin' to pull? Nobody's worn Badge No. 84 since Sam Lacy got killed two years ago. Chasin' a speed-crazy high school kid, who swerved and made him fall off his motor. Broke his neck!" He compressed his lips grimly. "You're tryin' to pull some kind of gag about *that?*"

"No! N-no . . . !" Bob rose shakily to his feet. "I . . . I . . . Maybe I just dreamed it all! That clonk on the head . . ." He laughed all at once, a wild sound, full of hysterical relief. "You're positive there was no little girl pinned under my wheel? No . . . no signs of . . . ?"

He started toward the wide-flung doors of the chapel, reeling with laughter. But it had all seemed so real! Those nightmare faces, the whispering voices: that macabre trial for a traffic fatality that had never happened anywhere but in his own overwrought imagination . . . !

Still laughing, he climbed into his convertible; found it undamaged by its dive into the ditch, and backed out onto the road again. He waved. Shrugging, grinning, the highway officer and the old sexton waved back, visible in a yellow circle of lanternlight.

Bob gunned his motor and roared away. A lone tourist, rounding a curve, swung sharply off the pavement to give him room as he swooped over on the wrong side of the yellow line. Bob blew his horn mockingly, and trod impatiently on the accelerator. Marian must be tired of waiting! And the thought of holding her in his arms, laughing with her, telling her about that crazy, dream-trial . . . Dead men! Trying him, the living, for the traffic-death of a child yet to be born! "The extreme penalty!" If not lynching, what would that be? He smiled, amused. Was anything that could happen to a man really "a fate worse than death . . . ?"

Bob's smile froze.

Quite suddenly his foot eased up on the accelerator. His eyes widened, staring ahead at the dark highway illuminated by the twin glare of his headlights. Sweat popped out on his cool forehead all at once. Jerkily his hands yanked at the smooth plastic of the steering-wheel, pulling the convertible well over to the right side of the highway . . .

In that instant, Bob thought he knew where he had seen the hauntingly familiar features of that lovely little girl lying dead, crushed, under the wheel of his car. "The extreme penalty?" He shuddered, and slowed down, driving more carefully into the darkness ahead. The darkness of the future . . .

For, the child's blond hair and long lashes, he knew with a swift chill of dread, had been a tiny replica of Marian's . . . and the tip-tilted pixy eyes, closed in violent death, had borne a startling resemblance to his own.

A descendant of John Rolfe, who was among the original settlers of the Jamestown Colony in 1607, Mary Elizabeth Counselman was born in Georgia in 1911 and grew up on a honest-to-Scarlett-O'Hara plantation. Educated at the University of Alabama and Montevallo University, she began selling fiction and poetry to such diverse publications as the Saturday Evening Post *and* Jungle Stories. *Her "The Three Marked Pennies" became the most popular story ever to appear in* Weird Tales. *The best of her supernatural writing, including "Night Court," is collected in* Half in Shadow *(Arkham House, 1978).*

Murlock's wife died from a fever. Or did she?

TWENTY-THREE

The Boarded Window

Ambrose Bierce

In 1830, only a few miles away from what is now the great city of Cincinnati, lay an immense and almost unbroken forest. The whole region was sparsely settled by people of the frontier—restless souls who no sooner had hewn fairly habitable homes out of the wilderness and attained to that degree of prosperity which today we should call indigence than, impelled by some mysterious impulse of their nature, they abandoned all and pushed farther westward, to encounter new perils and privations in the effort to regain the meagre comforts which they had voluntarily renounced. Many of them had already forsaken that region for the remoter settlements, but among those remaining was one who had been of those first arriving. He lived alone in a house of logs surrounded on all sides by the great forest, of whose gloom and silence he seemed a part, for no one had ever known him to smile nor speak a needless word. His simple wants were supplied by the sale or barter of skins of wild animals in the river town, for not a thing did he grow upon the land which, if needful, he might have claimed by right of undisturbed possession. There were evidences of "improvement"—a few acres of ground immediately about the house had once been cleared of its trees, the decayed stumps of which were half concealed by the new growth that had been suffered to repair the ravage wrought by the ax. Apparently the man's zeal for agriculture had burned with a failing flame, expiring in penitential ashes.

The little log house, with its chimney of sticks, its roof of warping clapboards weighted with traversing poles and its "chinking" of clay, had a single door and, directly opposite, a window. The latter, however, was boarded up—nobody could remember a time when it was not. And none knew why it was so closed; certainly not because of the occupant's dislike of light and air, for on those rare occasions when a hunter had passed that lonely spot the recluse had commonly been seen sunning himself on his doorstep if heaven had provided sunshine for his need. I fancy there are few persons living today who ever knew the secret of that window, but I am one, as you shall see.

The man's name was said to be Murlock. He was apparently seventy years old, actually about fifty. Something besides years had had a hand in his aging. His hair and long, full beard were white, his gray, lustreless eyes sunken, his face singularly seamed with wrinkles which appeared to belong to two intersecting systems. In figure he was tall and spare, with a stoop of the shoulders—a burden bearer. I never saw him; these particulars I learned from my grandfather, from whom also I got the man's story when I was a lad. He had known him when living nearby in that early day.

One day Murlock was found in his cabin, dead. It was not a time and place for coroners and newspapers, and I suppose it was agreed that he had died from natural causes or I should have been told and should remember. I know only that with what was probably a sense of the fitness of things the body was buried near the cabin, alongside the grave of his wife, who had preceded him by so many years that local tradition had retained hardly a hint of her existence. That closes the final chapter of this true story—excepting, indeed, the circumstance that many years afterward, in company with an equally intrepid spirit, I penetrated to the place and ventured near enough to the ruined cabin to throw a stone against it and ran away to avoid the ghost which every well-informed boy thereabout knew haunted the spot. But there is an earlier chapter—that supplied by my grandfather.

When Murlock built his cabin and began laying sturdily about with his ax to hew out a farm—the rifle, meanwhile, his means of support—he was young, strong, and full of hope. In that eastern country whence he came he had married, as was the fashion, a young woman in all ways worthy of his honest devotion, who shared the dangers and privations of his lot with a willing spirit and light heart. There is no known record of her name; of her charms of mind and person tradition is silent and the doubter is at liberty to entertain his doubt; but God forbid that I should share it! Of their affection and happiness there is abundant assurance in every added day of the man's widowed life; for what but the magnetism of a blessed memory could have chained that venturesome spirit to a lot like that?

One day Murlock returned from gunning in a distant part of the forest to find his wife prostrate with fever, and delirious. There was no physician within miles, no neighbor; nor was she in a condition to be left, to summon help. So he set about the task of nursing her back to health, but at the end of the third day she fell into unconsciousness and so passed away, apparently, with never a gleam of returning reason.

From what we know of a nature like his we may venture to sketch in some of the details of the outline picture drawn by my grandfather. When convinced that she was dead, Murlock had sense enough to remember that the dead must be prepared for burial. In performance of this sacred duty he blundered now and again, did certain things incorrectly, and others which he did correctly were done over and over. His occasional failures to accomplish some simple and ordinary act filled him with astonishment, like that of a drunken man who wonders at the suspension of familiar natural laws. He was surprised, too, that he did not weep—surprised and a little ashamed; surely it is unkind not to weep for the dead. "Tomorrow," he said aloud, "I shall have to make the coffin and dig the grave; and then I shall miss her, when she is no longer in sight; but now—she is dead, of course, but it is all right—it *must* be all right, somehow. Things cannot be so bad as they seem."

He stood over the body in the fading light, adjusting the hair and putting the finishing touches to the simple toilet, doing all mechanically, with soulless care. And still through his consciousness ran an undersense of conviction that all was right—that he should have her again as before, and everything explained. He had had no experience in grief; his capacity had not been enlarged by use. His heart could not contain it all, nor his imagination rightly conceive it. He did not know he was so hard struck; *that* knowledge would come later, and never go. Grief is an artist of powers as various as the instruments upon which he plays his dirges for the dead, evoking from some the sharpest, shrillest notes, from others the low, grave chords that throb recurrent like the slow beating of a distant drum. Some natures it startles; some it stupefies. To one it comes like the stroke of an arrow, stinging all the sensibilities to a keener life; to another as the blow of a bludgeon, which in crushing benumbs. We may conceive Murlock to have been that way affected, for (and here we are upon surer ground than that of conjecture) no sooner had he finished his pious work than, sinking into a chair by the side of the table upon which the body lay, and noting how white the profile showed in the deepening gloom, he laid his arms upon the table's edge, and dropped his face into them, tearless yet and unutterably weary. At that moment came in through the open window a long, wailing sound like the cry of a lost child in the far deeps of the darkening wood! But the man did not move. Again, and nearer than before, sounded that unearthly cry upon his failing sense. Perhaps it was a wild beast; perhaps it was a dream. For Murlock was asleep.

Some hours later, as it afterward appeared, this unfaithful watcher awoke and lifting his head from his arms intently listened—he knew not why. There in the black darkness by the side of the dead, recalling all without a shock, he strained his eyes to see—he knew not what. His senses were all alert, his breath was suspended, his blood had stilled its tides as if to assist the silence. Who—what had waked him, and where was it?

Suddenly the table shook beneath his arms, and at the same moment he heard, or fancied that he heard, a light, soft step—another—sounds as of bare feet upon the floor!

He was terrified beyond the power to cry out or move. Perforce he waited—waited there in the darkness through seeming centuries of such dread as one may know, yet live to tell. He tried vainly to speak the dead woman's name, vainly to stretch forth his hand across the table to learn if she were there. His throat was powerless, his arms and hands were like lead. Then occurred something most frightful. Some heavy body seemed hurled against the table with an impetus that pushed it against his breast so sharply as nearly to overthrow him, and at the same instant he heard and felt the fall of something upon the floor with so violent a thump that the whole house was shaken by the impact. A scuffling ensued, and a confusion of sounds impossible to describe. Murlock had risen to his feet. Fear had by excess forfeited control of his faculties. He flung his hands upon the table. Nothing was there!

There is a point at which terror may turn to madness; and madness incites to action. With no definite intent, from no motive but the wayward impulse of a madman, Murlock sprang to the wall, with a little groping seized his loaded rifle, and without aim discharged it. By the flash which lit up the room with a vivid illumination, he saw an enormous panther dragging the dead woman toward the window, its teeth fixed in her throat! Then there were darkness blacker than before, and silence; and when he returned to consciousness the sun was high and the wood vocal with songs of birds.

The body lay near the window, where the beast had left it when frightened away by the flash and report of the rifle. The clothing was deranged, the long hair in disorder, the limbs lay anyhow. From the throat, dreadfully lacerated, had issued a pool of blood not yet entirely coagulated. The ribbon with which he had bound the wrists was broken; the hands were tightly clenched. Between the teeth was a fragment of the animal's ear.

A dark genius of American letters, Ambrose Bierce was born in Ohio in 1842 and served in the Union army during the Civil War. A bitter and fearless man known for his witty writing (in one book review he wrote, "The covers of this book are too far apart"), he had a long, successful journalism career in San Francisco. His life ended with an eerie touch of mystery: he disappeared somewhere in Mexico in 1914.

Hobo Harold Skidmore was very sick, and when farmer Plone offered Harold use of his old log cabin, Harold eagerly accepted, even if the cabin had this odd habit of disappearing.

TWENTY-FOUR

The Ghosts of Steamboat Coulee

Arthur J. Burks

I

A heartless brakeman discovered me and kicked me off the train at Palisades. I didn't care greatly. As well be dropped here in Moses Coulee like a bag of spoiled meal as farther up the line. When a man knows he has but a short time to live, what matters it? Had I not been endowed with a large modicum of my beloved father's stubbornness I believe I should, long ere this, have crawled away into some hole, like a mongrel cur, to die. There was no chance to cheat the Grim Reaper. That had been settled long ago, when, without a gas mask, I had gone through a certain little town in Flanders.

My lungs were just about done. Don't think I am making a bid for sympathy. I know a sick man seldom arouses in the breast of strangers any other emotion than disgust.

But I am telling this to explain my actions in those things which came later.

After leaving the train at Palisades I looked up and down the coulee. Where to go? I hadn't the slightest idea. Wenatchee lay far behind me, at the edge of the mighty Columbia River. I had found this thriving little city unsympathetic and not particularly hospitable. I couldn't, therefore, retrace my steps. Besides, I never have liked to go back over lost ground. I saw the train which had dropped me

415

crawl like a snake up the steep incline which led out of the coulee. I hadn't the strength to follow. I knew that I could never make the climb.

So, wearily, I trudged out to the road and headed farther into the coulee, to come, some hours later, to another cul-de-sac. It was another (to me impossible) incline, this time a wagon road. I have since learned that this road leads, via a series of three huge terraces bridged by steep incline, out of Moses Coulee. It is called The Three Devils—don't ask me why, for it was named by the Siwash Indians.

At the foot of this road, and some half-mile from where it began to climb, I saw a small farmhouse, from the chimney of which a spiral of blue smoke arose lazily into the air. Here were folks, country folks, upon whose hospitality I had long ago learned to rely. Grimy with the dust of the trail, damp with perspiration, red spots dancing in the air before my eyes because of the unaccustomed exertion to which I had compelled myself, I turned aside and presently knocked at the door of the farmhouse.

A housewife answered my knock and nervously motioned me enter. I was shortly pointed to a seat at the table to partake of the tasty viands brought forth. When I had finished eating I arose from my place and was about to ask her what I might do in payment for the meal, when I was seized with a fit of coughing which left me faint and trembling; and I had barely composed myself when the woman's husband and a half-grown boy entered the house silently and looked at me.

"How come a man as sick as you is out on the road afoot like this?" demanded the man.

I told them my story, and that I had neither friends nor family, nor abode. While I talked they exchanged glances with one another, and when I had finished the husband looked at me steadily for a long moment.

"Is there a chance for you to get well?" he asked finally.

"I am afraid not." I tried to make my voice sound cheerful.

"Would you like to find a place where nobody'd bother you? A place where you could loaf along about as you wished until your time came?"

I nodded in answer to the question. The man strode to the door and pointed.

"See there?" he asked. "That's the road you came here on, against that two hundred foot cliff. Opposite that cliff, back of my house, is another cliff, thirteen hundred feet high. Matter of fact, my place is almost surrounded by cliffs, don't need to build fences, except where the coulee opens away toward Columbia River, which is some lot of miles away from here. Cliffs both sides of it, all the way down. No other exit, except there!"

As he spoke he swung his extended forearm straight toward the cliff to the north.

"See what looks like a great black shadow against the face of the cliff, right where she turns to form the curve of the coulee?"

"Yes, I see it."

"Well, that ain't a shadow. That's the entrance to another and smaller coulee which opens into this one. It is called Steamboat Coulee, and if you look sharp you can see why."

I studied that black shadow as he pointed, carefully, running my eyes over the face of the cliff. Then I exclaimed suddenly, so unexpectedly did I discover the reason for the name. Right at the base of that black shadow was a great pile of stone, its color all but blending with the mother cliff unless one looked closely; and this mass of solid rock, from where we stood in the doorway of the farmhouse, looked like a great steamboat slowly emerging from the cleft in the giant walls!

"Good Lord!" I exclaimed. "If I didn't know better I would swear that was a boat under steam!"

"It's fooled a lot of folks," returned the farmer. "Well, that coulee entrance is on my land, so I guess I have a right to make this proposition to you. Back inside that coulee about two miles is my old log cabin that could easy be made livable. Just the place for you, and I could send in what little food you would need. It's kind of cool at night, but in the daytime the sun makes the coulee as hot as an oven, and you could loaf all day in the heat. There are plenty of big rocks there to flop on and—who knows—maybe you'd even get well!"

"I thank you, sir," I said, as politely as I could; "you are very kind. I accept your offer with great pleasure. May I know to whom I am indebted for this unusually benevolent service?"

The man hesitated before answering.

"What difference does a name make? We don't go much on last names here. That there is Reuben, my boy, and this is my wife, Hildreth. My own name is Plone. You can tell us what to call you, if you wish, but it don't make much difference if you don't care to."

"My name is Harold Skidmore, late of the U. S. Army. Once more allow me to thank you, then I shall go into my new home before it gets so dark I can't find it."

"That's all right. Reuben will go along and show you the place. Hillie will put up a sack of grub for you—enough to last a couple of days—and tote it in tomorrow. You'll probably be too sore from your walk to come out for a while—and we may be too busy to take any in to you."

The woman dropped her arms to her side and moved into the kitchen to do the bidding of Plone. Plone! What an odd name for a man! I studied him as, apparently having forgotten me, he stared moodily down the haze-filled coulee. I tried to see what his eyes were seeking, but all I could tell was that he watched the road by which I had come to this place—watched it carefully and in silence, as though he expected other visitors to come around the bend which leads to the Three Devils. He did not turn back to me again; and when, ten minutes or so later, Reuben touched my arm and started off in the direction of Steamboat, Plone was still staring down the road.

I studied the territory over which we traveled. Though I knew absolutely nothing about farming, I would have sworn that this ground hadn't been cultivated for many years. It had been plowed once upon a time, but the plowing had been almost obliterated by scattered growths of green sagebrush which had pushed through and begun to thrive, while in the open Reuben and I struggled through regular matted growths of wild hollyhocks, heavy with their fiery blooms. Plone's farm was nothing but a desert on the coulee floor.

We were approaching Steamboat Coulee entrance, and the nearer we strode the less I liked the bargain I had made, for the huge maw looked oddly like a great open mouth that might take one in and leave no trace. But those red spots were dancing before my eyes again and may have helped me to imagine things.

When we reached the gap its mouthlike appearance was not so pronounced, and the rock which had looked like a steamboat did not resemble a steamboat at all. The floor of this coulee was a dry stream-bed which, when the spring freshets came, must have been a roaring torrent.

Before entering I looked back at the house of Plone, and shouted in amazement.

"Reuben! Where is the house? I can see all of that end of the coulee, and your house is not in sight!"

"We come over a rise, a high one, that's all," he replied carelessly; "if we go back a piece we can see the house. Only we ain't got time. I want to show you the cabin and get back before dark. This coulee ain't nice to get caught in after dark."

"It isn't?" I questioned. "Why not?"

But Reuben had begun the entrance to Steamboat Coulee and did not answer. I was very hesitant about following him now, for I knew that he had lied to me. We hadn't come over any rise, and I should have been able to see the farmhouse!

I liked this coulee less and less as we went deeper into it. Walls rose straight on either hand, and they were so close that they seemed to be pressing over upon me. The stream-bed narrowed and deepened. On its banks grew thickets of wild willow, interspersed with clumps of squaw-berry bushes laden with pink fruit. Behind these thickets arose the talus slope of shell-rock.

I studied the slopes for signs of pathways which might lead out in case a heavy rain should fill the stream bed and cut off my retreat by the usual way, but saw none. I saw instead something that filled me with a sudden feeling of dread, causing a sharp constriction of my throat. It was just a mottled mass on a large rock; but as I looked at it the mass moved, untwisted itself, and a huge snake glided out of sight in the rocks.

"Reuben," I called, "are there many snakes in this coulee?"

"Thousands!" he replied without looking back. "Rattlers, blue racers and bull whips—but mostly rattlers. Keep to your shanty at night and stay in the stream-bed in the daytime and they won't be any danger to you!"

Well, I was terribly tired, else I would have turned around and quitted this place—yes, though I fell dead from exhaustion ten minutes later. As it was I followed Reuben, who turned aside finally and climbed out of the stream-bed. I followed him and stood upon a trail which led down a gloomy aisle into a thicket of willows. Heavy shadows hung in this moody aisle, but through these I could make out the outline of a squatty log cabin.

Ten minutes later I had a fire going in the cracked stove which the house boasted, and its light was driving away the shadows in the wall. The board floor was well laid—no cracks through which venturesome rattlers might smell me out. I made sure of this before I would let Reuben get away, and that the door could be closed and bolted.

"Well," said Reuben, who had stood by while I put the place rapidly to rights, "you'll be all right now. Snug as a bug in a rug—if you ain't afraid of ghosts!"

His hand had dropped to the doorknob as he began to talk, and when he had uttered this last sinister sentence he opened the door and slipped out before I could stop him. Those last six words had sent a chill through my whole body. In a frenzy of fear which I could not explain, I rushed to the door and looked out, intending to call Reuben back.

I swear he hadn't had time to reach that stream-bed and drop into it out of sight; but when I looked out he was nowhere to be seen, and when I shouted his name until the echoes rang to right and left through the coulee, there was no answer! He must have fairly flown out of that thicket!

I closed the door and barred it, placed the chair back under the doorknob, and sat down upon the edge of the bed, gazing into the fire.

What sort of place had I wandered into?

For a time the rustling of the wind through the willows outside the log cabin was my only answer. Then a gritty grating sound beneath the floor, slow and intermittent, told me that a huge snake, sluggish with the coolness of the evening, was crawling there and was at that moment scraping alongside one of the timbers which supported the floor.

I was safe from these, thank God!

The feeling of security which now descended upon me, together with the cheery roaring of the fire in the stove, almost lulled me to sleep as I sat. My eyes were closing wearily and my head was sinking upon my breast. . . .

II

A cry that the wildest imagination would never have expected to hear in this place, came suddenly from somewhere in the darkness outside.

It was a cry as of a little baby that awakes in the night and begs plaintively to be fed. And it came from somewhere out there in the shell-rock of the talus slopes.

Merciful heaven! How did it happen that a wee small child such as I guessed this to be had wandered out into the darkness of the coulee? Whence had it come? Were there other inhabitants in Steamboat? But Plone had not mentioned any. Then how explain that eery cry outside? A possible explanation, inspired by frayed nerves, came to me, and froze the marrow in my bones before I could reason myself out of it.

"If you ain't afraid of ghosts!"

What had Reuben of the unknown surname meant by this remark? And by what means had he so swiftly disappeared after he had quitted my new home?

Just as I asked myself the question, that wailing cry came again, from about the same place, as near as I could judge, on the talus slope in rear of my cabin. Unmistakably the cry of a lost baby, demanding by every means of expression in its power, the attention of its mother. Out there alone and frightened in the darkness, in the heart of Steamboat Coulee, which Reuben had told me was infested by great numbers of snakes, at least one kind of which was venomous enough to slay.

Dread tugged at my throat. My tongue became dry in my mouth, cleaving to the palate. I knew before I opened the door that the coulee was now as dark as Erebus, and that moving about would be like groping in some gigantic pocket. But there was a feeble child out there on the talus slope, lost in the darkness, wailing for its mother. And I prided myself upon being at least the semblance of a man.

Mentally girding myself, I strode to the door and flung it open. A miasmatic mist came in immediately, cold as the breath from a sunless marsh, chilling me anew. Instinctively I closed the door as though to shut out some loathsome presence—I know not what. The heat of the fire absorbed the wisps of vapor that had entered. I leaned against the door, panting with a nameless terror, when, from the talus slope outside, plain through the darkness came again that eery wailing.

Gulping swiftly, swallowing my terrible fear, I closed my eyes and flung the door wide open. Nor did I close it until I stood outside and opened *my* eyes against an opaque blanket of darkness. When Plone had told me the coulee was cold after nightfall, he had not exaggerated. It was as cold as the inside of a tomb.

The crying of the babe came again, from directly behind my cabin. The cliff bulked large there, while above its rim, high up, I made out the soft twinkling of a pale star or two.

Before my courage should fail me and send me back into the cheery cabin, thrice cheery now that I was outside it, I ran swiftly around the cabin, nor stopped until I had begun to clamber up the talus slope, guided by my memory of whence that wailing cry had come. The shell-rock shifted beneath me, and I could hear the shale go clattering down among the brush about the bases of the willows below. I kept on climbing.

Once I almost fell when I stepped upon something round, which writhed beneath my foot, causing me to jump straight into the air with a half-suppressed cry of fear. I was glad now that the coulee was cold after nightfall, else the snake, were it by chance a rattler, could have struck me a death-blow. The cold, however, made the vile creature sluggish.

When I thought I had climbed far enough I bent over and tried to pierce the heavy gloom, searching the talus intently for a glimpse of white—white which should discover to me the clothing of the baby which I sought. Failing in this, I remained quiet, waiting for the cry to come again. I waited amid a silence that could almost be felt, a silence lasting so long that I began to dread a repetition of that cry. What if there were no baby—flesh and blood, that is? Reuben had spoken of ghosts. Utter nonsense! No grown man believes in ghosts! And if I didn't find the child before long the little tot might die of the cold. Where had the child gone? Why this eery silence? Why didn't the child cry again? It was almost as though it had found that which it sought, there in the darkness. That cry had spoken eloquently of a desire for sustenance.

If the child did not cry, what was I to believe? Who, or what, was suckling the baby out on the cold talus slope?

I became as a man turned to stone when the eery cry came again. It was not a baby's whimper, starting low and increasing in volume; it was a full-grown wail as it issued from the unseen mouth. And it came from at least a hundred feet higher up on the talus! I, a grown man, had stumbled heavily in the scramble to reach this height; yet a baby so small that it wailed for its milk had crept a hundred feet farther up the slope! It was beyond all reason; weird beyond the wildest imagination. But undoubtedly the wailing of a babe.

I did not believe in ghosts. I studied the spot whence the wail issued, but could see no blotch of white. Only two lambent dots, set close together, glowing like resting fireflies among the shale. I saw them for but a second only. Undoubtedly mating fireflies, and they had flown.

I began to climb once more, moving steadily toward the spot where I had heard the cry.

I stopped again when the shell rock above me began to flow downward as though something, or somebody, had started it moving. What, in God's name, was up there at the base of the cliff? Slowly, my heart in my mouth, I climbed on.

There was a rush, as of an unseen body, along the face of the talus. I could hear the contact of light feet on the shale; but the points of contact were unbelievably far apart. No baby in the world could have stepped so far—or jumped. Of course the cry might have come from a half-witted grown person; but I did not believe it.

The cry again, sharp and clear; but at least two hundred

yards up the coulee from where I stood, and on about a level with me. Should I follow or not? Did some nocturnal animal carry the babe in its teeth? It might be; I had heard of such things, and had read the myth of Romulus and Remus. Distorted fantasies? Perhaps; but show me a man who can think coolly while standing on the talus slopes of Steamboat after dark, and I will show you a man without nerves—and without a soul.

Once more I took up the chase. I had almost reached the spot whence the cry had come last, when I saw again those twin balls of lambent flame. They seemed to blink at me— off and on, off and on.

I bent over to pick up a bit of shale to hurl at the dots, when, almost in my ears, that cry came once more; but this time the cry ended in a spitting snarl as of a tomcat when possession of food is disputed!

With all my might I hurled the bit of shale I had lifted, straight at those dots of flame. At the same time I gave utterance to a yell that set the echoes rolling the length and breadth of the coulee. The echoes had not died away when the coulee was filled until it rang with that eery wailing—as though a hundred babies cried for mothers who did not come!

Then—great God!—I knew!

Bobcats! The coulee was alive with them! I was alone on the talus, two hundred yards from the safe haven of my cabin, and though I knew that one alone would not attack a man in the open, I had never heard whether they hunted in groups. For all I knew they might. At imminent risk of breaking my neck, I hurled myself down the slope and into the thicket of willows at the base. Through these and into the dry steam-bed I blundered, still running. I kept this mad pace until I had reached the approximate point where the trail led to my cabin, climbed the bank of the dry stream and sought for the aisle through the willows.

Though I searched carefully for a hundred yards on each hand I could not find the path. And I feared to enter the willow thicket and beat about. The ominous wailing had stopped suddenly, as though at a signal, and I believed that the bobcats had taken to the trees at the foot of the talus. I studied the dark shadows for dots of flame in pairs, but

could see none. I knew from reading about them that bobcats have been known to drop on solitary travelers from the
limbs of trees. Their sudden silence was weighted with ponderous menace.

I was afraid—*afraid!* Scared as I had never been in my
life before—and I had gone through a certain town in Flanders without a gas mask.

Why the sudden, eery silence? I would have welcomed
that vast chorus of wailing, had it begun again. But it did
not.

When I crept back to the bank of the stream-bed a pale
moon had come up, partly dispelling the shadows in Steamboat Coulee. The sand in the stream-bed glistened frostily
in the moonlight, making me think of the blinking eyes of a
multitude of toads.

Where, in Steamboat, was the cabin with its cheery fire? I
had closed the door to keep my courage from failing me,
and now there was no light to guide me.

It is hell to be alone in such a place, miles from the nearest other human being.

I sat down on the high bank, half sidewise so that I could
watch the shadows among the willows, and tried mentally to
retrace my steps, hoping that I could reason out the exact
location of the cabin in the thicket.

Sitting as I was, I could see for a hundred yards or so
down the stream-bed. I studied its almost straight course for
a moment or two, for no reason that I can assign. I saw a
black shadow dart across the open space, swift as a breath
of wind, and disappear in the thicket on the opposite side. It
was larger than a cat, smaller than the average dog. A bobcat had changed his base hurriedly, and in silence.

Silence! That was the thing that was now weighing upon
me, more even than thought of my failure to locate the little
cabin. Why had the cats stopped their wailing so suddenly,
as though they waited for something? This thought deepened the feeling of dread that was upon me. If the cats were
waiting, for what were they waiting?

Then I breathed a sigh of relief. For, coming around a
bend in the stream-bed, there strode swiftly toward me the
figure of a man. He was a big man who looked straight
before him. He walked as a country man walks when he

hurries home to a late supper. Then there were other people in this coulee, after all!

But what puzzled me about this newcomer was his style of dress. He was garbed after the manner of the first pioneers who had come into this country from the East. From his high-topped boots, into which his trousers were tucked loosely, to his broad-brimmed hat, he was dressed after the manner of those people who had vanished from this country more than a decade before my time. An old prospector evidently, who had clung to the habiliments of his younger days. But he did not walk like an old man; rather he strode, straight-limbed and erect, like a man in his early thirties. There was a homely touch about him, though, picturesque as he was; for he smoked a corncob pipe, from the bowl of which a spiral of blue smoke eddied forth into the chill night air. I knew from this that, did I call to him, his greeting in return would be bluffly friendly.

I waited for him to come closer, hoping that he would notice me first. As he approached I noticed with a start that two huge revolvers, the holsters tied back, swung low upon his hips. People nowadays did not carry firearms openly. In an instant I had decided to let this stranger pass, even though I spent the remainder of the night on the bank of the dry stream. Sight of those savage weapons had filled me with a new and different kind of dread.

Then I started as another figure, also of a man, came around the selfsame bend of the watercourse, for there was something oddly familiar about that other figure. He moved swiftly, his body almost bent double as he hurried forward. As he came around the bend and saw the first man who had come into my range of vision, he bent lower still.

As he did so the moonlight glowed dully on something that he carried in the crook of his arm. I knew instantly that what he carried was a rifle. Once more that chill along my spine, for there was no mistaking his attitude.

He was stalking the first man, furtively, and there was murder in his heart!

It did not take his next action to prove this to me. I knew it, even as the second man knelt swiftly in the sand of the watercourse and flung the rifle to his shoulder, its muzzle pointing at the man approaching me.

I cried out with all the power of my shattered lungs. But the man ahead, all unconscious of the impending death at his heels, paid me absolutely no attention. He was no more than twenty yards from me when I shouted, yet he did not turn his head. For all the attention he paid me I might as well have remained silent. It was as though he were stone-deaf.

I shouted again, waving my arms wildly. Perhaps he could not see me because of the shadows at my back. Still he did not see me. I whirled to the kneeling man, just as a sheet of yellow flame leaped from the muzzle of his rifle. The first man was right in front of me when the bullet struck him. He stopped, dead in his tracks. I guessed that the bullet had struck him at the base of the skull. Even so, he whirled swiftly, and both his guns were out. But he could not raise them to fire. He slumped forward limply, and sprawled in the sand.

I had not heard the report of the rifle, for simultaneously with that spurt of flame the bobcats had begun their wailing once more, drowning out the sound.

With a great cry, whose echoes could be heard in the coulee even through the wailing of the bobcats, I sprang to my feet and ran, staggering, down the watercourse, in the direction of what I thought was Steamboat's entrance.

Long before I had reached it my poor body failed me and I fell to the sandy floor, coughing my lungs away, while scarlet stains wetted the sand near my mouth.

III

When I awoke in the sand the sun was shining. Some sixth sense told me to remain motionless, warning me that all was not well. Without moving my head I rolled my eyes until I could see ahead in the direction I had fallen. In falling my right hand had been flung out full length, fingers extended.

Imagine my fear and horror when I saw, coiled up within six inches of my hand, a huge rattlesnake! His head was poised above the coil, while just behind it, against the other arc of the vicious circle, the tip of the creature's tail, adorned with an inch or more of rattles, hummed its fearful warning.

With all my power I sprang back and upward. At the

same time the bullet head, unbelievably swift, flashed toward my hand and—thank God!—safely beneath it! Stretched helplessly now to its full length, the creature's mouth, with its forked tongue, had stopped within a scant two inches of where my face had been.

Before the rattler could return and coil again I had stepped upon the bullet head, grinding it deep into the sand, and when the tail whipped frantically against my leg I seized it and hurled the reptile with all my might, out of the stream bed into the shell-rock. Even as I did it I wondered where I had found the courage; and what had kept me from moving while unconscious. Had I moved I might never again have awakened.

I climbed the bank of the dry stream to look for the entrance to my log cabin which I believed to lay ahead of me, but kept well away from the thickets for fear of snakes. With the sun high in the heavens, turning the coulee into a furnace, the snakes came out by hundreds to bask upon the shale, and as I passed, they coiled and warned me away with myriad warnings. I did not trespass upon their holdings.

After I had plodded along for fully an hour I knew that I must be quite close to the rock which gave Steamboat its name; but still I had not found the pathway leading to the log cabin. Evidently I had already passed it.

Even as I had this thought I came upon a path leading into the shadows of the willow thicket—a path that seemed familiar, even though, from the stream bed, I could not see the cabin. With a sigh, and much surprised that I had, last night, traveled so far in my hysterical terror, I turned into this path and increased my pace.

I came shortly to pause, chilled even though the sun was shining. For at the end of the mossy trail there was no cabin; but a cleared plot of ground adorned with aged mounds and rough-hewn crosses! Rocks were scattered profusely over the mounds and, I guessed, had been placed to foil the creatures which otherwise would have despoiled the bodies resting there. There was a great overhang of the cliff wall, bulging out over the little graveyard, and from the overhang came a steady drip of moisture. Slimy water lay motionless in a pool in the center of the plot. Mossy green were the stones. Mudpuppies scurried into the deeps as I stopped and stared, turning the water to a pool of slime.

How uneasy I felt in this place! Why had such a remote location been chosen as a cemetery, hidden away here from the brightness of God's sunshine? Nothing but shadow-filled silence, except for the dripping of the water from the overhang.

I hurried back to the stream bed and continued on my way.

Another hour passed, during which, my body racked with continual coughing, I suffered the torments of the damned. Those red dots were dancing before my eyes again, and nothing looked natural to me. The sunning snakes in the shale seemed to waver grotesquely—twisting, writhing, coiling. Here, on the cliff, was a row of ponderous palisades; but they seemed to be ever buckling and bending, as though shaken by an earthquake.

Then, far ahead, I saw the rock at the entrance. With a sob of joy I began to run—only to stop when I reached the pile, with a cry of hopelessness and despair. For the rock, unscalable even to one who possessed the strength to climb, now filled the coulee from lip to lip, while on my side of the pile there nestled a little lake, clear and pellucid, into which I could look, straight down, for what I guessed must have been all of twenty feet!

Some great shifting of the walls, during the night, had blocked the entrance, entombing me in Steamboat Coulee with all its nameless horrors!

There was no one to see me, so I flung myself down at the edge of the pool and wept weakly, bemoaning my terrible fate.

After a time I regained control of my frayed nerves, arose to my knees and bathed my throbbing temples. Sometime, somehow, I reasoned, Plone would find a way to reach me. There was nothing to do now but return and search again for my cabin. Plone had said that Hildreth would bring supplies to me—and I felt that they would know how to get in by some other way. They had lived in the coulee and should know their way about.

Wearily I began the return march. It never occurred to me to note that the sun went ahead of me on its journey into the west. I can only blame my physical condition for not noting this. Had I done so I would have realized at once that I had gone in the wrong direction, and that straight ahead of me lay freedom. I had gone to the head of the coulee, straight in from Steamboat Rock, and when I found the coulee blocked at the end had thought the entrance closed against me.

But I did not note the sun.

I strode wearily on, and found the cabin with ridiculous ease.

Inside, awaiting my coming, sat Hildreth, the wife of Plone! She said nothing when I opened the door, just sat on the only chair in the house and looked at me. I spoke to her, thanking her for the sack of provisions which I saw on the rickety shelf on the wall beyond the door. Still she said nothing. Just stared at me, unblinking.

I asked her about leaving this place and she shook her head, as though she did not catch my meaning.

"For God's sake, Hildreth!" I cried. "Can't you speak?"

For it had come to me that I had never heard her speak. When I had first entered the farmhouse she had placed a meal for me, and had bidden me eat of it. But I remembered now that she had done so by gestures with her hands.

In answer now to my question she opened her mouth and pointed into it with her forefinger. Hildreth, the wife of Plone, had no tongue!

Did you ever hear a tongueless person try to speak? It is terrible. For after this all-meaning gesture there came a raucous croak from the mouth of Hildreth—wordless, gurgling, altogether meaningless.

I understood no word; but the eyes of the woman, strangely glowing now, were eloquent. She pointed toward the door, trying to warn me of something, and stamped her foot impatiently when I did not understand. I saw her foot move as she stamped it—but failed to notice at the time that the contact of her foot with the board floor made no noise! Later I remembered it.

When I shook my head she arose from her chair and strode to the door, flinging it wide. Then she pointed up the coulee in the direction I had entered originally. Again that raucous croak, still meaningless. Once more I shook my head.

Was there something by the entrance that menaced me?

I was filled with dread of the unknown, wished with all my soul that I could understand what this woman was trying to say to me.

I stepped back, to search about the place for paper, so that, with the aid of a pencil which I possessed, she might write what she had to tell me. I found it and turned back to the woman, who had watched me gravely while I searched. Noting the paper she shook her head, telling me mutely that she could not write.

Then Plone, his face as dark as a thundercloud, stood in the doorway! To me he paid no attention. His eyes, glowering below heavy brows, burned as he stared at the woman. In her eyes I could read fright unutterable. She gave one frightened croak and turned to flee. But she could not go far, for she fled toward the bare wall opposite the open door. Plone leaped after her, and when I jumped between them, he flung me to the floor, where I bumped my head and lay stunned for a moment.

In that horrifying instant I realized why the murderer looked familiar last night. It was Plone! I half arose and whirled around to see what aid I could offer Hildreth. But they had vanished just like Reuben had the night before.

Trembling in every fiber of my being I strode to the back wall and ran my hand over the rough logs. They were as solid, almost, as the day the cabin had been built. To me this was a great relief. I was beginning to fear that I had stumbled into a land of wraiths and shadows or was hallucinating and I should not have been surprised if the logs had also proved to be things of shadow-substance, letting me through to stand amazed upon the shell-rock behind the cabin.

But here was one place in the coulee of shadows that was real.

I went to the door, locked and barred it. Then I returned and lighted the stove to disperse the unnatural chill that hovered in the room. After this I searched out my food and wolfed some of it ravenously. Another thought came to me:

if Reuben, Plone and Hildreth were nothing but fantasies, where had I procured this food, which was real enough and well cooked? Somewhere in my adventures since being kicked off the train at Palisades there must be a great gap I had tried to fill in. What had happened, really, in that blank space?

Having eaten, I stepped to the door and looked out. If I again went forth into the stream bed in any attempt to get out of the coulee, I should never reach it before dark. What would it mean to my tired reason to be caught in the open, in the midst of this coulee, for another terrible night? I could not do it.

Again I secured the door. Nothing *real* could get in to bother me—and even now I reasoned myself out of positive belief in ghosts. The hallucinations which had so terrified me had undoubtedly been born of my sickness.

Convinced of this at last I lay down on the rough cot and went to sleep.

IV

When I awoke suddenly in the night, the fire had burned very low and a heavy chill possessed the cabin. I had a feeling that I was not the only occupant of my abode; but, striving to pierce the gloom in the cabin's corners, I could see nothing.

In the farthest corner I saw the pale, ghostly lineaments of a woman! Just the face, shimmering there in the gloom, oddly, but neither body nor substance. The face of Hildreth, wife of Plone! Then her hands, no arms visible, came up before her face and began to gesture. Her mouth opened and I imagined I again heard that raucous croak of the tongueless. Again her eyes were eloquent, mutely giving a warning which I could not understand.

Fear seizing me in its terrible grip, I leaped from my bed and threw wood on the fire, hoping to dispel this silent shadow. When the light flared up the head shimmered swiftly and began to fade away; but not before I saw a pair of hands come forth from nowhere and fasten themselves below that head, about where the neck should have been.

Hands that were gnarled and calloused from toil on an unproductive farm—the work-torn hands of the killer, Plone!

Then the weird picture vanished and I was alone with my fantasies.

I had scarcely returned to my seat on the bed, sitting well back against the wall so that my back was against something solid, when the wailing of lost babies broke out again on the talus slopes outside. I had expected this to happen after nightfall; but the reality left me weak and shivering, even though I knew that the animals that uttered the mournful wails were flesh and blood. The wailing of bobcats, no matter how often it is heard, always brings a chill that is hard to reason away. Nature certainly prepared weird natural protections for some of her creatures!

Then the wailing stopped suddenly—short off. And the silence was more nerve-devastating than the eery wailing.

Nothing for many minutes. Then the rattle of sliding talus, as the shale glided into the underbrush.

This stopped, and a terrible silence pressed down upon me.

Then my cabin shook with the force of the wind that suddenly swooped through the coulee. It rattled through the eaves, shook the door on its hinges, while the patter-patter on the roof told me of showers of sand which the wind had scooped up from the bed of the dry stream. The wind was terrific, I thought; but ever it increased in power and violence.

The patter on the roof and the rattle in the eaves began to take on a new significance; for the patter sounded like the scamper of baby feet above my head, while the wailing about the eaves sounded like the screaming of people who are tongueless. The door bellied inward against the chair back as though many hands were pressed against it from outside, seeking entrance. Yet I knew that there was no one outside.

Then, faint and feeble through the roaring of the wind, I caught that eery cry in the night. It was the despairing voice of a woman, and she was calling aloud, hopelessly, for help! I shivered and tried not to hear. But the cry came again, farther now, as though the woman were being dragged away from me.

In God's name! What woman could be abroad in such a night?

The cry again. No man, fear the shadows as he might, could ignore that pitiful plea and call himself a man again.

I gritted my teeth and ran to the door, flinging it open. A veritable sea of flying sand swept past me; but through the increased roar came plainly that cry for help. I left the door open this time, so that the light would stream out and guide my return.

On the bank of the dry stream I stopped.

And before and below me I saw Hildreth, wife of Plone, fighting for her very life with her brutal husband! She was groveling on her knees at his feet—his hands were about her throat. As she begged for mercy I could understand her words. She had a tongue, after all! Then Plone, holding Hildreth with his left hand, raised his right and, crooking it like a fearful talon, poised it above the face of Hildreth.

He did a ghastly, unbelievable thing. I can not tell it. But when his hand came away her words were meaningless, gurgling—the raucous croaking of a person who had no tongue.

Frenzied with horror at what Plone had done, I leaped into the dry stream and ran forward—to bring up short in the middle of the sandy open space, staring aghast.

For I was all alone—no Hildreth, the tongueless—no Plone with the calloused hands! Once more a hallucination had betrayed me.

Screaming in fear I sprang out of the stream-bed and rushed toward the cabin, only to dart off the trail as I saw another man walk out of the cabin's light. He was dressed very much as had been the man whom I had seen fall before the murderous rifle of Plone last night. But he was older, stooped slightly under the weight of years. I heard him sigh softly, as a man sighs whose stomach is comfortably filled with food.

He walked toward the stream-bed, following the path through the thicket.

He had passed me when a malevolently leering figure followed him from the cabin—and that figure was Reuben, the feral son of Plone! Reuben, as his father had stalked that other unfortunate, stalked the aged man who preceded him. The latter passed a clump of service berry bushes and paused on the lip of the dry stream. He had scarcely halted when out of the clump of service berries stepped Plone himself, moving stealthily, like a cat that stalks a helpless, unsuspecting bird!

The older man half turned as though he heard some slight sound, when Plone, with the silent fury of the bobcat making a kill, leaped bodily upon his back and bore him to the ground, where the two of them, fighting and clawing, rolled into the sand below.

Reuben began to run when his father closed with the stranger, and I was right at his heels when he leaped over the edge to stop beside the silent combatants. Then he bent to assist his father.

The end was speedy. For what chance has an aged man, taken by surprise, against two determined killers? They slew him there in the sand, while I, my limbs inert because of my fright, looked on, horror holding me mute when I would have screamed aloud.

Their bloody purpose accomplished, Reuben and Plone methodically began to turn the pockets of the dead man inside out. The contents of these they divided between themselves. This finished, in silence, the murderers, taking each an arm of the dead man, began to drag the body up the sandy stretch toward the end of the coulee—the closed end.

Still I stood, as one transfixed.

Then I became conscious of a low, heart-breaking sobbing at my side. Turning, I saw the figure of Hildreth standing there, tragedy easily readable in her eyes, wringing her hands as her eyes followed the figures of her husband and her son. Then she extended her hands in a pleading gesture, calling the two who dragged the body.

She began to follow them along the stream-bed, dodging from thicket to thicket on the bank as though she screened her movements from Plone and Reuben. I watched her until her wraithlike form blended with the shadows in the thickets and disappeared from view.

As I watched her go, and saw the figures of Plone and

Reuben passing around a sharp bend in the dry stream, there came back to my memory a mental picture of a grave-yard located in perpetual shadow, adorned with rotting crosses upon which no names were written. Slimy stones at the edge of a muddy pool populated by serpentine mud-puppies.

Turning then, I hurried back to the cabin, whose door remained open—to pause aghast at the threshold, staring into the interior.

At a table in the center of the room—a table loaded with things to eat, fresh and steaming from the stove—sat an-other stranger, this time a man dressed after the manner of city folk. His clothing bespoke wealth and refinement, while his manner of eating told that he was accustomed to choicer food than that of which necessity now compelled him to partake. Daintily he picked over the viands, sorting judi-ciously, while near the stove stood Hildreth, her eyes wide with fright and wordless entreaty.

Reuben stood in a darkened corner and his eyes never left the figure of the stranger at the table. As he stared at this one I saw his tongue come forth from his mouth and de-scribe a circle, moistening his lips, anticipatorily, like a cat that watches a saucer of cream.

Plone, too, was silently watching, standing just inside the door, with his back toward me. As I watched him he moved slightly, edging toward the table.

Then Plone was upon the stranger, a carving knife, snatched from the table, in his hand.

But why continue? I had seen this same scene, slightly varied, but a few minutes before, in the sand of the dry stream.

Crouching there in the darkness I guessed what the wraith of Hildreth had tried to tell me. Going back in my memory I watched her lips move again. And as they moved I read the words she would have uttered. As plain as though she had spoken I now understood the warning.

"As you value the life God has given you—*do not stay in this cabin tonight!*"

The cabin was a trap! The ghosts of Reuben and Plone—for surely they must be ghosts—knew where it was, and could shimmer through its walls, to slay me at their will. By chance, I had escaped being murdered by going outside both nights. But until I escaped the coulee, I could be found and killed.

For hours I trembled in the shadows, afraid to move, while Reuben and Plone carried forward their ghastly work. Many times during those hours did I see them make their kill. Ever it was Plone who commanded, ever it was Reuben who stood at his father's side to assist. Ever it was Hildreth who raised her hand or her voice in protest.

Then, suddenly, she was back in the cabin with Reuben and Plone. She told the latter something, gesturing vehemently as she spoke. These gestures were simple, easy to understand. For she pointed back down the coulee, in the direction of Steamboat Rock. Somehow I knew that what she tried to tell him was that she had gone forth and told the authorities what he and Reuben had done. Plone's face became black with wrath. Reuben's turned to the pasty gray of fear which is unbounded. Both sprang to the door and stared down the coulee. Then Plone leaped back to Hildreth, striking her in the face with his fist. She fell to the floor, groveling on her knees at his feet. He dragged her forth into the trail, along it to the stream bed and, as I crept toward the edge, repeated that terrible scene I had witnessed once before.

Reuben advanced to the lip of the dry stream as Plone fought with Reuben's mother. He paid them no heed, however, but shaded his eyes with his hand as he gazed into the west in the direction of Steamboat Rock. Then he gestured excitedly to Plone, pointing down the coulee.

Plone was all activity at once. With Reuben at his heels and Hildreth stumbling farther in the rear, they rushed to the cabin and began to throw rough packs together, one each for Reuben and Plone.

But in the midst of their activities they paused and stared at the doorway where I stood transfixed. Then, slowly, though no one stood there except myself, they raised their hands above their heads, while Hildreth crouched in a corner, wild-eyed, whimpering.

Plone and Reuben suddenly lurched toward me, haltingly, as though propelled by invisible hands. Their hands were at their sides now as though bound there securely by ropes. Outside they came, walking oddly with their hands still at their sides.

They stopped beneath a tree which had one bare limb, high up from the ground—a strong limb, white as a ghost in the moonlight. Reuben and Plone looked upward at this limb, and both their faces were gray. Hildreth came out and stood near by, also looking up, wringing her hands, grief marring her face that might once have been beautiful.

Reuben and Plone looked at each other and nodded. Then they looked mutely at Hildreth, as though asking her forgiveness. After this they turned and nodded toward no one that I could see, as though they gestured to unseen hangmen.

I cried aloud, even though I had foreseen what was to come, as both Plone and Reuben sprang straight into the air to an unbelievable height, to pause midway to that bare limb; their necks twisted at odd angles, their bodies writhing grotesquely.

I watched until the writhing stopped. Until the bodies merely swayed, as though played upon by vagrant breezes sweeping in from the sandy dry stream.

Then, for the last time, I heard the piercing, wordless shriek of a tongueless woman. I swerved to look for Hildreth, and saw a misty, wraithlike shadow disappear among the willows, flashing swiftly out of sight up the coulee.

Hildreth had gone, and I was alone, swaying weakly, nauseated, staring crazily up to two bodies which oscillated to and fro as though played upon by vagrant breezes.

Then the bodies faded slowly away as my knees began to buckle under me. I sank to the ground before the cabin, and darkness descended once more.

When I regained consciousness I opened my eyes, expecting to see those swaying bodies in the air above me. There were no bodies. Then I noted that my wrists were close together, held in place by manacles of shining steel.

From the cabin behind me came the sound of voices— voices of men who talked as they ate—noisily. Behind the cabin I could hear the impatient stamping of horses.

I lay there dully, trying to understand it all.

Then two men came out of the cabin toward me. One of them chewed busily upon a bit of wood in lieu of a toothpick. Upon the mottled vest of this one glistened a star, emblem of the sheriff. The second man I knew to be his deputy.

"He's awake, I see, Al," said the first man as he looked at me.

"So I see," said the man addressed as Al.

Then the sheriff bent over me.

"Ready to talk, young man?" he demanded.

It must have mystified this one greatly when I leaped suddenly to my feet and ran my hands over him swiftly. How could they guess what it meant to me to learn that these two were flesh and blood?

"Thank God!" I cried. Then I began to tremble so violently that the man called Al, perforce, supported me with a burly arm about my shoulders. As he did so his eyes met those of the sheriff and a meaningful glance passed between them.

The sheriff passed around the cabin, returning almost at once with three horses, saddled and bridled for the trail. The third horse was for me. Weakly, aided by Al, I mounted.

Then we clambered down into the dry stream and started toward Steamboat Rock.

I found my voice.

"For what am I wanted, sheriff?" I asked.

"For burglarious entry, son," he replied, not unkindly. "You went into a house in Palisades, while the owner and his wife were working in the fields, and stole every bit of food you could lay your hands on. There's no use denying it, for we found the sack you brought it away in, right in that there cabin!"

"But Hildreth, the wife of Plone, gave me that food!" I cried. "I didn't steal it!"

"Hildreth? Plone?" The sheriff fairly shouted the two names.

Then he turned and stared at his deputy—again that meaningful exchange of glances. The sheriff regained control of himself.

"This Hildreth and Plone," he began, hesitating strangely, "did they have a son, a half-grown boy?"

"Yes! Yes!" I cried eagerly. "The boy's name was Reuben! He led me into Steamboat Coulee!"

Then I told them my story, from beginning to end, sparing none of the unbelievable details. When I had finished, the two of them turned in their saddles and looked back into the coulee, toward the now invisible log cabin we had left behind. The deputy shook his head, muttering, while the sheriff removed his hat and scratched his poll. He spat judiciously into the sand of the dry stream before he spoke.

"Son," he said finally, "if I didn't know you was a stranger here I would swear that you was crazy as a loon. There ain't a darn thing real that you saw or heard, except the rattlesnakes and the bobcats!"

I interrupted him eagerly.

"But what about Plone, Hildreth and Reuben?"

"Plone and Reuben," he replied, "were hanged fifteen years ago! Right beside that cabin where we found you! Hildreth went crazy and ran away into the coulee. She was never seen again."

I waited, breathless, for the sheriff to continue.

"Plone and Reuben," he went on, "were the real bogy men of this coulee in the early days. They lived in that log cabin. Reuben used to lure strangers in there, where the two of them murdered the wanderers and robbed their dead bodies, burying them afterward in a gruesome graveyard farther inside Steamboat Coulee. Hildreth, so the story goes, tried to prevent these murders; but was unable to do so. Finally she reported to the pioneer authorities—and Plone cut her tongue out as punishment for the betrayal. God knows how many unsuspecting travelers the two made away with before they were found out and strung up without trial!"

"But how about Plone's farm in Moses Coulee, outside Steamboat, and the farmhouse where I met the family?"

"It's mine," replied the sheriff. "There's never been a house on it to my knowledge. I foreclosed on it for the taxes, and the blasted land is so poor that even the rattlesnakes starve while they are crawling across it!"

"But I saw it as plainly as I see you!"

"But you're a sick man, ain't you? You never went near the place where you say the house was. We followed your footprints, and they left the main road at the foot of the Three Devils, from which they went straight as a die, to the mouth of Steamboat Coulee! They was easy to follow, and if I hadn't had another case on I'd have picked you up before you ever could have reached the cabin!"

Would to God that he had! It would have saved me many a weird and terrifying nightmare in the nights which have followed.

There the matter ended—seemingly. The sheriff, not a bad fellow at all, put me in the way of work which, keeping me much in the open beneath God's purifying sunshine, is slowly but surely mending my ravished lungs. After a while, there will come a day when I shall no longer be a sick man.

But ever so often, I raise my eyes from my work, allowing them to wander, against my will, in the direction of that shadow against the walls of Moses Coulee—that shadow out of which seems slowly to float the stony likeness of a steamboat under reduced power. And I wonder.

Born on a farm in Washington state in 1898, Arthur J. Burks served in the Marines in World War I. During the 1930s, he began writing for the pulp magazines, becoming so prolific that he became one of the fabulous "million-words-a-year writers." His novelette, Salute for Sunny, *was the most popular story Sky* Fighters *ever ran. His stories collected in* Black Medicine *(1966) are based on his experiences in the Carribean as an aide-de-camp to Gen. Smedley Butler. He died in 1974.*

Karl had to take care of his mother—no matter what happened to him.

TWENTY-FIVE

He Walked By Day

Julius Long

Friedenburg, Ohio, sleeps between the muddy waters of the Miami River and the trusty track of a little-used spur of the Big Four. It suddenly became important to us because of its strategic position. It bisected a road which we were to surface with tar. The materials were to come by way of the spur and to be unloaded at the tiny yard.

We began work on a Monday morning. I was watching the tar distributor while it pumped tar from the car, when I felt a tap upon my back. I turned about, and when I beheld the individual who had tapped me, I actually jumped.

I have never, before or since, encountered such a singular figure. He was at least seven feet tall, and he seemed even taller than that because of the uncommon slenderness of his frame. He looked as if he had never been warmed by the rays of the sun, but confined all his life in a dank and dismal cellar. I concluded that he had been the prey of some insidious, etiolating disease. Certainly, I thought, nothing else could account for his ashen complexion. It seems that not blood, but shadows passed through his veins.

"Do you want to see me?" I asked.

"Are you the road feller?"

"Yes."

"I want a job. My mother's sick. I have her to keep. Won't you please give me a job?"

We really didn't need another man, but I was interested in this pallid giant with his staring, gray eyes. I called to Juggy, my foreman.

"Do you think we can find a place for this fellow?" I asked.

443

Juggy stared incredulously. "He looks like he'd break in two."

"I'm stronger'n anyone," said the youth.

He looked about, and his eyes fell on the Mack, which had just been loaded with six tons of gravel. He walked over to it, reached down and seized the hub of a front wheel. To our utter amazement, the wheel was slowly lifted from the ground. When it was raised to a height of eight or nine inches, the youth looked inquiringly in our direction. We must have appeared sufficiently awed, for he dropped the wheel with an abruptness that evoked a yell from the driver, who thought his tire would blow out.

"We can certainly use this fellow," I said, and Juggy agreed.

"What's your name, Shadow?" he demanded.

"Karl Rand," said the boy but "Shadow" stuck to him, as far as the crew was concerned.

We put him to work at once, and he slaved all morning, accomplishing tasks that we ordinarily assigned two or three men to do.

We were on the road at lunchtime, some miles from Friedenburg. I recalled that Shadow had not brought his lunch.

"You can take mine," I said. "I'll drive in to the village and eat."

"I never eat none," was Shadow's astonishing remark.

"You never eat!" The crew had heard his assertion, and there was an amused crowd about him at once. I fancied that he was pleased to have an audience.

"No, I never eat," he repeated. "You see"—he lowered his voice—"you see, I'm a ghost!"

We exchanged glances. So Shadow was psychopathic. We shrugged our shoulders.

"Whose ghost are you?" gibed Juggy. "Napoleon's?"

"Oh, no. I'm my own ghost. You see, I'm dead."

"Ah!" This was all Juggy could say. For once, the arch-kidder was nonplussed.

"That's why I'm so strong," added Shadow.

"How long have you been dead?" I asked.

"Six years. I was fifteen years old then."

"Tell us how it happened. Did you die a natural death, or

were you killed trying to lift a fast freight off the track?" This question was asked by Juggy, who was slowly recovering.

"It was in the cave," answered Shadow solemnly. "I slipped and fell over a bank. I cracked my head on the floor. I've been a ghost ever since."

"Then why do you walk by day instead of by night?"

"I got to keep my mother."

Shadow looked so sincere, so pathetic when he made this answer, that we left off teasing him. I tried to make him eat my lunch, but he would have none of it. I expected to see him collapse that afternoon, but he worked steadily and showed no sign of tiring. We didn't know what to make of him. I confess that I was a little afraid in his presence. After all, a madman with almost superhuman strength is a dangerous character. But Shadow seemed perfectly harmless and docile.

When we had returned to our boarding-house that night, we plied our landlord with questions about Karl Rand. He drew himself up authoritatively, and lectured for some minutes upon Shadow's idiosyncrasies.

"The boy first started telling that story about six years ago," he said. "He never was right in his head, and nobody paid much attention to him at first. He said he'd fallen and busted his head in a cave, but everybody knows they ain't no caves hereabouts. I don't know what put that idea in his head. But Karl's stuck to it ever since, and I 'spect they's lots of folks round Friedenburg that's growed to believe him— more'n admits they do."

That evening, I patronized the village barber shop, and was careful to introduce Karl's name into the conversation. "All I can say is," said the barber solemnly, "that his hair ain't growed any in the last six years, and they was nary a whisker on his chin. No, sir, nary a whisker on his chin."

This did not strike me as so tremendously odd, for I had previously heard of cases of such arrested growth. However, I went to sleep that night thinking about Shadow.

The next morning, the strange youth appeared on time and rode with the crew to the job.

"Did you eat well?" Juggy asked him.

Shadow shook his head. "I never eat none."

The crew half believed him.

445

Early in the morning, Steve Bradshaw, the nozzle man on the tar distributer, burned his hand badly. I hurried him in to see the village doctor. When he had dressed Steve's hand, I took advantage of my opportunity and made inquiries about Shadow.

"Karl's got me stumped," said the country practitioner. "I confess I can't understand it. Of course, he won't let me get close enough to him to look at him, but it don't take an examination to tell there's something abnormal about him."

"I wonder what could have given him the idea that he's his own ghost," I said.

"I'm not sure, but I think what put it in his head was the things people used to say to him when he was a kid. He always looked like a ghost, and everybody kidded him about it. I kind of think that's what gave him the notion."

"Has he changed at all in the last six years?"

"Not a bit. He was as tall six years ago as he is today. I think that his abnormal growth might have had something to do with the stunting of his mind. But I don't know for sure."

I had to take Steve's place on the tar distributor during the next four days, and I watched Shadow pretty closely. He never ate any lunch, but he would sit with us while we devoured ours. Juggy could not resist the temptation to joke at his expense.

"There was a ghost back in my home town," Juggy once told him. "Mary Jenkens was an awful pretty woman when she was living, and when she was a girl, every fellow in town wanted to marry her. Jim Jenkens finally led her down the aisle, and we was all jealous—especially Joe Garver. He was broke up awful. Mary hadn't no more'n come back from the Falls when Joe was trying to make up to her. She wouldn't have nothing to do with him. Joe was hurt bad.

"A year after she was married, Mary took sick and died. Jim Jenkens was awful put out about it. He didn't act right from then on. He got to imagining things. He got suspicious of Joe.

"'What you got to worry about?' people would ask him. 'Mary's dead. There can't no harm come to her now.'

"But Jim didn't feel that way. Joe heard about it, and he got to teasing Jim.

" 'I was out with Mary's ghost last night,' he would say. And Jim got to believing him. One night, he lays low for Joe and shoots him with both barrels. 'He was goin' to meet my wife!' Jim told the judge."

"Did they give him the chair?" I asked.

"No, they gave him life in the state hospital."

Shadow remained impervious to Juggy's yarns, which were told for his special benefit. During this time, I noticed something decidedly strange about the boy, but I kept my own counsel. After all, a contractor can not keep the respect of his men if he appears too credulous.

One day Juggy voiced my suspicions for me. "You know," he said, "I never saw that kid sweat. It's uncanny. It's ninety in the shade today, and Shadow ain't got a drop of perspiration on his face. Look at his shirt. Dry as if he'd just put it on."

Everyone in the crew noticed this. I think we all became uneasy in Shadow's presence.

One morning he didn't show up for work. We waited a few minutes and left without him. When the trucks came in with their second load of gravel, the drivers told us that Shadow's mother had died during the night. This news cast a gloom over the crew. We all sympathized with the youth.

"I wish I hadn't kidded him," said Juggy.

We all put in an appearance that evening at Shadow's little cottage, and I think he was tremendously gratified. "I won't be working no more," he told me. "There ain't no need for me now."

I couldn't afford to lay off the crew for the funeral, but I did go myself. I even accompanied Shadow to the cemetery.

We watched while the grave was being filled. There were many others there, for one of the chief delights in a rural community is to see how the mourners "take on" at a funeral. Moreover, their interest in Karl Rand was deeper. He had said he was going back to his cave, that he would never again walk by day. The villagers, as well as myself, wanted to see what would happen.

When the grave was filled, Shadow turned to me, eyed me pathetically a moment, then walked from the grave. Silently, we watched him set out across the field. Two mis-

447

chievous boys disobeyed the entreaties of their parents, and set out after him.

They returned to the village an hour later with a strange and incredible story. They had seen Karl disappear into the ground. The earth had literally swallowed him up. The youngsters were terribly frightened. It was thought that Karl had done something to scare them, and their imaginations had got the better of them.

But the next day they were asked to lead a group of the more curious to the spot where Karl had vanished. He had not returned, and they were worried.

In a ravine two miles from the village, the party discovered a small but penetrable entrance to a cave. Its existence had never been dreamed of by the farmer who owned the land. (He has since then opened it up for tourists, and it is known as Ghost Cave.)

Someone in the party had thoughtfully brought an electric searchlight, and the party squeezed its way into the cave. Exploration revealed a labyrinth of caverns of exquisite beauty. But the explorers were oblivious to the esthetics of the cave; they thought only of Karl and his weird story.

After circuitous ramblings, they came to a sudden drop in the floor. At the base of this precipice they beheld a skeleton.

The coroner and the sheriff were duly summoned. The sheriff invited me to accompany him.

I regret that I cannot describe the gruesome, awesome feeling that came over me as I made my way through those caverns. Within their chambers the human voice is given a peculiar, sepulchral sound. But perhaps it was the knowledge of Karl's bizarre story, his unaccountable disappearance that inspired me with such awe, such thoughts.

The skeleton gave me a shock, for it was a skeleton of a man *seven feet tall!* There was no mistake about this; the coroner was positive.

The skull had been fractured, apparently by a fall over the bank. It was I who discovered the hat near by. It was rotted with decay, but in the leather band were plainly discernible the crudely penned initials, "K.R."

I felt suddenly weak. The sheriff noticed my nervousness. "What's the matter, have you seen a ghost?"

I laughed nervously and affected nonchalance. With the best off-hand manner I could command, I told him of Karl Rand. He was not impressed.

"You don't—?" He did not wish to insult my intelligence by finishing his question.

At this moment, the coroner looked up and commented: "This skeleton has been here about six years, I'd say."

I was not courageous enough to acknowledge my suspicions, but the villagers were outspoken. The skeleton, they declared, was that of Karl Rand. The coroner and the sheriff were incredulous, but, politicians both, they displayed some sympathy with this view.

My friend, the sheriff, discussed the matter privately with me some days later. His theory was that Karl had discovered the cave, wandered inside and come upon the corpse of some unfortunate who had preceded him. He had been so excited by his discovery that his hat had fallen down beside the body. Later, aided by the remarks of the villagers about his ghostliness, he had fashioned his own legend.

This, of course, may be true. But the people of Friedenburg are not convinced by this explanation, and neither am I. For the identity of the skeleton has never been determined, and Karl Rand has never since been seen to walk by day.

Lawyer Julius Long took to writing fiction to supplement his income during the Great Depression. Until his death in 1955 at the age of forty-eight, he was a steady contributor of more than two hundred short stories. Nearly all his work was in the detective genré. "He Walked by Day" first appeared in Weird Tales.

John fell in love with the farmer's daughter, even though everyone told him that the farmhouse and the family who lived there had been destroyed years ago.

TWENTY-SIX

The Phantom Farmhouse

Seabury Quinn

I had been at the New Briarcliff Sanitarium nearly three weeks before I actually saw the house.

Every morning, as I lay abed after the nurse had taken my temperature, I wondered what was beyond the copse of fir and spruce at the turn of the road. The picture seemed incomplete without chimneys rising among the evergreens. I thought about it so much I finally convinced myself there really was a house in the wood. A house where people lived and worked and were happy.

All during the long, trying days when I was learning to navigate a wheelchair, I used to picture the house and the people who lived in it. There would be a father, I was sure; a stout, good-natured father, somewhat bald, who sat on the porch and smoked a cob pipe in the evening. And there was a mother, too; a waistless, plaid-skirted mother with hair smoothly parted over her forehead, who sat beside the father as he rocked and smoked, and who had a brown work-basket in her lap. She spread the stocking feet over her outstretched fingers and her vigilant needle spied out and closed every hole with a cunning no mechanical loom could rival.

Then there was a daughter. I was a little hazy in my conception of her; but I knew she was tall and slender as a hazel wand, and that her eyes were blue and wide and sympathetic.

Picturing the house and its people became a favorite pas-

451

time with me during the time I was acquiring the art of walking all over again. By the time I was able to trust my legs on the road I felt I knew my way to my vision-friends' home as well as I knew the byways of my own parish; though I had as yet not set foot outside the sanitarium.

Oddly enough, I chose the evening for my first long stroll. It was unusually warm for September in Maine, and some of the sturdier of the convalescents had been playing tennis during the afternoon. After dinner they sat on the veranda, comparing notes on their respective cases of influenza, or matching experiences in appendicitis operations.

After building the house bit by bit from my imagination, as a child pieces together a picture puzzle, I should have been bitterly disappointed if the woods had proved empty; yet when I reached the turn of the road and found my dream house a reality, I was almost afraid. Bit for bit and part for part, it was as I had visualized it.

A long, rambling, comfortable-looking farmhouse it was, with a wide porch screened by vines, and a whitewashed picket fence about the little clearing before it. There was a tumbledown gate in the fence, one of the kind that is held shut with a weighted chain. Looking closely, I saw the weight was a disused ploughshare. Leading from gate to porch was a path of flat stones, laid unevenly in the short grass, and bordered with a double row of clam shells. A lamp burned in the front room, sending out cheerful golden rays to meet the silver moonlight.

A strange, eerie sensation came over me as I stood there. Somehow, I felt I had seen that house before; many, many times before; yet I had never been in that part of Maine till I came to Briarcliff, nor had anyone ever described the place to me. Indeed, except for my idle dreams, I had had no intimation that there was a house in those pines at all.

"Who lives in the house at the turn of the road?" I asked the fat man who roomed next to me.

He looked at me as blankly as if I had addressed him in Choctaw, then countered, "What road?"

"Why, the south road," I explained. "I mean the house in the pines—just beyond the curve, you know."

If such a thing had not been obviously absurd, I should have thought he looked frightened at my answer. Certainly his already prominent eyes started a bit further from his face.

"Nobody lives there," he assured me. "Nobody's lived there for years. There isn't any house there."

I became angry. What right had this fellow to make my civil question the occasion for an ill-timed jest? "As you please," I replied. "Perhaps there isn't any house there for you; but I saw one there last night."

"My God!" he ejaculated, and hurried away as if I'd just told him I was infected with smallpox.

Later in the day I overheard a snatch of conversation between him and one of his acquaintances in the lounge.

"I tell you it's so," he was saying with great earnestness. "I thought it was a lot of poppycock, myself; but that clergyman saw it last night. I'm going to pack my traps and get back to the city, and not waste any time about it, either."

"Rats!" his companion scoffed. "He must have been stringing you."

Turning to light a cigar, he caught sight of me. "Say, Mr. Weatherby," he called, "you didn't mean to tell my friend here that you really saw a house down by those pines last night, did you?"

"I certainly did," I answered, "and I tell you, too. There's nothing unusual about it, is there?"

"Is there!" he repeated. "*Is* there? Say, what'd it look like?"

I described it to him as well as I could, and his eyes grew as wide as those of a child hearing the story of Bluebeard.

"Well, I'll be a Chinaman's uncle!" he declared as I finished. "I sure will!"

"See here," I demanded. "What's all the mystery about that farmhouse? Why shouldn't I see it? It's there to be seen, isn't it?"

He gulped once or twice, as if there were something hot in his mouth, before he answered:

"Look here, Mr. Weatherby, I'm telling you this for your own good. You'd better stay in nights; and you'd better stay away from those pines in particular."

Nonplussed at this unsolicited advice, I was about to ask an explanation, when I detected the after-tang of whisky on his breath. I understood, then. I was being made the butt of a drunken joke by a pair of race course followers.

"I'm very much obliged, I'm sure," I replied with dignity, "but if you don't mind, I'll choose my own comings and goings."

"Oh, go as far as you like"—he waved his arms wide in token of my complete free-agency—"go as far as you like. I'm going to New York."

And he did. The pair of them left the sanitarium that afternoon.

A slight recurrence of my illness held me housebound for several days after my conversation with the two sportively inclined gentlemen, and the next time I ventured out at night the moon had waxed to the full, pouring a flood of light upon the earth that rivaled midday. The minutest objects were as readily distinguished as they would have been before sunset; in fact, I remember comparing the evening to a silver-plated noon.

As I trudged along the road to the pine copse I was busy formulating plans for intruding into the family circle at the farmhouse; devising all manner of pious frauds by which to scrape acquaintance.

"Shall I feign having lost my way, and inquire direction to the sanitarium; or shall I ask if some mythical acquaintance, a John Squires, for instance, lives there?" I asked myself as I neared the turn of the road.

Fortunately for my conscience, all these subterfuges were unnecessary, for as I neared the whitewashed fence, a girl left the porch and walked quickly to the gate, where she stood gazing pensively along the moonlit road. It was almost as if she were coming to meet me, I thought, as I slacked my pace and assumed an air of deliberate casualness.

Almost abreast of her, I lessened my pace still more, and looked directly at her. Then I knew why my conception of the girl who lived in that house had been misty and indistinct. For the same reason the venerable John had faltered in his description of the New Jerusalem until his vision in the Isle of Patmos.

From the smoothly parted hair above her wide, forget-me-not eyes, to the hem of her white cotton frock, she was as slender and lovely as a Rossetti saint; as wonderful to the eye as a medieval poet's vision of his lost love in paradise. Her forehead, evenly framed in the beaten bronze of her hair, was wide and high, and startlingly white, and her brows were delicately penciled as if laid on by an artist with a camel's hair brush. The eyes themselves were sweet and clear as forest pools mirroring the September sky, and lifted a little at the corners, like an Oriental's, giving her face a quaint, exotic look in the midst of these Maine woods.

So slender was her figure that the swell of her bosom was barely perceptible under the light stuff of her dress, and, as she stood immobile in the nimbus of moon rays, the undulation of the line from her shoulders to ankles was what painters call a "curve of motion."

One hand rested lightly on the gate, a hand as finely cut as a bit of Italian sculpture, and scarcely less white than the limed wood supporting it. I noticed idly that the forefinger was somewhat longer than its fellows, and that the nails were almond shaped and very pink—almost red—as if they had been rouged and brightly polished.

No man can take stock of a woman thus, even in a cursory, fleeting glimpse, without her being aware of the inspection, and in the minute my eyes drank up her beauty, our glances crossed and held.

The look she gave back was as calm and unperturbed as though I had been nonexistent; one might have thought I was an invisible wraith of the night; yet the faint suspicion of a flush quickening in her throat and cheeks told me she was neither unaware nor unappreciative of my scrutiny.

Mechanically, I raised my cap, and, wholly without conscious volition, I heard my own voice asking:

"May I trouble you for a drink from your well? I'm from the sanitarium—only a few days out of bed, in fact—and I fear I've overdone myself in my walk."

A smile flitted across her rather wide lips, quick and sympathetic as a mother's response to her child's request, as she swung the gate open for me.

"Surely—" she answered, and her voice had all the sweetness of the south wind soughing through her native pines—"surely you may drink at our well, and rest yourself, too—if you wish."

She preceded me up the path, quickening her pace as she neared the house, and running nimbly up the steps to the porch. From where I stood beside the old-fashioned well, fitted with windlass and bucket, I could hear the sound of whispering voices in earnest conversation. Hers I recognized, lowered though it was, by the flutelike purling of its tones; the other two were deeper, and, it seemed to me, hoarse and throaty. Somehow, odd as it seemed, there was a queer, canine note in them, dimly reminding me of the muttering of not too friendly dogs—such fractious growls I had heard while doing missionary duty in Alaska, when the savage, half-wolf malemutes were not fed promptly at the relay stations.

Her voice rose a trifle higher, as if in argument, and I fancied I heard her whisper, "This one is mine, I tell you; mine. I'll brook no interference. Go to your own hunting."

An instant later there was a reluctant assenting growl from the shadow of the vines curtaining the porch, and a light laugh from the girl as she descended the steps, swinging a bright tin cup in her hand. For a second she looked at me, as she sent the bucket plunging into the stone-curbed well; then she announced, in explanation:

"We're great hunters here, you know. The season is just in, and Dad and I have the worst quarrels about whose game is whose."

She laughed in recollection of their argument, and I laughed with her. I had been quite a Nimrod as a boy, myself, and well I remembered the heated controversies as to whose charge of shot was responsible for some luckless bunny's demise.

The well was very deep, and my breath was coming fast by the time I had helped her wind the bucket-rope upon the windlass; but the water was cold as only spring-fed well water can be. As she poured it from the bucket it shone almost like foam in the moonlight, and seemed to whisper with a half-human voice, instead of gurgling as other water does when poured.

I had drunk water in nearly every quarter of the globe; but never such water as that. Cold as the breath from a glacier, limpid as visualized air, it was yet so light and tasteless in substance that only the chill in my throat and the sight of the liquid in the cup told me that I was doing more than going through the motions of drinking.

"And now, will you rest?" she invited, as I finished my third draught. "We've an extra chair on the porch for you."

Behind the screen of vines I found her father and mother seated in the rays of the big kitchen lamp. They were just as I had expected to find them: plain, homely, sincere country folk, courteous in their reception and anxious to make a sick stranger welcome. Both were stout, with the comfortable stoutness of middle age and good health; but both had surprisingly slender hands. I noticed, too, that the same characteristic of an over-long forefinger was apparent in their hands as in their daughter's, and that both their nails were trimmed to points and stained almost a brilliant red.

"My father, Mr. Squires," the girl introduced, "and my mother, Mrs. Squires."

I could not repress a start. These people bore the very name I had casually thought to use when inquiring for some imaginary person. My lucky stars had surely guided me away from that attempt to scrape an acquaintance. What a figure I should have cut if I had actually asked for Mr. Squires!

Though I was not aware of it, my curious glance must have stayed longer on their reddened nails than I had intended, for Mrs. Squires looked deprecatingly at her hands. "We've all been turning, putting up fox grapes"—she included her husband and daughter with a comprehensive gesture. "And the stain just won't wash out; has to wear off, you know."

I spent, perhaps, two hours with my new-found friends, talking of everything from the best methods of potato culture to the surest way of landing a nine-pound bass. All three joined in the conversation and took a lively interest in the topics under discussion. After the vapid talk of the guests at the sanitarium, I found the simple, interested discourse of these country people as stimulating as wine, and when I left them it was with a hearty promise to renew my call at an early date.

"Better wait until after dark," Mr. Squires warned. "We'd be glad to see you any time; but we're so busy these fall days, we haven't much time for company."

I took the broad hint in the same friendly spirit it was given.

It must have grown chillier than I realized while I sat there, for my new friends' hands were clay-cold when I took them in mine at parting.

Homeward bound, a whimsical thought struck me so suddenly I laughed aloud. There was something suggestive of the dog tribe about the Squires family, though I could not for the life of me say what it was. Even Mildred, the daughter, beautiful as she was, with her light eyes, her rather prominent nose and her somewhat wide mouth, reminded me in some vague way of a lovely silver collie I had owned as a boy.

I struck a tassel of dried leaves from a cluster of weeds with my walking stick as I smiled at the fanciful conceit. The legend of the werewolf—those horrible monsters, formed as men, but capable of assuming bestial shape at will, and killing and eating their fellows—was as old as mankind's fear of the dark, but no mythology I had ever read contained a reference to dog-people.

Strange fancies strike up in the moonlight, sometimes.

September ripened to October, and the moon, which had been as round and bright as an exchange-worn coin when I first visited the Squires house, waned as thin as a shaving from a silversmith's lathe.

I became a regular caller at the house in the pines. Indeed, I grew to look forward to my nightly visits with those homely folk as a welcome relief from the tediously gay companionship of the over-sophisticated people at the sanitarium.

My habit of slipping away shortly after dinner was the cause of considerable comment and no little speculation on the part of my fellow convalescents, some of whom set it down to the eccentricity which, to their minds, was the inevitable concomitant of a minister's vocation, while others were frankly curious. Snatches of conversation I overheard now and then led me to believe that the objective of my strolls was the subject of wagering, and the guarded questions put to me in an effort to solve the mystery became more and more annoying.

I had no intention of taking any of them to the farmhouse with me. The Squires were my friends. Their cheerful talk and unassuming manners were as delightful a contrast to the atmosphere of the sanitarium as a breath of mountain balsam after the fetid air of a hothouse; but to the city-centered crowd at Briarcliff they would have been only the objects of less than half scornful patronage, the source of pitying amusement.

It was Miss Leahy who pushed the impudent curiosity further than any of the rest, however. One evening, as I was setting out, she met me at the gate and announced her intention of going with me.

"You must have found something *dreadfully* attractive to take you off *every* evening this way, Mr. Weatherby," she hazarded as she pursed her rather pretty, rouged lips at me and caught step with my walk. "We girls really *can't* let some little country lass take you away from us, you know. We simply can't."

I made no reply. It was scarcely possible to tell a pretty girl, even such a vain little flirt as Sara Leahy, to go home and mind her business. Yet that was just what I wanted to do. But I would not take her with me; to that I made up my mind. I would stop at the turn of the road, just out of sight of the farmhouse, and cut across the fields. If she wanted to accompany me on a cross-country hike in high-heeled slippers, she was welcome to do so.

Besides, she would tell the others that my wanderings were nothing more mysterious than nocturnal explorations of the nearby woods; which bit of misinformation would satisfy the busybodies at Briarcliff and relieve me of the espionage to which I was subjected, as well.

I smiled grimly to myself as I pictured her climbing over fences and ditches in her flimsy party frock and beaded pumps, and lengthened my stride toward the woods at the road's turn.

We marched to the limits of the field bordering the Squires' grove in silence, I thinking of the mild revenge I should soon wreak upon the pretty little busybody at my side, Miss Leahy too intent on holding the pace I set to waste breath in conversation.

As we neared the woods she halted, an expression of worry, almost fear, coming over her face.

"I don't believe I'll go any farther," she announced.

"No?" I replied, a trifle sarcastically. "And is your curiosity so easily satisfied?"

"It's not that." She turned half round, as if to retrace her steps. "I'm afraid of those woods."

"Indeed?" I queried. "And what is there to be afraid of? Bears, Indians, or wildcats? I've been through them several times without seeing anything terrifying." Now she had come this far, I was anxious to take her through the fields and underbrush.

"No-o," Miss Leahy answered, a nervous quaver in her voice, "I'm not afraid of anything like that; but—oh, I don't know what you call it. Pierre told me all about it the other day. Some kind of dreadful thing—loop—loop—something or other. It's a French word, and I can't remember it."

I was puzzled. Pierre Geronte was the ancient French-Canadian gardener at the sanitarium, and, like all doddering old men, would talk for hours to anyone who would listen. Also, like all *habitants*, he was full of wild folklore his ancestors brought overseas with them generations ago.

"What did Pierre tell you?" I asked.

"Why, he said that years ago some terrible people lived in these woods. They had the only house for miles 'round; and travelers stopped there for the night, sometimes. But no stranger was ever seen to leave that place, once he went in. One night the farmers gathered about the house and burned it, with the family that lived there. When the embers had cooled down they made a search, and found nearly a dozen bodies buried in the cellar. That was why no one ever came away from that dreadful place.

"They took the murdered men to the cemetery and buried them; but they dumped the charred bodies of the murderers into graves in the barnyard, without even saying a prayer over them. And Pierre says—Oh, Look! *Look!*"

She broke off her recital of the old fellow's story, and pointed a trembling hand across the field to the edge of the woods. A second more and she shrank against me, clutching at my coat with fear-stiffened fingers and crying with excitement and terror.

I looked in the direction she indicated, myself a little startled by the abject fear that had taken such sudden hold on her.

Something white and ungainly was running diagonally across the field from us, skirting the margin of the woods and making for the meadow that adjoined the sanitarium pasture. A second glance told me it was a sheep; probably one of the flock kept to supply our table with fresh meat.

I was laughing at the strength of the superstition that could make a girl see a figure of horror in an innocent mutton that had strayed away from its fellows and was scared out of its silly wits, when something else attracted my attention.

Loping along in the trail of the fleeing sheep, somewhat to the rear and a little to each side, were two other animals. At first glance they appeared to be a pair of large collies; but as I looked more intently, I saw that these animals were like nothing I had ever seen before. They were much larger than any collie—nearly as high as St. Bernards—yet shaped in a general way like Alaskan sledge dogs—huskies.

The farther one was considerably the larger of the two, and ran with a slight limp, as if one of its hind paws had been injured. As nearly as I could tell in the indifferent light, they were a rusty brown color, very thick-haired and unkempt in appearance. But the strangest thing about them was the fact that both were tailless, which gave them a terrifyingly grotesque look.

As they ran, a third form, similar to the other two in shape, but smaller, slender as a greyhound, with much lighter-hued fur, broke from the thicket of short brush edging the wood and took up the chase, emitting a series of short, sharp yelps.

"Sheep-killers," I murmured, half to myself. "Odd. I've never seen dogs like that before."

"They're not dogs," wailed Miss Leahy against my coat. "They're not dogs. Oh, Mr. Weatherby, let's go away. Please, please take me home."

She was rapidly becoming hysterical, and I had a difficult time with her on the trip back. She clung whimpering to me, and I had almost to carry her most of the way. By the time we reached the sanitarium, she was crying bitterly, shivering, as if with a chill, and went in without stopping to thank me for my assistance.

I turned and made for the Squires farm with all possible speed, hoping to get there before the family had gone to bed. But when I arrived the house was in darkness, and my knock at the door received no answer.

As I retraced my steps to the sanitarium I heard faintly, from the fields beyond the woods, the shrill, eerie cry of the sheep-killing dogs.

A torrent of rain held us marooned the next day. Miss Leahy was confined to her room, with a nurse in constant attendance and the house doctor making hourly calls. She was on the verge of a nervous collapse, he told me, crying with a persistence that bordered on hysteria, and responding to treatment very slowly.

An impromptu dance was organized in the great hall and half a dozen bridge tables set up in the library; but as I was skilled in neither of these rainy day diversions, I put on a waterproof and patrolled the veranda for exercise.

On my third or fourth trip around the house I ran into old Geronte shuffling across the porch, wagging his head and muttering portentously to himself.

"See here, Pierre," I accosted him, "what sort of nonsense have you been telling Miss Leahy about those pine woods down the south road?"

The old fellow regarded me unwinkingly with his beady eyes, wrinkling his age-yellowed forehead for all the world like an elderly baboon inspecting a new sort of edible. "*M'sieur* goes out alone much at nights, *n'est ce pas?*" he asked, at length.

"Yes, Monsieur goes out alone much at night," I echoed, "but what Monsieur particularly desires to know is what sort of tales have you been telling Mademoiselle Leahy. *Comprenez vous?*"

The network of wrinkles about his lips multiplied as he smiled enigmatically, regarding me askance from the corners of his eyes.

"*M'sieur is anglais,*" he replied. "He would not understand—or believe."

"Never mind what I'd believe," I retorted. "What is this

story about murder and robbery being committed in those woods? Who were the murderers, and where did they live? *Hein?*"

For a few seconds he looked fixedly at me, chewing the cud of senility between his toothless gums, then, glancing carefully about, as if he feared being overheard, he tiptoed up to me and whispered:

"*M'sieur* mus' stay indoors these nights. There are evil things abroad at the dark of the moon, *M'sieur.* Even las' night they keel t'ree of my bes' sheep. Remembair, *M'sieur,* the *loup-garou,* he is out when the moon hide her light."

And with that he turned and left me; nor could I get another word from him save his cryptic warning, "Remembair, *M'sieur; the loup-garou.* Remembair."

In spite of my annoyance, I could not get rid of the unpleasant sensation the old man's words left with me. The *loup-garou*—werewolf—he had said, and to prove his goblin-wolf's presence, he had cited the death of his three sheep.

As I paced the rain-washed porch I thought of the scene I had witnessed the night before, when the sheep-killers were at their work.

"Well," I reflected, "I've seen the *loup-garou* on his native heath at last. From causes as slight as this, no doubt, the horrible legend of the werewolf had sprung. Time was when all France quaked at the sound of the *loup-garou's* hunting call and the bravest knights in Christendom trembled in their castles and crossed themselves fearfully because some renegade shepherd dog quested his prey in the night. On such a foundation are the legends of a people built."

Whistling a snatch from *Pinafore* and looking skyward in search of a patch of blue in the clouds, I felt a tug at my raincoat sleeve, such as a neglected terrier might give. It was Geronte again.

"*M'sieur,*" he began in the same mysterious whisper, "the *loup-garou* is a verity, certainly. I, myself, have nevair seen him"—he paused to bless himself—"but my cousin, Baptiste, was once pursued by him. Yes.

"It was near the shrine of the good Sainte Anne that Baptiste lived. One night he was sent to fetch the curé for a

463

dying woman. They rode fast through the trees, the curé and my cousin Baptiste, for it was at the dark of the moon, and the evil forest folk were abroad. And as they galloped, there came a *loup-garou* from the woods, with eyes as bright as hell fire. It followed hard, this tailless hound from the devil's kennel; but they reached the house before it, and the curé put his book, with the Holy Cross on its cover, at the doorstep. The *loup-garou* wailed under the windows like a child in pain until the sun rose; then it slunk back to the forest.

"When my cousin Baptiste and the curé came out, they found its hand marks in the soft earth around the door. Very like your hand, or mine, they were, *M'sieur*, save that the first finger was longer than the others."

"And did they find the *loup-garou*?" I asked, something of the old man's earnestness communicated to me.

"Yes, *M'sieur*; but of course," he replied gravely. "T'ree weeks before a stranger, drowned in the river, had been buried without the office of the Church. W'en they opened his grave they found his fingernails as red as blood, and sharp. Then they knew. The good curé read the burial office over him, and the poor soul that had been snatched away in sin slept peacefully at last."

He looked quizzically at me, as if speculating whether to tell me more; then, apparently fearing I would laugh at his outburst of confidence, started away toward the kitchen.

"Well, what else, Pierre?" I asked, feeling he had more to say.

"Non, non, non," he replied. "There is nothing more, *M'sieur*. I did but want M'sieur should know my own cousin, Baptiste Geronte, had seen the *loup-garou* with his very eyes."

"Hearsay evidence," I commented, as I went in to dinner.

During the rainy week that followed I chafed at my confinement like a privileged convict suddenly deprived of his liberties, and looked as wistfully down the south road as any prisoned gypsy ever gazed upon the open trail.

The quiet home circle at the farmhouse, the unforced conversation of the old folks, Mildred's sweet companionship, all beckoned me with an almost irresistible force.

464

For in this period of enforced separation I discovered what I had dimly suspected for some time. I loved Mildred Squires. And, loving her, I longed to tell her of it.

No lad intent on visiting his first sweetheart ever urged his feet more eagerly than I when, the curtains of rain at last drawn up, I hastened toward the house at the turn of the road.

As I hoped, yet hardly dared expect, Mildred was standing at the gate to meet me as I rounded the curve, and I yearned toward her like a hummingbird seeking its nest.

She must have read my heart in my eyes, for her greeting smile was as tender as a mother's as she bends above her babe.

"At last you have come, my friend," she said, putting out both hands in welcome. "I am very glad."

We walked silently up the path, her fingers still resting in mine, her face averted. At the steps she paused, a little embarrassment in her voice as she explained, "Father and Mother are out; they have gone to a—meeting. But you will stay?"

"Surely," I acquiesced. And to myself I admitted my gratitude for this chance of Mildred's unalloyed company.

We talked but little that night. Mildred was strangely distrait, and, much as I longed to, I could not force a confession of my love from my lips. Once, in the midst of a long pause between our words, the cry of the sheep-killers came faintly to us, echoed across the fields and woods, and as the weird, shrill sound fell on our ears, she threw back her head, with something of the gesture of a hunting dog scenting its quarry.

Toward midnight she turned to me, a panic of fear having apparently laid hold of her.

"You must go!" she exclaimed, rising and laying her hand on my shoulder.

"But your father and mother have not returned," I objected. "Won't you let me stay until they get back?"

"Oh, no, no," she answered, her agitation increasing. "You must go at once—please." She increased her pressure on my shoulder, almost as if to shove me from the porch.

Taken aback by her sudden desire to be rid of me, I was picking up my hat, when she uttered a stifled little scream and ran quickly to the edge of the porch, interposing herself between me and the yard. At the same moment, I heard a muffled sound from the direction of the front gate, a sound like a growling and snarling of savage dogs.

I leaped forward, my first thought being that the sheep-killers I had seen the other night had strayed to the Squires place. Crazed with blood, I knew, they would be almost as dangerous to men as to sheep, and every nerve in my sick-ness-weakened body cried out to protect Mildred.

To my blank amazement, as I looked from the porch I beheld Mr. and Mrs. Squires walking sedately up the path, talking composedly together. There was no sign of the dogs or any other animals about.

As the elderly couple neared the porch I noticed that Mr. Squires walked with a pronounced limp, and that both their eyes shone very brightly in the moonlight, as though they were suffused with tears.

They greeted me pleasantly enough; but Mildred's anx-iety seemed increased, rather than diminished, by their presence, and I took my leave after a brief exchange of civil-ities.

On my way back I looked intently in the woods bordering the road for some sign of the house of which Pierre had told Miss Leahy; but everywhere the pines grew as thickly as though neither axe nor fire had ever disturbed them.

"Geronte is in his second childhood," I reflected, "and like an elder child, he loves to terrify his juniors with fear-some witch-tales."

Yet an uncomfortable feeling was with me till I saw the gleam of the sanitarium's lights across the fields; and as I walked toward them it seemed to me that more than once I heard the baying of the sheep-killers in the woods behind me.

A buzz of conversation, like the sibilant arguments of a cloud of swarming bees, greeted me as I descended the stairs to breakfast next morning.

It appeared that Ned, one of the pair of great mastiffs attached to the sanitarium, had been found dead before his kennel, his throat and brisket torn open and several gaping wounds in his flanks. Boris, his fellow, had been discovered whimpering and trembling in the extreme corner of the doghouse, the embodiment of canine terror.

Speculation as to the animal responsible for the outrage was rife, and, as usual, it ran the gamut of possible and impossible surmises. Every sort of beast from a grizzly bear to a lion escaped from the circus was in turn indicted for the crime, only to have a complete alibi straightway established.

The only one having no suggestion to offer was old Geronte, who stood Sphinx-like in the outskirts of the crowd, smiling sardonically to himself and wagging his head sagely. As he caught sight of me he nodded, sapiently, as if to include me in the joint tenancy to some weighty secret.

Presently he worked his way through the chattering group and whispered, "*M'sieur,* he was here last night—and with him was the other tailless one. Come and see."

Plucking me by the sleeve, he led me to the rear of the kennels, and, stooping, pointed to something in the moist earth. "You see?" he asked, as if a printed volume lay for my reading in the mud.

"I see that someone has been on his hands and knees here," I answered, inspecting the hand prints he indicated.

"*Something,*" he corrected, as if reasoning with an obstinate child. "Does not *M'sieur* behol' that the first finger is the longest?"

"Which proves nothing," I defended. "There are many hands like that."

"Oh—yes?" he replied with that queer upward accent of his. "And where has *M'sieur* seen hands like that before?"

"Oh, many times," I assured him somewhat vaguely, for there was a catch at the back of my throat as I spoke. Try as I would, I could recall only three pairs of hands with that peculiarity.

His little black eyes rested steadily on me in an unwinking stare, and the corners of his mouth curved upward in a malicious grin. It seemed, almost, as if he found a grim pleasure in thus driving me into a corner.

"See here, Pierre," I began testily, equally annoyed at myself and him, "you know as well as I that the *loup-garou* is an old woman's tale. Someone was looking here for tracks, and left his own while doing it. If we look among the patients here we shall undoubtedly find a pair of hands to match these prints."

"God forbid!" he exclaimed, crossing himself. "That would be an evil day for us, *M'sieur.* Here, Bor-ees," he snapped his fingers to the surviving mastiff, "come and eat."

The huge beast came wallowing over to him with the ungainly gait of all heavily-muscled animals, stopping on his way to make a nasal investigation of my knees. Scarcely had his nose come into contact with my trousers when he leaped back, every hair in his mane and along his spine stiffly erect, every tooth in his great mouth bared in a savage snarl. But instead of the mastiff's fighting growl, he emitted only a low, frightened whine, as though he were facing some animal of greater power than himself, and knew his own weakness.

"Good heavens!" I cried, thoroughly terrified at the friendly brute's sudden hostility.

"Yes, *M'sieur,*" Geronte cut in quickly, putting his hand on the dog's collar and leading him a few paces away. "It is well you should call upon the heavenly ones; for surely you have the odor of hell upon your clothes."

"What do you mean?" I demanded angrily. "How dare you—?"

He raised a thin hand deprecatingly. "*M'sieur* knows that he knows," he replied evenly; "and what I also know."

And leading Boris by the collar, he shuffled to the house.

Mildred was waiting for me at the gate that evening, and again her father and mother were absent at one of their meetings.

We walked silently up the path and seated ourselves on the porch steps where the waning moon cast oblique rays through the pine branches.

I think Mildred felt the tension I was drawn to, for she talked trivialities with an almost feverish earnestness, stringing her sentences together, and changing her subjects as a Navajo rug weaver twists and breaks her threads.

At last I found an opening in the abatis of her small talk.

"Mildred," I said, very simply, for great emotions tear the ornaments from our speech, "I love you, and I want you for my wife. Will you marry me, Mildred?" I laid my hand on hers. It was cold as lifeless flesh, and seemed to shrink beneath my touch.

"Surely, dear, you must have read the love in my eyes," I urged, as she averted her face in silence. "Almost from the night I first saw you. I've loved you! I—"

"O-o-h, don't!" Her interruption was a strangled moan, as if wrung from her by my words.

I leaned nearer her. "Don't you love me, Mildred?" I asked. As yet she had not denied it.

For a moment she trembled, as if a sudden chill had come on her, then, leaning to me, she clasped my shoulders in her arms, hiding her face against my jacket.

"John, John, you don't know what you say," she whispered disjointedly, as though a sob had torn the words before they left her lips. Her breath was on my cheek, moist and cold as air from a vault.

I could feel the litheness of her through the thin stuff of her gown, and her body was as devoid of warmth as a dead thing.

"You're cold," I told her, putting my arms shieldingly about her. "The night has chilled you."

A convulsive sob was her only answer.

"Mildred," I began again, putting my hand beneath her chin and lifting her face to mine, "tell me, dear, what is the matter?" I lowered my lips to hers.

With a cry that was half scream, half weeping, she thrust me suddenly from her, pressing her hands against my breast and lowering her head until her face was hidden between her outstretched arms. I, too, started back, for in the instant our lips were about to meet, hers had writhed back from her teeth, like a dog's when he is about to spring, and a low, harsh noise, almost a growl, had risen in her throat.

"For God's sake," she whispered hoarsely, agony in every note of her shaking voice, "never do that again! Oh, my dear, dear love, you don't know how near to a horror worse than death you were."

"A—horror—worse—than—death?" I echoed dully, pressing her cold little hands in mine. "What do you mean, Mildred?"

"Loose my hands," she commanded with a quaint reversion to the speech of our ancestors, "and hear me. I do love you. I love you better than life. Better than death. I love you so I have overcome something stronger than the walls of the grave for your sake, but John, my very love, this is our last night together. We can never meet again. You must go, now, and not come back until tomorrow morning."

"Tomorrow morning?" I repeated blankly. What wild talk was this?

Heedless of my interruption, she hurried on. "Tomorrow morning, just before the sun rises over those trees, you must be here, and have your prayer book with you."

I listened speechless, wondering which of us was mad.

"By that corncrib there"—she waved a directing hand—"you will find three mounds. Stand beside them and read the office for the burial of the dead. Come quickly, and pause for nothing on the way. Look back for nothing; heed no sound from behind you. And for your own safety, come no sooner than to allow yourself the barest time to read your office."

Bewildered, I attempted to reason with the mad woman; begged her to explain this folly; but she refused all answer to my fervid queries, nor would she suffer me to touch her.

Finally, I rose to go. "You will do what I ask?" she implored.

"Certainly not," I answered firmly.

"John, John, have pity!" she cried, flinging herself to the earth before me and clasping my knees. "You say you love me. I only ask this one favor of you; only this. Please, for my sake, for the peace of the dead and the safety of the living, promise you will do this thing for me."

Shaken by her abject supplication, I promised, though I felt myself a figure in some grotesque nightmare as I did it.

"Oh, my love, my precious love," she wept, rising and taking both my hands. "At last I shall have peace, and you shall bring it to me. No," she forbade me as I made to take her in my arms at parting. "The most I can give you, dear, is this." She held her icy hands against my lips. "It seems so little, dear, but oh! it is so much."

Like a drunkard in his cups I staggered along the south road, my thoughts gone wild with the strangeness of the play I had just acted.

Across the clearing came the howls of the sheep-killers, a sound I had grown used to of late. But tonight there was a deeper, fiercer *timbre* in their bay; a note that boded ill for man as well as beast. Louder and louder it swelled; it was rising from the field itself, now, drawing nearer and nearer the road.

I turned and looked. The great beasts I had seen pursuing the luckless sheep the other night were galloping toward me. A cold finger seemed traced down my spine; the scalp crept and tingled beneath my cap. There was no other object of their quest in sight. I was their elected prey.

My first thought was to turn and run; but a second's reasoning told me this was worse than useless. Weakened with long illness, with an uphill road to the nearest shelter, I should soon be run down.

No friendly tree offered asylum; my only hope was to stand and fight. Grasping my stick, I spread my feet, bracing myself against their charge.

And as I waited their onslaught, there came from the shadow of the pines the shriller, sharper cry of the third beast. Like the crest of a flying, wind-lashed wave, the slighter, silver-furred brute came speeding across the meadow, its ears laid back, its slender paws spurning the sod daintily. Almost, it seemed as if the pale shadow of a cloud were racing toward me.

The thing dashed slantwise across the field, its flight converging on the line of the other two's attack. Midway between me and them it paused; hairs bristling, limbs bent for a spring.

All the savageness of the larger beasts' hunting cry was echoed in the smaller creature's bay, and with it a defiance that needed no interpretation.

The attackers paused in their rush; halted, and looked speculatively at my ally. They took a few tentative steps in my direction; and a fierce whine, almost an articulate curse, went up from the silver-haired beast. Slowly the tawny pair circled and trotted back to the woods.

I hurried toward the sanitarium, grasping my stick firmly in readiness for another attack.

But no further cries came from the woods, and once, as I

glanced back, I saw the light-haired beast trotting slowly in my wake, looking from right to left, as if to ward off danger.

Half an hour later I looked from my window toward the house in the pines. Far down the south road, its muzzle pointed to the moon, the bright-furred animal crouched and poured out a lament to the night. And its cry was like the wail of a child in pain.

Far into the night I paced my room, like a condemned convict when the vigil of the death watch is on him. Reason and memory struggled for the mastery; one urging me to give over my wild act, the other bidding me obey my promise to Mildred.

Toward morning I dropped into a chair, exhausted with my objectless marching. I must have fallen asleep, for when I started up the stars were dimming in the zenith, and bands of slate, shading to amethyst, slanted across the horizon.

A moment I paused, laughing cynically at my fool's errand, then, seizing cap and book, I bolted down the stairs, and ran through the paling dawn to the house in the pines.

There was something ominous and terrifying in the two-toned pastel of the house that morning. Its windows stared at me with blank malevolence, like the half-closed eyes of one stricken dead in mortal sin. The little patches of hoarfrost on the lawn were like leprous spots on some unclean thing. From the trees behind the clearing an owl hooted mournfully, as if to say, "Beware, beware!" and the wind soughing through the black pine boughs echoed the refrain ceaselessly.

Three mounds, sunken and weed-grown, lay in the unkempt thicket behind the corncrib. I paused beside them, throwing off my cap and adjusting my stole hastily. Thumbing the pages to the committal service, I held the book close, that I might see the print through the morning shadows, and commenced: "I know that my redeemer liveth—"

Almost beside me, under the branches of the pines, there rose such a chorus of howls and yelps I nearly dropped my book. Like all the hounds in the kennels of hell, the sheep-killers clamored at me, rage and fear and mortal hatred in their cries. Through the bestial cadences, too, there seemed to run a human note; the sound of voices heard before beneath these very trees. Deep and throaty, and raging mad, two of the voices came to me, and, like the tremolo of a violin lightly played in an orchestra of brass, the shriller cry of a third beast sounded.

As the infernal hubbub rose at my back, I half turned to fly. Next instant I grasped my book more firmly and resumed my office, for like a beacon in the dark, Mildred's words flashed on my memory: *"Look back for nothing; heed no sound behind you."*

Strangely, too, the din approached no nearer; but as though held by an invisible bar, stayed at the boundary of the clearing.

"Man that is born of a woman hath but a short time to live and is full of misery—deliver us from all our offenses—O, Lord, deliver us not into the bitter pains of eternal death—" and to such an accompaniment, surely, as no priest ever before chanted the office, I pressed through the brief service to the final *Amen.*

Tiny grouts of moisture stood out on my forehead, my breath struggled in my throat as I gasped out the last word. My nerves were frayed to shreds and my strength nearly gone as I let fall my book, and turned upon the beasts among the trees.

They were gone. Abruptly as it had begun, their clamor stopped, and only the rotting pine needles, lightly gilded by the morning sun, met my gaze. A light touch fell in the palm of my open hand, as if a pair of cool, sweet lips had laid a kiss there.

A vaporlike swamp-fog enveloped me. The outbuildings, the old, stone-curbed well where I had drunk the night I first saw Mildred, the house itself—all seemed fading into mist and swirling away in the morning breeze.

"Eh, eh, eh; but *M'sieur* will do himself an injury, sleeping on the wet earth!" Old Geronte bent over me, his arm beneath my shoulders. Behind him, great Boris, the mastiff, stood wagging his tail, regarding me with doggish good humor.

"Pierre," I muttered thickly, "how came you here?"

"This morning, going to my tasks, I saw *M'sieur* run down the road like a thing pursued. I followed quickly, for the woods hold terrors in the dark, *M'sieur.*"

I looked toward the farmhouse. Only a pair of chimneys,

rising stark and bare from a crumbling foundation were there. Fence, well, barn—all were gone, and in their place a thicket of sumac and briars, tangled and overgrown as though undisturbed for thirty years.

"The house, Pierre! Where is the house?" I croaked, sinking my fingers into his withered arm.

"'Ouse?" he echoed. "Oh, but of course. There is no 'ouse here, *M'sieur;* nor has there been for years. This is an evil place, *M'sieur;* it is best we quit it, and that quickly. There be evil things that run by night—"

"No more," I answered, staggering toward the road, leaning heavily on him. "I brought them peace, Pierre."

He looked dubiously at the English prayer book I held. A Protestant clergyman is a thing of doubtful usefulness to the orthodox French-Canadian. Something of the heartsick misery in my face must have touched his kind old heart, for at last he relented, shaking his head pityingly and patting my shoulder gently, as one would soothe a sorrowing chid.

"Per'aps, *M'sieur,"* he conceded. "Per'aps; who shall say no? Love and sorrow are the purchase price of peace. Yes. Did not *le bon Dieu* so buy the peace of the world?"

The creator of one of the most famous of all occult detectives, Dr. Jules de Grandin, Seabury Quinn was born in Washington, D.C., in 1889. A man of several careers, Quinn was a lawyer, editor of trade journals for funeral directors, and was an expert on mortuary science. Most of his more than 160 stories appeared in Weird Tales, *and many of his de Grandin tales have been collected in six volumes, beginning with* The Adventures of Jules de Grandin. *The best of his non-de Grandin works are collected in* Is the Devil a Gentleman?

John Jeremy could recover any body from the river, but he kept his methods secret. Twelve-year-old Peter was determined to find out why.

TWENTY-SEVEN

Stillwater, 1896
Michael Cassutt

They are big families up here on the St. Croix. I myself am the second of eight, and ours was the smallest family of any on Chestnut Street. You might think we were all hard-breeding Papists passing as Lutherans, but I have since learned that it is due to the long winters. For fifty years I have been hearing that Science will take care of winters just like we took care of the river, with our steel high bridge and diesel-powered barges that go the size of a football field. But every damn November the snow falls again and in spring the river swells from bluff to bluff. The loggers can be heard cursing all the way from Superior. I alone know that this is because of what we done to John Jeremy.

I was just a boy then, short of twelve, that would be in 1896, and by mutual agreement of little use to anyone, not my father nor my brothers nor my departed mother. I knew my letters, to be sure, and could be trusted to appear at Church in a clean collar, but my primary achievement at that age was to be known as the best junior logroller in the county, a title I had won the previous Fourth of July, beating boys from as far away as Rice Lake and Taylors Falls. In truth, I tended to lollygag when sent to Kinnick's Store, never failing to take a detour down to the riverfront, where a Mississippi excursion boat like the *Verne Swain* or the *Kalitan*, up from St. Louis or New Orleans, would be pulled in. I had the habit of getting into snowball fights on my way to school and was notorious for one whole winter as the boy who almost put out Oscar Tolz's eye with a missile into which I had embedded a small pebble. (Oscar Tolz was a

God damned Swede and a bully to boot.) Often I would not get to school at all. This did not vex my father to any great degree, as he had only a year of schooling himself. It mightily vexed my elder brother, Dolph. I can still recall him appearing like an avenging angel wherever I went, it seemed, saying, "Peter, what in God's name are you doing there? Get away from there!" Dolph was all of fourteen at the time and ambitious, having been promised a job at the Hersey Bean Lumberyard when the Panic ended. He was also suspicious of my frivolous associates, particularly one named John Jeremy.

I now know that John Jeremy was the sort of man you meet on the river—bearded, unkempt, prone to sudden, mystifying exclamations and gestures. The better folk got no further with him, while curious boys found him somewhat more interesting, perhaps because of his profession. "I'm descended from the line of St. Peter himself," he told me once. "Do you know why?"

I drew the question because my given name is Peter. "Because you are a fisher of men," I told him.

Truth, in the form of hard liquor, was upon John Jeremy that day. He amended my phrase: "A fisher of dead men." John Jeremy fished for corpses.

He had been brought up from Chicago, they said, in 1885 by the Hersey family itself. Whether motivated by a series of personal losses or by some philanthropic spasm I do not know, having been otherwise occupied at the time. I found few who were able or willing to discuss the subject when at last I sprouted interest. I do know that a year did not pass then that the St. Croix did not take at least half a dozen people to its shallow bottom. This in a town of less than six hundred, though that figure was subject to constant change due to riverboats and loggers who, I think, made up a disproportionate amount of the tribute. You can not imagine the distress a drowning caused in those days. Now part of this was normal human grief (most of the victims were children), but much of it, I have come to believe, was a deep revulsion in the knowledge that the source of our drinking water, the heart of our livelihood—the river!—was fouled by the bloating, gassy corpse of someone we all knew. There was nothing rational about it, but the fear was real nonetheless: when the whistle at the courthouse blew, you ran for it, for either the town was on fire, or somebody was breathing river.

Out would go the rowboats, no matter what the weather or time of night, filled with farmers unused to water with their weights, poles, nets, and hopes. It was tedious, sad, and unrewarding work . . . except for a specialist like John Jeremy.

"You stay the hell away from that man," Dolph hissed at me one day. "I've seen you hanging around down there with him. He's the Devil himself."

Normally, a statement like this from Dolph would have served only to encourage further illicit association, but none was actually needed. I had come across John Jeremy for the first time that spring, idly fishing at a spot south of town near the lumberyard. It was not the best fishing hole, if you used worms or other unimaginative bait, for the St. Croix was low that year, as it had been for ten years, and the fish were fat with bugs easily caught in the shallows. I had picked up a marvelous invention known as the casting fly and had applied it that spring with great success. And I was only too happy to share the secret with a thin, pale, scruffy fellow who looked as if he had skipped meals of late. We introduced ourselves and proceeded to take a goodly number of crappies and sunfish during the afternoon. "That's quite a trick you got there," John Jeremy told me. "You make that up all by yourself?"

I confessed that I had read about it in a dime novel, though if Oscar Tolz had asked me, I would have lied. John Jeremy laughed, showing that his teeth were a match for the rest of his ragged appearance.

"Well, it works good enough. Almost makes me wish I'd learned how to read."

By this point, as I remember it, we had hiked up to the Afton Road and were headed back to Stillwater. As we walked, I was struck by John Jeremy's thinness and apparent ill health, and in a fit of Christian charity—I was just twelve—I offered him some of my catch, which was far larger than his.

John Jeremy regarded me for a moment. I think he was amused. "Aren't you a rascal, Peter Gollwitzer. Thank you, but no. In spite of the fact that it's been a long dry spell, I'm still able to feed myself, though it don't show. I'll grant you that. In fact, in exchange for your kindness"—his voice took on a conspiratorial tone—"I shall reward you with this." And into my hand he pressed a five-dollar gold piece. "For the secret of the fly, eh? Now run along home."

My father was unamused by my sudden wealth, especially when he learned the source. "That man is worse than a grave robber. He profits through the misfortune of others." It was then that I learned John Jeremy's true profession, and that he had been known to charge as much as *five hundred dollars* for a single "recovery," as it was called. "One time, I swear by the Lord," my father continued, "he *refused* to turn over a body he had recovered because the payment wasn't immediately forthcoming! A man like that is unfit for human company." I reserved judgment, clutching the eagle in my sweaty palm, happier than I would have been with a chestful of pirate treasure.

June is a month to be remembered for tornados, with the wind screaming and trees falling and the river churning. In this instance there was a riverboat, the *Sidney,* taking a side trip from St. Paul—and regretting it—putting into town just as one of those big blowers hit. One of her deckhands, a Negro, was knocked into the water. Of course, none of those people can swim, and in truth I doubt Jonah himself could have got out of those waters that day. The courthouse whistle blew, though it was hard to hear over the roar of the wind, and Dolph (who had been sent home from the yard) grabbed my arm and tugged me toward the docks.

The crowd there was bigger than you'd expect, given the weather—not only townspeople, but many from the *Sidney,* who were quite vocal in their concern about the unfortunate blackamoor. Into our midst came John Jeremy, black gunnysack—he referred to it as his "bag of tricks"—over his shoulder. People stepped aside, the way they do for the sheriff, letting him pass. He sought out the *Sidney*'s captain. I took it that they were haggling over the price, since the captain's voice presently rose above the storm: "I've never heard such an outrage in my life!" But an agreement was reached and soon, in the middle of the storm, we saw John

Jeremy put out in his skiff. It was almost dark by then and the corpse fisher, floating with the wind-whipped water with all the seeming determination of a falling leaf, disappeared from our sight.

The onlookers began to drift home then while the passengers from the *Sidney* headed up the street in search of a warm, dry tavern. Dolph and I and the younger ones—including Oscar Tolz—stayed behind. Because of my familiarity with the corpse fisher I was thought to have intimate and detailed knowledge of his techniques, which, they say, he refused to discuss. "I bet he uses loaves of bread," one boy said. "Like in Mark Twain."

"Don't be a dope," Oscar Tolz said. "Books are not real. My old man says he's got animals in that sack. Some kind of trained rats—maybe muskrats."

"Like hell," said a third. "I saw that sack and there was nothing alive in it. Muskrats would be squirming to beat the band."

"Maybe they're *drowned* muskrats," I offered, earning a cuff from Dolph. Normally, that would have been my signal to shut my mouth, as Dolph's sense of humor—never notable—was not presently on duty. But that evening, for some reason, I felt immune. I asked him, "Okay, Dolph, what do *you* think he uses?"

One thing Dolph always liked was a technical question. He immediately forgot that he was annoyed with me. "I think," he said after a moment, "that John Jeremy's got some sort of compass." Before anyone could laugh, he raised his hand. "Now just you remember this: all the strange machines people got nowadays. If they got a machine that can make pictures move and another one can say words, how hard can it be to make a compass that instead of finding north finds dead people?"

This sounded so eminently reasonable to all of us that we promptly clasped the idea to us with a fervor of which our parents—having seen us bored in Church—thought us incapable. The boy who knew Mark Twain's stories suggested that this compass must have been invented by Thomas Edison, and who was to dispute that? Oscar Tolz announced that John Jeremy—who was known to have traveled a bit—might have busted Tom Edison in the noggin and stolen the compass away, which was why he had it and no one else did. "Especially since Edison's been suffering from amnesia ever since," I said. I confess that we grew so riotous that we did not notice how late it had gotten and that John Jeremy's laden skiff was putting in to the dock. We took one good look at the hulking and lifeless cargo coming toward us and scurried away like mice. Later I felt ashamed, because of what John Jeremy must have wondered, and because there was no real reason for us to run. A body drowned, at most, three hours could not have transformed into one of those horrors we had all heard about. It was merely the body of a poor dead black man.

I learned that John Jeremy had earned one hundred dollars for his work that afternoon, plus a free dinner with the captain of the *Sidney*. Feelings in Stillwater ran quite hot against this for some days, since one hundred dollars was the amount Reverend Bickell earned in a year for saving souls.

Over the Fourth I successfully defended my junior logrolling title; that, combined with other distractions, prevented me from seeing John Jeremy until one afternoon in early August. He was balancing unsteadily on the end of the dock, obviously drunk, occasionally cupping his hand to his ear as if listening to some faroff voice, flapping his arms to right himself.

He did not strike me as a mean or dangerous drunk (such a drinker was my father, rest his soul), just unhappy. "Florida!" he announced abruptly. "Florida, Alabama, Mississippi, Missouri, Illinois, Michigan, Wisconsin, here." He counted the state on his hand. "And never welcome anywhere for long, Peter. Except Stillwater. Why do you suppose that is?"

"Maybe it is better here."

John Jeremy laughed loudly. "I wouldn't have thought to say that, but maybe it is, by God." He coughed. "Maybe it's because I've kept the river quiet . . . and folks appreciate it." He saw none-too-fleeting disdain on my face. "True! By God, when was the last time the St. Croix went over its banks? Tell me when! Eighteen eighty-four is when! One year before the disreputable John Jeremy showed his ugly face in the quiet town of Stillwater. Not one flood in that time, sir! I stand on my record." He almost fell on it, as he was seized with another wheezing cough.

"Then the city should honor you," I said helpfully. "You should be the mayor."

"Huh! You're too innocent, Peter. A corpse fisher for mayor. No, sir, the Christian folk will not have *that*. Better a brewer, or a usurer—or the undertaker!"

He had gotten quite loud, and much as I secretly enjoyed my friendship with him, I recognized truth in what he said.

"You wouldn't want to be mayor, anyway."

He shook his head, grinning. "No. After all, what mayor can do what *I* do, eh? Who speaks to the river like I do? No one." He paused and was quiet, then added, "No one else is strong enough to pay the price."

Though I was far from tired of this conversation, I knew, from extensive experience with my father, that John Jeremy would likely grow steadily less coherent. I tried to help him to his feet, quite an achievement given my stature at the time, and, as he lapsed into what seemed to be a sullen silence, guided him toward his shack.

I was rewarded with a look inside. In the dark, I confess, I expected a magic compass, or muskrat cages, but all that I beheld were the possessions of a drifter: a gunnysack, a pole, some weights, and a net. I left John Jeremy among them, passed out on his well-worn cot.

Four days later, on a Saturday afternoon, in the thick, muggy heat of August, the courthouse whistle blew. I was on my way home from Kinnick's, having run an errand for my father, and made a quick detour downtown. Oscar Tolz was already there, shouting, "Someone's drowned at the lumberyard!" I was halfway there before I remembered that Dolph was working.

The sawmill at the Hersey Bean Lumberyard sat on pilings well into the St. Croix, the better to deal with the river of wood that floated its way every spring and summer. It was a God dammed treacherous place, especially when huge timbers were being pulled in and swung to face the blades. Dolph had been knocked off because he had not ducked in time.

The water was churning that day beneath the mill in spite

of the lack of wind and current. I suspect it had to do with the peculiar set of the pilings and the movements of the big logs. At any rate, Dolph, a strong swimmer, had been hurled into an obstruction, possibly striking his head, so observers said. He had gone under the water then, not to be seen again.

The shoreline just to the south of the yard was rugged and overgrown. It was possible that Dolph, knocked senseless for a moment, had been carried that way where, revived, he could swim to safety, unbeknownst to the rest of us. Some men went to search there.

I was told there was nothing I could do, and to tell the truth, I was glad. My father arrived and without saying a word to me went off with the searchers. He had lost a wife and child already.

John Jeremy arrived. He had his gunnysack over his shoulder and an oar in his hand. Behind him two men hauled his skiff. I stood up to meet him, I'm ashamed to say, wiping tears on my pantaloons. I had the presence of mind to know that there was business to be conducted.

"This is all I have," I told him, holding out the five-dollar gold piece I had carried for weeks.

I saw real pain in his eyes. The breath itself seemed to seep out of him. "This will be on the house," he said finally. He patted me on the shoulder with a hand that was glazed and hard and went down to the river.

My father's friends took me away then and put some food in me and made me look after the other children. I fell asleep early that warm evening and, not surprisingly, woke while it was still dark, frightened and confused. Had they found him? I wanted to know, and with my father still not home, I had no one to ask.

Dressing, I sneaked out and walked down to the lumberyard. The air was hot and heavy even though dawn was not far off . . . so hot that even the bugs were quiet. I made my way to the dock and sat there, listening to the lazy slap of the water.

There was a slice of moon in the sky, and by its light it seemed that I could see a skiff slowly crossing back and forth, back and forth, between two prominent coves to the south. A breeze came up all of a sudden, a breeze that chilled but did not cool, hissing in the reeds like a faraway voice. I fell forward on my hands and shouted into the darkness: "Who's there?"

No one answered. Perhaps it was all a dream. I do know that eventually the sky reddened on the Wisconsin side and I was able to clearly see John Jeremy's distant skiff

Hungry now and deadly sure of my own uselessness in the affair, I drifted home and got something to eat. It was very quiet in the house. My father was home, but tired, and he offered nothing. I went out to Church voluntarily, and prayed for once, alone.

Almost hourly during that Sunday I went down to the St. Croix. Each time, I was able to spot John Jeremy, infinitely patient in his search.

It finally occurred to me about mid-afternoon that I had to do something to help, even if it came to naught. Leaving the house again, I walked past the lumberyard toward the brushy shallows where John Jeremy was, hoping that in some way my sorry presence would encourage a merciful God to end this. I was frankly terrified of what I would see—a body drowned a goodly time and in August heat at that—yet anxious to confront it, to move *past* it and get on with other business.

Two hours of beating through the underbrush, occasionally stepping into the green scum at water's edge, exhausted me. I believe I sat down for a while and cried, and presently I felt better—better enough to continue.

It was almost sunset. The sun had crossed to the Minnesota side and dipped toward the trees on the higher western bluffs, casting eerie shadows in the coves. Perhaps that is why I did not see them until I was almost upon them.

There, in the shallow water, among the cattails and scum, was John Jeremy's skiff. In it was a huge white thing that once was my brother Dolph. The sight was every bit as horrific as I had imagined, and even across an expanse of water the smell rivaled the pits of Hell . . . but that alone, I can honestly say, did not make me scream. It was another thing that made me call out, an image I will carry to my grave, of John Jeremy pressing his ear to the greenish lips of my brother's corpse.

My scream startled him. "Peter!" he yelled. I was as incapable of locomotion as the cattails that separated us. John Jeremy raised himself and began to pole toward me. "Peter, wait for me."

I found my voice, weak though it was. "What are you doing to my brother?"

He beached his nightmare cargo and stumbled out of the skiff. He was frantic, pleading, out of breath. "Don't run. Peter, hear me out."

I managed to back up, putting some distance between us. "Stay away!"

"I told you, Peter, I talk to the river. I *listen* to it, too." He nodded toward Dolph's body. "They tell me where the next one will be found, Peter, so I can get them out, because the river doesn't want them for long—"

I clapped my hands over my ears and screamed again, backing away as fast as I could. The slope was against me, though, and I fell.

John Jeremy held out his hand. "I could teach you the secret, Peter. You have the gift. You could learn it easy."

For a long second, perhaps a heartbeat and a half, I stared at his grimy hand. But a gentle wave lapped at the skiff and the God-awful creaking broke his spell. I turned and scurried up the hill. Reaching the top, I remembered the gold piece in my pocket. I took it out and threw it at him.

At twelve your secrets do not keep. Eventually, some version of what I'd seen and told got around town, and it went hard with John Jeremy. Stillwater's version of tar-and-feathering was to gang up on a man, kick the hell out of him, and drag him as far south as he could be dragged, possessions be damned. I was not there. Sometimes, as I think back, I fool myself into believing that I was . . . that John Jeremy forgave me, like Christ forgave his tormentors. But that did not happen.

Eventually, we learned that John Jeremy's "secret" was actually a special three-pronged hook attached to a weight that could be trolled on a river bottom. Any fool could find a body, they said. Maybe so.

But the flood of '97 damned near killed Stillwater and things haven't improved since then. A day don't go by now that I don't think of John Jeremy's secret and wish I'd said yes. Especially when I go down to the river and hear the water rustling in the reeds, making that awful sound, the sound I keep telling myself is not the voices of the dead.

A new writer whose stories are few but carefully crafted, Michael Cassutt is a California native who works for a television network. His first published story, "The Streak" (1977), is about murder on a baseball diamond; his later tales, nearly all science fiction, have appeared in Omni *and* Isaac Asimov's Science Fiction.

Although Joe Indian believed he didn't believe the Indian religion he was brought up to respect, he had to prove it to himself. . . .

TWENTY-EIGHT

Ride the Thunder
Jack Cady

A lot of people who claim not to believe in ghosts will not drive 150 above Mount Vernon. They are wrong. There is nothing there. Nothing with eyes gleaming from the roadside, or flickering as it smoothly glides not quite discernible along the fence rows. I know. I pull it now, although the Lexington route is better with the new sections of interstate complete. I do it because it makes me feel good to know that the going-to-hell old road that carried so many billion tons of trucking is once more clean. The macabre presence that surrounded the road is gone, perhaps fleeing back into smoky valleys in some lost part of the Blue Ridge where haunted fires are said to gleam in great tribal circles and the forest is so thick that no man can make his way through.

Whatever, the road is clean. It can fall into respectable decay under the wheels of farmers bumbling along at 35 in their '53 Chevies.

Or have you driven Kentucky? Have you drive that land that was known as a dark and bloody ground. Because, otherwise you will not know about the mystery that sometimes surrounds those hills, where a mist edges the distant mountain ridges like a memory.

And, you will not know about Joe Indian who used to ride those hills like a curse, booming down out of Indiana or Southern Illinois and bound to Knoxville in an old B-61 that was probably only running because it was a Mack. You would see the rig first on 150 around Vincennes in Indiana. Or, below Louisville on 64, crying its stuttering wail into the wind and lightning of a river valley storm as it ran under the darkness of electricity-charged air. A picture of desolation riding a road between battered fields, the exhaust shooting coal into the fluttering white load that looked like windswept rags. Joe hauled turkeys. Always turkeys and always white ones. When he was downgrade he rode them at seventy plus. Uphill he rode them at whatever speed the Mack would fetch.

That part was all right. Anyone who has pulled poultry will tell you that you have to ride them. They are packed so tight. You always lose a few. The job is to keep an airstream moving through the cages so they will not suffocate.

But the rest of what Joe Indian did was wrong. He was worse than trash. Men can get used to trash, but Joe bothered guys you would swear could not be bothered by anything in the world. Guys who had seen everything. Twenty years on the road, maybe. Twenty years of seeing people broken up by stupidity. Crazy people, torn-up people, drunks. But Joe Indian even bothered guys who had seen all of that. One of the reasons might be that he never drank or did anything. He never cared about anything. He just blew heavy black exhaust into load after load of white turkeys.

The rest of what he did was worse. He hated the load. Not the way any man might want to swear over some particular load. No. He hated every one of those turkeys on every load. Hated it personally the way one man might hate another man. He treated the load in a way that showed how much he despised the easy death that was coming to most of those turkeys—the quick needle thrust up the beak into the brain the way poultry is killed commercially. Fast. Painless. The night I saw him close was only a week before the trouble started.

He came into a stop in Harrodsburg. I was out of Tennessee loaded with a special order of upholstered furniture to way and gone up in Michigan and wondering how the factory had ever caught that order. The boss had looked sad when I left. That made me feel better. If I had to fight tourists all the way up to the lake instead of my usual Cincinnati run, at least he had to stay behind and build sick furniture. When I came into the stop I noticed a North Carolina job, one of those straight thirty or thirty-five footers with the attic. He was out of Hickory. Maybe one of the reasons I stopped was because there would be someone there who had about the same kind of trouble. He turned out to be a dark-haired and serious man, one who was very quiet. He had a load of couches on that were made to sell but never, never to use. We compared junk for a while, then looked through the window to see Joe Indian pull in with a truck that looked like a disease.

The Mack sounded sick, but from the appearance of the load it must have found seventy on the downgrades. The load looked terrible at close hand. Joe had cages that were homemade, built from siding of coal company houses when the mines closed down. They had horizontal slats instead of the vertical dowel rod. All you could say of them was that they were sturdy, because you can see the kind of trouble that sort of cage would cause. A bird would shift a little, get a wing-tip through the slat and the air stream would do the rest. The Mack came in with between seventy-five and a hundred broken wings fluttering along the sides of the crates. I figured that Joe must own the birds. No one was going to ship like that. When the rig stopped, the wings drooped like dead banners. It was hard to take.

"I know him," the driver who was sitting with me said.

"I know of him," I told the guy, "but, nothing good."

"There isn't any, any more," he said quietly and turned from the window. His face seemed tense. He shifted his chair so that he could see both the door and the restaurant counter. "My cousin," he told me.

I was surprised. The conversation kind of ran out of gas. We did not say anything because we seemed waiting for something. It did not happen.

All that happened was that Joe came in looking like his name.

"Is he really Indian?" I asked.

"Half," his cousin said. "The best half if there is any." Then he stopped talking and I watched Joe. He was dressed like anybody else and needed a haircut. His nose had been broken at one time. His knuckles were enlarged and beat-up. He was tall and rough-looking, but there was nothing that you could pin down as unusual in a tough guy except that he wore a hunting knife sheathed and hung on his belt.

The bottom of the sheath rode in his back pocket. The hilt was horn. The knife pushed away from his body when he sat at the counter.

He was quiet. The waitress must have known him from before. She just sat coffee in front of him and moved away. If Joe had seen the driver beside me he gave no indication. Instead he sat rigid, tensed like a man being chased by something. He looked all set to hit, or yell, or kill if anyone had been stupid enough to slap him on the back and say hello. Like an explosion on a hair-trigger. The restaurant was too quiet. I put a dime in the juke and pressed something just for the sound. Outside came the sound of another rig pulling in. Joe Indian finished his coffee, gulping it. Then he started out and stopped before us. He stared down at the guy beside me.

"Why?" the man said. Joe said nothing. "Because a man may come with thunder does not mean that he can ride the thunder," the driver told him. It made no sense. "A man is the thunder," Joe said. His voice sounded like the knife looked. He paused for a moment, then went out. His rig did not pull away for nearly ten minutes. About the time it was in the roadway another driver came in angry and half-scared. He headed for the counter. We waved him over. He came, glad for some attention.

"Jesus," he said.

"An old trick," the guy beside me told him.

"What?" I asked.

"Who is he?" The driver was shaking his head.

"Not a truck driver. Just a guy who happens to own a truck."

"But, how come he did that." The driver's voice sounded shaky.

"Did what?" I asked. They were talking around me.

The first guy, Joe's cousin, turned to me. "Didn't you ever see him trim a load?"

"What!"

"Truck's messy," the other driver said. "That's what he was saying. Messy. Messy." The man looked half sick.

I looked at them still wanting explanation. His cousin told me. "Claims he likes neat cages. Takes that knife and goes around the truck cutting the wings he can reach . . . just enough. Never cuts them off, just enough so they rip off in the air stream."

"Those are live," I said.

"Uh huh."

It made me mad. "One of these days he'll find somebody with about thirty-eight calibers of questions."

"Be shooting around that knife," his cousin told me. "He probably throws better than you could handle a rifle."

"But why . . ." It made no sense.

"A long story," his cousin said, "And I've got to be going." He stood up. "Raised in a coal camp," he told us. "That isn't his real name but his mother was full Indian. His daddy shot coal. Good money. So when Joe was a kid he was raised Indian, trees, plants, animals, mountains, flowers, men . . . all brothers. His ma was religious. When he became 16 he was raised coal miner white. Figure it out." He turned to go.

"Drive careful," I told him, but he was already on his way. Before the summer was out Joe Indian was dead. But by then all of the truck traffic was gone from 150. The guys were routing through Lexington. I did not know at first because of trouble on the Michigan run. Wheel bearings in Sault Ste. Marie to help out the worn compressor in Grand Rapids. Furniture manufacturers run their lousy equipment to death. They expect every cube to run on bicycle maintenance. I damned the rig, but the woods up there were nice with stands of birch that jumped up white and luminous in the headlights. The lake and straits were good. Above Traverse City there were not as many tourists. But, enough. In the end I was pushing hard to get back. When I hit 150 it took me about twenty minutes to realize that I was the only truck on the road. There were cars. I learned later that the thing did not seem to work on cars. By then it had worked on me well enough that I could not have cared less.

Because I started hitting animals. Lots of animals. Possum, cat, rabbit, coon, skunk, mice, even birds and snakes . . . at night . . . with the moon tacked up there behind a thin and swirling cloud cover. The animals started marching, looking up off the road into my lights and running right under the wheels.

Not one of them thumped!

491

I rode into pack after pack and there was no thump, no crunch, no feeling of the soft body being pressed and torn under the drive axle. They marched from the shoulder into the lights, disappeared under the wheels and it was like running through smoke. At the roadside, even crowding the shoulder, larger eyes gleamed from nebulous shapes that moved slowly back. Not frightened; just like they were letting you through. And you knew that none of them were real. And you knew that your eyes told you they were there. It *was* like running through smoke, but the smoke was in dozens of familiar and now horrible forms. I tried not to look. It did not work. Then I tried looking hard. That worked too well, especially when I cut on the spot to cover the shoulder and saw forms that were not men and were not animals but seemed something of both. Alien. Alien. I was afraid to slow. Things flew at the windshields and bounced off without a splat. It lasted for ten miles. Ordinarily it takes about seventeen minutes to do those ten miles. I did it in eleven or twelve. It seemed like a year. The stop was closed in Harrodsburg. I found an all night diner, played the juke, drank coffee, talked to a waitress who acted like I was trying to pick her up, which would have been a compliment . . . just anything to feel normal. When I went back to the truck I locked the doors and climbed into the sleeper. The truth is I was afraid to go back on that road.

So I tried to sleep instead and lay there seeing that road stretching out like an avenue to nowhere, flanked on each side by trees so that a man thought of a high speed tunnel. Then somewhere between dream and imagination I began to wonder if that road really did end at night. For me. For anybody. I could see in my mind how a man might drive that road and finally come into something like a tunnel, high beams rocketing along walls that first were smooth then changed like the pillared walls of a mine with timber shoring on the sides. But not in the middle. I could see a man driving down, down at sixty or seventy, driving deep towards the center of the earth and knowing that it was a mine. Knowing that there was a rock face at the end of the road but the man unable to get his foot off the pedal. And then the thoughts connected and I knew that Joe Indian was the trouble with the road, but I did not know why or how. I was shaking and cold. In the morning it was not all bad. The movement was still there but it was dimmed out in daylight. You caught it in flashes. I barely made Mount Vernon, where I connected with 25. The trouble stopped there. When I got home I told some lies and took a week off. My place is out beyond LaFollette, where you can live with a little air and woods around you. For awhile I was nearly afraid to go into those woods.

When I returned to the road it was the Cincinnati run all over with an occasional turn to Indianapolis. I used the Lexington route and watched the other guys. They were all keeping quiet. The only people who were talking were the police who were trying to figure out the sudden shift in traffic. Everybody who had been the route figured if they talked about it, everyone else would think they were crazy. You would see a driver you knew and say hello. Then the two of you would sit and talk about the weather. When truckers stop talking about trucks and the road something is wrong.

I saw Joe once below Livingston on 25. His rig looked the same as always. He was driving full out like he was asking to be pulled over. You could run at speed on 150. Not on 25. Maybe he *was* asking for it, kind of hoping it would happen so that he would be pulled off the road for a while. Because a week after that and a month after the trouble started I heard on the grapevine that Joe was dead.

Killed, the word had it, by ramming over a bank on 150 into a stream. Half of his load had drowned. The other half suffocated. Cars had driven past the scene for two or three days, the drivers staring straight down the road like always. No one paid enough attention to see wheel marks that left the road and over the bank.

What else the story said was not good and maybe not true. I tried to dismiss it and kept running 25. The summer was dwindling away into fall, the oak and maple on those hills were beginning to change. I was up from Knoxville one night and saw the North Carolina job sitting in front of a stop. No schedule would have kept me from pulling over. I climbed down and went inside.

For a moment I did not see anyone I recognized, then I looked a second time and saw Joe's cousin. He was changed. He sat at a booth. Alone. He was slumped like an old man. When I walked up he looked at me with eyes that seemed to see past or through me. He motioned me to the other side of the booth. I saw that his hands were shaking.

"What?" I asked him, figuring that he was sick or had just had a close one.

"Do you remember that night?" He asked me. No lead up. Talking like a man who had only one thing on his mind. Like a man who could only talk about one thing.

"Yes," I told him, "and I've heard about Joe." I tried to lie. I could not really say that I was sorry.

"Came With Thunder," his cousin told me. "That was his other name, the one his mother had for him. He was born during an August storm."

I looked at the guy to see if he was kidding. Then I remembered that Joe was killed in August. It made me uneasy.

"I found him," Joe's cousin told me. "Took my car and went looking after he was three days overdue. Because . . . I knew he was driving that road . . . trying to prove something in spite of Hell."

"What? Prove what?"

"Hard to say. I found him hidden half by water, half by trees and the brush that grows up around here. He might have stayed on into the winter if someone hadn't looked." The man's hands were shaking. I told him to wait, walked over and brought back two coffees. When I sat back down he continued.

"It's what I told you. But, it has to be more than that. I've been studying and studying. Something like this . . . always is." He paused and drank the coffee, holding the mug in both hands.

"When we were kids," the driver said, "we practically lived at each other's house. I liked his best. The place was a shack. Hell, my place was a shack. Miners made money then, but it was all scrip. They spent it for everything but what they needed." He paused, thoughtful. Now that he was telling the story he did not seem so nervous.

"Because of his mother," he continued. "She was Indian. Creek maybe but west of Creek country. Or maybe from a northern tribe that drifted down. Not Cherokee because their clans haven't any turkeys for totems or names that I know of . . ."

I was startled. I started to say something.

"Kids don't think to ask about stuff like that," he said. His voice was an apology as if he were wrong for not knowing the name of a tribe.

"Makes no difference anyway," he said. "She was Indian religious and she brought Joe up that way because his old man was either working or drinking. We all three spent a lot of time in the hills talking to the animals, talking to flowers . . ."

"What?"

"They do that. Indians do. They think that life is round like a flower. They think animals are not just animals. They are brothers. Eveything is separate like people."

I still could not believe that he was serious. He saw my look and seemed discouraged, like he had tried to get through to people before and had not had any luck.

"You don't understand," he said. "I mean that dogs are not people, they are dogs. But each dog is important because he has a dog personality as same as a man has a man personality."

"That makes sense," I told him. "I've owned dogs. Some silly. Some serious. Some good. Some bad."

"Yes," he said. "But, most important. When he dies a dog has a dog spirit the same way a man would have a man spirit. That's what Joe was brought up to believe."

"But they kill animals for food," I told him.

"That's true. It's one of the reasons for being an animal . . . or maybe, even a man. When you kill an animal you are supposed to apologize to the animal's spirit and explain you needed meat."

"Oh."

"You don't get it," he said. "I'm not sure I do either but there was a time . . . anyway, it's not such a bad way to think if you look at it close. But the point is Joe believed it all his life. When he got out on his own and saw the world he couldn't believe it any more. You know? A guy acting like that. People cause a lot of trouble being stupid and mean."

"I know."

"But he couldn't quite not believe it either. He had been trained every day since he was born, and I do mean every day."

"Are they that religious?"

"More than any white man I ever knew. Because they live it instead of just believe it. You can see what could happen to a man?"

"Not quite."

"Sure you can. He couldn't live in the camp anymore because the camp was dead when the mines died through this whole region. He had to live outside so he had to change, but a part of him couldn't change . . . Then his mother died. Tuberculosis. She tried Indian remedies and died. But I think she would have anyway."

"And that turned him against it." I could see what the guy was driving at.

"He was proving something," the man told me. "Started buying and hauling the birds. Living hand to mouth. But, I guess everytime he tore one up it was just a little more hate working out of his system."

"A hell of a way to do it."

"That's the worst part. He turned his back on the whole thing, getting revenge. But always, down underneath, he was afraid."

"Why be afraid?" I checked the clock. Then I looked at the man. There was a fine tremble returning to his hands.

"Don't you see," he told me. "He still halfway believed. And if a man could take revenge, animals could take revenge. He was afraid of the animals helping out their brothers." The guy was sweating. He looked at me and there was fear in his eyes. "They do, you know. I'm honest-to-God afraid that they do."

"Why?"

"When he checked out missing I called the seller, then called the process outfit where he sold. He was three days out on a one day run. So I went looking and found him." He watched me. "The guys aren't driving that road."

"Neither am I," I told him. "For that matter, neither are you."

"It's all right now," he said. "There's nothing left on that road. Right outside of Harrodsburg, down that little grade

496

and then take a hook left up the hill, and right after you top it . . ."

"I've driven it."

"Then you begin to meet the start of the hill country. Down around the creek I found him. Fifty feet of truck laid over in the creek and not an ounce of metal showing to the road. Water washing through the cab. Load tipped but a lot of it still tied down. All dead of course."

"A mess."

"Poultry rots quick," was all he said.

"How did it happen?"

"Big animal," he told me. "Big like a cow or a bull or a bear . . . There wasn't any animal around. You know what a front end looks like. Metal to metal doesn't make that kind of dent. Flesh."

"The stream washed it away."

"I doubt. It eddies further down. There hasn't been that much rain. But he hit something . . ."

I was feeling funny. "Listen, I'll tell you the truth. On that road I hit everything. If a cow had shown up I'd have run through it, I guess. Afraid to stop. There wouldn't have been a bump."

"I know," he told me. "But Joe bumped. That's the truth. Hard enough to take him off the road. I've been scared. Wondering. Because what he could not believe I can't believe either. It does not make sense, it does not . . ." He looked at me. His hands were trembling hard.

"I waded to the cab," he said. "Waded out there. Careful of sinks. The smell of the load was terrible. Waded out to the cab hoping it was empty and knowing damned well that it wasn't. And I found him."

"How?"

"Sitting up in the cab sideways with the water swirling around about shoulder height and . . . Listen, maybe you'd better not hear. Maybe you don't want to."

"I didn't wait this long not to hear," I told him.

"Sitting there with the bone handle of the knife tacked to his front where he had found his heart . . . or something, and put it in. Not in time though. Not in time."

"You mean he was hurt and afraid of drowning?"

"Not a mark on his body except for the knife. Not a break anywhere, but his face . . . sitting there, leaning into that knife and hair all gone, chewed away. Face mostly gone, lips, ears, eyelids all gone. Chewed away, scratched away. I looked, and in the opening that had been his mouth something moved like disappearing down a hole . . . but, in the part of the cab that wasn't submerged there was a thousand footprints, maybe a thousand different animals . . ."

His voice broke. I reached over and steadied him by the shoulder. "What was he stabbing?" the man asked. "I can't figure. Himself, or . . ."

I went to get more coffee for us and tried to make up something that would help him out. One thing I agreed with that he had said. I agreed that I wished he had not told me.

Ohio-born Jack Cady has enjoyed a wide and varied literary career. Newspaper editor and owner, university teacher and visiting professor of English are among his accomplishments. He has won such writing awards as a "First" from the Atlantic Monthly *for his short story, "The Burning" (which also received the Governor's Award and the Iowa Award in 1972) and the National Literary Award for his short story "The Shark" (1971). Much of his work has supernatural themes, such as the ghost novel* The Jonah Watch *(1982) and* The Man Who Could Make Things Vanish *(1983).*

Sometimes an archaeologist finds more than pot shards and arrowheads.

TWENTY-NINE

The Resting Place
Oliver LaFarge

The possibility that Dr. Hillebrand was developing kleptomania caused a good deal of pleasure among his younger
colleagues—that is, the entire personnel of the Department
of Anthropology, including its director, Walter Klibben. It
was not that anybody really disliked the old boy. That would
have been hard to do, for he was co-operative and gentle,
and his humor was mild; he was perhaps the greatest living
authority on Southwestern archaeology, and broadly
learned in the general science of anthropology; and he was
a man who delighted in the success of others.

Dr. Hillebrand was the last surviving member of a group
of men who had made the Department of Anthropology
famous in the earlier part of the twentieth century. His ideas
were old-fashioned; to Walter Klibben, who at forty was
very much the young comer, and to the men he had
gathered about him, Dr. Hillebrand's presence, clothed with
authority, was as incongruous as that of a small, mild bron-
tosaurus would be in a modern farmyard.

On the other hand, no one living had a finer archaeological technique. Added to this was a curious intuition,
which caused him to dig in unexpected places and come up
with striking finds—the kind of thing that delights donors
and trustees, such as the largest unbroken Mesa Verde
black-on-white jar known up to that time, the famous
Biltabito Cache of turquoise and shell objects, discovered
two years before and not yet on exhibition, and, only the
previous year, the mural decorations at Painted Mask ruin.
The mural, of which as yet only a small part had been uncovered, compared favorably with the murals found at

499

Awatovi and Kawaika-a by the Peabody Museum, but was several centuries older. Moreover, in the part already exposed there was an identifiable katchina mask, unique and conclusive evidence that the katchina cult dated back to long before the white man came. This meant, Dr. Klibben foresaw gloomily, that once again all available funds for publication would be tied up by the old coot's material.

The trustees loved him. Several years ago, he had reached the age of retirement and they had waived the usual limitation in his case. He was curator of the museum, a position only slightly less important than that of director, and he occupied the Kleinman Chair in American Archaeology. This was an endowed position paying several thousand a year more than Klibben's own professorship.

Dr. Hillebrand's occupancy of these positions, on top of his near monopoly of publication money, was the rub. He blocked everything. If only the old relic would become emeritus, the younger men could move up. Klibben had it all worked out. There would be the Kleinman Chair for himself, and McDonnell could accede to his professorship. He would leave Steinberg an associate, but make him curator. Thus, Steinberg and McDonnell would have it in mind that the curatorship always might be transferred to McDonnell as the man with senior status, which would keep them both on their toes. At least one assistant professor could, in due course, be made an associate, and young George Franklin, Klibben's own prized student, could be promoted from instructor to assistant. It all fitted together and reinforced his own position. Then, given free access to funds for monographs and papers. . . .

But Dr. Hillebrand showed no signs of retiring. It was not that he needed the money from his two positions; he was a bachelor and something of an ascetic, and much of his salary he put into his own expeditions. He loved to teach, he said—and his students liked him. He loved his museum; in fact, he was daffy about it, pottering around in it until late at night. Well, let him retire, and he could still teach a course or two if he wanted; he could still potter, but Klibben could run his Department as he wished, as it ought to be run.

Since there seemed no hope that the old man would give out physically in the near future, Klibben had begun looking for symptoms of mental failure. There was, for instance, the illogical way in which Dr. Hillebrand often decided just where to run a trench or dig a posthole. As Steinberg once remarked, it was as if he were guided by a ouija board. Unfortunately, this eccentricity produced splendid results.

Then, sometimes Hillebrand would say to his students, "Now, let us imagine—" and proceed to indulge in surprising reconstructions of the daily life and religion of the ancient cliff dwellers, going far beyond the available evidence. The director had put Franklin onto that, because the young man had worked on Hopi and Zuñi ceremonials. Franklin reported that the old boy always made it clear that these reconstructions were not science, and, further, Franklin said that they were remarkably shrewd and had given him some helpful new insights into aspects of the modern Indians' religion.

The possibility of kleptomania was something else again. The evidence—insufficient so far—concerned the rich Biltabito Cache, which Dr. Hillebrand himself was enumerating, cataloguing, and describing, mostly evenings, when the museum was closed. He was the only one who knew exactly how many objects had been in the find, but it did look as if some of it might now be missing. There was also what the night watchman thought he had seen. And then there was that one turquoise bead—but no proof it had come from that source, of course—that McDonnell had found on the floor near the cast of the Quiriguá stela, just inside the entrance to the museum.

The thefts—if there had been any—had taken place in April and early May, when everyone was thinking of the end of the college year and the summer's field trips. A short time later, and quite by accident, Klibben learned from an associate professor of ornithology that old Hillebrand had obtained from him a number of feathers, which he said he wanted for repairing his collection of katchina dolls. Among them were parrot and macaw feathers, and the fluffy feathers from the breast of an eagle.

Klibben's field was not the American Southwest, but any American anthropologist would have been able to draw an obvious conclusion: turquoise, shell, and feathers of those sorts were components of ritual offerings among the modern Hopis and Zuñis, and possibly their ancestors, whose remains Dr. Hillebrand had carried on his lifework. Dr. Kilbben began to suspect—or hope—that the old man was succumbing to a mental weakness far more serious than would be evidenced by the mere stealing of a few bits of turquoise and shell.

The director made tactful inquiries at the genetics field laboratory to see if the old man had been seeking corn pollen, another component of the ritual offerings, and found that there the question of the evolution of *Zea maiz* in the Southwest was related to the larger and much vexed question of the origin and domestication of that important New World plant, so interesting to archaeologists, botanists, and geneticists. Dr. Hillebrand had been collecting specimens of ancient corn from archaeological sites for a long time— ears, cobs, and grains extending over two millenniums or more, and other parts of the plant, including some fragments of tassels. It was, Klibben thought, the kind of niggling little detail you would expect to find Hillebrand spending good time on. Dr. Hillebrand had been turning his specimens over to the plant and heredity boys, who were delighted to have them. They, in turn, had followed this up by obtaining—for comparison—seed of modern Pueblo Indian, Navajo, and Hopi corn, and planting it. It was natural enough, then, that from time to time Dr. Hillebrand should take specimens of seed and pollen home to study on his own. It might be clear as day to Klibben that the old boy had gone gaga to the point of making ritual offerings to the gods of the cliff dwellings; he still had nothing that would convince a strongly pro-Hillebrand board of trustees.

Even so, the situation was hopeful. Klibben suggested to the night watchman that, out of concern for Professor Hillebrand's health, he keep a special eye on the Professor's afterhours activities in the museum. Come June, he would arrange for Franklin—with his Southwestern interests, Franklin was the logical choice—to go along on Hillebrand's expedition and see what he could see.

Franklin took the assignment willingly, by no means unaware of the possible advantages to himself should the old man be retired. The archaeologist accepted this addition to his staff with equanimity. He remarked that Franklin's knowledge of Pueblo daily life would be helpful in interpreting what might be uncovered, while a better grounding in Southwestern prehistory would add depth to the young man's ethnographic perceptions. Right after commencement, they set out for the Navajo country of Arizona, accompanied by two undergraduate and four graduate students.

At Farmington, in New Mexico, they picked up the university's truck and station wagon and Hillebrand's own field car, a Model A Ford as archaic as its owner. In view of the man's income, Franklin thought, his hanging on to the thing was one more oddity, an item that could be added to many others to help prove Klibben's case. At Farmington, too, they took on a cook and general helper. Dr. Hillebrand's work was generously financed, quite apart from what went into it from his own earnings.

The party bounced over the horrifying road past the Four Corners and around the north end of Beautiful Mountain, into the Chinlee Valley, then southward and westward until, after having taken a day and a half to drive about two hundred miles, they reached the cliffs against which stood Painted Mask Ruin. The principal aim of the current summer's work was to excavate the decorated kiva in detail, test another kiva, and make further, standard excavations in the ruin as a whole.

By the end of a week, the work was going nicely. Dr. Hillebrand put Franklin, as the senior scientist under him, in charge of the work in the painted kiva. Franklin knew perfectly well that he was deficient in the required techniques; he would, in fact, be dependent upon his first assistant, Philip Fleming, who was just short of his Ph.D. Fleming had worked in that kiva the previous season, had spent three earlier seasons with Dr. Hillebrand, and was regarded by him as the most promising of the many who had worked under him. There was real affection between the two men.

Two of the other graduate students were well qualified to run a simple dig for themselves. One was put in charge of the untouched second kiva, the other of a trench cutting into the general mass of the ruin from the north. Franklin felt uncomfortably supernumerary, but he recognized that

that was an advantage in pursuing his main purpose of keeping a close watch on the expedition's director.

After supper on the evening of the eighth day, Dr. Hillebrand announced rather shyly that he would be gone for about four days, "to follow an old custom you all know about." The younger men smiled. Franklin kept a blank face to cover his quickened interest.

This was a famous, or notorious, eccentricity of the old man's, and one in which Drs. Klibben, McDonnell, and the rest put great hope. Every year, early in the season, Dr. Hillebrand went alone to a ruin he had excavated early in his career. There was some uncertainty as to just where the ruin was; it was believed to be one known to the Navajos as Tsekaiye Kin. No one knew what he did there. He said he found the surroundings and the solitude invaluable for thinking out the task in hand. It was usually not long after his return from it that he would announce his decision to dig in such-and-such a spot and proceed to uncover the painted kiva, or the Kettle Cave fetishes, or the Kin Hatsosi blanket, or some other notable find.

If Franklin could slip away in the station wagon and follow the old man, he might get just the information he wanted. So far, Dr. Hillebrand's activities on the expedition had evidenced nothing but his great competence. If the old man ever performed mad antique rites with stolen specimens, it would be at his secret place of meditation. Perhaps he got up and danced to the ancient gods. One might be able to sneak a photo. . . .

Dr. Hillebrand said, "I shan't be gone long. Meantime, of course, Dr. Franklin will be in charge." He turned directly to his junior. "George, there are several things on which you must keep a close watch. If you will look at these diagrams—and you, too, Phil. . . ."

Franklin and Fleming sat down beside him. Dr. Hillebrand expounded. Whether the ancient devil had done it intentionally or not, Franklin saw that he was neatly hooked. In the face of the delicacy and the probable outcome of the next few days' work, he could not possibly make an excuse for absenting himself when the head of the expedition was also absent.

Dr. Hillebrand took off early the next morning in his

throbbing Model A. He carried with him a Spartan minimum of food and bedding. It was good to be alone once more in the long-loved reaches of the Navajo country. The car drove well. He still used it because, short of a jeep, nothing newer had the clearance to take him where he wanted to go.

He drove slowly, for he was at the age when knowledge and skill must replace strength, and getting stuck would be serious. When he was fifty, he reflected, he would have reached T'iiz Hatsosi Canyon from this year's camp in under four hours; when he was thirty, if it had been possible then to travel this country in a car, he would have made even greater speed, and as like as not ended by getting lost. He reached the open farming area outside the place where T'iiz Hatsosi sliced into the great mesa to the south. There were nearly twice as many hogans to be seen as when he had first come here; several of them were square and equipped with windows, and by some of them cars were parked. Everything was changing, but these were good people still, although not as genial and hospitable as their grandparents had been when he first packed in.

He entered the narrow mouth of T'iiz Hatsosi Canyon in the late afternoon, and by the exercise of consummate skill drove some four miles up it. At that point, it was somewhat wider than elsewhere, slightly under two hundred feet across at the bottom. The heavy grazing that had so damaged all the Navajos' land had had some effect here. There was less grass than there used to be—but then, he reflected, he had no horses to pasture—and the bed of the wash was more deeply eroded, and here and there sharp gullies led into it from the sides.

Still, the cottonwoods grew between the occasional stream and the high, warmly golden-bluff cliffs. Except at noon, there was shade, and the quality of privacy, almost of secrecy, remained. In the west wall was the wide strip of white rock from which the little ruin took its name, Tsekaiye Kin, leading the eye to the long ledge above which the cliff arched like a scallop shell, and upon which stood the ancient habitations. The lip of the ledge was about twenty feet above the level of the canyon, and approachable by a talus slope that was not too hard to negotiate. Some small evergreens grew at the corners of the ledge. From the ground, the settlement did not seem as if it had been empty for centuries, but rather as if its occupants at the moment happened not to be visible. The small black rectangles of doorways and three tiny squares of windows made him feel, as they had done over forty years ago, as if the little settlement were watching him.

South of the far end of the ledge, and at the level of the canyon floor, was the spring. Water seeped richly through a crack in the rock a few feet above the ground and flowed down over rock to form a pool at the base. The wet golden-brown stone glistened; small water growths clung to the crevices. In the pool itself, there was cress, and around it moss and grass rich enough to make a few feet of turf.

Here Dr. Hillebrand deposited his bedroll and his food. He estimated that he had better than two hours of daylight left. He cut himself a supply of firewood. Then he took a package out of his coffeepot. The package was wrapped in an old piece of buckskin. With this in hand, he climbed up the slope to the ruin.

The sense of peace had begun once he was out of sight of the camp at Painted Mask Ruin. It had grown when he entered T'iiz Hatsosi Canyon; it had become stronger when he stepped out of the car and glimpsed through the cottonwoods his little village, with its fourteen rooms. By the spring, it had become stronger yet, and mixed with a nostalgia of past times that was sweetly painful, like a memory of an old and good lost love. These feelings were set aside as he addressed himself to the task of climbing, which was not entirely simple; then they returned fourfold when he was in the ruin. Here he had worked alone, a green young man with a shiny new Doctor's degree, a boy-man not unlike young Fleming. Here he had discovered what it was like to step into a room that still had its roof intact, and see the marks of the smoke from the household fire, the loom ties still in place in the ceiling and floor, the broken cooking pot still in the corner.

He paid his respects to that chamber—Room 4-B; stood in the small, open, central area; then went to the roofless, irregular oval of the kiva. All by himself he had dug it out. Could Dr. Franklin have been there, spying unseen, he would have been most happy. From under a stone that appeared firmly embedded in the clay flooring Dr. Hillebrand took an ancient, crude stone pipe fitted with a recent willow stem. He filled it with tobacco, performed curious motions as he lit it, and puffed smoke in the six directions. Then he climbed out of the kiva on the inner side and went behind the double row of habitations, to the darker area under the convex curve of the wall at the back of the cave, the floor of which was a mixture of earth and rubbish. Two smallish, rounded stones about three feet apart inconspicuously marked a place. Sitting by it on a convenient ledge of rock, he puffed at the pipe again; then he opened the buckskin package and proceeded to make an offering of ancient turquoise beads, white and red shell, black stone, feathers and down, and corn pollen.

Sitting back comfortably, he said, "Well, here I am again."

The answer did not come from the ground, in which the bones of the speaker reposed, but from a point in space, as if he were sitting opposite Dr. Hillebrand. "Welcome, old friend. Thank you for the gifts; their smell is pleasing to us all."

"I don't know whether I can bring you any more," the archaeologist said. "I can buy new things, of course, but getting the old ones is becoming difficult. They are watching me."

"It is not necessary," the voice answered. "We are rich in the spirits of things such as these, and our grandchildren on earth still offer them to us. It has been rather for your benefit that I have had you bringing them, and I think that that training has served its purpose."

"You relieve me." Then, with a note of anxiety, "That doesn't mean that I have to stop visiting you?"

"Not at all. And, by the way, there is a very handsome jar with a quantity of beans of an early variety in it where you are digging now. It was left behind by accident when the people before the ones who built the painted kiva moved out. It belonged to a woman called Bluebird Tailfeather. Her small child ran off and was lost just as they were moving, and by the time she found him, the war chief was impatient.

However, we can come back to that later, I can see that you have something on your mind."

"I'm lonely," Dr. Hillebrand said simply. "My real friends are all gone. There are a lot of people I get on nicely with, but no one left I love—that is, above the ground—and you are the only one below the ground I seem to be able to reach. I—I'd like to take your remains back with me, and then we could talk again."

"I would not like that."

"Then of course I won't."

"I was sure of that. Your country is strange to me, and traveling back and forth would be a lot of effort. What I saw that time I visited you was alien to me; it would be to you, too, I think. It won't be long, I believe, before I am relieved of attachment to my bones entirely, but if you moved them now, it would be annoying. You take that burial you carried home ten years ago—old Rabbit Stick. He says you treat him well and have given him the smell of ceremonial jewels whenever you could, but sometimes he arrives quite worn out from his journey."

"Rabbit Stick," Dr. Hillebrand mused. "I wondered if there were not someone there. He has never spoken to me."

"He couldn't. He was just an ordinary Reed Clan man. But he is grateful to you for the offerings, because they have given him the strength he needed. As you know, I can speak with you because I was the Sun's Forehead, and there was the good luck that you were thinking and feeling in the right way when you approached me. But tell me, don't the young men who learn from you keep you company?"

"Yes. There is one now who is like a son to me. But then they have learned, and they go away. The men in between, who have become chiefs, you might say, in my Department, have no use for me. They want to make me emeritus—that is, put me on a pension, take over my authority and my rewards, and set me where I could give advice and they could ignore it. They have new ways, and they despise mine. So now they are watching me. They have sent a young man out this time just to watch me. They call him a student of the ways of your grandchildren; he spent six weeks at Zuñi once, and when even he could see that the people didn't like him, he went and put in the rest of the summer at Oraibi."

"New Oraibi or Old Oraibi?" the Sun's Forehead asked.

"New Oraibi."

The chief snorted.

"So, having also read some books, he thinks he is an ethnographer, only he calls himself a cultural anthropologist. And he is out here to try to find proof that my mind is failing." He smiled. "They'd certainly think so if they saw me sitting here talking to empty air."

The Sun's Forehead chuckled. "They certainly would. They wouldn't be able to hear me, you know." Then his voice became serious again. "That always happens, I think. It happened to me. They wanted to do things differently, when I had at last come to the point at which an Old Man talked to me. I reached it in old age—not young, as you did. They could not take my title, but they wanted to handle my duties for me, bring me enough food to live on, hear my advice and not listen to it. Struggling against them became wearying and distasteful, so finally I decided to go under. At the age I reached—about your age—it is easy to do."

"And now you say that you are about to be detached from your bones entirely? You are reaching the next stage?"

"Let us say that I begin to hope. Our life is beautiful, but for a hundred years or so now I have been longing for the next, and I begin to hope."

"How does it happen? Or is it wrong for me to know?"

"You may know. You are good, and you keep your secrets, as our wise men always did. You will see a man who has become young, handsome, and full of light. When we dance, he dances with great beauty; his singing is beautiful, and you feel as if it were creating life. Then one time when the katchinas themselves are dancing before us—not masks, you understand, the katchinas themselves—you can't find him among the watchers. Then you seem to recognize him, there among the sacred people, dancing like them. Then you think that the next time our grandchildren on the earth put on the masks and dance, that one, whom you knew as a spirit striving to purify himself, who used to tell you about his days on earth, will be there. With his own eyes he will see our grandchildren and bless them." The chief's voice trailed off, as though the longing for what he was describing deprived him of words.

"To see the katchinas themselves dancing," Dr. Hillebrand mused. "Not the masks, but what the masks stand for. . . . That would keep me happy for centuries. But then, I could not join your people. I was never initiated. I'd be plain silly trying to dance with them. It's not for me."

"For over forty years I have been initiating you," the Sun's Forehead said; "As for dancing—you will no longer be in that old body. You will not be dancing with those fragile, rheumatic bones. There is room for you in our country. Why don't you come over? Just lie down in that crevice back there and make up your mind."

"You know," Dr. Hillebrand said, "I think I will."

Both the Kleinman Professor of American Archaeology and the spirit who once had been the Sun's Forehead for the settlements in the neighborhood of T'iiz Hatsosi were thoroughly unworldly. It had not occurred to either of them that within six days after Dr. Hillebrand had left camp Dr. George Franklin would organize a search for him, and four days later his body would be found where he had died of, apparently, heart failure. Above all, it had not occurred to them that his body would be taken home and buried with proper pomp and ceremony in the appropriate cemetery. (But Philip Fleming, close to tears, resolutely overlooked the scattering of turquoise and shell in the rubbish between the crevice and the kiva.)

Dr. Hillebrand found himself among people as alien to him as they had been to the Sun's Forehead. They seemed to be gaunt from the total lack of offerings, and the means by which they should purify and advance themselves to where they could leave this life for the next, which he believed to be the final one, were confused. He realized that his spirit was burdened with much dross, and that it would be a long time before he could gather the strength to attempt a journey to the country of his friend.

His portrait, in academic gown and hood, was painted posthumously and hung in the entrance of the museum, to one side of the stela from Quiriguá and facing the reproduction of the famous Painted Kiva mural. Dr. Klibben adroitly handled the promotions and emoluments that fell under his control. Philip Fleming won his Ph.D. with honor, and was promptly offered a splendid position at Harvard. Moved by he knew not what drive, and following one or two other actions he had performed to his own surprise, Fleming went to Dr. Hillebrand's grave, for a gesture of respect and thanks.

It had seemed to him inappropriate to bring any flowers. Instead, as he sat by the grave, with small motions of his hands he sprinkled over it some bits of turquoise and shell he had held out from a necklace he had unearthed, and followed them with a pinch of pollen given him by a Navajo. Suddenly his face registered utter astonishment; then careful listening.

The following season, Fleming returned to Painted Mask Ruin by agreement with Dr. Klibben, who was delighted to get his Department entirely out of Southwestern archaeology. There he ran a trench that led right into a magnificent polychrome pot containing a store of beans of high botanical interest.

Within a few years, he stopped visiting the grave, but he was sentimentalist enough to make a pilgrimage all alone to Tsekaiye Kin at the beginning of each field season. It was jokingly said among his confreres that there he communed with the spirit of old Hillebrand. Certainly he seemed to have inherited that legendary figure's gift for making spectacular finds.

Winner of the Pulitzer prize (1929) for his Laughing Boy, *a novel of Navajo Indian life, Oliver La Farge was born in New York in 1901, educated at Groton and Harvard, and became a distinguished anthropologist and fiction writer. Serving as president of the Association on American Indian Affairs from 1933 on, he was known as an able advocate for Indian rights. Several of his best works are collected in* The Door in the Wall *(1969). He died in 1963.*

Acknowledgments